"My dear lord, could we not be alone?" said Katherine. "*I* can serve you."

"Of course," he said instantly, and dismissed the servant.

Suddenly across the table she gave him her tenderly wistful and seductive smile. "Will you be gentle with my whims?"

She was all beauty as she sat there in her white dress. Her red lips were parted, her gray eyes dark with love. He trembled and going to her, knelt beside her.

"I shall not always be gentle, Katrine," he said looking up into her face. "But by the soul of my mother, I shall love you until I die."

She bent over and opening her arms drew his head against her breasts. A gull mewed again outside the fortress, the fresh tang of the sea crept through the windows to mingle with the warmth of jasmine.

He raised his head from her breast and they looked, without fear or striving, deep into each other's eyes.

ett Crest Books
Anya Seton:

DEVIL WATER

KATHERINE

THE WINTHROP WOMAN

# Katherine

Anya Seton

FAWCETT CREST • NEW YORK

Exalted be thou and thy name.
Goddess of Renown or of Fame!
* * *
"Madam," said they, "we be
Folk that beseechen thee
That thou grant us now good fame."
* * *
"I warn you it," quoth she anon;
"Ye get of me good fame none,
By God! And therefore go your way."
"Alas!" quoth they, "and weylaway!
Tell us what your cause may be?"
"For me list it not," quoth she.
THE HOUSE OF FAME By Geoffrey Chaucer

A Fawcett Crest Book
Published by Ballantine Books

Copyright © 1954 by Anya Seton Chase

ISBN 0-449-21117-7

This edition published by arrangement with
Houghton Mifflin Company.

Printed in Canada

First Fawcett Crest Edition: February 1969
First Ballantine Books Edition: June 1983
Third Printing: November 1985

# CONTENTS

## Edward III ~ m.~
### (1312 ~ 1377)

Edward of Woodstock _m._ Joan of Kent (The Black Prince)

Isabel _m._ Enguerrand de Couci

Lionel _m._ Elizabeth de of Antwerp Burgh Duke of Clarence

Edward died young

Philippa _m._ Edmund Mortimer Earl of March

Richard II ~ _m._ 1st Anne of Bohemia (1367 ~ 1400) _m._ 2nd Isabelle of France murdered at Pontefract

Mortimer claim

---

## John of Gaunt _m._ 1st Blanche of Lancaster ─ ─ ─ ─ ─ ─ ─
### (1340 ~ 1399)
Duke of Lancaster King of Castile

Philippa _m._ João of Portugal (1360 ~ 1415) 8 children, including Henry the Navigator

Elizabeth ~ _m._ 1st Earl of (1364 ~ Pembroke 1426) _m._ 2nd John Holland

Henry of Bolingbroke ~ _m._ 1st ─ ─ ─ Mary de Bohun (1367 ~ 1413) Earl of Derby

Henry V (of Monmouth) Henry VI

~~~~~~~~~~~~~~~~~~~~~~~~~~~~~~~~~~~~~~~~~~~~

## Sir Payn de Roet ─ ─ ─ ─

Philippa _m._ Geoffrey Chaucer (1348 ~ 1387) (1340 ~ 1400)

Thomas?

## Sir Hugh Swynford _m._ 1st ─ ─ ─ ─ ─ Katherine ~ ~ ~ ~
### (1350 ~ 1403)

Blanchette (1367 ~ ?)

Thomas (1368 ~ 1432)

_m._ 1st Jane Crophill _m._ 2nd Margaret Darcy

---

John Beaufort _m._ Margaret (1372 ~ 1409) Holland

Henry (1375 ~ 1447) Cardinal Beaufort

Thomas Beaufort _m._ ("Tamkin") (1377 ~ 1427) no issue

Henry VII, Henry VIII, Elizabeth I, Mary Queen of Scots, James I, etc.

# ~Philippa of Hainault~

Edmund of ~ m. ~ Isabella
Langley          of
Earl of Cambridge  Castile
Duke of York

       Yorkist claim

Thomas of Woodstock m. Eleanor
Earl of Buckingham        de
Duke of Gloucester       Bohun
(murdered by Richard II)

~ m. 2nd Costanza of Castile ~ ~ ~ ~ m. 3rd Katherine
                                              Swynford
Catherine m. Enrique of Castile        (see below)
(Catalina)

   The Royal Line of Spain

SWYNFORD     ROET     LANCASTER

~ m. 2nd John of Gaunt (see above)
            (1340 ~ 1399)
        Duke of Lancaster, King of Castile

Joan Beaufort ~ m. 1st ~ Sir Robert Ferrers
(1379 ~ 1440)  m. 2nd ~ Ralph Neville of Raby, 1st Earl of
                                                 Westmoreland

   Edward IV, Richard III

# AUTHOR'S NOTE

In TELLING THIS STORY of Katherine Swynford and John of Gaunt, the great Duke of Lancaster, it has throughout been my anxious endeavor to use nothing but historical fact when these facts are known—and a great deal *is* known about the fourteenth century in England. Since I have based my story on history, I have tried never to distort time, or place, or character to suit my convenience.

For those few who are interested in sources, I append my main ones below; while for those who may wish to know something of the book's background and the writing of it, here are some brief notes.

My interest in Katherine began one day nearly five years ago when I read mention of her in Marchette Chute's charming biography, *Geoffrey Chaucer of England* (New York, 1947). I subsequently came to know Miss Chute and am extremely grateful for her encouragement.

I then began my research on the fourteenth century, preparatory to the necessary trip to England for more intensive delving and a view of the places associated with Katherine. Four years of my life have been spent in England, my father was English-born, and I have always dearly loved the country, but this special research trip in 1952 was particularly delightful, for it combined the beauties of an English spring with the zest of a treasure hunt.

I visited each of the counties; I studied the remains of John of Gaunt's numerous castles, and searched ever—in the British Museum, in town libraries and archives, in rectory studies, in local legend—for more data on Katherine's life.

Of her little was known, except when her life touched the Duke's and there are few details of that. The *Dictionary of National Biography* sketch is inadequate, the contemporary chroniclers were mostly hostile (except Froissart), and in the great historians Katherine apparently excited scant interest, perhaps because they give little space to the women of the period anyway.

And yet Katherine was extremely important to English history. When on the English tour I visited Lincolnshire, I was rewarded with new light. And here I must express my fervent thanks to J. W. F. Hill, Esquire, for his cordial help and for his scholarly, comprehensive book, *Medieval Lincoln* (Cambridge, Eng., 1948).

I wish also to thank all the kind people in Lincoln who interested themselves in my project, and especially the owners and the occupants of Kettlethorpe Hall, where I spent charmed days in Katherine's own home, trying to reconstruct the past. Though but a portion of the gatehouse and cellars remains from Katherine's time, the rectory contained one of those invaluable local brochures that are compiled by learned clerical gentlemen. *The Manor and Rectory of Kettlethorpe* by R. E. G. Cole, M. A., Prebendary of Lincoln, had a wealth of new information on the early Swynfords and on Hugh and Katherine, and dates—such as the one I have used for Hugh's death—which differ from the accepted ones but seem incontrovertibly documented. The death date for Hugh suggested the explanation I have used for his mysterious end.

The names of the major characters in this book will be familiar to students of English history, but I have also tried whenever possible to use actual people for the minor ones. John of Gaunt's own registers were invaluable in this respect. For instance, Brother William Appleton's official capacity and eventual fate were as I have shown them. Hawise Maudelyn was Katherine's waiting woman, Arnold was the Duke's falconer, Walter Dysse his confessor and Isolda Neumann his nurse. I have given him no retainers, officers or vassals who are not listed in the Registers.

To the development and motivations of the story it has sometimes of course been necessary to bring my own interpretations, but I trust they are legitimate, and backed by probability.

John of Gaunt has been much vilified by historians who have too slavishly followed the hostile chroniclers, particularly the Monk of St. Albans' consistently spiteful *Chronicon Angliae*. I have naturally preferred the view of his character which was held by his great biographer, Sydney Armitage-Smith, and certainly an impartial look at the facts seems to warrant it.

My "psychological" treatment of the changeling slander arose from several clues. Most of the historians have been puzzled by the Duke's actions at the Good Parliament and sudden reversal thereafter; one source ties this in with the probable deep unconscious effect on the Duke of that type of slander, and it seemed to me logical.

In covering a field so vast as the history and politics of this period, I have had to confine myself to those events which would have affected Katherine, but in showing national events I have tried to extract the truth from the welter of conflicting data and points of view. For the actual accounts of the Good Parliament and the Peasants' Revolt, I have read all the authorities, but have leaned chiefly on *The Anonimalle Chronicle* of St. Mary's Abbey, York, which gives information not available to the earlier historians.

The existence of Blanchette has been entirely overlooked, but it is documented by Armitage-Smith in the appendix, and also by the Registers.

These Registers have also, by inference, provided me with much of the story, since many entries bear on the personal life of Katherine and the Duke, such as their parting in 1381, attested by a Latin Quit Claim—as well as by those assiduous monkish chroniclers who never lost a chance to attack the Duke, for reasons I have tried to show.

My Latin was not adequate for all this research and various amiable people have helped me, but with Middle French and Middle English I have perforce become familiar and one of the great personal pleasures in writing this book has been the reading of much medieval literature—and Chaucer. It has occurred to me, and here I know I am treading on dangerous ground, that Chaucer may have had his beautiful sister-in-law in mind in occasional passages, particularly in the *Troilus and Criseyde.*

That I have not invented Katherine's beauty for fictional purposes is borne out, I think, by the references. John of Gaunt's epitaph in St. Paul's (now destroyed) referred to her as ". . . eximia pulchritudine feminam," an unusual tribute on a tombstone, while the disapproving monk of St. Mary's Abbey called her "une deblesse et enchanteresse."

Lady Julian of Norwich was one of the great English mystics. All her quotations are verbatim from her *Revelations of Divine Love,* edited by Grace Warrack (London, 1949). I hope it has been possible to rebuild the little church to which her anchoress's cell was once attached; when I visited it, it was in a pathetic state of demolition as a result of enemy action.

In closing I do want to thank again all those who have helped me, and particularly my dear friend Isabel Garland Lord, and my English cousin, Amy C. Flagg of Durham.

I have consulted all standard histories and source books for the period, and most of the Chronicles, but my debt to the following is greatest: *John of Gaunt's Register.* Camden Third Series, 4 vols., covering 1372–83. These volumes comprise the actual French (occasionally Latin) documents issued by the Duke. *Genesis of Lancaster* by Sir James H. Ramsay (Oxford, 1913), 2 vols. *John of Gaunt* by Sydney Armitage-Smith (London, 1904), the definitive biography. *Chaucer's World,* compiled by Edith Rickert (New York, 1948). *The Anonimalle Chronicle, 1333–1381, of St. Mary's Abbey, York,* edited by V. H. Galbraith (Manchester, Eng., 1927). *Sir J. Froissart's Chronicles,* translated by Thomas Johnes (London, 1810).

It would be tedious to list all the other chronicles, or the biographies of Chaucer, Wyclif, the queens, the Black Prince, Henry IV, Richard II, etc. But I must mention a few of the background books like J. J. Jusserand's *English Wayfaring Life in the Middle Ages,* translated by L. T. Smith (New York, 1950), J. Huizinga's *The Waning of the Middle Ages* (London, 1924), all of Eileen Power's vivid and exhaustive works, particularly *Medieval English Nunneries* (Cambridge, Eng., 1922), all the fine books by G. G. Coulton; H. S. Bennett's *Life on the English Manor* (Cambridge, Eng., 1937) and Sir Walter Besant's fascinating and beautiful volumes on *Mediaeval London* (London, 1906).

# PART ONE

(1366–1367)

"If no love is, ah God, what feel I so?
And if love is, what thing and which is he?
If love be good from whence cometh my woe?
If he be wicked, a wonder thinketh me. . . ."

TROILUS AND CRISEYDE

# I

IN THE TENDER GREEN TIME of April, Katherine set forth at last upon her journey with the two nuns and the royal messenger.

The invisible sun had scarcely risen as they quitted the little convent of Sheppey, and guiding the horses westward towards the Kentish mainland, rode gingerly down the steep hill. Dripping dun clouds obscured the minster tower behind them and thick mists blew in from the North Sea.

The bell began tolling for Prime and Katherine heard through its familiar clangor, the bang of the priory's gate and the faint voice of the little wicket nun calling again through the mist, "Adieu dear Katherine, adieu."

"Farewell, Dame Barbara, God be with you," Katherine answered, hoping that her tone was not too gay. She had tried to make herself feel the requisite doleful pang at parting from this convent where she had spent over five years, but her heart would not obey. It bubbled, instead, with excited anticipation.

She had been a puny child when the good Queen had sent her to Sheppey Priory as a boarder, and now she was a marriageable woman, for she would be sixteen next October sometime after Michaelmas. And she had had her fill of the cloisters and the hovering nuns, kindly as most of them were. She was sick of the inexorable bell that ruled their lives, tolling for Matins and Lauds and then every three hours throughout the day until Compline at eight o'clock and bed. She was sick of lessons and plain song, and the subdued admonishing murmurs of women.

No matter how dutiful one tried to feel, it was impossible to be sad at leaving this behind, not when the blood ran hot and rich in the veins, and when out in the world there were all the untried beckoning enchantments: dancing, sensuous music, merriment—and love.

Now at last it had come, the summons to court, when Katherine had almost given up hope, and it seemed that the Queen had totally forgotten her early interest in the little orphan. Perhaps the Queen had forgotten but at least Philippa had not. Katherine thought of the coming meeting with the sister whom she had not seen in all these years and gave a sudden bounce of joy, which the old white horse instantly resented. He stumbled in a muddy rut, recovered himself, then stood stock still, his long lips thrust out.

The Prioress Godeleva resented the bounce too, for Katherine was riding pillion behind the prioress.

"What possessed you to jump like that, Katherine!" snapped Godeleva over her shoulder, while she flapped the reins and tried to induce the horse to move. "Bayard hates double weight, and you're not a child to play the fool. I thought we'd trained you better." She flapped the reins again futilely.

Dame Cicily, the other nun, came fluttering up to them crying, "Oh dear, oh dear. Reverend Mother, what's the matter?" She was riding a decrepit nag borrowed from the convent's bailiff and had perforce dropped behind.

"As you see," said the prioress coldly, digging her heels into the horse's belly and slapping his neck with her small white hand, "Bayard is balking."

Dame Cicily nodded mournfully. "I knew there'd be bad luck when Dame Joanna killed that spider this morning— Lord, Lord, whatever shall we do?" She stared owl-eyed at her superior. Dame Cicily was afraid of horses and moreover had been in such a quiver since the prioress's choice of her as companion on this journey into the world that her wits were quite addled. "Maybe if we pray to Saint Botolph?" she wailed, clasping her hands. But the horse would not budge.

Long Will Finch, the Queen's messenger, who had been riding on ahead and singing a bawdy song to himself, suddenly noticed the silence behind him. He turned his roan and peering through the mists came back to investigate. "God's nails—" he muttered when he saw the trouble, "these holy old hens should stay in cloister. We'll not reach Windsor till Whitsun at this rate."

He dismounted, hit Bayard a powerful swat on the rump with the flat of his dagger while savagely jerking the bridle.

The horse gave an indignant snort but he jumped forward and Katherine clung to the prioress's plump waist.

"You need a switch, Reverend Mother," said Long Will, breaking a branch from a hazel bush and handing it to Godeleva.

The prioress inclined her head in gracious thanks. She was the daughter of a Saxon knight, proud of her lineage, and most anxious that the royal messenger should not think them ill-bred for all that they came from such an insignificant convent.

Long Will was not thinking of the prioress, he was looking at Katherine. Sunlight, now glinting through the fog that hung above the Swale, gave him his first good view of her. A tasty wench, he thought, cocking a practiced eye at the face beneath the green hood.

He noted large gray eyes fringed by dark lashes; and two glossy burnished braids, near thick as his waist, and so long that they swung against the horse's croup, while the loose tendrils, dark red as an autumn oak leaf, clung to a broad white forehead. That one wouldn't have to pluck back her hair to broaden her brow like the court ladies. Nor would she have to rub lead paste on her face. The girl's skin was milky smooth with a rose flush on the cheekbones—and no blemishes. Her full mouth was wider than the pouting lips admired at court, yet it betokened a lustiness any man would find challenging, as did the flare of her nostrils and the cleft in her round chin.

She'd be a fine wench for bed-sport, once she'd learned a bit, Long Will thought, as he walked along beside the white cob and stared at Katherine. Ay—she was exceeding fair, though as yet somewhat thin and small-bosomed. If only her teeth were good. Missing or rotted teeth spoiled many a beauty. He determined to make her smile. "Have ye visited the fine new castle, damoiselle?" he asked, pointing to the north where the crenelated towers of Queenborough loomed against the clearing sky.

"Certainly not," cut in the prioress. "I've permitted none of my house to go near the castle, swarming as it has been with lecherous men—workmen and soldiers—and but three miles from the convent."

"To be sure, Reverend Mother," said Long Will grinning, "holy flocks must be guarded, but I thought the Damoiselle Roet being a secular, perhaps she'd wandered that way—"

He winked at Katherine but the girl lowered her eyes as she
had been taught. She was thinking that this Will Finch's bold
stare was a little like that of the young squire who had come
to the convent to see her a year ago. It made one feel warm
and embarrassed but not unpleasantly so. The only other men
she had ever talked to, the old bailiff and an even older convent priest, had no such look in their eyes.

"Then ye didn't see the great Duke of Lancaster when he
came himself to inspect the building last year?" persisted the
messenger. "A pity. He's the most knightly and many think
handsomest too of our King's sons, except, to be sure Edward, Prince of Wales, God gi' him grace."

Katherine was not interested in the Duke of Lancaster, but
there was a question she ached to ask. So she leaned forward
whispering, "May I speak, Reverend Mother?" and peered
around to see that the prioress's round face was again bland
beneath the fluted white wimple. Godeleva nodded, torn between the impropriety of gossiping with a servant, albeit a
royal one, and her own curiosity about what would await
them at Windsor.

Katherine turned to Long Will. "Do you perhaps know my
sister, Philippa de Roet? She's one of the Queen's damoiselles."

"By cock's bones—of course I do," said Long Will. "Since
it was she gave me the Queen's purse and sent me on this
trip."

"What's she like, then, now?" asked Katherine timidly.

"Small, dark and plump as a woodcock," said Long Will.
"They call her La Picarde. She's a bustling little body who
has charge of the pantry maids and rules them stoutly. *She's*
not light-minded as some of the Queen's ladies, by God!"

"That sounds like Philippa," said Katherine, smiling at last.
"She ruled me stoutly enough when we were children."

"In truth you aren't much alike," cried Long Will, having
just discovered that when she smiled Katherine was the fairest maid he had ever seen. Her teeth were small and white
as daisy petals, her smile had a radiant charm, and yet a wistfulness that would melt your heart. It was a sad pity she
could hope for no great marriage. No doubt the Queen had
some one of her young yeomen in mind or a squire. Long
Will knew little of the background for his mission to the little
Kentish priory except that it was like a dozen others he had
performed for Queen Philippa, whose heart and charities

were large. She always concerned herself with orphaned children, particularly those, like the de Roet girls, whose fathers had been her own countrymen.

"Are many of the royal family now at Windsor?" asked Katherine presently. She thought of them as clothed in misty glitter, King Edward and Queen Philippa, and their princely sons and daughters; vague names seldom heard at Sheppey, where the talk was all of the proper observance of saints' days, the shiftlessness of the priory serfs or the recurrent fits, perhaps divinely inspired, which afflicted one of the novices.

"Most of 'em'll be at Windsor for the Saint George Day's feasting and jousting," said Long Will, "but I don't know just which ones. They all move so much from place to place, and now there's this new talk o' war."

"War?" cried the prioress sharply. "But we've been at peace with France these six years." Blessed Mary—not war again, she thought, knowing from bitter experience how war increased her administrative problems. Labor was scarce and grudging enough on the manor as it was. After the terrible Black Death in 'forty-eight there had been no strong serfs left at all to do the work. The nuns had labored in the fields themselves—those of them that survived the plague—and Sheppey had nearly gone under. Godeleva had been a novice then, and too young to realize the stark anxieties of her superiors. But they had struggled through. A new generation of serfs had grown up, though not the gentle biddable types of the old days, for these new ones flocked off to war by preference instead of waiting to be called. It had been so before the Peace of Brétigny, it would be so again if war came and no one left to labor except feeble old men and gloomy women.

"Not war with France, but with Castile, I hear," answered Long Will. "The Prince o' Wales, God gi' him grace, interests himself in the matter at Bordeaux." Suddenly bored with the women and his mission, Long Will spurred his horse and rode on ahead, cursing the plodding priory nags. If war came he'd not be sent on silly errands like this—herding virgins through the countryside.

"Come up, come up, my reverend dames," he called back impatiently, turning in his saddle. "I see the ferry waiting."

Long Will's patience was further tried by the crossing of the Swale. Bayard balked again, refusing for half an hour either to swim or board the ferry. Dame Cicily, who was even more afraid of water than she was of horses, managed to slip off the foot plank and was hauled out weeping, her black robes soaked and clinging to her skinny legs. And the ferryman, seeing the royal badge on Long Will's tunic, naturally tried to extort double fares. The Queen was thrifty like all Flemings and the purse she had provided for the journey would barely cover expenses so that the messenger had to subdue the ferryman with a rough and practiced tongue.

Katherine sat on a mossy stone on the farther bank of the Swale and listened dreamily to a spate of oaths she had not known existed while waiting for their guide to finish with Bayard and the ferryman. She was happy to be on the mainland at last, and a little frightened too. The April sun shone warm on her back, blackbirds sang in a wild cherry tree, and from over the hill on the road to London she heard the confused baaing of sheep and the tinkle of the bellwether.

She gazed across the Swale at the Isle of Sheppey where she had spent most of her conscious years. She could see the battlements of the unfinished castle but not the priory's squat little minster, nor hear the bell which must now be calling the nuns to Tierce, and she thought of the first day she had heard that bell over five years ago when she had been delivered at the convent from a cart, along with a side of beef and a half a ton of wine sent as gifts to Sheppey by the Queen. The Queen sent three gold nobles as well for Katherine's keep and Prioress Godeleva had been jubilant.

True, Katherine was neither a royal ward nor a well-dowered novice, nor even nobly born; she was simply a child, like many others, for whom the motherly Queen felt responsibility; but the prioress had been elated by this unexpected mark of royal interest, for Sheppey had never before been so honored. Usually it was large aristocratic foundations like Barking or Amesbury that were chosen.

It was because of Queenborough Castle, to be rebuilt on an old Saxon stronghold to guard the Thames, that the Queen had thought of the nearby priory—thought of it, and then apparently forgotten all about it again.

Katherine grew tall and strong, she had soon eaten up the gold nobles, and become an expense to the convent, but nothing more came from the Queen or from Philippa, Katherine's sister, except the young squire's message last year.

Royal personages, however kind, may be forgetful, Katherine had learned early, yet the Queen had said that she would never fail in remembrance of her compatriots and especially one who died in battle, as Katherine's father had.

Payn de Roet came from Hainault, the Queen's wealthy little Netherlands country, but he had married a French girl from Picardy who had died in childbed. After her death Payn had left his two little daughters with their grandparents when he followed the Queen to England. Payn had been a dashing, handsome man inclined to dress above his station and thus well fitting his nickname of Paon, the peacock.

He found favor with King Edward, who appointed him one of the royal heralds—King-of-Arms to represent the province of Guienne—then finally so distinguished himself fighting in France just before the peace in 1360 that King Edward had knighted him on the field along with many other deserving soldiers.

Sir Payn did not live long enough to enjoy either his knighthood or the truce, for a Norman arrow pierced his lungs during a skirmish outside the walls of Paris, and he expired with an anguished prayer for the future of his two little daughters in Picardy.

Queen Philippa heard of this later when the King returned to England, and was saddened. Soon she had occasion to send a messenger across the Channel with letters to Bruges and she entrusted him with various other commissions along the way.

So the messenger stopped off at the farm in Picardy and found that Sir Payn's family was indeed desperate for help. The plague, as it returned that winter for its second great smiting, had recently struck the household. The grandparents had died of it and all the servants. No one was left but Payn's two small daughters, and one, the younger, had been stricken too but miraculously recovered, though she continued to ail. They were being reluctantly tended by a neighbor.

These little girls were aged thirteen and ten. The elder was named Philippa, for the queen who had been her father's patroness, and the younger was Katherine. Finding them thus completely orphaned, and knowing the Queen's good heart, the messenger carried the children back to England with him on his return trip.

Of this voyage across the Channel and her arrival in a foreign country, or of the jolting ride through pouring rain to the royal palace at Eltham, and eventual reception by the Queen, Katherine remembered almost nothing. For she had been ill the whole time with a wasting fever and bloody flux.

Katherine had dim memory of a kind fat face topped by a gold circlet, and of a thick comfortable voice speaking to her first in Flemish then French, but though her sister Philippa admonished her sharply to answer the Queen, Katherine could not, and she remembered nothing else.

The Queen had had her carried to a forester's cottage where the goodwife, skilled with herbs, had managed to nurse the child back to health. By that time the Queen had moved to her favorite palace of Woodstock and taken little Philippa with her in her household, and when reminded that Katherine had most surprisingly recovered, she sent letters arranging for the child's admission at Sheppey.

How unhappy I was, and how homesick, the last time I crossed this river, thought Katherine, looking down at the muddy waters of the Swale.

"Viens, Katrine—dépêches-toi!" called the prioress from the road, preparing to hoist herself onto the white horse. Katherine jumped up. The prioress used French only in moments of ceremony or admonition and she spoke it with a flat Kentish twang, so that Katherine had not understood one word when she first came to the convent, but now this uncouth French was as familiar to her as the English the nuns always spoke among themselves.

Long Will, having subdued both Bayard and the ferryman, was waiting for them to start again.

Katherine jumped up behind Godeleva, and the little procession jogged off. Dame Cicily at the rear was still sniffling and shivering, and at intervals she called on St. Sexburga, the patroness of their convent, to protect her from more such mishaps. But the sun grew warmer, the muddy road dried, the soft Kentish air was bright with fragrance and bird song, and when they met a flock of sheep coming *towards* them—a very good omen—Dame Cicily cheered up and began to look about her at the changing countryside.

Long Will was singing again—a rippling ballad of alewives and cuckoldry, the words fortunately not quite audible to his charges. Even the prioress expanded under the rare pleasure of going on a journey, and said to Katherine, "Oh, child, may Saint Mary and our Blessed Lord forgive me, and They know I would never leave my convent except for such very good reason, but it *is* pleasant to be out in the world."

"Oh it is, it is, dear Mother!"

Katherine, startled by this human confession, looked affectionately down at the small black-covered head in front of her. The prioress had relaxed austerity for once and made some concessions to feminine vanity. Her wimple was glossily starched, she had directed that Dame Joanna, the chambress, refurbish the black cloak and rub cinnamon into the folds to stifle the inevitable odor of mildew and sweat. Her silver signet ring, badge of office, had been burnished with wood ash until it twinkled like a star on her plump white forefinger, and she had made the sacrist restring her finest coral rosary with gold thread.

Godeleva usually obeyed the Benedictine rule as well as anyone, but there are practical considerations too. On this trip to court, it should be possible to pick up a well-dowered novice for Sheppey, and those who live in the world are regrettably apt to be influenced by appearance. Parents did not like to confine their daughters to impoverished provincial houses, and the competition was strong, since there were in England some hundred and forty convents besides Sheppey, and all of them anxious for benefices.

The prioress twisted around to look at her charge, and thought that Katherine would do Sheppey credit. The girl had grown beautiful. That act the convent perhaps could not lay claim to, except that they had obviously fed her well; but her gentle manners, her daintiness in eating—these would please the Queen as much as Katherine's education might startle her. Katherine could spin, embroider and brew simples, of course; she could sing plain chant with the nuns, and indeed had a pure golden voice so natural and rich that the novice-mistress frequently had to remind her to intone low through her nose, as was seemly. But more than that, Katherine could read both French and English because "Sir" Osbert, the nuns' priest, had taken the pains to teach her, averring that she was twice as quick to learn as any of the novices. He had also taught her a little astrology and the use of the abacus, somewhat to the prioress's disapproval. Useless learning is a snare of the devil's and last year, when Katherine's beauty became obvious, Godeleva had had moments of worry about "Sir" Osbert's zeal for teaching. She had repented of her shameful doubts, however; the priest was a man, to be sure, but a very old one, and the watchful prioress eventually decided that he found in the hours he spent teaching Katherine only intellectual interest, and the alleviation of boredom.

"Drop your chin and straighten your back, child, as we've taught you," said the prioress, arranging the folds of her own habit, which had become tangled in the stirrups.

Katherine obeyed as well as she could on Bayard's jiggling rump, then leaned forward eagerly. "Oh, look, Reverend Mother—a spire over there and a castle and houses. Oh, is it London?"

Long Will heard this and let out a roar of laughter. "No more London than a rush dip is the sun. Yon's only Rochester."

Katherine blushed and said nothing more, but Rochester seemed to her a very great city. Besides the high spire there were at least a hundred chimneys pricking the sky above the massive encircling wall.

"They've a passable ordinary here, madam," said Long Will riding back to the prioress. "My gullet's dry, my belly empty as a tabor, and yours, too, very like. We'll dine at the Three Crowns?"

The prioress shook her head. "Not seemly," she said, pursing her lips. "We will go to the abbey guest house. One of my nuns, Dame Alicia, is cousin-german to the abbot."

Long Will and Katherine were much disappointed; Long Will because he liked the ale and the serving maid at the Three Crowns, Katherine because she had quite enough of religious houses and longed to see what a tavern was like; but the little prioress was accustomed to rule. Will grumpily led the way through the city gates towards the abbey.

They aroused interest in the streets, not because of the nuns, for on this way-stop to Canterbury one saw plenty of pilgrims, ecclesiastic and secular, but because of the royal badge on Will's tunic, and the lovely face that gazed down from behind the prioress. Katherine's hood had slipped back, her ruddy hair sparkled in the sun and her cheeks were like appleblossoms.

The citizens of Rochester shrank against the overhanging houses to let the three horses pass by on the narrow street, and they were free with their comments. "God's bones," cried a leathermonger, spitting amiably towards Will, "have ye been raping a nunnery, Longshanks?" "Worse 'n that," answered a passing pedlar sepulchrally. "He's taking the women to be hanged on London bridge for treason, what else!" Guffaws greeted this sally, and a baker thrust his head

through his shop window. "Their bones'll be picked clean in
a trice then, for 'tis well known vultures like virgin meat."

"Virgins they may be," cried the leathermonger, "but the
girl's too fair for that. Pray don't close her in a nunnery,
madam." He swept Godeleva a mock, beseeching bow. "Find
yourself another novice, ill-favored and snag-toothed. This
fair maid must warm some lucky man's bed."

"A murrain on the lot of you," cried Long Will, grinning.
"The Queen herself'll find this maid a husband. Make way,
make way," he shouted to a tangle of dogs and children playing at Hoodman Blind in the street ahead.

The prioress rode imperturbably through the chaffing. She
had heard plenty of rough talk in her girlhood at Sandwich
and, in fact, scarcely noticed it, being occupied with plans for
their accommodations that night. If the abbey could not receive them, they must push on to the priory at Lilliechurch.
But Dame Cicily was frightened; her long ferret nose quivered, her eyes grew pink, and she again regretted that she had
come.

Katherine was not frightened, but she was embarrassed
and pulled her hood close around her face. Can I be really
fair? she thought. No one had ever said so before and there
was no looking glass, of course, at Sheppey. She had heard
mention of fair women by some of the older nuns and a few
of the travelers who knocked at the priory wicket. They had
spoken of great beauties like Joan of Kent, wife to the
Prince of Wales, and warmly admired in this her native shire;
and some said that Blanche of Lancaster, John of Gaunt's
Duchess, was nearly as beautiful. But those two were blondes,
with hair like gold silk and eyes as blue as the Virgin's robe.
Dame Sybilla said so. She had seen both ladies at a tournament in Smithfield ten years ago, before she came to Sheppey
as a novice. Dame Sybilla had read many romances too, before she put away worldly things, and she said the lovely her-
oines were always fair-haired and blue-eyed, with pursed rosebud mouths.

Katherine could see that her own hair was only of a reddish
hue like a horse chestnut, but she wasn't sure about her eyes,
so she had consulted the de Northwode novice. Little Adela
de Northwode had examined Katherine's eyes conscientiously. "A sort of speckled gray, like—like a rabbit's fur,"
she had said at last. "Or maybe more like thin fog, just before the sun breaks through. But they are very large," she

added kindly as Katherine looked dashed, "near as large as a sheep's"—which was not reassuring. Further questioning elicited that neither did Katherine have a tiny, pouting mouth, and she had dejectedly given up all claims to vanity.

All the same, today she had felt a strange sense of power, and she had felt this thing last year when she had met the young squire.

Katherine had plenty of time that night to think about the squire, for she and the nuns stayed in the abbey's female hostel, and after attending Compline that night they went at once to bed on pallets in the dorter, and soon the fetid air was filled with feminine snores and coughs, just like Sheppey. Moreover, the bugs and fleas which lived in the stale rushes on the floor, scenting new flesh, fastened themselves with avidity on Katherine's tender naked body, so that between scratching and excitement, she could not sleep.

It was in May, nearly a year ago, that the squire had come riding up to the priory gatehouse asking for the Damoiselle de Roet, and he brought Katherine a message from her sister at court. This was the first message from Philippa since Katherine had come to Sheppey, but the young squire explained that Philippa was sorry about that; she had not had the advantage of a convent education and could not write, so there had been no opportunity before.

Katherine had received her visitor in the prioress's dim parlor, and she had been in such a state of confused pleasure that she had not been able to say much.

The squire's name was Roger de Cheyne and he was one of the Duke of Lancaster's retinue. The great Duke himself was at Queenborough that night, making a visit of inspection to the castle under construction, and Roger had obtained leave to ride to the priory and see Katherine. "Your sister, Philippa la Picarde," said the young man, twirling his jeweled felt hat and peering at Katherine with startled interest, "sends you God's greetings and hopes you are in health, as she is. She bids me ask you"—here he bowed and smiled charmingly towards the prioress—"if it is the Reverend Mother's and your intent that you be now entered here as a novice."

"Oh no! no!" cried Katherine violently, forgetting propriety in her horror.

The prioress frowned. "Mademoiselle de Roet will of course do as the Queen wishes—" She paused wondering if she was to be asked to receive Katherine without dowry.

The squire smiled at Katherine, and her heart jumped. He was so fresh and young, his skin fine like a girl's and barely shadowed with a golden down. His short chestnut curls clustered about his ears, his surcote of blue wool was embroidered in gold around the Lancaster red rose badge, he had a jeweled dagger and elegant pointed red shoes, but despite his elegance, his neck was thick-muscled and his shoulders broad. Totally innocent though she was, Katherine felt in him a virility lying beneath the courtly manner, as a tough branch supports the blossoms on a cherry tree.

"I cannot speak for the Queen," he said in his soft, wooing voice. "I've not seen her in months for she suffers much with the dropsy and keeps at Woodstock, but I understood your sister to mean that whether you choose marriage or the cloister, she would endeavor, in time—" he paused, knowing well how long such matters often took, "to suggest your wishes to our sovereign lady, God give her health."

"Oh," said Katherine faintly. So after all she must continue at the convent and await the Queen's pleasure, as before. She turned, biting her lips, to stare through the tiny unglazed window towards the sea.

The squire walked over beside her and touched her bare arm, so light and quick a caress that the prioress did not see it. "Ma belle," he whispered in rapid French, "hast thou yet felt Cupid's arrows that pierce the heart with honey fire?" At Katherine's quick indrawn breath and startled eyes, he went on louder in English, "I may tell your sister, then, that you wish to be wed?"

Katherine blushed scarlet and bowed her head. She knew nothing of the stylized game of courtly love and the young man's question about Cupid and honey fire was gibberish, but a shiver raced through her veins when he touched her and spoke in the almost forgotten accents of her childhood.

"Are you not English, Sir Squire?" she asked breathlessly.

Roger de Cheyne laughed. "English enough since my grandfather came here from Artois with Isabella of France and I was born at our manor in Oxfordshire; but my mother still has lands in France, so I've spent much time there."

"And your father?" asked the prioress. She, too, was interested in this springtime breath from the great world.

"Killed at Crécy, by his own French kinsman, as it turned out," said Roger cheerfully. "My father, of course, was in King Edward's company, but he had many relatives on the other side. Well, that's war. I was born, by the way, on the same day as the battle, so I never saw my father—God rest his soul."

Katherine was counting back. The English victory at Crécy had been in late August of 1346, so the young squire was nearly nineteen and born under the sign of Virgo. That meant for a man high ideals of chastity and nobility; often the natives of that sign went into holy orders, like the blessed St. Cuthbert.

She stole an anxious glance at Roger through her long lashes. He did not look like a young man inclined towards the priesthood, but then what did she know of young men and their inclinations, she thought, depressed. Nor would she find out anything now, it seemed, for the prioress had risen, holding out her hand for the squire to kiss her ring.

"It was good of you to come with your message, young sir," said the prioress far less cordially. She had suddenly realized that, charming as young de Cheyne might be, his visit had proved nothing. Katherine was apparently to remain on here as a charity boarder, her future still unsettled; besides Godeleva did not like the languishing glances the youth's bold eyes cast on her charge. There had been no seductions or scandal during her rule at the convent and there would not be—even of a secular. So the prioress herded Katherine back to the mistress of novices and personally supervised the serving of bread and ale to the squire before Godspeeding him under the gatehouse.

Katherine did not see him again, but as she lay that night amongst the novices she had heard trumpets blaring from the castle, and fancied that she could also hear the voices of men singing and laughing. The Duke of Lancaster and his meinie would be reveling, and Roger de Cheyne playing perhaps on the lute that she had seen strapped to his saddle. And Katherine had cried softly for a time, stifling the sound with her hair so as not to disturb the sleeping novices.

Sainte Marie, what a baby I was, thought this older Katherine lying on the strange hostel pallet, for now that release had come at last, all past disappointments seemed trivial. I will be good and please Philippa and the Queen, she thought vaguely, quite unable to envision either of them. Of the husband who would be allotted to her she scarcely thought at all, except that it would be delightful if he were young and handsome like Roger de Cheyne.

# II

IT TOOK THEM four more days to reach Windsor, and only for Katherine were the small mishaps and adventures of the road consistently interesting. The two nuns grew weary of strange beds and food, their middle-aged bones ached, their muscles cramped from all this riding. Moreover Dame Cicily had caught a cold after her ducking in the Swale, and her doleful sneezes grew as monotonous as the slow clop of the horses, or Long Will's increasingly exasperated oaths. He was on fire to get back to Windsor where the festivities would be already under way; the preliminary joustings in the lists, bullbaitings and cockfights by the river, while fair Alison of Egham had promised to give her old husband the slip and be waiting at the alehouse to join Will in merry dalliance. Yet by Sunday the party from Sheppey had traveled no farther than Southwark, and there was no means of hurrying them. Dame Cicily's nag limped, the prioress's cob shied and then balked at anything that annoyed it, which meant pedlars, dogs, puddles, geese and particularly the sound of bagpipes, which they encountered with frequency while they were on the Pilgrim's Way, since most groups bound for Canterbury included amateur musicians.

So Long Will chafed and endured a journey of nearly six days, though it had taken him less than three alone. And at Southwark he would not allow his charges to cross the Bridge and enter London, which would have meant more delay.

The tired nuns did not care. The prioress had twice been to London before this, once as a girl with her family, and once on pilgrimage to the shrine of St. Edward the Confessor at Westminster; as for Dame Cicily, she had reached a stage of sniveling apathy, longing only for the safe quiet of Sheppey and the ministrations of the infirmaress.

But for Katherine it was different. To be here at last by London town, which lay just across the river with its teeming traffic of wherries, wine-laden galleys from Gascony and gor-

27

geously painted private barges; to glimpse the shining walls
and the stately four-turreted White Tower, the bustling Bridge
hung with banners, to hear the hum and rhythm of the city
before the jangling of a hundred different church bells—and
to be allowed no nearer, that was a bitter disappointment.
Still, she was by temperament reasonable and by training
obedient, so she contented herself with a few timid questions.

That tremendous high spire to the left, so strong and up-
thrust above the city? Why, St. Paul's Cathedral of course,
said the prioress. And that great gray pile of masonry down
by the water's edge? The prioress did not know, but Long
Will took pity on the girl. "That's Baynard's Castle, damoiselle; it belongs to the Earls of Clare. Nearly all the nobles
have city houses, but the finest of all is the Duke of Lancaster's Savoy. Look—"

He swung his horse around and directed Katherine's gaze
upriver, a mile or so beyond the city walls. "Can ye see it?"

She squinted into the noon light and made out a huge mass
of cream-colored stone and many crenelated turrets from
which fluttered tiny splashes of red and gold, and one sharp-
pointed gilt spire that marked the private chapel, but she
could see few details, and no premonition seized her that the
great Duke's palace might ever be more to her than an object
of curiosity and awe. Indeed, she passed on quickly to strain
her eyes farther in the direction of Westminster, but she
could not see it because of the bend in the river, and Long
Will, though usually tolerant of Katherine, was hurrying
them on again. They turned south to pick up the Richmond
road, and tall oaks hid all on the north bank from sight.

"Yes," said Will, riding beside Bayard to keep a minatory
eye on the horse, and having pursued his own train of
thought, "John o' Gaunt's a lucky man—lucky in bed, that is.
He's naught but the King's third son, yet I vow he has more
lands and castles than his father."

"How is that?" asked the prioress, sighing. It had begun to
drizzle and there was still much road ahead before they
reached the convent where she intended to stop that night.

"By the marriage bed, madam," said Long Will, laughing,
"and by deathbeds, too. The Lady Blanche of Lancaster, bless
her sweet face, brought him the greatest inheritance in the
kingdom, once her father and sister were dead, may their
souls rest in peace. They died of plague five years ago, both
of 'em, and so the Lady Blanche got all." Katherine, mildly

interested, would have questioned further, but the prioress, who had just developed a crick in her back, sharply told her not to talk so much, and Katherine subsided.

Long Will kicked his roan, which leaped ahead. He hurried them on until they passed near the royal palace at Sheen, deserted now except for a few varlets, since King Edward seldom used it as residence, preferring Windsor, Woodstock or Eltham when he was not at Westminster. But Sheen was a small, pretty castle floating like a swan on its broad shining moat, and it put Will in a fine humor, for the gatekeeper's daughter was a buxom lass, coy enough to make good sport, and she would doubtless be found at Windsor for the merry-making.

On the following afternoon, Monday the twentieth of April, they finally reached Windsor, and during the last hour's ride, the road was so thronged they could scarcely move at all. Long Will's voice grew hoarse from shouting, "Make way! Make way for the Queen's messenger!"

From all the nearby shires, from as far away as Northumberland and Devon and Lincolnshire, the people were flocking to celebrate St. George's Day at Windsor. Weeks ago the King's heralds had galloped throughout the country proclaiming the great tournament and inviting all valorous knights to come and participate. There would be tilting at the quintain and other knightly games; there would be jousts and challenges, and there would be a climaxing tourney, or melee, for all contenders. Most of the knights had arrived at Windsor some days ago, and the lesser ones who could not be accommodated in the castle were already encamped on the plain below the walls in a bivouac of multicolored tents; many had brought their ladies, and all, of course, their squires.

But the common people, though not specifically invited, were welcome, too. For these, five hundred oxen were roasting at charcoal fires dotted around the fields, vats of beer had been set up, and a thousand loaves of barley bread already baked for distribution.

While Long Will expertly wormed his way through the streets of Windsor towards the castle gate they were jostled by prosperous merchants, beggars, palmers with cockleshells in their broad hats, whores in hoods of scarlet ray, respectable goodwives with their children, mummers and gleemen, all clamorous with holiday mood.

Katherine was a little frightened by the noise and confusion, and Dame Cicily was in tears as usual. Her habit had been caught by the gold spur of a passing knight as he shoved his horse impatiently through the press and now a jagged rip divided the black wool and shamefully exposed her skinny leg, fumble as she might to hide it. Even Long Will was disconcerted as he maneuvered his charges, and said, "God's bones, ladies, I don't know where they'll lodge you for I swear there'll not be a cranny vacant in the castle."

Only the little prioress was imperturbable. "We will wait inside the gates," she said majestically, "until you make known our arrival to the Damoiselle de Roet's sister, who will doubtless have made provision for us."

So they rode through the portcullis to the lower ward and huddled in a corner by the Curfew Tower near a black-gowned clerk who fidgeted impatiently while he also awaited answer to some message he had sent.

Long Will, dismounted, threw his reins to a stable urchin and disappeared.

This great paved courtyard was as full of confusion as the streets. Mounted knights and squires continually came and went, servants ran panting from building to building, a noble lady arrived in a gilt and blazoned chariot, was received by a bowing chamberlain and vanished through one of the myriad doors. Suddenly there was a greater flurry and a flourish of trumpets. Two boys in white livery marched through the gate, one bearing a jeweled miter and the other a crozier.

They were followed by a plump, red-faced man in gold-embroidered robes, riding on a large gray horse. The Prioress Godeleva uttered an exclamation. She slid down off Bayard, pulling Katherine with her. " 'Tis the Bishop of Lincoln," she whispered and knelt on the paving stones. Dame Cicily copied her prioress while tugging frantically at her torn habit.

Here and there throughout the courtyard others knelt too. John Buckingham, the bishop, smiled vaguely around, raising two fingers in blessing. Then his eye caught sight of the nuns and he looked startled. He rode over to them.

"Whence come you, Reverend Mother?" he asked Godeleva sharply, having noted her ring of office. "Are you of my flock?"

"No, my lord," said Godeleva. "We come from Sheppey Priory in Kent."

"Oh, the south," said the bishop, losing interest. Had they come from his own diocese it would be necessary to inquire into the appearance of two nuns in such worldly surroundings, but he was relieved that no steps need be taken, for he was hungry and impatient to be housed.

"We have permission, my lord," said Godeleva. "I bring this girl here at the Queen's command."

"Ah." The bishop glanced down at Katherine, of whom he could see nothing but a cheap green woolen hood, for her head was properly bowed. But he noted her hands, which were very dirty and ringless.

"Some charity wench of the good Queen's no doubt," he said with a condescending laugh, dismissing them all. He murmured *"Benedicite,"* and rode back to his waiting coterie.

Katherine flushed. There was enough truth in the bishop's careless statement to sting. I'm not a charity wench; my father was knighted, she thought hotly and she rose from her knees, staring after the bishop with no proper Christian humility. There were lesser priests around him, all fluttering and fawning except one, who stood apart. This priest wore doctoral robes and a four-cornered hat, and his brooding eyes, deep-set above a huge hooked nose, were fixed on the magnificent Lord Bishop of Lincoln with a certain irony, visible even to Katherine, who therefore felt sudden interest.

"I wonder who that is?" she said to Godeleva, pointing discreetly; but before the prioress, who did not know, could answer, the clerk behind them spoke.

" 'Tis Master John Wyclif, that was King's chaplain."

"Blessed Virgin!" cried the prioress crossing herself. "Not that priest who's dared defy His Holiness the Pope? Katherine, don't look at him! He's tainted with vile heresy. By Sainte Marie, I've even heard that he wishes to English the Gospels—is't true, Sir Clerk?"

The clerk laughed. "I've heard so. His Lollards, the poor preachers, make all manner of shocking statements to the people."

*"Deus misereatur!* 'Tis no matter for laughing!" The prioress frowned at the clerk's amused face. She drew Katherine and Dame Cicily off away from him, and lectured Katherine apprehensively on the many dangers that must be guarded against in the world. And they continued to wait.

During the next half-hour the girl had ample time to compare her own appearance with that of court ladies who flitted by and to become increasingly uncomfortable. The chambress at Sheppey had done the best she could for Katherine, con-

sidering that there was no money forthcoming, but the hood
and cape were now deplorably travel-stained, and the girl's
brown serge kirtle hung loose and baggy like the nuns' habits
and was unredeemed by lacings or fur or embroidery. Katherine's courage ebbed very low as time went on. The great folk
passed by without even a glance in their direction, and she
began inwardly to echo Dame Cicily's lamentations.

"Oh Reverend Mother, they've forgotten us! Perhaps it was
all a jest or a mistake! We were never meant to come! Would
that we were safe back at Sheppey! O Merciful Blessed Lady
and kind Saint Sexburga, don't desert us!"

"Hush," said the prioress sharply. "Here is Long Will
now."

Long Will loped down the ward and behind him there hurried a small plump girl with a worried smile. She was dressed
in a blue robe trimmed with squirrel and her dark hair was
looped in tight braids on either side of her round earnest
face.

She curtsied to the prioress, then peered at Katherine.
"Est-ce vraiment toi, ma soeur?" she said uncertainly.

Katherine leaned down, threw her arms around her sister's
neck and burst into tears.

The two girls clung to each other murmuring little choked
French endearments while Long Will looked on with sentimental approval, Dame Cicily sniffed in sympathy and even
the prioress's controlled face softened.

Philippa drew away first and returned to practical problems. "I fear we've no suitable accommodations up here for
you, Reverend Mother," she said apologetically, "but Long
Will can guide you to respectable night's lodgings in the
town, unless you wish to ride on to Ankerwyck Priory, perhaps?"

Godeleva flushed. "But surely I was to see the Queen. I understood I might have audience with the Queen." In spite of
herself her voice trembled, for it was easy to read dismissal in
the girl's proposal, and then where were all the golden hopes
of royal favor and tardy gratitude for the care of Katherine?
Where the hopes of picking up new novices?

"The Queen, Our Lady be merciful, is ill, Reverend
Mother," answered Philippa uncomfortably, for she was used
to supplicants at court and quite understood what the prioress
wanted. "The dropsy which plagues her is very bad and she
keeps to her bed, tended only by two of her ladies. I myself

have not seen her in a week—as soon as she's better, perhaps—"

"But she sent for Katherine," protested the prioress. "She must have known I could not let the girl travel alone with a messenger!"

Philippa sighed, knowing that the Queen had given no thought to the matter at all, once she had assented to Philippa's timid request for an Easter boon.

"Yes, my little Pica, of course we must send for your sister, and get her married, too," the Queen had said kindly. "Tell Will Finch to go for her and apply to the steward for —let me see—" She had wrinkled her scanty brows. "Half a mark—that should be ample for expenses." She had patted Philippa's shoulder and added playfully, "Shall we find her another worthy squire like yours, Pica, and marry you off together?"

But that had been the Queen's last good day. Since then she had suffered grievously with pains in her head; her legs had swollen big as pillows and her mind had grown cloudy and fretful, though this the Queen's faithful ladies thought, should not be attributed to the swellings but to another more shocking cause—that cursed scheming Alice, thought Philippa indignantly.

"We will stay in the town then," said the prioress with recaptured calm, "until the Queen is well enough to receive me. Katherine—" She looked at the girl and paused, with a smile which did not quite hide the anxious question in her eyes.

Katherine responded to the unspoken plea with a rush of warmth, and astonishment that the austere little ruler of Sheppey days should be pleading and in need.

"I won't forget, Reverend Mother," she said gently, kneeling and kissing the plump white hand. "Not all you've done for me, nor your wish for audience with the Queen. I won't forget."

The prioress murmured a blessing. "You've been a good girl," she said, turning away. "Continue to be." She mounted Bayard, Dame Cicily clambered up on her horse, and Long Will shrugged, catching up Bayard's bridle. He led the two nuns towards the gate.

"Well," said Philippa briskly, "now we must hurry. 'Tis near the hour for supper. Holy Michael and his angels, but we'll have to clean you up first and find you something fit to wear. You're not a slattern, I trust!" Philippa, hustling her

sister past the Round Tower to the upper ward and into the
passage that led to the Queen's apartments, had just taken a
startled survey of Katherine.

"I trust not," said Katherine trying to laugh, "but we've
been on the road since dawn and I've no change of clothes.
I'm sorry—"

Philippa made an impatient clucking noise. "We must borrow a decent gown; only Matilda Radscroft is tall enough
and she's not overgenerous, but if you offer to do something
for her—She's behind with her tapestry—can you embroider?"

"A little," answered Katherine humbly, stumbling up steep
stone stairs after her sister. She understood that Philippa
loved her of course, but that the moment of sentiment had
passed. She understood too that Philippa would do her
efficient duty no matter how she might dislike a disruption of
her well-ordered life.

But Katherine's eyes filled. She was hungry and tired and
she felt an amazing pang of homesickness for Sheppey.

Philippa opened a stout oak door and ushered Katherine
into the solar. Here in this small low-vaulted room lived six
of the Queen's damoiselles when they were in residence at
Windsor. The two who were closest to the Queen—Matilda
Fisher and Elizabeth Pershore—were now in constant attendance since the illness, and slept on the other side of the wing
in the anteroom near their mistress, while the others slept
here in three beds; except Alice Perrers, and there was little
doubt unfortunately as to where *she* slept, though in theory
she shared a bed in this solar.

Alice was here now, however, when Philippa and Katherine came in. All of the Queen's damoiselles were primping
for supper. They hovered near the fire, and held candles for
each other as they searched for finery in open coffers which
dotted the rush-strewn floor. Only Alice Perrers sat alone,
away from the others, and she was tended by the two tiring
maids who were assigned to all of them. One maid held a
candle and the other a looking glass while Alice rubbed cochineal paste into her high cheekbones and hid her wiry black
hair in a net of seed pearls.

She turned her pointed cat face towards Philippa and
Katherine, widened her shrewd dark eyes, and called, in the
caressing voice for which she was famous, "Ah, Pica, my
sweet, so is this the little sister, at last?"

Philippa stiffened, made the barest noise of assent and pulled Katherine to the other side of the fire as far as possible from Alice, who gave a laugh like chiming bells, and holding out her perfumed hand admired the sparkle of her new ring. It was of Saracen make, two rubies set in heavy worked gold, and had belonged to the King's mother, Isabella of France.

Katherine was puzzled, but had no time to wonder why Philippa was so rude, for the other ladies closed around them, greeting and exclaiming. They were solid young women and accustomed to work. They were not nobly born, except for Agnes de Saxilby, because the Queen sensibly chose her ladies for the embodiment of the Flemish housewifely virtues, and their positions were in nowise honorary. They gave active service. The wives of great noblemen would not do menial chores, even for the Queen. So these were the daughters or wives of gentry and they welcomed Katherine with rough kindness.

"Oh, so dirty! What frightful clothes! God's nails but they must be lousy. Burn them!" The ladies summarily stripped Katherine and threw her clothes into the fire while the girl stood naked and shivering, trying not to cry as Philippa brought water and a coarse towel and scrubbed her little sister until the beautiful skin turned fiery red and Katherine shrank and tried to protect her delicate round breasts from Philippa's determined scourings; Johanna Cosin unbraided and combed the burnished masses of Katherine's hair; they put on her a spare shift of Philippa's which was much too short, and Matilda Radscroft, carried away by the concerted undertaking, actually pulled her third-best gown from a coffer and slipped it over Katherine's head. The gown was of coarse and rather shabby velvet, trimmed with narrow bands of rabbit fur, and it hung loosely on Katherine's far more slender body, but its color was violet, and above it the girl's long neck glowed white as pearls and her still unbound hair, rippling below her knees, caught violet lights from the dress and gold ones from the fire.

"So much hair to make neat and to hold up in the cauls," Philippa grumbled, "and she hasn't even a proper girdle or a surcote for warmth."

"She has something else—a great deal else," said Alice Perrers' soft laughing voice from the corner, "and if you ladies are too stupid to see it, the men won't be. Thanks to

God that the King is short-sighted, I can fill his entire vision
—and shall."

Philippa stiffened, the other women's heads jerked back.
"The bawdy slut," whispered Johanna. They sent Alice looks
of hatred but they dared say nothing. Mysterious punish-
ments afflicted those who engaged the creature in open warfare. Agnes de Saxilby had last month spoken her mind to
Alice, calling her whore and witch—for it must be witchcraft
that would make the King so forget all his former duty and
affection for the Queen. Alice, saying nothing, had smiled her
sleepy smile, but only yesterday poor Agnes had heard that
the King had authorized a ruinous new levy on her father's
manor.

The ladies finished with Katherine and put the last touches
on their own toilets; they gave her a drink of wine which
must revive her, before they all flocked down the steps towards the Great Hall for supper. "Stay near me," whispered
Philippa. "Don't speak unless you're spoken to."

Katherine needed none of these admonitions, which simply
echoed her convent training, and she clung to her sister, feeling very nervous and wishing that she were not so tall and
might hide in that plump little person's shadow.

The Great Hall with its stone vaulting and tinted windows
was large enough to have contained the entire convent of
Sheppey. Katherine was dazzled by the light from a hundred
candles and torches, enchanted by the gay music of the
minstrels and amazed by the sweet scent that vanquished the
usual aroma of sweat, smoke and food. The floor was strewn
with aromatic herbs and a cartload of violets had been mingled with them. At the far end of the Hall on a dais, a line of
glittering, gorgeously jeweled men and women sat at the high
table and Katherine at once saw the King under the central
canopy before she politely lowered her eyes. He looks so old,
she thought, startled by the straggling white hair and thin
beard and shrunken shoulders. Edward was actually fifty-four
but he had the lean Plantagenet frame and years of cam-
paigning and intermittent fever had aged him.

The Queen not being present, the chamberlain waved Philippa and the other ladies in waiting towards a side table with
scant ceremony, and Katherine sat on the bench beside her
sister.

Servants sprinted back and forth on the free side of the
table, with flagons of mead or Gascon wine and more varlets

followed bearing platters of stag haunch, roast swan and larded boar's head. Katherine let Philippa help them both into the bowl they shared. There had been no such selection at Sheppey and Katherine was not even sure of the identity of these meats, blanketed as they were by thick sweet sauces. She played with her trencher of white bread and listened to the waves of laughter and loud talk which echoed around the vaulting of the Hall and nearly drowned out the minstrels' harps and lutes.

Suddenly a head was thrust between the sisters and a quick voice said, "So *there* you are, my fair Pica. I've been searching for you."

Philippa looked up and blushed. Her serious little face was lightened by a smile almost coquettish. "Good even, sir," she said. "I was afraid you might be serving the King tonight. Katherine, this is my betrothed, Geoffrey Chaucer, esquire."

"Betrothed!" echoed Katherine amazed. "You didn't tell me—God's greetings to you, sir," she added hastily, remembering her manners.

Geoffrey smiled, clambering over the bench and wedging himself between the two girls. "Her betrothed is perhaps a matter of small importance to Pica," he said in a tone of faint mockery. "You're the little sister from the convent, of course." He motioned to a servant, who brought him a bowl and cup.

"There was no *time* to tell her," protested Philippa, "so much to do, receiving her and the nuns and getting her ready to appear here. You can't imagine the condition she was in and—"

"To be sure," interrupted Geoffrey smiling. "I know you were busy as a little wren." He patted Philippa's hand and his hazel eyes twinkled as at some private joke.

Katherine decided that she liked him, though he was by no means the romantic figure she hoped would fall to her own lot. He was short, not much taller than Philippa herself and though he was only twenty-six, already inclined towards stoutness. He was more soberly dressed than the other King's squires; his tunic of a clerical mouse-gray wool was so scantily furred, and his belt and dagger were of simple silver. His fingers were ink-stained and there was a spot on his long sleeve. His stubby brown beard was neither creamed nor perfumed and his hair was cut unfashionably short above his ears; but there was sweetness and humor in his firm lips and a quiet amusement behind his alert gaze. Katherine felt instinctively, as had her betters before her from the King down, "Here is someone trustworthy and intelligent, a man truly debonair."

"You do not eat, ma belle?" Geoffrey said presently to Katherine, wiping his mouth on a napkin and taking a long draught of wine. "The goose patty's excellent."

"I can't—" she said, "it's all so bewitching and strange." Her eyes flew back to the royal table. Philippa, used to this sight, did not understand how like a summer dream it was, how impossible to believe that one was actually beholding them in their golds and scarlets, their ermines and coronets, their gauzy veils and jewels; the Plantagenets, a dozen or more of them, laughing, talking, eating, just like all the lesser folk along the side of the Hall.

But Geoffrey understood. "Yes, they're real," he said smiling. He put down his spoon. "You see the King—"

Katherine nodded. The King wore a small gold-pointed crown and the Queen's great empty throne was next to him. The King was half turned from the table and talking to someone a little behind him, someone with a small black head bound by a pearl fillet. "Why, it's Alice Perrers!" cried Katherine. "She's sitting on the arm of the Queen's chair."

"Hush!" whispered Philippa angrily. "You little ninny!"

Geoffrey chuckled. "There are some things we don't say out loud at court. We but whisper them to each other, my dear. But your natural curiosity about your rulers shall be gratified. Look, now—see the dark overblown lady in gold with the smoldering gaze which she keeps fixed on her liege lord next her?"

Katherine nodded.

"That is the Princess Isabel and her husband, Lord Enguerrand de Coucy. She dotes on him, having captured him late, and being perhaps none too sure of his affection. She is just up from childbed, a daughter, alas, another Philippa. There's profusion of Philippas named for the good Queen—that's why we call this one 'Pica.' " He smiled at his betrothed.

"Ay," she said nodding, "the Queen used to call me Philippa la Picarde every time, but she shortened it."

"And the King's sons—" continued Geoffrey, "do you know which they are?" Katherine shook her head, and he continued, "They're all home now, except the Prince of Wales, of course, who is at his court in Aquitaine."

He pointed out the royal princes to Katherine. There was Thomas of Woodstock, the youngest, a boy of eleven, who sat with his elbows on the table, scowling into his gilded cup with an expression of surly boredom. He and Isabel showed their mother's heavy Flemish blood. And there was Lionel of Antwerp, who was eldest of the sons, except for Edward, Prince of Wales. Lionel was a ruddy blond giant and the Queen's favorite. He was good-natured, stupid, a fairly recent and not too disconsolate widower, whose marriage to the Italian merchant princess, Violante Visconti, was in negotiation.

Lionel had just returned from a most uncongenial sojourn in Ireland, where he endeavored to rule the lands inherited from his late wife, Elizabeth de Burgh. He detested the Irish and, being now very drunk, was roaring a scurrilous song about them to the tune the minstrels were playing. Chaucer, while pointing him out to Katherine, regarded his former master with amused affection. Geoffrey had entered the household of Lionel, Duke of Clarence, as a page and progressing to squire had served him loyally. But Geoffrey had been much relieved at his recent transfer to the King's own service, having no liking at all for exile in Ireland.

Edmund of Langley, Earl of Cambridge, sat near Lionel and was much paler and smaller than his brother. Edmund at twenty-four was still a pretty boy, with sloping, almost beardless chin. He smiled often as he chatted with Lady Pembroke on his right, while now and again he looked nervously towards his father, who paid not the slightest attention to him nor to anyone except Alice Perrers. The King sat with his grizzled head twisted up towards Alice, sharing his ruby-studded cup with her, listening to her whispers and breaking now and then into a shout of laughter.

"I think I have them straight now," said Katherine, having followed Geoffrey's identifications breathlessly. "But the King has another son. Which is the Duke of Lancaster?"

Chaucer ran his eyes down the line again and shook his head. "He's not come in yet, though there is his most lovely Duchess, God give her joy."

Katherine heard the drop to seriousness in the squire's voice, which had been, throughout his previous recital, tinged with light irony, and she was startled by the expression in his eyes as they rested on Blanche, Duchess of Lancaster. Katherine glanced instinctively at her sister. But Philippa was discussing the proper distillation of lavender water with Dame Elizabeth Pershore, and not listening.

So Katherine examined the Duchess with avid interest, wondering at first, why she had so great a reputation for beauty. From this distance, at least, the Lady Blanche appeared muted and overshadowed by the other vivid and bejeweled ladies at the High Table. Her blond braids were partially concealed by a simple gauze veil and her pale oval face, calm and passionless as a lily, was turned from the others, while her sea-blue eyes gazed out across the Hall with gentle contemplation.

But as Katherine watched, the Lady Blanche responded to some remark from the Earl of Pembroke and she smiled a smile of piercing sweetness, while inclining her shining head in a gesture both humble and gracious. Katherine was suddenly awed. She is like the painting at Sheppey of the Blessed Virgin, she thought.

"Yes," said Geoffrey, who had been watching the girl's face, "she is a very great lady. The greatest in the land, not excepting the Queen."

"Can she have—has she children?" asked Katherine timidly, for it did not seem possible that this exalted lady might have known the dark urgings of the body, the stir of blood Katherine felt dimly in herself.

Geoffrey nodded slowly. "She has had three—Philippa, who is six, a baby, John, who died at birth, and Elizabeth, who is two years old, I believe."

Katherine considered this and was led on to another question. "Is there true love between the Duke and Duchess, do you think?" she whispered, not unaware of naïveté and boldness but knowing instinctively that she dared ask anything of this wise young man.

A shadow crossed his face, but then he smiled. "Ay, I believe there is and you don't yet know, child, how rare a thing love is at court, and in a royal marriage."

Katherine would have asked more but was diverted by a commotion of running feet outside the entrance to the Hall, and the blare of trumpets, followed by a herald's voice shouting a gabbled string of titles, "John, Duke of Lancaster, Earl of Richmond and Derby, of Lincoln and Leicester, enters here!"

All the company in the Hall, including those at the royal table except the King and Lionel, rose to their feet. "The noble Duke arrives," said Chaucer somewhat dryly, "with, of course, due ceremony and recognition."

Seven or eight young men strode into the Hall together but nobody could have had difficulty in identifying the Duke.

He was magnificent in a red and azure tunic quartered with the lilies of France and the leopards of England. A gold girdle, fastened by the ruby rose of Lancaster, hung on his narrow hips and around his wide muscular shoulders lay the SSS golden collar of Lancaster. John of Gaunt, who had just turned twenty-six last month, was the best made of all the King's sons. He was tall, though not so uncouthly large as Lionel, and he was slender, but not with the meager delicacy of Edmund. In John's face the Plantagenet stamp of long nose, narrow cheeks and deep eye sockets had been softened but not coarsened by the Flemish heritage. His eyes were as bright blue as his father's once had been, his thick hair was tawny yellow as a lion's pelt. His beard was clipped short and his face shaven to disclose a full and passionate mouth.

As he strode down the hall between the kneeling varlets and the bowing courtiers, Katherine felt the impact of a ruthless vitality and pride. He is more king than the King himself, she thought, staring fascinated. And many others thought so too, though not with her uncritical admiration. It was the Lady Blanche's vast inheritance that had raised the King's third son to such power and there were some who thought him dangerously edging towards royal prerogatives and negligent of the proper respect due his elder brothers, the Prince of Wales and Lionel.

The King had turned from Alice Perrers when his son's advent was announced and waited, frowning a little, until the Duke came up to the royal table and, kneeling, quickly kissed his father's hand and whispered something at which the King's face grew grim; he banged his fist upon the table, nodding slowly.

The Duke stood up again and raised his hand towards the minstrels, who hushed their instruments. He threw back his shoulders and though addressing the royal table, spoke in ringing tones designed to reach everyone throughout the Great Hall.

"A message has just come from our royal brother, the Prince of Wales. There is monstrous news. Henry Trastamare the Bastard has foully usurped the throne of Castile and was crowned on Easter Day!"

A shocked murmur ran around the Hall; it swelled to a chorus of dismay.

The Duke waited for the sensation to subside, then went on, "King Pedro, the rightful, most Christian and unhappy monarch has applied to us for aid against the shameful traitor!"

Now many knights jumped forward and there were exultant shouts. Katherine, who understood nothing of this but was gazing entranced at the handsome Duke, heard Chaucer say, "Welladay, so here we go again, poor England."

"What do you mean?" she asked, peering around at him.

He shrugged. "That the King and my Lord Duke will be on fire to right so grievous a wrong, particularly a wrong backed by France, and we shall fight again."

"Don't you want to fight?" said Katherine with some disapproval.

He chuckled in his throat. "I *have* fought, been captured and ransomed, too. I no longer need to prove myself the flower of chivalry, and I dare say I can serve my King better on missions."

"Missions," repeated Katherine, raising her chin and feeling a little sorry for Philippa. Her eyes flew back to the Duke of Lancaster. He had seated himself beside his wife and was talking animatedly across her to his father and brothers. She could no longer hear what was said but she saw that they were all in a buzz of excitement and indignation. Their royal blue eyes were flashing, and even little Thomas had lost his surly boredom and was hanging over the Duke asking eager questions.

How splendid they were, thought Katherine, and her heart swelled with hero worship, directed towards the lovely Lady Blanche as much as towards the Duke. Of all the handsome people, those two were the best-looking, and a fairy enchantment surrounded them like a nimbus.

"Ah, yes," said Chaucer, watching her, "the Plantagenets dazzle like the noonday sun—but the Lancasters," he added on a lower note, glancing up at the Lady Blanche, "that one there doesn't dazzle, she glows, gentle as the Queen of Heaven. I think, my dear—" he interrupted himself abruptly, "that you are causing some interest across the Hall."

Katherine had been entirely unaware of herself during the last hour. Now she followed Chaucer's gaze and reddened. Several of the Duke's retinue, after accompanying him into the Hall, had seated themselves at a table directly opposite.

Two of the young men were looking hard at Katherine and whispering.

For the one who stared with such intentness that he seemed to be scowling at her, she felt an immediate antipathy. He had an ugly florid face, square as a box, and kinky hair, short and dusty, buff in color like sheep's wool. His beard was of the same stubborn texture, so that it did not part neatly in the middle like that of other men, but jutted in a fringe. A jagged purple scar puckered his right cheek and contributed to the repulsion Katherine felt. The small scowling eyes were staring across at her with frank purpose, a look that even Katherine recognized as desire.

"Sir Hugh Swynford finds you appealing, it would seem," said Chaucer with grim amusement. "And so does the elegant young de Cheyne. Pica—" he said on a lower note to his betrothed, "we shall have some ado to guard your little sister's maidenhead."

Now Katherine recognized the young man who sat beside Sir Hugh, for he smiled at her and kissed his hand when he at length caught her eye.

"Why, it's the squire who came last year with the message from you, Philippa," cried Katherine, delighted. She smiled and waved back. "He's changed a lot, his beard has grown."

"Katherine!" cried Philippa sharply. "Behave yourself! De Cheyne's no squire now, he's been knighted—and knights are no concern of yours. You'll get into trouble, my girl, if you encourage any of the courtiers, especially of the Duke's retinue. They're only after one thing. You should know that much, even at convent." Philippa gave an exasperated sigh, foreseeing many complications from Katherine's arrival which had not previously occurred to her. She herself did not think the girl's looks particularly striking, indeed she had not yet substituted this new Katherine for her memories of the scrawny, sickly child she had last seen. But Alice Perrers' detestable cooing voice had given one warning and it seemed now that Katherine was attracting an undue amount of attention for a humble little convent girl in an ill-fitting dress. Even Geoffrey, her own betrothed, had spent the whole suppertime answering the girl's silly questions and displaying undue warmth.

Philippa had no sentimental illusions about her betrothal, nor the temperament for sighings and moanings and courtly love games. Her marriage to Chaucer was eminently fitting.

The Queen had suggested it, having in her maternal way considered various yeomen and squires in the royal entourage, picked out a handful of possibilities and given Philippa her choice of these and also the assurance of a dowry of ten marks yearly and continued patronage.

Philippa had preferred Geoffrey Chaucer to the other possibilities, though he was but the son of a vintner. Still, he had been attached to the royal family since childhood and was much liked by them. He was also educated as well as monk or clerk, and a sensible, good-humored man, quite ready to marry and found a family, being already twenty-six. The betrothal pledge had been exchanged on Shrove Tuesday under the Queen's benign eye and the marriage planned for Whitsuntide.

It was all orderly and seemly as Philippa liked it, though during the last weeks of greater intimacy she had come to know some unexpected things about her betrothed. He spent a ridiculous amount of money on buying books and time on reading them and also on scribbling verses—these traits she intended to regulate after marriage. And she had discovered that he had a romantic attachment for the Duchess of Lancaster, which troubled Philippa not at all, though she thought it silly. Some great ladies might amuse themselves by dalliance with humble squires but not Lady Blanche, who had never spoken more than a dozen words to Geoffrey, for all that he had translated a devotional poem to the Holy Blessed Virgin and presented it to the Duchess. There was nothing disquieting in that to a sensible woman, which, thought Philippa, reverting to her worry, Katherine apparently was not. There was but one obvious course. Philippa decisively mopped up a dab of honey paste with the last morsel of her bread, and decided to approach the Queen tomorrow on the matter of Katherine's marriage, no matter how ill the poor lady might be. Symkyn-at-Woode, one of the sergeants-at-arms, would do. He was a bluff, hearty soul, widowered twice over, so would have experience enough to keep a giddy young wife in line.

Philippa's plans for Katherine were destined to be thwarted. No sooner had the royal family arisen and filed out to their own apartments, thus releasing the rest of the compay, than the two young men from across the Hall darted over to present themselves. Geoffrey performed the introductions. "Sir Hugh Swynford, Sir Roger de Cheyne—the Damoiselle de Roet."

"Those beautiful eyes that slay me with cruel arrows I have seen once before," said Roger softly in French to Katherine. "More enchanting now even than in the little convent parlor. I've longed to see you again, ma toute belle."

Katherine felt a sharp pinch on her arm and heard Philippa give a warning cough, so that though she flushed and her heart beat fast with pleasure, she lowered her lids and did not answer. He was more charming than ever, she thought, with his red lips and warm brown eyes. She contrived to look up at him through her lashes with an artless coquetry, seductive enough to the experienced Roger but entirely devastating to the other man, the florid, scowling Sir Hugh, at whom she had not even glanced.

Geoffrey had drawn back a little and was watching them all with a cocked eyebrow and his air of quiet amusement, but Philippa, aware of turgid currents that were quite out of place, was not amused at all.

"You speak gallantly to my sister, Sir Roger," she said stonily. "You must not tease her, she's very ignorant." As Roger paid no attention to Philippa but continued to gaze amorously at Katherine, Philippa threw her betrothed a beseeching look.

Geoffrey came to her rescue. "You have recently married, I think, Sir Knight," he said, bowing to Roger. "How do you leave your lady wife?"

"Oh," whispered Katherine involuntarily. She twisted her fingers tight in a fold of her velvet gown, feeling that her disappointment burned on her face like a brand.

"Why she's well enough," said Roger lightly. "She stays on the manor, of course, since she is enceinte—Ma damoiselle," he smiled at Katherine, "will you not come out in the pleasaunce with me? There's a troupe of jugglers and a performing bear you might like to see."

Before Philippa could voice her sharp interdiction, Katherine raised her eyes and said quietly, "No, thank you, Sir Roger. I'm journey-tired. I've been traveling for days."

There was a sudden mature dignity in her low voice that startled all of them. Roger, who was accustomed to overeasy conquests, laughed good-humoredly and his melting eyes caressed her with added interest. Geoffrey thought, Good. The beautiful country mouse is not so simple after all. Philippa gave a relieved grunt and said briskly, "Well, then, let's go to bed. By your leave, sirs, may we pass."

But it was not Roger who blocked the way. It was the other

knight, Hugh Swynford. "Damoiselle," he said, swaying a little and frowning at Katherine, "I shall escort you safely across
the courtyard, by God."

His speech was thick, with a heavy pause between each
word, and Katherine, despite her dismay over Roger and the
repulsion she felt for this other knight, had a momentary desire to giggle. He must be drunk, she thought, this scowling
lout with the ram's wool hair.

"By all means, Sir Hugh," said Geoffrey. "Let's all see the
ladies to their staircase."

"And sing as we go——" laughed Roger. "Ma belle amie, que
voit la rose——" he caroled, taking Katherine's arm, while
Hugh strode silently on her other side.

Chaucer and his betrothed followed behind, since the
knight's rank must precede them from the Hall. "This is most
interesting," he said to Philippa, watching the three figures
ahead as they crossed the courtyard, which was illumined by
both moon and torchlight. "Your little Katherine has 'le diable au corps.' Both these noble knights wish to bed her."

"It's disgusting——" snapped Philippa. "We must get her
married *at once*. I think Symkyn-at-Woode, you know that
sergeant, he wants a wife and——"

"I think not, m'amie," said Geoffrey. "I think she may look
higher than Symkyn. This Sir Hugh is not married and he de-
vours her with his eyes. If Katherine is careful and chaste——"

"Oh, no——" interrupted Philippa, "that's impossible! She
has no dowry and the Swynfords are of old lineage, great
landowners in Lincolnshire. Katherine wouldn't presume."

Geoffrey smiled a bit sadly to himself. He patted Philippa's
plump little hand and said nothing, but he had heard the unconscious note of jealousy in the protesting voice. Ay, he
thought, it would be hard to marry a simple squire, a tradesman's son and a scribbler, while one's little sister captured a
landed knight. This had not happened yet, of course, but with
Katherine, he thought, looking at the graceful violet figure
moving ahead between the two knights, anything might happen. There was a mark of destiny on her, quite apart from her
beauty. He wondered what her horoscope foretold, perhaps a
conjunction of Venus and Neptune that explained the rare
and subtle quality she emanated.

She made one think of hot, tumbling love and sensual sport,
but she made one think of spiritual matters, too, like the mystic rose of tinted glass in St. Paul's window. A strangely fasci-

nating young creature but not for him. His heart was laid at the feet of the lovely white Duchess and his practical future lay with Philippa, who suited him well enough.

# III

DURING THE NEXT two days at Windsor, Hugh Swynford afforded much amusement to certain of the Duke's men.

Roger de Cheyne had hastened to share the joke with his friends, that Swynford whom they privily called the Battling Saxon Ram, had at last been touched by a softer passion than hunting or fighting: that he had become infatuated with Philippa la Picarde's little sister from the convent.

"He gawps at her," said Roger, chuckling, "like a slaughtered ox, sniffs after her like a starveling hound. It's incredible! Did you see him at Mass this morning? When the lovely little de Roet dropped her beads, Swynford stumbled headlong all over old Lady Atherton, rushing to pick them up, and the girl never noticed. Picked them up herself. Most diverting— not that I blame him. I too, find the maiden tempting."

His audience laughed, and bets were laid on Swynford's chance of success in seducing Katherine.

Katherine herself was almost unaware of Sir Hugh. She saw him occasionally and knew that he stared at her a great deal, but so did other young men, and she was so much absorbed in the excitements presented to her that she had thought for nothing else.

From morning to night there was music to listen to and pageantry to watch. Each afternoon a troupe of mummers set up a stage in the lower ward and gave an episode from the play of St. George, while Katherine gazed wide-eyed at the knight's entrancing adventures. St. George battled with a fearsome Turk who shouted bloodcurdling maledictions, he slew a green dragon from whose nostrils issued real smoke, he vanquished Beelzebub, whose red tail and obscene gestures made the crowd roar with mirth, and he rescued a weeping maiden played by a pretty boy with false breasts and a yellow silk wig.

Almost as interesting as the plays were the tumblers and jugglers; one of the latter, a Florentine, could keep six golden balls in the air at once and sing a love song in his own strange language at the same time. Katherine thought it marvelous.

Each day too there was jousting at the lists outside the castle walls. The ladies' loges were so crowded with the relatives and sweethearts of the contending knights that there was no room for Katherine. Geoffrey, seeing her disappointment, promised that he would smuggle her in somewhere to see the great tournament on Saturday, the last day of the festivities.

Philippa kept strict watch over her sister and saw to it that she herself or another of the Queen's women should always be with the girl, but even Philippa had relaxed into the general atmosphere of gaiety.

She discharged her duties every morning at six when she marshaled the pantry maids: tallied loaves of bread, unlocked and portioned out the day's allotment of the precious spices which would be used in the Queen's apartments, but after that, the Queen being still abed, Philippa was free. She noted that Katherine behaved modestly in public, that Roger de Cheyne did not press his attentions and that Hugh Swynford made no further attempt to speak to Katherine. So she felt that her fears had been unjustified and decided to wait until after the holiday to broach the girl's marriage to Symkyn-at-Woode.

Hugh, however, was awaiting opportunity. He was obsessed by Katherine, and dismally confused by this new sensation. Heretofore his occasional quick lusts had been as quickly satisfied, by whore or peasant, and had certainly never disturbed the tenor of his life.

But this girl, though she had no strong male protector, was yet a knight's daughter and attached, however nebulously, to the Queen. She might not be tumbled in a haymow or tavern, and in the face of her obvious indifference he did not know how to approach her. He watched for chances to see her alone, but there were none, and for the first time in his life he felt diffidence and regret that he was ugly.

On Wednesday evening, his fate relented. There had been showers all afternoon, but after vespers the dying sun sprayed crimson light along the western battlements. In the Queen's ladies' solar there was the usual bustle of preparation for appearance at supper and the clack of women's tongues.

Alice Perrers these last nights had no longer bothered to appear in the solar at all, and the gossip was mostly of her. Katherine was quick to learn, and she now quite understood the reason for Alice's unpopularity. But it did not concern her. The royal family were still only glittering figures to be glimpsed at the High Table, and the Queen only a name. Katherine had nothing to wear except the violet gown borrowed from Matilda and no finery to put on, so she sat idly for a while on the bed that she shared with Philippa and Johanna Cosin, listening to the excited female gabble and longing to be out in the spring dusk. Then she heard the sound of singing outside, a gay lilting air newly come from France.

> *Hè, dame de Vaillance!*
> *Vostre douce semblance,*
> *M'a pris sans defiance—*

Katherine jumped up and, murmuring something to Philippa about a necessary trip to the garderobe, instead ran down the stone stairs and out into the courtyard. There Hugh, who had been waiting, saw her, but she did not see him. She breathed deep of the soft air and followed the singing voices to the walled pleasaunce behind the eastern state apartments. The postern gate was open and she wandered through. The garden smelled of violets and rosemary, and the yew hedges, some as high as her head, had been clipped at the corners of the paths into peacock and lion shapes. There was no one in that part of the garden. The voices, now changed to a sadder tune, came from farther in by the fountain, whose splashing mingled with the plinking of a glittern.

Katherine loved flowers and was particularly sensitive to odors. She stooped to pick a daffodil and pressing the blossom to her nose, inhaled the sweet scent, when she heard the clanking of a sword and dropped the flower guiltily, suspecting that she had no right to be in the royal pleasaunce.

It was Hugh who strode around the corner of the hedge. He still wore his hauberk of chain mail, his sword and his spurs, for he had been jousting that afternoon, and had caught sight of Katherine in the courtyard before he had had time to divest himself of all his armor.

"Good evening, damoiselle," he said in so harsh a voice that she was more puzzled than frightened.

"I'm sorry," she said. "Perhaps I shouldn't be here, but the music was so lovely—and the garden." She smiled, a slow radiant smile, its wistfulness belied by the cleft in her chin and a dimple at the corner of her mouth.

"I'll go back now," she said nervously, for the knight was blocking her way as he had on the first evening, scowling at her beneath his bushy crinkled eyebrows, the scar suddenly livid on his cheek. He breathed like a winded stag and his chunky thick-set body seemed to be trembling.

"Don't stare at me so, Sir Hugh," she cried, trying to laugh. "I'm not a witch or a ghost."

"Witch," he repeated thickly. "Ay, that's it. Witchcraft. You've cast a spell on me."

She saw his mouth working, heard the rasp of his breath, and before she could move, he lunged for her. He grabbed her around the waist with one arm while his other hand tore down the shoulder of her dress. The worn velvet ripped like gauze, exposing her arm and one breast. He crushed her furiously against him and the sharp links of his chain mail ground into her flesh. He bent her backward until her spine cracked. She struggled for breath, then fought him with frantic terror. She beat him in the face with her fists and clawed with her nails until one of her frenzied blows hit his left eye. He tossed his head and loosed her just enough so that she could let out one long agonized scream.

"Don't Katherine, don't—" he panted, his grip on her tightened again. "I want you, I must have you—" He forced her against a hedge, bearing her down towards the ground.

A hand grasped Hugh's shoulder and a powerful arm jerked him upright, off Katherine, who fell to her knees on the path.

"Good God, Swynford," said a voice. "Must you pursue your little amours here?"

Katherine raised her head. One of her braids had come unbound and the cascade of hair half hid the naked shoulder and white breast that was imprinted with bloody flecks from the chain mail. Panting and shivering, she stared up at her rescuer.

It was the great Duke of Lancaster who stood between them on the path, his handsome mouth curled with distaste, his tawny gold hair bright in the dusk. His eyelids drooped over his vivid blue eyes as they always did when he was angry. He looked at his red-faced sweaty knight and spoke in a voice of biting calm. "I find your conduct displeasing, sir.

You disturb the beauty of the evening. Who is this lady, who moreover seems not to share your lust?"

He turned to Katherine and examined her. He saw that she was very young and frightened and that in a pale tearstained face two enormous eyes stared up at him with passionate gratitude. His arrogant mouth softened, he leaned down and gave her his hand. She clung to it as she stumbled to her feet and instinctively she moved near to the Duke, leaning almost on his arm. "My lord," she whispered, "thank you." Her mouth was tinder-dry with fear, her heart pounding in her throat, but she pulled her hair and the torn violet cloth across her breast and stood quietly beside the Duke.

John of Gaunt was touched, alike by her instinctive bid for his protection and by her dignified recovery from sobs and dishevelment. Her beauty he had not yet clearly seen, but he felt the girl's magnetism and turned with increased anger to Hugh. "Who is this lady you've insulted?"

Had it been anyone else but his Duke, Hugh would have replied with equal anger; as it was, he glowered at the ground and said sulkily, "She's naught but sister to Philippa la Picarde, one of the Queen's waiting women. I've not insulted her. She's cast a spell on me. Witchcraft!"

"By Saint George's spear—what nonsense! A spell of your own lust, you tomcat. I say you've most grievously insulted this poor child and—"

"Nay, my lord," interrupted Hugh. He raised his little greenish eyes and gazed at Katherine with a dumb misery. "I wish to marry her," he said heavily, staring at the ground. "She has neither lands nor dowry, but I would marry her."

Katherine gasped and shrank closer to the Duke, but he was staring at his knight with astonishment. "Would you indeed, Hugh?" he said slowly, and Swynford bowed his head.

That changed matters. If this girl were indeed portionless this offer was amazing. Swynford was of good blood and possessed of considerable property. To the Duke, as to all his family, marriage was a commercial transaction, a peacetime weapon for the acquisition of new lands and the extension of power. Love of one's mate was entirely fortuitous, and lovable as was the Lady Blanche, the Duke might not have felt for her such keen devotion had she not brought him vast possessions.

Though like all feudal lords he concerned himself with the marriages, deaths and begetting of his vassals, he would cer-

tainly not have pursued this tawdry little incident further tonight had it not been for the girl and the curiosity she was
beginning to arouse in him. He made one of his quick decisions and spoke in a tone of easy command. "Well, Hugh, go
back to your tent. We can talk of this tomorrow. And you,
damoiselle, come with me to the Duchess. I wish her to see
you."

Swynford bowed, turned on his heel and disappeared down
the path. Katherine was dazed and still said nothing. She obediently followed the Duke through the garden gate and up to
the Lancaster apartments.

The Lady Blanche was sitting on a cushion in the window
seat of her private solar; across her lap there lay a square of
pale blue satin on which she had been embroidering trefoils
in emerald silk. She was dressed in her favorite creamy white,
and as she had not yet changed for the evening her pale gold
head was uncovered and shone against the darkness outside.

Elizabeth and Philippa, her two little girls, played on a
Persian rug by the fireplace, near a minstrel who gently
twanged his harp and sang snatches from the "Chanson de
Roland."

Audrey, the Duchess's chief tiring-woman, moved silently
about her duties, perfuming water in a hand basin and carrying clothes from sundry chests in the solar to the hanging
brackets in the garderobe which served as antechamber to the
latrine.

The room was bright from twenty wax candles and jeweled
with color. The lights glowed on the crimson and olive of the
wall tapestries and twinkled off the bed hangings of silver
brocade.

When the Duke strode in with Katherine, the little girls
ceased playing and stared round-eyed at their father. The
minstrel hushed his harp and pulled his stool into a corner,
waiting for dismissal or command to continue.

The Lady Blanche rose with slow grace and smiled at her
husband. "I did not expect you so soon, my lord." Her serene
blue gaze rested on him tenderly. "I thought you were with
the messenger from Bordeaux."

"I was," said John, "and bad news it is, too—but then I
summoned some gleemen to sing for me in the garden and
banish care for a while. I was disturbed—" He shrugged and
indicated Katherine, who curtsied nervously, conscious of the
curious stares of the tiring-woman and the two little girls.

"Disturbed?" repeated Blanche. "By this child?" She put out her slender white hand to Katherine, smiling kindly, then she leaned forward. "But what's happened? Her gown is torn and there's blood on it. Audrey, fetch warm water and some wine. You're hurt, maiden?"

"Not much, Your Grace," said Katherine, very low. "My Lord Duke did save me."

"From what?" exclaimed Blanche, putting her arm around the girl.

"From rough love-making," said John, laughing suddenly. "But honorable it seems, in the end. Sir Hugh Swynford, you know the Lincolnshire knight they call the Saxon Ram, wishes to wed this young lady—an interesting idea."

"Oh, no," cried Katherine, sending the Duke a look of piteous bewilderment. "I'm sure he didn't mean it—and I couldn't, you must see I couldn't!"

"Hush, child," said the Lady Blanche, surprised that anyone should dare gainsay the Duke, whom she saw to be uncomfortable and wishful of escape. Indeed the girl, now brightly illuminated by the candles, had suddenly made an unpleasant impression on John, though he did not know why. True, many might call her beautiful, but to his taste she seemed overcolored and earthy next to the exquisite Blanche. He disliked the flaunting profusion of bronze hair, the redness of her bruised mouth, the black abundance of her lashes, and particularly her eyes that stared at him with urgent pleading. They were too large and gray and gleamed with golden flecks in the candlelight. Her eyes disturbed him, evoking an unreasoned confusion of far-off anger and pain. For an instant he knew that someone else had stared at him like that long ago, and there had been betrayal, then the impression vanished, leaving only sharp resentment.

He turned his back on Katherine and said to Blanche, "I'll see you later, lady." He touched his little daughters' curls and strode out of the room, banging the heavy oak door behind him.

"My lord is hasty sometimes," said Blanche, noting the girl's dismay. "And he has grave matters to worry him." She was well used to John's impulsive acts, as to his occasional dark moods, and knew how to temper them, or bide her time until they passed. She hastened now to minister to the unhappy maiden he had brought her and motioned to Audrey to bring the basin and a towel. Then she lifted the torn strip of violet cloth and the strands of hair from Katherine's shoulder and found the rows of tiny bleeding cuts on the breast beneath. "Tell me about it, my dear," she said quietly, bathing the cuts and salving them with marigold balm.

Hugh sat in his tent on the field near the lists while Ellis his squire removed his armor, but Hugh was unaware of Ellis or his surroundings. His blood ran thick as hot lead in his veins and he suffered desire, shame and confused torment that nothing in his life had prepared him for.

Hugh Swynford was of pure Saxon blood except for one Danish ancestor, the fierce invading Ketel who sailed up the Trent in 870 pillaging and ravishing as he went. A Swynford girl was amongst those ravished, but she must have inspired some affection in her Dane since she lured him from his thorpe in Lincolnshire to her own home at the swine's ford in southern Leicestershire, where he settled for some years and adopted her family's name.

The Swynfords were all fighters. Hugh's forefathers had resisted the Norman invasion until the grown males of their clan had been exterminated, and even now, three hundred years later, Hugh stubbornly rejected any tinge of Norman graces or romanticism. He went to Mass occasionally as a matter of course, but at heart he was pagan as the savages who had once danced around Beltane's fire on May Night, who worshiped the ancient oaks and painted themselves with blue woad—a plant indeed which still grew on Hugh's manor in Lincolnshire.

He was an ungraceful knight, impatient of chivalric rules, but in real battle he was a shrewd and terrifying fighter.

Hugh's branch of the Swynford family had long ago left Leicestershire and returned to Lincolnshire by the river Trent south of Gainsborough; and when Hugh was a child, his father, Sir Thomas, had fulfilled a long-time ambition and bought the manor of Kettlethorpe where Ketel the Dane had first settled. For this purchase he used proceeds from the sale of his second wife Nichola's estates in Bedfordshire, at which the poor lady wept and lamented woefully, for she was afraid of the towering forests around Kettlethorpe, and of the marshes and the great river Trent with its stealthy death-dealing floods. The Lady Nichola was also afraid of the dark stone manor house, which was said to be haunted by a demon dog, the pooka hound. Most of all she was afraid of her husband who beat her cruelly and constantly reproached her for her barrenness. So her wailings and laments were done in secret.

Hugh thought little about Kettlethorpe one way or the other, beyond accepting it as his home and heritage, and he was a restless youth. At fifteen he struck out into the world. He joined the army under the King, when Edward invaded Scotland, and there met John of Gaunt, who was then only the Earl of Richmond. The two boys were of the same age and Hugh conceived for the young Prince, whose charm and elegance of manner were so unlike his own, a grudging admiration.

At sixteen, Hugh, thirsting for more battle, had fought under the Prince of Wales at Poitiers. Hugh had killed four Frenchmen with his battle-axe, and shared later in the hysterical rejoicing at the capture of King Jean of France.

Hugh won his spurs after that and returned to Kettlethorpe to find that his father had suffered an apoplectic stroke in his absence. Hugh stayed home until Sir Thomas finally died and Hugh became lord of the manor. But as soon as his father's body had been laid in a granite tomb near the altar of the little Church of Sts. Peter and Paul at Kettlethorpe, Hugh made new plans for departure.

He detested his stepmother, the Lady Nichola, whom he considered a whining rag of a woman overgiven to fits and the seeing of melancholy visions, so he left her and his lands in charge of a bailiff. He outfitted himself with his father's best armor and favorite stallion, then engaged as squire young Ellis de Thoresby, the son of a neighboring knight from Nottinghamshire across the Trent.

Thus properly accoutered, Hugh rode down to London, to the Savoy Palace. He owed knight's service to the Duke of Lancaster by reason of Hugh's manor at Coleby, which belonged to the Duke's honor of Richmond, but he had not the money for the fee, and in any case much preferred to become the Duke's retainer, well pleased that his feudal lord should also be the youth he had campaigned with in Scotland.

Though the intervening years had made many changes in John of Gaunt's personal life, for he had married the Lady Blanche and thereby become the wealthiest man in the land, Hugh's own interests remained unchanged. He fought when there was war, and when there was not he pursued various private quarrels, and hunted. Hawking bored him with its elaborate ritual of falconry, for he liked direct combat and a dangerous opponent. The wild stag and the wild boar were the quarries he liked best to pursue through the dense forests. He was skilled at throwing the spear and could handle the longbow as well as any of the King's yeomen, but in close fighting he was supreme.

It was said of him that he had strangled a wolf with his bare hands in the wilds of Yorkshire, and that it was the wolf's fangs which had laid open his cheek and puckered it into the jagged scar, but nobody knew for certain. The Duke's retinue now numbered over two hundred barons, knights and squires, and a man so morose and uncourtly as Hugh excited little curiosity amongst his fellows. They disliked him and let him alone.

But when his extraordinary wish to marry the little de Roet became known, he inspired universal interest at last.

Katherine's frantic protests and tears were of no avail against Hugh's determination and everyone else's insistence that she had stumbled into an unbelievable piece of luck.

The Queen's ladies said it, even Alice Perrers said it, and Philippa scolded morning, noon and night.

"God's nails, you little dolt," Philippa cried, "you should be down on your knees thanking the Blessed Virgin and Saint Catherine, instead of mewling and cowering like a frightened rabbit. My God, you'll be *Lady* Katherine with your own manor and serfs, and a husband who seems to dote on you as well!"

"I can't, I can't. I loathe him," Katherine wailed.

"Fiddlefaddle!" snapped Philippa, whose natural envy increased her anger. "You'll get over it. Besides he won't be around to bother you much. He'll soon be off with the Duke to fight in Castile."

This was pale comfort but there was little Katherine could do except plead illness, hide in the solar and avoid seeing Hugh.

The Lady Blanche on hearing of the girl's aversion to the marriage had broached the matter to her husband and found him unexpectedly obdurate and impatient. "Of course Swynford's a fool to take her, I believe he could have had that Torksey heiress whose lands adjoin his, but I think he *is* bewitched. Since he lusts so for her, let him have the silly burde."

"You dislike her?" Blanche was puzzled by his vehemence. "I find her quite charming. I remember her father, a gallant soldier. When I was a child he once brought me a little carved box from Bruges."

"I don't dislike the girl. Why should I? I dislike wasting time or thought on such a trivial matter when we're going to war. And the sooner they marry the better, since Swynford will sail for Aquitaine this summer. He might as well beget an heir before he goes."

Blanche nodded. She was no more sentimental about marriage than anyone else, but she was sorry for Katherine and sent a page over with a generous present to help alleviate the girl's unhappiness.

During the days of Katherine's rebellion, when neither Philippa's annoyance nor the teasing of the other damoiselles could budge her from the solar, Katherine naturally thought of the prioress. Surely, thought Katherine, convincing herself against all reason, Godeleva would help her resist this horrible fate everyone else wished to force on her, and though in mortal terror of seeing Hugh, she determined to sneak somehow down to the village and find the prioress. But before this opportunity came, Long Will Finch appeared at the door of the solar with a letter from Godeleva to Katherine. It was crisply worded and contained a suggestion of reproach as it said that since the Queen was apparently still ill, Godeleva and Dame Cicily had decided to return to Sheppey, having heard of a safe party of Canterbury pilgrims with whom they might travel part way.

She trusted that Katherine was doing credit to her convent training and obeying her betters and would not forget to remind the Queen of Sheppey's needs when it was possible.

She ended with blessings and affection in Christ.

"So she's gone," said Katherine desolately, looking up at Will Finch.

"Yes, damoiselle," said the messenger with respect, touching his forehead. The tiring-maid had told him all the gossip. How one of the Duke's knights wanted to marry the little de Roet and of how she had received special favor and notice by the Duke and Duchess themselves. "I hear you've found good fortune already," he said diffidently. "May I wish you happiness."

She looked at him sadly and gave him a half groat for his services. Thanks to the Lady Blanche's present, she had a purse full of silver now and a new dress hastily made over from one of the Duchess's worn ones. It was of green brocade and the surcote was richly furred with miniver; also, Blanche had presented a woolen cloak, a silver girdle and netted cauls for the hair.

This finery lay across the bed untouched. It was impossible to resent the kind Duchess's generosity; indeed how, except by presents, could a girl in Katherine's position exist at all? Yet she had shrunk from putting them on, as she recoiled from all the evidences of Hugh's interest, direct and indirect.

But she could not go hiding herself forever in the solar, where she by no means had privacy, and the Queen's ladies twitted her continually about her conquest.

Katherine was alone now because it was the day of the final tournament, and everyone in the castle except the sick Queen and the scullions had gone down to the lists. Though the ladies had urged her and Philippa had commanded, Katherine, who three days ago had so joyously looked forward to this spectacle, would not go.

She was fifteen and incapable of self-analysis. She knew only that this gorgeous new world, at first so entrancing, had resolved itself into a chaotic mass of helplessness and fears, against which she struggled blindly, finding no weapon but evasion. She was much frightened of meeting Hugh again, but vaguely she knew too that this unhappiness was reinforced by a more subtle one. She longed to see the Duke, and this longing upset her as much as Hugh's obsession, for the Duke had not been her champion after all; he had seemed to show her sympathy and as suddenly withdrawn it, and during that moment in his wife's bower he had looked at her with cold distaste, with, in fact, an undoubted and inexplicable repulsion.

Katherine went to the slitted window and gazed down to the plain far below, by the river, where she could see the lists, and the forked pennants of the contending knights as their identifying flags fluttered from the pavilions. It was high noon now and the hot sun flashed off the silver armor; great clouds of dust obscured the actual field, but she could hear the roars of excitement from a thousand throats, and the periodic blare of the heralds' trumpets.

She turned into the room and throwing herself across the bed, hit her bruised breast. She winced and though the tiny cuts were healing the pain seemed to strike through to her heart. If I pray to the Blessed Virgin, she thought, maybe she'll help me, and the forlorn hope brought guilt, for she had missed Mass these two days of hiding in the solar. True, some of the courtiers did not go every day to Mass, Philippa often skipped herself, but the convent habit was strong.

Katherine slipped to her knees on the prie-dieu and began, *"Ave Maria gratia plena,"* but the whispered words echoed bleakly in the empty solar. Then she heard a heavy knock on the oak door.

Katherine, clad only in her linen shift, threw the woolen cloak around her and nervously called, "Come in."

The door opened and Hugh Swynford stood on the threshold looking at her somberly. He was dressed in full armor, for he was to be an afternoon contender in the lists. His chain mail hauberk was covered by the ceremonial white silk jupon embroidered with three golden boars' heads on a black chevron, his coat of arms. He looked formidable, and cleaner than she had yet seen him, his crinkled hair as light as straw, his square beard close-trimmed.

He advanced into the room and Katherine stifled a moan and then hot anger rose in her. Holy Blessed Mother, she thought, I pray to you and this is how you reward me!

She wrapped the cloak around her and stood tall and stiff against the wall, her face hardened like the carved stone corbel. "Yes, Sir Hugh," she said. "I'm quite alone and helpless. Have you come to ravish me?"

Hugh's eyes dropped. Dull red crept up from his mailed gorget. "Katherine—I had to see you—I—I bring you this."

He opened his clenched hand, holding it out stiffly, his eyes on the rush-strewn floor. On his calloused palm there lay a massive gold ring, carved claws around a sea-green beryl.

"Take it," he said hoarsely, as she did not move. "The betrothal ring."

"I don't want it," she said. "I don't *want* it!" She folded her arms tight against her chest. "I don't want to marry you."

His hand closed again over the ring; she saw the muscles of his neck quiver, and the scar on his cheek go white, but he spoke with control.

"It is arranged, damoiselle. Your sister consents, the Duke of Lancaster consents—and the Queen."

"The Queen?" repeated Katherine faintly. "You've seen the Queen?"

"I sent her a message through Lady Agnes. The Queen is pleased."

It was then that Katherine gave up hope. The Queen, the concept of the Queen, had always ruled her destiny as it had her father's. She owed her life to the Queen, and all her loyalty. Of what use was rebellion anyway, for, as Philippa kept asserting, no woman followed her own inclination in marriage. She knew better than to doubt Hugh's word. Brutal and stupid as he might be, he would also be bluntly honest. And now at her continued silence his ready anger flared.

"The Queen thinks me lack-wit to take you, no doubt! They all do. I see them sniggering behind their hands—that scurvy fop de Cheyne—" He scowled towards the window and the noises of the jousting. "His pretty womanish face. Pthaw!" And he spat on the floor.

"Why do you want to marry me?" said Katherine quietly. "Since I bring you nothing but my unwilling body."

He looked at her startled. Certainly he had not meant marriage until the Duke interrupted them in the garden. His assertion then had astonished himself. Was it an aura cast over her by the ducal protection, was it a cool integrity in the girl herself, and the increasing effect on him of her beauty, or was it the hunter's instinct for capture and total subjugation? His slow mind balked at reasons. He knew only that his longing for her was an anguish tinged with fear. It would never have occurred to him to speak of love, so he found refuge again in the excuse he had given the Duke.

"By Saint Anthony and his temptations, maiden, I don't know. You've cast a spell on me—or slipped me a love philter."

From weariness and futility, Katherine suddenly laughed. "I wish that I _had_ a love philter, so I might drink it too."

At her laugh his heavy face brightened, his little eyes sought hers in sudden pleading. "The ring, Katherine, put on the ring," he whispered, holding it out to her again, "and say the vows with me."

She bowed her head and held her hand out slowly. His blunt fingers shook as he pushed the ring down her middle finger where it hung heavy and loose as an iron shackle. "I, Hugh, plight thee, Katherine, my troth, as God is my witness." He swallowed hard, crossing himself.

Katherine looked down at the ring and the square, freckled sweating hand that clasped hers. She exhaled her breath in a long sigh, "I, Katherine, plight thee, Hugh—my troth, as God is my witness."

So be it, she thought. Her aversion to him had not lessened, but she found a bitter new peace in the surrender. He leaned towards her for the betrothal kiss and she yielded her cool mouth, then drew back. He let her go, finding this quiet self-possessed girl far more awesome than the one who had fought him in the garden.

"My Katherine," he said humbly, "will you come to the lists and see me joust now? I—I should like to wear your colors—"

A sardonic voice spoke in her head. Ah yes, it said, this is what you dreamed of, little fool, those nights at Sheppey. This is the fairy tale come true—a knight who asks to wear your colors at the King's tournament.

"I fear I've nothing to give you, sir," she said flushing, "except—wait—" She looked at the Lady Blanche's brocade dress and, quickly decisive, ripped the long green silk tippet from the left sleeve. "Will this do?"

He took the bright flimsy streamer and held it as though it burned his fingers. "Thank you," he muttered. "I shall hope to do you credit. I'll send back a page to guide you to the lists." He turned stiffly in his armor and the door banged shut behind him.

Katherine sank on the window seat, staring at her betrothal ring. Her first jewel. Massive and unwieldy, it looked on her small roughened hand. It was a cabochon beryl carved with Hugh's boarhead crest and far too large, since he had worn it himself. The beryl, like all stones, had talismanic powers, it gave victory in battle and protection to the wearer, and it had cost Hugh something to part with it, though he had other amulets to rely on.

Though Katherine knew nothing of this, she could not help but take pleasure in the possession of a ring and feel, especially now that Hugh was no longer near, a great lightening of mood.

She wound thread around her finger to hold the ring and gradually her natural optimism returned. She was honorably betrothed, she had pretty clothes to wear, and she would see the tournament after all. What excuse then for moping, and bewailing that the conditions surrounding these admirable facts were not as she had wanted them? "A bas la tristesse!" said Katherine aloud, and while she washed she hummed the gay French song she had heard in the garden, "Hè, Dame de Vaillance!"

When she had dressed herself in the long green gown, fastened the girdle low on her slender hips and bound her hair into two silver-filleted cauls on either side of her face, much as Alice Perrers wore hers, Katherine looked in the hand mirror and was startled, not by her beauty, which still seemed to her negligible, but by her air of sophistication. Her high white forehead and the delicate arched eyebrows looked exactly like those of all the noble ladies. If she pursed her mouth it became the two crimson cherry halves so much admired. She could see that the miniver-trimmed surcote disclosed half-moons of bosom and clung to her long waist without a wrinkle. Even the Duchess had not so sinuous a line. I look like one of them, she thought proudly, a court lady. Except for her hands. They were yet reddened from the winter's chilblains, and the nails ragged and short, for she still sometimes bit them.

Alice Perrers had pomades and unguents as well as face paints in her chest beneath the window. Katherine brazenly rummaged in the chest until she found a rose-water cream which she rubbed into her hands, so as not to shame the betrothal ring.

Honesty compelled her to admit that it was to Hugh she owed the extent of her transformation from the shabby little girl at Sheppey, and when the page he had sent for her tapped on the door, she followed him down to the lists with eager anticipation.

# IV

WHEN KATHERINE and her guide arrived at the lists it was in the intermission before the final melee. Outside the stockades, the common folk who had not been fortunate or agile enough to find perches on top of the barrier were milling about, gulping winkles and pasties and jostling for position near the cracks between the boards where they might see something of the jousting when it recommenced.

The page led Katherine through a gilded gate and up wooden steps to the huge Lancastrian loge, as Hugh had bidden him, and he found for her space on a red-cushioned bench far off to one side and directly under the brightly painted canopy that sheltered the loge.

The bench to which the page led Katherine was already fulsomely occupied by two ladies connected with the Lancastrian retinue: Lady de Houghton, and Dame Pernelle, sister of Sir Robert Swyllington, who was the Duke's chamberlain at Pontefract Castle.

Both these ladies were women of mature years with a nice appreciation of their own consequence. As Katherine squeezed herself down beside them they received her flustered apologies with cold astonishment.

"Who in the world—" said Lady de Houghton to her friend, not bothering to lower her voice. Dame Pernelle shrugged and both stout ladies, breathing heavily, for it was warm under the canopy, looked down their noses at Katherine and waited.

"Katherine de Roet, sister to Philippa la Picarde, Queen's panterer. I've—I've just come to court, my ladies," said Katherine nervously, trying to shrink into the smallest possible bulk.

"Ah—" said Dame Pernelle in a tone of enlightenment. "The Guienne *herald*'s daughter, ah yes—one has heard something." She raised her eyebrows significantly and glanced down towards the dais where the Duchess sat in a carved gold armchair.

Katherine, quite aware of the disparaging emphasis on "herald," said quickly, "My father was knighted on the field at Brétigny, my lady. Shall I move to the end of the bench— it won't crowd you so?"

They accepted her courtesy with a grudging murmur and continued to give her affronted stares. By what right did this chit think herself entitled to share a bench with ladies of their rank! And even if gossip were true and one of the Duke's knights had actually proposed marriage, it hadn't happened yet, and the girl should have been placed with her sister in the space allotted to the royal servants. "Insinuating baggage," said Dame Pernelle in the air, "aping her betters." For she had just discovered that the quality of miniver which trimmed Katherine's surcote surpassed her own fur, while the proud and lovely line of the long white throat up to the small jaw and averted profile were equally infuriating.

Katherine's ears grew hot under the silver cauls, and she stared straight ahead, biting her lips.

Suddenly she was rescued, and in a way that silenced the ladies, though in no way decreased their resentment. The Duchess, turning her chair to accept a cup of wine from a page, caught sight of Katherine, smiled at the girl and seeing that she looked uncomfortable, raised her pale, bejeweled hand and beckoned.

Katherine, blushing hotly, for those on all the nearest benches craned around to see, most thankfully obeyed the summons and, clambering past the ample knees beside her, ran down the steps to the velvet-covered platform at the front of the loge.

"Your first tournament, my dear, isn't it?" asked Blanche gently. "Sit here where you can see well." She indicated a cushion on the corner of the platform near her chair.

Katherine's heart melted with gratitude.

The Duchess was today dazzling as the southern May, having dressed to please her husband's taste, in full magnificence of jewels and ermine. Her silver-gilt hair was twined with pearls and she wore her gold and diamond coronet. She smelt of jasmine and Katherine adored her. She had felt this adoration once before in far lesser degree for Dame Gisela, the youngest and prettiest of the nuns at Sheppey, but Dame Gisela had been too ascetic and pious to reciprocate. Since coming to England there had been for Katherine no one special to love, except of course the statues of the Blessed Virgin, and St. Sexburga and St. Catherine. Which the prioress said were quite enough.

Blanche was accustomed to adoration, but she had the warmth of a great lady and she was drawn to the girl. She glanced at the boar-crested betrothal ring on Katherine's childish hand, saw where the tippet had been ripped from the sleeve of her gift, and reconstructed what must have happened.

She leaned down, saying, "I wish you happiness, my dear," then turned quickly, her blue eyes focusing on the field as two heralds with trumpets marched solemnly towards each other. Blanche, whose famous father, Henry, Duke of Lancaster, had been the foremost knight in the kingdom, had wit-

nessed many tournaments and appreciated each point of ceremony and honor. She listened intently to the heralds who announced a preliminary joust between John, Baron de Mowbray, and a Gascon knight, the Sieur de Pavignac.

These names meant nothing to Katherine and during the
ceremonious exchange betwee the heralds and poursuivants
on each side, she had time to look around her.

The lists here at Windsor were very large, with stockades
enclosing the hundred-and-fifty-yard field, and permanent
loges built in tiers on either side for the spectators. The royal
loge, canopied in gold and red striped silk, was in dead center
of the southern side, so that the sun might not bother the
royal eyes. The King being present today, the lily and leopard
flag fluttered over the canopy.

The Lancastrian loge adjoined the royal one, and Katherine had a good view of the King, who seemed in high spirits,
laughing, calling out jests and drinking frequently from a
gold and ruby cup presented by one of his squires.

Geoffrey Chaucer was not in evidence because, as Katherine found out later, he had not been able to attend the tournament at all. William of Wykeham, the King's architect, had
heartlessly scnt Geoffrey on a quick trip to London after the
precious pieces of stained glass needed to finish the west window of Henry the Third's renovated chapel in time for the
high ceremonial Mass tomorrow.

Nor was Alice Perrers to be seen. The Queen's chair was
occupied by her daughter, the Princess Isabel de Coucy, and
all the surrounding lords and ladies were of the highest rank.

The Queen's waiting women were huddled together on the
last bench of an adjoining loge and Katherine could not have
distinguished Philippa at all except that her sister got up and
waved at her, accurately expressing by means of the wave her
astonishment and approval at seeing her.

Katherine's interest was jerked abruptly back to the lists as
there was a roar from the crowd, a fanfare of trumpets from
the heralds and a marshal waving his white baton, who
shouted, "In the name of God and Saint George, come forth
to do battle!" At either end of the lists the squires loosed bridles, and two great destriers thundered towards each other
down the field. Clods flew from the hoofs while the riders,
with lances poised to aim at the opposing shields, lowered
their helmeted heads and braced themselves for the shock.

The crash of wood and metal was deafening, sparks flew

from the armor, the crowd shouted approval, which soon changed to a groan of disappointment. At the moment of collision the Baron de Mowbray's charger had veered too far left, the Gascon knight's lance had thus glanced off Mowbray's shield onto his hauberk and, lodging in the joint of the iron roundel which protected his shoulder, prized him out of the saddle, while the stallion was thrown back on its haunches. The baron lay on the ground, a helpless mass of armor. The Gascon knight raised his visor and grinned complacently towards the royal loge.

"Well done!" cried the King, tossing a jeweled medal of St. George towards the victor. "A noble course."

But the crowd of peasants, servants and villeins who had hoisted themselves around the edges of the stockade were not so chivalrous. They booed the foreigner who had unseated their English baron and they booed the discomfited Mowbray, too, as his squires hoisted him onto his feet and he walked angrily off the field.

"That was bad luck for Mowbray—his destrier is not worthy," said the Lady Blanche judicially. "The beast was frightened." Several of her entourage crowded around agreeing and discussing the best strains for chargers. Katherine listened and learned. She had wondered where the Duke was, and now she heard that he was making ready in the tents. For he was to take part in the final melee.

"I begged him not to," said Blanche, smiling, "and the King nearly forbade it, since the Duke must not risk injury at this time when the Prince of Wales has such need of him, but my lord will not listen. He so loves deeds of arms." She smiled and spoke with a rueful pride, but her eyes were anxious.

"Is it dangerous, my lady?" asked Katherine timidly. "I—I thought the lances were blunted."

Blanche looked down at the girl and thought the concern was for her betrothed. "So they are," she said, "nowadays, but the melee is a mimic battle and there is always danger— when men fight, I suppose. Look, what's this—"

A knight in brightly polished silvery armor and a covering jupon of blue silk embroidered with tiny deer had ridden up to the barrier in front of the Lady Blanche's loge. His tournament heaume was crested with a stag's head, and he raised the visor as he bowed, disclosing the gay teasing face of Roger de Cheyne. "God's greetings, my Lady Duchess," he called. "I crave a gage from the Damoiselle de Roet to bring me luck in the melee."

Katherine turned red as fire. She had ignored Roger since the night she had found that he was married, nor indeed had he made any further overtures. His action now sprang as much from a spirit of mischief, and desire to tease Hugh Swynford, as it did from his admiration of Katherine.

"She *has* a knight to wear her colors already, Sir Roger," said Blanche, seeing that Katherine did not know what to do.

"I know, my lady," said Roger gaily, "but I still may crave a token from her."

This was quite true and proper. Blanche herself had at different times during the tournament flung flowers, ribbons and even scarves to various worthy knights. "Here, child," she said quickly to Katherine, as she plucked an iris from the bouquet by her chair, "stand up and give him this."

Katherine, her heart beating fast, obeyed the Duchess, tossing the blue flower in a graceful arc, and Roger caught it neatly in his gauntlet. He kissed the iris and tucked it into a joint of his heaume, where it waved jauntily beside the stag's head.

"Grand merci, ma toute belle damoiselle," he called, kissing his hand and lowering the pointed visor. He spurred his stallion and cantered easily down the field towards the other contending knights.

The King himself had watched this pretty byplay with approval. It had been gracefully performed with the requisite style and spirit. So many of the knights had grown lax in these degenerate days, impatient of ritual, and skimping the full chivalric observances. In fact it had been with a view to restoring these and bringing back the glorious days of King Arthur's Round Table that he had instituted the Order of the Garter twenty years ago. He inquired who the knight was, and his master herald, whose business it was to identify all coats of arms, replied that it was the young Sieur de Cheyne, one of the Duke of Lancaster's men; but the King's further inquiry about the favored damoiselle the herald could not answer.

Katherine had subsided into confusion, wishing very much that the debonair Roger of the merry eyes and charming smile could be her knight in earnest, and interested to realize that even the Duchess saw nothing improper in this public attention from a married man. It was all part of the courtly game and not supposed to be taken too seriously.

Hugh Swynford, however, did take it seriously. He had watched Roger's sally down the field with savage uncertainty, not quite sure at that distance exactly what had happened, and he awaited Roger at the barricade. "Who gave you that flower?" He pointed his lance at the nodding blue iris.

Roger raised his visor and grinned. "La petite de Roet, may Venus bless her."

"She's betrothed to *me*." Hugh's eyes narrowed, he looked at Katherine's green streamer which fluttered from his own helmet.

"Splendid, mon gar," said Roger cordially. "She's a beauty, a prize." He smacked his lips delicately and rode on, the blue iris bobbing in rhythm to the horse's trot.

Hugh wheeled his destrier and beckoned to his squire. Ellis de Thoresby eagerly held up the helmet and shield. He was a brawny lad of eighteen, doggedly devoted to his master. Ellis had been born at Thoresby Hall in the heart of Sherwood forest and he was quite as impatient as Hugh was of the finicking graces exhibited by many of the foreign knights.

"Not yet," said Hugh, refusing the helmet and shield. "Where's the Duke?"

"Over there, sir," said Ellis, pointing. "But it's time to buckle your helmet," he added anxiously, for the twenty knights who were to contend on this side of the general melee were starting to line up, while each squire hauled at the bridle of his master's destrier.

Hugh did not answer; he spurred his horse and cantered between the tents until he reached the Duke, who was drinking a last stirrup cup of spiced malmsey. John was magnificent in full tournament regalia. His helmet was topped by a crowned golden lion guardant, and around the lion was draped Blanche's scarf of silver tissue. His engraved brass armor shone like a mirror, and the gold lilies and leopards blazed against vermilion and azure on his jupon. Palamon, his great charger, was restive and two squires clung to the red tasseled bridle as Hugh came up crying, "My Lord Duke!"

John tossed his cup to a squire and looked at his knight in surprise. "What is it, Swynford? You're not ready? The melee's starting."

"I wish permission to fight on the other side, my lord."

"You *what!*" John cried, half laughing, staring at the

square angry face surmounted by the skullcap of brown cloth which would cushion the great helmet. "What foolishness is this?"

"I wish," cried Hugh furiously, "to tilt *against* Roger de Cheyne in a deed of arms."

The Duke was both amused and annoyed. The twenty rival contenders at the other end of the lists had been a fairly arbitrary choice. His brother the Duke Lionel headed that side, and there were Lancaster knights there as well as Frenchmen and a Scot. But these arrangements had been made for days, and a sudden change transgressed on proper tournament procedure.

"If you wished a private joust with de Cheyne, why didn't you challenge him earlier?" said John frowning and stroking his prancing horse.

"I did not know in time, my lord, and the tourney ends today." Hugh's eyes slid from the Duke's face and rested on his own helmet. Ellis de Thoresby, who had run after his master, held it cradled in his arms. John followed the glance and saw the green tippet. "Is that Katherine de Roet's?" he asked, enlightened.

Hugh nodded grimly. "And de Cheyne wears the flower she gave him."

"Oh," said the Duke, and he thought, with sudden anger, That maudite girl again. She's a nuisance and a trouble-maker, and has certainly bewitched this poor knight. "Go then," he said impatiently, anxious to be rid of the whole episode. "Explain to the Duke Lionel and have him send one of his men here to replace you—but remember," he raised his voice sternly as Hugh turned with muttered thanks, "this is no jousting à l'outrance—there'll be real fighting enough for all in Castile. This is but knightly sport today."

Hugh's lips tightened. He made no reply, but galloped around behind the lists and the galleries to the opposite end of the field while Ellis jumped on his own horse and hurried as best he could after him.

In the loges the spectators had become impatient at the delay. Even the Lady Blanche's long fingers fidgeted nervously with the sapphire clasp of her girdle, and she strained her eyes down the field to try to make out the helmet with the golden lion while her lips moved in prayer to St. John the Baptist, her husband's patron.

But at last the trumpets brayed, the marshals advanced

brandishing their white sticks and followed by the heralds
and poursuivants at arms. The crowd hushed and listened avidly to the announcement. It was to a general tournament
melee with twenty of the bravest knights on each side, and
fought for the honor of St George and the King. The prize
was to be a gold noble to each knight on the winning side,
and an additional prize of one of the King's best falcons to
the knight adjudged most worthy.

The combat was to start on horseback with the breaking of
spears, but might then be pursued on foot with the flat of the
sword as the only weapon. The lances must have coronal
heads to dull them, and the swords were all blunted by heavy
lead foils. A knight would be adjudged hors de combat if he
were unhelmeted, lost hold of his weapon or if any part of
his body touched the stockades around the lists.

The marshals finished shouting the rules, while the heralds
yelled, "Laissez al-l-le-e-r—," and scampered for safety
over the barricades as the gates were raised at either end.

Katherine gave a frightened cry when the forty opposing
horses thundered down the field towards her center loge with
the roar of an earthquake. The long lances streaked like light
while from many of the knightly throats came bloodcurdling
battle cries. The shock of their meeting shook the loges, there
was a tremendous crash of steel, the cracks of splintering
wood and the wild high whinnies of the stallions.

"Oh, Blessed Sainte Marie," whispered Katherine, shrinking and clenching her hands. "They'll all kill each other!"

Some of the knights were at once unhorsed, more unhelmeted. The field became a threshing mass of shields and broken lances, armored bodies and armored horses. She could
recognize nobody, but after a moment she heard the Duchess
say with quiet pride, "He's still in the saddle, and his helmet
untouched."

Then Katherine distinguished a tall knight with golden lion
crest and knew by the emblems on his shield that it must be
the Duke. He had broken a lance with his brother Lionel,
who was a gigantic figure in armor as black and shining as
that often worn by his older brother, Edward.

The two dukes, both furnished with fresh lances by darting
squires, had drawn to the far side of the field and separated
for a second course. They ran this course fast and decorously
and again at the shock of impact on the shields, their lances
splintered fairly. But Lionel's horse had twisted a tendon and

one of the girths on his saddle had parted. He moved to the
rear for a fresh mount while John pulled to one side of the
lists and waited.

"Oh, well done!" cried Blanche. "A fair joust." And she
sighed with relief at the momentary respite, her eyes roaming
over the rest of the field. Already it had thinned; some
knights unhorsed, had lost their helmets or swords and been
hauled off by their squires. Some fighting on foot had been
backed to the stockades and thus disqualified. The contestants
had narrowed down to a dozen or so, but in the confusion it
was impossible to see which side was winning.

Suddenly Blanche laid her hand on Katherine's shoulder.
"Look, child, your two knights are fighting each other! See,
over there near the Duke."

Katherine saw then the helmets, one with her green
streamer on it, and the other with the stag's head, though the
iris she had given de Cheyne had long since been knocked
off. The two men were afoot, having both been unhorsed in
the first violent collision. They were fighting with swords and
de Cheyne seemed to be giving inch by inch under the furious onslaughts of the shorter, stockier figure.

Before the melee the Duke had had time to warn Roger of
Hugh's intent, and Roger had been amused. "So the little ram
is fuming? By Saint Valentine, I'll be pleased to give him satisfaction, my lord!"

But now Roger was no longer amused. This was no chivalrous contest for a lady's smile in which he found himself engaged. The blows from the flat of the sword rained on his
helmet and hauberk with stunning force. Swynford handled
his sword as his ancestors had used the battle-axe. Through
the slit in the visor Roger could see the glint of murderous
eyes and hear a panting drone of fury.

Roger parried the blows as best he could, but the blood
was bursting in his ears and nose; he stumbled and fell to one
knee while the crashing shocks of steel redoubled on his helmet and shoulders. He struggled to his feet and made a
desperate lunge, and at the same moment he felt a flash of
fire in his neck. The lead foil had come off Hugh's sword.

Hugh, berserk with blood lust, did not know it, the marshals, watchful as they were of each separate combat, had not
seen it—but the Duke saw.

Lionel had not yet signaled for the beginning of the third
course, and John had been watching Swynford and de

Cheyne uneasily. He saw the younger knight stagger and a spray of crimson spurt through the joint between helmet and gorget, he saw the naked sword tip flash, and he galloped up, shouting, "Halt, Swynford!"

But Hugh did not hear. He knew only that his quarry was weakened at last, and he beat down harder.

John might have stopped Hugh with a blow from his lance except for the rule that a mounted man must not touch one afoot, so he flung himself out of the saddle and ran up, drawing his sword; then lifting it high, sliced it down between the two knights as barrier. Hugh staggered back for a moment, and Roger slumped prone on the ground. His squire darted over with a poursuivant, and the two men carried his limp body off the field.

But Hugh could see little through the visor slit, and his eyes were half blinded with sweat. He knew only that here in the moment of victory over de Cheyne there was somehow new battle. And he turned on the Duke.

There was a rumble of astonishment from those spectators who had noticed this particular engagement, whispers of "Lancaster's unhorsed—Who's he fighting? What happened?"

One of the marshals galloped up and then paused uncertainly. By the rules of combat any knight on the one side might singly engage any one of the opponents, but in actual practice nowadays this was unusual, and the two princely leaders were tacitly reserved for each other.

But Blanche knew what was happening. She stood up, marble-still, her eyes fixed on the figures across the lists. And Katherine knew. She had held her breath while she watched the fight between Roger and Hugh, but the spectacle had not seemed very real; it was like the banging, slashing battles the mummers played, and there had been room in her heart for a primitive female thrill, since the two knights fought over her.

But when she saw the Duke had somehow taken Roger's place her detachment fled and fear rushed in. She gasped at each of Hugh's lunges and tightened as though to receive them on her own body, her lips moved incessantly. "Make him win, Blessed Mother, make him win," and it was the Duke that she meant.

It lasted only three minutes. Hugh's crazy rage did not abate, but he was no match for John of Gaunt, whose cool head, lean, powerful body and chivalrous training from babyhood had made him the most accomplished knight at court.

John parried the vicious blows and waited until Hugh's right arm was raised, then he hit the gauntleted hand a tremendous blow. Hugh's sword went spinning down the field.

The Duke with studied deliberation lowered his own sword and thrust it into the ground, while thundering applause shook the loges, and the King, cupping his hands, shouted, "Well done, Lancaster! Well done, fair son!"

It was then that Hugh realized who his opponent was. He staggered backwards, raising his visor. "My Lord Duke, I'm honored."

John gazed at him with icy eyes. "You're not honored, Swynford, you're disgraced. Look at your sword—" He pointed with his mailed shoe at the unguarded point of Hugh's sword as it lay in the dust, "and you wounded young de Cheyne in unfair combat."

Hugh turned purple under the sweat-caked dust. "By God, sir, I didn't know. I swear it."

"Get out of the lists," said the Duke. "We'll deal with you later." Hugh turned and limped slowly off the field.

John dismissed the problem of Hugh and, mounting his horse again, accepted the lance from his squire and rested it in the socket, preparatory to running the final course with Lionel. He saw that this course would be the end of the tournament, since the lists were cleared of all but two combatants, a French knight and Sir Michael de la Pole, his own man. He beckoned to the marshal. "How has it gone? What is the tally?" he asked.

"It's a near thing, Your Grace. The Duke of Clarence was ahead until you bested that knight." The marshal indicated Hugh's retreating figure. "But now, I see, his forces are ahead *again*." For even as they conferred, the French knight dexterously backed Sir Michael against the far stockade, and the Englishman raised his sword hilt high in token of submission.

"By Christ's blood, then, we must try to even the contest," cried the Duke and he waved his lance in signal to Lionel.

The crowd, which had been restive, quieted and watched with delight as the two resplendent Plantagenets ran the final course against each other. Here was no blind unruly jousting, but an elegant deed of arms with each fine point of technique observed. The ceremonious bowing of the helmeted heads as the herald's trumpet sounded, the simultaneous start from the lines drawn at either end of the lists, the lances held precisely horizontal, the control over the snorting destriers who were always liable to swerve, the shivering impact of the lances square on the opposing shields and the final neat thrust sidewards of Lancaster's lance, which dexterously knocked the helmet up and off Lionel's head, where it dangled by the lacings from the gorget.

"Splendid, splendid!" cried the King, proud of his sons.

John and Lionel came riding up to their father's loge and bowed to him while the heralds, once more taking the center of the field, proclaimed that the great tournament in honor of St. George had ended in a draw. The crowd groaned with disappointment. But, continued the heralds, the prizes would be given anyway by lot tonight at the Feast of the Garter and the special prize for the knight adjudged to have been most worthy in the tournament would also be presented then.

"Lancaster! Lancaster!" yelled a hundred voices, and John flushed. "Lancaster's the worthiest knight!"

It was the first time he had heard himself acclaimed by the mob, and he found it unexpectedly sweet. The King, his father, was immensely popular, of course, and Edward, Prince of Wales, was an idol. Even Lionel, the great blond giant who now sat good-naturedly grinning at his brother, had always, except in Ireland, enjoyed public admiration.

But John was a third son, and the most reserved of all Edward and Philippa's brood. He could inspire deep devotion amongst his intimates, but he had not the gift of easy camaraderie. He knew that most people, and certainly the common folk, thought him haughty and cold. He had been quite indifferent to their opinion, but now at the continuing shouts he felt a pleasant warmth.

He rode over to Blanche's loge and looked up at her smiling. "Well, my dearest lady," he said, "did you enjoy the tournament?" He looked very boyish with his ruddy gold hair touseled by the helmet, streaks of dirt on his cheeks and a happy look in his brilliant blue eyes, which gazed only at Blanche. He had not seen Katherine down on the platform, and he ignored the other admiring ladies around his wife.

"You were wonderful, my lord," said Blanche softly, leaning over the parapet towards him. "Listen how they shout for you. Grand merci to the Blessed Saint John who protected you from harm."

Oh yes, thought Katherine fervently, gazing at the Duke. A strange pain twisted her heart, and she looked away quickly.

Blanche caught the motion of Katherine's head. "Is young de Cheyne all right?" she asked, leaning closer to her husband whose tired horse now stood quiet next to the parapet. "I couldn't understand just what happened, but Sir Hugh—"

"—is a dangerous fool," snapped John, his face darkening. "I shall deal with him. Though it's that wretched girl's fault."

"Hush, my lord," cried Blanche, glancing swiftly at Katherine. "The poor child's not to blame."

It was then that John saw her sitting below his wife's chair. Her gray eyes with their long shadowing lashes were gazing out over the lists towards the distant oaks. In one quick angry glance he saw the change her new clothes had made in her, the long creamy neck exposed and the velvet flesh in the cleft of her breasts, which were outlined by the tight green bodice. He saw the dimple in her chin and the voluptuous curve of her red lips, he saw the tiny black mole high on her cheek where the rose faded into the gleaming white of her innocent forehead. He saw the rough, reddened little hands, the great beryl ring on the middle finger. She was sensuous, provocative, glowing with color like a peasant, and it seemed to him an outrage that she should be ensconced here next to his Duchess.

"Apparently *you* have no interest in the fate of your chevaliers, ma damoiselle de Roet," he called in a tone of stinging rebuke.

Fresh dismay washed over Katherine. The unkindness of his voice did not hurt her as much as the stab of her own conscience. For it was true, she had been thinking not of her betrothed or the charming young man to whom at the convent she had given so much thought. She had been immersed in a sudden fog of loneliness, unable to look at the soft expression of the Duke's eyes as they gazed up at his lovely wife. What's the matter with me? she thought, and she turned her head with her own peculiar grace and said quietly, "I am indeed concerned for Sir Hugh and Sir Roger, my lord. How may I best show it?"

John was silenced. The girl's poise showed almost aristocratic breeding, though she came of yeoman stock. And it was true that she could not run down to the leech's tent amongst all the disrobing men and find out for herself. He beckoned to one of his hovering squires, but the young man already had the required information, having just come from the pavilions.

He said that Roger de Cheyne, though faint from loss of blood, would recover, the stars being propitious. The King's leech, Master John Bray, had poulticed the neck wound. Sir Hugh Swynford was uninjured except for a twisted wrist and a bone or two broken in his hand, as a result of the Duke's blow. He had refused the services of the surgeon and gone at once to his tent. Amongst the other combatants there were no fatalities yet, though Sir Gerald de Usflet seemed to have lost his wits and kept whimpering, his brains being doubtless addled from blows, since his helmet was badly dented. Sir Mauburni de Linieres had vomited a basinful of blood, though Master John could find no wound, and one of the Hainault knights had clumsily managed to break both legs in falling from his horse.

John and all those near enough to hear the squire listened attentively and nodded approval. A gratifying tournament, few casualties and probably no deaths. At least today. Everyone knew that injuries bred fever and putrefaction later, but the outcome would depend on a man's strength, the skill of the physician and his ability to read the astrological aspects aright.

"Farewell, my sweet lady," said the Duke to his Blanche. "I'll see you at the banquet." Ignoring Katherine and the rest of the Duchess's entourage, he trotted his horse off towards the pavilions. It was necessary to punish Hugh in some way for flagrant transgression of the rules, but the heat of John's anger had passed. Poor Swynford was bewitched and doubtless couldn't help his behavior. Besides, a fierce and vengeful fighter was invaluable in war, however improper at a tourney.

And war was now John's great preoccupation. War with Castile. A deed of arms so chivalrous as to reduce these little jousts and melees to the pale counterfeits they were.

That very morning four knights, Lord Delaware, Sir Neil Loring and the two de Pommiers had arrived at Windsor from Bordeaux bearing official letters from Edward the Prince. There had been no time for the King to digest these letters yet, but John had read them. They contained an impassioned plea from his brother, asking for help in righting a great wrong. All of England must help, all of Christendom *should* help in restoring King Pedro to his throne and driving out the odious usurping bastard, Henry Trastamare. King Pedro and his young daughters had been reduced to ignominious flight, and had to throw themselves on Edward's mercy

at Bordeaux and beg for help, reminding him most pitifully
of England's long-time alliance with Castile. That rightful
anointed kings should find themselves in such desperate plight
must move every royal heart to valorous response and to
arms! That was the gist of the Prince's letters, and certainly
John's own heart had responded at once.

He burned to distinguish himself in battle as his elder
brothers did. His military role so far had been unimpressive,
through no fault of his own, but he chafed under the memories.

At fifteen he had gone to France with his father, full of
hope that he might distinguish himself in another Crécy as
his brother Edward had done nine years before. But this
French campaign bogged down into a welter of plots and
counterplots. King Jean of France holed in behind the walls
of Amiens and would not fight; it was all anticlimax and disappointment. King Edward knighted young John anyway, but
there was no glorious deed of arms to give the ceremony
savor, and the King moreover was preoccupied with trouble
in Scotland.

The English returned home in a hurry, prepared to subdue
the impudent Scots who had, as usual, seized any opportunity
to capture Berwick. John was jubilant again. The Scots would
do as well as the French as a means to prove his courage and
new knighthood. Again he was disappointed. Berwick, unpre-
pared for a siege, gave up at once, and then the infamous
Scottish king, Baliol, surrendered his country to King Edward
for two thousand pounds, and the English marched unchecked to Edinburgh, burning and looting as they went.

There was nothing in this moment of Scotland's abasement
to thrill a boyish heart, fed on the legends of King Arthur's
days, and fretting to prove himself the perfect knight. But in
Edinburgh he at least had a glimpse of chivalry. His father,
the King, had intended to burn Edinburgh as a final and con-
clusive punishment for the Scots. But the lovely Countess of
Douglas flung herself weeping before the angry conqueror,
imploring him to spare the city.

And the King had listened, had raised the sobbing beauty
and kissed her on the forehead in token of gallant submission. Young John himself had been one of those sent to
check the soldiers and their flaming torches. That day he had
conceived affection for the city they had spared, and sur-

prised admiration for the Scots, whom he had previously
thought to be uncouth monsters.

He had been sorry to leave Scotland and deeply chagrined
later that year that his father had not allowed him to return
to France and join the Prince of Wales. For by Michaelmas
they heard the stupendous news in London. The Prince and
his remarkable general, Sir John Chandos, had not only won
a brilliant victory at Poitiers, but they had captured the
French king!

Young John rejoiced with all England. He took his part in
the triumphant pageants and tourneys that greeted the return
of the young conqueror and his royal prize, but he had had
to fight envy. Edward was a brilliant hero. Edward was heir
to the throne, the court adored him, the people quite properly
doted on him, but what was there left for a third son who felt
himself potentially as great a warrior?

Lionel didn't care. He liked sports and wenching and
drinking. He amiably tried to fill any role his father told him
to, and beyond that he had no ambitions. But John cared
very much and spent many bitter hours. His rebellion was entirely inward and soon subdued by his strong sense of loyalty,
both personal and dynastic. Gradually his seventeen-year-old
energy, that winter of 1357, balked of glory, flowed into
other channels. He developed an interest in art, music, reading, where his taste ran to the romantic and stirring tales of
olden time.

He also discovered passion. He became infatuated with one
of his mother's waiting maids, Marie St. Hilaire, a handsome
good-natured woman in her mid-twenties who initiated him
into the forthright pleasures of sex. This affair lasted over a
year, when she got pregnant. The Queen, who demanded a
high moral tone from her ladies, was disgusted, and angry
with her son, too. The King, however, and John's older
brothers, were amused. His father remarked jovially that at
least the boy was a truly virile Plantagenet, and this episode
turned the King's mind to finding John a suitable wife.

Marie was well provided for and bore her baby without
fuss in London. It was a girl, and she named it Blanche in
honor of the bride the King had picked out for the baby's
father.

By this time John was nearly nineteen and had quite out-
grown Marie. It was easy for him to fall in love with the
beautiful Blanche of Lancaster. He saw her first in her fa-

ther's rose garden at the Savoy Palace, and in her white robes with her silver-gilt hair unbound as she played a Provençal melody on her lute, she epitomized for him all the Elaines, Gueneveres, Melusines of which he had read.

His marriage brought him luck and a great measure of the power he wanted, yet now at twenty-six he had still not found the opportunity to achieve glory on his own.

Castile would do that. The very sound of "Castile" was like the martial clash of cymbals, and he repeated the seductive word to himself while he rode towards the pavilions after the tournament. His heart beat faster as he saw how he would answer his brother's need at the head of an avenging host, in a latter-day crusade to fight for justice and the divine right of kings.

He would issue the call to arms throughout his vast domains. He could raise an army of his own retainers almost overnight, and finance the expedition from his own pocket. This it was to be the Duke of Lancaster.

John's musing eyes grew brilliant and he flicked Palamon to a faster pace.

As he neared the pavilions a child darted out from behind one of the tents and waved her dirty little claws. "Great Duke," she whined, "gi' alms, gi' alms—we've naught to eat." Her slanting dark eyes peered up at him through a tangle of dusty black hair, lice crawled on the filthy rags that barely hid her skinny little body. The stallion moved away from her under the pressure of John's knees as he said, "There's food for all down by the river—bread, ale and roast oxen." He pointed to the crowd of feasting peasants.

She shook her head with a sly smile. "We darena, noble lord, we'm outlaws—me da's skulking in tha' forest."

John shrugged and gestured to Piers Roos, his young body squire who rode behind him with others of the Duke's men. Piers opened the purse at his waist and flung the girl two silver pennies. She caught them in mid-air and darted off like an otter to disappear in the bushes.

"I suppose the woods are full of runaway churls today," remarked Piers laughing to his companions. "Come as near as they dare to the feasting. And as for that ugly maid, she's a veritable changeling."

John was not listening, and yet the last word uttered by Piers' clear young voice penetrated his mind with an effect of shock. Changeling. What was there in that word to stir up turmoil? His heart of a sudden pounded heavily and his stomach heaved as though with fear. Gray eyes, gray woman's eyes seemed to stare at him from the sky—troubled, farseeing eyes like the de Roet girl's. No—eyes like Isolda Neumann's!

He turned in his saddle and spoke sharply to the young men behind him. "Go to your tents, all of you, and leave me alone. I wish to ride in the forest."

Piers Roos looked startled; solitude was a state rarely desired by the Duke or anyone else, except of course hermits and anchorites who used it for penance. He scanned his lord's face, which seemed angrily tense, and wondered if the jousting had inflicted some obscure injury. "You'll want your helm, my lord?" he said diffidently, holding it out. "There are outlaws in the greenwood—there might be danger."

"Bah—" said John, kicking Palamon's flank. "What danger to me could there ever be from a handful of renegade villeins!" He spurred the horse and cantered off through the holly bushes and elders on the fringe of Windsor great forest.

Piers watched the yellow head and the scarlet and azure jupon until they disappeared, then turned to his companions. "Palamon is winded and lathered from the tourney," he said, frowning. " 'Tis not like him to neglect the stallion, whatever strange mood has come to him—" The other young men merely laughed; and, delighted to be released from duty, shouted for the pages to bring them wine, as they clambered from the saddles.

John was not thinking of the stallion, but he allowed the tired horse to slacken pace and rode slowly beneath the dappled beeches while he suffered for the first time in years from memories so painful that it was impossible even now in his maturity to dwell on them calmly.

Isolda Neumann had been John's foster mother for eight years, from the moment of his birth at the Abbey of St. Bavon in Ghent. She had nursed him at her breast, while the baby she herself had borne soon died. John remembered of her clearly only her calm gray eyes, and the softness of her voice as she sang to him and that he had loved her more than anyone in the world. His parents, the King and Queen, had been remote gods, infinitely respected, but preoccupied with great affairs, seldom at home, and too, there were the other eight children to claim their attention. Isolda had belonged to him alone.

She was the handsome widow of a respectable Flemish burgher, and she had a remaining child, an only son four years older than John. This boy, Pieter, had naturally accompanied Isolda when Queen Philippa's whole household moved back from Flanders to England. Pieter had been born with a twisted leg, but otherwise he was healthy and large for his years. A sly, pimpled boy, given to spiteful tempers and talebearing, he had apparently felt from the beginning for little John, his mother's nurseling, a vicious jealousy. Perhaps Isolda had not bothered to hide the far greater love she bore her charge, while perhaps she neglected her own son, pushing him too soon from the bed to sleep with the stableboys and vagrants in the castle cattle sheds.

Whatever the reason, Pieter's shrewd little mind, which was as twisted as his leg, eventually concocted a subtle revenge.

It had happened here at Windsor in the fetid death-dealing summer when red crosses were painted on every other house in London and the plague bells jangled day and night; but to all the children isolated behind the great castle walls there seemed to be safety enough, and they played together in the courtyards and gardens with carefree joy augmented by the relaxed vigilance of their terrified elders.

John now could not remember exactly how Pieter's persecution began, except that when a score or so of the castle children were playing together, Pieter would contrive to sneer at John's small failures, and whisper words the child did not quite understand. If John fumbled the leather ballon ball thrown to him, or missed his mark when tilting at a miniature quintain, Pieter would limp up and under cover of sympathy add directly in John's ear that his lack of skill was not surprising, that no more could be expected of a changeling.

So quickly was this done that the eight-year-old child was only puzzled, then quickly forgot in the interest of play.

Pieter bided his time until an afternoon when they were alone except for John's younger brother Edmund, who was six, and his little sister Mary, who was four. It was a sultry August day and the royal children's three nurses gossiped in the shade under the Norman gate while their charges played in the garden at the foot of the Round Tower. Pieter, who had special privileges because of his lameness, lounged near

the children watching John. Mary amused herself floating
peony petals in the tiny pool, but John had his new gerfalcon
with him, of which he was exceedingly proud, and was showing her off to Edmund. She was a snowy northern bird
hatched in the royal mew and already well trained by the
King's falconer, so that she sat hooded and quiet on John's
embroidered gauntlet, or when at times she flew high into the
air to the length of her creance, which was fastened to John's
glove, her twin bells tinkled gently and she returned to him at
his call.

"Ah, sweet noble Ela," cried John, stroking his bird's neck
with a blade of grass. "In a few years, Edmund, maybe Father will give *you* one, too, on your saint's day," he added,
swaggering a little before his admiring younger brother.

Pieter suddenly threw a large pebble at the falcon, who
started and bated violently, her great white wings thrashing
the air.

John turned on his nurse's son with fury. "What possessed
you to do that, churl! You've frightened her."

Pieter shrugged. "Let me take her," he said in his thick
Flemish voice, and kicking off his soft-leather shoe, he thrust
his left hand into it to make a perch for the falcon; watching
John slyly, he extended his hand, "Geef her to me. I can
manage her."

John's mouth dropped open as surprise replaced his
anger. "Why, Pieter, you know you may not touch her," he
said in all seriousness, and with a hint of pity. "She's a royal
gerfalcon. You must get yourself a sparrow hawk."

The narrow rat face glinted, for now the opportunity had
come. Pieter knew as well as the Prince and everyone else in
England the ironclad laws of falconry: that smaller hawks
were each assigned to a different class of men, as were mer-
lins to noble ladies, peregrines to earls, but only those of
royal blood might own or touch a gerfalcon. He thrust his
face close up to John's and spoke not so loud that his mother
and the other nurses might hear. "I haf as much right to her
as you—changeling."

John jerked his head back from the hateful face—while
the falcon again bated her wings—and he felt his heart begin
a slow hard thumping. "What do you mean?" he said steadily
enough.

"That *you're* no King's son, nor Queen's neither. You're
naught but the brat uf a Flemish butcher. The Queen smug-

gled you into her bed when the child she bore died, and she feared to tell the King."

For John the bright August afternoon had dimmed, then blackened, while Pieter's voice swirled disembodied around his head, and the hissing words lost meaning. His belly heaved as it did when he had eaten too many gooseberry pasties, but he stood rigid, staring at Pieter and still holding the gerfalcon carefully on his outstretched hand.

"You lie," he said at last, and could not control a quaver. He shut his lips tight. Edmund, who had squatted down to splash Mary at the pool, looked up, hearing something strange in his elder brother's voice, but seeing nothing was happening to interest him, scooped water over Mary's legs.

Pieter shook his head, but he stepped back, a trifle frightened now of what he had said and of the other boy's white face. "You're naught but a Flemish butcher's brat, a changeling," he repeated more feebly, and almost believed it himself, forgetting that this invention had first sprung from a minstrel's lay he had heard at Whitsuntide.

"I shall go with this tale to the Queen, my—my mother," John said, holding his head high, "and to Isolda."

"Nay," said Pieter quickly, " 'twould be no use. They'd neffer admit it for fear of the King."

John stood yet one moment, then he made a sharp high sound as tears burst from his eyes, and he sprang forward, hitting out with all the strength of his right fist.

The other boy was four years older and a head taller, but between his lameness and the suddenness of the onslaught he fell backward on the slope of the mound, and John, on top of him, found a sharp stone in his hand and cut down wildly, opening a gash in Pieter's neck. Pieter let out such a bellow that the nurses and the guards from the Round Tower all came running. They rescued Pieter and staunched the blood that flowed from his neck wound.

Then was John in disgrace; the King his father scolded him harshly for two transgressions of the knightly code, hitting a cripple afflicted by God, and especially for damaging by his turbulence the royal gerfalcon, which had in the uproar torn one of her talons in her struggles to escape. A falcon such as Ela was worth a hundred marks, and King Edward took her away from his son as punishment.

John scarcely missed the falcon which had been his chief delight, for the poison Pieter had instilled spread slowly through his soul. He ceased to play with the other children, but kept to himself and grew silent and morose. He lost interest in food. Isolda saw the change at once and fear gripped her, for now there were cases of plague in the town just outside the castle walls. She dosed him with snake treacle, she tied a toadstone around his neck with his medal of St. John, she washed him in pig urine, she hung a plague amulet with "Abracadabra" inscribed above his bed and questioned him anxiously. But he turned away from her and would not tell what ailed him. Nor would he go to see his mother, who was lying-in of another son, little William.

John, the Duke of Lancaster, riding aimlessly through the forest dusk, thought of these matters in his childhood, and the agony of those summer weeks eighteen years ago gripped him again. He had been shaken from all he knew, no longer sure that he was a proud Plantagenet, no longer daring to assert himself or claim affection from the family he had thought his. Was he indeed baseborn, a butcher's son, a changeling? Perhaps he had not wholly believed the boy's story, even then, but the doubt had been enough. Pieter himself had disappeared, the very night that John knocked him down. He had stolen his mother's purse and the jeweled trinkets the Queen had given her, slipped through the castle gate and vanished. Nor did Isolda mourn for him; she knew him for what he was, warped in mind and body. And soon she guessed that the woeful change in her little Prince had something to do with her son.

And worse was yet to come, for it was Isolda who caught the plague, and caught it because her concern for John sent her into Windsor town to find a well-known leech-wife reputed skilled at treating mysterious vapors and humors. She came back with a secret philter which she persuaded John to take, and also insisted that he should sleep in her bed that night so she might watch its effect, and from his mutterings and troubled cries as he slept she began to understand. She drew him tight against her breasts, kissing his golden head and coaxing him with soft questions, until he began to weep and still half asleep told her all that Pieter had said.

Then Isolda jumped from bed, and, picking John up in her strong arms, carried him from that room where others were sleeping and down stone steps and through passages to the private chapel. She set the startled child down by the altar rail. It was cool in the chapel and dark except for votive lights burning before the statues of St. George and the Blessed Virgin.

"Look, my little lord," whispered Isolda, "do you see where you are?" He nodded wondering.

"Then listen and remember always. Pieter most damnably lied. I swear it. Holy Saint Mary and Saint George and the Blessed Body of Christ are my witnesses. You *are* the King's son, and were born to the Queen in March eight years ago on the eve of Lady Day, and I received you into my own hands as you came from your mother's womb."

John looked up, awed, into her shining gray eyes. He understood what she said, but the strangeness of the place and her urgency overpowered all else.

"Pieter wanted to hurt you," she said, putting her hand on his head. "In years to come there may be many people who try to harm you because of envy, and they will tell lies, many lies. You must be too strong for them, my sweet lordling, and yet you must be merciful, because you're strong—Will you remember? And will you vow it?"

He nodded solemnly. Her white face seemed to shimmer in the dusk and her eyes looked down at him with anxious love. He held his arms up to her as he used to do when he was a baby, and kneeling on the cushioned altar step, she gathered him close.

"But you'll be with me always," he had whispered confidently. "You'll keep them from harming me?"

"I will," she cried, "I will—I'll never leave you."

How long they knelt there by the altar rail together he did not know, but that was the last time he saw Isolda.

She put him back in his own bed with his brothers, and the next day when he looked for her they told him she was ill. When she died three days later, there could be no concealment. Even the smallest children knew that there was plague in the castle; besides Isolda two knights died of it, and five squires and many scullions and maid-servants. The stench of burning corpses hung over the castle, and the world was to jangle of church bells, hand bells and the beating of tin pans to break up the thick, deadly air.

The royal family was spared, all except the Princess Joan, who died of plague at Bordeaux on the eve of her marriage to the heir to Castile, but the strange hysteria of plague time so permeated Windsor that John scarcely understood what had happened to Isolda, who had promised never to leave

him, nor felt reassurance from that hour with her in the
chapel. Both shocks had been too violent for a child to ab-
sorb. Fear and loss and a sense of injustice attacked him in
nightmares for years. In these dreams it was as though Isolda
had betrayed him by her death when he so needed her, and
he would see her urgent eyes fixed on him in the darkness
until he called to them, when they shut against him and dissolved into the black eyesockets of a skull.

Palamon stumbled suddenly, and the Duke, jerking up the
jeweled reins, made a sound of exasperation, not at the horse
but at himself. What was he doing wandering in the forest,
when they awaited him at Windsor for the Garter feast? Why
had the pleasant mood left by the acclaim at the jousting and
the plans for Castile been so stupidly shattered by a memory
of childish fears touched off by Piers' chance word? It's that
de Roet maid, he thought in anger, but on this instinctive
anger he now turned a cooler look, having recognized part of
the cause. It was not her fault that her gray eyes were like
those of one of whom memory was laced with bitter pain.
Nor, doubtless, was it her fault that she was possessed of a
troubling beauty. And yet he still disliked the girl.

That clod of a Swynford's welcome to her, he thought, and
turning Palamon he rode out of the forest.

## V

KATHERINE AND HUGH were to be married in London, and
as soon as possible. Hugh said that as there were no
families on either side to be consulted, no jointures or
dowries to be arranged, there was no reason to wait. All the
more since he was useless for fighting until his broken hand
mended, and wished to visit his Lincolnshire manors before
he left for Bordeaux with the Duke's forces. So this was the
natural time for a bridal trip.

These practical arguments deceived nobody. Everyone

from the page boys to Katherine herself could see the jealousy that possessed him, and the fever to get the girl alone away from everyone.

Katherine accepted the imminence of her fate without further protest, and had little time to realize it, for the last days in Windsor were filled with the bustlings of departure. The King and his train left immediately for Westminster, where Parliament would sit on May 4, while the Queen decided to return to the healthier air of Woodstock.

Katherine saw no more of either the Duke or Duchess of Lancaster. Their great household was on the move, even before the King's, as they set off for the Savoy Palace, and Blanche had many things to think of besides Katherine. At the Savoy, the Lancasters kept regal state with an establishment of six hundred people: barons, knights, squires and servants, besides the feudatories from all over England who were beginning to assemble in response to the Duke's call to arms.

Hugh wished to be married at St. Clement Dane's, a little church near the Savoy where the priest was a Lincolnshire man, and Katherine's wishes, of course, were not consulted. Hugh went down to London some days ahead to make arrangements and left Ellis de Thoresby behind at Windsor to guard Katherine and conduct her to London with Philippa.

The Queen was a trifle better. When Philippa applied for leave of absence so that she might accompany her sister and see her married, the Queen, after granting permission, expressed a desire to meet Katherine at last. So on Katherine's final day at Windsor, Philippa guided her sister to the Queen's apartments.

From this interview Katherine received an impression of sadness and suffering. The Queen's room was darkened, quiet. A physician and the two most favored ladies hovered near the fire while the Queen's secretary, a young Hainaulter in clerical robes named Froissart, sat at a high desk scratching on parchment by the light of a single candle.

The Queen lay in a huge four-poster bed hung with gold brocade and gaudily painted with her ostrich-feather badges. The coverlet was of blue velvet embroidered with the Queen's motto, "Ich wrude muche." And she had indeed labored hard all her life, to produce her twelve children and rear the nine who survived infancy; she had labored to help the King, and for the advancement of her adopted country, but now she could no longer labor at anything except the daily struggle to exist in a prison of bloated aching flesh.

Katherine knelt to kiss the swollen hand extended to her. The fingers were taut and white as veal sausages, and the girl repressed a shudder. She raised her eyes to the mountainous figure under the coverlet, saw the balloon face with its small features nearly hidden by the puffed cheeks. But the sunken brown eyes looked kindly on the girl while the wheezing voice spoke in guttural French.

"So, la petite Katrine de Roet, you've already found yourself a husband! A brave knight! Your papa, whom may God absolve, would be very proud."

"Yes, madam," Katherine whispered and would have said more, but the Queen turned fretfully, beckoning to her physician. "Maître Jacques, it gives no relief yet." The Queen pointed to her belly, where the physician had applied both leeches and hollow needles in an endeavor to drain off the dropsical waters.

"It will, madam, it will in time," he said gravely, and he held against her nostrils a wad of wool saturated with the brain-soothing juices of lettuce, poppy and henbane. The Queen inhaled, sighed, and closed her eyes. She had forgotten Katherine, and the girl looked at her sister, wondering if they should go, but Philippa shook her head. She knew the wandering habits of the Queen's mind these days, and she had no intention of letting Katherine leave Windsor without a wedding present if she could help it.

The sisters drew back to the fireplace where Matilda Fisher and Elizabeth Pershore were embroidering tiny unicorns on a length of rose velvet. The room was still except for the fitful crackling of the fire and the Queen's labored breaths.

Then the wheezing voice called out. "Froissart!"

The young man threw down his quill pen and jumped to the bedside. "Read to me 'Calais' again," said the Queen faintly.

Froissart went back to the desk, leafed through his manuscript of chronicles and found the section the Queen wanted. Then he stood by the bed reading about the glories of nineteen years ago when King Edward had besieged and captured Calais. Calais, the precious opening wedge to enforce Edward's claim to the French throne. Froissart's fresh young voice rang with the enthusiasm stirring deeds of battle aroused in him, even though the Queen had made him read this account each day for weeks.

She listened and her distorted face relaxed. She relived the moments when she had been young and beloved by the King. And that most poignant moment when she had saved the six condemned burghers of Calais from her husband's vengeance.

And here she interrupted Froissart, as she always did, raising herself a little on her elbow. "Yes, yes," she said, breathing faster as the scene grew vivid again. "Sir Walter Manny pled, my young Edward pled, the poor hostages wept and screamed, yet my dear lord would not listen. I can see him now, his face black as iron when he beckoned to the headsman, and the brute ran forward with his axe upraised—but I stopped the wicked thing. I fell on my knees and begged for their lives. And my dear lord listened. He listened to me— then."

"It was wonderful, madam. A most merciful act!" said the young chronicler soothingly. "God will remember it, and you—"

The Queen sank back on her pillows. "Ah, I was strong in those days," she said in a quieter voice. "I'd crossed the Channel in a terrible storm and stayed with the King during the fighting and the surrender, though I was with child again —William that was, my little William." She sighed. Her swollen fingers fumbled at the gold rosary which was pinned to the coverlet.

"Was it not the Lady Margaret, madam, as you told me before?" suggested Froissart.

"No, no," said the Queen fretfully. "I'm sure it was William. He was born here in this bed, the following summer, the year of the Black Death, and he did not live to see a second Easter—But what does it matter which child it was? Margaret's dead, too—may the Blessed Mother cherish their little souls. Dead. Dead. Dead. Half my children are dead."

The group of women by the fireplace crossed themselves and Katherine felt a wondering pity, for weak slow tears oozed from the Queen's eyes and glistened on her cheeks. Could she still care so much, when she had so many left? Five sons and a daughter, and the Queen was old—over fifty. How strange that she should cry.

"Ah yes," the wheezing voice on the bed went on after a moment. "He listened to me, then—the King did, and he thanked me for it later—Ah tell me—" She looked up at Froissart. "Did *she*—" The Queen checked herself, her blurred eyes moved to the faces of her ladies by the fire. "Nay, you all wouldn't tell me, out of pity, but Philippa la Picarde—are you there?"

"Ay, dear madam," murmured Philippa, running to the bed.

"Tell me the truth, Pica. You have a blunt tongue and an honest heart. Did *she* go' to Westminster Sunday with the King?"

No one in the room had any doubt who "she" was. Froissart dropped his eyes and turned away. Hot color flooded Philippa's earnest face, but she answered very low. "Yes, madam, she went."

The Queen nodded slowly. "I knew it. No," she said to the physician, who leaned over with his restorative, "let me be. Don't you think I've stood far worse things than this! It isn't that she shares his bed—what can that matter to me now? It's that she has no tenderness for him, no heart. She's rapacious, evil, and she'll bleed him white. She'll bleed England white!"

"Madam," pleaded the physician, putting his hand on her wrist, "I beg you not to think of these things. There's nothing —" He stopped and bit his lips.

"Nothing I can do. You're right, Maître Jacques." Again she reached for her rosary, and her eyes closed. Suddenly they opened again and fell on Philippa. "Your sister," she said. "You brought your little sister here?" Philippa beckoned, and Katherine returned to the bedside.

"Come nearer, ma fille," said the Queen. She peered at Katherine and smiled. "You're like your father. Such a handsome man. I remember him at some—some procession, or was it a tournament—in the tabard of the Guienne King-of-Arms, azure and gold, I think it was—all the wenches flocked around him. He came with me from Hainault long ago, and served me well—as you do, Froissart," she added, turning affectionately towards her secretary.

"Madam," put in Philippa anxiously, seeing that the Queen's thoughts were beginning to wander again, "Katherine is leaving Windsor tomorrow. She's to be married soon, if it please Your Grace."

"Ah yes," said the Queen. "She must have a little marriage gift in memory of her brave father. What would you like, child?"

Philippa sighed with relief. She nudged Katherine. "Ask for a purse," she whispered, "money."

But Katherine had yet to learn the importance of money, and besides she still had the silver the Duchess had given her. At this long-awaited audience with the Queen, she thought only of her promise to the prioress, and the moment in the courtyard when the stern ruler of her childhood had looked at her with appeal.

"Your Grace is very kind," she said quickly, not knowing how to express herself. "Could you, would you help Sheppey? The little convent where Your Grace placed me five years ago. They were good to me and they are in need."

"You little fool," hissed Philippa.

The Queen looked startled. "Has Sheppey had no benefices? Did I send nothing for your keep?"

"Not since the day I came there, madam, and I fear I ate a great deal," said Katherine apologetically. "The convent is very poor."

The Queen sat up straighter and spoke with something of her old energy. "You show gratitude and loyalty, child. I'm pleased. Froissart, write an order. We will send Sheppey a tun of Gascon wine and——" she hesitated, "a gift of two marks. Also we will send them," she thought a moment, "the d'Aubricourt girl as novice. She'll bring a dowry of near a hundred pounds sterling."

Froissart wrote industriously.

"Oh dearest madam, thank you!" cried Katherine, thinking of the joy these generous gifts would bring to Sheppey. Gascon wine, when they had never been able to afford anything but home-brewed ale! While with the two marks they could repair the dangerous minster steeple, buy cloth for new habits, perhaps enough gilt to freshen all the shabby saints' statues.

"And for yourself, my dear," said the Queen, warmed by the girl's unselfishness, but also mindful of the perennial skimpiness of her privy purse, "you shall have something to wear on your wedding day. Matilda," she called, "bring me the little coffer."

Her waiting woman rose and fetched a small iron-bound casket from one of the great oak chests along the wall. In this were kept the Queen's second-best jewels, chiefly the ones she had brought with her from Hainault. Matilda put the casket on the bed and unlocked it with a key she carried at her belt, then she held a candle down so the Queen might see. The Queen poked in the casket, turning over buckles and clasps, and little tablets enameled with pictures of the saints. Several times she fished up a piece of jewelry and hesitated, reluctant to part with any of these souvenirs of her early life, and her interest was ebbing as her bodily discomforts increased. She needed the privacy of the drawn curtains again, and the ministration of her ladies.

"Here then, fillette," she said hurriedly, plucking out a small silver brooch of crudely wrought leaves and vines entwining a motto. "What does the raison say? I've forgotten. Can you read?"

"Yes, madam," said Katherine proudly. She peered at the lettering. "It says, 'Foi vainquera,' I think."

"Ah yes," murmured the Queen, "a good saying. The best. Faith will conquer. Live by it, petite, and take my blessing—"

Katherine would have kissed the swollen hand once more, but the Queen gave a moan and cried, "Matilda, quick!" The waiting woman ran to the bed and drew together the heavy brocade curtains.

Once back in their own solar, which was empty for the moment, Philippa began to scold. "Really, Katherine, you might have had a decent present instead of that trumpery little nouche. It isn't worth ten pence."

Katherine looked down at her brooch. Certainly it was an unimpressive piece of jewelry compared to the ones she had seen on the courtiers. It had neither sparkle nor elegance, and the motto was disappointingly trite, the sort of things the nuns said.

"But I helped Sheppey," said the girl dispiritedly, "as I promised."

"Oh, no doubt," Philippa shrugged. "Very noble, but you might have done both if you'd had any sense. One must know how to deal with great folk. Now the Queen gave *me* ten marks for my wedding. Geoffrey'll be delighted." Philippa, pleased by this thought and having rebuked her feckless sister, now turned briskly to her coffer and began to pack it in readiness for the move to London tomorrow.

Katherine watched her sister's efficient hands folding and stowing linen shifts, veils, hose and towels. She herself had nothing to pack, and her eyes wandered to the window where she could see the tilting field barren now of gaudy tents and pennants. She sighed. "I wish I were marrying someone like your Geoffrey, or—or, dear God, not marrying at all."

"What rubbish!" Philippa rolled a pair of scarlet wool stockings and stuffed them in a corner of the chest. "Don't start all that again! You wanted to get married. That's why you came to court, instead of taking the veil. And you've had the luck of the angels."

"I suppose so," said Katherine, gazing down at her betroth-al ring, "but—but—oh, Philippa—aren't you—aren't you ever afraid?" Quick rose stained her skin, and her head bent lower.

"Of what?" Philippa raised her face from the chest to ex-amine her sister. "Oh, you mean the wedding night? They say it isn't bad. Agnes de Saxilby says she just shut her eyes and thought of something else. One gets used to it quickly."

It occurred to Philippa then that her convent-bred sister might well be ignorant of certain pertinent facts, though no one at court could be. She got up from her knees and put her arm around Katherine's drooping shoulders. "You know what happens, of course?" she asked more gently.

Katherine winced. There had been bitches and dogs at the convent, there had been Philo, the manor bull, bellowing in a stockade to which the village cows were brought one by one. And there had been Fat Mab, the convent cook, who swilled ale the day long and loved nothing better than to bawl out hoarse descriptions of the bed sport of her younger years.

So Katherine was not entirely ignorant, though there was much she did not know and found that she did not wish to know. She said "Yes" hastily, and though grateful for her sis-ter's caress, slid off the bed and made pretense of poking the fire. Philippa did not understand; the unknown held for her no fears that she could not vanquish by common sense. She was handicapped neither by imagination nor a restless yearn-ing for beauty and fulfillment. The image of Hugh's face rose before Katherine, softened now by distance, but bringing with it the familiar repulsion and a faint tinge of pity. Holy Blessed Mother, help me to be a good wife, she thought, but the words were empty.

Katherine and Philippa set out for London on the last day of April with Ellis de Thoresby as escort, and a pack horse to carry Philippa's coffers. Despite occasional showers, the morning was soft and sweet as honey. The roadside bloomed yellow with buttercups and primroses, pale blue with forget-me-nots. In the pastures fluffy newborn lambs bleated after

their mothers, who grazed amongst the tiny white and rose
daisies. The caw of rooks fighting above their nests high in
the trees drowned out more melodious birdsong, except that
now and again they heard the cuckoo like a bell in the distant
copses.

In many of the villages through which they rode the young
lads had stolen time from work and were setting up May-
poles for the morrow. In other larger towns where they had a
permanent Maypole, the gilded wheel with its streaming colored ribbons had already been set on top of the stout oak
shaft, and children were practicing at twining the ribbons
while they danced and sang May carols.

How beautiful the world is, thought Katherine, forgetting
what lay before her. There had been little beauty and no
frolic at Sheppey. High on a bleak hill continually swept by
the North Sea winds, neither the convent nor its dependent
hamlet had had the spirit for merrymaking.

Much of Katherine's pleasure, too, came from the horse
she was riding. It was only a hired one, to be sure, like Philippa's, but it was a stout little brown mare and the first decent horseflesh she had ever mounted. When they passed
through the village of Hammersmith and came up with a
band of minstrels bound for Westminster Palace and singing
to the tinkle of their gitterns, Katherine began to hum with
them until she caught the tune and could not help joining in
with her fresh lovely voice.

> The hedges and trees they are so green,
> As green as any leek.
> Our heavenly Father, he watered them
> With his heavenly dew so sweet.
> The sun shines bright, and the stars will give their light
> A little before it is day.
> So God bless you all, both great and small,
> And send you a joyful May.

The gleemen laughed and waved approval, crying that the
maid had a voice as fair as her face. Philippa primmed her
lips to say, "Katherine, I cannot understand where you
learned to be so forward," though then she smiled a little and
beat time with her feet in the stirrups. Ellis de Thoresby paid
no attention except to clear a way through the gleemen for
his charges. He was a stolid young man and a squire's re-

sponsibilities lay heavy on him. He patterned himself on his master, and while a bear-baiting or even a cockfight might amuse him, he had no mind for singing.

When they passed Westminster Palace, the great Abbey bell was tolling for Nones, so it was yet midafternoon, and they had made good time. Katherine, excited at the prospect of seeing London at last, gaped at the royal buildings like any country girl, but thought them small and unimpressive after Windsor. And when a mile farther downstream they came at the bend of the river to the gleaming white walls of the Savoy, Katherine saw that the Lancastrian palace was more magnificent than the King's. The Savoy was crenelated but not fortified, having been built less than a hundred years ago, and its windows were of good size, and most of them glazed. It was built in a series of quadrangles, turreted at the corners and covering three acres between the Strand and the river. Pennants, imprinted with the red rose, fluttered from the turrets, but from the tall gilt spire of the private chapel there hung a flag with Lancaster's own arms—France ancient and England quarterly under a label of three points ermine—to show that the Duke himself was in residence.

"Sir Hugh was to meet us here," muttered Ellis, drawing his horse up by the Savoy's Strand gate, "but we're early."

Katherine, in no hurry to see her betrothed, drew back into the shadow of the great white wall and watched the traffic clatter by on the newly paved Strand.

There were country folk in leather jerkins returning to their villages and pulling empty carts, having sold their produce at markets in the Chepes. There were richly dressed city merchants, sometimes accompanied by their wives, ambling back to town for supper. There was a splendid painted chariot drawn by two horses and containing an enormously fat and bejeweled Benedictine abbot. There were crippled beggars and noisy young prentices, and there was a street vendor tinkling a bell and urging his wares. "Hot pies! Hot pies! Good sirs and dames, buy me hot pies!"

Katherine looked longingly at the little meat pastries on the pieman's tray and said to Philippa, "Couldn't we get some? I'm so hungry. I have pennies."

But Philippa shook her head. "Save what few pennies you've left from the Duchess's bounty—and if you'd listened to me you might have had *more* than pennies from the Queen. We'll sup soon, when Sir Hugh comes."

Katherine sighed. Her healthy young stomach growled with hunger.

When Hugh finally came galloping up the Strand towards them he was in a black temper from a brawl with a horse dealer in Smithfield from whom he had just bought a palfrey for Katherine. He was also in some pain from his wounded hand, and he did not greet them courteously, though his eyes lightened when they saw Katherine. He merely said, "So you're here! Well, come along, all of you. You're to lodge at Chaucer's. We'll sup there now and I'm in sore need of it." He whacked Katherine's mare on the rump. The horse jumped forward, nearly unseating the girl. He's a churl, she thought furiously. I detest him. God help me.

Hugh leaned over from his saddle and clasped his good hand tight on her thigh. She could feel the heat of it through the green silk of her skirt. "Katherine," he said roughly, "d'you see that church?"

She moved her leg and pulled the horse away from Hugh's. She said nothing, though she looked at the small wooden parish church ahead.

"That's Saint Clement's Dane," he said. "That's where we'll be married Saturday."

"Saturday!" she cried, whitening. "Not *this* Saturday! It's too soon. What of the banns?"

Saturday was the day after tomorrow. A shiver ran down her back, she stared at the church again and her throat closed.

"I had the banns all cried at once on Saint Mark's Day," said Hugh, frowning. "The priest's a Lincoln man and beholden to Swynfords for his living. It's *all* arranged for Saturday morning—Katherine—" He put his hand out towards her again, but on seeing her stony profile, he let it drop. He knew not how to woo her, he knew only that with her he became even more harsh and clumsy than usual. He had not even wit enough to explain his tardiness, which had been caused for her sake. He suffered bitterly from her repugnance to him, though it increased his desire for her, but he had persuaded himself that once he possessed her she would turn yielding and warm. Young virgins always did, they said. He himself had had nothing to do with decent women, let alone virgins.

They rode along in silence, with Philippa and Ellis behind them. Katherine was turning wild, impossible plans over in her mind. Tonight, from the Chaucer house, she might escape, after everyone was asleep; she would hide somewhere until the city gates opened in the morning, take cover in the greenwood, in Epping forest; she saw it now, a dark sea of emerald to the north. There must be berries there to eat and maybe kindly outlaws who would help her. She would first find a knife and cut her gown off at the knees so as to run better. She looked down at the Duchess's gift and thought how shocked that gracious lady would be if she knew these wicked plans.

"You've seen my Lady Blanche—and the Duke?" said Katherine coldly at last as they squeezed through Ludgate into the narrow streets of London town.

"No," said Hugh and clapped his lips together. Though he slept in a loft with other knights in a corner of the vast Savoy he had seen nothing of his lord and lady because the Duke was punishing him for his behavior at the tournament. He had sent Hugh word by a page that Hugh was forbidden to eat in the Great Hall, nor might he wait upon the Duke until after returning from his manor of Kettlethorpe in August. That Hugh must then report at Plymouth, ready to embark for Bordeaux. This punishment was not severe, but Hugh found it galling to his pride and had no intention of telling it to Katherine.

They rode past St. Paul's and Katherine had no heart to admire the great cathedral of which she had heard so much. The London she had longed to see now seemed to her very cramped and dark and noisy with an earsplitting din from the rattling of carts, street criers and bells clanging for vespers from the hundred and fifty parish churches. She was conscious chiefly of foul smells and increasing weariness. They turned down Thames street and in to the Vintry where Geoffrey's father, Master John Chaucer, lived in a large half-timbered house, near St. Martin's church. A cargo of Gascon wine had that day been delivered from off a galley at Dowgate slip, and piled barrels still cumbered the street outside the Chaucer door.

Hugh dismounted and helped Katherine down, though he left Philippa to his squire. He knocked loudly. They waited long for an answer while Philippa looked worried and Hugh remarked under his breath that it was a pity Geoffrey was so little eager to see his own betrothed. Hugh banged again on the door, this time with the hilt of his dagger. A window was thrown open above, and a woman's voice cried, "Hush, for the love of Jesu, hush—there's grave sickness here."

Philippa gave a little cry and crossed herself and they all stood silent for a moment, until at last the door opened softly and Geoffrey himself stepped out. "No, it's not I who is ill, sweet heart," he said to Philippa in answer to her expression. He took her hand and held it in his, then turned to the others. "God's greetings to you, Katherine, Sir Hugh and Ellis de Thoresby. I'm sorry to give you such poor welcome, but my father has this day suffered a strange kind of fit, he gasps for breath and moans with pain. I fear—" Geoffrey shook his head. His bright little hazel eyes were sad. "We've sent for the parson." He gestured towards the church, and at that moment the priest emerged, treading solemnly, his silver-gilt crucifix held at arm's length before him.

The priest's eyes were half shut and his lips moved in prayer. He was followed by a small acolyte who bore the sacred pyx on a pillow beneath a lace cloth. Geoffrey threw wide the door of his house and fell to his knees, with the girls, beside the doorstep. Hugh and Ellis uncovered and kneeled also. With bowed heads they all waited while the Sacred Body passed between them and up the stairs to the dying man.

Katherine arose with her rebellious heart somewhat chastened. It had seemed to her that there was a glow of unearthly light shimmering above the shrouded mystery as it passed her so near, and that a voice had spoken to her in reproof. She thought with shame of the mad plans she had made for escape, and guiltily murmured the words of contrition. She kept her head low and stood quietly by the house wall while the others made immediate arrangements.

Philippa, it seemed, would stay here where she could be of help to her future family in these critical hours, but Chaucer had thought Katherine would do better at a friend's house. The abode of death was no place for a bride. The Pessoners in Billingsgate awaited her now, and he directed Hugh to their home. Katherine silently kissed her sister and remounted her mare.

Guy le Pessoner was a wealthy fishmonger, and an important official in that all-powerful guild. His fine house, many-gabled and newly tiled, stood just past the entrance to London bridge and had its own dock on the river for the unloading of fish. He had a garden, too, though the roses and lilies that bloomed there made little impression on the all-pervading odor. The Pessoners did not mind; they were a jolly crew and enjoyed life whether it smelled of lilies or herrings, and they welcomed Katherine, Hugh and Ellis most heartily, leading them at once to the Hall where the family were still supping.

The oak board was loaded with joints of beef and mutton, with pigeon pies and boiled capons spiced with ginger and cinnamon. There was a mess of jellied eggs in a wooden dish, white loaves of bread, and great tankards of ale and mead. And for sweets there were honey and almond pastes, nutmeg custards and a basket heaped high with boiled raisins.

Nobody waited for ceremony, all reached and helped themselves, cutting chunks off the roasts with their hip knives, or ladling meat juices onto the bread trenchers with the great dipper. Katherine's hunger was such that she forgot all the prioress's careful schooling and soon was reaching, gulping, smacking with the rest of them. There were a score of people in the Hall, prentices in leather aprons not quite cleansed of fish scales, two maidservants and the large Pessoner family. Large in size as well as in number, from Guy himself, who was built like one of his own herring barrels, and Dame Emma, who was round, firm and red as an apple, through the eleven children to the baby, who brandished fat arms and suckled greedily at Dame Emma's ample bosom. Katherine had never seen such plump and merry people. She noted that even Hugh, who sat beside his host, looked less surly and once or twice when Guy made some ribald joke, Hugh gave a grunt of laughter.

Katherine herself sat on the bench beside Hawise, the eldest daughter, and when everyone had quenched his thirst and Hawise no longer had to keep running down to the cellars for more ale, she had leisure for Katherine, and turned to their visitor with sympathetic curiosity. Katherine satisfied it willingly, saying without visible tremor that she was to be married Saturday morning, and that yes, Sir Hugh, there, was her betrothed.

"Is it so?" said Hawise, examining the knight. "He's naught so bad, young enough too. I'd mislike an old man's bed—dry as bean straw. Is he rich?"

Katherine laughed. It appeared that all the Pessoners said right out whatever was in their minds. "I—I think so. I don't know rightly," she answered.

Hawise looked startled. Even in her own class no marriage ever took place without a complete airing of all financial matters, and amongst the gentry and nobility she knew that this airing went much farther into a pother of jointures and settlements and papers to be signed.

Hawise questioned more and found out all the lonely circumstances of Katherine's life and her warm heart was touched. She felt drawn to the girl and protective, though she was but two years older.

Suddenly she stroked Katherine's cheek with her finger. "How fair you are, damoiselle," she said without a trace of envy. "Sheen as a fairy woman, I trow."

She herself was neither shining nor fair, being a stout big-boned lass, sandy-haired, freckled as a thrush's egg, and with a front tooth missing. Yet there was about her the wholesome strength of a healthy animal, and a mind for fun and color that made her very likable.

After Hugh had taken an inarticulate leave of Katherine, and he and Ellis had returned to the Savoy for the night, Katherine mounted thankfully to the loft over the fish shop, where she climbed into a big bed beside Hawise and two younger sisters, who were already asleep. She would not see Hugh again until they met at the church door, because it was not seemly to meet during the twenty-four hours before their marriage; and she resolutely tried to forget him.

Hawise started to talk of the wedding, but on seeing that Katherine fell silent and sighed often, the older girl let the topic alone and spoke instead of her own young man. This was Jack Maudelyn, weaver's apprentice, and Hawise loved him dearly, though they were not betrothed. The Pessoners were people of consequence in London, and Master Guy was loath to give his daughter to a mere prentice. Moreover, though the weavers had a fine enough guild, her father looked down on them and thought them not a patch on the wealthy victualing mysteries such as the fishmongers, the vintners and grocers. "I misdoubt Dada'll ever give consent, until I get me with child by Jack," added Hawise cheerfully, snuggling her head into the goose-feather pillow.

"Blessed Sainte Marie!" cried Katherine, sitting up straight in bed. "You wouldn't do that, Hawise. 'Tis mortal sin, it's—it's *horrible!*"

The other girl chuckled, she put her arm around Katherine's slender naked shoulders and pulled her down again.

"Easy to see you're convent-bred, sweeting. 'Tis no such sin, an' ye get wedded in time. It happens often enough in London. I've no mind to keep me maidenhead much longer. God's bones, I'll be eighteen come Michaelmas!"

Katherine was shocked, but she was fascinated, too. Could there be different ways of looking at a thing, even mortal sin? And was it possible that this ordeal which awaited her Saturday could be viewed in this cheerful and matter-of-fact light, could even be pleasurable? Ah, but Hawise loved her Jack, surely that made a difference, though Philippa said not, Lady Agnes de Saxilby said not, too—that love had nothing to do with duty. Suddenly, there swam before her eyes an image of the Duke as he had smiled up at his wife at the tournament. She shut her eyes tight and fingering the wooden beads that hung around her neck, began the Pater Noster.

She was awakened before daybreak by Hawise's playful slaps. "Get up, get up, damoiselle, for we must bring in the May!"

The whole Pessoner household was astir. The maids were raking out the floor coverings of stale, matted rushes, and laying down sweet-smelling new ones to last the month. Dame Emma stood over the kitchen fire seething eels and pike in claret to make her famous galantine, for though this was Friday, she saw no reason to keep strict fast, so long as one touched no meat. Indeed it was one of the most joyous of holidays, and Katherine, scampering barefoot in a borrowed kirtle through the London streets with Hawise and a dozen other lads and lasses from their ward, forgot the dignity of her fifteen years, forgot that she would be a wife tomorrow, and giggled and danced and sang with the rest of them.

At every block they were joined by a new band of young people from other districts, and they all poured through Bishopsgate into the open fields and woods past St. Mary Bedlam's hospital. Now they scattered, darting in all directions, hunting for the thickest-blossomed hawthorns, for branches of apple and sycamore and flowering cherry. Through the fresh dew-sparkled dawning, the lads' jerkins and maidens' kirtles flitted like scarlet, yellow and green butterflies.

Katherine and Hawise, having found their May boughs, were sitting in a meadow, feverishly weaving a garland of primroses and bluebells, when someone threw a mistletoe ball at Hawise's head. It bounced into her lap amongst the flowers and she looked up giggling. " 'Tis Jack," she said to Katherine, "I'll pay him out!" She stuffed the heavy bannock her mother had given her against hunger dexterously into the mistletoe, and when a shock of brick-red hair peered around the trunk of the nearest beech, she flung her missile hard. It hit Jack full on the mouth; he let out a roar of mock fury, and rushing for Hawise tumbled her backward upon the grass, tickling her until she howled for mercy.

Katherine drew a little aside during this rough play, but she laughed, too, and when Jack finally released his victim with a smacking kiss, she saw that he was a big hulking lad, as freckled and sandy as Hawise herself.

His eye lit on Katherine, and thinking her naught but a pretty barelegged maid, he seized her around the waist, pinched her little rump and nuzzled her neck. Katherine struggled and twisted, which he took for coyness, and he twined his hands in her long shining hair.

"Nay, nay, Jack!" cried Hawise. "Let her be. She's not one o' us. She's convent-bred! She's betrothed to a *knight*."

Jack's lantern jaw dropped; he released Katherine's hair, then peered fearfully around the quiet meadow.

"Her knight's not lurking here, you great booby!" laughed Hawise. "Come help us with our garland, quick!" It brought extra good fortune to bring in the May before the sun was fairly up. And when the garland was finished, Katherine had already forgiven Jack. The three young people ran back together into town, singing in round, as they skipped down Bridge street, the oldest of all the springtime greetings, "Sumer is icumen in, lhude sing cuccu."

In after years when Katherine thought of this last day of her girlhood she saw it lit up with a golden gaiety.

Spring bloomed in all the dark houses, every rafter and every post was festooned with greenery. The girls wore wreaths of flowers in their hair, the men tucked flowers behind their ears and under their belts. They drank the May wine, perfumed with wild thyme and violets. And they went to dance and sing around the enormous gilded Maypole which each year was erected by St. Andrew's church in Cornhill. So famous was this Maypole that it had given its name to the church, St. Andrew-under-Shaft, at which some of the stricter clerics frowned, deeming the May frolics pagan things that lured the folk to license. But most of the clergy thought no harm, and in the smiling ring of onlookers about the Maypole there was many a passing friar or parson, and even the black-garbed Benedictines stopped to watch.

Ah, Katherine should have been May Queen, cried Hawise, for she was fairer than any other maiden! But the queen had been chosen long ago, and already sat on her flowery throne beside the dancing. The May Queen's father was a goldsmith, and his metal seemed to shimmer in his daughter's hair, while her eyes were round and blue as forget-me-nots, so that Katherine knew Hawise was but being kind in calling her the most fair. Still, this kindness warmed her, and added to the glory of the golden day the feeling that she had found a true friend.

She did not forget Philippa mewed up in the house of illness. Once they stopped in the Vintry to inquire and found that Master John Chaucer seemed neither better nor worse. Philippa, full of pleasurable importance, had taken charge of the kitchen, so as to release Dame Chaucer for the nursing. Katherine felt guilt that she should be enjoying herself so much while her sister toiled. But Philippa wanted no help, it was plain that she was too busy to think of Katherine, who therefore continued to enjoy her freedom, which ended at last when they all danced the hay-de-guy around a bonfire in the wide square near the Guildhall.

How different was Katherine's awakening on Saturday morning. The lovely weather had dissolved into a steady rain. She awoke long before Hawise, against whose sturdy shoulder she had slept fitfully, and lay staring at the rafters and listening to the drip. It seemed as though a cold hand was gripping her heart, and she dared not move for fear the cold would spread and freeze her whole body.

The kindly Pessoners tried to rally her spirits with sly jests and rough teasing. They were sorry for this bride who had no mother to weep with her, and no kin to dress her. Hawise indeed took over the latter rite, tending Katherine lovingly and anointing her with a fragrant essence of gillyflowers, dressing her in the Duchess's green gown, which had been cleansed and freshened yesterday by one of the Pessoner maids. She brushed the curling dark auburn hair until it gleamed like Bohemian garnets, and left the mantle of hair to flow loose down to Katherine's knees in token of virginity. She set a bridal wreath of garden flowers on the girl's head, volubly cursing the rain as she did so. "But don't ye mind, my sweeting, mayhap it'll clear, thanks be to Saint Swithin!"

Her heart ached for this still, quiet figure who allowed herself to be dressed and tended like a wax image, when yesterday she had been all rosy laughter. Bad luck, thought Hawise sadly, that it should rain, always an ominous wedding portent, and worse luck yet to be married in May. Blessed Mary grant the girl didn't know that, being yet so unworldly, or it might further depress her spirits.

The Pessoner parish church, St. Magnus, had but just finished ringing for Tierce when there was a knock at the door. It was Philippa with Geoffrey, come to conduct the bride to St. Clement's.

"She's ready," said Hawise, drawing the hood carefully over Katherine's wreath to protect it from the rain and fastening the cloak at the neck with the Queen's brooch.

"And a most beautiful bride," said Geoffrey, chucking Katherine gently under the chin; but his gaze lacked its usual alertness. He had been up the last two nights with his father, who still lingered. He and Philippa both were tired and distraught. Philippa, in fact, could scarce keep her mind on the marriage, because now Dame Agnes Chaucer had taken ill, too, with vomiting and purging, and the neighbor who had come in to tend house in their absence seemed doltish as a sheep.

It was a silent, dripping-wet little company that plodded on foot along Thames street towards Ludgate. Hawise came with them, and Jack Maudelyn, who had sneaked off from his loom. Katherine had asked them both yesterday, when the world had been joyous and gay.

When they reached St. Clement's Dane they saw Hugh and Ellis, on horseback, awaiting them by the lych gate. Katherine raised her eyes once to Hugh. She saw a kind of fearing relief in his taut face, and that he was close-shaven; his stubborn beard subdued with oil, his crinkled hair, too, smoothed down and closer cut. She saw the scar across his cheek stand out purple on his flushed skin, and that his lips trembled. She saw all these things as though she looked through mist. Hugh seemed not real, she herself seemed not real, and she moved obediently and gave her hand and murmured answers like a docile child.

They stood first in the church porch, outside the iron-hinged door. There was a priest, called Father Oswald. There were vows. Geoffrey, Philippa, Ellis, Hawise and Jack pressed close, crowded under the porch to keep out of the rain. The priest then opened the door and they all went into the church. It was dank and musty and smelled of burning mutton fat from the votive candles at St. Clement's shrine. There were two wax tapers lit at the altar. A fitful gray light came through the coarse glass windows. Hugh and Katherine knelt at the altar rail, the others on prie-dieus behind. A runny-nosed little acolyte darted out from the vestry, and the priest turned to start the celebration of Mass.

Katherine heard a commotion in the nave, the sound of footsteps on the stone floor, the clink of metal, the rustle of garments. The priest faltered and paused, he swallowed nervously, staring into the back of the church, then he went on hastily with the Mass. Katherine did not turn her head; she felt no curiosity; she fixed her eyes on the gilded dove above the tabernacle, and her lips moved mechanically.

But Hugh turned to see, and she heard him make an exultant sound under his breath. She wondered vaguely why. The Mass went on, the bridal couple communicated. It was over. The priest spread his hands and said, *"Benedicite.* Go in peace, my children," then surreptitiously cuffed the altar boy who had forgotten his duties and stood staring openmouthed into the nave.

Hugh should have kissed her then, but he did not. He still held her hand as the priest had joined them, and his grasp tightened as he pulled her sharply around and after him down the aisle.

It was the Duke and Duchess of Lancaster who stood there by the west door. They were most splendidly appareled in crimsons and gold and jewels, and they each wore their ducal coronets, for they were going to a state banquet later. They lit up the gray church like torches.

"We're deeply honored, my lord and lady," stammered Hugh, dragging Katherine after him. She pulled her hand from his and curtised low.

The Duchess smiled. "We thought to wish you well at your wedding." It had been by chance that she had heard of it, through the gossip of one of her ladies who knew Ellis de Thoresby, but then her interest in Katherine had revived. She had asked the Duke to accompany her to the church, since it would be a matter of a few minutes only, and been a trifle surprised that he consented so readily, but thought he had decided to reinstate Hugh as a wedding boon. Yet now he did not look at Hugh, nor return his greeting. Instead he stood staring fixedly at Katherine.

"You've not kissed your wife, Swynford," said the Duke in a deep mocking voice. "It seems you need example." He leaned over, with a certain swift grace peculiar to him. He drew Katherine into his arms and kissed her slowly, deliberately, on the mouth. Fire shot through her, and as she gasped, her lips opened under his. In that instant she felt the hardness of his body under the velvet surcote and melting sweetness flowed through her bones, depriving her of strength. The Duke, feeling her yield, tightened his arms to support her. Then he released her, and laughed. "Her mouth tastes of honey, Swynford. Fortunate you are that you may drink your fill." He spoke thus tauntingly, and gazed at Hugh with careless arrogance, to hide a perplexing emotion he had felt as the girl's lips opened under his. Not desire, nor surprise that her body should be so tender, though both these thoughts had come to him, but a strange new impulse to protect.

Hugh's face was flushed with anger, knots stood out on his jaw, but he dared say nothing. He grabbed Katherine and gave her a rough, clumsy kiss. She scarcely noticed it. Her whole mind was bent on recovery, on controlling the trembling of her knees, and hiding tears that had stung her eyes as the Duke released her. For shame she could not raise her eyes towards the Duchess. But the Lady Blanche saw nothing out of the way. There were always kissings and sport at a wedding.

And now that they had honored the couple, the Duchess was anxious to hasten on to the banquet which could not start until they arrived. She held her long white hand out to Katherine, kissed her on the cheek and said, "May God bless your marriage bed, my dear, and make it fruitful. I'll see you again, no doubt, later this year in Lincolnshire, for I intend going to Bolingbroke when my Lord Duke sails for Aquitaine." Her gracious smile drifted from Hugh and Katherine over the rest of the wedding guests, who stood silently respectful farther up the nave. She slipped her hand through the Duke's arm.

The Duke said, "Farewell," and bowing slightly, turned on his heel, his gold spur clinking against a stone column. He found that the thought of Katherine's marriage bed disgusted him. Nor did he feel as tolerant of Swynford as he had. Were it was not for the need of good fighters in Castile—He snapped off these confused thoughts, and with Blanche joined their mounted retinue which awaited them on the street.

In the church porch, the others clustered around the bridal pair and offered awed congratulations. Philippa was delighted at the honor done her sister, and said so repeatedly. "Nearly as grand as though the Queen herself had come! I couldn't believe my eyes!"

Hawise was much excited at having seen these great folks so near. "Was there ever so stalwart and fair a man as the Duke!" she cried to Jack, who did not share her enthusiasm, but scowled, and grumbled that gold, jewels and coronets would make any man look handsome to a foolish woman.

Hawise paid no attention to this and turning to Katherine cried giggling, "Cock's bones, I just wish it'd been *me* he kissed on the mouth so—so masterful—like he did you, my lady!"

*My lady*. Katherine heard her new title with shock. I'm the Lady Katherine Swynford, the wife of a knight. This is my husband. She stole a frightened glance at Hugh but he had turned his back and was conferring acidly with Ellis about a loose girth on his saddle.

Only Geoffrey made no comment on the unexpected appearance of the Lancasters. Perceptive as always, he had seen more in the Duke's kiss and Katherine's reaction to it than a careless gesture, and his eyes had flown in loyal anger to the Lady Blanche's lovely unconscious face.

No, she would never suspect evil. Remote and shining as the moon, no grosser passions touched her. Yet for the first time in his long worship, Geoffrey wondered what it would be like to be mated to the moon, so cool and predictable and exalted. And then he smiled and reproved himself for harboring foolish whimsies, because he had felt during that moment in the dingy church an odd fear, as though some turbulent, even menacing, force had been set in motion. One that none of the people, not even the all-powerful Duke and Duchess, might be able to withstand.

# VI

KATHERINE's wedding night was spent at a pilgrim inn near Waltham Abbey. Hugh had meant to go farther, but he listened to Katherine's timid plea that she might stop and see the famous shrine of the black cross as they passed by. He was himself now willing to postpone the hour when they should be alone. Nervousness diminished his desire for her and at the thought that he would soon make her wholly his, he grew afraid. She seemed to him unearthly beautiful sitting straight and quiet on the little dappled palfrey he had given her. She had thanked him for the mare with startled gratitude, her voice soft-toned as he had never yet heard it for him. This had caused his heart to quiver and jump like a hare's.

Hugh was not in the least devout; he had never bothered to visit any shrine before, but Waltham Abbey was of some interest to him because it was no Norman shrine. It held the bones of Harold, the last Saxon king, and its miraculous black marble cross had been placed here by Tofig, a Danish thane.

As he and Katherine took their place amongst other pilgrims in the abbey, the huge shadowed nave inspired Hugh with awe, while the brass spirals on the thick round columns seemed to writhe at him like snakes. No holy feeling did they engender, but rather a superstitious shrinking that stirred the hairs on the back of his neck. And after they mounted the pilgrim's steps, while he looked up at the black cross, a strange thing happened. Somehow the buckle which fastened his scabbard to the belt had loosened; as he bent his knee, his sword fell to the pavement with a great clatter, then rolled down the steps to the chancel floor, where it lay pointing towards the western door.

The other pilgrims shrank back, murmuring and exclaiming. It was a sign, they said, that the Holy Cross was angry with the knight. It wanted none of his worship and had flung off his sword to point in such a way that he must leave the sanctuary. And they looked askance at Hugh, wondering what secret sin he might be guilty of.

Then a fat monk hurried up from behind the shrine, and said that indeed it was a sign, almost a miracle, but they must be careful of interpretation. He deemed that the Holy Cross wished the sword offered to it as a gift, that only in this way could the knight appease divine wrath.

Hugh stood silent on the top step gazing down at his fallen sword. The scabbard was of silver-gilt intricately carved, the sword itself of finest Damascus steel, the hilt incrusted with small rough emeralds. This sword had been his father's and had saved Hugh's own life in France and in many a skirmish since. He looked down at it with fear, feeling that in some way his manhood, too, had fallen from him, and he shook his head, muttering, "I will *not* give up the sword."

The people jostled and exclaimed again, whispering that hell fire would claim the knight for such disobedience, and one old crone lifted her wheezy voice to cry that she had seen a great white hand dart through the air from the Holy Cross and strike the sword off the knight's girdle.

The monk peered into Hugh's shut face, and finally said that there might be another way to avert wrath. The shrine had need of embellishment. The Holy Rood at Bromholme, though but a mean inferior miracleworker, had a new cloth of woven gold, but there was none like that here. It might be that for the *price* of the sword the Blessed Cross would be appeased.

Hugh looked from the monk to the heavy black cross. A tiny image of the Saviour had been fastened to its gleaming surface, but the cross breathed neither of pity nor redemption. Like the stone idols his ancestors had worshiped, it towered dark and sinister above him. What portent was this for his marriage? He saw that Katherine had drawn aside from the other pilgrims and stood watching, her cheeks gleaming white in the darkness of her hood.

He opened his purse and put four marks into the monk's outstretched hand. The monk's splay fingers closed over them. He murmured benediction and walked quickly back behind the shrine. Now the people murmured again, some thinking the knight got off too easily, but most thought that so great a sum would surely propitiate the cross.

Hugh descended the steps, picked up his sword and strode from the church, while Katherine walked after him. She had been frightened at the shrine when the sword clattered down and the people cried it was a sign. But when she saw fear on Hugh's face, too, she had felt a twinge of doubt. Had it been the Blessed Virgin or a saint he had somehow offended, she would not have questioned, but this lumpish black stone which contained not even a relic of the true cross seemed to her an ugly thing. Might it not have been that the sword had fallen because Hugh, hindered by his wounded hand, had not fastened it properly? And the fat monk with greedy piggish eyes, had he not been overglib in his interpretations? Yet, she realized with sudden shame, these were impious thoughts, and perhaps she entertained them only so that she need not think of the moment which was fast approaching.

They went to a mean and shabby inn, The Pelican, because Hugh had given up nearly all the money that he had, nor would he seek free shelter for them at the abbey hostel, where they would have been separated into different dorters.

The stuffy little loft room assigned them at the inn was no fitting bridal bower. The straw was moldy on the square box bed and hidden but in part by stained old quilts. Smoke seeped up through the rough planking from the kitchen fire below and in the dusty corners black beetles scampered.

Hugh looked sideways at Katherine, then he shouted for Ellis to bring up a flagon of strong ale, and of this he drank cup after cup in frantic haste as though he drank for a wager. He offered some to Katherine, but she merely wet her lips, and gave him back the cup. She had become very still, and stood by the tiny window, gazing out into the twilight towards the abbey. It seemed to her like a crouching beast; the chancel was its head, the double transepts its arms and legs, the nave its massive tail. A monster, ready to spring at her through the dusk. She turned her head a moment when Hugh banged down the oaken strip that bolted the door. She saw that his face had grown dark red, and heard the sound of his breathing. She shrank nearer to the window, and her hand clenched on the sill.

He came up behind her, gripping her shoulders with furious strength. "Katherine!" he cried, his voice as though he hated her. "Katherine—" The pain of his grip on her shoulders almost made her scream, and yet she knew that his fury was not directed at her, and through her fear, pity flickered and was gone.

In the quiet dawn light after Katherine had been weeping for many hours, she heard the nightingales singing from a thicket behind the inn. She lay and listened to their carefree bubbling song and at first it seemed to her an unbearable mockery. She eased her bruised body into a new position as far on the straw from Hugh as possible. He lay on his back snoring heavily, the room stank of sour ale and sweat. But as she listened to the nightingales, her tears dried, some peace crept into her heart, with a tough strength. She thought that no matter how her body was violated, it could not affect her unless she let it. She was still Katherine, and she could withdraw with this knowledge into the secret chamber where no one else might penetrate by violence. She could surround herself with an impregnable wall of hidden loathing and contempt.

As she thought this the abbey bells began to call the monks to Matins. The clangor of the great-throated bells and then the chanting of male voices drowned out the nightingales. Her hand went to her beads, and she began the Ave, but the beads slipped from lax fingers. What can the spotless Queen of Heaven know of that which befell me this night, what can Saint Catherine know, who was a virgin martyr? Leaning down from their purity, they may be gracious, but they cannot truly understand. So I am alone. I need nobody else. All that must be, I can endure alone.

Hugh stirred and murmured in his sleep. He reached his arm out as though he searched for her. She lay motionless, watching him, coldly, through narrowed lids. He looked younger in his sleep, yet his mouth drew in tight at the corners as though he suffered. His groping hand found the spilled masses of her hair and grasping a strand he pulled it to his cheek so that the jagged scar lay on her hair.

His gesture did not touch her, he was as alien to her now as had been the panting, heaving beast earlier. But she would never be afraid of him again, nothing that he did could touch her. She would be a dutiful wife, she would accept the hard lot that fate had given her, but yet she would be free. Because he loved and lusted and floundered, while she did not, she would be forever free.

Thus Katherine thought on her first morning of wifehood
in the ugly loft room of the inn at Waltham Cross.

On their way up to Lincolnshire, Hugh, Katherine and
Ellis spent three more nights on the road. Katherine was neither happy nor sad. She treated Hugh in a cool, friendly
enough manner, acceded indifferently to his nightly demands,
and yielded nothing of her inward self. He marked with jealousy that she spoke to Ellis in the same polite aloof way she
spoke to him, and that all her warmth and tender pleasure
went to the little mare he had given her. She had named it
Doucette, saying that it was sweet as the doucettes of cream
and sugar she had tasted at Windsor, and she was forever
patting its neck and murmuring little love words to it. Hugh
felt hot anger at the horse, but this he tried to hide, being
afraid of Katherine's scorn.

He could not have put words to his feelings, but in a confused way he realized that when he had forced and then possessed her body she had somehow managed to escape him
completely. But still he thought that she would come closer to
him later, and he reminded himself often of how young she
was, though very young she did not seem to him. For he had
never seen her dance and romp as she had in London on
May Day, nor had he ever heard her joyous quick laughter.

At Wednesday noontime, when they were a few miles
south of Lincoln town, they turned off the Ermine way and
climbed the Ridge to see Hugh's smaller manor of Coleby,
which he held in fee from the Duke of Lancaster. This
manor was much neglected, its house nothing but a crumbling shell, where Hugh's reeve, a sottish drunken lump of a
man named Edgar Pockface, dwelt in the leaky hall with a
brood of fifteen children. The reeve came lurching out the
door as he heard horses in the weed-choked courtyard and
stood aghast at seeing his manor lord. He tugged his forelock
and began mumbling. Hugh dismounted, glaring around at
the tumbledown dovecote, the byres and stables half unroofed,
the scanty piles of fodder moldering unsheltered on the dank
earth.

"By God's blood, Edgar Pockface!" he cried. "Is this the
way you oversee the villeins, is this the care you give my
manor!"

Edgar mumbled something to the effect that the serfs were
unruly, that they refused to do their regular week-work for

their lord, let alone the boon-work, that it had been so long
since Sir Hugh or his bailiff had come here they had near
forgot they were not freemen.

Hugh raised his hand and struck the stupid face a vicious
blow across the mouth. "Then this will remind you that you
are not free!"

The man staggered back and fell in the muck beside the
drinking well. He sat up spitting blood from a loosened tooth
and weeping drunkenly.

Then as though he had settled the whole matter of the
manor's management, Hugh mounted his horse and, gesturing
to Katherine and Ellis, led the way back to the High road.

Katherine was pained and puzzled. Should Hugh not inspect his serfs? Should he not ride over the rest of his land to
see in what condition it was? Should he not above all eject
the drunken reeve, and find one who could manage the tenants and obtain from them the requisite labor? She rode in
silence for a while, then ventured, "Will you not get a new
reeve, Hugh, for Coleby?"

He shrugged. "Oh, Edgar'll do well enough now, he's
learned a lesson. Fear makes the best taskmaster."

Katherine doubted it, but she said no more. She did not
yet know that Hugh was the most indifferent of landlords,
caring nothing for husbandry, and interested in his manors
only enough to demand that they yield him sufficient rents
and fines so that he might satisfy his few needs. He had not
been home in three years and had left everything in the
hands of his steward at Kettlethorpe, whom he had good reason to trust. So long as Hugh gave knight's service to the
Duke, his wants and those of Ellis were provided for, and
soon his wartime wages from the Duke would commence.

It was on the prospects of these that he had raised cash
from a money-lending Lombard in London to finance his
wedding and buy Katherine's palfrey. But the forced gift to
the black cross at Waltham had so reduced him that now he
had but a few pence left. This troubled him not at all. Gibbon, his bailiff, must produce an accounting at Kettlethorpe
and replenish Hugh's purse, and that was all there was to it.

Katherine did not think long about the dilapidation of Coleby, assuming that all would be different at Kettlethorpe, the
home manor. Yet her yeoman blood had been disquieted. She
remembered a little of the great farm in Picardy where she
had spent her childhood. She remembered the reverent voices

of her grandparents as they spoke of their land, her grandmother's incessant orderly bustle to make, to tend, to repair. She remembered her grandfather, riding forth at all hours of the day or night to peer with shrewd weatherwise eyes at every field of grain and vegetable patch and pasture on his land. Katherine had loved them, too, those fertile sunlit acres, and the feeling of happy abundance after Michaelmas when the granaries were full, and the sweet hay stacked high in the lofts.

An ache for the past came to her as she looked out across the flat gray fenland. She thought the fens ugly and forlorn. It had been drizzling all day, but now the dun clouds dropped lower and the rain sliced cold and straight as knives. When at last they reached the little suburb of Wigford across the river Witham from Lincoln town, Hugh was in a great hurry to cover the remaining ten miles to Kettlethorpe and would not let Katherine linger to gaze up the hill at the cathedral. She could see it but dimly through the clouds and rain, but it seemed to her a wondrous fair site for a house of God. The three great spired towers floated up towards heaven as though they had no roots in the sinful world below.

And how comforting it was to see a hill again, and a town, after the miles of flatness, punctuated only by isolated hamlets. They had come to a remote world in these days of travel. London seemed to her now as far-off as France, as Rome, as the fairy land of Cockaigne. Their very speech was different here—it twanged and burred so she could scarcely understand it. She felt ungladness in the people. They smiled seldom and dressed in sober hues. So the glimpse of Lincoln heartened her, and she was pleased that Kettlethorpe was near.

But it was not. The ten miles dragged like thirty. Here and northward along the vale of the Trent it had been raining since St. George's Day, and the full moon tides had thundered up the down-rushing swollen river in an eagre; this sinister wave, high as a man, had burst many of the earthen dykes and flooded much of the land. And though now the water had receded and lay in pools and patches on the sodden fields, the highway was a mire of sticky red mud, so deep at times that the horses slipped and floundered; their hoofs sucked in and out like uncorked bottles. While they used the towpath along the side of the Fossdyke progress was not so difficult, for on this busy link of navigation the bargemasters had placed stones and branches to give their tow horses some footing, but when the road turned from the canal at Drinsey Nook, it became well-nigh impassable.

Katherine's little Doucette had begun to tire, and when beneath a puddle of water its hoof caught in a deeper hole, the mare gave a frightened snort and fell splashing on its side. Katherine jumped instinctively and landed unhurt beside Doucette, but covered with the cold sticky mud and near to tears.

Hugh, swearing furiously, first picked her up, then with Ellis' help tried to raise the kicking, plunging palfrey. This they could not do until Katherine spoke to the little beast and soothed it with her coaxing. Katherine would have gone on afoot, but Hugh commanded her to mount again, and finding that the water on the road came nearly to her knees, she obeyed. Hugh took Doucette's bridle and led the horse after him; Katherine clung to the pommel in sodden misery. The drenched hood and cloak no longer kept off the rain at all. She found that she had lost one leather shoe back there in the mud, but it made no difference, her stockinged foot in the stirrup was no colder than the shod one.

They plodded on, meeting nobody but a cowled barefoot friar who did not return Hugh's gruff greeting, but sloshed past them, head bowed, chanting to himself.

As they drew nearer the manor lodge the wind came up and blew the rain in their faces, but the footing improved a trifle, for now the road ran though light moorland soil and sand which comprised most of the parish. Yet it was dark when they saw upon the left a pair of tall iron gates, and a cottage just inside them.

"Kettlethorpe!" said Hugh. "We'll soon be dry and sheltered, Katherine."

But no one came to open the gate, though Ellis kicked it and hammered on it, and both men shouted. The lodgekeeper's thatched shanty remained dark, and no smoke came from its chimney.

"The devil and his foul fiends take this wretched churl. I'll have him put in the stocks, I'll lop off his deaf ears!" Hugh drew his sword and dealt the old padlock a violent blow. The chain that held it was near eaten through with rust and at the second blow it parted; the padlock dangled free. Ellis pushed back the creaking gates and said in surprise, "This road has not been used for long, Sir Hugh. 'Tis full overgrown."

There was, in fact, no road at all, though its place was marked by an avenue of magnificent wych-elms, tall as steeples, their branches writhing and tossing in the strengthening wind. Beneath the elms there was a tangle of weeds, bushes, long grasses and brambles that tore at Katherine's skirts. The horses balked, twisting and seeking some easier way. Ellis had to go ahead of them on foot, beating down the thicket with his sword.

Is there no end to this journey? Katherine thought, shivering, and she noted that Hugh did not meet this new hindrance with cursing, but had fallen silent while he constantly peered ahead. She could not see his face, but she felt his uneasiness, and her own discomfort grew.

For near a mile they fought their way along the abandoned road, then suddenly Katherine saw a church on her right, a dark shape of the cross against the darker sky, while to the left there was a huddle of buildings and a squat round tower. Still there were no lights, and no sound but the wind in the trees and the slash of rain.

They rode into the muddy outer court between the church and the house, and now Katherine saw the dull gleam of a small moat and a low stone gatehouse, its wooden bridge drawn up flat against the arch.

"Ho, Kettlethorpe!" shouted Hugh. "Gibbon le Bailey! Lady Nichola! Open up!"

Still the uncanny silence held. It was broken by a frenzied baying from the inner court, one deep menacing note over and over like a tocsin.

" 'Tis old Ajax," cried Hugh, with unconcealed relief. "Someone's in there."

"Unless it be the demon pooka hound," said Ellis, laughing nervously and crossing himself.

"Shut up, you bloody fool. You know well it's not been seen in Swynfords' time, 'twas of the old days. Open up! Open up in the name of the Trinity!"

At this a dim white head peered out of the peephole above the gatehouse, and a peevish old voice cried, "Who is't now that makes such clamor?"

"Toby Napper, by God, what ails you all? Don't you know me? A fine welcome this for the lord of the manor and his new lady!"

The white head disappeared, the windlass began to creak, until the rickety bridge flopped into the mud across the narrow moat. The horses crossed into the inner courtyard, where the hound came bounding and growling at them. But he knew Hugh's voice, and when Hugh gave him a powerful kick he slunk into the shadows.

Then Hugh turned on the gatehouse keeper, who stood holding a wavering horn lantern, his head wagging feebly. "Where're the stableboys? Where the house carls?" Hugh seized the old man's shoulders and tried to shake wits into him.

"Naught but me, m'lord, for this year past. M'lady turned 'em out. No one sleeps in the manor but me and m'lady—and—and Gibbon."

"Ay, ay, and what *of* Gibbon? Why isn't he here?"

"Ah, he's dying, is Gibbon," said the old man unctuously. "There's a worm gnawing of his bones. They've turned limper'n eels, his bones has. He lies abed all day and will not move. A young man was Gibbon, but now he's older than I be." The wheezing voice broke into a cackle of laughter.

Hugh made an exclamation, loosing the skinny shoulders, grabbed Toby's lantern and threw open the unbolted door to the Great Hall. Inside it was as dark and dank as out. There was no fire, nor sign of any, on the central hearth. The eating trestles, planks and benches were stacked high on the far wall. Rain splashed through a hole in the thatched roof onto a corner of the lord's dais.

"Ellis!" Hugh cried. "Gallop to the village and bring me back serfs. By God's nails, we must have food and warmth, no matter what's amiss here!"

The squire ran out and mounted his horse. Hugh put the lantern on the hard-packed earthen floor. He turned his face slowly from one end of the Hall to the other, remembering it in the days of his boyhood, when there had been torch and firelight, the smell of roasted meat, and ten servants running to attend the Swynford appetites.

Katherine crumpled down in one of the window embrasures, leaning her head against the stones, so cold and weary that she could not think. Her teeth chattered, and beneath her drooped lids the flickering shadows in the Hall swayed like water.

Then through her exhaustion she heard a rustling at the door, and opened her eyes. A woman stood there staring at Hugh. She was small and thin as a stick, her black gown flapped around her in the wind from the reopened door, and her triangular widow's coif was no whiter than her narrow face.

"Is it you—Hugh? Have you come?" She spoke in a high sighing voice in which there was neither surprise, nor pleasure nor dismay. "I thought you'd come. *They* told me so."

Hugh had jumped back as she appeared suddenly gliding into the hall. The contempt he had always felt for his stepmother and the anger at the havoc she had obviously wrought on his manor were both checked by the unfocused stare of her dull red-rimmed dark eyes.

"Ay, lady," he said warily after a moment, not moving towards her. "I've come home, with my bride." He pointed to Katherine, who slid slowly from the window and made a curtsy. "And I mislike the welcome you give to the new lady of Kettlethorpe."

The woman turned her mournful gaze on Katherine. "A bride?" she said, shaking her head in disbelief. "A bride at Kettlethorpe? *They* did not tell me that."

"*Who* did not tell you, madam?" Hugh snapped.

The Lady Nichola Swynford waved a bony hand vaguely towards the east. "The folk who live in the water, in the river, in the well. One mustn't say their name. They tell me many things."

"God's wounds," Hugh whispered, crossing himself and stepping close to Katherine. "She's lost the few wits she had."

The girl nodded and sat down again in the window niche. She looked at her husband, mud-spattered, his habitual scowl modified by the uneasy glances he threw his stepmother. He stood near the lantern, legs wide apart, his bandaged hand resting on his sword hilt. They both watched the Lady Nichola, who began to drift restlessly around the Hall. As the black-robed figure came to the water that streamed through the roof onto the dais, she stopped. She cupped her hands and caught some of the water, murmuring soft words to it as though in greeting.

Katherine shut her eyes again. A merciful blankness fell across her mind.

During the next days at Kettlethorpe, Katherine had opportunity for the exercise of many qualities she had not known she possessed. Her strong young body recovered soon from the drenching and exhaustion of her arrival; the recovery of her spirits and the acceptance of conditions so different from her imaginings took longer. Yet a sturdy common sense came to her aid. For better or worse this was now her home, and she the lady of the manor. She was child enough to feel pride in the sudden responsibilities thrust upon her. It was a little like the games of being grown-up ladies she had played with other girls at Sheppey, yet this feeling of play-acting did not preclude a hardheaded realism. She thought often of Philippa in those first days and wondered how her sister's orderly methods would have righted this muddle.

Kettlethorpe parish stood in the isolated corner of Lincolnshire at the southwest tip of Lindsey. It was bounded by the River Trent on the west, Nottinghamshire on the south and the angled Fossdyke on the east and north—a parcel of some three thousand acres including, besides the manor village, two hamlets called Fenton and Laughterton. It had formed part of the Saxon Wapentake, or Hundred, of Well, and owed feudal dues to the Bishop of Lincoln, under whom the Swynfords held this manorial right.

It had never been a populous or especially productive manor, the soil being suited only to the growth of hay, flax, hemp and such like, and most of the land being in virgin forest for the pleasure of its lords. Earlier owners, such as the de la Croys, had had large holdings elsewhere to supplement their rents, as indeed so had Hugh's father until mismanagement had dwindled off Nichola's dowry, leaving the Swynfords only Coleby and Kettlethorpe.

Yet these two would have supported them all in sufficient comfort, were they well administered, Katherine thought. Hugh still had over sixty serfs at Kettlethorpe, man, woman and child; plenty to give him week-work on his home farms, boon-work at the harvests and inside work to run the manor.

The trouble here, of course, was twofold: the Lady Nichola's eccentricities and the mortal sickness which had attacked Gibbon, the bailiff.

Three days after Katherine's arrival she felt well again and decided to see this man who lay in a wattle-and-daub hut at the end of the courtyard between the dovecote and the bakehouse.

The weather had at last cleared and Hugh, having bullied and whipped some sulky serfs from their own fieldwork and back into the manor kitchen, had taken Ellis and ridden off into the forest to hunt for sorely needed food. He was not

sorry to put off the countless tasks which awaited him. A
manor Court must be called, the serfs brought to punishment,
their overdue fines collected, a new bailiff found. But above
all the larders must be replenished; they were completely
empty. Lady Nichola lived on sheep's milk and stewed herbs
which she cooked herself in an iron pot in the tower room
where she spent all her time when she was not wandering
through the marshes and fields towards the river. Gibbon existed on the fitful donations of Margery Brewster, the village
alewife, who felt kindly towards him, having several times
shared his bed in the days of his strength, but whose tavern
duties and brood of babies left her little time for charity. No
one knew what old Toby lived on in the gatehouse, but he
was shrewd, despite his age, and there had been nobody to
notice the gradual depopulation of the lord's dovecote, nor
hear the squeal of snared rabbits in the lord's hunting pre-
serve.

Katherine had not asked Hugh's permission to visit the
bailiff. Already she had learned that the mention of painful
subjects induced in him an angry stubbornness which might
well have led to refusal.

She waited until she saw the tip of his longbow disappear
into the forest on the other side of the moat, then set herself
to a leisured inspection of her domain, much irked that she
still had no proper clothes except the travel-stained green
gown the Duchess had given her, not even a linen coif to
hide her hair and show her housewifely status. No matter,
she thought, braiding and looping the great ruddy ropes
neatly on either side of her face. She was determined not to
be discouraged, and to meet this new life with calmness.
Since there was no one to help her, she must depend on herself, and again, as it had on the morning after her marriage,
this thought gave her strength.

She decided to visit the Lady Nichola first in the tower
room. She had not seen her mother-in-law since the night of
arrival, but smoke and steam sometimes drifted through the
arrow-slit windows and twice she had heard a not uncheerful
crooning sound from up there.

The low defensive tower had been built, as had the manor,
a hundred and fifty years ago, in the reign of King John. It
was attached to the hall and solar, but there was no communication with these except by the outside staircase, which also
served the solar. The manor plan was simple and old-fash-

ioned. There was the thatched two-storied Hall, forty feet long, and the narrow solar where Katherine slept with Hugh was tacked high onto its western end. Beneath the solar lay an undercroft for stores. At the eastern end of the Hall there was a kitchen, and a half-loft above it where the servants slept. These and the tower with its ancient donjon and two round rooms above were all there was to Kettlethorpe. No private chapel, no spare chambers, garderobes or latrines. The demands of nature were answered in an open corner of the courtyard behind the dovecote.

It was a more primitive dwelling than any Katherine had ever known; even the convent at Sheppey and her grandparents' great farmhouse had been more luxurious, while the Pessoner house in London, and of course the great castle at Windsor, had shown her entirely different standards of comfort.

And the furnishings at Kettlethorpe she deemed shockingly plain and scanty for a knight's home. The planks and trestles and benches in the hall were barren of carving and as roughly hewn as those in a rustic's cot, while the solar was furnished only with a square box frame heaped with a moldering goose-feather bed and a flea-infested bearskin for a coverlet. It surprised her much that they should drink the small ale Hugh had commandeered from the village out of coarse wooden mazers and that there should be no object of the slightest value to be seen, not even a saint's statue, or a tapestry to keep out the constant draughts. She longed for explanation of this singular poverty, but did not dare ask Hugh, seeing that he felt shame at the condition of his estate and tried to hide it by loud rantings against his stepmother. All the more she could not ask him because she had brought him no dowry, nor had he reproached her with its lack. In justice, she owed him all her help to straighten out his affairs.

As she ascended the outside flight of wooden steps into the tower, her heart beat fast, for she heard the Lady Nichola's high murmuring float out onto the still air. The dairy maid said that the Lady Nichola had water-elf sickness, a fearsome spell; and none of the servants would go near her. Katherine paused to gather courage and looked across the courtyard wall and the moat, towards the cross on the church spire. She had not yet been over to the church, and there was no Mass except on Sundays. The parson, grown slack, as everyone else on this manor, was not even at home, but had gone some days ago to Lincoln on business of his own.

It seemed strange to Katherine to live without the sound of bells. She must learn now to guess at the time, but it mattered little, for here there were no regular hours for anything. All was haphazard.

She mounted the stairs and entered the tower's ancient guardroom. Many generations had passed since it had heard the clash of steel and the oaths of men-at-arms, and its slit windows, sunk seven feet deep into the walls, had never heard the whir of defending arrows. No other baron had coveted this isolated manor. The first lord had built the tower and dug the moat because it was the fashion of building in his day, and he had used Kettlethorpe chiefly as a hunting lodge. Katherine, glancing quickly about, saw that the room contained only two ironbound chests. In the center of the stone floor there was a rusty grille over the only airshaft to the donjon beneath. In the time of Hugh's father, Sir Thomas, this donjon had been used occasionally for the detention of serfs awaiting trial, but now it had long been empty of all but rats who tunneled upward from the surrounding moat. Katherine saw that dust lay thick as her hand on the chests and that a drift of dead leaves had blown into the corners.

She climbed the narrow stone steps that were built in the thickness of the wall and came to the top room. A mangy deerhide barred the doorway. The murmuring had stopped, there was a listening silence within.

Katherine cleared her throat and called softly, "My Lady Swynford! It's Katherine, Hugh's bride. May I enter?"

She heard a scuffling noise as though something were being quickly hidden, and a tiny stifled sound, sharp and high. Her heart beat faster, but she called again. Still there was no answer, but she heard the rasp of frightened breathing.

She pushed the deer hide and entered. "Ah no!" she cried when she saw the little black figure. "My poor lady, you mustn't be afraid of me!"

The Lady Nichola, her arms clasped tight across a lumped cloth on her breast, was cowering behind her bed. Her dark eyes were fixed on Katherine with dumb terror. When Katherine drew nearer, she flattened her shoulder blades against the wall as though she would break through its stones. From the lumpy cloth she strained to her chest there came again the stifled sound.

"Dear lady, I won't hurt you. I've come up to do you honor, as is right. See, I'll come no nearer. I won't move from here." Katherine's voice, low and soft as a viol, thrilled with pity.

Nichola, who had heard no kindness since she had come to Kettlethorpe ten years ago, stared unbelieving. "You'd take her away from me—" she whispered. "Don't take her away —she does no harm."

The girl shook her head and tried to smile reassurance. Though the Lady Nichola was over forty and her scant dark hair was streaked with gray, yet her little face, twisted by fear, was somehow childlike.

Katherine stood stock-still as she had promised and saw the clutch of the claw hands slowly relax on the bundle they protected. The cloth heaved and squirmed.

"What have you there, my lady?" said Katherine very gently. "I swear by Saint Mary and her Blessed Son that I'll not touch it, nor do anything you don't wish."

"But Hugh would—he'd take her away from me and beat me as his father did. Beat me because I'm barren."

Katherine stiffened. "No," she said, her jaw tight. "No one shall beat you."

The Lady Nichola crept forward to the bed, her wide-straining eyes fixed on Katherine's face. She put the bundle down on the coarse hemp coverlet. The girl waited quietly, though the flesh on her back tingled. The cloth heaved and from underneath there walked out a small bedraggled kitten. It was striped in pale buff and it wore a collar made of woven grass from which dangled a leash of plaited scarlet wool.

Almost Katherine laughed, for she had expected some shocking thing, a baby perhaps—crazed women did steal babies—or sign of witchcraft like a serpent. But pity quenched her smile as Lady Nichola snatched up the kitten and covered it with kisses, while it miouled feebly.

"Dear, my lady," said Katherine, " 'tis no sin for you to keep a kitten. No need to be so fearful."

"*They* gave her to me," said Nichola, stroking the little beast while she tied it to the bedpost. "She was drowning in the river, because they wanted her themselves to play with, down there amongst the reeds, but they let me have her.

Sometimes they're very kind. But they didn't tell me you were coming—Hugh's bride."

Suddenly the unseeing stare left Nichola's red-rimmed eyes, and the young wild look left her face. Now wrinkles dented around her drooping mouth and between her brows. "So there's a new Lady of Kettlethorpe," she said in a much lower voice. "How did you come to be here?" She sat down quietly on the bed.

Katherine was startled at the change. She saw that the madness had ebbed suddenly to disclose a dead weariness of spirit beneath. Now for a few minutes while there was sanity in Nichola's questions, Katherine told her something of her life and how she came to marry. Nichola nodded from time to time and listened sadly. "I too came from the south," she said, "to this most dismal place. But I was always afraid. He would not have hated me so, had I not been afraid. Even though I bore no children. He broke my arm once—see—" She pulled up her black sleeve to show a crooked lump of bone beneath the mottled skin. "But I was ugly—like a monkey, my lord said." She twisted her head and looked up at Katherine. "*You're* beautiful, fair as *they* are that I see in the water when the other life is on me. Yet you will molder here, even as I, and grow ugly and afraid unless—unless—" She jumped up, her voice soared to its high chanting note and she cried, "I'll weave a spell for you, Hugh's bride. I have the herbs; the hazel and the bloodwort and the secret ones. I have water here from the Holy Well in Rough wood. I'll make a potion that'll save you—"

She ran to the iron pot which hung on a tripod against the smoke-blackened wall, she blew the smoldering charcoal embers in the pan beneath and catching up a fistful of dried herbs began to cast them in the pot.

"Nay, lady," said Katherine gently, "I want no potion." But she saw that it was useless. The moment of reason had passed. Nichola did not hear her. The wild yet happier look came back into her face. She picked the kitten from the floor and, carefully untying its wool leash, held it to her breast and began to croon softly, "Ah my pretty one—my poppet, my sweeting, you too shall stir the potion—" And she held the kitten's paw on the ladle.

Katherine turned away and, lifting the deer hide, slipped from the tower room. She felt no fear now of the Lady Nichola, but she was heavy of heart. She descended the steps to the courtyard and let the sun stream on her uplifted face while trying to recapture the hopeful energy she had felt earlier. Ajax, the great mastiff, walked over to her stiff-legged from his kennel, sniffed her gown, then stalked away towards the stables. She followed him and entering went straight to Doucette's stall. The little mare greeted her with a whinny, and she threw her arms around its neck. Then her arms fell slack. One Lady of Kettlethorpe has nothing to love but a kitten and I— She looked at her horse and sudden anger possessed her.

She spied a stableboy's bare legs protruding from a mound of straw in the next stall. "Wake up, you lazy churl!" she cried sharp and loud. "Get up!" The lad jumped to his feet, knuckling sleep out of his eyes.

"What's your name?" Katherine surveyed him with disgust —his filthy hair, dangling red hands and torn dung-spattered smock.

"Wat—that be Walter—Wat's son, m'—lady," he stammered, not very sure who this tall angry maiden might be. He had heard that the new Lady of Kettlethorpe was but a soft child who had lain abed all yesterday.

"Well, Wat Watson!" cried Katherine. "Why have you not curried my palfrey? Why is the hayrick empty?"

Wat swallowed and, ignoring her first question, said that the hayrick was empty because there was no hay.

"There's green grass in the meadow beyond the moat," she snapped. "Go pull enough to fill the manger, then curry Doucette, water and saddle her. I will ride later."

"Ay, m'lady," said Wat.

"And—" added Katherine, "when you've finished that, clean out this foul stable. By God's sweet dignity you should be shamed!"

He stared, open-mouthed. Later in the alehouse he told the story with embellishments. He said that Katherine had belabored him with a pitchfork and roared at him with strange London oaths, that she had threatened him with ear-lopping, did he not do her bidding. Nobody believed all this, for Wat was known as a liar and a sluggard. But it confirmed the general apprehension that the easygoing days were over, and there were long faces in the alehouse.

Buoyed on the wave of her anger, Katherine quitted the stables, picked her way through ancient refuse past the empty granary set high on posts for safety against vermin, past the mammoth bake-oven where the serfs should have been bringing their loaves and paying the manor levy on each baking. The iron oven door was missing from the wrenched hinges. No doubt someone had found use for it, she thought grimly, and use for the iron locks which had plainly been prized from the doors of other buildings, dairy house, woodshed and loom room.

She came to the low daub-and-wattle hut where she knew the bailiff lay and tapped upon the door. A man's harsh voice said, "Who's there?" and she answered with firmness, "Katherine Swynford, the new Lady of Kettlethorpe."

"Enter then!"

The stench inside the hut near knocked her over, and she stood blinking in the darkness and retching uncontrollably while red fear smote her. Was this perhaps the stink of plague? Her nostrils still remembered the vileness of the night in Picardy when her grandparents died. But this man had lain here for months and plague victims did not linger. But there was worse than plague! She gasped and stepped back into the courtyard.

"Is he *unclean?*" she whispered, not knowing that she spoke.

"Nay, lady," said the bitter voice in the darkness, "I'm no leper. Would that I were, for in the lazaretto I'd be with others of my kind and tended by the brothers. I'd not be lying here alone in my own ordure."

Katherine's stomach heaved again, she put her hand tight against her mouth and came back within the door.

"Open the shutter, lady," said the voice, half sneering. " 'Twill sweeten the air for squeamish noses."

Katherine flung back the little window shutter. The cool spring breeze blew from the forest across the room and out the door. She looked down at the man who lay on a straw pallet on the floor. A russet mantle such as men had worn in the early days of Edward's reign covered all his body; she could see but his arms. On the sharp bones and knobbed joints the flesh hung slack as a bag. And in his ivory skull-head the eyes were sunk so that she scarce could see that they were blue. Only the long curling brown hair of his head and his matted beard showed that he had been a comely man. His lips drew back from his strong white teeth, and he shut his eyes, for light made them ache.

"Behold Gibbon, your steward, my lady," he said. "I can

move nothing but my head, and these fingers—see! He clenched his jaw, veins stood out on his forehead and his left hand jerked on the mantle.

"What is it, Gibbon?" she asked, steadily enough.

"I know not. It began two years ago with a weakness in my legs. They trembled much. The trembling crept from limb to limb, but now they do not even tremble."

"You've had a leech?"

"A barber from Torksey. He bled me often. It does no good. While I yet could get about I burned candles at Saint Hugh's shrine in Lincoln minster. That did no good, either, nor will it—this is punishment for the sin of my begetting."

"Does no one tend you, Gibbon?"

"Oh, ay—when they remember. Old Toby at times, big Margery Brewster from the vill, the parson when he's not chaffering in Lincoln for fine meats and wines to fill his fat belly."

Katherine frowned and lifted her chin. "There must be many changes on the manor!" she cried. "*I'll* see that you're tended properly—a serf to care for you night and day. Then you'll get better."

He looked at her then with some attention. A feeble smile narrowed his sunken lids. "You're full young to be so resolute," he said. Young and very fair, he thought. Shining with indignation, burning to set wrongs right, and certain that it could be done. Like Saint Michael with the sword and scales. Ay, he thought, and shut his eyes again—once I would not have compared so female a creature to Saint Michael. He felt the weight of his dead body that hung to his neck like a sack of stones. Soon the neck too would be dead, and then the head.

"Is there much pain?" she said softly. There was a flagon of ale on the floor and a piece of bread. She poured ale into a wooden cup and held it to his lips. Almost, she felt courage to pull back his mantle and cleanse him, but yet she could not. She had seen no man naked save Hugh, and at him she had not looked.

He shook his head to the ale. "Margery was here this morning. I was fed. No, there's no pain." He added in a stronger voice, "Where's Hugh gone? I heard the horses in the courtyard."

"Hunting in the forest. We need meat." She said it lightly, that he might not think it a reproach to his stewardship. She had meant to ask him many questions about the manor, but now she felt she could not disturb so ill a man with her ignorance. She would like, too, to question him about himself; his turn of speech astonished her. Here was no peasant twang or clumsy grammar; he spoke as well as any knight at Windsor court, better, in fact, than Hugh. What then did he as bailiff here?

Gibbon had become intuitive during these months when nothing seemed to live in him but his brain. He felt her thoughts. "Hugh told you naught about me, did he?" He looked up at her with the faint smile. It had been long since anyone had lingered to talk to him.

"No," she said, "he spoke never of you, nor of his manors."

"Ay, it was always that way. Hugh has little interest in his lands, but *I* had. I fended for him, and I ruled his villeins. I collected his rents and fines and though I paid out each Michaelmas the twenty pounds service fee Kettlethorpe owes the Bishop of Lincoln and the fees due from Coleby, yet we were prospering. Soon here we might have furnished and made the manor worthy of Swynfords. I had even thought to build a pleasure garden, between the tower and the moat, in case Hugh got him a bride." His lips twisted from his teeth. "Now there is a bride—but no pleasure garden, no handsome furnishings to greet her. And the manor—I can guess what condition it's in."

"I've wondered," she said, hesitating, "why there are no furnishings here, except the rudest."

"Hugh sold them all at his father's death. He had to pay relief and heriots to *his* feudal lords, of course, before he could claim his inheritance. You must know that," he added in surprise.

She shook her head. "I know nothing."

"Hugh should find a new bailiff at once, and you will need help to administer your dowry."

"I bring no dowry," said Katherine quietly. "Hugh *would* have me, nonetheless."

Gibbon fell silent. This seemed to him very bad news. Since he had known of Hugh's return home with a wife he had passed some of the interminable black hours in wondering what dowry she brought, and how it could be best expended for the rehabilitation of the manor which had to him been wife, family and salvation for years. That the girl was fair and intelligent he saw, that she had some tenuous connection with the court he had heard from Ellis, but none of this offset the lack of dowry. In fact, he had hoped that Hugh, when he finally returned home, might see the wisdom of wooing the Lady Matilda, sister to Philip Darcy, the lord of Torksey. True, Matilda was a widow, and something brown and shriveled in looks, having lost most of her teeth, but she had borne children and was not yet past the age to bear others. Besides, Hugh had never seemed the man to be finicky about the women he bedded. The Torksey lands were rich and adjoined Kettlethorpe on the north; the marriage would have recouped the Swynford fortunes.

"It irks you that I bring no property," said Katherine, flushing. His silence hurt her so that she fogot his illness and added sharply, "Is it the custom in Lincolnshire for the hired bailiff to concern himself so deeply in his master's affairs as this!"

Gibbon turned his eyes back to her. "Ah, but you see, madam, I too am a Swynford, and debarred by birth from owning land myself. I yet make shift to serve my house—or did."

The hot stain faded from Katherine's forehead, she looked down at him amazed. "*You* are a Swynford, Gibbon?"

"Ay. Hugh and I are half brothers."

"But I don't understand—"

He made a derisive sound in his throat. "Simple enough, for I'm a bastard."

She could not prevent a shocked sound. Bastardy had always seemed to her the most pitiable of states!

Gibbon's sardonic voice went on. "Ay—our most dear father, Sir Thomas, strew others like me from Grimsby to Grantham, though his only true-born son was Hugh. Yet was I a special case, for my mother was a nun at the Fosse Priory, not two miles from here."

Katherine swallowed. "Sweet Jesu," she whispered.

"Two days after she bore me, she drowned herself in the Trent, but this I did not know until my father died. He had me reared by the Gilbertines at Sempringham, and not knowing then I was a bastard I once thought to join their order. When my father made full confession on his deathbed, the gentle Gilbertines were scandalized. They prayed for my mother's lost soul, and my father's black one, but they turned me out."

The muscles of his throat ached from so much talking, and he sighed. "What then, Gibbon?" Katherine whispered, putting her hand on his inert arm.

"Why, then Hugh was the heir, and he summoned me to aid him on the land, swearing that none here should taunt me with the infamy of my birth. It was generously done, and I was grateful." His tongue thickened and grew numb, the pulse in his neck began to tremble and beat, he felt himself drifting into the half-world of mists.

"Ay, it was generously done," Katherine murmured, turning this new aspect of her husband over in her mind. Generous yet expedient, too; Hugh had needed someone he could trust to run the manor.

"Gibbon," she said, "will you help me when you can, tell me what must be done here?"

His lips moved in assent, then fell slack.

She went quickly out of the hut into the sunny courtyard and shut the door. Dear God this is now my *home*, she thought. Soon Hugh and Ellis will go to Aquitaine and I shall be here alone with a crazed woman, a dying man and a pack of rebellious serfs. Of a sudden she thought of Hawise with a desperate longing, the tough, shrewd, bouncing girl with the merry tongue and the warm heart. If I had her here to help me, to laugh with as we did on May Day.

Hawise had said as she kissed Katherine goodbye outside the church porch, "Remember I'd do anything for ye, my lady. Ye've but to let me know." Katherine had neither listened nor responded, had mounted Doucette in a daze—bemused, drunken—because of the Duke of Lancaster's contemptuous kiss.

"You little fool," said Katherine aloud to the deserted courtyard. "Ah, I hate him. He meant to make a fool of me."

She walked the length of the manor house and past the tower where Nichola could still be heard crooning to her cat. Katherine opened the low postern gate and forced her way through brambles and nettles onto the miniature peninsula which had once held a garden. It jutted into the nearly stagnant waters of the moat. The brambles scratched her arms, a lazy cloud of midges hovered over her head. The moat was scummed with pollen and smelled of swamp mud. She watched a water rat swim from beneath the wall and, mounting the soggy bank, scuttle away.

Then from the forest she heard a wild hallooing like a battle cry, and the fainter winding of a horn. At least, she thought, there would be meat for dinner.

# VII

ACCORDING TO the Duke's instructions, Hugh left Kettlethorpe for Southampton in the middle of August, on the day after the Feast of the Assumption. They had managed to celebrate this feast with some of the traditional lavishness, thanks to Hugh's and Ellis' skill at hunting. There had been venison enough for all the village and a wild boar that Hugh had slain across the Trent in Sherwood forest.

The sun shone, there had been dancing on the green, while to the little church for blessing the people had brought their samples from the harvest: oats, barley, peas, beans and flax plants, in woven baskets.

It was at Gibbon's suggestion that the Swynfords made special effort to celebrate the feast day for their tenants. Hugh, intent on his departure, would never have thought of it.

In June the manor Court had been held in the Great Hall, and Hugh had dealt out irritable punishment to his serfs, saying that as all had grown lax there was no use inquiring into the merits of each case. He exacted immediate payment of the overdue rents and fines and clapped those who asked for time into the stocks, besides personally flogging others. He decreed boon-work at once on his home fields and would have withdrawn every able-bodied man, woman and child from necessary work on their own plots, had not Gibbon intervened, pointing out that total failure of the tenants' crops would hardly benefit the major.

Katherine had had a litter made for Gibbon, and he had been carried into the Hall to attend the Court, and when he found the strength to give advice, Hugh, after the first impatient objections, usually heeded.

So now in August, the administration of the manor had improved. New officers had been appointed from amongst the villeins, a hayward to guard the fields and pastures, and a reeve, Sim the tanner, the shrewdest man in the village. Sim was cold-eyed and slippery as a mackerel, but he was proficient at figuring on the abacus and would brook no lame excuses from the villeins it was now his duty to oversee. From having been a leader of the malcontents, and adept at petty swindling from the lord's possessions, Sim now reversed himself to guard Hugh's interests, being mightily pleased with his position and the small wage that went with it.

Gibbon had foreseen this, too, and suggested that the tanner be chosen. No life had returned to the bailiff's useless limbs, but, cared for now by a husky lad and often consulted by Katherine and the reeve, his mind had lightened and a trace of color come into his bone-pale skin.

No new bailiff had been found, and in truth Hugh would not have known how to look for one, nor spare the money for his wages. And there was another reason, scarce acknowledged to himself, why Hugh sought no new bailiff, who might be a lusty man and would inevitably see much of Katherine.

On the night of the feast, when Hugh and Katherine went to bed, he, being hot with ale and suddenly aware of how sorely he would miss her, pulled her roughly towards him and began to fumble with her breasts.

"Let me be, Hugh," she said sharply, pushing him away. "I'm queasy and tired."

His anger flared at the reminder that always she submitted to him in tense endurance, making no sound except a sigh of relief when he quitted her. But she had never before denied him outright. "By God's blood!" he shouted. "How dare you shove me from you!" And as she stiffened, turning her head from his drink-soured breath, he struck her, though not hard, across the cheek.

"Ay," she said with biting contempt, sitting up in bed and pulling her long hair around her nakedness, "like father, like son. But *you* will not need to beat *me* with a blackthorn stick for that I'm barren."

"And why should I not! Why should not *he* have beat that mewling rag of a—" Then he caught her meaning. His clenched fists fell open and he, too, sat up, trying to see her face in the darkness. "Are you with child, Katherine?"

"So I believe," she said coldly. She had had no one to consult, and her knowledge of the signs was sparse, yet the lewd talk of Fat Mab, the Sheppey cook, had been enlightening.

"When think you it'll be born?" Hugh's voice cracked with gladness. He had hoped for this, not so much that it would provide him with an heir as that breeding would make her unattractive to other men, and surely it would change her indifference to himself.

"In May, I suppose," she answered him in the same chill tone. It seemed to her impossible, even ridiculous, that a new life had started growing in her belly, especially one in which Hugh had a share, for she felt herself as alone and untouched as ever; but she could not ignore the changes in her healthy young body, nor the new exhaustion and distaste for food.

"In May?" said Hugh eagerly. "No doubt I'll be back with you. It won't take us long to beat the Castilian bastard's rabble." He flexed his broken hand to try it, as he did many times a day. It had healed well and was strong as ever.

"I hope you'll be back, Hugh." She spoke more gently, though in truth she could not imagine how it would be in May, and longed to have him go. It seemed to her that it would be bliss to be alone in bed, and freed from the importunities of this hairy, naked man.

"There must be a midwife on the manor," said Hugh. "I believe 'tis the parson's wench, Molly. Ask Gibbon. And mind you keep away from that crazed bitch Nichola; she might upset you with her ravings, might mark the child."

"I'll be careful, Hugh." She was faintly touched by his solicitude. And when he again pulled her towards him, but now with clumsy forbearance, she suffered the scrape of his coarse beard while he kissed her hungrily and the weight of his heavy head on her breast when he fell into snoring sleep.

The next morning, before the dew was off the grass, the church bell rang and all the villagers assembled to Godspeed their manor lord. They gathered in the outer court beyond the moat, and Katherine stood amongst them holding the stirrup cup of strong ale.

Hugh was dressed in gleaming armor, from which Ellis had polished every trace of rust or stain. Katherine herself had mended the linen jupon which covered his hauberk of chain mail like a tight-fitting shirt. The jupon's embroidered blazon proclaimed Hugh's identity, as did his silvered shield with black chevron and three gold boars' heads painted on the leather. His fighting helmet was of iron, shaped like a beehive, yet far lighter than the great ceremonial heaume he had worn at the tournament.

Ellis followed him, dressed in Lincoln green with his master's badge sewn on his arm. Wat, the stableboy, led the two great destriers, their harnesses ajingle with tiny brass bells.

As Hugh came through the gatehouse and crossed the drawbridge, his serfs gave a polite cheer; there were a few invocations to St. George and the Blessed Mother for Sir Hugh's safe return from the wars. Though there was no special enthusiasm, and their well-wishing came rather in response to immemorial feudal custom than to any personal interest in Hugh, the little demonstration nevertheless proved that the feast yesterday had mollified them; at least they were no longer openly rebellious.

They made way for the parish priest, who lumbered through the lych gate to give final blessing. Hugh and Ellis knelt on the ground to receive it. The priest asperged them with holy water.

Hugh arose and clambered into the saddle from the mounting block, then he sat stiff and high to look down at Katherine. "Farewell, lady," he said below his breath, and into his small truculent eyes there came a look, as though he would say more, but could not. He was at his best on horseback, where one saw neither his bandy legs nor his chunkiness. His ram's-wool hair, trimmed by Ellis, lay neat and close to his head as wartime fashion demanded, and when Katherine, smiling, proffered him the stirrup cup, he took it from her and drank with a sober grace. "God keep you, my Katherine," he said, very low.

"And you, my lord and husband," she returned. "Guard him well, Ellis," she added, her dazzling smile moving to Hugh's squire. That stolid young man started and bowed. He had never had personal interest in his master's lady, seeing her simply as one of Sir Hugh's possessions, like his horses and his manor. He had not even wondered at Hugh's choice of a dowerless maiden, for it was not his way to wonder. But now as Katherine's smile rested on him, several impressions penetrated his slow wits. One was the astonished recognition of her beauty. Tall and slender like a young queen, she stood there in her shabby green fur-trimmed robes. Her cleft chin was held high, her great eyes shone like crystals between the thick black lashes. And her smile was brilliant and gracious as an April morning. But should there have been a smile, however gracious? This girl, so young and untried, upon being left alone by her war-bound lord, should she not have wept?

Women, thought Ellis, relinquishing the matter, were hard to fathom. He tested the loose buckle on the strap that held his master's gear behind the cantle and, soothing his impatient horse, frowned towards the southern sky. If those were not thunderheads gathering, they should reach Grantham by dark.

Katherine dutifully waved goodbye until the two trotting horses faded from sight down the avenue of wych-elms that led to the Lincoln road. The villeins noted that she had shown decorum throughout the speeding, and they drew back respectfully now, that she might rush into the house and let loose her grief in private. But Katherine felt neither grief nor the slightest doubt that Hugh would return. Her certainty of his safety beyond the seas in Aquitaine arose not so much from her ignorance of war as from a blind unrecognized trust in the overlord he would serve. Because the Duke of Lancaster was invulnerable, lofty and beyond the touch of mischance, so would his men be. Hugh would certainly return, and in the meantime she had respite.

"The day grows warm, lady," said the priest, mopping his shining red face with a corner of his claret-colored gown. He moistened his thick lips and glanced towards the manor house. " 'Twill soon be Prime."

Katherine took the hint. "Come in and break your fast with me, Sir Robert. I believe there's still some mead left over from the feast."

Sim Tanner, the reeve, who stood waiting to hustle the peasants back to their proper tasks, gave a derisive snort. Nobody believed that the priest ever denied his belly, or even went fasting to the Blessed Sacrament. A greedy and lazy man was Robert de Northwode, but well liked by the village nonetheless. He came from the parish and was the only son of a freeman blacksmith who lived near Fenton village by the North wood from which the family had taken its name.

The blacksmith prospered enough to finance his son's rise in the world. Robert took minor orders, and when the old rector died, Hugh at Gibbon's suggestion appointed Robert to the living. Certainly there were no other eager candidates. The glebe lands were poor, the tithes hard to collect and the rectory in bad repair.

Robert, however, was pleased. It was agreeable to be addressed by the priest's honorary title of Sir and to have become the chief person in the parish after the manor lord. Being young and lusty, he soon picked himself a hearth-mate, a stout good-natured wench from the village, and with his Molly and their four placid infants he made himself very comfortable. Though canon law denied her the title of wife, Molly was not ill thought of. Celibacy might be asked of monk or friar but hardly from so natural a man as a village parson, nor did the Bishop of Lincoln trouble himself about irregularities in poor parishes.

So Sir Robert led an agreeable life. Molly earned extra pennies by serving as midwife, and he pottered about his garden where he raised raspberries and peas for his table. He bred hounds and sold the puppies at Lincoln fairs and he spared his parishioners the boredom of sermons, the discomforts of strict penance and any criticism whatsoever of their morals or spiritual lives.

Katherine, while she sat at the High Table in the Hall, watching him smack his lips over his mead and the spiced venison pasty, was both shocked and amused. Except for the thicket of little black curls which encircled his tonsure, he looked like an amiable pink sow, dressed in claret robes, which were egg-stained and much patched because his hound puppies were forever clawing at them.

Katherine had hoped for spiritual and intellectual guidance from her manor priest, since Sir Osbert at the convent had been a man of high thought and learning. But she soon discovered that Father Robert could neither read nor write, and that to her timid confessions he scarcely listened, but granted absolution in a hurried gabble before she had finished, while his flat Lincolnshire accent made the Latin he had learned by rote almost ludicrous.

On the last day of October, All Hallow's Eve, Katherine, having supped alone as usual at the High Table in the dark dreary Hall, sat idly watching Ajax, the mastiff, nosing for bones in the littered rushes below the dais. The house carls had fastened hazel branches across the doors and the windows to keep out the witches and bogles which infested this particular night, and from across the moat she could hear the chanting of the villagers who were circling their homes with lighted candles for the same purpose. The servants, having flung her food on the table, had early sneaked off to the village for apple-bobbing and fortunetelling.

Katherine's despondency reached a point where she felt that she would have welcomed goblins or any other weird visitant which might break the monotony and isolation of Kettlethorpe, when Ajax suddenly abandoned his bones, stiffened and growled.

She crossed herself, staring fearfully at the protecting hazel withes, then she heard the halloo of a human male voice and old Toby's quavering answer, while Ajax precipitated himself against the door, barking and growling.

She spoke to the dog, held him by his collar and opened the door waiting eagerly. No visitors had come to Kettlethorpe since a wandering friar after Michaelmas. But it was only Sir Robert, who had just returned from amusing himself in Lincoln for three days.

Katherine was so disappointed that tears spilled down her cheeks, a display she knew to be revoltingly childish. "The smoke—" she said. " 'Tis so smoky in here." As indeed it was. A goblin wind had blown up and puffed all the fire smoke back into the hall through the open roof hole.

"Ay, a wuthering night," said the priest, brushing twigs and mud off his robes. He shuddered. "I mislike Hallow E'en, there's things abroad—best not thought on. I'd not of come back today but for the Feast of All Saints tomorrow. There be some in the vill want Mass said."

"I should certainly hope so—I know I do," said Katherine shortly. Father Robert's idea of his parochial duties was exceedingly flexible. Which pleased Hugh well enough.

"I was calling at the George 'n' Dragon, in the town, ye know where it is? The big tavern near the castle uphill from what folks used to call the Jewry, not in our time, nor our gaffers' time either though—"

"Yes," murmured Katherine. There was never any hurrying the priest's thick ramblings, especially when he was bursting with ale like an overripe plum. She glanced wearily at the roof over the dais, where the thatcher had not properly repaired the leak. It must have started to rain, for the usual trickle plink-plunked on the table.

"Tavernkeeper—Hambo o' Louth he's called, he knows I drop in from time to time—he told me, Hambo did, there was a pedlar come from Lincoln, three days back, on his way to Grimsby. Pedlar what carries mostly ribbons, threads, gewgaws for the women. Seems he'd started in London and bore a letter. He left it with Hambo, for when someone from here'd drop by."

"Letter!" Katherine jumped up. "Letter for Kettlethorpe! Jesu, Father, give it to me!"

The priest's fat fingers fumbled with maddening slowness at the buckle of his pouch. Finally he held out a sealed piece of parchment. "Is it sent to *you?*" he asked, having puzzled for some time over the looks of the inscription, and this being the first letter he had ever seen close.

"Yes, yes," she said, tearing at the seal. "Why it's from Geoffrey!"

She read rapidly, while her mouth trembled, and her eyes darkened. "No bad news about Sir Hugh?" cried the priest.

"No," Katherine said slowly. " 'Tis not bad news. It's from a King's squire called Geoffrey Chaucer; he and my sister were married in Lammastide. They're living in London, in the Vintry, until my sister returns to service with the Queen."

Father Robert was impressed. So glib she talked about the King and Queen. He pursed his thick lips and looked at her with new respect.

"London," said Katherine, on a long sigh, gazing around the dark bare hall, "seems very far away."

"Well and it *is,*" said the priest, rising reluctantly, for she was staring at the letter and obviously not going to offer him anything to drink for his pains.

When he had gone, she reread her letter, and one sentence especially. Geoffrey had written, "Philippa bids you not grow overworldly in the luxury and High Estate which you now enjoy—but I dare add I hope you amuse yourself right well, my little sister."

Katherine smiled bitterly when she read that and put the letter at the bottom of her coffer.

More and more during the autumn months as her pregnancy advanced, lethargy came over Katherine, and she drew into herself. Her mind felt as though it grew thick as pottage, and she was continually benumbed by cold. Her initial interest in the manor waned, she scarce found the energy for talks with Gibbon any more, and he, seeing this, did not trouble her, having established a fair working relationship with the reeve.

The Lady Nichola was no companion. Now that the

weather was bad, she kept always to her tower room with her cat and seemed to be confused by Katherine's rare visits. Besides, the girl was not unmindful of Hugh's command. Who knew what might not mark the child? The two maids were prodigal of warnings. Katherine must not gaze directly into the fire, she must shut her eyes quickly and say an Ave if she saw a spider, a rat or a toad. She must always put her right shoe on first and never sleep with her legs crossed. And as for riding Doucette, the perils of any such folly were impressed on her by the entire manor staff and even Gibbon.

After the leaves fell and the freezing November rains began, Katherine stayed almost entirely in her room, either shivering by the smoking fire or huddled in the great bed beneath the bearskin, trying to shut her ears to the howling of hungry wolves in the forest. Sometimes she roused herself and plied a listless needle to make swaddling clothes for her baby. But the baby still seemed imaginary. Even though her belly and her breasts had swollen and grown hard, she had no sense of its presence within her.

"It'll be different when you quicken, lady," said Milburga. This was the servant Katherine had chosen as personal waiting maid, because she was cleaner and less stupid than the others. But Milburga was old, being over thirty and a widow, and she treated Katherine with a blend of oily deference and petty bullying that the girl found annoying.

On St. Catherine's Day, November 25, Katherine awoke to find that she had been crying in her sleep, and knew that she had dreamed of her childhood. In the dream she had been little "Cat'rine" again, crowned with gilded laurel leaves and perched on cushions in the middle of her grandparents' kitchen table at the farm in Picardy. There were laughing faces around her, and hands stretched out towards her with gifts—straw dolls and shining stones and apples—while many voices sang, "Salut, salut la p'tite Cat'rine, on salut ton jour de fête!"

Then in the dream her big handsome father lifted her from the cushions and kissed her while she snuggled in his arms, and he pressed a little gingerbread figure of St. Catherine into her mouth. She tasted the heavenly sweetness of it until someone wrenched her jaws apart and snatched the sweetmeat away. And she awoke weeping.

There had been light snow in the night, the wind had blown a fine drift through the loosened shutter and there was a ridge of white along the bare stone floor beneath the iron perch where her cloak hung.

The fire had died to ashes. Katherine looked at the cold gray ashes and her tears changed to a loud and passionate sobbing. When Milburga bustled in from the outside stairs with the morning ale, the maid exclaimed, "Mistress, what ails ye!"

As the girl merely hid her face in her arms and continued to sob, the woman drew back the covers and made a quick examination. "Have ye pains, here or here?" she demanded. Katherine shook her head. "Leave me be. Go away," and she sobbed more violently.

Milburga's sallow face tightened. "Stop that rampaging at once, lady! Ye'll harm the child."

"Oh, a murrain on the child!" cried Katherine wildly, rearing herself on the bed.

"Saint Mary protect us—" gasped Milburga, backing away. Her pale mouth and pale eyes were round with horror. She receded to the door and stood gaping at her mistress.

The wild angry grief fell off Katherine like a mantle, leaving her afraid. "I didn't mean it—" She put her hands on her belly, as if to reassure the dark outraged little entity inside. "Send for Sir Robert. Tell him he must celebrate a Mass—This is my saint's day—my sixteenth—that's why—why—"

But of what use to explain to that tight shocked face that she had been sobbing for her own childhood, for the dear lost days of special cherishing and festival. Even at Sheppey, where she had been the only Katherine, the nuns had made a little atmosphere of fête and congratulation for her on this saint's day. Here there was nobody to either cherish her or care.

The north wind blew sleet through the crack in the shutter and whistled down the smoke hole. She pulled the bearskin around her shoulders and crouched into the only warm spot on the damp sheet, but she might not stay there long, for she must cleanse and dress herself to receive the priest, and she must wrestle to bring her hard rebellious spirit to penitence.

Milburga, bound on her errand to the rectory, paused in the kitchen below to regale the other servants with their mistress's shocking behavior. They clustered around exclaiming, the cook, and the servitor and the dairy maid. All work stopped at once, except that little Cob o' Fenton, the tow-headed spit-boy, crouched in his niche in the great fireplace, automatically turning the handle with his toes while he longed to be out in the raw misty air fishing in the Trent. They were roasting a lean old ewe, and her scanty grease smelt rancid as it hissed into the fire. In truth the manor food was poor, and slackly prepared, for there was no one at the High Table now that Lady Katherine kept to her room so much and was growing as strange and solitary as the Lady Nichola.

" 'Tis the curse, no doubt, creeping on them both," said Milburga, shaking her head with gloomy relish. "Soon we'll hear the pooka hound abaying in the marshes."

"Jesus save us!" squealed Betsy, the dairy maid, her child mouth quivering. They all crossed themselves.

"Nay," said the cook sourly, shaking his knobby gray head. "I believe 'tis no *Swynford* curse, though well they deserve it. The demon hound was sent by the devil to haunt the de la Croys for their grievous sins. That's why they sold us and the manor to Swynfords." He eased his rheumatic joints onto a bench.

The others listened respectfully. Will Cooke was over fifty and well remembered the old days under the de la Croys. He and his fathers before him had always been manor cooks, yet he had no liking for the lords or his work. During the years of Hugh's absence he had moved into his daughter-in-law's cot in the vill and taken happily to woodcarving.

He had been the most defiant of the serfs when at the manor Court Hugh had ordered him back to his hereditary duties, and Hugh had flogged him so hard that his shoulders oozed blood for days. Will would have run off to hide in Sherwood forest, had he been younger, but his stiffened knees hampered him, as did the dead weight of custom. Kettle-thorpe lords had always been so. Sir Hugh was no worse than the de la Croys who had thrown his father into the tower dungeon for the inadvertent scorching of a spiced capon.

"If ye're to call the parson," he said, scowling at Milburga, " 'twill mean that fat ox'll feed here after, and our fine young lady be down for once, God damn her finicking foreign ways." He picked up his sharpest knife and on the worn chopping block began to slice the old sheep's entrails for a mortrewe.

The initial good will Katherine had aroused on the manor by reason of her beauty, youth and the promptness with which she had done her duty in conceiving an heir had soon

died down. After all, she was a foreigner, not only alien to
Lincolnshire, but actually born in the country which they
held to be their hereditary enemy. She spoke an English they
had trouble understanding. "Norman English," said Will
Cooke contemptuously. And yet she was neither nobly born
nor rich. She was no lady they could boast of to the serfs on
near-by manors, at Torksey or Stowe. And moreover she was
a nuisance. Were it not for her, the house carls might all
have returned to their village cots and own pursuits, as they
had before Sir Hugh's brief visit. Defying the nearly helpless
Gibbon and the reeve, they might well have mutinied against
her, even braving Hugh's displeasure later. But they were de-
terred by the usage of generations. Satan grinning from his
hellish flames waited eagerly to pounce upon the serf who
disobeyed his feudal lord, and while Katherine might be unpopular, she yet carried within her the Swynford heir to
whom they would all some day do homage.

Katherine, sunk in sickliness and torpor, knew that they
gave her grudging service, but had not the spirit to care. The
chill dampness which crept upward from the moat seemed to
have got in her bones. She shivered often and coughed; of
nights her throat grew so sore that it awakened her to swallow.

On the fourth Sunday in Advent the December day was
clear and bright for a change. Katherine dragged herself up
and, feeling a trifle better, crossed over to the church for
Mass. She sat alone in the lord's high boxed pew by the chancel and leaning her heavy head against a carved oaken boss,
vaguely watched the priest lurch and gabble through the service. She could not see the villagers in the choir, but she
heard their responses, and heard, too, the chaffering and giggles and gossiping that went on in the nave below. The dark
little church grew steamy with the peasant smell of sour
sweat, leeks and manure. She tried to fix her thoughts upon
the Elevation of the Host, yet all she could think of were the
rolls of pink fat on the priest's neck and the quivering of oily
curls around his tonsure.

It was at that moment that she felt the baby quicken, and
was frightened. This tapping and fluttering in her belly
seemed to her monstrous. Suddenly she thought of a tale she
had heard at Sheppey of a boy who had swallowed a serpent's egg, the egg had hatched inside him and the snake,
frantic to escape, gnawed—

Katherine stifled a cry and rushed from the pew through the side door of the church into the open. She sank on the coffin bench beneath the lych gate and drew great lungfuls of the cold sparkling air. Two of Margery Brewster's children were sliding on an iced puddle beside the church path and they stopped to stare at her in wonderment. Her terror receded and she grew ashamed. She must go back in church and apologize to the Blessed Body of Jesus for her irreverence. She got slowly to her feet, then turned round in amazement, for a horse came galloping down the frozen road beneath the wych-elms.

The children turned from gaping at her and gaped at the horseman. He reined his mount before the drawbridge to the manor, and Katherine with a great leap at her heart saw that he wore on his tunic the Lancaster badge.

She ran across the court and greeted him fearingly. "Whence do you come? Is there news of the war?"

The lad was Piers Roos, the Duke's erstwhile body squire, who had been left at home to serve the Duchess. He had a fresh freckled face and a merry eye. He pulled off his brown velvet cap to disclose a mass of tow curls, and grinning at Katherine said with some uncertainty, "My Lady Swynford?"

She nodded quickly, "What news do you bring?"

"Nothing but good. At least we know no war news yet from Castile. I come from Bolingbroke, from the Duchess Blanche. She sends you greeting."

"Ah—" Katherine's drawn little face softened with pleasure. She had never dared hope that the Lady Blanche would indeed remember her; and during these months at Kettlethorpe, the London and Windsor days had gradually faded into fantasy.

"She bids me escort you to Bolingbroke for the Christmas festival, if you'd like to come."

Her indrawn breath and the sudden shining of her shadowed eyes were answer enough, and Piers Roos laughed, seeing that she was even younger than he was himself and not the solemn, weary woman she had seemed as he dismounted.

"We'll go tomorrow then, if you wish. The ride'll take but a day."

"I—I cannot go fast," faltered Katherine, suddenly remembering, and blushing. "I—they—think I should not ride at all."

"What folly," said Piers cheerfully, understanding at once. "The Lady Blanche is larger than you and she still rides out daily."

"The Lady Blanche!" Katherine repeated, wondering that she should be amazed, and why the young squire's information came as a small unpleasant shock. "When?"

"Oh, March or April, I believe. I know naught of midwifery." He laughed outright, and Katherine after a minute joined him.

The energy Piers' invitation brought her buoyed Katherine through all difficulties. She ordered Doucette curried and groomed and ignored the gloomy disapproval of her household.

The next day her sore throat had disappeared, the fluttering in her belly she did not notice; she smiled and hummed as she crossed the inner court to take leave of Gibbon.

"Ay, mistress," he said sadly, as he stared up at her from his pallet. "You're in a fever to be quit of Kettlethorpe."

"Only till Twelfth Night," she cried. "Then I'll—I'll be back. And I'll not pine any more, I promise. I'll help you on the manor again."

"Godspeed," he said and closed his eyes against the light. Hugh would not like it, and yet even Hugh would not have made Katherine refuse an invitation from the Duchess. I could not stop her from going, thought Gibbon, and sighed. Could not, since he had neither strength nor power, and would not for she was still such a child, and he knew well how much maturity it took to withstand loneliness and boredom. He did not believe with the villeins that she was wilfully imperiling her baby, but many nameless forebodings came to him in the long night hours, and he wished as heartily as the rest of the village that Hugh had seen fit to marry the noble Darcy widow, of Torksey.

# VIII

BOLINGBROKE LAY clear across the county near the eastern
coast of Lincolnshire. It was a small fair castle set in
meadowlands and encircled by the protecting wolds.
Even in winter the meadows were green beneath their coating
of hoarfrost; and the little turrets and high central keep, all
beflagged in scarlet and gold, had a gay welcoming look. It
was the Lancasters' favorite country castle; there Blanche had
spent much of her girlhood, and there she and John had
come for seclusion in the first days of their marriage.

It held for her many happy memories, and she had returned to it now, knowing that its homely shelter would help
her bear the anxiety of her lord's absence, and the anxiety of
awaiting the new baby. This time her prayers and pilgrimage to the Blessed Virgin of Walsingham *must* be answered.
It would be a boy, and it would live, as the other baby boy
had not.

From the moment when the Lady Blanche herself met
Katherine in the Great Hall and, taking the girl's hand,
kissed her on the cheek, through the twelve days of Christmas, Katherine managed to forget Kettlethorpe. With the rest
of the Duchess's company, Katherine immersed herself in the
serene and gracious aura which surrounded Blanche.

The Duchess, thickened by pregnancy, no longer made one
think of lilies yet she was no less beautiful in her ripe golden
abundance, and Katherine admired her passionately.

There were few guests, for Blanche smilingly explained
that she had enough of company at the Savoy or at court and
wished for quiet. The Cromwells from near-by Tattershall
Castle rode over Christmas night, and the Abbess of Elstow,
who was cousin to Blanche, spent the days between St. Ste-
phen's and New Year's, but so intimate was the castle gathering that Katherine wondered much, while she rejoiced, that
she had been invited.

She put it down to kindness of heart, and tried to repay the Duchess in every way she could. The Duchess responded with affection and growing interest in the girl. And yet it was a sentence contained in a letter she had received from her husband which had prompted the invitation.

The Duke had written soon after landing in Brittany; and assembling his command of four hundred men-at-arms and six hundred archers for the march south to join his brother and the exiled Castilian king at Bordeaux. He wrote in a happy confident mood, telling his "très-chère et bien-aimée compagne" many items of news: that the fair Joan, Princess of Wales, was enceinte again and near to term; that King Pedro, God restore him to his rightful throne, had with him at Bordeaux his handsome daughters, and that the desolate plight of these wronged princesses had captured the sympathy of all the English, who would certainly triumph over that baseborn fiend Trastamare, and the lilies and leopards of England would float at last above Castile and fulfill Merlin's age-old prophecy.

Descending into less exalted vein, the Duke had shown his usual consideration for Blanche's comfort, asking if the steward at Bolingbroke had repaired the bridge over the outer moat yet, and how the masons were progressing with the stone portraits of the King and Queen on the refurbished church, for "it is there, dearest lady, that our child will be christened, and I pray I may return in time."

Blanche kissed the parchment when she read this, and sinking to her knees on the prie-dieu beside the great bed had communed with a jeweled image of the Blessed Virgin which stood flanked by candles and holly greens in the niche above.

When she returned to the letter she found in the last paragraph the question, "Have you seen aught of the little Swynford? Her clodpoll knight is here in camp and confides (as though it were a rare and difficult feat) that he has got her with child. It might be kindness to see how she does, alone, on their manor."

Blanche had not wondered that of all their acquaintance, her lord had mentioned by name only this little bride; neither suspicion nor speculation had ever troubled the purity of her love, and she hastened to obey without question and in generous measure. She was rewarded, for she enjoyed Katherine's visit.

The girl's admiration touched her. Though there were ten

years between their ages, besides the greater gulf of Blanche's lineage and experience, she found Katherine companionable. The two women sat together and embroidered through the winter dusks, and Blanche noted how the girl's red chilblained little hands tried to imitate the skill of her own long white fingers. Sometimes Blanche picked up her lute or gittern and they sang—plaintive love songs, or Christmas carols to the Virgin. And at the singing Blanche knew herself surpassed, for her high passionless voice, like a choir boy's, sometimes flatted, while Katherine hit true and round on every note, and once she had overcome her timidity and learned the songs, they poured like honey from her slender throat.

"Do you make much music at Kettlethorpe?" inquired Blanche idly one evening when they had finished singing Adam de la Halle's rondeau, "Fais mari de vostre amour."

"No, madam," said Katherine after a moment, the pleasure dying from her face. She had, from pride and a desire to forget the place, always evaded the Duchess's few polite questions about her manor.

"Are your minstrels unskilled?" asked the Duchess in some surprise.

Katherine thought of her hall, which was barer and meaner than the cow-byres here, and could not help laughing. "We have no minstrels, madam. It's not," she added quickly, "a manor quite like any you have known."

The Duchess raised her pale arched brows, and seeing Katherine's unwillingness, said no more. Bred to unlimited wealth, reared in a succession of castles of which this one was the simplest, it was true that she could not imagine a manor such as Kettlethorpe. She was familiar with the hovels of the poor where she dispensed lavish charity, but that a landed knight's home might be almost as meager and uncomfortable had never occurred to her. Nor did it now, but her sky-blue gaze focused and she noted for the first time the shabbiness of Katherine's clothes, though she was far from recognizing or remembering the let-out and altered green dress she had given Katherine at Windsor. But she determined to make the girl some presents on New Year's Day and, dismissing the matter, she turned smiling, as her two little girls ran into the Ladies' Bower to announce that a new batch of mummers from Lincoln had arrived and had playfully chased

the children around the courtyard. Elizabeth, the baby, was
squealing with excitement.

"Dragon, Mama! All fire!" she shrieked, dancing on her
little red shoes and pointing to the window. "Big dragon!
He'll eat us up!"

"It's not a real dragon, Mother," explained Philippa earnestly. "It's only a man in a disguise. You mustn't be frightened."

Katherine, watching, thought how like the good little Philippa that was. At six and a half, she was already a blurred
copy of Blanche, well-mannered and considerate. She never
had tantrums, never disobeyed. She was as blond as her
mother too, though she gave no promise of Blanche's beauty.
Her flaxen hair hung in lank strands either side of her narrow
Plantagenet face, and her skin, owing, no doubt, to her recurrent bilious attacks, had a sallow greenish tinge.

She was a devout child and had already made her first
Communion; she could read the psalter very well, and when
she played, it was always a solemn re-enactment of one of
the saints' lives.

Elizabeth, who was not yet three, outshone her elder sister
on all counts. She was wilful, demanding and extremely
spoiled, for she had charm. She had red cheeks and a mop of
russet curls which would one day darken to brown. She was
said to resemble her sinister great-grandmother, Queen Isabella of France, and certainly she was not like her fair-haired
parents.

Elizabeth soon gave up trying to pull her mother off to
meet the dragon. Blanche, who had seen quantities of mummers, merely smiled her lovely calm smile and said, "Presently, my poppet—" not stirring from her carved armchair.
She was larger with this pregnancy than she had ever been,
and more indolent.

So the baby danced over to Katherine singing, "Dragon,
dragon, come see 'Lisbet's dragon!"

Katherine was more than willing. She looked to the Duchess for permission, then she took the children's hands. Elizabeth tugged and tumbled ahead of her down the winding
stone stairs, but Philippa followed sedately, clutching Katherine's hand in a damp, careful clasp.

When they reached the courtyard, it was full of retainers
and villagers who had come to see the fun. The mummers let
out a shout of greeting to the ducal children and cavorted

around the trio, singing "Wassail, wassail!" hoarsely through their masks. There were a score of them, each disguised as an animal—goats, rabbits, stags, dogs and bulls—except their leader, the Lord of Misrule, who wore a fool's costume tipped with jingling bells and whose face was splotched with blobs of red and blue.

The dragon was indeed a wonderful object, he writhed realistically on the stones and, opening and shutting his painted canvas jaws, emitted clouds of evil-smelling brimstone. When the dragon seized the small rabbit-headed figure in his mouth and pretended to eat him up while the capering Fool emitted falsetto screams and beat at the dragon with a peacock feather, Katherine laughed as heartily as all the others in the courtyard and even little Philippa gave a round-eyed, nervous smile.

But then the mummers' play grew bawdy. The fool shouted that since the dragon was on fire, good Christians all must sprinkle water on him, and began to do so in the most natural manner. Katherine, though she could not help laughing, gathered up the wildly protesting Elizabeth and shepherded Philippa back to their mother.

By the time they reached Blanche's fire-lit bower, Katherine had silenced the baby with a firm command and then the crooning of a little French nursery song from her own childhood; and when she went to put her down beside her mother, Elizabeth clung fast to Katherine's neck.

"You're truly good with the children, my Katherine," said the Duchess, seeing this, and also that Philippa clung trustingly to the girl's skirts. "But you should not carry that heavy child in your condition—Elizabeth, let my Lady Swynford go!"

"Won't," cried the child, clinging harder to Katherine, and as she saw her mother's face darken with a rare frown, she shrieked, "I like her best, I like her best!"

It was only a piece of baby naughtiness; it ruffled the Duchess not at all, who merely raised her voice and called Elizabeth's nurse from the anteroom, yet it gave Katherine a strange guilt as though she had somehow stolen from the Duchess, and unwittingly hurt this lady who had been her kindest friend.

She thrust Elizabeth at the nurse, who vanished with her howling charge, and while Philippa still remained and gave her mother a solemn account of the mummers, Katherine picked up her embroidery and went to the far corner of the bower, out of sight, while she fought off the unease that had come upon her.

It passed, of course. She reasoned it away, telling herself that women in her state were given to fancies and that it was a piece of presumption for her to think she might affect the Duchess in any way at all, just as her cheeks grew hot with shame when she remembered what a ridiculous dither she had been in at the Duke's perfunctory kiss in the church.

Here in his castle with his wife and children, she saw her folly in its true light, and in some way allied to this, she began to think more kindly of Hugh and her duties at Kettlethorpe.

In this the Duchess unconsciously helped, by assuming that Katherine must be pining for her husband, even as she was for her own lord. And by stressing quite without intent the remarkable good fortune which had transformed Katherine from a charity orphan into a lady of quality. "The Blessed Saint Catherine must have you under special protection, my dear."

"Yes, madam," said Katherine humbly.

"Some day," continued Blanche, "you should make the pilgrimage to Our Lady of Walsingham in Norfolk, she gives great sanctity and is especially kind and merciful to mothers." She paused, and a misty light shone in her eyes. "I went to Her in June—from Her bounteous grace She has rewarded me." She glanced towards her lap and added very low, "And I know She'll give me a healthy son."

"Ah, dearest lady," cried the girl. She took the Duchess's hand and laid it to her cheek, looking up at the fair white face, the high placid brow and the ropes of golden hair entwined with tiny pearls. "You who are like the Queen of Heaven Herself, of course She has rewarded you!"

"Hush, child," Blanche turned her hand and put it gently over Katherine's mouth. "You mustn't say foolish things. But indeed I love you well, too—we must see each other after our babes are born. It saddens me to part with you."

Katherine sighed agreement, for the parting was on the morrow, Epiphany Day. And the hope Katherine had briefly held, that the Duchess would ask her to stay on a while, had long ago vanished. Blanche thought the girl eager to get back to the manor for which she was now responsible, and the Swynford heir, of course, must be born on its own lands. This

was the code, and as the Duchess herself never hesitated to
put duty before inclination, so it never entered her mind that
a girl of Katherine's obvious worth could do so.

Katherine duly returned to Kettlethorpe in Piers Roos'
charge, but the Duchess, having decided that the roads were
too icy for horseback, sent her in one of the great ducal char-
iots. It was drawn by four horses and was as lavishly carved,
gilded and painted as Blanche's own bridal chests. Katherine
lay inside on a velvet couch and despite the jouncing and
lurching of the springless wheels, she found that this piece of
generosity somewhat alleviated her sorrow at leaving Bolingbroke. So did the other evidences of Blanche's kindness which
lay stacked in coffers at the rear of the long carriage. Katherine had two dresses now, and a length of Flemish woven
wool with which to make a third. There was fine linen for
baby clothes, and there were a lute, an English psalter and an
ivory crucifix.

The Duchess, after consultation with Piers, had finally realized something of conditions at Kettlethorpe and done her
best to mitigate them.

Katherine had poignantly grateful thoughts on the long
ride and made many good resolutions for her future. She
would be as much like the Duchess as possible—always gracious, charitable and devout. She doubted her power to force
Sir Robert to celebrate daily Mass as did the Duchess's chaplain, but at least she could pray every day and she need not
wickedly skip Sunday Mass because of trifling illness, as she
had through the autumn. She saw now clearly that she had
grown guilty of the sin of accidie—spiritual sloth. The nuns
had talked much of that sin at Sheppey.

She had time for conscience-searching, as the ride home
took fifteen hours. The lumbering carriage traveled slowly,
and after they had rested the horses at Lincoln, it began to
snow, and the last miles to Kettlethorpe were nearly as wearisome as they had been when she first came there in May with
Hugh. And her welcome was scarcely better. The manor
house was dark, the servants, not expecting her, had gone to
bed in the kitchen loft and when routed out by Piers were
surly and unhelpful and scarcely attended to Katherine in
their wonder at the great painted carriage and their resentment of the supercilious ducal postilions.

Katherine went up to her dank musty-smelling solar. She
did not undress but crept as she was between the clammy

sheets. The night candle flickered and blew out in a gust from the east wind through the shutter. The east wind also carried sound from the tower. An intermittent wailing chant, with sometimes a sharper call as of a question. The Lady Nichola talking to her cat, or to the snowflakes, or to some ghostlier figment of her sick mind—what did it matter?

Nothing had changed. Katherine pulled the bearskin around her ears and clenching her teeth prayed violently for resignation.

The winter snows melted in the strengthening sun. Its light moved southward and now awakened Katherine through the solar window that gave on to the forest, where nesting rooks began their incessant cawing. A film of ice no longer glazed the moat each morning, and as the pastures turned a tender green, the newborn lambs, white as swan's-down, filled the fragrant air with plaintive bleats.

April came in with soft cloudless days, and gentle nightly showers—prime growing weather; and as the danger to the new-sown crops from freezing or floods abated, the grim faces of the serfs grew softer. They sang often in the fields and the dairies and the malthouse; they even smiled at Katherine while they bobbed their heads to her.

The whole manor pulsed with spring, and Katherine spent most of her time outdoors basking on a bench in the courtyard or strolling dreamily through the lanes, listening to the thrushes and blackbirds. She could not walk far now before her back ached and her ankles swelled, but she was no longer sickly or unhappy. She existed from day to day, peacefully expectant as any fecund animal, yet so accustomed now to her burden that she could not remember how it felt to be free.

In Holy Week, a wandering Gray Friar turned up at the manor to beg a night's hospitality for his small shaggy donkey and himself. Katherine was delighted to accommodate him, and all the more so as he brought news. Brother Francis was bound north into the wilds of Yorkshire on a preaching expedition, but he had come from Boston town, near Bolingbroke. He told Katherine that on April 3, eleven days ago, the Duchess Blanche had been safely delivered of a fair, healthy son who had been christened Henry after her father. "All the countryside rejoiced," added the friar. "I thought our bell at Saint Botolph's church would crack from the wild pealing, and the bonfires in our streets set alight two houses."

"Oh I'm glad!" cried Katherine, "so very glad!" Tears came to her eyes, of honest joy for Blanche, but of hurt too. "All the countryside rejoiced"—and yet she had known nothing of it, had worried and prayed for her friend, who might have sent some messenger from amongst her retinue to tell the news. And yet why should she? The Duchess lived in the midst of vast concerns, made vaster now by the birth of a male heir at last; she knew nothing of loneliness or isolation. Doubtless she thought Katherine had heard the news long ago, if she ever thought of her at all. But the hurt persisted.

"This new little Henry of Lancaster," pursued the friar, a small merry man who enjoyed gossiping, "is born to great inheritance, but he has no hope for the English throne, especially since the birth of his new cousin."

"What cousin?" said Katherine, pouring ale for the friar.

"Why, Richard, of course! He that was born at Bordeaux to the Princess of Wales on Epiphany Day." He looked at her quizzically. "Surely, lady, you live here close as the kernel in a nut—most proper though in your state and with your lord away!"

Katherine was nearly stung into telling him that she was not such a country bumpkin as he thought her, that she had visited the Duchess and had stayed at court where her sister waited on the Queen; but the impulse died, for he might think her boastful or lying and, besides, his chatter rippled on without a pause.

"When King Edward dies, God give him grace, our glorious Prince of Wales will reign, and after him come his two sons, little Edward—a sickly lad though and given to fits—but now we also have the tiny Richard. If aught should happen to all of them," he raised his hand and murmured, "*Christus prohibeat!*—there's the Duke Lionel and his get, present and future, for I hear he's to marry again, and *then* the Duke of Lancaster and finally our little Henry Bolingbroke, fifth in line if no new ones are born." He shook his head. "Nay, lady, we'll never have a *Lincolnshire*-born king —a great pity."

"Indeed," said Katherine somewhat dryly. She was growing tired, and her love for Lincolnshire was not such as to make her appreciate this angle of young Henry's birth. Besides, her heart was still very sore and she desired to hear no more about the Lancasters.

On the last day of April, Katherine awoke early and was filled with restless energy. She dressed and went downstairs to the courtyard before the sun was fairly up. She awakened Toby to make him lower the drawbridge, and, walking into the woods, gathered armfuls of flowers and flowering branches. She carried them to the Hall and began to prop them in corners, and in the window embrasures. Then seeing that the long oak table was spattered with candle wax and other grease, she called into the kitchen for Milburga.

The maid found her mistress violently polishing the table, and noting the flowers and branches already placed in the Hall, nodded sagely. "Ay lady, I see yere hands're restless and ye feel the need for busyness. For sure your time be nigh."

Katherine looked up startled. "Nay, I feel well, better than for long. I but wanted to bring the May into the house ready for tomorrow." Her voice wavered, for she thought of May Day a year ago in London, with Hawise.

"I'll go tell Parson's Molly ye'll be needing her later on," said Milburga stolidly. As usual she managed to convey a subtle contempt for Katherine.

"Nonsense, the baby isn't due yet. Get a rag and help me with this table." Katherine didn't know for sure when the baby was due, but Milburga always aroused her to opposition.

"Ay, I'd best warn Parson's Molly," repeated the woman as though Katherine had not spoken, "or she might be off at sundown to light the fires and launch Ket's boat on the river."

Katherine bit her lips. Her palm itched to slap the smug sallow face. Milburga well knew that Katherine had forbidden the outlandish ritual performed by her tenants on this St. Walburga's Eve. Gibbon had warned her of it, and described it as a brutish heathen festival which had come down from Druid times and had to do with sacrifice to some dark goddess they called Ket, though some said it was in honor of the Dane, Ketel. No matter which, the proceeding seemed outrageous to Katherine.

The serfs, it seemed, always lit fires in a small circle of ancient stones on a hill near the Trent and after an orgy of dancing, guzzling and worse, they then launched a coracle on the river. The coracle would contain three newborn slaughtered lambs—slaughtered, with wild cries and leapings, on a stone they called an altar. The whole ceremony was called the "Launching of Ket's Ark," Gibbon told her, and his objection to the function sprang not so much from moral indignation at this pagan folderol but from the wanton waste of the lambs and waste of two days' work, one of preparation, and one of recovery from the drinking throughout the night.

But Katherine had been shocked and rushed at once to the priest demanding that he stop the preparations. "Oh, I cannot, lady," said Sir Robert, astonished. "They've always done so here. 'Tis custom. I've often gone myself to launch Ket's ark."

"But it's *heathen!*"

The priest shrugged and looked honestly bewildered.

Then Katherine calling all her housefolk together, and the reeve, had issued a command forbidding them to hold Ket's rite this May Eve. They had said nothing, merely listened to her and dispersed silently. But she had heard the reeve's mocking laugh and Milburga's high-pitched whinny in the courtyard.

"I *told* you, Milburga, that I forbid this thing tonight," said Katherine, trying to speak with dignity. "I expect to be obeyed."

The maid's lips twitched. "To be sure, lady. So I needn't warn Molly?"

"Certainly not!"

Thus it was that night, an hour after sundown, that Katherine felt her first pains and found herself alone, deserted by all the housefolk. They had fed her her supper, and Katherine, not dreaming that they would defy her and being still in a restless mood, had gone up to the solar and, sitting by the window with her lute, strummed random chords while she tried to remember a song she had sung at Bolingbroke.

She took pleasure in her music, and though mostly self-taught, had become a fair player, so that at first she did not notice the growing sharpness of an ache in her back. But the pain grew more insistent, and she stood up, thinking to ease the cramp. Sure enough, it ebbed. She leaned out of the window, gazing idly into the dark forest beyond the moat and thinking on Hugh. She had had no news of him except that given her by the Duchess in January of his arrival overseas, but she had expected none. Even if he had found someone to write a letter for him, whom could he have sent to deliver it?

Yet he had hoped to be home in May and perhaps he might be. It seemed to her that if he came she would be neither sorry nor glad, though she would feign gladness.

She sighed, then tensed, holding on to the rough stone of the embrasure and hearing her own startled breathing. The ache in her legs and back had returned more strongly, and this time before ebbing sent a stab of pain up through her loins.

She ran to the door and down the stairs calling "Milburga!" There was no answer; no lights in Hall or empty kitchen, where the embers had been raked under the curfew for the night. She went out into the quiet court and clenched her hands while another pain came and went. "Toby!" she shouted underneath the gatehouse windows. Though the bridge was down the keeper was not here.

She stumbled to Gibbon's hut, and flung the door open.

"God's wounds, what is it?" cried the man's slow voice in the darkness. "Is it you, my lady? Open the shutter." After a moment she obeyed, and he saw her in the gloaming light. She was crouching, her arms laced tight across her belly.

"Jesu—" whispered the sick man. "Poor creature, so your time has come—but lady, go up to bed, send for the midwife. Oh ay—I'd forgot—God blast them all—they've gone to Ket's hill." A spasm twisted his yellow face. "Is no one here?"

"No—one—" she gasped, "and I dare not try to reach the village."

" 'Twould do no good, there'd be nobody there, I heard them go—they were laughing, shouting drunken songs—" The veins corded on his forehead. "Devil take this stinking useless body of mine—"

"What shall I do, Gibbon?" she asked dully.

"Go to your bed." He spoke briskly to hearten her. "It can't be long before they come back. I'll listen and shout, send someone to you. Be brave for a little while, it won't be long." Though he knew well that last year they had stayed the night through at their wicked rites.

"Ay," she said, "I'll go to bed. That would be best." She could not think for herself, and Gibbon's words brought her relief. "The pains're not so bad," she added, trying to smile. "Not near so dreadful as I'd heard."

Not yet, poor lady, he thought, turning his head from her innocent face. She groped her way through the door. She crept up to the solar and throwing off her gown lay on the sheet in her shift. The night was warm, but had it not been, she would have needed no covering, for soon the sweat began to pour off her heaving body.

Towards midnight Gibbon, lying in the hut, heard the first scream shrill down across the courtyard, and slow tears oozed from beneath his shut lids. In her tower room, the Lady Nichola too heard the scream, and raised her head, wondering. She had been dripping water from a flagon into a clay pot and carefully greeting the drops as they fell.

> *This water for self, this water for elf,*
> *Nixie, pixie, kelpie, sylph.*

She was about her own May Eve rites. The cat, a full-grown tabby now, lay curled on the bed, purring lazily.

When Nichola heard the strange sound again, she put the flagon down on the hearth and spoke to the cat. "Are they calling me, sweeting, d'you think? Is it She Who Lives in the Holy Well?"

Then she shook her head; into her staring dark eyes there came a look of anxiety, for dimly through the floating mists she felt the hard stab of human urgency. She smoothed down her rumpled widow's weeds and bound her graying hair into a must-stained coif. She picked up a twisted rush and lit it at the fire. "I must see what they want," she said, stroking the cat. "I'll not be long—"

She wandered down the stone steps in the tower and across the guardroom to the outside stairs, when she heard the sound again. She knew it came from the solar and was puzzled. She pushed the door slowly open and stood holding the rush dip high, gazing into the dark room.

The sounds came from something on the bed where she had once slept herself with her lord. What was it on the bed that writhed and tossed, and ever and again gave forth a wailing cry?

She moved nearer and saw a mass of tangled hair and two wild eyes in a glistening face.

"Hugh's bride?" she whispered, unbelieving. She blinked, leaned over the bed and seeing red stains, cried, "What has been done to you, Hugh's bride?"

"For the love of God, lady!" cried Katherine, " 'tis my baby that will not be born." She grabbed at Nichola's hand,

clenching it until the bones cracked, and with the pain from
that desperate grip the shadows receded in Nichola's mind.

She had borne no child herself but she had seen birth once
long ago on her father's manor. She sat on the bed and held
Katherine's hands, nor winced when the girl pulled on them
frantically; and between the pains she murmured soothing
words and wiped the sweat-drenched face with a corner of
the sheet.

Presently Katherine quietened a little, falling into an exhausted doze until the gray dawn light filtered into the solar
and the larks and thrushes trilled beneath the forest window.
Then the girl's laboring body renewed its struggle.

The sun had climbed above the forest top when she was
delivered at last.

"Oh, what is it?" Katherine cried when she could speak
again. "Does it live? Is it all right?" She tried to raise herself
and fell back panting.

" 'Tis a girl, a baby girl," said Nichola slowly, staring down
at the bed. "It seems all right, I think—but—I remember—
there is something needs be done—" She fumbled at her girdle, where she kept the little knife she used for cutting herbs.
She bound the cord tight with a strip torn from the sheet,
then clipped sharply. The baby gasped and let out a wavering
cry. Nichola started when she heard the cry. She pulled the
linen coif from her head and wrapped the baby in it, then
cradled the little bundle against her chest.

"Ah, let me see her," Katherine whispered, holding out her
arms. "Give her to me—"

Nichola drew back a step, uncertainty came into her face,
which had been sure and intent before. "What do you want,
Hugh's bride?" she asked in a high singing tone, shaking her
head. "What is it that you want?"

"I want to see my baby, bring her here, lady—" The girl,
all dazed and numb, could not understand why this woman,
who had been her only comfort the night long, should back
away and shake her head. Neither of them heard a commotion in the courtyard below, men's voices and the clop of
horses' hooves.

The baby whimpered and Nichola, bending quickly, kissed
its face. "Ah there, my darling—" she crooned, "my pretty
one, you want to see *them,* don't you? We'll go now to the
river—"

Deadly fear smote Katherine. "Lady!" she cried. "Come

here!" Nichola backed yet another step towards the door. She looked at Katherine slyly and said, "You'd take her from me but she's mine—"

"Jesu, Jesu—" Katherine whispered; she lurched upright on the bed and would have leaped onto the floor, but she dared not, for she saw Nichola glance sideways at the door and that she strained the bundle ever tighter to her chest. Katherine mastered the chattering of her teeth. "And if she's yours, lady," she said and forced a coaxing tone, while she tried to hold the black eyes with her own, "you must tend her carefully; she may be cold, you know, so put her down a moment and stir up the fire that you may warm her—"

Nichola stood hesitant, looking from Katherine to the dark fireplace, then she shook her head again. "Nay, I think not. *They* of the river want to see her first, I must hasten—" She put her hand on the door latch. Katherine stumbled from the bed—and screamed and lurched across the room. She screamed again, for Nichola ran through the door, while footsteps clattered up the stairs.

The woman shrank by the open door, cowering over the baby. A man stood on the landing staring at them with amazement.

"Oh, stop her, stop her!" Katherine sobbed. "She's stealing my baby!" Swift as light the man leaned down and took the bundle from Nichola, who let out a long quivering moan. He put the baby on the bed, then turned to the panting girl who had fallen to her knees on the floor. "In God's name, Katherine!" he cried, and picking her up in his arms he laid her on the bed beside the baby. She stared up at him, seeing vivid blue eyes frowning with concern in a sun-bronzed face. "My Lord Duke," she whispered in feeble wonder, and then his eyes and the room and Nichola's moaning faded into grayness.

It was past high noon when Katherine came to herself again and heard the subdued muttering of women's voices, and at first she could not think what had happened, but lay in a vague dream watching through heavy lids the dance of dust motes in a sunbeam. She turned a little in the bed and her hand fell on her flat belly, then she remembered and started up with a cry, "My baby!"

The kind round face of Parson's Molly bent over her. "Here, lady, here's the tiny maid, all snug and swaddled and content." She put the infant in the crook of Katherine's arm. "As fine and fair a babe as I ever see," and over Molly's shoulder Milburga's frightened peering face nodded agreement.

Katherine looked down at the tiny head covered with darkish fuzz, the crumpled nose and moist pink lips. "Put her to the breast," said Molly, pulling down the sheet, "let her suck to bring the milk in." Katherine felt the hungry tug of the little mouth, and a wave of delight such as she had never known washed through her body. She felt that they two were floating in a golden bath together. The dark doings of the night before seemed but a foul dream long past, neither fear nor pain could touch her ever again, for here was love come at last, incorporate in this tiny thing that breathed and nestled and belonged to her alone.

When the baby fell asleep, she moved it so that its head lay against her cheek and slept too. The women let her be while they whispered fearingly together.

No one knew what the Duke would do to them. His anger had been terrible as he came down the solar stairs into the courtyard when the housefolk came stumbling and lurching back across the drawbridge from Ket's rites. He had not whipped them nor berated, but his eyes had flashed like swords and the tone of his voice as he gave them orders banished their drunkenness like a purge.

They had run frantically to obey him, themselves appalled when they found out what had happened in their absence. The Lady Nichola, sobbing and beating her breasts, had been already chained to her bed in the tower by the Duke's men, for he had brought five with him.

And when Parson's Molly came running to the manor from the village, they found what sad plight their little mistress was in, wallowing unconscious in fouled sheets and the stench of birth-blood, while the babe lay naked, though unhurt—praise be to the Blessed Virgin!

The women now heard the shouts of men-at-arms below, and a squeal of pain from Toby as one of the Duke's retainers cuffed him; and they huddled by the fire glad of the sanctuary of the birth room. Then they heard footsteps on the wooden landing and a knock outside. Molly's fat cheeks mottled, but she went to the door and opened it bravely. She curtsied as she said low, "Our lady sleeps, my Lord Duke, but we've washed her and the babe."

John pushed her aside and strode to the bed. He stood looking down at Katherine. White and spent as a plucked windflower she seemed to him, lying there defenseless with her baby next her cheek. And the small happy smile on her pale lips increased his pity. It was pity that he felt and again that strange urge to protect that he had known when he kissed her a year ago, but now there was no desire mingled with this other feeling. She seemed to him as child-like and pure as his own daughters. Her long lashes quivered and she opened her eyes. They no longer reminded him of Isolda's for there was in them no urgency, no appeal—clear and untroubled they looked up at him.

She saw him through a dreaming haze, so big and shining with his tawny head, a topaz velvet tunic over powerful chest and shoulders, and eyes blue as speedwells against his sunburned skin.

"I don't wish to disturb you, Katherine," he said gently. "I came to see how you did—and the babe." He took her hand, noting with tender amusement that it was still somewhat rough and the nails bitten.

"I do well, my lord," she let her hand lie trustingly in his, scarcely aware that it did. "Is she not lovely?" She nuzzled the baby's head.

John smiled assent, though the infant looked like all others to him and not near so comely as his own son, who had lost the newborn pulpy redness.

"How came you here, my lord?" she asked, drawing her arched brows together. "It seems strange—now I begin to—to wake."

"Having business in Lincoln, I thought to pay you a May morn visit, and—I scarce expected to be so opportune." He frowned, glancing at the frightened women by the fire. "I thought you might like news of Hugh."

"Ay—where *is* Hugh?" she murmured.

"Still in Castile, at Burgos with my army but unharmed. I'll send him back soon. I see you sorely need him."

"But you're here," she whispered smiling, drugged with the torpor of exhaustion and peace.

"Not for long—my ship waits for me at Plymouth. I came back because I have a son."

"Ah yes—" she said. "I knew—I had forgot—how does my Lady Blanche—"

"Fairly," he said and no more, seeing that Katherine was

not fully awake and making an effort to be courteous. He dropped her hand and turned to the window.

Blanche was not churched yet. He had returned to find her very ill with milk fever and one of her legs so red and throbbing that she cried out when it was touched. But the blissful shock of his unexpected return had improved her at once.

She had been well enough for him to leave Bolingbroke and make this hasty trip to Lincoln to inspect its castle, which he owned. Conferences with the constable had taken little time and it had been on impulse that he decided this fine May Day morning to ride on to Kettlethorpe and see Katherine. In truth, he had not thought of her at all these last months—months of triumph, culminating in the glorious victory at Nájera on Saturday April 3. The memory of that arid sun-baked Castilian plain gave him sharp joy.

With the always able help of Sir John Chandos, and his English bowmen, the Duke had led the shock troops in the vanguard of the Prince of Wales' army, and they had loosed a barrage of whirring arrows that turned the tide almost at once. The Castilians fell back, they disintegrated, they ran, and, forced into the flood-swollen river Najerilla, they drowned—twelve thousand of them. The rushing waters had turned red as wine. By noon the battle was over and King Pedro, sobbing with gratitude, had kissed his champions' hands, had knelt on the blood-soaked earth before the Prince of Wales and the Duke of Lancaster.

It was unfortunate that amongst the bodies of the Castilian slain they could not find that of the bastard Trastamare, but otherwise the victory had been complete even to the capture of the redoubtable Sir Bertrand du Guesclin. All the victors had held high feast in Burgos, Castile's fair capital. And there when the messenger from Bolingbroke found him ten days later, John discovered that he had fresh cause for exultation. His son Henry had been born on the same day as the triumph at Nájera, surely a most auspicious bit of fortune. He gave thanks in the cathedral and determined to make a quick trip home to see his son—and Blanche. But neither sentiment nor paternal pride alone could justify the time expended on such a voyage, for there were still angry matters to smooth out in Castile and his brother needed him. So John bore letters to the King at Westminster and, more important, had seized the opportunity to replenish his purse from funds held by his receiver general at the Savoy. The campaign, however glorious, had been expensive.

These matters passed through his mind as he stood by the window and he almost regretted the impulse that had sent him here this morning; for he saw that he could not leave at once as he had planned, while Katherine lay helpless, at the mercy of her serfs and the mad woman Nichola. Yet he was sorely pressed for time and turned plans over in his mind which might best insure her safety until he could send Hugh back.

He returned to the bed and saw that she had awakened, and was softly kissing the baby's head. "Your villeins must be punished, Katherine," he said, smiling at her. "I understand from your bailiff that you and he forbade their extraordinary rites last night and yet they left you here alone."

"That was *my* fault, my lord." Through this dreaming bliss she felt no anger towards anyone. "The midwife would have stayed with me but I wouldn't let Milburga fetch her."

The two listening women looked at each other. Molly whispered, "Our little mistress is kind—" Milburga shrugged. They held their breaths.

John shook his head impatiently. "These serfs cannot be permitted to defy you—there's no strong arm on this manor, that I see well, nor can I forgive Swynford for leaving you in charge of such a bailiff—a dead man—it was dangerous folly —" His anger rose at Hugh, though in Castile he had felt none, for Hugh had again proved himself a powerful fighter.

"Poor Gibbon does the best he can," said Katherine softly. "It's I who have been lax."

"Nonsense, child! It's only that you're far too young to have learned the arts of ruling and you must have help. I've decided what shall be done."

"Yes, my lord," said Katherine, humbly. Though he was but twenty-seven he seemed to her the embodiment of unquestioned authority as he stood there, his shining head thrown back, his eyes stern. He spoke to her as her father had used to long ago. There was no tension between them now, nor did she remember that there ever had been. He was but her overlord and her rescuer.

"I shall leave one of my men here to guard you. A Gascon named Nirac de Bayonne and—for a Gascon—trustworthy." John smiled suddenly. Nirac amused him with his quick tongue, nimble wits and sly humor. Nirac was a man of many

parts, he could concoct licorice potions or spice hippocras; he
could fight with the dagger and sail a ship, the latter accom-
plishment learned during years of smuggling and freebooting
between Bayonne and Cornwall. Though Gascony and
the rest of Aquitaine belonged to England, Nirac had not
troubled himself about allegiance, until the Prince of Wales'
officers caught him and pressed him into military service in
the recent Castilian war. And that temporary allegiance
would have dissolved as soon as he had been paid, except for
the entirely fortuitous circumstance that John had saved his
life at Nájera.

This was no deed of chivalry—the Duke had simply interposed his well-armored body between Nirac and a Castilian
spear; but the fiery little Gascon had been passionately grateful and attached himself doggedly to the Duke.

John was a shrewd judge of those who served him and he
knew that Nirac would obey his commands loyally, and he
thought too that of the men with him today, Katherine would
be safest with this one. Nirac belonged to that type of man
who had but tepid interest in the love of women.

John glanced towards the courtyard window where the sun
already slanted above the church spire and said, "Yes—I'll
leave you Nirac. He'll keep your churls in order until Swynford gets home. And, Katherine—"

She looked up at him and waited.

"Your baby must be christened—now."

Katherine gasped and drew the baby closer. "Is there danger for her? The women said she was unharmed—does there
seem something wrong to you?"

"No, no—there's nothing to fear. But we'll christen the
babe at once, because I shall be its godfather."

"Oh—my sweet lord—" whispered Katherine, flushing
with delight. During the vague unreasoning months of her
pregnancy she had wondered once or twice who might be
found to sponsor the baby if it were actually born.

"It is a very great honor—" she whispered.

"Yes," said the Duke, "and will help insure your safety
and the babe's." It was for this reason he had suggested it.
The spiritual parentage of an infant was no light thing; it
linked the sponsor with the real parents in bonds of compa-
ternity, it incurred obligation for the infant's material as well
as religious nurture and, if as in this case the sponsor were of

royal blood and the most powerful noble in the land, it endowed the baby with an exalted aura.

A child so honored on earth and in heaven would be powerfully protected and even Katherine's unruly serfs should be intimidated.

The christening took place an hour later at the old Saxon font in the little church across the lane. The nave was crowded, because the Duke had sent his men to summon all the villagers, many of whom had been shaken and slapped from their drunken snorings. Parson's Molly held the baby and served as godmother since there was obviously no one else in the least suitable on the manor. At the baptismal questions, John took the baby from Molly and made the responses himself, though waiting with barely concealed impatience while the flustered Sir Robert tried to remember the Latin form, could not, and reverted to English.

The baby was christened Blanche Mary as Katherine had asked. And she wailed satisfactorily when the holy water doused her head and the devil flew out of her.

Katherine, lying tense and strained on her bed, heard the glad ringing of the church bell and dissolved into happy tears. My tiny Blanche, she thought, Blanchette, named for the lovely Duchess and the Blessed Queen of Heaven. She would be safe now forever from the horrors that menaced the unbaptized. And surely all the good fairies had hovered near this christening and brought the baby luck, though there was scarcely need for luck greater than sponsorship by the Duke. How good he is, she thought, and she felt for him the same gratitude and humble admiration she did for the Lady Blanche, and she felt too that she was purged completely from those other darker feelings towards him which now seemed to her incredible.

When the Duke preceded Molly and the baby back into the solar, Katherine greeted him with a soft little cry and, taking his hand, kissed it in a childlike gesture of homage.

The Duke, receiving it as such, bent over and kissed her quickly on the forehead. "There, Katherine, your babe is now a Christian and you and I have become spiritual brother and sister. So I must leave you. I can scarce reach Bolingbroke tonight as it is."

She nodded. "I know, my lord. I'm sorry. And when you see Hugh—"

"Ay," he broke in with sudden curtness, "I'll tell him all and send him back. In the meantime, here is Nirac."

The little Gascon had been hovering in the doorway and skipped in at his master's call crying "Oc! oc! seigneur—" followed by a further string of liquid syllables which Katherine could not understand. The man was like a blackbird with his bright round eyes, his cocky strut and a cap of hair like glossy blue-black feathers. He wore the Duke's blue and gray household livery, and the tunic clung like a glove to his spare wiry body.

John laughed and said to Katherine, "Nirac speaks the langue d'oc, but much else as well, some Spanish, the barbarous Basque, French of course."

"And English, seigneur, also—I am a man of many tongues and many talents."

"Daily you prove that Gascon bragging shames even the devil," said John a trifle sternly, "but I'm entrusting you here. You will guard this lady—"

"With my life, seigneur, with my honor, with my soul, I swear by the Virgin of the Pyrenees, by Sant' Iago de Compostela, by the English Saint Thomas, by—"

"Yes, well, that's enough, you little jackanapes. I trust you'll never be forsworn. I've told the serfs that I leave you here in my place until their rightful lord comes home. You'll know how to make them obey?"

The bright beady eyes sobered and gazed intently up at the Duke's face. "Oui, mon duc." He nodded once. "Your wishes shall be done in every sing—long as Nirac de Bayonne has breat' in body—" His narrow brown hand fingered the hilt of his dagger.

"No, mon ami," said the Duke, glancing at the dagger, "you must be chary of violence. The English have laws on the manor, 'tis not like your wild mountain country. You must be guided by the Lady Katherine."

The Gascon's hand dropped, he looked at the pale girl on the bed, then back into the Duke's face as though reading something there. He ran to the bedside and knelt. "Votre serviteur, belle dame," he said. "I shall guard you for the Duke."

Neither of them gave any deeper meaning to these words or guessed that Nirac had misconstrued the situation. He came of a primitive southern race where emotions were as simple as they were violent. There was love and there was hate, and no nuances between. He loved the Duke; therefore he would love this girl whom he took to be the Duke's leman, else why should his master waste all this time attending to such trivial matters as baptisms and peasants. Perhaps the baby was the Duke's—that would explain matters, and explain too why the young mother never spoke of her husband in the days that followed, but spent all her time nursing and petting her baby.

She listened though, when Nirac spoke of the Duke, while a smile half-wistful and half-awed would light her gray eyes. Nirac, eager to please her, sang often of the Duke's bravery at the battle of Nájera. Sir John Chandos' herald had made up a song after the battle, and it began,

> *En autre part le noble duc*
> *De Lancastre, plein de vertus*
> *Si noblement se combattait.*
> *Que chaqu'un s'en émerveillait. . . .*

She listened and she took pleasure in Nirac's company. They often spoke French together, he was gay, and of some help to her on the manor by his very presence, though the serfs resented him bitterly. Still, for the next weeks they gave no further cause for complaint, being thoroughly cowed by the ducal visit. But there were many whispered conferences in the alehouse and on the whole the distrust of Katherine increased, now that she was forever shadowed by this other foreigner that the terrifying Duke had foisted on them. Singing they were, the lady and that strutting little rooster at all hours in the Hall, in a gibberish no one understood. The manor folk longed for their rightful English lord to return.

Parson's Molly always defended her mistress when she heard the others reviling her. She pointed out how the lady had shown mercy in many ways and particularly in the matter of the Lady Nichola. She had ordered that the crazed woman be unchained and simply confined to her tower room behind a locked door, and Lady Katherine herself brought up milk and bread and spoke gently to the woman who had tried to steal her baby. But the Lady Nichola never answered, she crouched now day and night in a corner of her room while floating little pieces of straw in a pan of water, nor even cared about her cat. At Lady Katherine's orders, they carried Nichola down to the church during Mass and tied her to the rood screen that the evil spirits might be exorcised, and Lady Katherine saw to it that nobody poked or pinched the mad woman at these times, for the little mistress was clement.

And no woman, Molly said, could be a better mother than the Lady Katherine, that was plain for all to see.

"And what of it?" sniffed Milburga. "The ewes and the sows do as much, and she thrives on it herself—the quean." Even to the most reluctant eyes, Katherine's beauty could not be ignored. Her curly dark auburn hair shone with a new luster, as did her skin, where the healthy rose again stained the cheekbones. All girlish angularity had left her small-boned body. It had regained its supple slenderness, but now her arms were rounded and her breasts, once somewhat undeveloped, had swollen to globes that strained the bodice of her gowns.

When she walked to the church or down the village street, the menfolk eyed her sideways, and there were lip-smackings and uneasy jests when she had passed, yet despite this new voluptuousness there was something pure and unawakened in her yet, and even Milburga could find no excuse for accusing Katherine of light conduct.

The hours her mistress spent with the Gascon were always in the Hall or courtyard in full view of everyone, and at night not only was the solar door bolted but Katherine had taken little Betsy, the dairy maid, to sleep with her and help tend the baby.

The honor should by rights have gone to Milburga, and the slight augmented her ill will. But it seemed that the lady noticed little of the undercurrents on her manor, her whole thought centered in the baby and even when she talked or sang with the Gascon, she held her child in her arms and joyfully suckled it whenever it whimpered.

The twenty-ninth of June would be the feast day of Sts. Peter and Paul, and the most important one of the year for Kettlethorpe folk since it celebrated the dedication of their parish church. On this day, after morning Mass, the villagers had always held high carnival with sports and copious drinking, climaxed by the lighting of bonfires on Ket's hill and at the four corners of the parish. This year, they were uneasy about their celebration, having sharply in mind the unfortunate consequences of their May Eve rites and being uncertain of Lady Katherine's attitude or that of Nirac, the hateful little watchdog the Duke had set over them.

A week before the festival they deputied their reeve to approach Katherine and find out her wishes. On the afternoon when Sim Tanner, the reeve, walked on his wooden clogs from the village to the manor house, it was pouring cold rain from a dun-colored sky. He presented himself dripping at the door of the Hall, his leather jerkin stained with mud.

Katherine was in the Hall with Nirac and Gibbon, whom she often had carried there so that he might lie by the fire and have a change of view. She greeted the reeve courteously, thinking that he came to consult Gibbon on some farm matter, then seated herself again on her low chair and picked up her spindle.

Nirac had been amusing himself by whittling a set of chessmen from an alder slab. When they were finished he hoped to teach Katherine chess, of which game he had learned a smattering from one of the Duke's squires. Nirac found life at Kettlethorpe exceedingly dull and looked up eagerly at the reeve's entrance, then, disappointed that it was not some more interesting visitor, returned to his whittling.

Gibbon lay on a pile of deerskins near the central hearth. This was one of his good days when his mind was clear and he fancied that he could feel a faint tingling in his legs. His speech, however, had grown thicker and more halting in the last months and he seldom forced it. His eyelids flickered greeting to the reeve, then his veiled gaze returned to Katherine. Watching her was the last pleasure left him, and he always made the servants deposit him close to her chair.

She was not yet skilled at spinning, but since the baby had come she had forsaken lute playing and embroidery for more useful arts. She twirled the coarse gray fibers onto her spindle from the distaff and watched the process with a small frown of concentration that Gibbon thought bewitching. The baby lay gurgling in a plaited willow basket at her feet and whenever her eyes left the balky yarn, which frequently knotted or broke, they strayed downward towards the basket and a light came into them. If she ever looks at a *man* like that— thought Gibbon, what rapture she would kindle. But it'll never be Hugh. He sighed, and thought with some pity of his half brother.

Sim, who had been standing as near the fire as he dared while his jerkin steamed drier, now cleared his throat. "Prithee, m'lady, I come to ask ye summat. I speak for all your villeins."

"Aie—e!" cried Nirac, cocking his head and instantly alert. "And *now* what does that meaching canaille want of her?"

The reeve's slit mouth tightened, his cold haddock eyes flicked to the Gascon then back to Katherine, who laid down her spindle and waited. "Next Tuesday's our church day, lady," he continued. "Since the time of our great gaffers and long before, Kettlethorpe folk've held the day special for sport and feasting."

"Pardieu!" Nirac threw down his knife and jumped up to stand by Katherine. " 'Tis all they do here, these worthless churls—feasting and sporting. Never do they think of work!" This was manifestly unfair, for the serfs had had no time off since May Eve, but he despised the serfs and considered that anything that thwarted them advanced Katherine's interests.

"Tell him, madam," he said, lower, to Katherine, "to take his farouche fishface out of here and return to his tasks."

"Peace, Nirac!" said Katherine sternly. She didn't like the reeve, who treated her with the same veiled disrespect Milburga did, but Gibbon said he served the manor well. She glanced down at Gibbon, who was watching her with a faint smile on his bloodless lips. He did not try to answer her unspoken question because he felt that she must learn to handle manor matters herself and, besides, he knew not what advice to give. In strict justice, the villeins deserved their feast day as they had always had it, yet there would be drunkenness and brawling and probably deaths as there had been other years. The manor could ill afford to lose a single strong pair of arms, though the lechery that accompanied their celebration was beneficial to the manor. The more brats that were bred in the fields and haycocks the better, since on each one a cash fine of leyrwite would be due to Hugh. On the other hand, the "custom of the manor" decreed largesse from its lord with free ale and meat provided, and this would seriously tax the manor's slender larder. Since the serfs were forbidden to hunt game, and Nirac had no experience of lordly sports, there was no one to bring in meat, and Katherine's resources would be seriously depleted by the slaughter of a sufficient amount of oxen or sheep.

Katherine knew little of these practical considerations and she knew that the reeve's request was reasonable enough; but his insolent popeyes annoyed her and she said coldly, "And if I refuse permission, you might defy me as you did May Eve?"

Sim's long face flushed and before he could answer, Nirac sprang forward like a cat. "They cannot defy you, for they have *me* to reckon with—me, Nirac le Gascon! My sword is ready. I shall carve the miserable ladrones into mincemeat, I shall slice their ears and fingers—"

"Chut! Nirac—" Katherine cried impatiently. She was used to his extravagances, but the reeve had gone chalk-white and his voice was high and thin like a neighing horse. "And whilst you're brandishing your sword and dagger, you greasy meacock, what think you *we'll* be doing? We've pitchforks, and axes, and scythes—we can carve off ears and fingers too, ay and cods and stones—"

"Sim—Sim—" gasped Gibbon from his pallet. Nobody heard him. Katherine stood frozen, while a dangerous still-ness flowed over the Gascon. "You t'reaten me?" he said softly. "Do you forget, miserable serf, that I wear the livery of the Duke of Lancaster?"

The reeve's face convulsed, his furious breath flattened his nostrils. "He's not *my* overlord!" he shouted. "I spit upon your Duke of Lancaster!"

The instant the spittle left his mouth, the reeve was fright-ened, Nirac gave him no time for repentance, he scooped the whittling knife off the table and sprang.

"Holy name of God, Nirac!" Katherine screamed, as a spurt of blood jetted against the stone wall. "You'll kill him! He's unarmed." Neither of them heard her. The panting bod-ies struggled, knocking against the stools and table. Katherine grabbed the baby and ran onto the dais. "Help!" she cried, "for Christ's sake, help!"

A slow sob rose in Gibbon's throat and his left hand twitched. The fighting men rolled and stumbled over him as though he were part of the floor, his mantle became drenched with the reeve's blood.

The kitchen folk heard the noise and their mistress's cries. They crowded around the wooden screen, peering fearfully.

"Stop them, Will!" cried Katherine. "Hurry!" The cook did not move. He had not yet understood the scene except for a vague hope that the reeve was murdering the hated Gascon.

The men rolled near the corner of the dais and Katherine heard a bubbling liquid groan. Nirac was on top, his knees on the reeve's chest, his knife hand raised again. She put the baby in the center of the great table and, jumping from the dais, clenched her teeth and, grabbing a handful of Nirac's streaming black hair, jerked with all her might. "Halte!" she shouted, "au nom du duc!"

Nirac's grasp loosened, he shook his head in a dazed way, trying to free his hair. She pulled harder so that his face was forced upward and he saw hers. "You don't want that I kill him?" he panted. "Yet you heard what he said!"

"I think you *have* killed him. Get up!" She yanked him off the inert reeve who lay gasping and bleeding on the flags. She knelt beside the man, and distractedly wiped his face with the hem of her gown. "Milburga, bring water and linen—some-one get the priest. Hurry!"

"Bah!" said Nirac, smoothing his hair back and wiping his knife on a handful of rushes, "the salaud won't need the priest." He examined his victim with a practiced eye. "A few cuts, my knife is short—he's had no more than a good blood-letting. Had I had my dagger—"

Nirac was right, it appeared, for by the time Sir Robert and his Molly came puffing into the hall, Sim was recovering. There was no need for the priest nor even need of Molly's leechcraft. The cuts and stabs had hit no vital spot except for the artery in the arm and that stopped spurting when Katherine tied the liripipe of the reeve's own hood right about the wound.

The manor folk clustered around, glancing sideways at Katherine, who had rushed back to the dais to soothe her crying baby and remove it from the table. They did not look at Nirac, who had nonchalantly returned to his stool and his whittling. Will Cooke and old Toby helped the reeve to his feet and supported him out the door and back to his cot in the village. The reeve had not said a word nor raised his bloodshot eyes as he tottered away.

"Lord shield us, lady, but what took place here?" asked the priest, settling himself into a chair and toasting his wet shoes at the fire. "What has Sim Tanner done?"

"He insult *me!*" said Nirac, carving a flourish on the Rook, "and he insult mon seigneur le duc—" He shrugged and quirked his mouth in a contemptuous smile.

"Ah?" said Sir Robert, thoughtfully, and seeing that Katherine was suckling her baby and not likely to offer him any-thing, he helped himself to the remains of a cup of ale which Milburga had brought in for the reeve. Nirac's explanation satisfied him, and after all no great harm had been done.

The rain beat harder on the tile roof. Little Cob o' Fenton

came in with candles. He stoked the fire with applewood and began to fling knives and wooden trenchers on the High Table in readiness for supper. Ah, that Nirac! thought Katherine. His notions of serving her and his lord made him a dangerous nuisance, and yet she had grown quite fond of him.

Her gaze passed from Nirac to the priest, who sat dozing while he waited for food. His claret-colored robes overflowed his chair and from them rose a pungent odor of hound dog. Her eyes dropped to the last of the three men, and Gibbon was looking up at her, though as always she could see little of the expression beneath the sunken lids. She smiled at him, and thought sadly that he had failed in these last months and with compunction that she must tell Cob to cleanse him from the reeve's bloodstains and renew the fouled padding of hay beneath his hips. She had half risen, when her sharp ears heard unusual sounds through the beating of the rain.

"Hark!" she said. "What can that be?"

Ajax from his kennel let out his warning bay, and now they all heard the clack of horse hooves on the drawbridge. The Duke is back, Katherine thought, and a wild sweet joy exploded like a fiery shower in her breast, then vanished so fast she never knew she had felt it, for as she ran to the door she heard a voice in the courtyard.

"It's Hugh come home!" she cried to those within the Hall, her cry trembling with what passed for gladness. She flung wide the door.

Thanks be to God in His mercy, thought Gibbon, now at least she will be safe.

# PART TWO

## (1369)

To Danger came I all ashamed,
The which aforn me hadde blamed,
Desiring for to appease my woe;
But over hedge durst I not go,
For he forbade me the passage.
I found him cruel in his rage,
And in his hand a great burdoun.

ROMAN DE LA ROSE

# IX

THE YEAR of 1369 was one of disaster for England. John Wyclif's wandering Lollard preachers were not slow to point out that the corruption and wickedness of the clergy—and the court—had attracted God's wrathful eye. The four dread horsemen of the Apocalypse were let loose across the land to scourge it again with famine, war, pestilence and death. There had been all manner of sinister omens. A remarkable comet had flashed across the sky, its fiery tail pointing unmistakably towards France. In the south the earth had quaked and shuddered a warning, in Northumbria a woodman hacked into an oak that shrieked and shed human blood. And soon all England heard of the first disaster. The young Duke Lionel of Clarence, the King's second son, the great golden giant who had laughed and drunk and jousted his way into the hearts of the people, he was dead in Italy. He had died on his wedding trip after marrying the Milanese heiress, Violante, and there were some who spoke of poison.

The period of mourning for Lionel was scarcely over before the people heard disquieting news which affected their lives more nearly. There was rebellion in Aquitaine. The treacherous and disloyal English subjects of Guienne and Gascony had refused to pay the hearth tax that the Prince of Wales had levied, though it was obvious that only by thus raising money from them could their own soldiery be paid for fighting the Castilian campaign. Worse than that, Charles the Fifth, the sly mealymouthed king of France, had dared to meddle in these English affairs, and suddenly find flaws in the execution of the treaty of Brétigny. The Prince of Wales, and later King Edward himself, responded with hot countercharges. In April of 1369, after nine years of uneasy peace, war with France was declared again.

For a time in that catastrophic summer these national affairs scarcely affected Kettlethorpe, but the Swynfords shared more immediate troubles with the rest of England's rural population.

It had been a winter of vicious cold, and when a late spring unlocked the deep-frozen earth it brought with it weeks of unremitting rain. Day after day the sullen skies lowered, and no sun showed. In June at the moon tide, an eagre thundered up the swollen Trent and burst the dykes as far as Newton, then the swirling waters rushed over the sodden land, drowning and devastating as they advanced.

At Kettlethorpe, one of Sir Robert and Molly's little boys had been drowned, as he fished by the river; but the other villagers had taken refuge in the church, which was built on higher ground.

Around the manor house the moat merged with the flood waters until the building seemed to stand in the margin of a vast lake and the forest trees to the south pierced this lake like monstrous reeds. In the manor hall and courtyard, water had lain a foot deep for two days, and the manor folk had huddled in the solar or the tower guardroom, in chill and hungry fear, until the flood at last subsided to leave behind a coating of viscous black mud, drowned sheep, and ruined crops.

Besides the drowning of the priest's boy and the devastation of the land, the flood brought Kettlethorpe another tragedy. The sound of rushing waters so near to her had roused the Lady Nichola from the mindless stupor into which she had fallen after little Blanche's birth. She had become greatly excited and, cramming her wasted body into the embrasure of her window, called out words of wild greeting to the river sprites. The waters rose higher until from her window she could see nothing but a shining sea, and this had provoked her to spine-chilling laughter. For months afterwards Katherine heard the echo of that laughter and felt remorse that she had not gone to try and calm the poor lady but instead had stopped her ears and stayed in the solar soothing her two babies and thinking of nothing but their safety.

Somehow with the cunning and uncanny strength of madness, the Lady Nichola had loosened the bolt on her door. She had clambered up the stones to the roof of the tower and with one long triumphant cry had flung herself down into the waters below. It was many days before they found her body and brought it back to the little church for a Requiem Mass which the priest was reluctant to celebrate. Katherine overrode him fiercely, saying that it was the water elves that had bewitched the poor lady and driven her to suicide, and that therefore her soul could not be damned. Sir Robert, by no means certain of this theological point, finally gave in, and the Lady Nichola was laid to rest beneath the aisle slabs near the church altar—next to Gibbon.

Gibbon had faded slowly out of life, and last Christmas Eve had died in a manner as quiet and unassuming as the Lady Nichola's leave-taking had been frenzied. Katherine had mourned deeply for Gibbon, and Hugh had too. They had made a special trip into London to the cathedral to buy Masses for his soul, but Katherine had had no leisure for much mourning. Besides the care of little Blanche, there was the new baby, Thomas, there was the manor work, and there was Hugh.

On a searing hot afternoon in late August, Katherine sat on a heap of straw with the babies in the portion of her courtyard that was shaded by the gatehouse and listened to the tolling of their church bell from across the moat. It would toll for three hours in memory of yet another death, and though Katherine's tears did not flow as they had for Gibbon or even for Lady Nichola, she felt a poignant sadness, and she sat with folded hands and murmured, *"Requiescat in pace."*

On Lady Day, August 15, the good Queen Philippa had died at Windsor, when the laboring heart had no longer been able to struggle on beneath its burden of dropsical flesh. Sim, the reeve, had heard the news in Lincoln where he had gone to try and buy seed corn to replace the ruined crops. He brought back the doleful tidings about the Queen and also a letter from Geoffrey Chaucer which confirmed them and added more. Geoffrey wrote that there was plague in London and the south, an outbreak more virulent than any in eight years. Geoffrey was worried about his own Philippa, who was apparently pregnant at last, and much distraught over the Queen's death. After the funeral ceremonies and the Queen's interment in Westminster Abbey, Geoffrey thought to bring Philippa to Katherine in Lincolnshire, far from the dangerous London air, and leave her there, for he himself was ordered to France, on a mission for the King.

It had been over three years since the sisters had met, and

this prospect helped temper Katherine's sadness. She looked down at the Queen's little brooch, with which today she had fastened the neck of her gown. Foi vainquera, she thought, touching the motto, and wondered if the Queen's faith had truly sustained her through these last years. Even at Kettle-thorpe, one heard of the shameless Alice Perrers and the bejeweled splendor with which she openly flaunted her position as the King's mistress and advisor.

"Non, non, Blanchette!" cried Katherine, recalled from her abstraction by the straying of the eldest towards the stables. "Come back to Mama!" The baby giggled naughtily, her fat little legs ran faster. She was of an enterprising turn of mind, and she loved the stables and Doucette, her mother's palfrey; but there was danger from Hugh's stallions. Katherine flew across the courtyard and swooped the baby up in her arms, administering a gentle spank on the wriggling behind. "Méchante!" she whispered, burying her face in the plump little neck. Sometimes she talked French to the babies, though Hugh didn't like it. Blanchette pouted, then decided to nestle close to her mother. Katherine sat down again with the child on her lap. Blanchette was a vital, lively little thing, with a mop of marigold curls and round smoky gray eyes like her mother's, but darker. She was continually getting into mischief and Katherine adored her, as she had from the hour of her birth.

With little Tom it was different. Katherine looked down at the withe cradle where her son slept. He had been born in September on St. Matthew's Day nearly a year ago. He had given little trouble then, and he gave little now. He was a stolid child who seldom smiled and never gurgled or shrieked as Blanchette did. He had hemp-colored crinkled hair and was in fact remarkably like his father.

Katherine sighed when she thought of Hugh. This morning when he rose at dawn to hunt the red deer in the forest, his bowels had griped and run with bloody flux again, and he had been so weakened after an hour at the privy pit behind the dovecote that even with Ellis' help he had scarce been able to mount his horse. This dysentery that Hugh had brought back from Castile often seemed cured and yet each time returned, despite Katherine's nursing and all the remedies suggested by Parson's Molly. They had tried garlic and ram's gall clysters, they had bled Hugh regularly, sprinkled his belly with holy water, and even called in the leech monk from St. Leonard's priory in Torksey. This monk fed Hugh a potion made of powdered toadstone, bade the ailment begone in the name of the Trinity and gave him a paper to wear above his navel on which were written, "Emmanuel, Veronica," but still the seizures and the flux came back at intervals, and Hugh suffered grimly.

The mourning bell, after a pause, clanged out again the first of fifty-six long tollings, one for each year of the Queen's life. Katherine recited a prayer, then settled herself more comfortably on the straw and leaned her head against the gatehouse wall. Blanchette had gone to sleep and Katherine eased the child down beside her. Flies buzzed lazily over the stinking dung pile near the cow-byre, where several chickens scratched for seed, but otherwise the courtyard was quiet, its usual activities suspended out of deference to the Queen. The afternoon grew warmer and Katherine longed for a drink, but she feared to disturb Blanchette and in any case was too drowsy to walk across the court to the well, and she would not tap the keg of ale they kept in the undercroft beneath the solar, for they must eke out the little they had left. God alone knew when they could brew more, since the flood had ruined the barley crop, and the scanty replacement had been sown so late and under the wrong aspects of the moon.

Katherine sighed again. She had been up since daybreak, caring for the babies and trying to help poor Hugh before attending the Queen's memorial Mass. She pulled Tom's cradle close to Blanchette and, curling around her sleeping children, nestled into the straw.

It was thus that the Chaucers found her a half-hour later. They had dismounted by the church, tied their horses to the lych gate and walked across the drawbridge to inquire, because Philippa, on seeing the manor house, had been quite sure that there was some mistake. She was accustomed to royal castles and the palatial homes of noblemen, and nothing through the years of their separation had arisen to shake her conviction that her sister's enviable marriage to a landed knight presupposed baronial grandeur.

"I'll take oath this can't be Kettlethorpe Manor," she said to her husband as they entered the courtyard. "It must be the bailiff's home." Her high insistent voice penetrated Katherine's dreams, and the girl stirred and slowly raised her head.

The movement caught Philippa's incredulous eye, and she turned.

"Blessed Saint Mary—'tis Katherine! God's love, sister, do you sleep on straw, like a *beast,* here?" The shock momentarily outweighed Philippa's affection and she spoke in sharp dismay.

Since the day was so hot, Katherine had after church laid off her linen coif and bundled her masses of ruddy hair into a coarse hemp net—like a byre-maid, thought Philippa. Bits of straw were stuck amongst the damp curls that clung to the girl's cheeks. Her gown was of blue sendal but looked much like a peasant's kirtle, since Katherine had not covered it with the sideless furred surcote which befitted her rank; and worse than that, she had looped the long skirt up beneath her girdle so that it was plain to see that she wore no hose. Barc white ankles showed above the scuffed soft-leather shoes. Philippa was appalled.

Katherine blinked, still thinking that these two whom she had not seen for so long were part of her dream—a short plump young couple, both dressed in black, both gazing at her with surprise—then she scrambled to her feet with a glad cry and rushing to her sister threw her arms around her neck. Philippa returned the kiss, but Geoffrey, who knew the signs, saw what his wife's next words would be like, and, himself kissing Katherine on each cheek, said quickly, "By God's mercy, my dear—you're fairer than ever—and these are the babes? La petite Blanche, wake up, poppet! Your uncle has brought you trinkets from London! And *there's* a fine fat boy! We'll have one just like him, eh, Pica?" and he pinched his wife's round cheek.

"With Christ's grace," said Philippa glancing at the babies, but not to be diverted. "Katherine, is this the way you keep your state as lady of the manor—what example do you give your servants? And——" She glanced frowning around the littered courtyard and at the small building and one low tower; her sharp eyes noted the crumblings between the aged stones, the moldering thatch on the roof, the general air of dilapidation, and she finished more feebly, " 'Tis not what I thought."

Katherine smiled at her elder sister, even welcoming the old atmosphere of reproof and admonition which took her back to childhood. "Kettlethorpe is small," she said temperately, "but we did well enough until this summer. We had a fearful flood and all our crops washed away. Our flocks too. Were it not for produce from our holdings at Coleby, which is on higher ground, I don't know where we'd turn. Hugh is hunting in the forest, but game is hard to find, the wild things were all driven out by the waters."

"Ah, yes," said Geoffrey sadly, "throughout England there's the smell of doom. We saw as we came north fires, famine—but here at least you've no plague—"

Katherine glanced in sudden fear at her babies. Tom slept on, but Blanchette hid behind her mother and peered round at the strangers. "I've heard of none," she said, and crossed herself. "Is it so bad in the south—you—you haven't lost—" She faltered, glancing at their mourning clothes which were of a rich sable wool trimmed with velvet and strips of black fox. Philippa's tightly coiled dark braids were bound with an onyx and silver fillet, and beneath it her earnest face was round and neat as a penny.

"Oh, no," said Philippa, "we wear this for the Queen, God assoil her gentle soul. The suits were given us by the King's orders." She spoke with a certain complacence, though she sighed. She had been devoted to the Queen and now had no idea where her next permanent home would be, since Geoffrey was away so much on King's business and even now must return to Dover, then report to the Duke of Lancaster at Calais.

She was fond of Katherine, but in view of what she had already seen of Kettlethorpe, she could not but be doubtful about the protracted visit Geoffrey had planned for her. The Queen had left her a pension of a hundred shillings yearly, and Philippa suspected with natural annoyance that she might have to pay board instead of living in the luxurious elegance she had imagined, while saving her income for the benefit of her long-awaited baby.

"We had the Queen's Requiem Mass today—you hear the passing bell," said Katherine diffidently. "You mustn't think we don't sorrow for her here, though we *are* so far away."

Geoffrey's bright hazel eyes glanced at the girl and softened. Ever quick to catch human overtones, he heard the wistfulness in her voice, thought that she was more unhappy than she knew and bore herself with a rather touching gallantry. It was true that she was more beautiful than ever, her cheeks like red and white daisies, her lustrous eyes gray and soft as vair; she glowed with bright health though she was slender as a birch. Despite the two children and despite her eighteen years, there was still something virginal about her.

He reflected that it was not thus he had expected Katherine to be now, when he had first seen her at court three years ago, when he had said that she had "le diable au corps" and thought her a flame to light man's lust. He had thought that there was the mark of destiny upon her. And he had been wrong. The stars had held for her, it seemed, only the fate shared by thousands of other women; motherhood, housewifery, struggle and—as he at once discovered when Hugh returned—the endurance of a difficult, ailing husband.

By the time Hugh came in from hunting, the Chaucers had been settled in Lady Nichola's old tower room and were in the Hall awaiting supper.

Hugh made an effort to greet his guests cordially. He sent Cob to broach the last keg of ale. Little Cob, the erstwhile spit-boy, was now nineteen and had been promoted to servitor, though he was still flax-haired and undersized; also sulky, for he liked farming and loathed his kitchen duties. He brought up a flagon of ale to the Hall and spilled some, at which Hugh gave him a savage kick on the shins.

Then Hugh filled the wooden mazer, said "Wassail," drank and passed it to Philippa as hospitality demanded. She answered "Drinkhail" uncertainly before she sipped. These Saxon customs were seldom seen at court, and Philippa tightened her lips. The ale was inferior and besides, she was used to wine. If it weren't for the plague—she thought unhappily —but there was no other place for her to go, and anyway she dared travel no farther in her condition.

The wassail cup passed from Katherine to Geoffrey and back to Hugh, who took a deep draught, and spat most of it out on the rushes. Swallowing started up the gripes. "What news of the Duke in Picardy?" he said through his teeth to his brother-in-law. "How goes the war?"

Geoffrey shrugged. "A standstill, I believe. Our noble Duke makes alarums and excursions, but that wily Valois fox has run to earth and will not fight; his skulking fainéantise serves France well. He has but to wait until the Prince of Wales has insulted the last of our Gascon allies, then the whole of Aquitaine will revolt against us."

"You speak thus of the *Prince?*" Hugh said, frowning.

"My dear Hugh—I speak truth. In Aquitaine they call Edward 'the Black Prince,' and not only from the color of his armor. Since Castile he steeps himself in wrath, he plunders and kills without mercy. One by one he estranges his barons there, demanding that they maintain his magnificent English court at Bordeaux and yet allows them no positions of importance. They're proud, those Gascons, as proud as we are, I trow. Is it wonder they turn to the honied soothing welcome of the French king?"

"Phaw!" said Hugh, "the Gascons are scurvy riffraff—like any cur, they do better for a flogging!"

Katherine had retired to a corner behind the table while she suckled little Tom, but she looked at her husband when he said this, and wondered if he thought of Nirac.

There had been a fearful scene with Nirac, after Hugh's return two years ago. The wounded reeve had lost no time in taking his grievance to his lord, and he had slandered Katherine too. Hugh had gone berserk, accusing her of whoredom with the Gascon. Her own house servants had reluctantly come to her defense, and they and poor Gibbon had finally convinced Hugh of her innocence. But Hugh had struck Nirac a violent blow across the mouth and kicked him off the manor. Nirac had gone without saying anything except one soft aside to Katherine in French. "Adieu, madam, I obey the Duke—but I shall not *forget* your brave knight." And his black eyes had glittered like a lizard's.

Geoffrey saw nothing special in Hugh's remark beyond the normal English contempt for foreigners, and he thought with some pity that Hugh's irritability doubtless sprang from ill health. As, for that matter, did perhaps the new violence and unreason of the Prince of Wales, for they said that the Prince had picked up some baleful disease in Castile.

Hugh had aged much since Geoffrey had seen him last. There were white threads amongst the wooly drabness of his hair and beard. He had grown thin and had lost the chunky look he used to have. His high-necked, loose-sleeved blue cote-hardie hung on him slackly; deep furrows ran from his sharpened nose down either side of his clamped-in lips; the scar on his cheek lumped purple against the pallor of his skin. He could not be over thirty, but a young man's vigor had seeped out of him. Poor Katherine, thought Geoffrey, as Hugh with a muttered oath clutched at his belly and, doubling over, stumbled out into the courtyard. The jest that Geoffrey might, at another time, have made about this most ludicrous of human ailments, died as he thought of it, and instead he said, "Is it because of these attacks that Hugh has not gone to join the Duke in war service?"

Katherine wiped the baby's mouth and put him down in the cradle. "Nay, for sometimes he is well," she said slowly, buttoning her bodice. " 'Tis that my Lord Duke ordered him not to come. He wrote from the Savoy that Hugh must stay on our manor to—to care for it." Katherine colored and looked away from Geoffrey's sharp gaze. The Duke's letter had actually said, "You are ordered to remain at Kettlethorpe to give proper guardianship and care to your lady." Hugh had been hurt and angry. He had felt himself discarded, "put out to grass," though he made only that one comment. Nor had he ever said much about the ducal visit at the time of Blanchette's birth, except to express gratification at the honor done the baby.

"We've heard nothing else from Their Graces of Lancaster in all this time," said Katherine, "except that the Duke sent that hanap for Blanchette." She pointed to a silver-gilt chalice which stood on a wall bracket below Hugh's hanging armor. The cup had been specially engraved for the child with delicate foliage and tendrils supporting the Swynford blazon; on the knob of the richly carved cover there was a cabochon emerald—Blanchette's birthstone. "Nor should we expect to hear—" she added hastily, not wanting Geoffrey to think her presuming.

"Of course not," said Philippa, who knew better than Katherine the constant demands, confusion and movement from castle to castle that regal living entailed; and moreover there was war and the royal mournings. "I trust you were properly grateful for the Duke's favor, Katherine," she said crossly, looking at the cup. She had never received such a gift herself, and she thought it looked remarkably out of place against the damp sooty stones of this meager hall.

"I—we sent back thanks by the messenger," said Katherine uncomfortably. She had tried to write a letter to the Duke but had been ashamed to send it, though she had hunted for words to copy from the psalter. Writing was very different from reading, and the priest at the convent had taught her little of the art.

"The Duchess Blanche is this week to arrive at Bolingbroke," said Philippa. "She too flees from the plague."

"Is she, indeed?" A pang, half sweet, half bitter, shot through Katherine's heart. She thought of those twelve days of Christmas she had spent with the Duchess at Bolingbroke nearly three years ago and of the sympathy between them and the joy she had felt. She had not ceased to love the Duchess, even though the Lady Blanche forgot her.

"Why don't you ride over to Bolingbroke and wait on her, Katherine?" suggested Geoffrey. " 'Twould be fitting."

Hugh had come back into the Hall and crouched in his high-backed chair, his knees drawn up to ease the cramps. His dull eyes lifted now to his brother-in-law's face, and he frowned.

"By all means!" cried Philippa, having instantly seen the advantages. "She was fond of you, and once she sees you, will renew her favors—though heaven knows you were stupid enough in that regard with the Queen—God absolve her soul —but still, the Lancasters have always taken some interest, and if Hugh's out of favor with the Duke—"

"Nay, he is *not!*" cut in Katherine sharply, as she heard her husband make a sound. "What a foolish thing to say—"

"Pica didn't mean that," said Chaucer, as usual covering his wife's bluntness. "Everyone knows that Hugh fought most bravely in Castile and doubtless the Duke's giving him special consideration in return. But 'twould be courteous to wait upon our most lovely lady since she's so near. Hugh would accompany Katherine."

"No," said Hugh somberly. "I want no truckling in women's bowers. I'll abide here till the Duke sends. Ellis can escort Katherine since you think it seemly that she go." He leaned his chin on his hand and stared into space.

It was strange that Hugh never looked at his wife, Geoffrey thought. There seemed an excessive constraint or embarrassment, though perhaps explicable by his heavy nature or bodily discomforts.

"I'd like to go—" said Katherine hesitating. She sent towards Hugh an anxious smile to which he paid no attention. "For a few days—and take Blanchette, except not yet a while until Tom is weaned—and Hugh is better again—and, too, I—"

"Oh, peace to this babbling, Katherine!" said Philippa briskly. "You shall go next Monday before the whole of Lincolnshire knows that the Duchess is at Bolingbroke and the castle's swamped with supplicants. I'll take charge here and you may be easy in your mind. As for the baby, there must be some woman in the vill can give him suck. 'Tis time *you* stopped anyway, for you're thin as a rake handle. Blanchette is yet too young to go, besides, she'd hinder you from full attention to pleasing the Duchess. You must use your wits, Katherine."

"My wits?" the girl repeated, half amused. She saw the well-remembered zeal in Philippa's eye, and wondered what the house carls would think of the determined hand which would be laid on them.

"Your wits, of course, p'tite imbécile! The Duchess has given you fine gifts before—and by the rood, you could use some now. Besides, a wise wife will find way to further her husband's interests. You should plainly tell her you're in want at Kettlethorpe, that Hugh has sickness he caught in the Duke's service, and perhaps a pension—"

"I *want* no pension!" shouted Hugh furiously, "until I fight again."

"Bosh—Geoffrey has one from the King—twenty marks a year. 'Tis clear as glass to me, you two've no more sense than a couple of sheep."

Geoffrey chuckled. "Sheep or not, you'd best listen to Pica. Always she knows whereof she speaks."

" 'Tis fortunate," said Philippa, having accepted her husband's tribute and seeing that the Swynfords made no further protest but in their separate ways looked somewhat dazed, "that Katherine has had the plague and recovered. Maître Jacques, the Queen's leech, says that when that happens, and 'tis most rare, the Black Death never strikes again."

"Did I?" said Katherine, startled. "You mean in Picardy —I remember that I was very ill when our grandparents died of plague. But I thought children were spared."

"Most were, it passed *me* by, but you turned speckled brown as a thrush, you bled from the nose and you had a plague boil big as an apple in your armpit. I remember when it burst, for we were alone in the farmhouse, you and I— everyone had deserted us."

"Ay—" said Katherine slowly. "The pain comes back now, and the relief when the matter spurted out. You gave me milk to drink—you nursed me, child that you were yourself. My sister, you were good to me." Katherine leaned over and kissed Philippa. "But I didn't know before how brave."

"By Saint Sebastian, I knew no better," said Philippa matter-of-factly, patting Katherine's arm. " 'Tis different today. In London, I took no chances with the impure air. I stuffed my nostrils with borage and trinity flowers, I carried the bezoar stone, and Geoffrey did too."

He nodded gravely. "Few have courage when the plague bells jangle and red crosses brand the doors— Katherine, will you play your lute and sing to us? Some cheerful tune."

"I've not played for long," she said. "Do you, Geoffrey, read to us instead, for sure you have some books in your saddlebag?"

"That he has," snapped Philippa, "crammed so full of them, he'd no room for change of linen or a pair of seemly shoes! An ink horn, too, he's brought—and quills!"

Katherine met Geoffrey's eyes in a smile, as she remembered how her sister had thought to cure him of his perverse reading and scribbling.

"I've been trying to English 'Le Roman de la Rose,' " Geoffrey said with some diffidence. " 'Tis not near so good as Guillaume de Lorris' fair verses, but if you like to listen to that tale of courtly love—"

"Oh please!" cried Katherine. She gathered up Blanchette, who had grown tired of playing with a blackamoor puppet the Chaucers had brought her, and settled the child comfortably in her arms.

Philippa sniffed and seeing no help for it, picked up Katherine's neglected spindle and began to twirl yarn from the distaff.

Hugh gave a grunt of dissent, and saying that he wished to find Ellis, got up and went out of the hall.

Geoffrey drew close-written parchments from his pouch and pulled his stool near the window light. "It begins by telling of dreams," he said to Katherine, "like this—

> *For this trowe I, and say for me,*
> *That dreams signifiaunce be*
> *Of good and harm to many wights,*
> *That dreamen in their sleep a-nights*
> *Full many things covertly,*
> *That fallen after all openly.*"

Yes, that's true, thought Katherine. Many things fell out as she had dreamed them. Some nights ago she had dreamed of a coffin and a great horde of weeping mourners garbed in black—and lo, the Queen was dead. But the poem was about love, not death, and Katherine listened intently to the excerpts that Geoffrey read. With the dreamer of the story, she met Dame Idleness, Sir Mirth, the Lady Courtesy. She wandered in an enchanted garden so fair "that there is no place in paradise, so good in for to dwell or be, as in that garden." The God of Love, Lord of this garden, he was crowned with roses, and he had a young knight to serve him that was called "Sweet-looking." This young knight held two bows with which to shoot Love's arrows. There were five fair arrows and five foul arrows, and as Geoffrey read how the arrows were named, Katherine listened yet more eagerly, for it seemed to her that she might learn a little about this romantic love and its meanings.

The five golden arrows were called Beauty, Simplicity, Frankness, Companionship and Fair-semblance. Did these indeed make the blissful wounds of love? Katherine wondered, disappointed. She could not picture those arrows ever wounding her heart, nor yet the five black ones that were shot from a crooked bow—Pride, Villainy and Shame, Wanhope and Inconstancy. To none of these did she feel herself vulnerable either.

So I don't understand this sort of love, and never will, she thought sighing, and how foolish to think that it existed, since The Romance of the Rose was only a dream, Geoffrey had said so in the beginning. Real life was here in this Hall and imbued with quite different qualities—such as duty and endurance. The poem was like the jewel-toned tapestries of fairy beasts and misty glades that she had seen at Windsor, while life was like the rough gray yarn Philippa spun from the distaff. Yet—she thought suddenly, caught by a fleeting glimpse she could not quite perceive—the tapestry, *too*, exists. I saw it.

"You frown, Katherine!" said Geoffrey laughing, and folding up his parchments, "The Romaunt wearies you?"

"Nay, Geoffrey—it pleased me—but I think it sad that I can never find such a beautiful garden, nor hope to pluck the one red rose the dreamer yearned for."

"It may be you will yet, Katherine," said Geoffrey softly.

"Katherine will what?" Philippa had been mentally rearranging the Hall, stacking the trestles on the south wall instead of the north, putting up a more convenient torch bracket. "What red rose? Oh, I see—the poem—Geoffrey, in truth I think it sounded better in French, more elegant. The

Queen's minstrel, Pierre de Cambrai, used to recite it to us—English is no tongue for *poetry*."

"I expect you're right, my dear," Geoffrey said. He fastened the clasp on his pouch and stood up, stretching his legs. "Rhyme in English has much scarcity, and I am but an indifferent maker."

Katherine started to protest, out of courtesy, and because she had enjoyed the poem; but she saw that her opinion would touch him no more deeply than had Philippa's. For all his merriness and kindness, she felt in him an encircling wall behind which his true self dwelt alone, little affected by the outside world which it viewed with smiling detachment. And she admired this trait which was like the self-sufficiency she had fostered in her own heart. She glanced at little Tom and then down at the curly head against her arm. If I have these safe, she thought, what need of more?

# X

IT WAS the eleventh of September before Katherine set out on her journey to Bolingbroke. She had been unwilling to go until Tom was properly weaned. Then Blanchette had had some brief childish complaint that required her anxious nursing, but soon the little girl was hale as ever, so that Katherine left her to Philippa without anxiety, though with many a pang. "Sainte Marie!" cried Philippa seeing her sister's tears as she kissed the sleeping child goodbye, "one would think you were leaving for a year instead of a few days—'tis folly to dote so on a child."

Hugh too was better, his bowel gripes and flux lessened, though the other weakness that troubled him so bitterly had not improved. Katherine thought of this matter as she rode with Ellis along the Lincoln road to Bolingbroke.

Since the birth of little Tom, and for some months before that, Hugh had not been able to claim a husband's rights, and she felt some guilt that a circumstance which disturbed him

so profoundly should be to her a heartfelt relief. Freed from
his clumsy, hurried importunities, she could minister to his
other needs with far more tolerance. It was otherwise with
him: he got so that he scarcely spoke to her unless he must,
and in the rare times when she had caught him looking at
her, he turned his head quickly away, but not before she had
seen his bewildered anger and humiliation.

She knew that he had tried secret remedies. Ellis one day
innocently let slip mention of a visit to a witch who lived
near Harby in Nottinghamshire, Dame Grizel by name, who
was much patronized by folk of the surrounding countryside.
After that visit to the witch, Hugh privily drank a brown potion before he went to bed and kept beneath his pillow at
night two small shriveled black objects like dried plums; but
of this, neither of them ever spoke. Philippa expressed blunt
surprise that in view of Katherine's proven fecundity, a year
had passed since Thomas' birth and there was no sign of a
new baby. Katherine had shrugged it off with a laugh, saying
that Philippa had been laggard enough in starting her *first*
and need not taunt. Yet she felt contrition that in her prayers
for Hugh's health she neglected to pray for the return of that
part of it he wished the most.

But today she need think of no troublesome things, it was
joyous to be going on a journey, the wind blew in her face
and she hummed as she spurred Doucette into a gallop, while
the disapproving Ellis pounded along at the requisite three
paces behind her. "My lady, slacken!" he called finally,
"there's a party up ahead!" She pulled in Doucette. This narrow road through Bardney to Bolingbroke was not much fre-
quented and they had met nobody but a tinker and two journeymen woodcarvers who were bound for Lincoln Cathedral
to seek work on the new choir stalls.

The road ahead was blocked by a plodding procession of
heavy carts piled high with wool sacks and drawn by oxen.
An oxherd ran back and forth with his goad between each
pair of carts, and despite Ellis' shouts to make way, neither
the oxen nor the herds budged an inch.

Three well-dressed horsemen rode ahead of the carts and
one of them, hearing Ellis' shouts and seeing a young woman,
called a command to the nearest oxherd, who stolidly passed
it back. In due time the oxen hauled the carts to one side. "I
could have ridden through the field around them—" said
Katherine to Ellis as she edged past the carts.

"Oh, no, lady," Ellis was shocked, "not seemly to give the road to peasants. You must remember your rank."

Ay, thought Katherine, I suppose I must, for I'm out in the world again. She arched her neck, patted her hair and replaced her blown riding hood as she came up to the three horsemen.

The elder was a merchant and obviously a man of consequence. His surcote was of garnet velvet, parti-colored with saffron. He wore a high-crowned glossy beaver hat, a jeweled dagger at his belt, and his iron-gray beard was neatly forked. "God's greeting, lady," he said in gloomy tones. "We regret to have impeded your way." He turned from her and, flicking his horse's reins, resumed his slow amble.

Katherine was so accustomed to startled interest in men's eyes that her courteous disclaimer faltered. She glanced at the other two riders, and the youngest, having just taken a good look at her, checked his horse and guided it beside Doucette. "Are you traveling far, fair lady?" he asked, and the warmth in his tone restored her assurance. He too was finely dressed in velvet and a beaver hat, but his forked beard was chestnut brown.

"We go to Bolingbroke," said Ellis crowding up repressively, "and must be on our way, good sir."

"Why, we go there too!" cried the second merchant. "Best that you stay with us, there are outlaws in the forests on the wold."

"I've heard of none," said Ellis stiffly, "and I know well enough how to protect my lady. Allow us to pass."

"Wait, Ellis, we'll ride with them a little." Katherine had talked to no one outside of Kettlethorpe for so long, and Ellis was so dull a companion that she longed for novelty. "Do you also go to see the Duchess, sir?" she asked.

"Ay," he nodded and his smooth pink face grew as gloomy as the other merchant's had, "to ask her help, though we're bound later," he said with sudden force, "for that thrice-cursed town of Boston, may the foul fiend snatch it!"

"And what has Boston done?" said Katherine, trying not to laugh. She glanced at the third horseman, who was garbed in cleric's robes, his face, sunk beneath his black and purple twisted hood, was dismal and long-mouthed as were his fellow travelers'.

"But we are Lincoln men! We are the Suttons, lady!" cried

the young merchant, "so you need not ask what Boston has done."

"Indeed, sir, forgive me, but I do not know."

"Why, they've stolen our staple! The stinking whoresons, vilely wheedling and lying, they've persuaded the King—or more like they've bribed that infamous concubine of his—to wrest the staple from Lincoln and set it up for themselves."

"Ah, to be sure—" said Katherine. Hugh had indeed mentioned that the King had moved the staple from Lincoln to Boston and that it meant grave loss for Lincoln. No longer would all the wool and hides and tin of the country pass through Lincoln for export, no longer could she be the premier cloth town of the northeast, or its commercial center. By royal command, she had been debased. Katherine, knowing that this year at Kettlethorpe they would have trouble enough to support themselves and no surplus whatsoever to sell, had thought little of the news. But she looked sympathetically at the three gloomy men and said, "Do you think the Duchess can help you, sir?"

The young merchant hunched his shoulders. "We can but try. The Duke is our friend, we know him well. We hold manors under him near Norfolk and he has often dined at our house outside Lincoln."

Katherine considered this with interest. Mention of the Duke ever gave her a warm and trustful feeling since the day of Blanchette's birth, though he seemed to her incalculably remote. It was a little like the way one felt about God, a being all-powerful, stern but merciful (if you could catch his ear), yet naturally so engaged in vast enterprises that one would never dare to intrude one's self.

The intimacy with the Duke suggested by these Suttons therefore surprised her, and she asked polite questions while they rode slowly along towards the wold at the head of the wool train. She ignored the fuming Ellis, who liked neither the sluggishness of their pace nor the admiration in the younger merchant's eye.

The Suttons were wealthy burgesses and one of Lincoln's most prominent families. Master John, the older one, was the father, these the two sons, Robert, and Thomas the clerk. Master John had been Lord Mayor of Lincoln last year and now held a seat in Parliament. They belonged to a class she had never met, landholders, civic dignitaries and prosperous merchants, entirely pleased with themselves and their station, and yet neither noble nor knighted. They did homage and paid fees for the lands they held under the Duchy of Lancaster but otherwise they were toughly independent, awed by nothing, and Katherine was startled by the way Master Robert spoke of the King. "Taxes, taxes, taxes so the old dotard may satisfy his leman, or satisfy his itch to rule in France, as though we hadn't enough to do at home. First, it's a tax *in* wool, and then it's a tax *on* wool, and who's to pay the piper but us woolmen? Though never fear, we're not so dull as not to get 'round that a bit—eh, father?" He nudged Master John, who grunted morosely.

"How may that be?" asked Katherine.

Robert Sutton was delighted with so attentive and pretty a listener. He winked at her and chuckled. "Why, pass the tax on, as it were. Lower the price we *pay* for the wool. Our tax goes up? Then the price we pay the peasants goes down and down and down."

"Yes, I see—" said Katherine thoughtfully, "but couldn't they refuse to sell to you?"

"No other way *to* sell! We woolmen stick together, and with the staple, all wool must come to Lincoln—but we've lost the staple, curse it, unless the gracious Duchess can change the King's mind. Why do *you* go to Bolingbroke, lady?"

For the same reason you do, I suppose, to get something from the Duchess, Katherine thought with sudden shame. And yet that was not wholly true.

"I go to pay my loving homage," she said slowly. "Sir Hugh Swynford, my husband, is the Duke's man."

"Oh ay?" said Master Robert, "Swynford—of Coleby and Kettlethorpe? Have you much pasture? I don't seem to remember any lots of your wool."

"We seldom have surplus, and this year none at all. Most of our sheep were drowned in the flood. Nor had we many."

"Oh yes, the floods—a great pity," Robert looked at her with kindling eyes, "but you must get more sheep on your demesne farms, take land from your serfs if need be. Wool's the only crop to bother with! I can show you many ways to prosper from the sheep, advise you as to stock—when we all return to Lincoln, I'll do myself the honor to ride out to your manor and—"

"Robert!" said his father on a long descending note, which accurately indicated warning.

Robert, who had been edging his horse over so that his thigh encroached on Katherine's leg, while he looked down on her with moist enthusiasm, now drew away and held his tongue. There had been an unfortunate affair last year when he had been led astray by the languishing eyes of a leather-monger's wife and invested in a parcel of hides which later proved to be badly tanned and rotting. Nobody could regret this folly more than Robert himself, so he cleared his throat and said, "Why look—it seems the weather's changing. Fog blowing in from the sea."

It was scarcely past midday and the sun had been glowing fitfully from behind dark-massing clouds. Now wisps and curls of mist began to float by and lie white in the hollows. On the wooded upland of the wolds the treetops reared above a bank of lemon-gray vapor.

"Yon's an uncanny light ahead," said the young cleric, speaking for the first time. "Fog looks yellow as saffron, and I ne'er saw fog at midday so far inland." He pulled his silver beads up from his girdle and fingered them uneasily.

"Nay, Thomas!" cried his elder brother, laughing. "For you've seen little of the world at all. *All* things amaze you. My brother," he said to Katherine, "is but just come home from Oxford where I'll vow he never stuck his long nose outside Merton close, so bookish is he."

Katherine smiled but she too felt a mounting discomfort. The air was thick and still as though it held thunder, and when they reached the wolds and began to climb through heavy yellow mist, they heard the long-drawn hooting of an owl in the unseen forest.

"What can that be that hoots by day, except a soul in purgatory?" said Thomas, and he crossed himself. One by one the others followed suit, but Robert said, " 'Tis only that the fog has fooled the bird to thinking it is night."

They walked the horses along in silence after that, all of them watching the rutted way, for they could see ahead but a few feet. They mounted higher and the mist cleared though they saw that it lay thick as tawny wool below them across the fens to the southeast and in the cup where Bolinbroke must lie. When they began the descent, at once they plunged back into the fog. The shouts of the oxherds behind them grew muffled and distorted and seemed to come from all directions. Otherwise there was an eerie stillness until Master

John broke it. "I smell smoke," he said. He drew off his embroidered gauntlets and nervously chafed his gouty fingers.

They all sniffed the thick unmoving air. Yes, there was smoke, but in the faint pungency Katherine caught a trace of another odor, a fetid sickening fume that touched in her some uneasy memory.

"I smell nothing but the fog—Christ's maledictions on it —" said Robert. " 'Twill be luck an we can keep the road."

They plodded on in the still, yellow half-world—trees loomed up of a sudden on either side of them and as suddenly disappeared. It grew warmer and the strange stench grew stronger until they all felt it sting their nostrils. Then through the fog appeared an orange glow and they heard the crackle and hiss of flames and came upon a bonfire in the center of the road. The fire burned off some of the fog. They could see no one about, but small houses and an alestake showed that they had entered Bolingbroke village. The fumes came from the fire; its oily suffocating smoke writhed upward and drifted through the air.

"It smells of brimstone," cried John Sutton, pulling up his horse and coughing. "Why do they build this here! God's body, but this stink may harm my wool."

"There's another fire down over there," said Katherine, "by the castle wall, I think." She too coughed, her eyes watered. The horses snorted and, tossing their heads, began to trot, trying to rid themselves of the discomfort. No other living thing moved in the village street and, held by dazed uncertainty, they let the horses have their will. The road led around the castle walls and the dry moat. They reached the barbican and saw that the great wooden drawbridge was raised flat against the portcullis. The air was clearer here, the horses stopped, and their riders stood staring up at the looming mass of wall when suddenly the mist lifted.

"Jesu, look!" cried Ellis hoarsely. He pointed with his whip.

"God shield us," whispered Katherine. On the bottom of the drawbridge was painted a red cross four feet high. And now she knew that she had smelled a smoke stench like this eight years ago in Picardy.

"There's plague in the castle!" cried John Sutton, his voice quavering. "We must turn the wool carts—Robert, hasten, stop them—don't let them come nigh here!"

His son gave a cry and galloped down the street into the fog.

"We must get 'round the village away from this contagion," muttered Master John. "Lady, d'you know of another road—do you, young squire?" He turned distractedly to Ellis. "Oh weylawey, there's naught but misfortune and disaster for me lately. Thomas, pray to Saint Roch—to all the saints—for sure you have the Latin they can understand."

The young clerk started and dragged his eyes from the plague cross that glistened red as blood through the mist, his trembling fingers reached for his beads.

"Come, Lady Katherine, come—" whispered Ellis. He snatched at Doucette's bridle. A shutter opened in the guardroom of the gatehouse and a man's helmeted head showed at the window.

"Now who be ye what gabble and jangle out there?" the guard called out. "For sure ye see that we've no welcome to give ye at Bolingbroke except the kiss of the Black Death."

"Blessed Virgin, what has *happened?*" cried Katherine, clasping her hands tight on the pummel.

"Sixteen of us are dead, that I know of—God shrive them, for a priest has not! The chaplain died a-first, five nights gone, the friar after him."

"Unshriven!" She heard the wail from the two Suttons behind her, and the sudden panic clop of hooves as their horses were spurred.

Ellis grabbed her arm, and she shook it off. "The village priest!" she cried up to the window. "Get him!"

"How may we? Since he's run off hiding like the rest of the vill!"

"What of the Duchess and her babes?"

"I know not, mistress, for since yester e'en I've not quit the guardroom and I've barred the door." The voice in the window cracked into high-pitched laughter. "I've barred the door 'gainst the plague maiden and her red scarf and her broom. *She'll* not get in, to bed wi' me."

"Come away, lady—come—" Again Ellis seized Katherine's arm, his face had grown yellow as the smoke.

"No," she said, though her heart beat slow and heavy. "I cannot. I'm going in. Belike I'm safe from the contagion, Philippa said so, but whether or no, I must go in to the Duchess."

"You're mad, lady—Sir Hugh would kill me if I let you go—"

She saw that he meant to drag her off by force, his hand clenched on her arm so she near overbalanced in the saddle. Deliberately she called on anger.

"How dare you touch me, knave!" she said, low and clear. "How dare you disobey me?" And with her free hand she slapped him hard across the face.

Ellis gasped. His hand fell off her arm. His mind floundered in a coil of fear and uncertainty.

She saw this and in the same clear voice said, "You need not enter the castle with me, I release you from your duty, but this you must do. Ride fast to the abbey at Revesby, it's the nearest as I remember. Bring back a monk, at once! In the name of the Trinity, Ellis—*go!*" Such force did she put in her voice, such command in the look she gave him, that he bowed his head. "The road to Revesby lies that way," she said, pointing, "then to the west." He tautened the reins and spurred his horse.

"Guard! Ho, guard!" Katherine called turning to the castle. The helmet showed again in the window. "Lower the bridge and let me in!"

"Not I, mistress," again the man let loose a gust of laughter. "I'll not budge." His tone changed as he pushed closer to the window. "What, little maid, and do you lust to join our sports in here? By God's bones, the Black Death holds merry dances! The posern gate is open, since 'tis through there the castle varlets fled." He leered down at her.

Katherine guided Doucette along the dry moat past the south tower to a footbridge that led across to the postern. She dismounted and tied the mare loosely to a hazel bush that it might graze. She unbuckled her saddle pack and hoisting it in her arms crossed the footbridge. Between the battens on the low oak door another red cross was painted and beneath it in straggling letters, "Lord have mercy on us."

She went through the unlocked door in to the bailey. On the flagstones near the well another plague fire burned. An old man in soot-tarnished blue and gray livery threw handfuls of yellow sulphur on the smoldering logs. He raised his shaggy head and looked at her dully. Two other figures moved in the bailey. They were hooded and masked in black cloth and they held shovels in their hands. The flagstones had been lifted from a section of the western court near the barracks and she saw that a long ditch had been dug into the earth. Beside the ditch there stood a high mounded bumpy pile covered by bloodstained canvas, and the stench from this pile mingled with the fumes from the fire.

Katherine tried to turn her eyes away from the mounded pile but she could not. One man seized a little hand bell and, jingling it, muttered behind his mask. He put the bell on the ground, and the two hooded figures silently dragged a limp thing with long black hair from out the pile and heaved it into the ditch, where one blue-spotted wrist and hand protruded for a moment like a monstrous eagle's claw, then slowly sank from sight.

Katherine dropped the bag she carried. She ran stumbling towards the private rooms at the far end of the bailey. She reached the foot of the stone staircase that led up to the Duchess's apartments. Here it was that she had stood laughing at the mummers' antics with the two white girls in that Christmastime three years ago. She looked back into the smoke-filled silent courtyard and saw the hooded figures fumble again beneath the canvas on the mound.

Her stomach heaved, while bitter fluid gushed up into her mouth. She spat it out and turning, began to mount the worn stone steps. As she rounded the first spiral the hush that held the castle was broken by the sudden tolling of a bell. Muffled though it was by the stone walls around her, she knew it for the great chapel bell and she clung to the embroidered velvet handrail while she counted the slow strokes. Twelve of them before the pause—a child then, this time—somewhere in the castle and dimly through the knell she heard a long far-off wailing.

At once much nearer sounds broke out from above her, a wild cacophony of voices and the shrilling of a bagpipe. She listened amazed; in the discordant sounds she recognized the tune of a ribald song, "Pourquoi me bat mon mari?" that Nirac had taught her, and many voices were bawling it out to the squealing of the pipes and the clashing of cymbals.

As Katherine mounted slowly the noise grew more raucous, for it came from the large anteroom outside the Duchess's solar, and the door was ajar. There were a dozen halfnaked people in the room, all of them in frantic motion, dancing. Nobody noticed Katherine, who stood transfixed in the doorway. Despite the fog heat, a fire was blazing on the hearth and the painted wall hangings were illuminated by a score of candles. On the table, which had been pushed to the wall, there was the carcass of a roast peacock, a haunch of venison and a huge cask of wine with the cock but half shut; a purple stream splashed down on the floor rushes which had been strewn with thyme, lavender and wilting roses. To the falcon perch beside the fireplace, a human skull had been tied so that it dangled from the eye sockets and twisted slowly from side to side as though it watched the company who danced around and around upon the rushes. They jerked their arms and kicked their legs. When the minstrel who held the cymbals clashed them together, a man and a woman would grab each other convulsively and, kissing, work their bodies back and forth while the rest jigged and whirled and called out obscene taunts.

Katherine, held vised as in a nightmare, recognized some of these people, though their faces were crimson and slack with drunkenness. There was Dame Pernelle Swyllington, the stout matron who had protested Katherine's presence in the Lancaster loge at the tournament at Windsor. Her bodice was torn open so that her great breasts hung bare, and the cauls that held her grizzled hair had twisted loose and bumped upon her shoulders as she danced. There was Audrey, the Duchess's tiring-woman, dressed in a wine-stained white velvet gown, trimmed with ermine, the skirt held bunched up around her waist, though yet she tripped and stumbled on it. Her broad peasant face was wild as a bacchante beneath one of the Duchess's jeweled fillets. Audrey held Piers Roos by the hand and when the cymbals crashed, she flung herself against his chest, slavering. The young squire wore nothing but a shirt and was drunk as the rest, his pleasant freckled face drawn down into a goatish mask, his eyes narrow and glittering. A kitchen scullion danced with them, and a small pretty young woman—a lady, by her dress—who giggled and hiccuped and let any of the men fumble her who wished: Piers, or the scullion, or the minstrels—or Simon Simeon, the steward of Bolingbroke Castle.

It was the sight of this old man, his long beard tied up with a red ribbon, his portly dignity lost in lewd capers, a garland of twined hollyhocks askew on his bald head, that shocked Katherine from her daze.

"Christ and His Blessed Mother pardon you all," she cried. "Have you gone mad—poor wights?" A sob clotted in her throat, and she sank down onto a littered bench, staring at them woefully.

At first they did not hear her; but the piper paused for breath and the steward, turning to catch up a mazer full of wine, saw her and blinked foolishly, passing his hand before his bleared eyes.

"Sir Steward," she cried out to him, "where is my Lady Blanche?" Her despairing voice shot through them like an arrow. They ceased dancing and drew back, huddling like sheep menaced by sudden danger. Dame Pernelle clenched her hands across her naked breasts and cried thickly, "Who are you, woman? Leave us—begone." Piers' arm dropped from Audrey's waist and he shouted, "But 'tis Lady Swynford —by the devil's tail! I've often longed for this! Come dance with me, my pretty one, my burde, my winsome leman—" His nostrils flared on a great lustful breath, he shoved Audrey to one side and would have grabbed at Katherine, but the old steward stepped between and held his shaking arm out for a barrier.

"*Where is the Duchess?*" repeated Katherine, unheeding of Piers.

"In there," said the steward slowly. He pointed to the solar. "She bade us leave her—while we wait *our* turn."

"She's dead then—" Katherine whispered.

The steward bowed his head and through mumbling lips he said, "We know not."

Katherine jumped from the bench and ran past them to the solar door. They watched her dumbly. Piers drew back against the others. They made no sound as she went through the door but when it closed behind her a woman's voice cried out, "Give me the wine!" the pipes shrilled and the cymbals crashed anew.

In the great solar it was dim and quiet. Two huge candles burned on either side the vast square bed that was hung with azure satin. The Duchess lay there on white samite pillows. Her eyes were closed, but her body twitched, her breath was like the panting of a dog. Her arms were crossed on her chest below a crucifix, the white flesh mottled from the shoulder to the elbow with livid spots. A trickle of black blood oozed from the corner of her mouth and ran onto her outspread golden hair.

As Katherine gazed down, shuddering, the purple lips drew back and murmured, "Water—" The girl poured some into a

cup and the Duchess swallowed, then opened her eyes. She
did not know the face that bent over her, and she whispered,
"Where's Father Anselm? Tell him to come—I haven't long
—nay, Father Anselm's dead, he died the first—" Her voice
trailed into incoherent muttering.

Katherine knelt on the prie-dieu which stood beside the
bed and gazed up at the jeweled figure of the Blessed Virgin
in the niche. No fear for herself entered her mind, nor did
she pray that the Duchess would recover, for that would be a
miracle worked by God alone. She saw that the plague boils
had turned inward, and none that vomited blood ever lived.
She prayed only that Ellis would bring the monk in time. She
prayed while the candles burned down an inch, and the
Duchess shivered and moaned, and once cried out. Suddenly
Katherine's wits cleared and she saw that she must go back
outside the castle to guide the monk since he would be a
stranger, nor did Ellis know of the postern gate.

She knew that it was useless to ask help of those in the
anteroom. She slipped down the privy stairway that led to the
Duke's wardrobe and out on a corner of the battlements, and
down to the bailey.

It was dark outside now except for the glare from the
plague fire. The hooded black figures had gone and loose
earth covered the ditch. Katherine sped through the bailey
and out through the postern door. The fog had blown off into
a fine rain, yet at first she could see nobody outside the castle
walls. Then she heard the whicker of a horse over by the
church and she ran there, calling, "Ellis!"

Her squire and a tall Cistercian monk in white had taken
shelter from the rain in the church porch, having indeed been
unable to find a way into the castle. Katherine wasted no
time on Ellis and, giving the monk a murmur of gratitude,
seized the edge of his sleeve. Together they hurried back into
the castle and up the privy stair to the Duchess's room.

The Duchess still lived. She stirred as Katherine and the
white monk came to her bed, and when she saw the cowled
head and the crucifix the monk held out to her as he said
*"Pax vobiscum,* my daughter," she gave a long sigh and her
hand fluttered towards him. The monk opened his leather
case and laid the sacred parts of the viaticum out on the
table, then he motioned to Katherine to leave.

The girl crept down the stairs and turned off the landing
into the little room called the Duke's garderobe, because it

was in here that he dressed and that his clothes were kept when he was in residence. It was bare now except for two iron-bound coffers, a rack full of lances and an outmoded suit of armor that hung from a perch and shone silver-gray in the darkness. A faint odor of lavender and sandalwood clung to the room and there was here no plague stench.

Katherine sat on the coffer with her head in her hands until the monk called out to her.

The Duchess died next morning at the hour of Prime while a copper-red sun tipped above the eastern wolds against a lead sky. Katherine and the Cistercian monk knelt by the bedside whispering the prayers for the dying, and one other was with them—Simon, the old steward of the castle, who had recovered from his drunkenness and crept in to join them, his head bowed with heavy shame.

A little while before her passing, the Lady Blanche's torments eased, and it seemed that she knew them. She tried to speak to the steward and though the words were not clear, they knew she spoke of her dearest lord, John, and of her children; and Simon breathed something of reassurance while the tears ran down his face. Then Blanche's wandering gaze passed over the monk and rested on Katherine with a look of puzzled recognition. She remembered nothing of the night just gone but she felt the girl's love and saw the anguish in her eyes. She raised her hand and touched Katherine's hair. "Christ have mercy on you, dear child," she whispered, while the gracious charm of this most noble lady showed for a moment in her dimming blue eyes. "Pray for me, Katherine—" she added so faintly that the girl heard with her heart and not her ears.

Then the great room was quiet again except for the chanting of the monk. Lady Blanche sighed, her fingers closed around the crucifix on her breast. *"In manus tuas—Domine —"* she said clearly, in a calm, contented voice. And died.

It seemed that the Black Death, having slain the Duchess, had at last slaked its greed. The weather on that September 12 turned sharp and freezing cold, and the evil yellow fog vanished. There were a few more deaths throughout the castle, a scullion and a dairy maid, two of the guards and the head falconer's wife; but these had all been stricken before the Duchess died, and there were no new cases.

Of those who had danced in frenzy by the skull in the

anteroom, none died of plague but Audrey, the Duchess's tiring-woman, and she followed her mistress on the next day without even regaining her senses from the drunken stupor which had finally quietened all the revelers.

On Piers Roos, too, the dread black spots appeared, but God showed him mercy, for the plague boil in his groin swelled fast and burst like a rotten plum; and when the poison drained away, Piers recovered, albeit he lay for months in sweating weakness afterwards.

During those days of heavy sorrow and gradually lightening fear, Katherine remained at the castle. They had sore need of help, and old Simon was distracted by the terrible responsibilities thrust on him. Of those at Bolingbroke, thirty had died. Most of the varlets had run off in panic to the wolds and fens. There were few left to do Simon's bidding, and none to tell him what disposition should be made of the Duchess—until the messenger he had dispatched to the King at Windsor should return.

They sealed away the Lady Blanche in a hastily made coffin and placed it in the private chapel. There the good white monk said Masses for her soul, and many of her household came to pray; and there too, every morning after it seemed sure the plague had passed, Katherine brought the ducal daughters, Philippa and Elizabeth, to light candles and kneel by their mother's black velvet bier.

The children had all been safe in the North Tower throughout the scourge; the Holy Blessed Mother had watched out for them, since their own could not.

The baby, Henry, toddled merrily about the floor in his own apartments, playing with his silver ball and a set of ivory knights his father had sent him. When Katherine first went to see him he drew back as children do, and hid distrustfully behind his nurse's skirts, but he soon grew used to her and crowed with glee when she played finger games with him as she did with Blanchette.

The little girls occupied rooms higher up in the tower, and Katherine found them well enough in health, though Philippa was nine now and old enough to understand the terrible things that had befallen them; between the strands of lank flaxen hair, her long sallow face was runneled with tears, and nothing that Katherine could say lightened the stillness of her bearing. Yet she remembered Katherine and seemed to find some comfort in standing silently beside her.

Elizabeth at five was noisier than ever. She harried the servants and bullied the nurses and her sister, all of whom gave in to her rather than provoke a screaming rage. She was a brown little thing, all except her eyes, which were leaf-green and could flash like a cat's. When she was told of her mother's death, she howled loudly for a while because she saw those about her weeping, but in her visits to the bier in the chapel she found a not unpleasing importance. She liked Katherine because she smelled good and told her stories and had a low sweet voice unlike her Yorkshire nurse's, but she cared deeply about nobody.

Katherine longed for her own children and especially when she saw little Henry, who was so near to Blanchette in age and whose baby tricks wrenched at her heart. Almost she resented him because he was not Blanchette.

But her own babies were well at Kettlethorpe and did not miss her. Ellis had ridden home with all the frightful tidings of Bolingbroke, and returned some days later with a message from Philippa, who had made him repeat it so many times that through Ellis' voice Katherine could plainly hear her sister's.

"You're not to come home yet, on any account, lady," Ellis reported stolidly. "They're all well and wish to stay so. Dame Philippa says there's no telling but the plague might be hiding in your clothes waiting to smite those nearest you in revenge that *you* are safe. She said to tell you that they're singing Masses for the Duchess's soul at Kettlethorpe church, and all is being done seemly there, so you need have no care for anything; but you must not return until all danger from pestilence has passed."

They stood in the chill windswept bailey by the now lowered drawbridge, and Ellis, acting under orders, kept his distance from her.

"And what does Sir Hugh say?" Katherine asked slowly.

Ellis looked uncomfortable. Hugh had said very little beyond expressing shock at the Duchess's death. He had always been a morose man, but lately even Ellis thought him unduly brooding and withdrawn.

"He sends you greeting—" said Ellis, "and said you may do as you please."

Katherine nodded. That was like Hugh as he had become in the last year. It was as though he held himself away from her in all things, no longer gave her commands nor yet made clumsy efforts to gain her affection; and she thought that this was because of the thing that had happened to him. But Philippa's advice was sensible and though it pained her it also freed her for a different obligation.

"Do you then, Ellis," she said, "return now to Kettlethorpe and tell them I shall join the funeral cortege that'll escort our dearest Lady Blanche to London, for this is what the King commands. And perhaps I shall remain there to do her the last honors, when she is interred, after the Duke is back from France."

Ellis considered this and decided that it was a fitting course for her to follow and would not displease Sir Hugh.

"When will the Duke come back to England? Do y'know, lady?"

She shook her head. "They say he may not yet have heard the dreadful tidings since he fights deep in Picardy. I daren't think how it'll be with him, when he does," she said, remembering the look in the Duke's eyes as he had gazed up at his wife at the tournament. "In one month he has lost both mother and wife," she added as though to herself. The Queen perhaps he would not miss much, since they had seen so little of each other in years, but—

" 'Tis God's will," said Ellis briskly, having delivered his message and being anxious to be off. " 'Tis in nature that a mother dies; as for a wife, she can be soon replaced."

Ellis' chance and sensible words were like a spark to a hidden mine and Katherine was seized with sudden stabbing anger. "You fool, you heartless dolt!" she cried, her gray eyes blazing. "How dare you speak so! The Lady Blanche can *never* be replaced, nor would he want to!"

Ellis' jaw dropped. "I meant no harm, I simply thought that—"

"God's blood! Then stop thinking since it leads you into lunacy!"

He stood there gaping at her, and the scarlet faded from her cheekbones. "Never mind, Ellis," she said, "no doubt I spoke too sharp. How should you who hardly knew her understand— Adieu then, give them my love at home, I'll contrive to send a message soon."

She watched him mount his horse and cross the drawbridge, when he turned left for the village and the road across the wolds towards Kettlethorpe.

She walked slowly down the bailey and entered the private

chapel to kneel by the altar rail. Beneath the black and silver pall, the outline of the coffin could be faintly seen. Seven tapers burned beside it in memory of the seven works of charity.

Katherine buried her face in her hands on the rail and wept as she had not wept during all her time at Bolingbroke.

# XI

THE LADY BLANCHE of Lancaster's funeral cortege wound its solemn way down England all through the first days of November. For the greater part of the journey her bier rested at night in the abbeys and cathedrals which had sheltered the remains of another much mourned and beloved lady some eighty years ago—Eleanor of Castile, the "chère reine" to whose memory the first Edward had erected stone crosses at each stage of the sorrowful progress.

By this November of the Lady Blanche's last journey, the plague had passed on. Some said that it had flown to Scotland in search of fresh victims, some that it lurked still in the wild secret mountains beyond the Welsh border, but it no longer smote England. The people gathered everywhere by the roadside to watch the Duchess's hearse, sable-draped, and drawn by six black horses in silver harness, with nodding black ostrich plumes fastened to their heads. Folk fell to their knees and wept for this disaster which had robbed them of the second lady in the land so soon after their Queen, yet from the magnificence of the black-garbed procession with its lords and ladies, chanting monks and humble varlets, many folk drew a personal solace. During the time of terror and hideous death there had been no dignity of mourning, and now in the honors done the Duchess they could weep quietly for their own dead, too.

Behind the hearse rode the King's youngest son, Thomas of Woodstock, a dark thick-set lad of fourteen whose haughty look and sulky mouth disguised his complacence at having been assigned to his first princely duty. Since Lionel was dead, and his other three brothers were fighting in France, there had been no one else of fitting rank for the King to send.

Katherine had a place in the middle of the procession behind the members of the great Lancastrian administration—the chancellor, the chief of council, and the Duke's receiver general, all of whom had hurried to Bolingbroke after summons by messenger.

She lived much within herself during those days of the Duchess's procession. There was little to occupy her mind except the interest of the journey. She had no close contact with anyone she knew, since rigorous etiquette ruled every phase of the progress and was enforced by the Duke's officers. She no longer saw the ducal children except at a distance, for they rode in a chariot with their nurses behind their young uncle Thomas and far ahead of Katherine's place in the cavalcade.

On the last night the procession stopped at Waltham, where the Duchess's coffin rested below the shrine of the black cross, but Katherine had no wish to pay her reverence to the cross this time and did not enter the church.

On the next afternoon when the procession had turned right through Islington and nearly reached the charterhouse, there was a flourish of trumpets and a long muffled roll of tabors on the road ahead. The horses were halted and word ran back along the line that the King had come out to meet them. They all dismounted and continued on foot to the Savoy.

Katherine could see little of what went on, and it was not until the Duchess had been borne into her home chapel at the Savoy and the procession was broken up at last, that she saw the King. He wore a plain silver mourning crown and beneath it his lank hair shone silver too, though in his scanty drooping beard there were still some yellow traces. His lean face was deeply furrowed, his faded blue eyes were redrimmed; as he walked with dragging steps into the chapel, no one could doubt that he felt grief, as he had felt it for his Queen so short a time ago. And yet, not six paces behind him, taking precedence of all the lords and ladies, came Alice Perrers, her head respectfully bowed, but a faint smile on her thin red lips. Her mourning robe was stiff with seed pearls, the gauzy veil on her elaborately coiffed black hair was powdered with brilliants, while the odor of musk that she exuded overlay the scent of incense from within the chapel.

Katherine watched with disgust and wondered that the courtiers seemed to take so calmly this woman's flaunting presence there.

Many things shocked her that first night at the Savoy Palace. The King and his company remained for supper and Katherine from her seat at the side of the Great Hall observed the High Table with little of the wide-eyed admiration she had felt for royalty three years ago.

The supper began on a solemn enough note, the King's confessor offered a prayer in Latin, added, extempore, some remarks about the great lady they were mourning, and ended with admonitions for all to think of the state of their own souls since mortal life was fleeting. When he had finished, the Lancaster and King's heralds blew long dirgelike wails and the minstrels in the gallery above began a soft slow tune. But this seemly quiet lasted only until the first cups of rich vernage wine had been drained. Then Alice Perrers, who sat next to the King, leaned towards him and whispered in his ear, whereupon his melancholy mouth curved in a smile. She leaned over and picked up a fluffy yellow dog which wore a gold and ruby collar. She danced the dog on the table and crowned it with a ruffle of bread, and a feather pulled from the roast swan a kneeling squire presented to her. The King laughed outright and put his arm around Alice's naked shoulders.

At once the watchful minstrels changed to a merry tune, and a wave of ribaldry flowed unchecked along the High Table. One of the lords shouted out a lewd riddle, and all the company tried to guess it, each capping the other's sally with a yet coarser one. Katherine could not hear all the words, but she could see the laxness of their bodies as they lolled on the cushioned benches; and she could see the King and Alice drinking together from one cup, and that Prince Thomas teased the young Countess of Pembroke by dabbling wine between her breasts and tickling her plump arms with a leering precocity.

The interminable meal dragged on, and each course ended in a subtety: triumphs of the confectioner's art, cunningly contrived to fit the occasion. The first one represented the Black Death with his scythe standing above the body of a saffron-haired maiden. Death's figure was fashioned from spun sugar colored black with licorice. Katherine thought it marvelous and horrible; but at the High Table they scarcely looked at the subtlety except that Alice Perrers absently broke off a piece of Death's licorice robe and sucked on it as she talked to the King.

Katherine's head began to ache, her stomach revolted against the highly spiced and ornamental dishes. At last she murmured an excuse and slipped out into the cold dark night. So vast was the Savoy, such a honeycomb of buildings, alleys and courtyards that she could not remember her way back to the small dorter the chamberlain had assigned to her.

Except for the noise in the Great Hall and the bustle of servants running to it from the kitchens, the Savoy was now a sleeping city, dimly lit by a few bracketed wall torches. Katherine wandered through wrong turnings and into several dark courts before she saw anyone from whom she could ask directions. Then from a small gabled house near the state apartments she saw a tall friar emerge and knew him for a Franciscan by the gray of his habit and the long knotted scourge that dangled from his waist beside his crucifix. His cowled head was bent over a black bag. He was buckling the straps and did not see Katherine in the shadowy court until she went up to him.

"God's greetings, good Brother," she said. "I regret to trouble you, but do you know the palace?" She feared that he might beg alms of her as all friars did, and she had not three groats left in her pouch from the half-noble which Hugh had given her for pocket money at Bolingbroke over two months ago. But her weariness had increased while she wandered about and she ached for rest.

The friar looked at her keenly but could see little beneath her hood. He contented himself with saying, "Yes, mistress, I know the Savoy well." Brother William Appleton was a master physician, and a savant though he was still but thirty, and he stood high in the Duke's favor by reason of his discretion, as well as his skill with the probe and lancet.

"I've lost my way, Sir Friar," said Katherine with an apologetic smile. "I'm to lodge in the Beaufort Tower, but I cannot find it."

"Ah," said the friar, "mayhap you came from Bolingbroke today with the funeral train?"

Katherine bowed her head. Suddenly tears stung her eyes and her journey seemed to her both foolish and futile. Here she had no friends and no true place, nor could she forget the horror of those days at Bolingbroke and plunge to revelry as the others had. And the Lady Blanche had no further need of naïve prayers, now that she rested in her own chapel in the home of her ancestors, while six monks prayed for the repose of her soul.

"You're weary, mistress," said the monk in a kinder tone. "I'll guide you to the Beaufort Tower."

He led her through an arch and down some steps into the vaulted tunnel that ran along outside the ducal wine cellars, then up again towards the river into a court called the Red Rose, because in summer it was filled with roses of Provence.

"Yonder's your tower," said the friar, pointing to a massive round tourelle on which were blazoned, six feet high in gold and gules, the arms of Beaufort and Artois, for Blanche's grandmother. "'Tis the oldest part of the palace and has not yet been renovated and embellished by my Lord Duke as have the buildings around the Inner Ward. Did you notice the carvings and the traceried windows and that all of them are glazed?" He spoke at unaccustomed length because his trained eye noted the droop of Katherine's head, he had heard the choke in her voice, and he wished to examine her a moment by the torchlight. Though the plague seemed to be over, one knew how violently it had raged at Bolingbroke, and it was his duty as physician to be watchful.

"Yes, Sir Friar," she said, turning her face up to him in the light as he had hoped, "all here is wondrous fair."

Wondrous fair indeed! he thought, startled, gazing at the pure oval of her face, the wide gray eyes and the sharp chiseled line of forehead and nose. Her hair glowed dark copper against the black hood. She had the lovely face of a pagan Psyche that he had seen on his pilgrimage to Rome, and though he was an austere man, and none of your concupiscent degenerate friars who had sprung up of late to disgrace the barefoot orders, yet he *was* a man and had not quite subdued a sensitivity to beauty.

"You are not feverish, my sister?" asked the friar, suddenly recollecting why he had wanted to examine her face, and touched her forehead with his cool bony fingers.

"Nay, brother—I'm well enough—in body. 'Tis my heart that's heavy. Have you heard when our Lord Duke will come?"

"Why, very soon! For he has landed at Plymouth. A dark

and bitter thing 'twill be for him, his meeting with his poor
lady, God absolve her soul."

"I think He has no need to," said Katherine very low, "she
was without sin. Grand merci for your guidance, Sir Friar."
She gave him a faint smile and turned to the door of the
Beaufort Tower, where a sleepy porter answered to her
knock.

Brother William murmured *Benedicite* and walked
thoughtfully back through the courtyard, his horny naked
soles making no sound on the chill flagstones.

Tired as she was, Katherine could not sleep that night. She
shared a bed with some Derbyshire knight's fat sister, and
Katherine lay on her back listening to the lady's snores; to
the gurgle of the Thames from below their window; to the
periodic clang of church bells wafted upstream from London
town a mile away. Here at the Savoy they had a great
painted Flemish clock fixed to a tower in the Outer Ward. It
struck the hours by means of little dwarfs with hammers on a
gong, and she heard each hour's end pass by.

At four o'clock she rose and dressed herself quietly. A
maidservant slept on a pile of straw in the passage but she
took care not to waken her. It seemed to Katherine, that if
she could be alone in the chapel with the Lady Blanche, she
might be eased of her heavy heart and she might understand
why she felt grief and horror now far stronger than while she
had actually lived through the dreadful days of plague.

She lit a candle at the embers of their dorter fire, went
down the stone steps and let herself out into the Red Rose
Court. The torches had been extinguished. It was not yet
dawn and the black November sky twinkled with frosty stars.
She walked slowly, peering with her candle, and found her
way through the main court entrance into an alley, where a
dog barked at her and was hushed by a sleepy voice. She
went under another arch between the chancery buildings and
the turreted ducal apartments and so into the Outer Ward.
Beyond the barracks and the stables, the chapel lights flickered through its stained-glass windows and spread patches of
blue and green and ruby on the stones outside.

She pushed the chapel door and entered. The nave was
empty. The monks who were on duty chanted their prayers
far in the depths of the chancel behind the gilded rood
screen. Katherine crept up to the chancel step and knelt

there, gazing from the black bier in front to the silver image of the Blessed Virgin in a niche to her right.

As she looked back to the coffin her ear was caught by a sound from the chancel floor in the shadow of the bier. She looked more closely and gasped.

A man in black lay prone on the tiles, his arms outstretched towards the coffin. She saw the convulsive heaving of his shoulders and heard the sound again. Between his outstretched arms his hair gleamed gold against the shadowed tiles.

She clenched her hands on the pillar of the rood screen trying to raise herself and run from witnessing this that she had no right to see, but her muscles had begun to tremble and she stumbled on the edge of her skirt. At once the man raised his head and his swollen bloodshot eyes flashed with fury. "Who are you that dares come in here now? How dare you gape at me—you graceless bitch—" He stopped, and rising to his feet walked down beneath the rood screen. "Katherine?" he said in a tone of wonder.

Still on her knees she stared up at him mutely. Slow tears gathered in her eyes and ran down her face. The monks' voices chanted louder in the Miserere, then died away.

"Katherine—" said the Duke. "What do you here?"

"Forgive me, my Lord," she whispered, "I loved her too—"

His mouth twisted and he flung his clenched fists against his breast. "My God, my God—that she should leave me like this. These weeks since I heard I didn't believe, I couldn't believe—" He turned and looked at the coffin. "Go, Katherine," he said dully.

She fled down the nave and out of the chapel. She did not go back to the dorter, she wandered through the courts until she came to the great terraced garden by the river. She groped her way past the clipped box hedges, down marble steps until she reached the landing pier at the foot of the garden. It was chill there from the river breeze and she shivered a little in her cloak. She crouched on a stanchion at the edge of the pier and watched the inky slow-moving waters pass, pouring themselves eternally into the sea, and she no longer thought of the Lady Blanche, nor of the horrors of the plague: she prayed for the man who lay on the chancel tiles by the bier.

The Duchess was interred at last four days later. Her marble tomb was placed in a chantry next to the high altar in St. Paul's Cathedral, and two chantry priests were engaged to sing Masses for her soul in perpetuity. Her funeral procession from the Savoy down the Strand through Ludgate to St. Paul's was the most magnificent ever seen in England, it surpassed even Queen Philippa's recent obsequies in Westminster Abbey, but to the Duke it brought no comfort.

When he returned from St. Paul's he would speak to nobody and mounting straight to his private apartments, locked himself into the small chamber that was called Avalon because its English tapestry portrayed the enchanted burial of King Arthur.

John would not enter the great solar which he had shared with Blanche nor sleep in the bed where he had once lain in her arms; and for days he would not quit the Avalon Chamber at all. During this time there was only one person whom he would admit, Raulin d'Ypres, his young Flemish body squire who brought him food which he barely touched. No one else saw him.

Each morning in the high-vaulted Presence Chamber which adjoined the privy apartments, an anxious group of men gathered to await the squire's word as to whether they would be received, and each day Raulin came back, his broad face gloomy as he gave them a denial. On the Thursday after the Duchess's funeral he returned to the waiting men and said, "The Duke's Grace still vill not see you, my lords. He sits effer the same staring at the fire, except sometimes he writes on a parchment. This morning though he vishes Master Mason Henry Yevele sent for."

"God's wounds!" cried the great baron, Michael de la Pole, who was a blunt, burly middle-aged Yorkshireman, "then he wishes to consult Yevele on the alabaster effigy of the Duchess. If he can do that, he can spare us a moment! Has he quite forgot the war? Has he forgot the dangers his royal brothers face in France?"

The Duke's two highest domestic officials, his chancellor and receiver general, exchanged weary, resigned glances. Apparently on this day too, the Duke would transact no business and the chancery affairs must wait. They shrugged and went out.

De la Pole was devoted to his Duke, to whom he had taught many of the arts of war, but he did not understand this excessive grieving. He stalked over to the window to join

Lord Neville of Raby, who was irritably tapping his foot and drumming, with dirty heavily beringed fingers, on the stone sill while he stared out at a windy rainswept Thames.

"He," said de la Pole, frowning in the direction of the Avalon Chamber, "has not even reported to the King on our campaign in Picardy!"

"Nothing to report, I hear," growled Neville, "since you never joined in battle—body of Christ, why didn't you *force* the French bastards to fight?" He glared at de la Pole from beneath his bushy grizzled eyebrows. A harsh North Country man was the great Lord of Raby and never one to mince words.

De la Pole's ruddy face darkened, but he answered temperately. "How could we, since they hid from us? We did what might be, we burned the country from Calais to Boulogne; but ill luck hounded us, and the plague there too." He sighed, thinking of the many plague deaths in camp. "But what's our *next* move to be? The Prince of Wales is sore beset in Aquitaine, Edmund piddles away his forces in the Dordogne, that hot fool of a young Pembroke will listen to nobody and holds himself a better soldier than Chandos—we must plan a *new* attack—yet my Lord Duke sits in there moping alone."

Lord Neville blew his beaked nose loudly with his fingers and wiped them on his miniver-lined sleeve. "Ay," he said angrily, "but 'tis not of land *I* wish to speak to him, 'tis of the disposition of our ships." Neville had just been appointed Admiral of the Fleet and as a man of fifty and an arrogant one, it irked him to await the decisions of a man of twenty-nine, though it was his feudal overlord. There was a stir across the room, a yeoman held open the great oak and wrought-iron door. Two friars padded in.

"Ah, now we have the godly faction represented," said de la Pole dryly. "We'll see how they fare."

The two friars were as unlike as a gray heron and a plump hen. Brother William Appleton, the lean Franciscan physician, towered a head above Brother Walter Dysse, the Carmelite, whose snowy cope was woven of the softest Norfolk worsted and belled out to show glimpses of an elegant tunic, and a gold and crystal rosary dangling from a paunch as neat and round as a melon. And while the Franciscan Gray Friar was shod only by his own soles, the Carmelite had soft kidskin shoes and wore hose of lamb's wool.

"Nay, Brethren," said the young body squire to them,

flushing, for he was still unused to the new importance the Duke's behavior had thrust upon him. "His Grace will not see *you* either. He says his body and his soul must shift for themselves since he cares nought about them."

"*Christus misereatur!*" said Brother Walter lisping slightly as he palmed his plump white hands. "Sweet Jesu but that is a melancholy message."

"He cannot help himself," said the physician, thoughtfully. "His horoscope shows him much afflicted by Saturn. Yet, for that black bile from which he suffers he should be bled, and I have other remedies which might help, could I but try them."

"And how long will His Grace be ruled by Saturn?" said Baron de la Pole walking over to the Gray Friar. "By God, I hope not long!"

"The aspects are somewhat unclear, and yet it seems that soon Venus will ascend and mitigate the baleful Saturn," answered Brother William carefully.

"Venus forsooth!" cried the baron. "Don't prate to me of Venus, Sir Friar—it's Mars that we need! Mars!—look now, here come two *more* black crows!" he added as the great door again swung open. Court mourning for the Queen and the Duchess would last until Christmas and had peopled the palaces with black, which depressed de la Pole, who was fond of scarlet. The two newcomers were not Lancastrians however, and de la Pole drew close to Lord Neville, who still fidgeted by the window. Both men stiffened and watched the newcomers warily. These two noble young sprigs, the Earl of March and Richard Fitz Alan, heir of Arundel, were known to hold little love for the Duke.

Edmund Mortimer, the Earl of March, was great-grandson to the Roger Mortimer who had been Queen Isabella's paramour, but he had no likeness to that lusty man. This Mortimer was a weedy stripling of eighteen with pimples thick upon his beardless face. Insignificant as a stableboy, a stranger might have thought him, except for his pale eyes, which had a cold steady gaze; but no one in the Presence Chamber thought him insignificant. He was the ranking earl, he owned vast possessions in the Welsh marches and in Ireland, and he had recently wed young Philippa, the only child of Duke Lionel of Clarence, and thus become grandson to the King.

"I'm here," he announced in a high grating voice, "to see Lancaster. I have a message for him." He glanced at the

friars, then at the two barons. His companion, Fitz Alan,
nodded agreement and spread his stubby hands to the fire.

"No doubt you do—" said de la Pole, "but he's not to be
disturbed."

"By God's bones, indeed he's not!" growled Lord Neville.
Whatever bickering they might indulge in amongst themselves they were at one against outsiders.

"I come," said Lord March imperturbably, "from the
King. He summons the Duke to Westminster at once, for
conference. He's to accompany me *now*. Kindly have me announced." March's spotty little face was smug, and the two
barons were silenced. No one might disobey a summons from
the King, not even a favorite son, but de la Pole thought that
a more agreeable messenger might have been chosen. No
doubt the choice was Alice Perrers' doing. She blew now hot
now cold on this courtier or the other as her subtle mind conceived it to her advantage, and the King did as she wished.

Raulin departed on this new errand to the Avalon Chamber, and the company settled to wait for his return. The little
earl hunched himself in a gilded chair before the fire and
shivered, for his skinny body was always chilly. He stared enviously at two huge Venetian candlesticks which flanked the
fireplace. They discontented him with a pair he had recently
ordered for himself, as the Savoy discontented him with his
own city mansion, and the knowledge that, while he owned
ten castles, John of Gaunt had more than thirty. His thoughts
turned to the heir his countess was expecting. There at least
he bettered the Duke. This babe, whatever it was, stood
nearer to the English throne than Lancaster or any get of his.

"That churlish squire takes long to return," he said to Fitz
Alan, who was munching on a handful of raisins and spitting
the seeds out at an andiron. "That *Fleming*— Why must Lancaster ever show favor to foreigners!" March reached for a
raisin, then thought better of it. Two of his teeth were rotting
and sweetness hurt them. "By Saint Edmund!" he began pee-
vishly, "the Duke forgets my rank, this is outrageous—" He
stopped, for Raulin returned slowly through the door and
came up to him, bowing.

The squire fixed his eyes on a tapestry behind the earl's
head and said without inflexion, "My lord, His Grace sends
his love and duty to the King and prays His Majesty to bear
with him. He cannot come now but vill anon."

De la Pole watching from the window could not hold back

a chuckle at the little earl's expression. March got off the chair and drew himself as high as he could. "D'you mean to tell me it took all this time to produce this insolent message!" he shrilled at the squire, who closed his lips and stared stolidly towards the wall. It had taken no time at all for the Duke to give that message, the time had been taken by another matter which caused Raulin much hidden amazement.

"Well, my lord," cried de la Pole cheerfully, "you've had your answer!" His own discontent with Lancaster had melted into pride. The Duke was afraid of nothing, not even his father's famous Plantagenet temper, and de la Pole gave thanks that he owed his homage to the Duke instead of to this pimpled bantling, or any other overlord.

The earl and Fitz Alan left with what dignity they could, and Lord Neville said, " 'Tis strange the King makes much of the Mortimer spawn which caused his father's murder."

"Ay," said de la Pole lowering his voice. "But much is strange about our King these days, alack. The great chevalier who gave us Crécy and Poitiers has dwindled to a feeble lecher—it is his *sons* who must save England." He bowed to Neville. "Well, I see no use to stay here longer, I give you good day."

One by one they departed until the Presence Chamber was emptied of all but the squire. Raulin waited until there was no one on the stairs, then sped out into the courtyard and, obeying the Duke's orders, made for the Beaufort Tower.

The porter told him that Lady Swynford was not within. Her mare had been saddled and brought, and she had left some time ago.

"Did you hear naught of vere she might've gone?" pursued Raulin who knew nothing about the woman he was seeking and whose competent Flemish brain was mystified by the dark urgency his master had shown.

"I might of—" the porter paused and picked his nose thoughtfully, "were't to my interest."

Raulin opened his purse and held out a quarter noble. The porter bit it and said, "My Lady Swynford did ask the way to Billingsgate, summat abaht fishmongers it were—fishmongers wi' a fishery French name—Poissoner—Pechoner—she wanted to see."

Raulin, finding that the porter could give no other information, set off for the City on what seemed an unlikely quest. But the Duke had forbidden him to return without this

Lady Swynford. He rode to town and down Thames street towards the Bridge and began to make dogged inquiry.

Katherine had spent the last days in growing dejection.
Her grief and horror had worn themselves out at last and she
had stood amongst the hordes of mourners in St. Paul's and
felt only sadness. Since then, she had been planning how to
get home, but there were material difficulties. She had not
enough money for the journey, nor did she dare set off without escort. The wisest thing would be to get a message to
Hugh that he might send Ellis for her. But that would take
time. In that vast Savoy Palace she felt as lost and forgotten
as in a wilderness. The ducal children had been taken with
their household to the country air of Hertford Castle, and
most of the Bolingbroke people had dispersed after the funeral.

The decision to go to Billingsgate and seek Hawise had
been impulse, and once she had thought of it, she lost no
time and set off in a chill and windy drizzle.

In three and a half years the Pessoners had changed very
little except to grow rounder and noisier. An herb-strewn fire
roared on the hearth, where some of the children played at
rolling apples. Master Guy was not to be seen for he was
counting cod in his warehouse next door.

The low-raftered Hall smelt of fragrant smoke and fish.
Hawise was standing at the dairy room door vigorously
pounding the dasher in a large butter churn when one of the
young Pessoners let Katherine in.

Hawise gawked for a moment, her bare freckled arms
dropped from the churn, then a wide happy gap-toothed grin
spread over her big face. "God's beard!" she cried, " 'tis Kath
—m'Lady Swynford!" She rushed across the Hall and folding
Katherine in her arms kissed her heartily on the mouth. "Sit
down, sweeting, sit down—I'm that joyed to see ye! Be'ent we,
Mother? When I dropped the porridge ladle this morning I
knew we'd have a lucky caller, but I never dreamed of *you*,
love!" She pulled Katherine down beside her on a settle and
beamed at her with so much affection that Katherine felt a
pricking of gladness behind her lids.

Dame Emma bustled over with a pewter platter of honey
cakes and sugared ginger. "Welcome, welcome, eat hearty o'
these, lady, while I mull some ale for us. We'll have crabs

too—" added Dame Emma comfortably, "abobbin' o' their little pink cheeks in the ale."

Katherine laughed, basking in the warm kindly atmosphere and the goodwife's conviction that food was life's most important matter. She turned to Hawise with girlish eagerness and cried, "Tell all! How has it been with you, this long time?"

"Ay, but first of you," said the older girl, sobering to glance at Katherine's black gown. " 'Tis worn for the Duchess—nothing else, I pray?"

"Nay. We're all well at Kettlethorpe. *I've two babies*, Hawise!"

"And I one—" Hawise let out a snort of laughter and ran to the court calling, "Jackie, Jackie—come hither, imp—forever playing wi' the old sow, he is—'tis that he's but a piglet himself—" She hauled her offspring into the Hall and cuffed him gently on the ear, then wiped him off before presenting him proudly to Katherine.

Jackie was two years old and a true Pessoner, being fat, cheerful and sandy-haired. He grabbed a fistful of honey cakes and plumped himself on the rushes to enjoy them.

"Ay, he's Jack Maudelyn's right enough," said Hawise, seeing that Katherine did not like to ask, "and he was born in wedlock too, though only just. Father held out stubborn long, the dear old goat."

"Is Jack still weaver's prentice?"

"No prentice now, nor yet weaver neither. He went for a soldier to make us a fortune in booty, we hope. He's a fine archer, is Jack, and he joined the free companies under Sir Hugh Calverly. They fight for England now that we're at war again, to be sure."

"To be sure," said Katherine smiling. "So your man is gone, and you've come back home to wait like many another."

"Is't the same with you, lady dear—your knight abroad too?"

"Not now," said Katherine, turning her face away. But feeling that her curtness rebuffed Hawise, she made an effort and while they drank their hot pungent ale and sat close together on the settle, she told a little of what had passed with her since Hawise had waved tearful goodbyes beneath the porch of St. Clement's Dane on the wedding day.

In truth, there seemed not much to tell, nothing momen-

tous at all except the recent time of plague at Bolingbroke
and that Katherine slid over quickly. Yet during the bare recital of her years at Kettlethorpe, she noted that Hawise
looked at her with shrewd sympathy, and when Katherine
had done, Hawise said, "Have ye no woman there wi' you
save those North Country hinds?" The London-born Hawise
spoke as though Lincolnshire folk might be horned and
tailed.

"Well, now for a while there's Philippa too, you know,"
said Katherine laughing.

"In truth." Hawise gave a skeptical twinkling glance but
from politeness said no more. She had seen something of
Dame Philippa while Master Geoffrey still lived in London
with the Chaucers, and Hawise thought that Philippa was not
a woman to give over the mastery of any household she was
in and wondered how it would be when Katherine went
home. Again as she had when they first met, the girl aroused
in Hawise a tender feeling. Having no beauty herself she felt
no envy, but only a desire to serve it, and she recognized as
had no other person except Geoffrey a bitter loneliness in
Katherine that muted her shining fairness as dust films a silver chalice.

She could see that Katherine had had enough of living in
splendor at the Savoy, and being intuitive as well as practical,
she guessed that there was some embarrassment about getting
back to Kettlethorpe. She was turning the matter over in her
mind when there came another rap on the door.

" 'Tis doubtless the master o' that herring ship to see Father," she said to Dame Emma as she hastened to open it.

Raulin d'Ypres stood upon the doorstep and asked in his
gutteral voice, "Does anyone here know uff a Lady Swynford?"

Hawise, noting the Lancaster badge on the young man's
black tunic, drew back and looked at Katherine, who stood
up in surprise. "I'm Lady Swynford."

The squire bowed. "Please to come vit me to the Savoy.
Someone vishes to talk to you, my lady."

"Who does?" said Katherine, in surprise.

The squire glanced at Hawise and Dame Emma and the
tumbling children, then back to Katherine's puzzled resistant
face. "May I speak vit you alone, my lady?"

Katherine frowned and turned to Hawise, who looked
troubled. Hawise reminded herself that she did not know the

ways of court folk, but a blind mole could see something out of the way in this. "Shall I call Father to rid you of him?" she whispered in Katherine's ear.

Katherine looked back at the stolid squire. He met her gaze and stared down pointedly at the Red Rose embroidered on his breast. How strange, she thought, what could that mean? Most of the men in the palace below knight's rank wore that badge. "Well, come over here," she said stepping into the empty dairy room, and as the squire followed, she added, "What *is* this coil?"

"His Grace vants you to come to him, my lady," said Raulin very low.

She lifted her head, the pupils of her eyes dilated until the grayness turned as black as her gown. "The Duke?"

Raulin bowed.

"Why does he send for me in secret?" She pressed her hands tight against her breast to still the jumping of her heart, but she stood very quiet, leaning against the milk table.

"Because since the funeral he has seen nobody but me, nor does he vish to, my lady, except now—you."

The color ebbed slowly back into her face and still her great eyes stared at the squire in question, in disbelief, until he said brusquely, "But lady, hasten. It is already long since I vas sent to find you."

Katherine moved then, she walked back into the Hall and reached up to the perch where Hawise had hung her wet cloak. "I—I must go—" she said to the anxious Pessoners. "But I'll see you very soon."

"Not bad news—" cried Hawise, quickly crossing herself. "Lady, ye look so strange!"

"Not bad news." Katherine took a deep breath, smiled at Dame Emma and kissed Hawise, but it seemed as though she did not really see them. When the door had closed behind Katherine and the squire, Hawise turned frowning to her mother. "She was happy here afore wi' us— What *can* that gobble-tongued outlander've said to throw her into such a maze? 'Twas like she wandered in a fearing dream and yet feared more to wake."

"Fie, daughter," said Dame Emma, adding cinnamon and nutmeg to the hare she seethed over the fire. "Ye make too much o' naught. Do ye get on wi' the churning."

Hawise obeyed but as she pounded slowly in the churn, her

cheerful face was downcast and she sang a plaintive little
song that she had heard on London streets.

> Blow, northern wind, fend off from my sweeting.
> Blow, northern wind, blow.
> Ho! the wind and the rain they blow green pain.
> Blow, blow, blow!

# XII

KATHERINE and Raulin rode back to the Savoy in silence
until they had passed beneath the great Strand portcullis
into the Outer Ward, and dismounted at the stables. Then
Raulin said, "This vay, my lady," and led her towards the
river side, nearly to the boat landing. In the west corner of
the court between the bargehouse and the massive wing
which housed the ducal children's apartments, there was a
low wooden building surmounted by a carving of a large
flying hawk. This building contained the falcon mew, and one
of the falconers stood always on guard to prevent strangers
from entering, or any sudden happening which might upset
his highstrung and immensely valuable charges.

Raulin nodded to the falconer, skirted the mew and
plunged suddenly into a dark passage that lay hidden between
it and a stone water cistern. Here was a small wooden door
which he unlocked. "But the privy apartments are in the
Inner Ward," protested Katherine nervously as he motioned
her up narrow stone steps that were hollowed from the thickness of the wall.

"This leads to them," said Raulin patiently. "His Grace
does not vish that people see you. It vould make talk."

Katherine swallowed, and mounted the steps. They ended
on the next floor in a narrow passage that ran along the inside wall of consecutive chambers and ended in another
wooden door. This door was concealed by a painted cloth-

hanging. Raulin pushed it aside and they emerged into the Duchess's garderobe, a small oblong chamber.

Behind another painted hanging they entered the darkened solar, narrow chinks of light around the edges of the closed shutters showed that the vast bed had been draped with a black pall. They went through another chamber where the Duchess's ladies had used to sit and two more rooms until they turned a corner towards the river into a square tower. Here was the Avalon Chamber.

Raulin knocked on the carved oak door and gave his name. A voice said, "Enter!" Raulin held the door, then shut it after Katherine, and went away.

Katherine walked in quietly, her head lifted high, her cloak clutched around her. The Duke was sitting on a gold-cushioned window seat gazing out over the river towards the rocks and stunted trees of Lambethmoor. He did not move at once, and she stood on the woven silk rug that covered the tiles and waited.

He was clothed in plain black saye, without girdle or mantel, the tight-fitting cote and long hose molded his lean muscular body and were unrelieved by trimming. He wore no jewels excpt the sapphire seal ring that Blanche had given him. His thick tawny hair was cut short below his ears, and he was clean-shaven. This startled her, for it made him seem younger, and when he slowly turned his head towards her, she saw that his chin was square and had a cleft like her own.

"You summoned me, my lord?" she said, for he did not speak but stared at her with a remote brooding look. His skin had lost the sun-bronze that it had shown when he came to Kettlethorpe, and it was stretched taut across the sharp Plantagenet cheekbones, the narrow cheeks and long high-bridged nose. His mouth, wide-curved and passionate, was drawn thin at the corners like his father's, and his heavy eyelids seemed as though they would never wholly lift again to disclose the vivid blue beneath.

She knelt, as was seemly, and taking his hand, kissed it in homage. While she knelt, her cloak loosened and her hood fell back. He touched her curling rain-dampened hair. " 'Tis the color of carnelians," he said, "the gem that heals anger. Would that it might heal sorrow——" He spoke as though to himself, in a low faltering voice. His hand fell back onto his thigh, and she raised her head, wondering. Through every fiber in her body she had felt that light touch on her hair.

His gaze slid slowly over her face, then rested on the cream and umber tiles which floored the chamber. "I sent for you, Katherine, that I might thank you. Old Simon of Bolingbroke told me what you did for—for her. You shall know my gratitude."

Her cheeks stung with heat. She jumped up from her knees and pulled the cloak around her. "My lord, I told you that I loved her. I want no reward—no payment!"

"Hush! Leave be, Katherine. I know you're not venal. I've thought of you much these last days, thought of how you were with her at the end—while I—on the day she died—" He broke off and, getting up, walked to the fireplace.

The day she died, he thought, September twelfth, the day when the French had tricked and fooled him, drawn him into battle formation and then sneaked off into the night laughing at the gullible blundering English. A bootless costly mockery had been the whole campaign, and through no fault of his; but he guessed well what they said of his generalship here at home. Blanche would have known how to soften the humiliation. With her serene smile, she would have made little of so trifling a setback, and her faith in God's good will towards them would have communicated itself to him. He would have slept quietly again on her white breast and been calmed. Five months since he had lain in her arms for the last time—or the arms of any woman. Fastidiousness or fidelity had checked the clamors of his body, and he would not tumble camp trulls as the others did.

"Katherine," he said abruptly, "I cannot rid me of my grief. Each day it worsens, and yet I must rid me of it and take up my heavy duties."

She looked at him mutely. She could find no words of comfort, she did not know what he wanted of her; but she felt a closeness between them that had never been before.

"Put off your cloak and sit down," he said, smiling faintly. "You stand there like a hart that scents the hunter. I think you need not fear me."

She flushed. "I know, my lord." She walked across the room and hung her cloak on a silver perch that projected from the inner wall. It was a room of beauty and luxury such as she had never imagined. Two of the plaster walls were powdered with a pattern of gold stars and tiny flowerets like forget-me-nots. The hooded fireplace was of green marble deeply carved into medallions and foliage. The elaborate gilded furniture had been made by master craftsmen in Italy, the canopied bed was hung with ruby velvet embroidered with seed pearls, and ruby glowed again with amber and azure in the blazons of the leaded windowpanes. On the east wall hung the great Avalon tapestry in dark and mysterious greens. Deep in the woven forest, the Blessed Isle of Avalon rose palely, shining through a mist, and the figures of King Arthur and his queen lay bathed in a moony light. Tall and fateful in his druid's robes the wizard Merlin stood below the royal dead and pointed to far distant hills on which there was a fairy castle floating.

"Ay—that tapestry pleases me much," John said, following her gaze. "Merlin's castle puts me in mind of one I saw in Spain, after our victory at Nájera." His somber look lightened for an instant. Always at the thought of Castile he heard the shouts of triumph and rejoicing from his men and saw the face of the messenger who had brought him news of his son's birth to augment the thrill of victory.

"You were happy in Castile?" Katherine ventured. "You and the Prince of Wales righted the great wrong done the Castilian king."

"But, God's wounds, it didn't last!" he cried with sudden anger. "Don't you *know* what happened at Montiel last March? King Pedro foully murdered by his brother the bastard, who sits again upon the throne he has no right to!"

"Who has right then, since the poor king is dead?" she asked after a minute, thinking that it might be anger was better for him than brooding grief and that this coil about far-off kings could not touch him too nearly.

"The heiress is the king's daughter, the Infanta Costanza," he answered more quietly. " 'Tis she who is the true Queen of Castile." He thought of the times he had seen the exiled princesses at Bordeaux. Costanza was a skinny black-haired wench who must be about fifteen now: two years ago he had been amused at the haughtiness of her bearing and the vehemence of her Spanish as she had thanked him for the aid given to her father. "Pedro was often a cruel and crooked man," John said. "His promises were writ on water, but what matters that, for he was also the true-born anointed king— King of Castile."

He spoke the last three words with a solemnity that puzzled

Katherine, as though they were a charm or incantation, and yet she thought he scarcely realized this himself or that for a moment he had forgotten his grief. He sighed and turned from the tapestry. "Merlin had many prophecies about my house," he said listlessly. "They've come down by word of mouth throughout the centuries—Blanche cared naught for such things—she cared only for the things that came from Holy Writ." He flung himself down in a chair by the fire and leaned his forehead on his hand.

"My lord," said Katherine softly, "do you remember how she looked on the day of the Great Tournament at Windsor three years ago—so golden fair and laughing when you rode up to the loge? For sure, she will look thus in heaven while she waits for you."

He raised his head and said, "Ah, Katherine, you know how to comfort! So few know that I long to talk of her that's gone. Instead they start and look away and speak of foolish things to distract me—yet here is one other that understands."

He got up and went to the table, which was littered with vellum books and official missives which he had not glanced at. He picked up a folded parchment on which the seal and cords had been broken and opened the letter. "Listen," he said, and read very slowly:

> *"I have of sorrow so great wound*
> *That joy get I never none,*
> *Now that I see my lady bright,*
> *That I have loved with all my might,*
> *Is from me dead, and is agone.*
> *Alas, Death, what aileth thee,*
> *That thou should'st not have taken me,*
> *When thou took my lady sweet,*
> *That was so fair, so fresh, so free,*
> *So good, that men may well say*
> *Of all goodness she had no meet!*

> *"Right on this same, as I have said*
> *Was wholly all my love laid*
> *For certes she was, that sweet wife,*
> *My suffisaunce, my lust, my life,*
> *Mine hap, mine health and all my bless,*
> *My world's welfare and my goddess,*
> *And I wholly hers, and everydel."*

He sighed and put the parchment on his lap. "The maker has said it for me and with true English words. The maker is your brother-in-law, Katherine."

"Geoffrey!" she cried.

"Ay, I too was amazed for I had thought him a shrewd nimble little man, apt on King's service but not of temper or feeling to write like this."

"Geoffrey is deep of feeling, I believe," she said, and thought that the verses had been written perhaps to soothe his own sorrow as well as the Duke's, for she remembered the look in his eyes when he beheld the Lady Blanche. "Is he back then?" she asked, wondering that she had not seen him.

"Nay, at Calais on a mission. He says that he is writing more of this poem and with my permission will call it 'The Book of the Duchess,' which I've most readily granted. Katherine, you see new reason why I'm grateful to you and your kin."

"It is joy to serve you, my lord." She lifted her face and smiled at him. For John it was as though a shutter had been flung open, and the noon light had rushed in. He had never truly seen her beauty before nor had he ever seen a smile like that, compounded of a luminous tenderness in the gray eyes, and yet in the lift of her red lips, the short perfect teeth and the dimple near her voluptuous mouth there was a hint of seduction. His nostrils flared on a sharp breath and his thoughts darted hither and yon in confusion. Why had he summoned her today, why had he forgot that she had angered him back at Windsor, forgot that her eyes had once reminded him of anguish and betrayal? Why had he let her share in his grief now and kept her with him in this warm intimacy when a purse of gold would have amply repaid? Why must she sit there now in her clinging black gown that showed the outline of each round breast and the curve of the long supple waist? His eye fell on the pouch she carried at her girdle. It was of painted leather blazoned with the Swynford arms. He stared at the three little yellow boars' heads and said angrily, "Have you no blazon of your own, Katherine?"

Her tender smile faded. She was puzzled by the sudden harshness of his tone though well aware the question covered something else. "My father had no blazon," she said slowly. "He was King-of-Arms for Guienne, you know—he was knighted only just before his death."

He heard the quiver in her voice, and his anger vanished under the impulse to protect that she alone of all women had ever roused in him. He had indeed forgotten her low birth and the consciousness of the great gulf between them brought a subtle relief.

"But you may rightfully bear arms," he said in a light tone. "Come, what shall they be?" He motioned her over to the table where he sat down and picked up a quill pen and smoothed out a blank parchment. "You are too fair and rare a woman to be lost beneath those Swynford boars' heads," he added with a certain grimness. "Your name was Roet, was it not?" She nodded. "Well, that means a wheel," and he drew one on the parchment. They both stared down at it. Then John said, "But stay—it must be a *Catherine* wheel, of course, since it is yours!" And he added small jagged prongs to the wheel, as it always was in St. Catherine's symbol.

Katherine watched as he started afresh and drew the shield, then placed three Catherine wheels inside it, for three, he thought, made better balance and he had much feeling for all things in art. He drew with bold vigorous strokes and took pleasure in this small creation, which made a neater play on her name than many another of the nobles' canting arms— Lucy with his luce's heads, or that fool of an Arundel with his hopping hirondelles, or martlets. For like this, most blazons had been chosen, and in making this individual badge for Katherine he felt that he bestowed on her a special gift and one far more lasting than the money he intended to give her.

"The field shall be gules," he said, touching the shield lightly with his pen, "the wheels or, for those colors suit you. Lancaster Herald shall enter this in the Roll of Arms tomorrow."

"Thank you, my lord," she cried, truly delighted, as much for the interest that he had shown as for her own promotion to armiger, and as she leaned over to look more closely at the little shield, the warm flowery scent of her body assailed him. He glanced sideways, at her unconscious face so near his that he could see the separate black lashes on her lowered lids and the down on her cheeks. She moved a little, and he felt her soft fragrant breath.

He shoved the parchment, quill and sand pellmell across the table and jumped to his feet. She turned in fear, thinking him angry again; and as she looked up into his eyes, her hands grew cold with sweat and her legs began to tremble.

"Jesu—" he whispered. "Jesu—" He pulled her slowly toward him and she came as one who walks through water, each step impeded, until she leaned against him and yielded him her mouth with a low sobbing moan.

They stood thus pressed together in a mindless wine-dark rapture while the last reflected light faded from the Thames outside and vesper bells rang faintly down the river. The fire died down. A log cracked in two, and flames leaped up again. She felt him lift her in his arms and her heart streamed into his. She had no strength to pit against his will and her own need, yet as he laid her on the ruby velvet bed her hand turned against his chest and she felt the sharp pressure of her betrothal ring.

She twisted from him wildly and flung herself off the bed, "My dearest lord, I cannot. I cannot!" She sank to her knees by the bedpost and buried her face in her arms. He lay quiet as she had left him, and watched her, while his breathing slowed in time, and he said very low, "I want you, Katrine, and I believe you love me." He spoke her name in the soft French way—as she had not heard it since her childhood and so piercing sweet it sounded to her that the meaning of his other words came slowly.

Then she raised her head and cried with bitterness, "Ay—I love you—though I knew it not till now. I think I've loved you since that time in Windsor pleasaunce you beat off Hugh, who would have raped me, and it's for that, that I am married."

The fire hissed in the silent room, and against the wall below water lapped from the wake of a passing boat. John stirred and put his hand on her arm. *"I'll* not force you, Katrine—you shall come to me of yourself."

"I cannot," she repeated, though she dared not look at him. "Dear God, you know I cannot. Ay, I know adultery is so light a thing at court, but I'm of simple stock and to me 'tis sin so vile that I would hate myself as much as God would."

"And hate *me?*" He spoke low and gently.

"Sainte Marie, I could never hate you—dear my lord, don't torture me with these questions, ah let me go—" for his hand had tightened on her arm and he bent his face close to hers. She gathered all her strength and cried, "Have you forgot why we are both in black!"

He drew back sharply and got up off the bed. He went to the fire and twisting a rush lit the tapers on the table and in the silver wall sconces. He came back to her and lifted her roughly to her feet. "I scarce know what to think," he said, "except that I must forget *you*, it seems." His hands dropped from her shoulders. His blue eyes had gone hard between the narrowed lids, and he spoke with chill precision. "You have yourself reminded me that there are ladies of the court will help me to forget all manner of grief, and who will not think it shame to be desired by the Duke of Lancaster."

A spearthrust of pain streaked through her breast, but she answered as steadily as he, "I've no doubt of that, Your Grace. As for me I must return to Kettlethorpe at once."

"And if I refuse permission—what would you say?"

"That such a thing would ill befit a man reputed one of the most chivalrous knights in Christendom."

They stared at each other in a struggle that wracked them both, and she clung to the sudden enmity between them as a shield.

He turned first and walking from her to the window stood looking out at the night-darkened Thames. "Very well, Katherine, I shall arrange your escort back to Lincolnshire. You'll receive word at the Beaufort Tower. You still shall have no cause to reproach me for ingratitude."

She said nothing. Now that he no longer looked at her, her face grew anguished, she gazed at the tall black figure by the window, at the haughty set of his shoulders, the implacability she felt in his averted head.

She ran to the perch and seized her cloak and was out of the door and had shut it behind her before he understood. He turned crying, "Katrine!" to the shut door. Then staring at it, he sank down on the window seat as she had found him. His eyes, still grim, traveled from the door to the hollow on the ruby velvet coverlet where they had lain together so briefly and where he had been shaken by a passion such as he had never known. "There's a fire been lit that's not so easy to put out," he said aloud. He got up and going to the table picked up Chaucer's poem. He gazed at it, and made a strange hoarse sound. He put the poem carefully to one side. After a moment he began to rip the seals and tear the cords on the neglected official missives, his fingers moving with sharp violent jerks.

Katherine fled through the rooms behind the Avalon Chamber as she had come, passing Raulin as he sat in a recess waiting for summons. He cried "M'lady!" but she did not hear him and he was left to his own startled thoughts.

Through the Duchess's dressing room and down the stairs and out behind the falcon mew, Katherine ran, until in the Outer Ward she forced herself to slower steps and pulled her hood far down over her face. She went to the stables and ordered Doucette saddled. She flung herself on the mare and set forth through the great gate and down the Strand to London. The Savoy was hateful to her, nothing would induce her to return to the Beaufort Tower, and from instinct she fled back to the only warm unstressful affection she had ever known.

Hawise herself opened the door to Katherine's knock and her glad cry of welcome faltered as she got a good look at the girl's face.

"May I stay here tonight?" whispered Katherine, clutching Hawise. "Just tonight. I must leave for home at dawn."

"For sure, love, in my bed, and longer than that. Here, Mother, gi' me the wine—" for Katherine had begun to shiver uncontrollably. Hawise flung her strong young arm round Katherine's waist and held a cup to the girl's lips.

The Pessoners crowded around, kindly, murmuring. Master Guy rocking on his heels by the fireplace boomed out, "Hast seen some goblin, my little lady, that has 'frighted you? You're safe enough here, for the smell o' good fresh herring affrights goblins!" and he chuckled.

"Hush, clattermouth," snapped his wife, and beneath her breath she said, "God's nails, mayhap 'tis some breeding cramp, poor little lass," for she had seen that dazed glassy-white look on the face of many a woman that was to miscarry of a child.

"Come to bed, sweeting," said Hawise with firm authority. "You look fit to drop and soaked through too." She marshaled Katherine up the loft stairs to the sleeping room over the fish shop and sharply quieted two of the younger children who poked their heads up from bed. She undressed Katherine and wrapped her in a blanket and put her in her own bed, where little Jackie slept on the far side.

Katherine sighed, and her shivering stopped. "Thank you,"

she whispered. Hawise sat on the bed and held the candle near.

"Can you tell me, dear?" she said, her shrewd eyes scanning the upturned face, the bruised trembling lips. " 'Tis a man?" she said. "Ay, I see it is. And he has used ye ill?" she added fiercely.

"Nay—" Katherine turned her face into the pillow, "I don't know. Blessed Virgin, give me strength—I love him—I must get home—to my babies, to Hugh—I cannot stay so near—"

"Whist, poppet!" Hawise stroked the girl's arm. "You shall get home. Has't been arranged?"

"Nay, I'll go alone—I want no arrangements. I want nothing from him. I'll sleep in abbey hostels—they'll give food—I must go as soon as it's light."

"And so you shall, but not alone, for I'll come wi' ye."

Katherine, distracted, beset by fear and desperate yearning, did not understand at first, then she drew herself back and looked into Hawise's face. "God's love, and would you come with me, in truth?"

"Methinks ye've *need* of a good serving maid, m'lady," said Hawise twinkling.

"But I've no money, until I get to Kettlethorpe!"

"So I've guessed. I've silver enow put by to get us there, ye can pay me later, so ye needna look high-nosed about it."

"But Jackie—we couldn't take him!"

"Jackie'll be merry as a pie right here. Forbye he's fonder o' his granny than me anyhow. Nor can I bide wi' ye long if my Jack comes home from war. But I'll not let ye go the road alone."

"May Christ bless you!" Katherine whispered.

"Sleep now, mistress. I'll call ye before Prime, we can scarce start sooner."

Some whoreson knight or squire had brought her to this, thought Hawise, as she left the loft room, had caught her fancy with wheedling talk and sugary smiles such as she'd never get from Sir Hugh, poor fair lady. She heartily damned the unknown man and went downstairs to tell her parents of her decision.

The Pessoners were all up to see the girls start out. After the first protests against their daughter leaving them, the goodhearted couple had given in, and last night Master Guy had hired a horse from the livery stable down the street and routed out one Jankin, his best prentice, telling him to make ready to escort my Lady Swynford and Hawise at least until they might catch up with some safe company that was also Lincoln-bound. Dame Emma packed a hamper full of cheese, new-baked loaves and a leg of mutton, then crammed corners with saffron cakes before she helped Hawise make up a bundle of her own belongings. "And what o' Lady Swynford's gear?" asked the good dame, knowing that Katherine had fled to them with nothing but her cloak.

" 'Tis left at the Savoy; she said 'no matter,' there wasn't much and she's in such a dither to be off, she'll not send for it."

Dame Emma shook her head. " 'Tis beyond me. Well, daughter, I can see she needs ye, for ye're level as a pan o' milk and will take care o' her. Good speed, and don't stay overlong."

So the Pessoners all stood and waved cheerily on the doorstep. Little Jackie waved to his mother as gaily as any, for Dame Emma had promised him that he should have a gingerbread man for his breakfast.

Hawise rode pillion with Jankin on the hired horse, and Katherine preceded them on Doucette, who had been well curried and fed at the livery stable. Jankin was a great gangling lad of fifteen, strong enough to hoist a hundred weight of cod onto the scales and canny enough to haggle with fishermen at the dock, and he was delighted with this expedition. He and Hawise chattered as they rode along Bridge street to Bishopsgate, but Katherine rode in silence. Now that she was safely off, each of Doucette's hoofbeats was like a hammer on her heart. If I should never see him again—she thought, Blessed Mother, how could I live, and yet it was the fear of seeing him again which had driven her to this desperate haste. The fear that if he were there so near her she might have crept back to the Avalon Chamber, beseeching, begging —I was wrong, my darling, my dearest lord, nothing matters to me but you, forgive me, take me—

There in the London street she winced and gritted her teeth, clenching her hands on the pommel. During the night when she had slept a little, she had thought herself in the Avalon Chamber lying in his arms with his mouth on hers, she had heard again each dark shaken tone of his voice and in her dream he told her that he loved her—each time as she wakened she saw only the coldness of his eyes before he turned from her at the end and remembered that from him there had been no talk of love, but only desire. Then shame would flood her that she had dared to dream that he spoke of love while the Lady Blanche stood there between them, and bitter shame that she had cried out to him her own love. Yet it is true, God help me, Katherine thought, and such an anguish came to her that she jerked on Doucette's reins and stopped the mare in the middle of the road while she gazed back past London spires to where the Savoy lay.

"What is't, m'lady?" asked Hawise anxiously as she and Jankin jogged up. Now that she had become Katherine's servant she thought it seemly to use respectful address before others.

Katherine started. "Nothing," she said, trying to smile. "Can you go faster? We should be past Waltham at the nooning."

For to stop again in Waltham she could not bear. The twice she had covered this North road before she had thought herself unhappy, but it had been nothing like this.

"We can try," said Hawise, "if old cat's meat here'll hump himself." Jankin pricked the horse with his little iron spur and they lumbered into a trot.

It grew colder, the sun gleamed once or twice, then dwindled. The horses' hooves rang out on the freezing road. Their fellow travelers—friars, pedlars, merchants, journeymen and beggars—all huddled themselves deep into whatever covering they wore and omitted greetings to each other.

When they were three miles short of Ware, light snowflakes drifted down and melted on their cloaks. They were hungry and the hired horse stumbled from weariness. They stopped at an isolated alestake that thrust its long bush across the highway. They hitched the horses under a lean-to shed, and Jankin stayed to see that a tattered little knave watered and fed them while the two women entered the tavern with the hamper.

"God's nails!" muttered Hawise, frowning, "have they no brooms in Hertfordshire!" The low smoky room was littered with moldering straw which had matted on the trampled earth with strewn bones, eggshells, apple peel and chicken droppings from the hens that clucked under the one greasy table. Behind a trestle piled with kegs and flagons the alewife stood, her arms akimbo, staring malevolently. Two men sprawled at the table. They were black-bearded except where a running sore had bared the jaw of the younger one. They were clothed in sheepskin and torn leather breeches. Their feet were wrapped in filthy rags. Their heavy oak staves leaned against the wall. They had a long knife which they silently passed back and forth to cut chunks from a gray-furred loaf of dark bread they had brought. They glanced from Hawise to Katherine then at each other. One picked a louse off his knee and cracked it between his fingernails.

Hawise put the hamper on the farthest end of the table and wiped a space clean with the corner of her cloak. "I suppose we may eat our dinner here, goodwife?" she asked dubiously. "An we buy some ale."

The woman shrugged and made a gobbling noise in her throat.

"She has no tongue," said the younger of the two men grinning to show yellow stumps. "T'lord o' the manor yanked it out long since for evil talk—talked against him she did, when all he'd done was trample down her crops when he was out hunting one fair day. To be sure, he trampled down her babe too, that was playing in the corn, but 'twas no fault o' his."

"Hush thy clack, fool!" growled the other man angrily, casting an uneasy glance at Jankin, who came through the door.

" 'Tis but a lad," said the first man. Jankin flushed and fingered the little dagger Master Guy had given him. He sat stiffly down beside Hawise, who unpacked the hamper. The alewife leaned over the trestle and like the two bearded men watched each item that came out.

"You will share our food?" said Katherine faintly. "For sure I can eat none," she whispered to Hawise. The stink of the alehouse sickened her, and she loathed these ugly evil people.

"Why not?" said he of the running sore, grabbing at the hunk of mutton Hawise held out, "for are we not all created equal in the sight o' God? Did He ordain that you s'ld eat while we go empty?"

"What manner o' babble is that?" said Hawise briskly. "If ye are beggars ye can be fed at th' nearest abbey."

"Phuaw!" the man spat through his yellow teeth. "Moldy bread and a slice o' cheese the rats won't touch, whilst the monks sit on their fat arses swilling capon."

"Come, we must go," said Katherine rising. "Leave them the rest of the food." The two men watched intently while Hawise paid the alewife for the sour brew that they had hardly touched. The men stood watching while the trio mounted. Their eyes rested on Doucette and the brass-studded leather saddle, the carved bone stirrups.

Katherine flicked the mare, they started north again at as fast a trot as the hired horse could manage. "A pack of ribauds," said Hawise. "They'd thievery in their eyes."

"Suppose they come after us and waylay!" cried Jankin eagerly. He burned for battle and now that the unease of the alehouse was over, he felt disappointment.

"How could they, numskull—they've no horses!"

"A short cut," answered Jankin, considering. "They'd know of one through the fields; they might hide in yonder green wood and then jump out—"

"By the Mass, Jankin, you've too much fancy!" Hawise rapped him angrily on the skull with her knuckles. "D'you wish to frighten our lady?" But she frowned.

"I believe the foul creatures are runaway serfs, outlaws of some kind," said Katherine shuddering. She drew Doucette close to the others.

They entered the wood where trees grew close to the roadside. The snow, which had stopped, began to fall again in lazy, aimless flakes.

"There's something moving in th' thicket there," cried Jankin pointing unsteadily. With fast-beating hearts they looked, then Hawise said, "Naught but a stray hound!" and kicked their horse again. They were near out of the wood when they heard noise behind them. The pound of galloping hooves. Turning, they saw four helmeted men bearing down on them full tilt, shouting and waving their arms.

"What now!" cried Hawise. "Do they mean to run us down?" Jankin yanked their horse off the road, and Katherine swerved Doucette so hard that the little mare pranced angrily. But the men pulled up in a flurry of flying clods and jingling harness. A cold stillness descended on Katherine; on each of them she saw the Lancaster badge.

"Ho! men-at-arms, what would you of us?" cried Jankin in a high dauntless voice, while Hawise cried, "Saint Mary! That first one is th' outlandish squire came for my lady yesterday!" and new fear smote her. Katherine sat her horse stiff and straight as though she'd been carved from the oak behind her, and whatever these newcomers had in mind, 'twas plain Jankin could avail nothing against spears and swords and armored men.

"My Lady Swynford!" cried Raulin, riding directly up to Katherine and wiping his sweating face on a corner of his surcote. "A fine race you haff run us, by my fader's soul, ve haff pounded the road since Tierce!" He spoke with annoyance. Tracking down this extraordinary young woman to Billingsgate yesterday had been simple compared to the difficulties today when he had found she was not at the Beaufort Tower.

"What is it you want?" Katherine, angry at herself for the joy she had felt when she saw the badges, spoke with extreme coldness.

"His Grace promised you escort, I belief—yet you did not vait. He sends letters too."

"Letters! For me?" said Katherine faintly.

"Not for you, lady. For your husband, Sir Hugh, and for officers at Lincoln Castle."

Hawise looked sharply at the squire, then at Katherine, thinking, His Grace? the Duke of Lancaster? what is this? when suddenly she guessed the truth and was so startled she nearly fell off the horse.

"These men," said Raulin, indicating the sergeant and two soldiers behind him, "are your escort to Lincoln."

"By Saint Christopher, I'm glad to hear that!" exclaimed Hawise. She had begun to think Jankin far too slender a defense against the hazards of the road. She winked companionably at the sergeant, who winked back, grinning.

"Ay, we're glad of escort," said Katherine, but her irresolute heart was heavy again. He had kept his promise, nothing more. As it should be, of course.

Raulin dispatched the rest of his business quickly, for he was weary of running about the country after my Lady Swynford.

He repeated instructions to the sergeant, saw that he put the ducal letters for Lincoln safely inside his hauberk, and then agreed to take the deeply disappointed Jankin back to London with him. Raulin consigned Hugh's letter to Katherine's keeping and said, "There is vun more thing. His Grace send to you this." He held out stolidly a triangle of parchment, smaller than the palm of his hand. Katherine took it and turned it over. It was the shield the Duke had drawn for

her, her own blazon; the three Catherine wheels had now
been painted gold against the field of scarlet.

Oh, what does it mean? she thought. Was it a special message to remind her of that contented moment when they had
leaned together on the table and he had drawn this for her?
Did it mean forgiveness? Or was it only that he wished to be
rid of all thought of her?

She could not know, but after they had said farewell to
Raulin and Jankin, and the two women rode with the soldiers
on to Ware, she found opportunity to secretly kiss the shield
and slipped it in the bosom of her gown.

It was on a fine sunny morning that they rode through the
suburban village of Wigford, then across the Witham on the
High bridge and through the city walls under the great arch
of Stonebow and so into Lincoln town.

"God's teeth, could they find no steeper hill to build on?"
laughed Hawise gazing up what seemed to be a perpendicular
climb to the castle and the minster above. "Folk here must be
goats!" All through the journey her town-bred scorn of the
provinces had been leavened by a bright-eyed interest in new
sights. "Bustling little place," she added approvingly. It was
market day. The narrow streets were lined with booths, and
thronged with chaffering goodwives, most of them dressed in
the scarlet and green cloth for which Lincoln weavers were
famous.

"No bustle like there used to be afore they took the staple
away," said the sergeant, who had been to Lincoln before.
"Couple years back there'd be a reg'lar Tower o' Babel here
wi' heathen sailors from the German Ocean an' traders from
Flanders an' Florence all a jib-jabbering away like a hassel o'
magpies. 'Tis quiet now."

"A deal better than those dreary fens, forsooth. Hark!
There's music!" cried Hawise cocking her head. They had
climbed up through the Poultry with its squawking tethered
produce, past the skin market at Danesgate, and here in an
open court the tanners' guild was rehearsing for its procession
on St. Clement's Day. Fiddles, pipes and tabors had the tanners, and they scraped and whistled and drummed while one
of their number, dressed in violet Papal robes to represent
their patron saint, leaped up and down in rhythm and juggled

with a large tin anchor which stood for the instrument of St. Clement's martyrdom.

At a fresh spurt from the fiddlers and a loud tattoo on the tabors, the juggler threw his anchor high and missed it as it fell. It rebounded on the paved courtyard and bounced into the fish market just ahead, clattering down beside a woman at a stall.

Doucette shied, and while Katherine quieted the mare, she heard a familiar voice raised in sharp protest. "Have care, you clumsy jackanapes! You near broke my toe!"

The juggler sheepishly retrieved his anchor, while Katherine leaned over the mare's head and called "Philippa!" and then seeing a tiny figure clutching at the woman's skirts, Katherine jumped off the horse. She scooped Blanchette up in her arms, and rained kisses on the little face that screwed up in protest.

The child started to cry, but as Katherine crooned love words to her, and laughed and held her close, the little pink lips stopped quivering. Blanchette put her arms around her mother's neck.

Philippa had been standing by the fish stall pinching a large glassy-eyed mackerel, while a Kettlethorpe lad teetered behind her with a wicker basket already filled with honeycombs, leeks, stone jars and leather shoes. Philippa flopped the mackerel into the basket, walked up to Katherine and said calmly, "By Sainte Marie, enfin te voila! I've been wondering when you'd get back. Don't start spoiling that child again, the instant you get here."

Katherine set Blanchette down and embraced her sister, seeing that the weeks she had been gone and lived through a lifetime of terror, death, anguish and despairing love, had been placid fast-flying routine for those at home. "And little Tom, Philippa," she said urgently, "is he all right?"

"Of course, he's all right. Both babes grown fat *and* obedient, I've seen to that. Are all these people with you, Katherine?"

She pointed at the three soldiers and recognized Hawise with astonishment. "Why, it's the Pessoner lass!"

Katherine explained briefly that Hawise had come to be her servant for a while and that the Duke of Lancaster had sent escort, at which Philippa nodded with satisfaction, and turned to accompany Katherine and the others up to the castle. Katherine set her delighted little girl upon Doucette, and holding her in the saddle walked beside the mare.

"Hugh is in town today too," Philippa said, puffing hard, for the climb was steep and she had gained much weight now in her sixth month of pregnancy.

"How is Hugh?" asked Katherine quickly.

"Better in health, though grumpy and worried to death over the manor dues. He couldn't pay them at Michaelmas. He can't pay 'em yet. Twice he's been to Canon Bellers in the close to beg for time on Kettlethorpe, and now to the Duke's receiver in the castle about the Coleby rents." Philippa glanced at the men and Hawise, then lowered her voice. "Did you get something substantial from the Duke, or Duchess—God rest her soul?"

Katherine shook her head and such a shut, chill expression of warning hardened her beautiful face that Philippa's disgusted expostulation died unspoken. Instead she gave a weary sigh and said after a moment, "Then I don't know what's to be done. Hugh's borrowed all he can from that Lombard in Danesgate. The Duke's receiver, here, John de Stafford, is a mean hard-bitten man who threatens seizure of your lands and chattels." She did not add that she herself had been helping all she could and that the money expended on these market day purchases had come from her own pension, but Katherine heard the sigh and put her arm around her sister's shoulders. "I'm sorry, m'amie," she said sadly. "The sergeant there has some official letter to deliver to this Stafford. Perhaps I should go too and beg him for time."

"It might help," agreed Philippa sighing again. "I believe he doesn't like Hugh. Bite your lips to make them red, and here—" she patted a coppery tendril of Katherine's blown hair into place.

They had reached the East Gate of the castle walls, and the gateward did not even look up as their party streamed through. The castle bailey contained a dozen buildings including the shire house and the gaol, the residence of the constable and the Duchy of Lancaster's offices; and there was a constant coming and going of people on business.

They inquired of a hurrying clerk and walked the horses over to a low building that stood between the ancient Lucy keep and the shire house. The Lancaster coat of arms was nailed above the door, and lolling on a bench beside two tethered horses sat Ellis de Thorseby, Hugh's squire. He greeted

Katherine with some warmth, having conceived admiration for her courage in the time of plague at Bolingbroke. Katherine, though she concealed it, was startled at his unkemptness. His shock of greasy hair hung tangled to his shoulders beneath a moth-eaten felt cap. His rusty tunic was threadbare at the elbows and his once yellow hose were profusely patched. Katherine, used now to the sleek elegance of the Lancastrian retinue, was shocked into awareness of their own shabbiness.

Sir Hugh was inside, Ellis told them, had been there some time, pleading his case with the Lancastrian receiver for Lincolnshire.

"Well, I'm going in too," said Katherine resolutely. The sergeant followed her, holding his letters stiffly in front of him. One was for Oliver de Barton, the castle's constable, and had something to do with quarters for the sergeant and his men and an exchange of guards, but the content of the other letter to the receiver he did not know.

They walked through a roomful of scribbling clerks who stared at Katherine and made loud smacking noises behind their hands, and across to a door guarded by a page. While the page opened the door to announce them, Katherine heard an angry shouting voice within. "I'll not pay the Coleby rent because I haven't got it yet, and be damned to you! You know bloody well I've not been able to collect from the villeins since the crop failures."

"I know very well, Sir Hugh," interrupted a dry rasping voice, "that your Coleby manor is grossly mismanaged, but 'tis no concern of mine. Mine is to procure your feudal dues to the Duchy of Lancaster, which I shall do—we have several methods—" He turned irritably in his chair. "Well, what is it, what is it?" he said to the page and peered at Katherine and the sergeant in the doorway.

"Hugh," she said, running to him and putting her hand on his arm. She saw startled gladness soften his angry eyes. He made as though to kiss her, then drew back and said awkwardly, "How come you *here*, Katherine?"

"And *who* are you that comes here?" Stafford had a small toadface, with low sloping forehead and unwinking eyes, which regarded Katherine disagreeably.

She said, with her most charming smile, "I'm Lady Swynford, sir. I—I cannot think that you'll be too hard on us, for sure a little more time and Sir Hugh will find—"

"No more time at all," said Stafford, banging his small ink-grimed hand on the table. "Nor does it help your case, Sir Hugh, to drag in a wheedling woman. Tomorrow noon I'll have the rents, that's final. I've been too slack already in my duty to His Grace of Lancaster."

At this, the sergeant, who had been listening open-mouthed, cast a look of embarrassed sympathy at the flushed and worried Katherine, and by way of creating a diversion said, "Here, sir, here's a letter to you from His Grace, sent from the Savoy, sir. I've just come from there as escort to my Lady Swynford, sir."

Stafford took the parchment and examined the seal. Many such documents came to him from the chancery and he started to put it aside and dismiss the Swynfords, when he noticed the small privy seal next the large one and frowned. This he had seen but twice before, and it meant that the letter was sent directly from the Duke and sealed with his own signet ring. At the same time, he captured the echo of the sergeant's words, "escort of my Lady Swynford—from the Savoy—" He glanced up quickly at the tall girl in the black hood, at the truculent knight, whom he thoroughly disliked. A poor tenant, and a poor knight also, since it was well known the Duke had not called him back into service.

Stafford broke the seals and cords on the parchment, read it slowly while a deep mauve tint traveled up his flabby cheeks. He cleared his throat and read it again before saying to Katherine, "Do you know the purport of this order?" She shook her head and her heart beat fast. It was plain that Stafford did not believe her, but he turned to Hugh and said in the tone of one gritting teeth over a hateful duty, "My Lord Duke sees fit to rescue you from your embarrassment, it seems."

He glanced down at the parchment and read the official French aloud in a clipped tight accent. "We, John, Son of the King, Duke of Lancaster, etc., make known that from our especial grace and for the good and loving service which Lady Katherine Swynford, wife of Sir Hugh Swynford, has rendered to our late dearly beloved Duchess, whom God assoil, we do give and grant to the said Lady Swynford until further notice, all issues and profits from our towns of Waddington and Wellingore in the County of Lincoln to be paid at once upon receipt of this letter and thereafter in equal portions at Michaelmas and Easter. In witness, etc., given, etc., at the Savoy this twenty-seventh day of November, in the forty-second year of King Edward's reign."

Stafford looked up. The woman seemed astounded, and also as though she were going to weep. The knight looked puzzled and uneasy, obviously straining to understand the unfamiliar French legal words. "What does it mean?" he muttered, biting his lips.

"It means," said Stafford shrugging, "that your wife's revenues from the Duke's towns which he has granted her will pay your rents at Coleby *and* Kettlethorpe, I should judge, with plenty to spare. That's what it means."

"Huzzah!" cried the sergeant from near the door and met Stafford's glare imperturbably.

Hugh glanced at Katherine and then at the paved floor. "It is most generous of the Duke," he said.

"There's a postscript," said Stafford, tapping the parchment with an irritable finger, "which provides that whenever Sir Hugh Swynford shall be absent from home on knight's service one of the Duke's own stewards shall be appointed to ride to Coleby and Kettlethorpe to render assistance and manor supervision to Lady Swynford, the costs to be met by this office."

Ah, I have been well repaid—thought Katherine, with a bitter pang. The great powerful hand had been bountifully and negligently extended to rescue them. We're only little people, she thought, like the serfs, and what are we but serfs too? She glanced at the grim toad of a receiver. Had chivalry and justice not outweighed the anger that the Duke had felt for her when they parted—there would have been distraint, and punishment. Swynfords would have lost their horses, stock, all chattels—possibly imprisonment too, and the Duke would never have heard of it. But now they were safe.

"Tomorrow at noon," said Stafford, rising, "you will receive the moneys due you from this grant and will then pay your Coleby rent with interest. I give you good day, sir and lady."

The Swynfords walked out through the roomful of clerks and scarcely heeded when the sergeant congratulated them and took his leave to report to the constable. There was no one in the stone passage outside and before going into the court where Philippa and the others waited, Hugh suddenly stopped and looked at Katherine. His hand clenched on his sword hilt, his square face whitened, "For *what* of your services, my lady, has His Grace of Lancaster seen fit to bestow such reward?" He said, his voice croaking like a rook's.

Her gray eyes met his steadily and with pity, for now she knew what unanswered love was—and jealousy. "For none but what the grant said, Hugh, that I served the Duchess Blanche." She pulled her beads out from her purse and kissed the crucifix. "I swear it by the sweet body of Jesus and by my father's and mother's souls."

His gaze fell first and he sighed. "I cannot doubt you." He leaned towards her. She showed none of her inward shiver as he kissed her hungrily on the lips, but she felt sick fear. Was he then cured of the impotence that had afflicted him? Holy Blessed Mother, she thought, I could not endure it. But she knew she must endure it, if it were so. To escape from his rough grasp she made a business of putting her rosary back in her purse and saw the Duke's letter. "Here," she said quickly, "this is for you, from the Duke. I had forgot in all that trouble in there. Shall I read it to you?"

He nodded flushing. She broke the seal and scanned the letter. "It's an official order for you to report for knight's duty in Aquitaine. You're to join the company under Sir Robert Knolles, until the—until the Duke arrives himself—ah, that gladdens you!" she cried, for his face had brightened as she had not seen it in years.

"Ay, for I've been ill content to sit at home while others fight, you know that, and I've worried much that the Duke did not want me, it seemed a slight, a punishment, for what I know not. Yet I've but a slow mind and can't follow his."

Nor can I, thought Katherine. I don't know what he really feels towards me or Hugh.

" 'Tis not that I wish to leave you, my Katherine, but see he has relieved my mind by providing proper stewardship for you—not, thank God, one quartered at Kettlethorpe like that foul Nirac was after you bore Blanchette. Ay, 'tis of his god-child that he thinks no doubt in these grants to you, his god-child named for his poor lady. 'Tis of that he thinks."

"For sure it is, Hugh," she said gently. I shall never dwell on the Avalon Chamber again, she thought—it's finished. All debts are paid, all has been decently resolved. It shall be as though it never happened.

"Come, my husband," she said smiling. "We have much good news to tell Philippa." They walked arm in arm from the passage into the sunlit court.

# PART THREE

## (1371)

"... O Love, to whom I have and shall
Be humble subject, true in mine intent,
As I best can, to you Lord give I all,
For evermore, my heart's lust to rend."

TROILUS AND CRISEYDE

# XIII

IN THE DUSK of St. John's Day, June 24, 1371, three
portly middle-aged men enjoyed the freshening air in the
cloisters of the Abbey of St. Andrew at Bordeaux, which
was now the Duke's royal palace. Two of the men were great
lords of Guienne: one, Jean de Grailly, the powerful Captal
de Buch, and the other, Sir Guichard d'Angle, who owned
vast tracts in Saintonge and Angoulême. They were both tirelessly loyal to their English overlord and had resisted the
blandishments of the French king, though many of their fellow nobles had not. The third man was the big English
baron, Michael de la Pole, whose taste for action had been
well gratified since he chafed and cooled his heels while
awaiting the Duke of Lancaster nineteen months ago in the
Savoy.

The three gentlemen, dressed in brocaded satins, sat on a
marble bench, drinking the chilled delicate wine that came
from a near-by Médoc village. It was poured for them by a
hovering page. The day had been very warm but now a faint
breeze stirred the roses and jasmine and rippled the little fish-
pond in the cloister garth.

"Fine stirring deeds of arms today at the jousting!" said de
la Pole enthusiastically. "Our Duke covered himself with
glory against the Sieur de Puissances, *unhorsed* him, pardieu!" The baron spoke in dogged Yorkshire French because
it was more fluent than the Guienne lords' English.

"Aha," said the captal, belching pleasurably and rolling his
tongue around a sip of wine, "he's almost the knight his
brother is."

"Better, far *better!*" cried de la Pole instantly annoyed.
This was an old argument. The captal and Sir Guichard had
been the Prince of Wales' men and though they had obe-

diently transferred homage to Lancaster last January when the Duke took over Aquitaine from the sick and shattered Prince, de la Pole felt that they consistently underrated him.

"Sainte Vierge!" said the captal obstinately. "Lancaster can't hold a candle to his father! Or his brother Edward, the Perfect Gentle Knight."

"Perfect Gentle Knight be damned!" cried the baron, glaring "Look at Limoges! Was that the action of a perfect knight? Women, children massacred without mercy while the Prince lay gloating on his litter—blood, screams, tortures—the whole town slaughtered, except the few our Duke saved. What sort of knight is that?"

Sir Guichard d'Angle interposed, sighing, "Some demon seized upon the Prince, his illness is destroying him."

"And his line—" said the baron solemnly. The three men were silent, each thinking of the death of little Edward, the Prince's oldest son, here last winter. After the aged King and ailing Prince of Wales, the heir now to the English throne was Richard, a child of four so fair and frail that he seemed made from gossamer.

"Lancaster is dangerously ambitious!" said the captal, following the natural train of thought. "I feel in him a ceaseless urge to rule, a lust for power greater even than the power he has—fires barely held in check—"

"Yet they *are* held in check," cut in de la Pole. "I know him far better than you do. On his loyalty to his brother, ay and his nephew, little Richard, I'd stake my life and soul." He lowered his voice and, motioning the page to stand farther off, whispered behind his hand, "I believe 'tis not the *English* throne he covets."

"Ha-ha-ha!" Sir Guichard exploded into laughter half malicious, half indulgent. "Parbleu, mon baron, do you think you tell us news! It was I planted it in his head, though the idea found fertile ground. He has thought much about Castile."

"Has he then made formal suit to the Infanta?" said de la Pole, discomfited and a trifle hurt that the Duke had withheld his confidence.

"Nenni—I think not yet. Something seems to hold him back. A moody man and broods much, unless he's fighting."

"He needs a woman," said the captal shrugging his massive shoulders. He upended his gilt cup to let the last of the wine trickle down his throat. "Unhealthful to live like an anchorite, it must be months since that Norman whore went to his bedchamber at Cognac."

"And came out again so soon, one wonders there was time for sport," said Sir Guichard chuckling. "But soon he'll have a woman in his bed. The exiled and penniless Costanza'll not keep him waiting, once he asks her. 'Tis the best marriage she could ever hope for. All very well to be rightful Queen of Castile, but reigning is another matter when the throne's already filled. Our Duke will have hard task to get himself upon it."

"I think this marriage might be ill judged," said the captal shaking his head. "It will throw the weight of Castile definitely to France. Do you think the bastard King will do nothing to save his throne, when he hears the Duke's plans? We've trouble enough holding Aquitaine as it is—He'll simply embroil England in yet another war." He rose and hitched his gilt-bossed girdle below his vast belly. "But whatever we think, the Duke will do as he pleases. C'est un véritable Plantagénet."

On the second floor of the abbey John sat on a stool in the garderobe of his private apartments. He was naked, and Raulin was scrubbing off the sweat and grime from the tournament with a handful of lint dipped in hot rose water. Nirac de Bayonne hovered near with a razor and basin, waiting to shave his master. By the door to the anteroom, Hankyn, the Duke's chief minstrel, softly plucked a gittern while he sang a plaintive love tune from Provence.

John was tired, and he had twisted a muscle in his shoulder while steadying the heavy lance that had prized the Sieur de Puissances from his saddle. Nor had the shoulder quite recovered from the sword wound it had received at Limoges.

He beckoned to Nirac. The little Gascon sprang to the Duke and began to massage the lean hard muscles of the long back with knowing fingers. As he rubbed he whistled happily through his teeth, and his hands when they neared the red shoulder scar were gentle as a woman's. Raulin knelt on the sheet beneath the bath stool and began the methodical washing of the Duke's feet.

John shut his eyes and allowed his thoughts to drift. On this day his lieutenancy of Aquitaine was ended, he was no longer bound to sit upon the lid of the boiling caldron his brother had abandoned to him; no longer bound to fight his

brother's battles at his own costs as he had been doing for
months. Again, as always in this struggle with Charles the
Fifth, there was a stalemate. There had been victories, there
had been losses; the French king fought a war of niggling at-
trition that disgusted John.

But there was a bold and brilliant step awaiting. A glorious
chivalric deed blessed by God and rewarded by a prize so
dazzling that John's scalp tingled and his mouth grew dry
when he thought of it. Last night he had dreamed that he
knelt in the cathedral at Burgos—the gleaming white limestone cathedral where he had given thanks for Nájera and the
birth of his son—and in the dream, he had felt the touch of
the sacred oil as the archbishop anointed him and he had felt,
vivid as in waking, the holy pressure of  Castile's golden
crown.

"You smile, my lord!" said Nirac in delight, reaching for a
towel. "It is true, that always Nirac know 'ow to please his
lord!"

"I smile, you little monkey, not because you rub my back
but for a thought I had," said John with the indulgence he
always showed to Nirac and which annoyed Raulin, who did
not approve of levity, nor that this baseborn fellow should be
so much around the Duke. Raulin had enjoyed those months
in England when he alone had been close to his lord while
Nirac had been left behind in Picardy to convalesce from a
lung inflammation.

I shall send Guichard d'Angle to the Infanta tomorrow,
John thought, as he lifted his face that Nirac might shave
him, and he said, "Nirac, when you were in Bayonne last
month, you said you saw the Infanta Costanza at Mass? The
rightful Queen of Castile, that is."

"Si fait, mon duc, she was near to me as Hankyn there,"
Nirac pointed to the minstrel.

"How did she look?" said John as though absently.

"Shabby, 'er mantle was worn, 'er shoes—"

"Not her clothes, dunderhead! Her person!"

"Boney," said Nirac promptly, shaving the golden beard
with deft strokes, "breasts flat as plates, white skin, black
hair, long upper lip on a mout' not made for smiling, nor
parbleu for kissing. Castilian eyes—big, black, angry. She is
très dévote, they say she wears hair shirts so she'll not forget
'er father. I think she may be a little mad. Her young sister
Isabella is much prettier."

The Duke frowned and Nirac, seeing he had made a mistake, added quickly, "But the Infanta Costanza is vairy young, scarce seventeen, she'll improve sans doute, and I could not see clear, la cathédrale was dark."

There was a long silence in the garderobe except for the tinkling of the gittern. John allowed himself to be dressed by Raulin, lifting his arms into the white silk shirt, stepping into the short linen braies to which the long skintight yellow hose were fastened with points. The topaz velvet tunic was dagged into leaflike curls at hem and sleeves and buttoned with pearls. When he was ready dressed, the squire and valets stepped back expecting him to walk into the antechamber, where some of his gentlemen awaited to invest him with his ducal crown and regalia of Aquitaine. But he shook his head and breaking the long silence said to Raulin, "Leave me, all of you—except Nirac."

John walked to the open window and gazed out through the soft southern dusk across red tiled roofs to the curving Garonne. The river shone like pewter in the twilight, and two English ships with pennants fluttering above the crow's-nests were moving downstream, bound for home.

John watched the ships a moment and then he said, "Nirac!" The little Gascon was waiting, his bright lizard eyes on his master's face. "Do you remember the Lady Swynford of Kettlethorpe?" said John, turning slightly from the window.

"Sainte Vierge! 'Ow should I forget! Belle et gracieuse, la dame Cathérine." Nirac paused, then added, "I do not forget 'er knight—that *Swine*-ford, either."

John lowered his eyes and looked at Nirac as though he would rebuke his impudence. But instead he said slowly, "Knolles makes good report of Swynford, he's fought fiercely and been wounded twice."

"But 'e recovers, parbleu!" Nirac did not add What a pity! though his tone implied it, because he was puzzled by the Duke's mention of a lady he had thought forgotten long ago and mystified as to the tenor of these remarks; but yet he felt he need not hide his hatred of the Saxon knight who had so outrageously humiliated him at Kettlethorpe.

"Swynford arrived here at Bordeaux yesterday with the rest of Knolles' disbanded company," said the Duke. "He's bedridden from a leg wound. I sent him Brother William to bleed him and apply poultices."

The Duke's own physician for this swine of a knight, thought Nirac, more than ever mystified since he knew that the Duke had not seen Swynford in all these months in Aquitaine. The knight had been attached to Knolles' savage company up north where the fighting had been hardest, most vicious, most dangerous. As he thought this, a light flickered in Nirac's mind, but he was not sure. He glanced quickly at the Duke, but the blue eyes were veiled.

"I am going to ask for the Queen of Castile in marriage—all will be quickly arranged thereafter," said the Duke in the same remote voice. He raised his hand to quell Nirac's burst of excitement. "It is proper that my royal duchess be provided with English ladies here to attend on our marriage. I shall send off escort and messengers to summon them. You, Nirac, will return to Kettlethorpe and fetch my Lady Swynford."

"Ah-ha?" said the little Gascon, somewhat enlightened, but still uncertain; for Raulin, of course, had never mentioned the episodes with Lady Swynford at the Savoy, and Nirac knew that four years had passed since the Duke had been to Kettlethorpe. But his master's next words left no doubt. In an instant the austere control vanished from the sharp-etched handsome face, and John said passionately, as one who cannot help himself, "I must see her again before I marry."

So—thought Nirac—it is like that. But surely this desire was easily satisfied—and why then all the tohubohu about the husband? He saw from the softened look upon the Duke's face that he might venture a question, and he said, "Mon duc, then you will want to send Sir Hugh out of Bordeaux before she comes?" Send him far north again to fight, he thought, as dangerously as possible.

John's lips tightened, then he gave a half-angry laugh. "I fear she wouldn't come unless it were to join her husband."

"Merde! You mean she's *virtuous?*" cried Nirac, astounded, and seeing assent in the Duke's silence, understood at last that he had quite misread the situation when he had been at Kettlethorpe. "Oc," he added thoughtfully, "she 'as spirit and strength, cette belle petite dame—I saw it when I was there."

John having once broken through the barrier he had erected against Katherine, now felt great desire to go on talking of her, and to question Nirac for any memories of her during those months the Gascon had spent at Kettlethorpe.

Yet he resisted it. He was ashamed of his longing, ashamed that he had not forgotten her as he had willed himself to do and that the calculated slaking of his lust with two court ladies and the Norman whore had left him disgusted and uncured.

It angered him to suspect that she would disobey his summons—though rightly so, no doubt, considering what had passed between them—if he tried to bring her here solely under guise of serving his new Duchess. Swynford's authority must be invoked as well. By humiliating subterfuge, Hugh must be made to summon Katherine himself, his wound would serve as excuse. But there'd be no trouble managing Hugh, thought John, he'd be pleased enough at the honor done his wife in the appointment to lady in waiting and pleased enough to see her too, God rot him.

And when Katherine came—what then?

John turned and slammed the shutter on the window so hard that Nirac, who had been watching him anxiously, jumped.

Well, when Katherine came and he saw her again, he would be cured. No woman on earth had the beauty and the appeal he had gradually endowed her with since she ran from him in the Avalon Chamber. Doubtless by now she had grown fat or scrawny, her peasant blood would tell as she grew older, the earthy vitality which had first offended him at Windsor would do so again, as crudeness always had offended him. He would see the blemishes—her rough chilblained hands, the black mole on her cheekbone, the breathless headlong way she sometimes talked, even the sudden quiet dignity that came to her in stress could be seen as a ridiculous pretension—in short, he would be cured.

"I'll give you complete instructions tomorrow," he said to Nirac and walked out of the garderobe to the chamber where his fidgeting retinue was waiting.

On the tenth of August the *Grâce à Dieu,* four days out of Plymouth, ran into heavy seas past Finistère in Brittany, and the tricksy Biscayan winds hurled themselves at the little ship and threatened to blow her back to England. The master had been through worse weather on his many voyages between the home ports and Bordeaux, and after a few hearty curses he ordered the sail lowered and the sea anchor put out. He checked on the steersmen at the rudder, then retired to the castled poop with a keg of strong ale, prepared to ride out the storm until the Blessed Virgin should send them a north or westerly wind to blow them again in the right direction.

Though it might well be that St. James would take as much interest as the Blessed Mother in this voyage, since besides the party bound for Bordeaux at the Duke of Lancaster's orders, there were ten pilgrims for the holy shrine of St. James Compostela in Spain. These pilgrims had been stuffed in the hold with the freight and were constantly and abominably seasick, but their fares represented extra profit on the voyage and the Duke's receiver at Bordeaux would be pleased.

In the wainscoted, tapestried cabin below the castled poop, the women were seasick too. The Princess Isabel de Coucy lay in the largest bunk and groaned, occasionally raising a saffron face to vomit into a silver basin held for her by one of her sniffling, retching women. Lady Scrope and Lady Roos of Hamlake lay together in another bunk and each time the *Grâce à Dieu* wallowed and slid over a wave, Lady Scrope clutched her companion and whispered wildly, "Blessed Jesus, save us, we shall all be drowned!" Lady Scrope was Lord de la Pole's sister, but she was a timorous little wisp of a woman, quite unlike her brother.

For Katherine there was no bunk at all, she and a squire's lady were assigned two pallets on the broad-beamed floor. Katherine was a little frightened by the storm, though it exhilarated her too, and she longed to be out on deck away from the stench of vomit and other odors resultant upon the day and night confinement of eight women in so small a room, but the captain had barred the door so that his valuable passengers might come to no harm by running about the heaving deck or tumbling overboard.

There being no help for it, Katherine lay as quietly as possible on her pallet. Her head was turned away from the unpleasant sights and sounds behind her and she braced herself as best she might against the ship's rolling pitch. She had not been seasick in these days since leaving Plymouth, and she was not so now. This small superiority over the Princess Isabel gave her satisfaction. The Princess had been unremittingly patronizing from the moment of their meeting at Plymouth Hoe, before they ascended the gangplank into the *Grâce à Dieu*.

The King's daughter had been a spoiled beauty in her

youth, famous for her caprices and wanton extravagance. Now at forty she was no longer a beauty, though she considered herself one. She was fat and mustached and dark, for she took after her mother, Queen Philippa's people. Isabel's hair, though sedulously dyed with walnut juice and vinegar, had turned a streaky grizzled brown. And her cheeks, though rouged with cochineal, were mottled with liver spots. Katherine's pity might well have been aroused had the Princess's manner been pleasanter, for it was known to all on the ship that Isabel had seized avidly upon this opportunity to cross the sea so that she might try once again to find her runaway husband, the Lord Enguerrand of Coucy, who was many years her junior.

Isabel had twice before this tried to find him, in Flanders, and in Holland; but her elusive lord had always fled before she came. Now it was rumored that he lived in Florence, and Isabel, in talking to Lady Roos in the cabin, was frank enough about her intentions. "Since I'm suffering this frightful voyage to please my brother of Lancaster and attend his wedding, I shall demand that he give me escort and safe conduct on my way to Italy later." Though she spoke to Lady Roos, no one in the cabin could ever escape that loud penetrating voice, except now—thought Katherine gratefully—when it was diminished into groans.

The storm grew worse, and the noises. Between the poundings and crackings of the ship, and the shouts of the sailors, she could sometimes hear the curses and prayers of the pilgrims from below decks. Nirac was down there too, packed in with the other messengers and the Princess's squires and men-at-arms. The *Grâce à Dieu* was in battle trim with cannon mounted in the castles, for not only was there constant danger from pirates and French galleys, but the Flemings had suddenly taken to attacking English ships in the Channel.

An enormous wave hit the ship, which mounted, shivered and plunged with a shock that knocked Katherine against the bulwark. Lady Scrope screamed again, crying on St. Christopher, St. Botolph and the Blessed Virgin to save them, for the ship would surely sink.

Katherine thought it quite probable. She clutched her beads tight against her breast and tried to stem growing panic with Aves and Paternosters, while her thoughts beneath ran in confused images of home, especially of the day Nirac came with the puzzling letter from Hugh, dictated to a scrivener

and summoning her to Bordeaux, "at the Duke's command."
Her first feeling had been of anguished shock at the news of
the Duke's intended marriage. The violence of this feeling
had distressed her deeply, for gradually throughout the placid
days at Kettlethorpe, alone with her babies and Philippa, she
had almost trained herself not to think of the Duke except as
her feudal overlord where bounty had much eased their life.
The day after receipt of Hugh's letter she had reasoned herself from that first anguish into resignation and relief. For
now that the Duke was marrying the Queen of Castile, there
could be nothing more between them, ever, and she need not
fear that seeing him again might upset her hard-won equilib-
rium. Her second thoughts were of conscience-stricken concern for Hugh. Nirac was extremely uncommunicative about
the extent of Hugh's wounds or indeed on any matter per-
taining to Bordeaux, so that she knew little beyond the
sparsely worded letter.

But there was no question of her refusing to go. Philippa
settled that at once. Dual command from husband and Duke
must be obeyed. Philippa had her own baby now, also a little
Tom, and had been at Kettlethorpe so long that she felt she
owned it. Chaucer, still coming and going on official business,
was glad enough to leave her there.

So Katherine had set forth on her journey with Nirac,
stopping two days in London with Hawise, whose Jack had
returned from France and claimed her. The affection between
the two women was even stronger than it had been before the
moments Hawise had spent at Kettlethorpe, and Hawise had
shed many hearty tears at parting from Katherine. "Ay, my
sweeting, God shield ye on this voyage—I'll keep a candle
burning to Saint Catherine for ye, night and day—I had a
dream last night—nay, I'll not say it—would I could come wi'
ye, my dear lady."

But here Jack Maudelyn had frowned very black and said
his wife had had enough of strampaging about and must
abide in London at her own hearthfire, and he muttered
something more beneath his breath about the scurvy whims
of lords and ladies. Jack was not the merry hobbledehoy he'd
been five years ago on May Day. His years in the army had
changed him, he had become rough-tongued and brutal, a
malcontent, disinclined for steady work. Though he was a
master weaver now, he had scant interest in his loom, but
much in his guild privileges and he spoke often of the City's

rights, making angry allusion to "royal rogues and tyrants" who must be taught better if they dared to infringe on these rights.

Full of spite Jack was. Katherine had felt deeply sorry for Hawise and saddened that Jack should be jealous of the affection between them too.

Again the little ship quivered and plunged. The wind blew harder. The master abandoned his keg of ale and lost his fortitude, when he glimpsed through the driving rain squalls a dark mass of rock and tiny specks of moving light around its base. If that were the Isle of d'Ouessant and they were blown upon its shores, the bloodthirsty wreckers waiting on the beach would dispatch whatever souls the waves spared. And even if they escaped the island, the *Grâce à Dieu* could not long survive this pounding. Her seams were parting, and the naked sweating men in the hold had shouted that the pump no longer kept down the rising water.

The master crossed himself and touched the wooden image of the Virgin that was carved on the mast, then lurching and floundering through green water on the deck amidships, he unbarred the cabin door and stumbled in on a great blast of howling wind and rain. The women raised their heads, staring at him in terror, while the candles in the swaying horn lamps guttered, then flared up.

The master's bearded cheeks were pale as the women's as he said, "Noble ladies, we're in great danger. I doubt we'll outride this storm wi'out a miracle. Ye must pray and make vows."

Lady Scrope screamed and wrung her hands. "Which saint?" she cried, "which saint will help?"

The master shook his head. "I know not. We mariners pray to the Blessed Virgin of the Sea—in the hold they pray to Saint James—mayhap your own patrons will intercede for you. But without a miracle we're doomed."

The women stared at him yet another moment, then the Princess Isabel pulled herself to her knees on her bunk crying wildly, "I vow my ruby girdle and my gold hanap to you, Saint Thomas à Becket, if you will save me, and I vow to Saint Peter that I'll make pilgrimage to Rome as well."

From the others came a babble of frightened voices and a medley of vows.

Katherine knelt with the rest, bracing herself between the thwart and a bolted-down chest. Through her mind like a shout ran passionate words: Don't let me die, yet, don't let me die, for I have never really lived! Quick as light she felt a fearing shame that she could have so wicked and untrue a thought at this moment when her soul was in peril, and she clasped her hands, crying silently, Sweet Saint Catherine, save me! But her thoughts would not compress themselves into the vow. Candles yes, and money, yes—but she felt that Saint Catherine would not save her just for these. For what, then? Suddenly in this moment of danger she saw into a dark corner of her heart she had kept hidden, and she made her vow.

The miracle was wrought, by which saint or all of them together there was no means of knowing, though the master gave credit to the Blessed Queen of the Sea. At any rate, just as dawn broke over the bleakly distant shore of Brittany, one of the mariners had seen a strange light in the sky and a pinkish cloud beneath it shaped like a lily. This was a sign that their prayers were heard, for the wind died at once and they had drifted to the lee of the baleful little Isle d'Ouessant, where the water was calmer, and yet the outgoing tide kept them off shore while they calked their leaks and pumped the hold dry. On shore the frustrated wreckers danced and shook their fists at the ship, but they dared not try to board because of the cannon mounted on the decks and the archers who ranged themselves along the rail.

By noon a gentle wind had sprung up from the north, the *Grâce à Dieu's* great painted sail filled, and the ship resumed her course for Bordeaux.

Four days later, on the vigil of our Lady's Assumption, the *Grâce à Dieu* sailed up the broad Girone with the afternoon tide and veered south into the narrower Garonne while the village church bells along the banks rang for the beginning of the festival. It seemed excessively hot to the Englishwomen, who were seated on deck beneath a striped canopy. They had never seen a sun so white and glaring, nor river water so turbidly yellow, and even Princess Isabel's insistent voice was stilled. She sat in a cushioned chair while one of her perspiring women waved an improvised fan made from parchment. The Ladies Scrope and Roos crowded as close as possible so that their florid cheeks might also cool in the tiny breeze.

In anticipation of the landing at Bordeaux, all the ladies had dressed in their best; which entailed furs and velvets far too warm for the climate. Katherine's best was of dark Lincoln green with a sideless apricot surcote trimmed with fox.

The cauls which confined her hair on either side her face were woven of gold thread, which deepened the tone of her glossy bronze hair as they accented the golden flecks in her gray eyes. She knew that no colors suited her quite so well as the richness of dark green and gold, and she was happy in the possession of becoming clothes, but she had as always little consciousness of the challenging quality of her beauty.

Now at twenty the last angles of extreme youth had softened into rounded bloom, and she moved with languorous grace. Her beauty had an exotic flavor far more vivid than when Geoffrey Chaucer had first sensed it at Windsor. It was this flavor that caused Princess Isabel's angry whisper to Lady Roos, as she watched Katherine, who stood by the rail leaning her chin on her hand and gazing out at the strange white plaster houses, gilt crosses and red roofs of this new land.

"That woman's no true-born child of that herald de Roet! She's some bastard he got on a Venetian strumpet—or mayhap Saracen. Look how she holds her hips!"

"To be sure," said Lady Roos, striving to please, "and her teeth are most un-English—so small and white."

"Mouse teeth!" said the Princess angrily pulling her lip down over her own teeth, of which several were missing. " 'Tis not that I mean! But her effrontery—I shall tell my brother of Lancaster that I find her most unsuitable choice for a waiting woman—though in fact I believe she's invented that tale as excuse to worm her way over here, that and the pretty story of a wounded husband! I've seen a great deal of the world, and I can scent a designing woman quick as smell a dead rat in a wall, I can always—" The Princess's suspicions were cut short by a rushing of mariners and archers to the starboard rail amidships and a chorus of halloos while the watch in the crow's-nest dipped the Lancaster pennant and raised it again on the mast.

The Princess heaved herself up from her chair and went to the rail. "Why 'tis John—come to meet me!" she said complacently, peering down at the approaching eight-oared galley. Her younger brother was standing in the prow, his tawny head brilliant and unmistakable in the sunlight.

Katherine had discovered this fact some minutes earlier when the galley first glided in sight down the river, and the sudden violent constriction in her chest stopped her breath. Her first instinct was flight—down to the cabin. She controlled herself and remained where she was. Sooner or later this moment must be met, and she armored herself with the certainty of his indifference to her.

The galley drew alongside and the Duke ascended the ladder, followed by the Lords de la Pole and Roos. The Duke jumped lightly onto the deck and smiled at the assembled mariners and archers. Katherine, watching from above, saw Nirac dart out from the crowd of men and, kneeling, kiss his master's hand. The Duke said something she could not hear but Nirac nodded and drew back with the others. Then the Duke came up the steps to the poop deck and walking to his seated sister, kissed her briefly on both cheeks, while the other ladies curtsied. There was a further flurry of greeting when the other gentlemen clambered up. De la Pole greeted his sister, Lady Scrope, and Lord Roos his wife, while Katherine still stood rooted in the angle of the rail.

The Duke turned slowly, negligently, as though without intent until he saw Katherine. Across the heads of the fluttering, chattering ladies their eyes met in a long unsmiling look. She felt him willing her to come to him, and her lids dropped, but she did not move. After a moment he covered the space between them, and she curtsied again without speaking.

"I trust the voyage was not too disagreeable a one, my Lady Swynford," he said coolly, but as she rose her eyes were on a level with his sunburned throat and there she saw a pulse beating with frantic speed.

"Not too disagreeable, Your Grace," she said and rejoiced at the calm politeness of her tone. She felt the slight hush behind them and saw the Princess's watchful stare; lifting her voice a trifle she added, "How does my husband? Have you heard, my lord?"

"Better, I believe," John answered after a moment, "though still confined to his lodgings."

Katherine again meeting his gaze saw the color deepen beneath the tan of his cheeks. "I'm longing to see Hugh and care for him," she said. "May Nirac guide me to Hugh's lodging directly we disembark?"

A strange almost bewildered look tightened the muscles around his eyes, but before he answered a strident voice, called imperiously, "John, come here! I've much to tell you —you've not heard yet the peril we were in on this wretched ship—the King's Grace, our father, has sent special message

—and how long are we to be kept sweltering here in this infernal heat?"

"Ay, Nirac shall guide you, Lady Swynford," he said, then turning to his sister laughed sharply. "'Your commands, my sweet Isabel, plunge me back into the happy days of my childhood. In truth, you've changed but little, fair sister."

"So I'm told," said the lady nodding. "Lord Percy said but t'other day, I looked as young as twen—, as several years ago. By Saint Thomas, what's that caterwauling?" She broke off to glare indignantly around the deck. A medley of voices had arisen from all parts of the ship. A confusion of sound at first, until led by the high clear tenor of the watch, it resolved itself into a solemn melody, a poignant chant carried by some forty male voices.

"It is the hymn of praise to the Virgin of the Sea," said John. "'Tis sung on every ship of all nations when port is safely reached—for see, here is Bordeaux." He pointed to the white-walled town curving around its great crescent of river, and dominated by the high gilt spires of the cathedral.

"Here is Bordeaux" echoed Katherine's thought, and the words blended with the great swelling chorus of the Latin hymn the men sang: "Thanks to Thee, Blessed Virgin, for protection from danger, thanks to thy all abiding mercy which has saved us from the sea—" She shivered in the violent sunlight, staring at the garish savage colors on the riverbank: the white and scarlet houses, the purple shadows, the brilliant yellows, crimsons, greens of vegetation shimmering in heat beneath a turquoise sky, and she thought with foreboding of how far away was the cool misty northland, and all safe accustomed things. She fastened her attention on the city in front of her so that she might not turn again to look at him who stood behind her on the deck.

# XIV

HUGH'S LODGINGS were two rooms over a wineshop in an alley behind the cathedral. Nirac duly guided Katherine through the town from the pier, while a small donkey laden with her two traveling chests ambled with them. She had managed to avoid the Duke entirely, even taking it upon herself to tell Nirac of the Duke's permission and order Nirac to accompany her.

This order Nirac received with an enigmatic shrug and smile, "Comme vous voulez, ma belle dame," and she thought that the faithful, amusing little Gascon whom she had known so well in England had somehow changed here in his native land. She chided herself for thinking him suddenly sinister and secret, like the twilit town that turned blank walls to the street and hid its true life from passers-by.

It was not until they mounted the littered stone stairs above the wineship that Katherine thought of the angry treatment Hugh had shown to Nirac long ago at Kettlethorpe and wondered if the Gascon still resented it, but then she thought that if he did it would not matter; stronger than any other thing in life for Nirac was his adoration of the Duke, and that feeling would check all others.

"Are you sure this is it?" she asked dubiously as they stood on a cramped landing and she knocked at a rough plank door. There was no sound from within.

"La cabaretière said so, madame," answered Nirac who had inquired from the shopkeeper.

Katherine knocked again, then pushed open the sagging door, calling, "Hugh."

He lay on a rough narrow bed and had been dozing. The single shutter was closed against the heat, and in the dim light he blinked at his wife, who lit the doorway like a flame. Then he struggled to his elbow and said, uncertainly, "Is it really you, Katherine? But it's early—Ellis left to fetch you but a short time ago—we heard the ship was sighted in the river. Who's that behind you, is it Ellis?"

"No, Hugh," she said gently, going to the bed and taking his hand, "it's Nirac, the Duke's messenger. I hurried straight to you and have missed Ellis."

His hand clung to hers, it was hot and dry. His unshaven face was haggard between the matted wisps of his crinkled hair, and in his voice she had heard the querulous note of ill health. On a stool by the head of the bed there was a pile of torn linen strips, a bleeding basin and a small clay cup. Flies buzzed in the stuffy sour room, the dingy hempen sheet on which Hugh lay was wadded into lumps. She bent over and kissed him quickly on the cheek. "Ah, my dear, 'tis well I've come to nurse you. The Duke said you were better, are you?" She glanced at the bandaged leg, which was propped on a straw pillow.

"For sure 'e's better!" cried Nirac heartily, coming forward to the bed and bowing. " 'Is Grace's own leech 'as cared for 'im, an' now 'e 'as the best medicine in the world!" He smiled at Katherine, his bright black eyes were merry and charming, and she wondered what had made them seem sinister before.

Hugh said, "Oh, it's you, you meaching cockscomb. I'd forgot all about you." His dull gaze wandered from the Gascon to Katherine. "Ay, I'm better, the wound's near done festering. I'd be up now save for the griping in my bowels, it weakens me."

"Alack!" she said, " 'tis the flux again? But 'twill pass—you've got over it before."

He nodded, "Ay." He made effort to pull himself from the self-centered lethargy of his illness, yet in truth her beauty daunted him; and though he had much wanted her to come, now he felt the old discouragement and humiliation which always sought relief in anger. "So you *are* here," he said crossly. "I trust you're not too fine a lady to fetch us up some supper and wine from the woman's kitchen down below. Or has the Duke's appointment turned your head?"

Nirac made a faint hissing sound through his teeth, but she did not hear it as she answered, "I'm here to care for you, Hugh. Come, don't speak to me like that," she said smiling. "Don't you long for news of home—of our children?"

"I leave now, madame," said Nirac softly, and he added in swift French, "I wish you joy of your reunion." He was gone before she could thank him for his long care of her on the journey.

Through the rest of the day Katherine tended her husband. She took off her fine green gown and put on a thin russet kersey which she wore for everyday at Kettlethorpe; in this she tidied and cleaned the two bare little rooms. She made Hugh's bed, washed him and rebound his leg, hiding her revulsion at the look of his wound, which was puffed high with proud flesh and oozing a trickle of yellow pus. But Hugh said it had much improved, and Ellis, when he returned from his fruitless errand to the ship, also agreed.

"You should've seen the gash fortnight ago, my lady," he said twisting up his honest stupid face, "the leg was blackening and there was red streaks up to the groin."

Hugh nodded gravely. "A mercy we didn't cut it off. 'Twas Brother William saved it with his poulticing and his drugs, God be thanked."

She shuddered, holding fast to her pity and the certainty that under his ungracious manner he had need of her.

Gradually Hugh grew gentler, as the first shock of strangeness wore away. They slipped back into the groove inevitably worn by their five years of marriage. After they had supped and were more at ease and glowing from the delicious Gascon wine, Ellis sat by the window with his back turned to them, tinkering with some buckle on his master's gear, and Katherine curled up on the bed chattering of the babies—how lovely little Blanchette had grown and that she could sing three songs—here Hugh smiled proudly, seeming more interested than at the news that Tom could talk plainly and sit a horse alone and was near as big as his sister.

In this strange city five hundred miles away, it was almost as though they were home at Kettlethorpe, except for the heat and the smell of garlic and jasmine, and the sound of far-off singing—a wild nasal chant, darkly disturbing as was the Basque land from whence it came.

Katherine told many items of home news, particularly that the new flocks on the demesne farm were flourishing and that the Lincoln merchants, the Suttons, had been helpful with advice. She also told Hugh about the birth of Philippa's baby, proudly adding that she had done most of the midwifery herself, with Parson's Molly to assist. "But Philippa had an easy time—the babe popped into the world like a greased pig from a poke," she laughed, "not like the struggle I had to birth Blanchette."

"Ay, but you're no more like your sister than Arab filly is to plough horse, my Katherine," said Hugh gruffly, not looking at her but fumbling for her hand. He pulled her down so that her bright face rested against his coarse wooly beard. She held herself tight so as not to draw back, and thought of the three violent and unhappy nights in which he had once more claimed her during their last brief time together at Kettlethorpe when she came home from the Savoy and before he left to join Sir Robert Knolles.

Hugh thought of those nights too, and cursed the physical debility that once more unmanned him, knowing that without the vigor of drunken haste, a paralyzing doubt would set in —and fear, and then he would hate her and the lovely body which he well knew he had never truly possessed.

"I thought I had got you with child, before I left," he said, releasing her suddenly.

She sat up with an imperceptible sigh of relief. "Nay," she said lightly, "it didn't happen, doubtless because 'twas the dark of the moon then. Hugh, tell me of the fighting you've been through, tell me how you got this," she touched the bandaged leg. "Here I prate on of silly humdrum things at Kettlethorpe while you've done many a dangerous deed of arms."

She led him on to talk of the one subject which he understood and where he felt himself always sure, and under her admiring questions he expanded, words came to him more easily, his scowl vanished, and when he started to describe a hand-to-hand encounter with a Poitevin knight, in which the latter had cravenly cried for mercy, he actually laughed.

It was thus that Brother William Appleton found them when he pushed the door open and padded in on his bare feet. *"Deo gratias!"* cried the Gray Friar, standing at the foot of the bed and surveying his patient with kindly surprise, "Here is betterment indeed! Truly a wife is God's gift. *Benedicite*, my Lady Swynford." He placed his hand on her head. "How was the voyage?" He dropped his sack of drugs and instruments on the floor and smiled at Katherine.

"We had a great storm and I was much afraid," she said, hastening to pour the friar a cup of wine, "but our Blessed Lady and the saints vouchsafed a miracle and we were saved. It was a most wondrous and humbling thing." Her voice trembled, and Brother William glanced at her keenly, thinking that though she seemed made for the pleasures of the flesh, there yet was a sense of spiritual striving about her, and a healthiness of mind and body which pleased him who spent so much of his time with the sick. "Ay, it *is* a humbling thing when Heaven's mercy shields us from danger," he nodded his long cadaverous head, "and we may be sure God sends us every chance for salvation—how do you find your husband?"

"Most grateful to you, Sir Friar, he says you saved his leg and maybe his life."

"Well, well—I've some skill but 'tis not all my doing. His stars were propitious." As he spoke the friar deftly unbound Hugh's leg, and scooping a green ointment from a little pot plastered the wound. " 'Tis made of pounded watercress," he explained to Katherine, who exclaimed at the color. "A balm the wild Basques use in their mountains, and ignorant as they are—barely Christians—they know much of simples. I've healed many a wound on the Duke's men-at-arms with this."

"How soon do you think I can get about, Brother?" asked Hugh through clenched teeth as the friar probed and pulled back the proud flesh.

"You can hobble a bit now, since it seems your dysentery's lessening—Did you take all the bowelbinder I left you?" He peered into the clay cup on the stool and shook his head. "Lady, you must see that he takes this each time before he eats. Camphorated poppy juice alone will heal the flux."

"I'll see that he takes it, Sir Friar," she said smiling, and held the cup for him to fill it with a black mixture.

"We must have you strong and able to attend on the Duke's wedding, Sir Hugh," said Brother William, fishing a rusty lancet from the bottom of his sack and motioning to Katherine to hold the basin for the daily bleeding.

Hugh thrust out his pallid gnarled arm and said with a hint of pride, "Katherine has been appointed brideswoman to the marriage."

"I know," said the friar with a faint chuckle, "you've told me many times." He had learned that and much more during the days of high fever that Hugh had suffered after he first came to Bordeaux, and in addition the friar had served as Hugh's confessor. So there was little he did not know about this man and his groping, clumsy brain, his grossnesses and sulky angers, his inability to adjust himself to others, his superstitious fears, and yet with all this, his bitter, humiliating, pathetic love for this beautiful woman.

Poor souls, thought the friar, applying styptic and a wad of lint to the bleeding arm cut. Yet, no doubt, they would rub along somehow, no worse off than many a man and wife, until finally all passions died, and age or philosophy would bring surcease.

"Have you seen the Infanta Costanza?" said Katherine very casually while pouring the blood from the little basin into a slop jar. "Is she fair?"

"They say not," answered the friar. "Remember, my Lord Duke desires her to be spoken of as the Queen of Castile— nay, I believe she is not fair."

He saw a strange little quiver pass over Katherine's mobile face, and having much observant knowledge of women, thought it came from gratified vanity and was amused, for from this foible she had seemed quite free; but he said nothing more. He gave them blessing and departed to visit another of the Duke's sick fighting men, his mind quite at ease about Hugh.

Katherine slept that night on a straw mattress on the floor beside Hugh's bed, and Ellis slept as usual on a pallet near the outer door. In the soft gray dawn, Katherine rose and dressed to go to early Mass before the great crowds would come later. She yearned for the blissful comfort of the act of communion, when the sweet body of Jesus should enter into her own body and strengthen her, and she hoped that in the cathedral she might find a shrine to St. Catherine too. She felt great need to kneel before her own particular saint and refresh the moment of transcendent gratitude she had felt on the ship.

Hugh grunted sleepily as she told him where she was going, and she saw that he had improved in the night, his fever flush was gone and he breathed quietly.

In her green and gold gown, to do honor to the festival, and a fine silk hooded mantle, Katherine slipped downstairs past the wine shop into the cobbled street. It was hotter than it would ever be in England, but she gave thanks for the morning freshness and hurried to the cathedral, which was but a block away.

Early as it was, many others were astir. In the little *place* by the cathedral a dozen donkeys backed and filled carts loaded with country produce to be sold at the stalls, while a band of strolling players hammered on the platform which would later hold the Mystery they would produce.

The great west doors of the cathedral were wide open, the organ tones vibrated through the still air, while a line of peasants and rustics filed into the church bearing herbs, roots and fruits for blessing at the Virgin's shrine. Two mutilated beggars lolled on the cathedral steps and waving ulcerous stumps of legs and arms whined at Katherine, "Ayez pitié, belle dame, l'aumône, pour l'amour de Dieu—" She opened her purse and cast them silver pennies, then into the extended hat of a faceless leper, she flung more of her silver, crossing herself as he mumbled "Grand merci" and shuffled away, shaking his warning clapper.

The hideous mutilations of the beggars and the leper had shaken her and before entering the cathedral she paused to collect herself. An ancient Bordelaise in high fluted cap and white apron was spreading baskets of flowers on the steps and Katherine walked over to her, at once assuaged by the lovely unfamiliar flowers—gaudy peonies, jasmine, fat red roses and huge lilies, all strangely shaped and more highly perfumed than any she had ever known.

As she leaned down to buy a bunch of jasmine, she noted vaguely that a tall pilgrim stood on the step a little way off, leaning on his staff. She finished her purchase; holding the jasmine against her cheek and sniffling delightedly, she turned again towards the cathedral. The pilgrim turned too and mounted the steps. He carried a scrip covered with cockle-shells, and he was muffled to the mouth in a sackcloth cloak, his large round hat was pulled down low on his forehead so that little of his face showed. Katherine, assuming that it was one of those who were en route for St. James Compostela, gave him an indifferent glance. She walked into the cathedral porch, pausing to peer ahead into the dark nave and locate the candle seller amongst all the booths and hurrying celebrants.

She felt an urgent hand on her arm and turned in astonishment to see that it was the pilgrim who had clutched her. He raised his head a little so that she might see his eyes and said, "Katrine! I must talk to you."

"Sweet Jesu! My lord!" she cried, so astounded that she dropped the jasmine sprays all over the worn stone paving.

"Hush!" he said sternly. "Come with me, I know a place we can talk."

She bent over and picked up her jasmine, slowly, fighting for time to collect herself and marshal her resistance.

"I command it," he said, then with a swift change of tone, "nay—I beg you, I beseech you—Katrine."

She bowed her head and began to walk, following him a few paces behind. They went down the steps, across the busy *place* and up a street to a little inn, Auberge des Moulins. He took a key from his scrip and unlocking a low door in the pink plaster wall, motioned her to enter. It was the small inn garden to which he had brought her. It was planted with a few flowers and many herbs and furnished with wine-stained trestle tables and benches.

"We'll not be disturbed here," he said, flinging off his hat and loosening the sackcloth cloak, "I've feed the aubergiste lavishly. My God, Katrine—" he added with a wry laugh, "look to what straits you've brought the ruler of Aquitaine— skulking in sackcloth, bribing frowsy scoundrels for a place of assignation—like a wenching sergeant—you should be proud of your enchantments!"

"What have you to say to me, my lord?" She leaned against the trestle table because her knees shook, but her gray eyes were fixed on him steadily and their gaze held warning, yet she thought that, in the coarse brown sackcloth, he had never seemed so handsome nor so princely.

"What have I to say to you?" He broke off, biting his lips. Since before Prime he had been waiting near the cathedral, knowing that she would come to Mass, and praying that she would be alone. Yet if that dolt of a squire, Ellis de Thoresby, had accompanied her, the meeting would still have been managed. Since the sight of her on the ship yesterday, she had obsessed him to a point beyond reason—almost beyond caution.

He turned on her suddenly, with violence. "I love you, Katrine. I want you, I desire you, but I love you. I feel that I cannot exist without you. That's what I have to say to you."

The garden walls melted. A rushing wind lifted and hurled Katherine into a void, a wind—no, a river of fire. An agonizing painful joy in the whirling and rushing of this river of fire—

He threw himself down on the bench and seized her cold

hands, looking up at her white face. "My dear love," he said softly, humbly, "can you not speak to me?"

"What can I say, my lord?" Her eyes fastened themselves on the blue flower of a borage plant near his foot, she stared at the little blue star while the fiery river throbbed and scorched in her breast.

"That you love me, Katrine—you told me so once."

"Ay," she said slowly, at last, "nothing has changed since then. Nothing. And I am still Hugh's wife—however much I —I love you."

He gave a sharp gasp and bending his head covered her hands with kisses. "Sweet heart!" he cried exultantly, and put his hands on her waist to pull her down to him. She stiffened and shook her head. "Nay, but there is one thing changed since we two were in the Avalon Chamber—then you mourned a wife but lately gone, and *now* you are betrothed to one who will soon be yours."

"There's no love in that, it has naught to do with us. You know that I must marry again, for England—for Castile."

"Yes," she said tonelessly, "I know."

"Katrine, Katrine—come to me then—you're in my blood, in my bones, and in my heart there is naught but you."

She raised her eyes and tears slid quietly down her cheeks. "I cannot be your leman, my lord. Even if for love of you I could so shamefully dishonor Hugh, yet I cannot, for I have made a sacred vow."

"A vow?" he repeated. His hands dropped from her waist. "What vow, Katrine?"

"On the ship," Katherine said, each word dragging forth with pain. "Saint Catherine saved my life, for that I made the vow—" She stopped and swallowed looking past him in the sunny wall. She went on in a whisper, "To be true wife, in thought, in deed, to my husband who is the father of my babies."

Outside the garden, the cathedral bells began again to clang for the commencement of another Mass, while nearer from the *place* a bust of horns and clarions heralded the beginning of the mystery play, and nearer yet inside the inn there was a shout of drunken laughter. At last John said gently, reasonably, "My foolish Katrine—and do you think the whole ship was saved because you made this vow?"

"I don't know," she answered in the same muted voice. "I only know that I made it and will keep it unto death."

Unto death. The words rang irrevocably in his ears, even while a hundred persuasions sped through his mind. Arguments that might move her, perhaps the contentions of John Wyclif, how that saints and miracles and vows were but ignorant superstitions invented by venal popes and hypocritical monks to gull the simple folk. But he loved her, so these things he could not say, for he did not quite believe them himself and there was a commandment in the Bible—one the Blessed Jesus too had affirmed—and he knew well that even John Wyclif would never condone adultery. And stronger far than the new logic of the Lollards were the teachings of his childhood. Grinning fiends, devils and their obscene tortures, damnation eternal awaited those who sinned. For himself he did not care, but her he could not endanger. He turned his head away and did not speak.

"Now you will hate me again!" she cried on a sobbing breath, she could no longer maintain the frozen stillness of her body; though she had renounced him, she could not bear that he should never look at her again with passion—and the new tenderness. "Dear my lord, my heart will break if you hate me, and last time too we parted in anger—"

He shook his head. "I love you, Katrine—and while you're near me, I feel that your wish is mine." He stopped, thinking that this had never been true of him before. There had been no such testing with Blanche, nor need for conscience. "Yet I know myself—" he cried with sudden violence, "I shall not stay so tame, so conquerable—" He took a quick step towards her, then halted. "Go, Katrine—go," he said, and hot tears sprang into his eyes.

She fled from the garden and through the *place* to the cathedral. The Mass had just begun; she pushed her way through the people to a confessional where she murmured so rapid and confused an account of temptation and contrition in her northern French that the inattentive priest made little of it and granted quick absolution. Then she ran up to the choir, as near the High Altar rail as she could get. She knelt on the tiles. She heard no word of the Mass, but when she received the Holy Wafer on her tongue a sad peace came to her and she thought that glimmering around the Crucifix she saw a glow of benignant light.

While Katherine was at Mass, John of Gaunt, the pilgrim in sackcloth, strode with bowed head through the streets of Bordeaux to the palace-abbey, oblivious of interested glances or occasional timid questions, "Godspeed, Sir Pilgrim, art bound for Compostela or for Canterbury? Or mayhap the Holy Land?"

The Bordelais were gay today, the women dressed in scarlet shawls, wore flowers and combs in their hair. There was dancing in the streets and festival music spangled the warm air. But John saw and heard nothing.

He entered the abbey, not surreptitiously by the side door as he had slipped out, but through the main gate, flinging his pilgrim hat in the face of the astounded gateward, as the man questioned him. "Forgive me, Your Grace—" babbled the gateward, when he recognized the Duke, "I had not known you—" John strode on and through the Grande Salle, where a dozen varlets were scurrying with gold silk napery, silver saltcellars, mazers, hanaps, spoons, laying the great tables for dinner.

The salle opened on to the cloister garth, where a group were seated under the cool arcades. A Moorish dwarf, scarce two feet high, amused them with tumbling tricks and sly songs piped in such a squeaky voice that the Princess Isabel was rolling with laughter. So convulsed were all the lords and ladies—when the dwarf, who had a chained popinjay and a monkey with him, announced that he would perform a marriage between the two little beasts and, placing them on a miniature bed, forced the monkey into the liveliest imitation of amorous commerce with the squawking popinjay—that nobody saw the Duke until he had passed through the cloister and was mounting the steps that led to his apartments. Then Isabel jumped and said, "Could that be Lancaster? What an extraordinary garb!"

"It was, madam," said Michael de la Pole. "Some private penance maybe."

"Nonsense! He's no more pious than that monkey there. It seems to me he's acting very strange, I thought so yesterday, and to go out now, when Edmund has arrived in his absence —not that one ever considers Edmund much, to be sure—"

The baron, who knew the insistence of the royal lady's discourse and was not interested in her opinions on the personality of her brothers, asked a hasty permission to withdraw, since he wished to speak to the Duke.

He found the Duke in his solar, being dressed by his squires, while that little Gascon, Nirac, hovered around and clucked over him like a hen. Edmund of Langley, the Earl of Cambridge, lay sprawling on the jeweled coverlet of the State Bed, eating figs and watching his brother with his usual expression of amiable vacuity. Edmund had come overland down from Calais with a large force of his men and arrived an hour ago.

"Greetings, baron," Edmund said to de la Pole, biting into another fat green fig. "God's blood, but it's hot here in the south, I always forget that when I'm in England."

De la Pole bowed, acknowledged the greeting, and said, "My lords, I hope I don't intrude? There are certain arrangements about the wedding, my Lord Duke, that need your immediate attention."

John turned his head, and the baron was startled at the suffering look in his eyes, a look of actual wanhope, or despair, thought the baron, who was not imaginative. Bad news then? But what? Unless Cambridge had brought it. A glance at Edmund dispelled that thought. The earl's sensibilities were none too keen, but he certainly was not the bearer of ill tidings. His jaws moved placidly like the sheep he somewhat resembled and his pale blue eyes expressed only a mild gustatory pleasure.

Edmund had spent most of his thirty years docilely obeying and admiring all three of his elder brothers, but particularly this one who was so near him in age, and of whom he was a paler smaller copy, as though fashioned from John's leftover tints which had been insufficiently and consequently diluted. Where John's hair was a vigorous ruddy gold, Edmund's was silvery flaxen and sparse; the unmistakable Plantagenet strength of long nose and chin and cheekbone had in Edmund blurred to softness.

"I'll attend to you, presently, baron," said the Duke in a singularly flat voice. "Edmund tells me that His Grace, our father, approves that the Queen of Castile's sister Isabella be given to him."

" 'Struth," said Edmund, swallowing his fig and licking his fingers. "High time I got me some wife, they say the little Infanta 'Bella is grown quite appetizing, fifteen years old and firm as a plum." He giggled happily. "She'll suit my sweet tooth."

"Your marriage to her will make doubly sure our claim to the throne of Castile," said John sternly.

His brother at once drew his face into earnest agreement. "To be sure, to be sure."

"A double wedding then, my lord?" asked de la Pole in some surprise, thinking of the little time that was left—only a month—before the Duke's nuptials, and of the multitudinous details which must be settled. There were still indentures and contracts to be signed, some of the exiled Castilian envoys from Bayonne were even now waiting below for audience with the Duke, nor had the final decision been made as to the locale for the ceremony.

"No double wedding," said John, holding his hands out over a silver basin that Nirac might pour rose water on them. "Edmund can marry the Infanta later—Gentlemen," he glanced at his brother, the squires, Nirac and finally the baron, "before I receive the Castilians, or consult with you, Michael, I wish food—and I've not yet communed. Raulin, where is Brother Walter?"

"He vaits in the chapel, Your Grace," said the Flemish squire, fastening the last buckle on the Duke's gold and sapphire girdle, before adjusting it low on the hips.

The Duke nodded and quitted his solar for the narrow passage that connected it with the private chapel.

Nirac slipped unobtrusively out of the room and followed his master, unheard and unseen. It was he who had procured the pilgrim clothes and he, alone, who knew where the Duke had gone this morning, and though in this last hour there had been no privacy, and thus no way to find out what had happened, Nirac had been more shocked than the baron at the expression of his master's eyes. He intended to find out once and all for all the Duke's true inward wishes. And he availed himself of a discovery long since made.

In the days of the monks the private chapel had adjoined their infirmary. A square peephole had been made in the wall to the right of the altar so that the bedridden monks might participate in the Mass. A painted hanging of the Day of Judgment now covered the peephole but through the cloth one could hear all that took place. Nirac flattened himself to the wall behind the arras on the infirmary side and listened.

As he had expected, the Duke was confessing to the Carmelite friar, Brother Walter Dysse, who traveled with him everywhere. At first the Duke's voice was low. Nirac could hear

little, though in the pauses the plump friar's soothing voice
lisped about "sins of the flesh—lustful thoughts—deplorable
but human, God could easily forgive—true repentance—"

"But I'm *not* repentant!" The Duke's voice rose suddenly
high and passionate. "I love the woman—she is my life—all
my bliss. I care naught what you say, Brother, nor fear
God in this—"

"Then, why do you confess to me, my lord," said the unctuous voice reasonably, "since you wish no ghostly counsel?
Yet I feel God is not wroth—come, I'll grant you absolution—"

"Ay, you're a man of the world, good friar, 'tis no doubt
for your comfortable nature I keep you for confessor." The
Duke's voice had a bitter mocking edge. "Were I to tell you I
had abducted, ravished this woman, had forced her to adultery, what would you say then?"

There was a pause, Nirac could hear the rustling of garments as though the friar had shifted on his seat, and he pictured how the plump, white hands would smooth each other,
and how Brother Walter's white mouth had pursed as he
heard the soft voice answer, "With a few penances—my lord
—and contrition, of course—"

"Ay—and if I told you I had murder in my heart—murder
for the stupid clod that stands in my way—what then? Still a
few penances, still absolution?"

There was a longer pause. Nirac straining at the hole,
clenched the edges of the wall with his little brown hands, for
the Duke went on harshly, "Nay, I cannot do it! You need
not wrack your conscience for a compromise. The husband is
my liege man and feal to me, and he is sickly—wounded—
hating him as I do, yet I've helped him heal of his wounds,
but my God, why does he not *die!*"

Nirac silently withdrew from behind the arras. Alone in
the disused infirmary, he laughed softly from pure joy. "O
Sainte Vierge, je te remercie de ta grande bonté!" he whispered and made a reverent sign of the cross.

In the midafternoon while the Duke dined in the Grande
Salle with the English, Aquitainian and Castilian nobles,
Nirac set forth for the alley behind the cathedral. The little
Moorish dwarf trotted beside him swinging the popinjay in
its cage, while the chained monkey scampered along the
ground.

Everywhere they passed, the people crowded around laughing at the monkey, poking and feeling of the dwarf and urging that he do tricks, but Nirac would not let his charges pause until they came in to the courtyard below the Swynford lodging. There, Nirac told the dwarf to wait, while he clambered up the stone steps to the first floor.

Katherine opened to Nirac's knock. Her pale strained face lightened when she saw him perky and grinning on the threshold.

"Morbleu, but 'tis dark and morne in 'ere!" cried Nirac bowing to Hugh who was up, sitting on a chair beside a table littered with the remnants of dinner, his injured leg propped on a stool. Ellis had gone out to buy them some small purchases at the fair. "One should be gay on this jour de fête," continued Nirac, noting Ellis' absence with satisfaction. "I've brought you something to amuse you, pour vous distraire."

"That was kind of you, Nirac," said Katherine smiling. "It's a bit dismal in here, but Hugh is so much better, I believe he'll soon be out."

"Ah, bon!" Nirac looked now neither at Hugh nor Katherine, his quick eyes ran around the rooms, resting on the flagon of wine, then on the clay cup of medicine by the bedside. "The good Brother William prescribes fine drugs for you, hein?" he said. "They make you well, Sir Knight?"

Hugh grunted quite amiably. He didn't like Nirac, but he realized how dull it must be for Katherine cooped up here, and if the little jackanapes amused her— Also he was free from pain in the leg or gripes in the belly for the first time in weeks. "To be sure, the Gray Friar knows his craft," he agreed, "and my lady sees that I take his swill." He glanced at the clay cup which contained the black camphorated poppy juice. Nirac nodded, then turning quickly said to Katherine, "But are you not curious to know what I 'ave brought you?"

"A new song?" she smiled, knowing Nirac's many gifts, "or maybe a comic figure you've carved?"

"Nenni—belle dame! Those would not make you laugh so much. Come to the window."

Their only window gave on to the courtyard and Katherine leaning out cried, "Oh what is it? A manikin? Is he real? And the green bird, and a little beast jumping on the ground—oh, Hugh, you never saw so droll a sight!"

"But 'e *may* see it, madame. See, we'll 'elp 'im to the window, 'e can sit there and watch."

Hugh was himself curious, and while Katherine supported his leg Nirac shoved the chair over so Hugh might see out, then Nirac said, "But you, madame—you most see them close and 'ear the dwarf's so foolish jokes. Do you go down and I'll stay with Sir Hugh."

She hesitated, but Hugh said, "Go along, Katherine, tell him to do a trick. I saw a monkey once in Castile could juggle nuts like a Christian. Ask him can his monkey juggle."

Katherine ran downstairs into the courtyard, where already a small crowd had gathered around the dwarf, who began to tumble across the courtyard like a leather bouncing ball.

Hugh leaned far over the sill to see and hear what he could, and when the monkey strutted and stamped its feet and slapped its tiny hands on its backside in imitation of the dwarf, Hugh let out a hoarse guffaw.

Nirac's business took only a minute. The Gascon murmured excuse, to which Hugh paid no attention, and walked into the bedroom to relieve himself into the slop jar, then with a lightning motion he snatched a leaden phial from within his tunic, and emptied gray-white powder into the clay cup which was still half filled with Brother William's drug. Antimoine the alchemist had said the powder was monksbane, but would answer Nirac's specifications even though the recipient be no monk. Nirac did not touch the cup, but with one eye on Hugh's back, he stirred hard with a little stick he had brought. The powder swirled and disappeared into the black mixture. He slipped the stick and empty phial into his tunic and walked back to the window, crying over Hugh's shoulder, "Ah, but 'ow droll—mordieu! The monkey and the popinjay they marry—see! 'Tis that trick made the Princess Isabel scream with mirth." Nirac's voice trembled, a sudden brief fit of shaking seized on him and passed. Hugh noticed nothing.

When the dwarf had run through all his repertoire, Katherine came back, her face flushed with laughter, and cried, "Ah Nirac, how good of you it was to give us such a treat!"

Hugh nodded, still smiling a little. "Ay gramerci," he said. "'Twas courteously done. Here's silver for the dwarf," he fumbled in his purse and held out some pennies.

Nirac hesitated only a moment before he took the money. "I must return to 'Is Grace," he said, looking at Katherine. "'Is Grace cannot do without Nirac. Always 'e look for me, depend on me."

"To be sure," she said indulgently, but the happy flush faded and the gnawing pain she had forgotten for a few minutes returned.

"Le bon Dieu vous bénisse," said Nirac, still looking at Katherine, who was faintly surprised at this solemnity, but ever a creature of quick moods, the Gascon then grinned, executed a sweeping flourish of farewell, and trotted out the door with his usual nimbleness.

"Strange little man—" said Katherine, straightening up the table and rubbing off the wine stains with a cloth. "He's always been kind and pleasant to me, yet much as I've seen him, I feel I know him hardly at all."

"Bosh—these Gascons!" said Hugh. "There's naught in them *worth* knowing. Damn the man—he should have thought to wait and help me to bed. I grow weary."

"Ellis'll be back soon," she said soothingly, "or maybe I can manage if you lean on my shoulder. Nay, but there *is* Ellis."

The young squire clumped in and flung a basket on the table. He too had been enjoying himself, he had tilted at the quintain with a group of other squires on the outskirts of town, and then seen a most wondrous bullbaiting—no scurvy little sport such as it was in England but pulse-stirring contest in which three bulls had been stabbed and four men gored. Ellis was full of it, and Hugh asked interested questions, while Katherine unpacked the basket. Ellis had brought them peaches and figs and a loaf of flat white bread imbued with garlic. Later she would get hot pork sausage up from the kitchen of the wineshop and refill the flagon for their supper. Soon this day will have passed, she thought, and the next will pass too. She would forget this morning in the garden of the inn—seal it over with wax as the bees sealed over frightening intruders in their hive. As she thought thus sensibly, gray misery enveloped her, and her lips formed words that were pushed up from the place where her mind had no control. "My dear love," she whispered, and going to the pitcher where she had placed the crumpled, withering but still fragrant sprays of jasmine, she buried her face in them.

After Hugh was in bed and Katherine had dressed his wound, which seemed far less swollen, Hugh and Ellis still talked of bullbaitings: of one they had seen in Burgos after Nájera, and of a remarkable contest held at Angers in which two bears and two bulls had been let loose in the arena to destroy each other in a frenzy of claws and horns and teeth and stamping hooves.

Katherine prepared the supper. She intended to get a serving maid to help her in a day or so, but in the meantime increased leisure for thought would be no boon.

When the vesper bells chimed out from the cathedral, they all listened for a moment and Katherine said to her husband, "Our meal is ready, Hugh—can you relish it? See what fine fruit Ellis has brought us, there's naught like that in England."

"Ay," said Hugh. "I've appetite. Give me the wine, my dear. 'Tis not so good as honest ale, but it serves."

She started to pour for him, then stopped. "Your potion, Hugh," she smiled and shook her head, "first you must have your draught."

She gave him the clay cup. He took it grumbling but swallowed nearly all the contents. "Phaw!" he said with a wry face, "filthy stuff. I'll take no more of it."

"Oh, come," she said as she would have to Blanchette, "it's not so bad——" She took the cup and gazed into it idly, wondering as women always have that men who delighted in blood and slaughter should be so finicking in little things. She sniffed it, thinking the smell of camphor not unpleasant, and out of curiosity would have tasted it, but seeing that there was little left and there was no knowing exactly when Brother William would return with more, she put it down, and she and Ellis served their supper.

Shortly after they had blown the candles out and Katherine still lay sleepless on her pallet, she heard Hugh give a heavy groan; then he cried out sharply. She started up and stumbled to him in the darkness. "What is it, Hugh, what's the matter?"

"I had a dream——" he muttered in a thick hoarse voice. "I dreamed the pooka hound was baying for me—'twas at Kettlethorpe—the pooka hound with fire-red eyes, it's baying near Kettlethorpe—I heard it——"

She put her hand on his forehead, which was clammy, and said, "Hugh dear—'twas naught but a bad dream, and the pooka hound does not bay for Swynfords, don't you remember? It was of the old days——"

He groaned, "Sweet Christ, but I've a fearful pain—the gripes again."

She called to Ellis and when he woke, told him to fetch a

light from the kitchen fire. Hugh writhed and moaned. When
Ellis came back and lit a candle, she saw that Hugh's cheeks
had gone hollow, there was slime on his lips and his glistening
face was greenish. Then he began to vomit and purge. She
and Ellis worked frantically trying to ease him.

"What can have happened, lady?" whispered the squire.

"I know not—" she whispered back, distracted. "It's the
flux again but worse than I've ever seen it—dear God, Ellis,
can you find the Gray Friar?"

The squire tumbled downstairs and ran out through the
court. The violent bloody vomiting and purging eased a little,
Hugh lay back exhausted. She wiped the sweat from him and
murmured gentle sounds while her heart beat fast with fear.
Could it be the fruit, that had loosened his bowels? Hugh had
eaten several of the luscious figs and peaches. Oh Blessed
Mother, she thought, I should not have let him eat the fruit.
She put her arm under his head and raised it a little. "Hugh
dear—finish Brother William's draught—it *must* help you—
would to God there were more of it." She held the cup to his
lips and he swallowed mechanically, then he fell back crying,
"Water!" There was a little in the washing pitcher, she mixed
it with the wine to make it wholesome and gave it to him in
the clay cup.

Suddenly he started up and looked at her wildly. "Don't
you hear it?" he cried. "It's across the Trent in the forest. Listen! It comes nearer. It scents me now—it scents death."

"Hugh, my dear husband—" She put her arms around
him, trying to hold him down, while he twisted and turned,
regardless of his injured leg, unknowing of her.

Soon he gave a great cry of pain, and, doubling over with
spasm, began again to vomit. When the Gray Friar came
running in with Ellis, he stood by the bed and shook his
head. "God pity him!" he murmured sadly, feeling Hugh's
pulse, which was so feeble and lagging, and the wrist so
clammy-cold, the physician knew there was no time to be lost
in giving him the last rites.

Katherine knelt in the other room, while the friar's voice
intoned the prayer for the dying. She could not pray, she
could not think. She was vised in a great dazed disbelief.

The friar called her and they stood together by the bedside.
Hugh's eyelids fluttered, he said quite clearly, " 'Tis a bloody
struggle, the pooka hound and the bull—the hound has him
by the throat." His eyes opened wider and he looked up at

Katherine. "A bloody struggle, Katherine—" he said. "Christ have mercy—"

She bent and kissed the gray forehead. He was quiet for a few more minutes while Ellis kneeling on the other side of the bed wept with dry racking sobs.

Then Hugh gave a long shudder and his breathing stopped. The friar crossed himself, and Katherine followed suit. She felt nothing but the vast disbelief.

Brother William sighed heavily. "Poor soul, I can't understand it—I thought he was cured—yet these dysenteries—it must be there was a rotten spot in his bowel that burst. Ay —that happens." He turned and put his long thin hand on Katherine's arm. "My dear lady, 'tis a hard thing for you. Come sit down. You must take wine."

Staring at nothing, white-faced as the plaster wall, she suffered the friar to lead her to a chair.

# XV

BROTHER WILLIAM stayed the night in the Swynford lodgings. After summoning the old crones who laid out the corpse, he took pitying charge of Katherine and Ellis. To the former he gave a sleeping draught, but the young squire, who could not stop blubbering and moaning, he kept busy with many necessary tasks.

The Gray Friar was accustomed to the sad procedures attendant upon the death of an English knight abroad. In the morning he started to make arrangements for the Requiem Mass, temporary disposition of the coffin and passage for it on a homebound ship, when the friar bethought him that perhaps the Duke should be notified first. To be sure, His Grace had for some time shown no interest in Sir Hugh's welfare and also was of so impatient and puzzling a humor lately that the friar hesitated to bother him. Still, there was poor Lady Swynford to be considered, and her now undetermined position.

Having left Katherine sleeping under the opiate and Ellis hunched in a corner and drinking himself into oblivion, the friar set out for the palace.

The Duke was in Council. He sat listlessly on the gilded throne of Aquitaine, beneath the embossed lilies and leopards of the blazon. He had none of his usual alertness nor held his long body with the decorum he normally showed to the office his brother had bequeathed him. His legs crossed, his fingers worrying a loose fringe on the crimson velvet armrest, he listened moodily to the propositions and wrangles of his councilors.

Sir Guichard d'Angle, reporting on his most recent trip to Bayonne, informed them all wryly that the Castilian court there, sure now of England's eagerness for the marriage, was acting with ridiculous pride and greed. "One would think 'twere the daughter of the Holy Roman Emperor His Grace would wed! They demand yet another jointure settled on the Queen. They demand that she may bring twelve of her ladies with her and as many courtiers. They refuse to let her near Bordeaux until after the ceremony."

The Captal de Buch twirled the cup of wine that stood ever at his elbow and gave a great laugh. "Bluster, mon vieux," he said to Sir Guichard, "nothing but bluster. The Castilians can haggle as well as the Jews, you know."

"Then," broke in de la Pole hotly, "we must use a firm hand."

The Duke leaned forward. "Nay," he said in a tone of angry command. "Give them what they want. And the marriage may take place at Roquefort."

De la Pole subsided, frowning. The other Englishmen said nothing. Their interests were martial; they waited for the tiresome matter of the marriage to be over so that they might take up a far more worrying topic—the continual depredations of the great French constable, du Guesclin, in the north.

The captal, shrugging, buried his formidable beak in his cup. Sir Guichard bowed to the Duke and, beckoning to the clerks who waited with parchment spread at a smaller table, said, "Then we will draft a letter, my lord."

This business was proceeding when they were interrupted by a commotion near the door. The yeoman-on-guard expostulated with someone, until a shrill determined voice cried, "But it is vairy important, le duc will agree!"

John frowned and again raised his heavy lids. "By Our Lady, Nirac!" he called irritably, "what is it?"

The little Gascon slithered past the door and ran to his master. He knelt on the dais and gabbled very low, in the langue d'oc, "Brother William Appleton is here, 'e has something to tell you."

"In God's name—you little fool—do you burst in here to tell me *that!*—ah?" John stared down with startled question into Nirac's unwinking black eyes. The Gascon raised his brows slowly—with meaning.

"I'm sorry, gentlemen," John said, rising. "A matter I must attend to."

"But Your Grace," cried Sir Thomas Felton, "there's grave trouble in the north, Bertrand du Guesclin—"

"I'll return shortly, Sir Thomas, but I think you forget I resigned full power here. 'Tis now in *your* hands to administer Aquitaine, you and the captal. No doubt you'll do far better than I have." He gave the two men a cold nod and, followed by Nirac, walked out of the Council room. The men stood up and bowed as he passed them, then reseated themselves in some consternation.

"Mauvaise humeur," said the captal, chuckling. "His temper grows as thorny as the poor Prince of Wales'. Nom de Dieu—these Plantagenets! They should laugh more—enjoy life. What that one needs," he jerked his plump chins towards the door, "is a woman!"

"So you keep saying," growled de la Pole. "He's getting one, isn't he?"

"A warm complaisant wench," said the captal imperturbably, "not a yellow bag of bones who thinks of naught but avenging her dead papa. I could find him a woman—I know a little dancer, a Navarrese—round thighs—breasts like pillows —lips juicy as mulberries." The captal, ticking off these attractions on stubby fingers would have continued, but the Englishman snorted impatiently, and Sir Guichard interrupted with a smile.

"Enfin, captal—no doubt she's superb, your little Navarrese. But to a determined man, all cats are gray at night. Also Costanza is proud—mon Dieu, how proud! And jealous too, I'll warrant. If the Castilians got wind of dalliance now, it might wreck the marriage."

"A plague on the marriage!" cried Sir Thomas Felton. "The question is what are we to do about du Guesclin!"

John stood by the empty fireplace in the antechamber of his private suite and heard the Gray Friar speak in a calm and sorrowful voice the incredible words, "And so, my lord, the poor knight is dead, God absolve his soul!"

"What—" said the Duke so low that it was scarcely a whisper, "what did you say?"

"I said, my lord, that Sir Hugh Swynford suffered a violent attack of dysentery and is dead."

"But he can't be—he was getting well. He can't be!"

This cry was uttered on so strange a note and the Duke turned his back on the friar so violently that Brother William took it for anger and said humbly, "Your Grace, forgive me. I did my best. I applied all the skill God has granted me, but it was not His Will, that the knight should live."

Nirac stood unnoticed near the door, his arms crossed on his chest, now he hugged them tight around himself, for he could see his master's face though the friar could not. He saw the look of dazed incredulity give way to awe, and then the blue eyes blazed wide open. The Duke repeated, slowly and in a shaking voice, "It was not His Will, that the knight should live!"

"The funeral arrangements, Your Grace—" persisted the friar, puzzled by the Duke's averted back and choked speech. "I can attend to all that, but 'tis a melancholy situation for the widow, and the squire. I thought perhaps you might wish to direct your chamberlain or some other of your household officers to call?"

"The widow," said the Duke. "Ay, the widow, you said, Brother. I shall attend to that myself," and now as the Duke turned, the astounded Gray Friar saw what Nirac had seen —the face of joy—the young, eager, tremulous face of joy.

Brother William started back frowning. "My lord, what would you of her! She is in great grief, unprotected, and I believe a truly virtuous woman—"

"I know that. And I shall not forget. But there are things *you* do not know." The Duke smiled with a tenderness that astonished the Gray Friar and added softly, "God has heard my prayers and given me blessing. Nay, good Brother, don't look so sour, you're not my confessor. You've done all you need. Wipe out this matter from your mind. Here, take this."

He opened the purse at his belt and thrust into the friar's unwilling hand a dozen gold nobles. "For the poor, for the sick,
for the lepers, for anything you like. Now leave me alone!"

For the next three days the court was mystified by their
ruler's behavior, though the younger lords and ladies were delighted. Between one breath and the next, it seemed, the
Duke had thrown off all the heavy brooding and ill temper he
had shown for months.

Each day he rode out hawking by the river with a party of
congenial courtiers and shouted triumph when his great white
gerfalcon, Oriana, brought down wild duck and heron. Each
day he took part in joustings and small deeds of arms with
one or another of his knights. And there was dancing and
singing in the Grande Salle at night.

The Princess Isabel was annoyed at this inexplicable
change but her grumblings met with little sympathy. Even
her younger brother Edmund, who was apt to agree with any
opinion expressed to him, said, "Oh, don't fuss about John. I
expect he's having a last fling before he marries, and anyway,
'twas time we had some mirth."

Amongst the courtiers, only the Captal de Buch knew the
reason for this volte-face on the part of the Duke, who had
consulted him on a certain matter. The captal, of course,
highly approved, chuckled often to himself, but kept his
counsel as he had been told to do.

On the fourth day after Hugh's death, the Duke sent word
to the Princess Isabel that he would be absent for a while and
that she and Edmund were to preside over the High Table in
his place.

At dusk the Duke and Nirac left the palace by the privy
stair, both of them enveloped in dark gray cloaks and hoods
without insignia, and though John rode his strongest and favorite charger, Palamon, the horse's trappings were simple
enough to befit a plain Bordelais burgher. They rode silently
through the streets past the cathedral to the Swynford lodgings, where the frowsy courtyard was deserted except for a
snuffling pig and some chickens that scratched at the manure
pile.

Upstairs, Katherine sat by the empty bed, staring at the
note from the Duke which she had received earlier that day.
Nirac had brought it and waited for her answer. "I'll be here

at vesper time and will receive my Lord Duke," she had said to Nirac. "But tell him that is all. It must be farewell."

After Nirac had bowed and gone, she had sat on, scarcely moving, forgetting food and drink, as she had for days. It seemed as though someone else inhabited her body while the real Katherine still slept under the opiate the friar had given her. Her body, swathed and veiled in black, had attended the Requiem Mass and the brief ceremony when the coffin was consigned to the cathedral crypt to await transportation home. Her eyes had even wept as her hands took off the clumsy Swynford betrothal ring and placed it in the coffin. Later she had tended Ellis, who had passed through roaring drunkenness into stupor. But no special thought had accompanied any of these things.

Even the Duke's note had not awakened Katherine, though somwhere within her there had been a shivering. Like the distortions dimly heard and seen through that yellow plague fog at Bolingbroke, life came to her muffled.

When the noise of horses clattered up from the courtyard, Ellis had been burnishing Hugh's armor, rubbing off every fleck of rust. At times when he was less drunk than others, this occupation gave him some comfort. " 'Twill do for little Tom—" he said to Katherine. "Little Tom'll soon grow to it, now he must fill his father's shoes."

She nodded, but her babies seemed as remote as everything else.

The courtyard sounds augmented, and Ellis peered out of the window. "There's two horsemen coming upstairs," he said, putting down Hugh's hauberk. "What can they want?" He opened the door, and Katherine stood up.

A tall man walked in, and threw back his hood.

"My Lord Duke!" cried Ellis, dropping to his knees. His bloodshot befuddled eyes squinted up uncertainly. Nirac hovered on the landing.

"I've come for you, Katrine," said John quietly, ignoring Ellis and looking over his head at the girl.

"No, my lord—" she whispered, but some of the muffling veils around her dissolved, her breathing quickened. Ellis stumbled to his feet and stood, swaying a little, his jaw thrust out, peering from his lady to the Duke, who spoke again.

"Ay—dear heart. You're coming with me. There's nothing now to keep us apart." Lifting his arms, John took a step towards her as she stood mute and still by the bed.

"You dare not touch her!" shouted Ellis, his wits clearing. "You dare not touch my lady!" Lunging suddenly his great hamlike fist shot out and blundered harmlessly past John's shoulder. The Duke stepped sideways, then with swift negligent motion hit Ellis squarely on the chin. The squire reeled, tottered over backward and lay gasping on the floor. Katherine gave a cry and would have run to the squire, but John forestalled her with another swift movement. He picked her up in his arms and held her so cruelly tight that she could not move. He laughed exultantly and kissed her on the mouth until she ceased to struggle; still holding her pinioned he walked downstairs with her and, mounting Palamon, placed her in front of him on the saddle, half covered by the folds of his cloak. The horse jumped forward at the spur.

The saddle, which had been built for a man in full armor, easily held them both, and Katherine made no further protest. Her head fell on John's chest, where she heard the beating of his heart.

The horse cantered for many miles before it slackened, then John, looking down at the head on his breast, shifted her weight a little on his arm and said with a gentle laugh, "And do you sleep, Katrine?"

"No, my lord," she said looking up at him in the darkness. "I think I am happy. It's very strange."

He bent and kissed her. "You will be happy, and always."

A cool salt-laden wind sprang up, she felt it on her face, and at the same time Palamon slowed to a walk while the sound of his great hooves grew dull and plodding. She roused herself and hearing the shrill cry of a gull said, "Are we near the sea, my lord?"

"Ay," he said, "we're in Les Landes, Katrine. We go to the captal's Château la Teste. Do you know where that is?"

"No," she said quietly. "I only know that from wherever it is that we're going there can be no turning back."

He tightened his arm around her, they rode on in silence.

Les Landes was the weirdest and most desert portion of France. On its sand and tufa wastes nothing grew except the stunted furze or bracken, and reeds in the salt marshes. Here the airs were thick with mist and the ever encroaching ocean pushed the sand dunes back and back over the undetermined land.

There was one track marked by white stones across these marshes. It was maintained by the Captal de Buch, whose an-

cestors, centuries ago, had built themselves a secluded fortress
on the Gulf of Arcachon. It was but thirty miles from Bordeaux, yet deep in an isolation desirable to a tribe of sea barons.

As they neared the castle, two of the captal's retainers,
mounted men-at-arms holding torches, came down the road
to meet them and guided them the rest of the way. They
went beneath the raised portcullis through massive walls and
stopped by the door of a round donjon tower. Katherine was
so cramped and chilled that she could scarce stand. John put
his arm around her waist and they ascended the rough winding stairs to the Hall.

Here, though no servants were visible, the captal's varlets
had ably followed his orders, as relayed from the Duke. An
enormous driftwood fire blazed on the hearth, in the iron
brackets a dozen perfumed candles burned. The moldering
stone walls had been covered with painted silk hangings and
arras brought from Bordeaux, the floor was strewn with
sweet rushes and rose petals, while the single small damask-
covered table was banked with jasmine.

John, watching Katherine tenderly, saw the deep breath
with which she drew in the delicious fragrances, and he
smiled. He had created beauty for her here, in this dank old
fortress, and he had forgotten nothing which would add to
the sensuous enhancement of their joy.

"Take off your black robe, Katrine," he said, "and refresh
yourself, my dear heart. You'll find everything needful here."
He led her to a small room adjacent to the Hall. Here too a
fire blazed, and the bed which had been brought by wagon
from Bordeaux was furnished with silk sheets and pillows
and hung with gold taffeta powdered with tiny jeweled ostrich
feathers and crowns.

A fat tiring-woman curtsied as they entered, and holding
out a basin of warm water to Katherine, waited with dull incurious eyes. The Duke withdrew saying, "Hurry!" on an
eager laugh.

While the girl washed, the tiring-woman brought her a
gown from the garderobe. "For you to wear—le captal
wants," she said. Actually the Duke himself had ordered the
gown made for Katherine, but the tiring-woman had never
left La Teste and knew of no lord but the captal.

The robe was of cream-white sendal trimmed only by an
embroidered gold and green cipher on the low-cut bosom.

The cipher was a J and K intertwined with leaves and set in a heart. Katherine looked at the cipher and her eyes filled with bitter-sweet tears. She slipped the gown over her head and the woman girded it, then unbinding Katherine's hair, she began to comb out the long shimmering auburn strands.

John came back to the door as Katherine started to replait her hair. "Nay!" he cried, "don't bind it, my love. Leave it loose!"

"Like a bride?" she whispered, half smiling, yet troubled.

He came to her and seizing a handful of the gleaming hair carried it to his lips. The tiring-woman backed away, John made a quick gesture, and she turned and waddled off to the stairs.

They supped together at the table near the fire in the Hall. Nirac would have waited on them, but as he bent over to fill the gold hanaps with pale delicate wine from the captal's cellars, a shrinking repulsion penetrated Katherine's enchantment. When the little Gascon had retired to the serving table she said softly, "My dear lord, could we not be alone? I can serve you."

"Of course," he said instantly, and dismissed Nirac, though John was faintly surprised. He had thought that his choice of servitor was the precise one which would save her all embarrassment. "You don't dislike Nirac, do you?" he asked when they were alone.

She shook her head, not knowing herself what had caused the shrinking. "A whim, my dearest lord," she said. "Women have them—" Suddenly across the table she gave him her tenderly wistful and seductive smile. "Will you be gentle with my whims?"

She was all beauty as she sat there in her white dress. Her hair fell nearly to the rushes and glistened like the carnelians he had once compared it to, her red lips were parted, her gray eyes dark with love. He trembled, and going to her knelt beside her.

"I shall not always be gentle, Katrine," he said looking up into her face. "But by the soul of my mother, I shall love you until I die."

She bent over and opening her arms drew his head against her breasts. A gull mewed again outside the fortress, the fresh tang of the sea crept through the windows to mingle with the warmth of jasmine.

He raised his head from her breast and they looked without fear or striving but quietly, deep into each other's eyes.

They stayed three days at the captal's old fortress in Les Landes and during that time they never left the Hall and the bedchamber.

The ecstasy of their union brought to each of them a wondering awe. Katherine had nothing but dreams with which to compare this sweet agony of passion, unslaked even by the bliss of fulfillment, and the total merging of herself into another, so that even for the moments they were away from each other's arms she felt him as much part of her flesh as its throbbing veins.

John had known love before, but not like this. How palely gentle and courteous now seemed that far-off time with Blanche! Then there had been reticences and dignity, and quietly maternal indulgence, and always, on his part, gratitude.

Now there was no need for reticence or gratitude. Here in the sea-scented bedchamber, there was a man and a woman who came together naked and unashamed, proudly bestowing on each other the beauty of their bodies and thereby finding ineffable joy.

On the third evening they sat on piled cushions before the fire, drinking wine from a single cup, laughing at nothing and whispering little words such as lovers have always used.

Then John reached out his arm for the lute which hung by a red velvet ribbon from a hearth peg and said, "Lovely, listen. *Now* I think I have the tune for the song I wished to sing you—"

She drew a little from his arms that he might play unencumbered, and they smiled at each other as he rippled his fingers tentatively across the strings. "You, my Katrine, are all lovesome things," he said softly, "and I am the man who says—

> *She is coral of goodness, ruby of rightness.*
> *She is crystal of cleanness, and banner of beauty.*
> *She is lily of largesse, periwinkle of prowess,*
> *She is marigold of sweetness, and lady of loyalty.*
> *For her love I cark and care,*
> *For her love I droop and dare,*

> *For her love my bliss is bare*
> *And I wax all wan.*
> *For her love in sleep I slake,*
> *For her love all night I wake,*
> *For her love I'd mourning make*
> *More than any man."*

He sang the old English words to a haunting melody that had come to him, and when he repeated the chorus she joined him, changing only the pronoun to, "For *his* love I cark and care, for *his* love I droop and dare," singing in her rich golden voice.

So lovely was their duet that the Captal de Buch who had paused, panting from the stairs, outside the door of the Hall, turned with startled emotion to Nirac who had followed him. "Nom de Vierge! Can that be the Duke? They sing like angels in there together. Are they then so happy?"

Nirac shrugged and answered with harshness, "No doubt they are, captal. I've not seen them in three days. The tiring-woman waits on them."

The captal raised his bushy eyebrows and laughed. "Oh la belle chose, hein?" he said winking at Nirac. "One forgets all else!" He thumped with his fist on the door, but they were finishing their song and did not hear him, so he opened the door. Earthy libertine though he was, the captal's roguish greeting died in his throat when he saw them.

The two on the cushions seemed to be bathed in light. The girl was but half clothed yet so pure was the beauty of her arms and breasts gleaming like alabaster between strands of long auburn hair, and so adoring the expression on the Duke's face, that the captal saw no lewdness, but felt instead, a bitter stab of nostalgia. Thirty years ago there had been a moment almost like this for him too, but it had lasted only a little while, when the woman had died.

"Your pardon, my lord—lady—" he stammered, backing off. He saw the measure of the entrancement which held the Duke, in that he did not flash with fury at this interruption. Instead he put his arm around the girl and held her against him in a gesture so tender and protective that the captal swallowed hard.

"What is it, my good de Grailly?" John said. "Have you come to be thanked for your wondrous hospitality?" He smiled and bending his head laid his cheek for a moment against Katherine's hair. "We will not need paradise, I think, my Katrine, after Château la Teste."

The girl raised her brilliant eyes and moved in her lover's arm, as though she nestled closer.

The captal cleared his throat. "I came, my lord, because you told me to. I—it is now Thursday night. There are—are many urgent matters awaiting you at Bordeaux." He saw the wincing that passed over the girl's face and added uncomfortably, "May I have a few words with you, my lord?"

The Duke started to refuse, but Katherine, clutching her white robe around her, slipped from his arm, and giving the captal a proud tremulous smile, walked back into the bedchamber.

"She's of a great beauty, your little Swynford, mon duc," said the captal recovering his aplomb, now that Katherine was gone. "I congratulate you on a delicious interlude. I deeply regret to wrest you out of it."

The Duke looked at him strangely, and said, "She is my heart's blood. My life. I want nothing but her."

"Doux Jésu!" murmured the captal. He walked to the wine flagon and pouring himself a goblet full, drank it hastily. "The Castilian commissioners have returned with the signed contracts and ring, Your Grace. You are now formally betrothed to the Queen of Castile. The marriage is set for the Feast of Saint Matthew in the church at Roquefort as you commanded."

The Duke said nothing. Lines drew themselves around his mouth. His eyes grew harsh, the face which had been glowing and young as Katherine's showed all of his thirty-one years.

"Yesterday," pursued the captal, "John Holland of Kent arrived from England with wedding presents and letters from the King's Grace, your father, and the Prince of Wales. I have brought them to you—I had—" he added, "a bad time hiding your whereabouts. At last I told them you were fulfilling a secret vow. It *is* a vow to Saint Venus, pardieu!" He chuckled and slapped his thigh, then sobered at the look in the Duke's eyes.

The captal opened his pouch and extracting two folded parchments, each impressed with red ribbon and large royal seals, held them out to the Duke, who stared at them in silence without taking them.

The man is bewitched, thought the captal, uneasily. "Be

reasonable, my lord. One must never let one's little pleasures interfere with the really important affairs of life. Nor have I ever known you do so before. John Holland says that in England they buzz with excitement about your marriage. The people seem much pleased at the alliance."

"The devil take the commons—what care I for them? And the devil take my marriage," said the Duke. He looked towards the arras which covered the door of their bedchamber. "The thought of Costanza sickens me!"

The captal was shocked. He gulped the rest of his wine while wishing passionately that some eloquent man like Guichard d'Angle or even de la Pole could deal with this dangerous frame of mind.

"Costanza is but means to an end, mon duc," he said at last. "She means Castile. You will be King." Aha, touché, thought the captal as he saw the blue eyes flicker. He belched with relief, settled his girdle over his paunch and continued. "Once married and in England, you may naturally do as you please. The little Swynford need not leave you. It isn't as though she were someone you might marry."

The Duke's tall body slumped. He flung himself in a chair and gazed down at the fresh jasmine petals which were strewn amongst the rushes. "You speak twofold truth, captal," he said after a silence. "I could never marry her and she must never leave me."

"Ah bon, so all will arrange itself," laughed the captal. He tore the leg off a raisin-stuffed capon that stood untouched on the table, amused to see that little of the excellent food his cook had sent up to the lovers had been eaten. "We'll set out for Bordeaux, then, at daybreak? Your Council will be waiting you at nine."

"No," said the Duke. "I'll not go to Bordeaux tomorrow. Nor for a fortnight."

The captal put down his capon leg. "But my lord—"

"For two more weeks, Katrine and I shall be alone together. I'm going to take her to the Pyrenees."

"Pitié de Dieu! But you can't!" stammered the captal. "What would people say! And there's no time, the wedding arrangements—this is folly?"

John got up from the chair and lifted his eyebrows. "You forget, de Grailly, whom you are addressing?"

The captal flushed and murmured apology while he thought, These English—they are mad. Sentimental, stiff-necked fools, God pity them. He *cannot* go running around the country with his harlot just now, it's imbecile. Fraught with danger too, political and personal.

But the captal found there was no help for it. The Duke gave him minute instructions and ended the intrusion by calling "Katrine" in a voice of poignant longing.

The lovers left Château la Teste the next noon, headed for the south, and dressed as a nondescript couple of pilgrims, John in the brown sackcloth he had used earlier when he found Katherine at the cathedral, and she in a short green kirtle and cape which had come from a chest in the keep. Green was the color of true love and they were delighted with the find. With them on the journey went two of the captal's men, a shepherd and a blacksmith, both sturdy fellows well acquainted with the nearly trackless wastelands they must traverse, but of wits too dull to question this expedition or the couple they escorted.

Nirac did not accompany his master, as he had expected to do when he heard of the plan. Even had Katherine's lightest request not been law to John at that time, he himself felt less affection for Nirac than he used to. The little Gascon had lost his charm and impudent smile, he had received the Duke's orders to return to Bordeaux in heavy silence. His eyes were bloodshot, his sallow skin had a gray tinge, so that John had said kindly, "Have you a fever, Nirac? You don't look well. You must rest till I return. Here——" and he gave him a gold noble, "a little reward for your many services."

"For my services, mon duc," Nirac repeated in a peculiar tone. The Duke glanced at him, but though he heard something like "You know not *what* service I've rendered you," he dismissed it as a vagary.

When they left the courtyard of La Teste, Katherine rode pillion behind John on Palamon. As she glanced back in farewell towards the round tower where she had known rapture, she saw Nirac standing against the wall apart from the stableboys who had gathered in the court.

Nirac's little monkey face was twisted as though he were crying. It was turned up towards the oblivious Duke, but when the Gascon felt Katherine's gaze, his glance shifted to her and she waved to him in sympathy, feeling something of Nirac's miserable jealousy. He did not wave back and at that distance she could not be sure, but it seemed as though his eyes glinted at her with sudden bleak hatred.

This distressed her for only a second, then she forgot him. Her arms tightened around John's waist and she leaned her cheek on his shoulder. Beneath the musty harsh sackcloth she sensed the warmth of his skin and its cleanly male tang of bergamot.

He raised one of her hands from his girdle and kissed the palm, then turned and smiled at her. "You are happy, sweet heart?"

"Happy, my dearest lord."

"Nay, Katrine, for these——" He could not bear to put a term to the time they would be like this together, nor had she asked. They spoke of nothing but each other and their love. "For this journey I am not your 'Lord,' we are but John and Katherine, a respectable couple bound like many another on pilgrimage to Compostela. We are nothing else."

She laughed joyously. "Do we keep a shop, John? Are we clothiers? Pastry cooks? In Bordeaux, perhaps? Nay, I think not for we neither of us have the Gascon accent. From farther north then? My own natal Picardy, or your Ghent?"

"Why, no," he cried startled. "We are *English,* Katrine!"

"Of course," she said, ashamed that England had so instinctively seemed to her a land of unhappy memories which she wished forever to forget.

"Look!" he cried quickly, understanding her with his heart, "See the two white herons rising? What a place these marshes are for wild fowl. Ah, that I had Oriana! What sport we'd have! You've never hawked? But I shall teach you, darling."

When, she thought, and where? But this and many other things she dared not think of.

"And you've never seen the mountains," he went on, as they followed their plodding guides on a path of sunken logs and across little tufted ridges between the salty swamps. "I long to show them to you."

He did not know himself why he yearned to take her to the wildness and grandeur of the Pyrenees. Perhaps it was that he wished to be alone with her in lands which did not owe him suzerainty and where no one could know him. Perhaps it was the more primitive instinct of seeking the most beautiful of natural frames for their love.

And on the second day as they crossed Les Landes, when they saw the Pyrenees, ragged crests of purple shadows tinged with silver, sharp-etched against the southern sky, Katherine caught her breath. Tears came to her eyes. She shared at once with him the mystic exaltation that called out to them like a great chord of music from these mountains, and as they penetrated through the strange Basque lands into Navarre, climbing ever upward amongst rushing streams, rock cliffs and the darkness of pines, their love deepened. No longer frenzied in its physical hunger but sustained and quietened by a spirit higher than themselves.

One day they reached Roncevalles at the top of the pass near the Pas de Roland where Charlemagne's great paladin had been killed six hundred years before. Here there was a large abbey built for the accommodation of travelers and pilgrims between Spain and France. But they avoided the abbey with its curious priests and summer load of wayfarers and pushed on some miles to a tiny mountain inn.

This inn was a rendezvous for smugglers and accustomed to receiving all manner of guests. The black-eyed landlady asked no questions, responded with a shrug to John's halting Basque, bit the silver coin he gave her, and allotted them a small clean chamber over the storage room, while the captal's two servitors were quartered in one of the many caves hollowed out of the cliff.

The days that John and Katherine spent at the inn were a timeless enchantment. They slept on a pile of sweet-smelling hay. They drank the strong heady wine that was poured from goatskins, and ate trout and écrevisses and hot tasty dishes brewed with the red peppers that dangled like strings of great rubies along the creamy inn walls. They wandered off amongst the mountains and found a small pastured valley by a waterfall where Katherine picked wild flowers: the tiny lemon-colored saxifrages, violet ramondia, white spiky asphodel, and alpenrose. She wove them into garlands while John lay on the velvet greensward beside her, pelting her lazily with the flowers, or content to watch her. Sometimes they sang together, and he often recited to her poems and ballads he had learned in his youth.

In this bright secret valley which they had made their own, there was a ruined chapel, abandoned long ago by the mountaineers, who thought it haunted by the wild mountain spirits. Two of the chapel walls had fallen into rubble, but against a portion of the east wall the rough square altar still stood. It was carved with odd runic scrolls and supported a stone crucifix.

They loved the little chapel, as indeed they had endowed each feature of the valley, even the tinkling goats that strayed into it, with the magic of their own dream. The sun shone each day on this, the gentle "soulane" side of the Divide, and each night the frosty stars blessed them through the sparkling air.

When nearly a week had passed there came a night that Katherine felt a change. A new dark urgency and restlessness was on her lover, he embraced her with more violent, even brutal, passion. Several times he started to speak to her but checked himself, and she was afraid.

She fell at last into heavy, miserable sleep. When she awoke the first rays of the sun came through the window. She started up with a cry, for he was not beside her. She waited and called, for there was no answer. She dressed with clumsy shaking fingers, ran down through the deserted inn and outside into the cool sunrise.

Palamon was in the stable. He whickered gently as she spoke to him, so she guessed where John had gone, and ran up the stony hills and through the beech and pine copses until she reached their valley. At first she could not find him, then she looked upward and saw a tall solitary figure standing on top of a little peak that guarded the valley to the south.

She slowed her pace and climbed up to him silently. He did not move as she joined him on the summit; she thought he had not heard her. His head was lifted, his tawny hair stirred in the wind, while he gazed with fixed somber intensity over distant plains that lay spread out far below them to the dim horizon.

Her heart beat hard and painfully, seeing that he had indeed gone from her, and there was no welcome.

Yet as she turned to go he spoke, without looking at her, his gaze still fastened on the horizon. "That is Castile, far yonder where the gold light falls on the hills."

Castile. The word hissed like an adder. "I hate it, hate it!" she cried. The hoarse shaking voice was not her own, she tried to stop it and could not. "I hate it, and I hate her, the Castilian woman! Tell me, my Lord Duke-who-would-be-king, when will the Castilian wench become a bride?"

His nostrils flared, he jerked around on her with a violence to match her own, "You dare to speak to me like that! You forget, Katrine—"

"Forget! Can I ever forget that this is pretense! Can I ever forget your royal birth or your royal hopes? Yet I do dare to say I hate them. I am no duchess, no queen, but I have been your equal in love, for this I dare to tell you how I feel."

Anger died from his eyes. He bent his head and stepped towards her. "Dear heart, we *are* equal in love. You've no cause for hatred, for you shall never leave me. I've been thinking, and have decided what's to be done. You shall go back to England at once and wait for me at the Savoy—"

"And I'm to be your leman for all the world to see, like Alice Perrers to the King? And what of your new Duchess, the Queen Costanza? How will she like this arrangement?"

He stiffened and said coldly, "You have little knowledge of courts. It is a common arrangement. Be reasonable. After all, we have been lovers this past fortnight without scruples."

"This past fortnight, my lord, we have hurt or dishonored no one. We are both—still—free." Her voice broke. She looked at him with anguish and fled down the hillside, stumbling and tripping on the rough ground until she reached the valley, where moved by blind impulse she ran into the little ruined chapel and flung herself down to her knees with her hands clasped on the altar.

She felt him kneel down beside her and then, after a moment, a touch on her arm. He said very low, "Look at me."

She raised her head slowly and obeyed. Tears stood in his eyes, and his arrogant mouth quivered. He took her right hand in his and spoke solemnly, "Here on consecrated ground I, John, do plight thee, Katrine, my love and in token do give thee this ring, in the name of the Father, and of the Son, and of the Holy Ghost." He drew from his finger the sapphire seal ring that Blanche had given him and slipped it on Katherine's middle finger. She stared down at it and a sob tore up from her chest.

They both turned to the blunted little stone crucifix, and through the roofless chapel their prayers floated out to mingle with the murmur of the waterfall.

On September 18, three days before the Feast of St. Matthew, Katherine sat alone in a guest chamber of the Bendictine nunnery at Bordeaux. Her traveling chest had been brought here to her, and she was again dressed in her black

mourning robes, her braided hair bound into black velvet
cauls and covered with a thin veil. A breeze pungent with the
tang of fresh-trampled grapes from a hundred villages carried
the distant shouts of the peasants working in the vineyards.
Katherine sat quietly by the window looking out over the
harbor where a cluster of masts dipped and swung with the
ripples of the Garonne. Her face was white and still. Though
her eyes were swollen from nights of stifled weeping, now she
had no more tears.

She waited for the summons she knew would come, and
wondered without interest on which of those ships out there
she was to sail on the morrow.

A little nun knocked on the door, entered, flustered and
blushing, to say that madame had a most important caller—
the Duke's own physician, the Franciscan, Brother William.
He was awaiting her in the parlor.

Katherine smiled thanks and rose. The little nun peered up
at her admiringly. If the prioress knew anything about this
beautiful widow who seemed so unhappy and gave no information about herself, she was the only one at the convent
who did.

Cause enough to be unhappy, said the cellaress acidly, with
the poor lady's husband dead and she so far from home. Yet
the nuns were not satisfied, there was some mystery about
Lady Swynford and a glamor that intrigued them. They whispered about her as they sat at work or walked in the cloisters
and found her nearly as interesting as the topic that excited
all Bordeaux. The royal wedding in three days. When the
Duke and new Duchess returned from the marriage at Roquefort there would be a procession right down the street
past the convent; by hanging out of the windows they would
see the handsome Duke, golden as the sun, strong as a lion,
people said, and see his Castilian bride—a queen, for all she
was but seventeen.

" 'Tis such a pity, madame, that you do not stay for the
wedding," said the little nun, as she accompanied Katherine
down to the parlor. "It will be so gay with fifty trumpeters,
they say, and jongleurs from Provence!"

Lady Swynford did not answer.

Brother William had been chatting with the portress, he
turned as Katherine entered and bowed. Beneath his black
cowl his eyes were severe, he did not smile at her as he used
to do.

He glanced at the portress and the nun, who vanished. Katherine sank down on a stool, clasping her hands tight on a fold of her skirt, but she raised her face to the friar and waited with mute dignity for him to speak.

His gaze softened only a trifle as he stared down at her and saw the shadows beneath her wide gray eyes and the lines of suffering that pulled at her mouth. Then he shook his head. "I had never thought to come to such a woman as you, with the sort of message I bring. The Duke awaits you in his presence chamber. He can not receive you except as one of the many who are filing through for audience, because at present great discretion is required." Brother William stopped, frowning.

"I know," she said. Dull red flowed up her cheeks. Her gaze rested on the knotted scourge that girded the friar's gray habit, then dropped to his dusty bare feet.

"It would be wise," continued the Brother with chill distaste, "for you to remove that ring you wear. It would be as familiar to many at the palace as it is to myself."

She took off the sapphire seal ring and slipped it in her bosom.

"The Duke will manage that you have a few minutes alone together, but the time must necessarily be brief so as not to arouse suspicion. I am therefore directed to repeat the arrangements His Grace has made for you and to which he commands and also implores your final consent."

Katherine swallowed and said dully, "I am sailing tomorrow on whatever ship he has selected."

"Ay, and when you land you will proceed to the Savoy bearing official letters which will grant you fifty marks at once and appoint you Resident Governess of His Grace's two little daughters, the Ladies Philippa and Elizabeth. You may send for your sister, Mistress Chaucer, and your own two children from Lincolnshire to join you at the Savoy, where they will also be provided for. You will remain at the Savoy until the Duke returns." The friar paused, before adding with biting emphasis, "When, I gather, further intimacies will continue to be suitably rewarded."

"Brother William!" Katherine jumped to her feet. "You've no right to speak to me like that! I've already refused these arrangements, I *did* refuse them, though now—now—" She bit her lips until the blood surged back into them purple. "You've no right to judge! What can you know of love, or of a woman's heart? Do you think I've no pride? Do you think I don't suffer?"

The friar drew a long sigh. "Peace, child," he said, "peace! I don't judge you, that is for God to do. He knows what's in your secret heart. I see only a guilty love. Guilty," he repeated half to himself and gazed at her intently with his keen physician's eyes. "Nirac de Bayonne is ill," he said.

"Nirac—" she cried in an amazement that the watchful friar knew was innocent and unfeigned. "Why do you speak of him, now? Oh, I'm sorry he's ill, poor little scamp. He'll cure soon enough if the Duke is kind to him, I warrant."

So, I believe that I am quite wrong, thought the friar with deep relief. This girl at least knew nothing, if there were truly anything to know. Nirac had had two attacks like fits of madness, in which the Gray Friar had been called to tend him and soon discovered that these fits came from the taking of drugs obtained from some disreputable alchemist in the Basque quarter of town. During these fits Nirac had shouted out strange words and vague sinister allusions, coupled with Katherine and Hugh Swynford's names but actually nothing more than what an excited brain might invent. The friar was ashamed of the dreadful suspicions that had come to him.

He spoke more kindly to Katherine as they hurried towards the palace together.

To reach the Presence Chamber they had to traverse the palace cloisters. In the central garth a crowd of lords and ladies amused themselves, some tossing a gilded leather ball, some wagering piles of silver coins on the roll of ivory jewel-studded dice. The Princess Isabel sat on a blue velvet chair in the shade of a mulberry tree, munching candied rose petals and gossiping with Lady Roos of Hamlake. Her brother, Edmund of Langley, lounged beside her chair while he tickled the sensitive nose of Isabel's spaniel with an ostrich feather.

The Princess's sharp eyes missed very little. She spied Katherine's black-robed figure as the girl approached the Great Stairs and called out peremptorily, "My Lady Swynford!"

The girl started and glanced at the Gray Friar in distress. He said, "You must go to her," with some sympathy, for he did not like the Duke's sister.

Katherine moved slowly across the turf and curtsied to the Princess, who said, "I've heard some rumor that your knight has died, God rest his soul. I see," she glanced at Katherine's gown, "that it is so. A pity. Was it not some time ago?"

"A month, madam," said Katherine faintly. Edmund having made the spaniel sneeze looked up, his mouth fell open as he stared at Katherine. He scrambled to his feet and waving the ostrich feather cried, "And where have you been since, my lovely burde? So fair a widow should not go unconsoled." He leered at her with mawkish gallantry, and Katherine looked away, stricken by the caricatured resemblance to his brother in this weak, foolish face.

"Quiet, Edmund," said the Princess as though she addressed the spaniel. "Where are you bound now?" she pursued to Katherine, her instinctive resentment sharpening her voice, though in truth she had forgotten Lady Swynford since she saw her on the boat and had no motive but curiosity.

"To crave leave of departure from my Lord Duke, madam. It—it has been arranged that I sail home tomorrow."

"Ah—" said Isabel satisfied, "back to that North Country whence you came? Some village with a silly name, a kettle in it, what was it?"

"Kettlethorpe, madam," said Katherine, and stood waiting while Isabel chortled and Edmund giggled amiably and continued to eye the girl with warmth. "Have I your leave to depart now, madam?"

Isabel nodded and crammed another fistful of sugared comfits into her mouth. Katherine curtsied again and rejoined Brother William, who had been watching the way she bore herself and thinking that she was hard to condemn as wholeheartedly as his conscience bade him do for this scandalous intrigue she had plunged into while her husband lay but four days dead. As she stood before those two Plantagenets in the garden, she had seemed more royal than they and fashioned of a finer metal. Yet she was weak, debased by the sins of the flesh, and he must guard himself from excusing her because of the beauty of her flesh: a lure devised by the ever guileful Devil.

They entered the crowded anteroom past the yeoman-on-guard, and Brother William introduced her to the chamberlain, who said that my Lady Swynford would be received in her due turn. Katherine sat on a bench between one of the Castilian envoys and a Florentine goldsmith who held on his lap a casket of jeweled trinkets which he hoped to sell to the Duke as gifts for the bride.

The Gray Friar bowed to Katherine gravely and said, "I'll leave you now, my child, and shall pray that Christ and His Holy Mother strengthen you. *Benedicite.*"

She bowed her head.

Her head remained bowed while those ahead of her filed into the Presence Chamber: an abbess from Perigueux, a distressed knight and his lady from the Dordogne, the Castilian, the goldsmith, a messenger with letters from Flanders. At last the chamberlain spoke her name and a page resplendent in dazzling blue and gray livery came to usher her. An unknown squire received her at the door of the Presence Chamber and opened it for her to enter.

The Duke sat in a gilded canopied chair that was raised on a low dais. On his head he wore a coronet studded with cabochons, rough lumps of emeralds, balas rubies. His surcote of crimson velvet was furred with ermine and above the gold Lancastrian SSS collar his face was tired and bleak.

They looked at each other then looked away while the Duke said in his voice of chill command, "I will see this lady alone." The squire and a clerk who had been seated at a table silently withdrew.

She stood where she was in the middle of the floor, until he reached out his hand and said, "Come to me, Katrine."

She went over to the dais and kissed his hand. He drew her slowly up against him and kissed her on the lips.

"Brother William gave you my message?"

"Yes, my lord."

"You'll not refuse again, my dear one. I must know that you'll be there, waiting for me."

"I cannot refuse again," she said in a strangled voice, "for I believe I bear your child."

"Jesu!" he cried, his eyes blazed with light. "My child! My son! You will give me a son, Katrine. Another royal Plantagenet!"

"A bastard," she said, turning her head.

"But my son. He shall never suffer from it. Katrine, now you *cannot* leave me! I'll give you the world and all that's in it, I'll cherish you, care for you, you'll never know a hardship or a worry! You shall see what it is to be loved by the Duke of Lancaster!"

"And in return, my lord, I give you my good name—"

"Nay, darling, it need not be. No one need know. I'll do all to protect your good name. 'Tis fitting enough that you should be appointed Governess to my daughters, they're fond of you. And everyone knows I care for my people, that your husband died in my service and that you were—" he paused, "were beloved of the Duchess Blanche."

She looked at him sadly, thinking that men saw only what they wished to see, and that it would be no easy thing to conceal their love or the fruit of it. In truth he did not realize how they would shrink from the furtive, from a prolonged course of lies and subterfuges. In that they were alike, both imbued with reckless pride.

"I cannot see far ahead, my dear lord," she said sighing, "but I'll do as you say until you return, and I'll do my best for our children." And mine, she added silently, for in these last days that she had been alone in Bordeaux, she had thought much with painful yearning of her true-born babies, as though to reassure them that her love for them was untouched by this other all-compelling love that had come to her, nor changed by the new baby that she carried in her womb.

A flourish of trumpets sounded from the outside windows. They both started.

"The heralds practice for your wedding march," she said, the words dropping like stones on a wooden dish. "Adieu, my lord."

"Katrine," he cried. He pulled her close to him. "You *must* be careful, you will be *safe* on this journey. 'Tis the best master we have, the staunchest ship. I'll have two priests pray for your safety night and day in the cathedral. Oh my Katrine, do you love me?"

The bitterness left her eyes, she put her arms around his neck, and met his hot demanding lips with a gentle kiss. "Ay, my lord, I love you," she said with a laugh that was half a sob. "I think you need not ask."

# PART FOUR

## (1376–1377)

There saw I first the dark deceptions
Of Felony, and all the counterplots;
Cruel anger, red as any coal;
Pickpockets, and eke the pale Dread. . . .

THE KNIGHT'S TALE

# XVI

ON THE AFTERNOON before St. George's Day, 1376, April
bloomed in Warwickshire. The young lambs bleated
from the pastures beyond the mere, while a hazy gold
light turned the sandstone of the battlements to the color of a
robin's breast. All Kenilworth Castle, cleansed and garlanded
for the festivities, waited for the Duke to come again.

Katherine sat on a sunny stone bench in the Inner Court
near the old keep, lending an indulgent ear to the happy
shouts of the children as they romped through the courtyards. From this bench she could watch the entrance to the
castle at Mortimer's Tower and be ready when the trumpet
sounded and the first member of the Duke's company should
gallop through from the causeway. This time she had not
seen him for two months.

She was dressed in the gown he preferred to most of the
others he had ordered for her: an amber tunic beneath a
clinging sideless surcote of apricot velvet, furred with ermine.
Her golden girdle was inlaid with enamel plaques blazoning
her own arms—the three Catherine wheels or, on a gules
field. A thin topaz-studded fillet encircled her high arched
forehead, her eyebrows were plucked, her lips lightly reddened with cochineal paste as the Duke liked to see them.
Her dark auburn hair was perfumed with costly ambergris,
imported from Arabia, that he had appropriated for her in
some hastily abandoned castle on his Great March through
France, three years ago.

That march had been a foolhardy deed of courage. He had
forced his weakening and finally starving army through
enemy territory the length of France, from the north to Bordeaux. He had exposed his own person to danger time and
again, and suffered with his men. Even the French thought

this chevauchée a triumphant feat, spectacular as any his
brother the Black Prince had ever achieved, and yet in the
end there was loss, not gain. The lands through which he
marched had bowed under the trampling feet like long grass,
and sprung up again when he had passed.

When John had returned to England, embittered, his
dream of conquering all France and then Castile once more
postponed, he had found himself the target of an angry, puzzled England. For there was unrest everywhere and dissatis-
faction with conditions. The people clamored for another
Crécy, another Poitiers, but times had changed. A new and
wilier king sat on the French throne, and the once great English king was senile, his policies unstable, blowing now hot
now cold, obedient to the greedy whims of Alice Perrers, and
caring only to please her.

Yet now there was a truce with France, a precarious amnesty negotiated by the Duke at Bruges last year. The
thought of John's months at Bruges brought sharp pain to
Katherine, though it was a pain to which she was well accustomed.

John had taken his Duchess with him to Flanders and
there at Ghent, his own birthplace, Costanza had been delivered of a son—at last.

But the baby did not live! Katherine crossed herself as she
sat on the bench in Kenilworth courtyard and thought, *Miserere, Domine,* as she had when she first heard the news that
the baby had died—for shame of the fierce joy she had felt.

My sons live, thought Katherine. She glanced up to the
windows of the Nursery Chamber in the South Wing. A
shadow passed behind the clear tiny panes, and Katherine
smiled. That would be Hawise, or one of the nurses, tending
the infant Harry in his cradle, or perhaps fetching some toy
to distract little John as he ate his supper—for he was a fussy
eater and prone to dawdle. Healthy rosy boys, both of them,
golden as buttercups, with their father's intense blue eyes.

A high jeering singsong shattered the peace of the courtyard. "Scardey cats! Scaredy cats! Cowardy cowardy custard,
go get thyself some mustard—Ye *durstn't* do what *I* do—"
That was Elizabeth, of course. Katherine jumped up prepared
for trouble and hurried through the arch to the Base Court.
Though the Duke's younger daughter was twelve years old
and near to womanhood, Elizabeth's reckless enterprises still

had to be restrained before they led herself and the younger children into actual danger.

This time Elizabeth was hopping on one foot upon the slate roof of the ducal stable and clinging to the weather vane. Tom, Blanchette and the three little Deyncourts were all cramped into various stressful positions on the slippery slates as they tried to climb up to the taunting figure above them. Blanchette, her mother saw at once, was crying while she teetered on a window ledge, and fumbled for fingerholds in the stone gutter.

"Elizabeth!" called Katherine sharply, to the stable roof. "Come down at once!" She ran to rescue Blanchette by climbing on a mounting block and holding her arms up to the child, who dropped thankfully into them. "Little simpleton," scolded Katherine, kissing her, "When will you learn you *cannot* and *must not* do all Lady Elizabeth says?" She ran on from Blanchette and pulled down the Deyncourt children. But her own Thomas wanted no help. He turned a sulky face to his mother and said, "Let me be, lady. I shan't go to the roof, but I shall get down as I please," which was as typical of Tom at eight as it had been all his life. Never openly disobedient, but a headstrong sulky boy who reminded her often of his father, Hugh.

"Well, Bess," called Katherine to the culprit on the roof, "I told you to come down——"

"Can't," quavered the child. Her swarthy little face had paled, she clung so hard to the weather vane that its veering cock shook as in a high wind.

"Then be brave a few more minutes and hold tight," called Katherine more gently. She clapped her hands crying, "Groom! Here!" A stableboy ran out, brought a ladder and soon had Elizabeth safe on the ground——safe and defiant. "I wasn't scared, I was just gammoning you, my lady."

Katherine wasted no time in dispute, Elizabeth was forever getting into pickles from which she could not extricate herself. "Beat her!" advised Dame Marjorie Deyncourt, wife to the castle's constable. "You spare the rod too much." The Deyncourt children were beaten as regularly as they attended Mass. Five years back, when Katherine first assumed responsibility for the rearing of the Duke's two daughters, she had had recourse to frequent switchings as the only way to handle Elizabeth——Philippa needed no such measures, ever——but gradually Katherine had learned that firm kindness and the minimum of punishment better controlled the child. And John would seldom have her punished either, this giddy little daughter could always cozen him by climbing on his lap, shaking her dark curls and pouting her red lips, which were plump as cherries and gave promise of disquieting sensuality.

"Go, Bess, and find one of your maids," said Katherine sternly. "Tell her to wash you, you cannot greet your father in this state. Then stay in your chamber till you're summoned."

Elizabeth shrugged, but she went off to the castle, scuffing her feet. She liked Lady Swynford well enough and knew her to be just, but lately she had been puzzled by the situation between this lady and her father, which before she had accepted without interest. That the two baby boys called John and Harry Beaufort were her half brothers, she knew, and that her father loved Lady Swynford she had seen often enough with jealous eyes; but no one had ever explained these matters and mention of them was shushed. Servants' gossip overheard last week had awakened her to the knowledge that there was something strange about her governess, something the tiring-women snickered about behind their hands, and Nan, the laundry maid, had cried dramatically, "Ah, me heart bleeds, indeed it do, for that poor betrayed Duchess, a-pining away at Hertford or in them North Country wilds at Tutbury. 'Tis a mortal shame."

But Elizabeth had not liked her father's Spanish wife at all, the time that she and Philippa had been taken to Hertford to call on her. The Duchess had glittering eyes like pieces of jet, while the touch of her bony hand was cold and moist as a fish. Nor would she speak one word of English. She had given Elizabeth and Philippa an unsmiling scrutiny, then turned to talk in Spanish with the Castilian ladies who hovered near. Elizabeth had been sent to play with little Catalina, who was her half sister, too. Catalina was four years old like Lady Swynford's John Beaufort, but three months younger than he. This fact had been part of the servant's mysterious sniggers.

Katherine had felt a change in Elizabeth's attitude towards her of late, and thought with the flinty resignation she had been learning, She's beginning to realize, and it may be will rebel against me completely. But there was nothing to be done. It is as it is, thought Katherine. This Plantagenet motto gave her somber comfort; to John's amusement she had asked that it be graven on the gold rim of the diamond brooch he had given her last New Year's. She wore the brooch today on her apricot velvet bodice, and had long since put away the old Queen's trumpery little silver nouche with its saccharine "Foi vainquera."

Katherine walked back towards the Inner Court, while Blanchette skipped happily beside her. The other children had run off to the tiltyard outside the walls to watch the making of St. George's effigy for the games tomorrow. But Blanchette stayed with her mother whom, at nine, she already greatly resembled. She will be prettier than I could ever be, thought Katherine rumpling the silky curls that were bright as new-scoured copper. The little girl's eyes were gray too, but darker than Katherine's, even as her hair was lighter. The round eyes looked up at her mother now with confiding sweetness, and Katherine kissed her again.

How strange that Blanchette, begotten by an unloved father, born in anguish and loneliness, should still be the dearest of all her children, precious though John's babies were. Was there always a special tenderness for the firstborn? Yet John was less fond of his Philippa than of any of the others. Was it then that Blanchette was a girl and Katherine saw there her own childhood, or was it that because of John's arrival that morning of her birth, Blanchette had seemed like his own child? No use to question the mysterious alchemy of the heart, and certain it was that amongst the tormenting things her equivocal situation had brought to her, she had found solid material compensations, too. There was not one of her family who had not benefited, and John had provided lavishly for his godchild.

Last year he had granted to Katherine for Blanchette the wardship of the lands and heir of Sir Robert Deyncourt, cousin to the constable here at Kenilworth, and the marriage of this heir with all its fees and appurtenances. The wardship alone brought income to build Blanchette a handsome dowry. But Katherine thought with relief, it would be some years before one had to think of Blanchette's marriage.

"Here comes Lady Philippa," announced the child, who had crawled up on the bench beside her mother and was playing with a kitten she had fished out from the throng of mewing cats that were gathered hungrily about the door of the great kitchens. Katherine looked up to greet this elder of her two ducal charges and felt, as so often with Philippa, a touch of exasperated pity. Here was a girl about whom one must indeed think of marriage for she was full sixteen, and the Duke had entered into tentative negotiations with the courts of Flanders, Hainault, and even Milan.

Yet it was impossible to imagine Philippa bedded. She was pale, devout, submissive and so sexless as to make virginity seem inevitable.

"Good even, Lady Katherine," she said curtsying and speaking in her whispering little voice. She glanced rather anxiously at the Mortimer Gate Tower, "No sign yet of my lord father?"

"No," said Katherine, making room for the girl on the bench. "Didn't you think to wear the new crimson gown he had sent you?" Philippa was swathed in a dun-colored robe that spared none of her bad points, the flat chest and clumsy waist.

"I—I didn't—" said the girl fingering her sagging girdle nervously. "I feel so discomfited in crimson. Will he be angry with me?"

Katherine smiled reassurance, knowing that Philippa feared her father as much as she admired him. But he would not be pleased, and she would have to protect the girl from his annoyance that reduced Philippa to tears and long hours of penitence on the prie-dieu in her chamber.

Katherine might have insisted that Philippa go back and change, but she hadn't the heart. The ornate red dress was even less becoming than her ordinary garb, it made of her a figure of fun, like the garish tinsel puppet the mummers called Mrs. Noah.

"You're so beautiful, Lady Katherine—" said Philippa wistfully. "He's never angry with *you*."

"Ah, but he is!" Katherine laughed. "At times. One must wait until it passes, it soon does."

Philippa pulled from her reticule a square of samite, part of the chapel altar cloth she was embroidering. She was shortsighted and, bending her long serious face close to the needleful of gold thread, said without rancor, "Ay, for he loves you."

Katherine started. The blush that still plagued her, despite her twenty-five years, stained her fine skin. Philippa had never said anything so frank, though a girl of sixteen could be in no doubt as to the situation. Still, it had been tacitly ignored.

In the beginning, when John brought Costanza back from France and for some years thereafter, the lovers had been very discreet. For little John's birth, Katherine had gone to Lincolnshire, not indeed to Kettlethorpe—that would have shamed her doubly, as a slur on Hugh's memory—but to Lincoln itself, to a house on Pottergate, privily secured for her by the Duke. And for a time, the exact date of Hugh's death abroad having been left uncertain, they had fostered the assumption that this was Hugh's posthumous child.

No such covering assumption was possible when little Harry was born. It was plain enough for all to see that Lady Swynford had no husband; and the Duke, welcoming his new son, had renounced all further pretense and bestowed on the little boys one of his territorial titles, Beaufort, for lands in Champagne, long since lost to France and unlikely ever to prejudice the interests of his legitimate heirs.

Katherine had been glad when concealment of their relationship was no longer possible and relieved that at the two of his castles where she chiefly stayed with the children, Kenilworth and Leicester, all the retainers from the stewards and constables down, continued to treat her with obedient deference. The Duke would have seen to that, had not her own dignity quelled any overt disrespect. But there were times when something pierced the tough shell she had grown, and Philippa's calm statement filled her with unease.

She glanced at the girl, then at Blanchette, who had wandered off with her kitten towards the kitchens; she held her head high and stiff and said in a thickened voice, "Do you mind, Philippa?"

"Mind what, Lady Katherine?" The mild eyes stared. "Oh, that my father should love you? No. For I have loved you myself, ever since the time at Bolingbroke when you did get shriving for my blessed mother on her deathbed, God keep her soul in peace." She crossed herself and, bending close, took a slow stitch on her embroidery. "And you've been good to us since our father put us in your charge. But—" She moistened her lips, looked unhappily at Katherine, then away.

"But what, Philippa?"

" 'Tis mortal sin you live in—you and my father!" she whispered. "I'm frightened for you. I pray—pray for your souls."

Katherine was silent, then she put out her hand and

touched the girl's pale hair gently. She got up from the bench
and walked across the courtyard towards the gate that led out
to the mere and the pleasaunce where she herself had directed the planting of new flower beds and a boxwood maze.
The garden was alight with daffodils, lilies and violets; in moments of disquiet she sought its comfort as instinctively as
Philippa sought the chapel. She put her hand on the iron
gate latch, then turned with a glad cry. Clear on the spring
air there came bugle notes and the rumble of many galloping
hooves from the south where the road skirted the mere.

She started to run towards the entrance, wild as any hoy-
denish girl, but checking herself, walked with a shaking heart
to stand quietly, as was proper, next to Philippa on the first
step of the Grand Staircase that led up to the Hall.

Lancaster Herald cantered first through the arch and sa-
luted them with a dip of his trumpet and its pendent Lancaster arms. The court filled with jostling, shouting horsemen,
with stableboys and pages, who must be alert to catch
dropped bridles and run with mounting blocks.

Thirty or more had accompanied the Duke. In the confusion she noted only the clerics: a tall black-robed priest,
vaguely familiar, and the Carmelite, Walter Dysse, sleekly
plump as a white tomcat, who made her an unctuous salute
as he dismounted. Again there was no sign of Brother William, the Gray Friar. Though he was still the Duke's chief
physician, Katherine knew that Brother William avoided her.
The few times that they had met perforce, in the years of her
connection with the Duke, the friar had looked at her with
sad inscrutable eyes. Once he mentioned Nirac, who had died
over there in Bordeaux sometime after she left it, but he had
seen how little Nirac interested her now, and after listening
to her conventional murmur of regret, had hurried away.

A flicker of relief that the Gray Friar had not come was
quickly lost in her trembling anticipation.

The Duke's favorite hounds, Garland and Echo, came
gamboling through the arch, they leaped at her in greeting
and she patted their narrow gray heads, while she waited.

At last she saw him on Palamon as he paused to call back
some instructions to Arnold, his head falconer, who rode on
towards the mew bearing the great hooded white gerfalcon,
Oriana, on his gauntlet.

Each time that she saw John after deprivation, her body
flamed and seemed to melt. She thought him comelier, more

princely than ever, and loved him the more for the increasing
reserve he showed to the world, because it heightened the
rare sweet moments of their intimacy. Though he was now
thirty-six, he had grown no heavier—indeed what true Plantagenet could ever be stout? His hair, cut shorter than it used
to be, had dulled from gold to sun-bleached sorrel, but it was
thick as ever; and while Raulin d'Ypres, the Flemish squire,
held the stirrup, John jumped down from Palamon with the
easy grace of his youth.

He walked to the stairs, while Katherine and Philippa curtsied. Farther up the steps John Deyncourt, Kenilworth's
constable, bowed low and cried, "God's greeting, Your
Grace."

The Duke smiled briefly at his daughter, his eyes passed
over her dress with a faint frown, then, resting on Katherine,
widened in a private signal of greeting. "You look well, my
lady," he said softly and taking her hand, bore it to his lips.

"I am, now that you're here—" she whispered.

"The little lads?" he asked.

"Hearty as puppies. The babe has grown much since you
saw him, he speaks ten words."

"God's blood! And does he!—Henry!" the Duke, chuckling, called over his shoulder. "I'll vow *you* never were so
forward as your new brother. He speaks as many words as he
has months! Come pay your duty to Lady Swynford!"

Today the Duke had brought his heir with him, the nine-
year-old Henry of Bolingbroke, who was a thoughtful, matter-of-fact child, somewhat short for his years but sturdily
built so that he did well at knightly sports. His hair and eyes
were russet-toned, his snub nose was peppered with freckles.
He favored his grandfather and namesake, the first Duke of
Lancaster, rather than his handsome parents, yet from them
he had his character: from Blanche, a sweetly courteous dignity, from John, ambition and a lightning temper usually controlled. From them both he had pride, and consciousness of
rank.

Katherine smiled at Henry as the boy obediently bowed
before her. She seldom saw him, for he lived at the Savoy in
a separate wing with his own retinue of squires, tutors and
household officers, but she loved him for his father's sake,
and he responded, as did most children, to the sincere interest
she accorded them.

The Duke mounted the grand outer staircase to the Hall,

which he had as yet but partially rebuilt, though it was finished enough to show that in grace of proportion, airiness of tinted windows and carving of stone it deserved its growing reputation as one of the most magnificent rooms in England. Usually upon his arrival at Kenilworth the Duke's first act would be eager inspection of the work done by the master masons since his last visit; but today, though the oriel in the Sainteowe Tower had been completed, and in the Hall a window of stained glass depicting the garden from the Roman de la Rose had been installed since he was here, he gave these changes but an abstracted look, and Katherine saw that some matter was disturbing him.

She knew better than to question. In any case they would have no privacy until late that night, when he would come from the great White Chamber, up the hidden stairs to her solar—and her bed. Until then she must wait and do her duty as chatelaine towards all the company he had brought. She must find out whether the chamberlain had readied sleeping quarters for them all, and she was already certain that not enough of the precious spices had been doled out to season food for so many.

John at once retired to the White Chamber with Raulin in attendance. While the guests were occupied with drinking in the Hall, Katherine went upstairs to fetch the keys which would unlock the spice chest. In her solar she found Hawise industriously shaking a rowan branch over the bed and muttering some sort of charm.

"Holy saints, wench!" cried Katherine laughing. "What *are* you doing?" She looked at this dear maid and companion with amused affection. They had been through much together since Hawise had come back into her service before little John was born. Well-paid service now; the days had passed when Katherine must accept her maid's own money to exist. Hawise's present wages were equal to the Pessoners' yearly income from fish, and the fishmonger marveled at this, proud that his daughter had such good fortune, particularly as her husband, Jack Maudelyn, had turned of sour puzzling temper, neglectful of his looms and prone to traipse off into Kent after the Lollard preachers and come back full of their heretical mouthings against the monks, the bishops, and God's manifest plan of rich and poor, lord and commoner.

Hawise's stout arm continued to weave the branch over the bed, until she concluded the magic words which whistled a little through her gapped teeth before she turned and favored her mistress with a stern look. "I'm fixing it so ye'll not conceive again now that my Lord Duke's back wi' ye. Two bastards is aplenty for ye to bear, my poppet, and you so bad wi' the milk leg after Harry, I thought I'd lost ye."

"Oh, Hawise—" Katherine laughed, coloring a little. "I must take what God sends, I suppose." She bent and peered at herself in a silver-backed mirror, rubbed a little more red salve on her lips, frowned at a roughening she thought she saw on her chin.

"Ye needna fret," said Hawise watching. "Breeding's not harmed your looks, I'll grant that, ye've still a waist like a weasel." She spoke tartly because it hurt her to see her beloved mistress frowning at the mirror and reddening her lips like any of the lewd court women, and there were other small changes too in her lady. God blast him, Hawise thought, as many times before. Since he couldn't marry her why didn't he let her be! *She's* too fine for this game, however many play it. It'll kill her if he tires. Though as yet there were no signs of his tiring.

"The Duke is concerned about something, I fear," said Katherine gesturing for Hawise to bring her the bunch of keys from their hiding cranny beside the chimney. " 'Tis perhaps that the Prince of Wales is worsening and may not live the summer out? Yet that's no new thing."

"Nay, more like 'tis this matter of Parliament next week," said Hawise, who had been down to London to see her husband for Easter, and there heard much angry talk. "The commons are in savage mood. No doubt His Grace has wind of what they'll ask, and by cock's bones, they don't see eye to eye, commons and His Grace!" Indeed she had checked her Jack sharply for the hateful things he repeated of the Duke, but this she did not tell her mistress.

Katherine nodded, vaguely relieved. Inclination as well as good taste kept her from interest in national affairs. She was no Alice Perrers, whose greed for power and money were all but wrecking England, so they said. Katherine's only desire was to live quietly removed from the hurly burly of the court, to keep herself and her children from public scrutiny and receive John when he came as any lady would her rightful wedded lord who must be often absent on man's business.

This meant ignoring a great part of his life. It also meant ignoring Costanza and that other child of his at Hertford

Castle—Catalina—which meant Katherine in English. The Duchess Costanza had wished to name her child for a favorite Spanish saint, not knowing, in the summer of 1372, of Katherine Swynford's existence. John had laughed when he told Katherine of this. It amused him that his wife should name their daughter for his mistress, all unknowing, and part of his unkind laughter had come from his anger with Costanza for producing a girl, and no suitable heir for the throne of Castile. Katherine had felt faint pity for that other woman, all the easier to feel since she had never seen the Duchess.

Costanza had heard of Katherine's existence now, no doubt, though Philippa Chaucer said there was no telling *what* the Duchess knew, always jib-jabbering in her own heathenish tongue to those Spaniards, but mum as a clam to her English household.

The Duke had appointed Katherine's sister as one of the English waiting women to his new Duchess, and granted her a handsome annuity of ten pounds. Philippa had been delighted and looked upon the appointment as heaven's just reward for the dull years of hardship at Kettlethorpe. That she owed this windfall to Katherine's peculiar connection with the Duke, she accepted with brisk realism, though seldom alluding to it. Ever shrewd judge of a bargain, Philippa considered that the manifold benefits now enjoyed by all Katherine's family, nicely balanced off moral qualms. And she frequently thanked God that Hugh had died so opportunely, "Or you might have been shackled till Doomsday to that grumbling ha'penny husband, Katherine, and we'd all still be pigging it at Kettlethorpe."

Philippa's attitude had hurt Katherine, at first; she had felt her love cheapened by it, and for some time mention of Hugh gave her dull pain, like remorse, oddly mixed with anxiety. But that was in the beginning, now when she thought of Hugh, there was nothing but a blank.

Katherine rose from the dressing stool and fastening the keys to her girdle smiled at Hawise. "I must see to our guests. I scarce know who has come with His Grace."

The company assembled in the Great Hall were culled from the Duke's retainers or close friends and were mostly men, of course. Katherine was accustomed to that. Still, a couple of the young knights had brought their wives, and Lord Latimer, the King's chamberlain—a sly-eyed man,

long-nosed as a fox—had his lady with him up from London.
An honor so unusual that Katherine, as she received Lady
Latimer's subdued civilities, thought that his lordship must
need very special favor from the Duke. And she was increasingly aware of tension beneath the surface of this gathering.

Lord Michael de la Pole was his bluff hearty self and
greeted Katherine with the semipaternal pinch of the cheek
he always gave her; but then he drew to the corner by the
north fireplace and, scowling, whispered with the huge glowering Lord Neville of Raby. Both barons glanced sideways at
Latimer, then with deepened frowns their eyes turned to the
tall priest in the black doctoral robes, as though they wondered what he did there.

Katherine wondered too, for the priest was John Wyclif,
leader of the heretical Lollards. Wyclif had responded to her
greeting with a slight bow and left her at once to stand by
himself near the Roman de la Rose window, which he examined with apparent interest. Katherine too looked at the new
window, admiring the blaze of emerald light surrounding the
god of love and the ruby rose.

"Do you understand Love's Garden better now than once
you did, little sister?" said a voice in her ear.

She whirled around crying, "Geoffrey!" and caught his
hand in pleasure. "I didn't see you nor know you were coming. I thought you at Aldgate."

"I was. But since His Grace was so good as to include me
in Saint George festivities, I came. I grow dull alone with my
sinful books, my wool tallies."

His hazel eyes twinkled as they always had, faintly mocking. In the months since she had seen him, he had grown
stouter, and there was gray in his little forked beard. His
gown was deeply furred like any prosperous burgher's; he
wore a gold chain that had been given him by the King, but
there were still inkstains on his fingers and a battered pen
case hung at his neck with the chain.

"Nay, Geoffrey," she said. "You know you're never dull
alone, you like it."

They smiled at each other. Though Philippa sometimes got
leave from her duties to the Duchess Costanza and visited her
husband in his lodgings over Aldgate, where she cleaned and
clucked and harried him out of his easygoing bachelor habits,
these visits sprang largely from a sense of obligation, and the

Chaucers were both more contented apart. Their little son stayed with his mother, so Geoffrey lived alone.

"How goes your work at the Custom House?" Katherine asked. "Somehow I never thought to see *you* smothered in wool."

"Don't sneer at wool, my dear," he said lightly, " 'Tis the English crown's chief jewel. God bless those glittering fleeces that pour through the port of London out to a wool-hungry world. I value them high as ever Jason did. Our kingdom'd be bankrupt without them. If—" he added, frowning suddenly, and glancing at Latimer, "it isn't so already."

"What is it with Lord Latimer?" she asked in a low voice. "I sense unease here today, and my Lord Duke seems heavy of mind."

Well he may, thought Chaucer. There was trouble seething over a perilous fire. No telling how far the Commons were prepared to go in attacking the crown party, in this first Parliament called in three years; but they would not tamely grant the new subsidy which would be demanded by the King. That no one who had come from London could ever doubt. They would not dare attack the old King directly, nor yet perhaps the Duke, unpopular as he had grown. But they might conceivably fly for game as high as Latimer, who was King's chamberlain, keeper of his privy purse and the Duke's associate as well. Doubtless Latimer was an unscrupulous opportunist who had been feathering his own nest at crown expense like many another; but they said worse of him, far worse than that.

"Why, Latimer is the butt of many rumors. What man in high place is not?" said Geoffrey to Katherine, shrugging as though the matter were of no consequence. He understood the Duke enough to know that he preferred that Katherine should be kept apart from the turmoil of his public life. In truth, Geoffrey thought that the protective tenderness his patron showed to Katherine was one of the most admirable traits in a complex character.

A rustle of attention by the Sainteowe door to the Hall, and the glimpse of a coroneted head, showed that the Duke had entered. Katherine, her eyes clearing at once from the frown with which she had asked of Latimer, hurried down the Hall to meet him.

Geoffrey settled himself inconspicuously on a cushioned window seat and surveyed the company. He looked at the ra-

diant Katherine as she sat near the Duke, in her velvet and
ermine and new jewels. So he had been right when he saw
her first at Windsor and thought her destined to rise high in
life by reason of her rare beauty. The drabness of her years
at Kettlethorpe had after all been but a transient step. Yet
this relation with Lancaster was not the role he had vaguely
imagined for her either. This was too frank, too crude in its
flouting of the chivalric code which demanded above all a
delicate secrecy in the pursuance of illicit love. More fitting
far if they had managed to conduct their love like that of
Troilus and Criseyde, unsuspected by the censorious world.
His thoughts played with the story of Criseyde, and almost he
could see Katherine as the lovely Trojan widow.

Nay, thought Geoffrey, smiling at himself, my mind has
gone a-blackberrying. And he looked at the Duke, who was
now in earnest converse with Wyclif and obviously far from
love-longings. It was no soft bond that linked these two, the
great Duke and the reformer whose teachings now infiltrated
England. This bond was indignation. Between them, though
no doubt for different motives, they were agreed on debasing
and despoiling the fat monks and fatter bishops who were
bleeding the land.

Wyclif—so spare, so dedicated to his startling theories of
communal property, to his attacks on the Pope, to his denial
of the need for confessions, saints or pilgrimages—seemed a
strange colleague for Lancaster, whose orthodoxy had never
been in question.

Yet they seemed to have respect for each other, thought
Chaucer, and it was folly ever to listen to the slanders put out
by their many enemies. The house of fame, he thought, is
built on melting ice, not steel, and rumbles ever with a sound
of rumors, while the goddess of fame is as false and capricious as her sister—Fortune.

Geoffrey's hand went to the pen case that hung at his neck
and, forgetting the Duke and Wyclif, his eyes darted around
the Hall. Seeing no writing materials, he slipped quietly
through the North door to the office of the constable. Here,
as he'd hoped, a clerk was working on the castle accounts
which would be submitted to the Duke's auditor tomorrow.

Geoffrey borrowed what he needed and huddling on a
stool beside the clerk, noted the words, and the rhymes they
presently suggested. " 'The great sound . . . that rumbleth up

and down, in Fame's House, full of tydings, both of fair speech and chidings, and of false and truth compound.' "

He wrote on. The verses he had had in his head for many weeks began to shape as he wished them.

That night when the guests had all retired, Katherine lay waiting between silken sheets for her lord to come. Her naked body glowed from the sweet herbs with which Hawise had cleansed her, her skin was fragrant with the amber scent, and she rejoiced that it was firm and fresh as it had ever been. She thought how the responses of this body had increased and that her passion now was equal to his, though for modesty she tried sometimes to hide it. Yet carnal love was no sin, she thought stoutly, if the love be true-hearted. A hundred romances had taught her this, and since no strict confessor exhorted her, she no longer felt the sense of sin. Brother Walter Dysse, the Carmelite friar, listened with placid indulgence to her infrequent confessions, as he did to the Duke's. And she went to Mass only as an example to the children and the castle folk.

The room grew chill in the April dawn before John came, sliding without a word into her bed while her arms closed about him hungrily; but later he did not fall asleep on her breast. He lay staring up at the shadowy bed canopy that was strewn with tiny diamond stars.

She put her hand softly on his forehead, for sometimes he liked to have her stroke his hair, but he turned his head away.

"What is it, my dear heart?" she whispered. "The Blessed Mother forfend you are not displeased with *me?*"

"No, no—lovedy," he drew her tight against him so that her cheek was in the hollow of his neck, but still he stared up at the canopy. He would not speak, lest the baffled rage which fermented in his soul should sound like fear.

It was Raulin, his stolid Flemish squire, who had given him a hint of what they said in London. John had listened in contempt, unmoved at first, so ridiculous were the slanders. Corruption, disloyalty, designs against his brother, the dying Prince, against little Richard, the heir apparent—this was but monkey talk, the spiteful chatter of the rabble which would never dare say these things to his face. But then Raulin went on. "Another thing they visper, Your Grace—ach—such folly, 'tis not vorth repeating."

But John had commanded him to speak, knowing that he would be better armed to protect the crown for the coming fight in Parliament if he knew all their preposterous weapons.

"Some cock-and-bull tale that Your Grace is a changeling, not of royal birth."

"Bah! How feeble—"John had laughed. "Their other inventions are better. What more do they say of this? What particulars?"

" 'Tis all I heard," said Raulin, "no von beliefs it."

John had shrugged and spoken of something else, but in his stomach it was as though a cannon ball had gutted him, and his whole body trembled inwardly like that of the child who had first heard the word "changeling" nearly thirty years ago. Beneath his intercourse with others, beneath his joy at seeing Katherine, he had been trying to turn cool logic on this shameful fear. The King of Castile and León, the Duke of Lancaster, the most powerful man in England, to be overwhelmed by a vague whisper, to feel like a whimpering babe —cowering in terror of treachery, and injustice and loss. Last night he had dreamed of Isolda, and that he, a child again, looked up to her for comfort; but her gray eyes held naught but contempt and she sneered at him saying, "And did you believe me, my stupid lordling, when I said Pieter had lied? He did *not* lie, and you are hollow, empty as a blown egg, no royal meat within you."

"My dearest, what *is* it?" cried Katherine again, for the muscle of his arm jerked and the hand that had lain along her thigh clenched into a fist.

"Nothing, Katrine, nothing," he cried, "except I shall deal with my enemies! The hellish monks and the ribauds of London town—I'll crush them till they crawl on their bellies, sniveling for mercy; and I'll show none!"

She was frightened, for she had never heard him like this, and she said timidly, "But great men such as you, my lord, always have enemies and ever you have been above them— just and strong."

"Just and strong—" he repeated with a bitter laugh. " 'Tis not that they call me—ay—Do you know what they think, Katrine? They think I have no loyalty to my father and my brother. They think I plot to seize the English throne. The curse of God be on the fools!"

He shut his mouth, scowling into the darkness. His father and his brother—the idols of the nation, both feeble, ailing, moribund and at loggerheads just now. The Prince of Wales, frantic to conserve the kingdom for his son, little Richard, and to soothe the dangerous unrest of the English people, had called this Parliament and caused it to be subtly known that he would back the Commons in its attack upon the corruption around the doddering King. The Prince from his sickbed looked to John for support in this. The King too, caring only to giggle and toy with Alice Perrers, yet looked with childish faith to John to spare him discomfort and uphold the divine rights of the crown. Mediator! scapegoat! John thought violently. I bow my head to obey them both, to fight for what they each demand, and hear myself called traitor for my pains.

Yet this injustice but bred a clean contemptuous anger, not like that other squirming shameful fear which he now subdued again, helped by the unquestioning love of the woman beside him. What use to fear a vague slander which might well have been a chance shot and a not uncommon one in history, when fears were felt for the rightful succession? Doubtless as Raulin said, few knew of it and none believed it.

He breathed deeply and turning to Katherine, kissed her. "By Saint John, my love—" he said in the light tender voice he kept for her alone, "I've been tilting with a phantom. I'll cease my folly."

She understood nothing of this, except that his dark mood had passed and that in her he found comfort.

But while he slept at last in her arms, it was as though his distress had passed to her and she suffered that there was so much of his life she did not know.

## XVII

ST. GEORGE'S DAY was a happy one at Kenilworth. The Duke was his gayest, his most charming.

He jousted with his knights and shouted encouragement to Henry and Tom Swynford when the two boys joined in mimic battle, armored like their seniors and mounted on ponies. At night in the Great Hall, he danced with all the ladies and with Elizabeth, twirling and spinning the child until she shrieked with laughter. He was kind to the staid Philippa, forbearing to tease her for her solemn ways or chide her for not wearing the crimson gown. Nor was Blanchette forgotten. He had brought his goddaughter her heart's desire, a little lute made of wood and ivory with green tassels, like her mother's. Blanchette loved music and had learned to play from the same minstrel who taught the ducal children.

For two days and two more nights John and Katherine knew poignant joy, poignant in that it must be so brief; then on Friday morning the horses were again assembled by the keep, and the heavy carts and wagons lined up below in the Base Court, while varlets scurried to them from the castle bearing traveling coffers.

At six, Lancaster Herald blew a long plaintive blast of farewell. Katherine, standing on the stairs, bade them all godspeed—to little Henry of Bolingbroke, who, of course, returned to London with his father, to Geoffrey on his bony gray gelding, to the Lords Neville and de la Pole on their brass-harnessed destriers; to Lord Latimer, whose long vulpine nose was red from the chill morning wind as he stood beside his lady's litter. And to John Wyclif, the austere priest, who alone of this company had held himself apart from the merrymaking. Not discourteously, but as one whose thoughts were elsewhere, and whose interest lay only in moments of earnest converse with the Duke.

They had all mounted before the Duke turned to Katherine, who waited with bowed head, holding out to him the gold stirrup cup.

"God keep you, my love," he said very low, taking the cup and drinking deep of the honied mead. "It'll not be long this time, I swear it by the Blessed Virgin," he added in answer to the tears in her eyes. "You know I ache for you when we're apart."

She turned away and said, "Do you stop now at Hertford?" This question had been gnawing at her heart, and she had not dared voice it.

"Nay, my Katrine," he said gently, "I go straight to London to be ready for Parliament, you know that. You may be sure the Queen Costanza's no more eager for my company than I for hers."

She did not know whether he lied to her, out of kindness, but her heart jumped at the cold way he spoke of his Duchess, and she looked at him in gratitude, yet lifting her chin proudly, for she would not be a dog fawning after a bone for all the watching meinie to see.

He kissed her quick and hard on the mouth, then mounting Palamon cantered through the arch.

On the twenty-ninth of April, shortly before the hour of Tierce, as the Abbey bells were ringing, the King opened Parliament in the Painted Chamber at Westminster Palace. Then he seated himself on his canopied throne, while his sons disposed themselves according to rank on a lower level of the dais. But the Prince of Wales lay on a couch, half concealed by his standard-bearer and a kneeling body squire. The Prince was a shocking sight. His belly was swollen with the dropsy as his mother's had been, his skin like clay and scabrous with running sores. Only his sunken eyes at times shone with their old fierce brutality, as he turned them towards the King, or to his brother of Lancaster, or out past the bishops and lords to the crowd of tense murmuring commoners at the far end of the long hall.

King Edward held himself erect at first and gazed at his Parliament with something of the calm dignity of his earlier years; but gradually he drooped and shrank into his purple robes of state. His palsied fingers slipped off the scepter, and his face grew wrinkled and mournful like a tired old hound's. Except when he glanced towards the newel staircase in the corner behind the dais and saw the painted arras quiver. Then he brightened, and tittered behind his hand, knowing that Alice was hidden there on the turn of the stair.

The Duke of Lancaster sat on a throne too, one emblazoned with the castle and lion, for was he not—however far from his kingdom—the rightful ruler of Castile and León? Next sat Edmund of Langley, his flaxen head nodding with amiable vagueness to friends here and there amongst the lords, while he cleaned his fingernails with a little gold knife.

On the King's left his youngest son, Thomas of Woodstock, dark and squat as his Flemish ancestors, scowled at the wall where there was painted a blood-dripping scene from the Wars of the Maccabees. Thomas was not yet of age and never consulted by his father or brothers. He resented this but bided his time in wenching and gaming, and quarreling with his wealthy young wife, Eleanor de Bohun.

The morning was indeed dull. It opened with the expected speech by Knyvett, the chancellor, who droned on for three hours while exhorting the Houses to be diligent in granting the kingdom a new subsidy; money urgently needed, said the chancellor, for the peace of the realm, defense against possible invasion and resumption of the war in France, also—here he glanced at the Duke—in Castile.

As Parliament was invariably called for like reason, the speech held no surprises and those on the royal dais and the lords on their cushioned benches muffled yawns.

The Commons were ominously quiet. At the conclusion they asked permission to retire to the Abbey chapter house for consultation. The King, who had been drowsing, sat up and quavered happily, "So it's all settled. I knew there'd be no trouble. The people love me and do my bidding." He rose and glanced towards the arras. He wanted his dinner, which would be served him in a privy chamber with Alice, and he wandered towards the stair. His two elder sons looked at each other, John in response to a gesture walked over to his brother's couch.

"Let him go—" whispered the Prince. "He'll not be needed now." He fell back on the cushions, gasping. His squire mopped his temples with spirits of wine and after a moment the Prince spoke again, "Nor am I needed. Christ's blood, that I should come to this—useless, stinking mass of corruption! John, I must trust you. I know your loyalty—whatever they say. Conciliate them—listen to them. Hold this kingdom together for my son!" Tears suddenly spurted down his cheeks and a convulsion shook his body.

John knelt by the couch. His own eyes were moist, while he silently kissed his brother's swollen hand.

The convulsion ebbed into one of the woeful swoons which had afflicted the Prince for months. They carried him sadly from the Painted Chamber and took him home by barge to Kennington across the river, where Princess Joan and their little Richard awaited him.

Very soon the Commons began to show its mettle. A delegate requested that certain of the lords and bishops might join with them in conference in the chapter house. The Duke agreed graciously and waited with sharp interest to hear their choice, nor was surprised that amongst the twelve men named were two of his bitterest enemies, his nephew-in-law, the Earl of March, and Bishop Courtenay of London.

The earl, still at twenty-five pimply and undersized, had never forgiven the slight Lancaster had put upon him after the Duchess Blanche's death, when he had been kept cooling his heels in the Savoy. Each year his jealousy had grown and was now reinforced by fear. March's two-year-old son, Roger Mortimer, was heir presumptive to the English crown, after Richard. Unless the dastardly Lancaster should plot to force the Salic law on England and grab the crown himself. For Roger's claim came through his mother. This fear added fresh fuel to March's loathing; and the earl, upon hearing his name called, looked up at the Duke with a sly triumphant sneer, which Lancaster received with a shrug. March was a poor weedy runt whose spite was worth no more return than bored contempt.

Courtenay was more formidable. As Bishop of London he was the most powerful prelate in the country after Canterbury, and the Duke's well-known views on Episcopal wealth and his association with Wyclif had long ago incurred Courtenay's hatred.

The Commons' choice of these two lords to bolster up their coming attack against the crown gave some measure of the difficulties ahead, but was not startling. The choice and the acceptance of Lord Henry Percy of Northumberland, however, was dismaying.

The Duke, standing rigid on the dais, watched with a tight mouth while the twelve hostile bishops and lords filed out to the Abbey chapter house to join the Commons.

The lords remaining in the Painted Chamber settled back in an uneasy rustle of silks and velvets and let loose a buzz of consternation. Michael de la Pole detached himself from his fellows and coming up to the Duke said with the familiarity of long friendship, "By God's blood, Your Grace, what's got into Percy? The blackguard's gone over to the enemy! Yet a month ago he swore passionate love to you and the King!"

The Duke laughed sharply. "He has no enduring passion except for himself and his wild Border ruffians. He's swollen with pride and no doubt March has been puffing it with the hot air of promises."

He sighed, and de la Pole looking at him with sympathy said, "There's a vicious battle ahead, and I don't envy you the generalship."

In the ensuing days, the Commons' line of attack became

abundantly clear. The first mine was sprung with the election
of Peter de la Mare as their Speaker. De la Mare was the
Earl of March's stewart. He was also a blunt fearless young
man who wasted little time in presenting reply to the chancellor's demand for a subsidy. What, he asked, had become of
all the money already granted?

The people, de la Mare went on, were grievously dismayed
at the shocking waste and corruption in high places, and they
wished the guilty parties brought to justice. He stopped.

There was a long silence in the Painted Chamber. Everyone looked at the Duke, who finally said, inclining his head,
"Indeed if this be so, the people are within their rights. Who
are those whom you would name, and what are their alleged
crimes?" And he smiled with perfect graciousness.

The smaller fry were dealt with first: a customs collector,
and the London merchants John Peachey and Richard Lyons,
both accused of extortion, monopoly and fraud. These men
were summarily tried, found guilty and sent off to prison.

Then as the Duke and his friends had suspected, the Commons went for Lord Latimer. They accused him of a dozen
peculations, of having helped himself to twenty thousand
marks from the King's privy purse and finally of treason in
Brittany.

Here John momentarily lost his calm and spoke out in
anger, for Latimer, however unattractive a personality, had
been his friend, and though quite probably guilty of malver-
sation, the accusation of treason the Duke considered to be
outrageous, and said as much. It was thereupon withdrawn,
but Latimer was found guilty on the other charges, and the
Duke, biting his lips and avoiding the convicted peer's frightened foxy eyes, made no further effort to save him.

The Commons exulted openly: they had for the first time
in history succeeded in impeaching a minister of the crown!

John had been to Mass that morning and there prayed that
he might be guided by justice in the coming trials and that he
might be given strength to conciliate the people as his brother
had implored him to do. Revolt, civil war—like the evil smell
of brimstone in plague time—pervaded the air of the Painted
Chamber, indeed the air of all England. The Prince thought
compromise the best way of clearing it, and he might be
right.

The indictment of Lord Latimer had been expected, the
identity of their next quarry had not.

A collective gasp rose from the lords' benches as de la Mare called, "Lord Neville of Raby!"

"What's this!" cried Neville jumping to his feet and turning purple. His fierce little boar's eyes glared at the Speaker and then at his hereditary enemy, Percy of Northumberland. He strode down the hall towards the Commons, his great chest swelling. He shook his fist shouting, "How dare you churls, ribauds, scum—to question *me,* a premier peer of the realm!"

Some eighty pairs of eyes stared back at him defiantly. He swiveled and charged through the center of the Chamber past the four woolsacks up to the dais. "You *cannot* permit this monstrous act, Your Grace!"

The Duke's nostrils indented and he breathed sharply. For Latimer he was not responsible, but Neville was his own retainer who had served him for years. A rough, violent man of war, like the other Border lords, yet ever loyal to Lancastrians. The Duke hesitated, then he said quietly, "It seems that we must hear, my Lord Neville, what they would say."

The Speaker bowed and launched forth at once, raising his voice over Neville's uproarious objections. The Commons' charges of illicit commissions were trivial, a matter of two marks a sack in some wool transaction which Neville furiously denied, but he could not sustain his innocence. Their next accusation, that four years ago he had produced an insufficient number of men to serve in Brittany and then allowed these men to conduct themselves licentiously while awaiting shipment, Neville contemptuously refused to answer at all.

Commons, considering that the charges were proved, requested that he be removed from all his offices, and heavily fined.

This is ridiculous, thought John, 'tis only to insult me that they attack Neville. Though there had been slight dishonesty proved, what man among the Commons, what man among the twelve turn-coat lords had not done as much? But he tightened his jaw and held his peace. He waited for the next accusation in grim suspense and was relieved at the object of their final and most virulent attack—Alice Perrers.

There was truth in what they said of Alice: that she was rapacious, venal and a wretched influence on the King; that she bribed judges, forged signatures, and helped herself to crown funds and jewels. Moreover they said, it had been discovered that she was married and thus wallowing in flagrant

adultery and that her hold on the King could only be the result of witchcraft. A Dominican friar had given her magic
rings which produced enslavement.

Nay, belike it wasn't witchcraft, John thought, as he listened to this accusation. Her hold was simply that of gaiety,
and a warmth, however spurious, to light an old man's bones.
Fear of death had come upon the King. What wonder that he
fled from the gloomy monks who spoke only of the dangers
of hell fire? Or that he clung to Alice, who told him witty
stories and listened sweetly to his meandering tales of long
past battle? Evil as she might be, it would go hard with the
old man to have her banished from England, as Commons
demanded. For I think he cannot live without her now, nor
live long anyway, thought John sadly. And he thought too of
Katherine with the sharp twist of longing she always roused
in him, and how miserable a thing it would be should outsiders try to part him from her.

Yet Katherine and the Perrers were as unlike as a rose and
a jackdaw and it were shame to think of them in the same
breath.

He equally acceded to the Commons' wish and had Alice
summoned to the bar. She came before them soberly dressed
and demure, her little cat face hidden by a veil, her head
meekly bowed, which did not prevent her from casting voluptuous, imploring glances sideways at the Duke.

He had her sentence softened to banishment from court,
and they forced her to swear on pain of excommunication
and forfeiture of all her property that she would never again
go near the King. Then they appointed two sergeants-at-arms
to go with her and see that she obeyed.

"And now, by God," said Lord de la Pole to the Duke, on
the day that Commons finished dealing with Alice, "I think
we're out of this stew. See—that sharp-toothed young de la
Mare's jaded at last, there's no more bite in him. I was proud
of you, my lord. 'Twas no easy thing to let them override
your inmost wishes and your loyalty. And yet I think it had
to be, some of their claims were just and it may be wise to
sacrifice royal prerogative at times, if it gain the love of the
people."

"Ay, so my brother of Wales thinks," said John, smiling
into the bluff, affectionate eyes of the older man. "But by
Christ's sweet blood, now they must be contented. Is it too

much to hope they may even be content with *me?*" He
looked at his friend with a sudden wistfulness.

Before the baron could answer they were interrupted by a
messenger who rushed into the Painted Chamber and, throwing himself to his knees before the Duke, panted out urgent
words. The Duke shook his head with a look of deep sorrow.
He rose and held his hand out to still the hubbub. "Lords and
commoners all," he said, "we must adjourn. The Princess of
Wales has sent from Kennington. This time there is no hope
of his rallying."

Edward of Woodstock, the Black Prince, died on Trinity
Sunday, the eighth of June in his forty-sixth year. The King
his father, and the Duke his brother, knelt by the bedside,
and to those two he confided the care of his wife, Joan, and
the nine-year-old Richard. The King and Duke kissed the
Bible held out to them by the Bishop of Bangor to seal their
oath.

Then the old King beat his breast with the loud lamentations and fell into a pitiable childish weeping, until the Princess Joan led him away.

The Duke and the bishop remained with the Prince until
the end came, when John leaned down and kissed the brow
which had been contorted with pain and was now suddenly at
peace. As the Bishop of Bangor folded the gnarled warrior
hands across the still breast, John left the bedside and walked
into the antechamber, where the old King whimpered in his
chair and stared with frightened eyes at the crucifix that was
fastened to the wall.

Princess Joan knelt on a rich carpet beside her little son,
holding him close and crooning to him tender mother words
of reassurance. Richard's body was stiff in her arms, his delicate girlish face was glassy from the horror of hearing his father's last agonized cries.

"It is finished," said John crossing himself. "God give his
soul rest." The three in the antechamber made the sign of redemption, while the Princess gave a low shuddering sob.

John slowly sank to one knee before the child. He took the
icy little hand and laying his forehead on it, said, "I, John,
King of Castile and León, Duke of Lancaster, do swear allegiance to thee, Richard, who art now the heir of England."
The child's round cornflower eyes stared down at his uncle's

bowed head. The big magnificent man had always seemed a being as godlike and remote as King Arthur.

Richard turned whispering to his mother. "Why does my uncle of Lancaster kneel to me?"

"Because you will be King of England, Dickon—when—" She glanced at the old man humped over in his chair. "Some day." She looked down at her brother-in-law, and her tear-blurred eyes were beseeching. "God pity us, John," she said, "and *you* must pity us. Who is there but you that can protect us now that my dear lord is dead!"

"I have vowed to protect you, my sister, and Richard shall be—by reason of his holy birthright—ever first with me and before my own son."

"I believe you," she said after a moment.

Little beauty remained to Joan of Kent, who had once been the fairest maid in England. Her forty-eight years had coarsened her. She had grown fat and the pure golden hair was brassy now with dye. Yet the feminine charm which has captured and held the Prince of Wales' resistant heart had not faded. Despite her anguish for her husband and the fears she felt for the future of her son, she smiled at John and she touched his shoulder caressingly with her plump ring-loaded hand.

"Christ and His Holy Mother guide us all," she said very low. She looked from the handsome stern-faced Duke to the old King and then to the frail trembling child beside her.

For Katherine, the summer months were slow and heavy with longing. Kenilworth, scarce three days' journey from London, was not isolated. Messengers went back and forth to the Savoy, and Katherine had the comfort of brief letters from the Duke, but she did not see him. She knew that he loved her, yet she knew too that he threw himself into whatever aspect of his life was uppermost with single-minded vehemence, and the news that came through from London made clear the enormous pressure put upon him now.

Parliament sat on until mid-July. And there were the multitude of duties and arrangements resultant from the Prince of Wales' woeful death. And the King was ill, had taken to his bed at Havering-at-Bower, pining for the banished Alice more than for his dead son, so the people whispered. The Duke was virtually regent of England.

Katherine strove to be reasonable. She played with her babies; she supervised the studies and games of the older children; she sat embroidering with Philippa and their women; and often they all rode out with hounds and bows and the Duke's foresters to hunt the roebuck. Katherine had become a fair shot herself under the Duke's tutelage, and even Philippa enjoyed the chase.

The months passed, and Katherine lived for the receiving and writing of letters. She had mastered writing now, had practiced with the children while they learned from an elderly friar. She wrote to John of the children, and frankly of her love and longing, and she wearied him with no reproaches.

Yet each time she picked up the quill and at many other moments too she wondered if he found time to visit Hertford, which was but a morning's ride from London. And knowing that he must, her chest would churn with sick jealousy of this woman she had never seen. Costanza shared his bed, his name, his rank, however cold and foreign she might be, however little he might love her.

When these thoughts overwhelmed Katherine, she would fight them with a frantic busyness—ripping out embroidery she had set and starting anew in a snarl of silks, or scandalizing the little Beauforts' nurses by a total upset of routine when she seized her babies and carried them off to her solar for hours of impassioned cuddling.

There were two at the castle who suffered with Katherine when they saw the strained feverish fits come on her: the two who loved her best, Hawise and Blanchette. The maid suffered in full awareness of her mistress's heart, and the child from instinct; yet in both the result was the same—a resentment of the Duke. Hawise did not express it, knowing that would but hurt her lady more, and Blanchette was not aware that she hated the great powerful figure whom her mother loved. But it was during that summer that the little girl first took to weeping without reason and to wandering off by herself to hide in remote nooks of the castle or the grounds, nor would come out, until at last she heard her mother's frightened voice, when she would let herself be found, and cling sobbing to Katherine.

At last at the beginning of September, a messenger arrived from the Savoy and bore joyful news. The Duke summoned Katherine and some of the household down to London.

"Ma très chère et bien-aimée," the Duke wrote to her in

French, as he always did, and told her that he could not yet
leave London; but it would not be improper if she as governess accompanied his daughters on the occasion of the annual
obituary service for their mother, the Duchess Blanche, at St.
Paul's. He directed that she leave her Swynford children and
the two Beaufort babies at Kenilworth with their nurses,
since the London air was not so healthful for little ones as
that of Warwickshire; and he ended with an enigmatic little
quotation which was private to them.

"Il te faudra de vert vestir," he wrote, and she finished it
aloud laughing softly, "c'est la livrée aux amoureux," thinking of the first time they had said it to each other at the
Château la Teste when she had worn the green kirtle as they
started for the Pyrenees.

"Ay, now ye'll be merry as a popinjay again and juicy with
love like a plum," said Hawise, acidly coming into the solar
with an armful of Katherine's white silk shifts and glancing
at the letter. "Well, when does he come?"

"He doesn't. We're going to the Savoy instead."

"Peter! That's a new betaking!" Hawise's sandy eyebrows
shot up. "Will it not cause talk, an ye go to London?"

Katherine's glowing face hardened. "What more fitting
than that I should pay respect to the memory of my beloved
Duchess?"

Ay, you've no cause to fear *her,* Hawise thought, but what
of the other Duchess? And she said, "There may be discom-
fortable things for ye to meet down there, sweeting."

Katherine lifted her chin. "I must chance it. Dear God,
Hawise—" she turned with sudden passion, "do you not remember how long I've been parted from him?"

Katherine, the two ducal daughters, Hawise and a score of
household servants journeyed down to London four days
later.

Blanchette cried frantically when her mother left, but Tom
did not even bother to say farewell, having embarked at
dawn on a rabbit-snaring expedition with one of the Deyncourt boys.

Katherine worried about Blanchette for some time as they
rode along the causeway and around the mere to cross the
Avon. Beside the river bridge there stood a tavern, on its
swinging sign was painted the Duke's arms. She gazed at
them lingeringly, thinking that despite the thousands of times

she had seen it this blazon never failed to give her a thrill of
delight. And she forgot Blanchette.

At first the arrival at the Savoy was dismaying. She had
not remembered how vast it was, how filled with people and
commotion. Numerous as were the household officials, those
of the chancery were greater. And too at the Savoy, most of
the Duke's retinue were quartered. Katherine was given a
chamber to herself near the falcon mew and close to the
ducal suite, but she felt nearly as remote from him as she had
when first she stayed here at the Beaufort Tower seven years
ago.

Hawise helped to dress her in green satin trimmed with
seed pearls, and then Katherine waited two hours in her
room without word before a page tapped on her door to say
that His Grace wished her to come to the Avalon Chamber.

He sat writing at the well-remembered carved-oak table,
frowning at a private missive to Wyclif, which he did not
wish to dictate to a clerk. But he flung his pen into the sand
cup and jumped up to give her greeting. He held out his arms
and she ran to him with a low cry of joy.

He laughed, holding her from him, looking at her so that
her pulses pounded. "And so you're wearing green, dear
heart, as I asked—and I too." He pointed to the lining of the
dagged sleeves of his brocaded robe. "We'll do full justice to
love's color, won't we, Katrine!" He put his hand on her
breast and kissed her avidly.

He lifted her and carried her to the great crimson velvet
bed which stood by the Avalon tapestry.

Before the honied oblivion overwhelmed her, she thought
of that other time so long ago when he had carried her to
this bed, and she had denied him with fear and anger. How
strange that she had done so. For the space of the thought's
flash she could not remember the reason. But it was because
of *Hugh*, was it not? The answer seemed to her as flatly
meaningless as a problem on the abacus. More than Hugh
though, she had been full queasy of conscience in those days,
a priggish child. But she could not remember what that girl had
felt.

When their bodies were close they often caught echoes
from each other's minds, and John, seeing the faint shadow
in her languorous eyes, said, "Ay, darling, I never thought
we'd be here like this, that other time when you ran from
me." He laughed low in his throat. "Nor did I guess how hot

a love my pope-holy little nun could show, though 'tis true she has the hidden mark of Venus." He kissed a certain small brown mole.

Quick rose dyed her cheeks, she pushed him away from her with mock anger, yet her voice trembled as she said, "You reproach me, my lord? You would have me more coy? Maybe I should check your desire with stern looks and remind you that this is a fast day, and for conscience' sake we must abstain!"

At this he laughed again, with tenderness. "Do you think my love could have been held so close by a cold and canting woman?" He seized her hands as they shoved against his chest and holding them pinioned wide apart, looked down at her teasingly, and then with the darkening grimness of passion until her lips parted and she ceased to struggle.

The Duchess Blanche's Requiem Mass was to be held on her death day, September 12. A week at the Savoy had passed in a delicious haze. Taking their cue from their lord, the courtiers showed no recognition of Katherine's actual position, but there was an undercurrent of indulgent approval of the lovers. And except for the few of the ladies who were jealous of her beauty and would have liked to enjoy the Duke's favors themselves, she was treated with respect.

It was a happy week. One day they held a fête champêtre in the famous gardens. Tables strewn with thyme and loaded with simple country fare were set up beneath the rose arbors, and later the lords and ladies, glowing from the ale they had drunk, girded up their velvet robes to dance the hay and cut other rustic capers.

On another sparkling morning the Duke ordered out his barges. All seven of them, garlanded, and canopied with tapestries, started down the Thames on a junket to Deptford. The Duke rode in his great barge of state with his two daughters, a half-dozen of his gentlemen—and Katherine. She sat on a cushion beside the Duke, and her hand curled into his beneath a concealing fold of his outspread satin mantle, and dreamily watched the London banks stream by. Above the gabled houses the church spires pierced the violet sky like arrows, and the music of their bells nearly drowned out the gay songs from the minstrels' barge.

They floated swiftly with the tide like the cluster of white swans that followed them. The four oarsmen barely skimmed the water, the helmsman alone was brisk as he swung his wooden tiller to steer them amongst the teeming water traffic, produce and fishing boats, the pleasure barges of other nobles, and the ferries plying to and from the Surrey bank.

They came to the Bridge with its load of higgledy-piggledy houses so squeezed it seemed that some must slide into the rushing current, nor was Katherine's dreamy peace disturbed by the row of severed heads that were stuck on iron pikes along the Bridge. Though one young curly head was fresh and still dripped blood, she felt but a dim pity. There were always rotting heads on London bridge, and she neither knew who these men were nor for what crimes they had suffered.

The sun sparkled on the water and the warm firm hand clasped hers tenderly beneath the mantle fold. Today John was relaxed and pleased to share with her his knowledge of the scene around them. He pointed out a galley from Venice, spice-laden so that the pungency of cloves and nutmeg drifted to them across the river, and an English ship, Calais-bound, with a cargo of the precious wool. Once they laughed together at a drunken monk so fat he overweighted the wherry he was crossing in, and howled with rage each time his great rump splashed in the water.

It was her last day of merriment.

That evening they returned with the tide as the Savoy chapel bell rang for vespers. They disembarked at the barge landing and followed the Duke through the arch to the Outer Ward. Katherine saw at once from the throng of horses and people that some new company had arrived, but beyond noting that they must be foreigners, for there was something odd about their clothes and she heard words in a strange tongue, she thought nothing of so usual an occurrence. Except for a pang because the arrival of important guests would necessitate prolonged entertainment and inevitably postpone the hour when she and John might be alone.

As she followed behind him she saw him start and heard him say "Christ's blood!" in an angry tone before he strode ahead into the crowd of newcomers.

She stood uncertainly by the bargehouse when suddenly her arm was clutched and she looked down at her sister.

"Philippa!" she cried staring at the plump face beneath the neat white coif. "What do you here?"

"My duty, naturally!" said Philippa shrugging. "But I expected warmer greeting after the time we've been apart."

Katherine bent and kissed her sister on each cheek. "I was startled, I thought you at Hertford with—with—" She faltered, glancing towards the newcomers. Bitter coldness checked her breath.

"Ay, so," nodded Philippa. "The Duchess is here. To visit her wedded lord. She took the notion in the night, from a dream. Her father the murdered King Pedro appeared to her and told her to come. Or so I've gathered from the only one of her ladies who'll speak English to the rest of us. Faith, Katherine," she added patting the girl's hand, "you're white as bleached linen. You'll have to make the best of it. Show me to your chamber. I dare say I can sleep with you?"

"Where will the Duchess sleep?" asked Katherine very low.

"In the ducal suite, of course. She always does when she comes here."

Katherine turned and silently led the way up to her chamber, where Hawise was drowsing by the fire waiting for her mistress. Hawise and Philippa greeted each other in the offhand manner of long but tepid acquaintanceship.

"This'll not be easy for my lady," said Hawise, glancing at Katherine, who had moved to the window to stare out through the tiny leaded panes at the silver Thames below.

"Bah! She needn't fret." Philippa hung her serviceable squirrel-trimmed mantle carefully on a perch and bent to adjust her coif in Katherine's mirror. "The Duchess hasn't come for bed-sport, that I'll warrant."

"How d'ye know that?" Hawise saw Katherine's slender back stiffen.

"Because," said Philippa briskly, "she cannot, if she would; which sport I think was never to her liking. But since she gave birth at Ghent last winter an infirmity has gripped her in her woman's parts."

Katherine turned slowly, her dilated eyes were dark as slate. "Then if this is true, she will but hate me the more, as I know I would."

"What whimsy!" Philippa had no use for morbid speculations. "I dare say she never thinks of you at all. What wonder to her that the Duke should have a leman, indeed what great noble has not?"

Katherine flinched, her nails dug sharply into her palms. She turned back to the window and leaned her cheek against the stone mullion.

"Ye shouldna've said that." Hawise scowled at Philippa,

who was searching in Katherine's little tiring coffer to find a
pin.

"Whyever not? 'Tis simple truth. By the rood, Hawise—
can you not keep your mistress's gear in better order! This
coffer's like a pie's nest. Hark—there's the supper horn. You
must hurry, Katherine."

"I'll not come down," she said in a muffled voice.

But to such folly Philippa would not listen. She flattened
Katherine with stern elder sister edicts. And her common
sense, though devoid of imagination, was not untinged with
sympathy. Katherine was here, the Duchess was here, sooner
or later they must meet, best to get it over.

Katherine, hastily attired by Hawise in the splendid apricot
velvet gown, accompanied Philippa down and across the
Inner Ward to the Great Hall, where the chamberlain separated them and seated each according to rank. Philippa went
to the long board by the door where were fed the mass of
commoners: heralds, squires, waiting women, friars, the low-
lier chancery officials and their wives. Katherine, no longer
entitled to her usual seat, since all room at the High Table
was pre-empted by the Castilian retinue, was put amongst the
knights and ladies at the board below the windows. She slid
quickly into place but could not raise her eyes from her pewter trencher which the varlets heaped with gobbets of smoking brawn. Yet soon she was forced to notice the knight beside her, Sir Esmon Appleby. He rubbed his foot against
hers, he made play of brushing her arm as he reached across
her to dip into the salt, he cast sideways looks into her
bosom. She moved away on the bench, though wedged as she
was between him and the elderly clerk of the Duke's privy
expenses this was difficult.

Sir Esmon gripped his hand on her velvet-covered knee
and whispered with wine-soaked breath, "No need to be so
prim tonight, sweet burde. His Grace is occupied, pardee!"

"Leave me alone!" she said, shaking with anger.

"Nay, sweet heart," the knight's hand crept upward along
her thigh, "Play not the virgin with me! I can show you
many a lusty trick, I'll vow His Grace ne'er thought of!"

She seized the meat knife from her trencher and slashed it
down across the groping hand.

"Jesu!" yelped the knight, jumping up and staring at his
welling blood. The lady next him squeaked with laughter,
even the old clerk snorted into his cup as Sir Esmon, dabbing

at his hand with his napkin, picked up his trencher and angrily moved to a place at the far end of the board.

Katherine sat stiff and faint with humiliation, staring at her untouched food. At last she raised her head and looked at the High Table, at the great high-backed golden chair beside the Duke which had always been empty till now.

Dear Mary Mother, she thought. The misery which had receded with Philippa's revelation in the chamber washed over her in a muddy flood.

The Duchess was small and young. She was not ugly as they had said.

Katherine, like one who cannot cease from pressing on an aching tooth, strained her eyes down the Hall. Young. Four years younger than I! Costanza was still but twenty-one. For all that Katherine had known this, yet she had resolutely pictured the Duchess as middle-aged, and big with a haughty maturity. She had not guessed the smallness.

The Duchess was dressed in somber gray. Katherine could see no jewels except her crown and a long sparkling pendant at her neck, which must be the reliquary she wore always and which Philippa said contained one of St. James' fingers.

Katherine looked from the glossy black wings of Costanza's netted braids beneath the golden crown, to the dark eyes below. Even at this distance, one could see that they were large and brilliant, and they seemed to gaze out with brooding intensity from the long narrow face, even when the little head tilted towards the Duke.

Katherine, watching in anguish, saw that they spoke but seldom together. His face that she knew so well in all its moods was set into the stern mask which she passionately told herself always hid boredom. But she could not escape noting another quality she had never seen in him—deference. The Duke and Duchess ate from the same gilt salver, drank from the same hanap, and Katherine saw that he held back from each sip and morsel, so that Costanza might partake first, and that every motion of his body and the carriage of his head showed obeisance.

For Christ's sweet mercy—will he not look towards me once! Her fingers ripped a hunk from the soft white bread and kneaded it like clay.

"You eat nothing, my lady?" said the old clerk on her left. He looked at her curiously.

"Nay, sir—I—I have a touch of fever." She seized her

wine cup and drained it. The thick heady vernage burned in her stomach. She picked up a breast of roast partridge, dipped it in the sweet pepper sauce then put it down again untasted. The meal dragged on.

Katherine sat and waited for the moment when she might be released. He had no thought for her, he had forgotten the sweetness of last night, of this very day in the barge. She drank more of the vernage, and her bitterness grew close to hatred. Ah, Katherine, where can you run to now, as once you ran from him? Where in the whole of England could you hide from him now, he who pretends to love you? Cold, cruel, heartless—so deep was she in her turmoil that she paid no heed to an announcement by the herald.

She caught its echo only because of the buzzing of the people around her. The Duke had commanded that all those who had not previously been presented to the Queen of Castile should come up now as their names were called.

This too, she thought—he wishes to humiliate me, to see me pay homage to his wife. And she steeled herself in anger. One by one, lords, knights, and their ladies were summoned by the chamberlain.

Then she heard "Lady Katherine Swynford." She walked stiff-kneed down the Hall, her cheeks like poppies. There were snickers quickly checked, and she felt the slyness of spearing eyes.

She reached the Duchess's chair and curtsied low, touching the small cold hand extended to her, but she did not kiss it. She raised her eyes as Costanza said something quick and questioning in Spanish, and she heard the Duke answer, "Sí."

The women looked at each other. The narrow ivory long-lipped face was girlish and not uncomely, but seen close like this one felt only austerity. The black eyes glittered with a chill fanatic light. They seemed to appraise Katherine with the scrutiny of a moneylender examining a proffered trinket, and again Costanza spoke to the Duke.

He leaned slightly towards Katherine, saying, "Her Grace wishes to know if you are truly devout, my Lady Swynford. Since you have the care of my daughters, she feels it essential that you neglect no religious observance."

Katherine looked at him then, and saw behind the sternness of his gaze a spark of amusement and communion.

Her pain ebbed.

"I have tried not to neglect my duties towards the Ladies Philippa and Elizabeth," she said quietly.

The Castilian queen understood the sense of this, as indeed she understood far more English than she would admit. She shrugged, gave Katherine a long enigmatic look, and waved her hand in dismissal as the chamberlain called another name.

Katherine quitted the Hall, walked slowly across the courtyard. Oh God, I wish I hadn't seen her, she thought, yet he doesn't love her, I know that. No matter that she is so young and a queen, it's me that he loves, and it does her no real wrong—and she doesn't care—one can see it, and *she* cannot even bear him a son. Yet, Blessed Virgin, I wish I had not seen her.

Throughout the sleepless night in her lonely bed, Katherine's thoughts ran on like this.

# XVIII

THE DUCHESS COSTANZA that night announced to the Duke that she wished to make pilgrimage to Canterbury at once. It was for this that she had come to London. Her father, King Pedro, in her dream had directed her to go, and also told her certain things to tell the Duke.

"He reproaches you, my lord," said Costanza to John when they were alone in the state solar. Her Castilian women had been dismissed for the night, having attired her in the coarse brown robe she now wore to bed. Her large black eyes fixed sternly on her husband, she spoke in vehement hissing Spanish. "I saw my father stand beside me, groaning, bleeding from the hundred wounds that traitor made in him. I heard his voice. It cried, 'Revenge! When will Lancaster avenge me!' "

"Ay," said John bitterly, "small wonder he cries out in the night. Yet twice I've tried—and failed. The stars have been set against us. I cannot conquer Castile without an army, nor raise another one so soon."

"Por Dios, you must try again!"

"You need not speak thus to me, lady. There's nothing beneath heaven I want more than Castile!"

"That Swynford woman will not stop you?" she said hoarsely. Into the proud cold face came a hint of pleading.

"No," he said startled, "of course not."

"Swear it!" she cried. She yanked the reliquary from beneath her brown robe. "Swear it now by the sacred finger of Santiago!" She opened the lid and thrust the casket at him.

He looked at the little bleached bones, the shreds of mummified flesh and thick, ridged nail. "My purpose needs no aid from this."

She stamped her foot. "Have you been listening to that heretic—that Wyclif? In my country we would burn him!" Her shaking hand thrust the reliquary into his face. "Swear it! I command you!" Her lips trembled, red spots flamed on her cheekbones.

"Bueno, bueno, doña," he said taking the reliquary. She watched, breathing hard, as he bent and kissed the little bones.

"I swear it by Saint James," he made the sign of the cross. "But the time is not ripe. The country is weary of war, they must be made to see how much they need Castile. They must —" he added lower and in English, "regain their faith in me as leader. Yet I think the people begin to look to me for guidance. They say that in the city yesterday they cheered my name."

She was not listening. She shut the reliquary and slipped it back under her robe. "Now I shall go to Canterbury," she said more quietly. "My father commanded it. It must be that since I am in this hateful England, an English saint is needed also for our cause. I shall see if your Saint Thomas will cure me of the bloody flux, so I may bear sons for Castile."

The Duke inclined his head and sighed. "May God grant it, lady." But if, he thought wryly, 'tis not God's will that I should lie soon with her again, I shall submit with patience.

He held out his hand to Costanza, and with the ceremony she exacted and which he accorded to her rank, he ushered her up the steps to her side of the State Bed. He held back for her the jeweled rose brocade curtains. She thanked him and shutting her eyes, began to murmur prayers. Her narrow

face was yellow against the white satin pillow, and his nostrils
were offended by her odor. Costanza's private mortifications
included denial of the luxury of cleanliness. Beneath the requisite pomp of her position, she tried to live like a holy
saint, contemptuous of the body.

In the first years of their marriage she had not been so unpleasing. Though she had brought to their bed only a rigid
endurance of wifely and dynastic duty, still she had allowed
her ladies to attire and cleanse her properly at all times, and
taken pride in the smallness of her high-arched feet, the
abundance of her long black hair. She had been quieter, gentler, and though they had soon ceased, there had been moments when she showed him tenderness, had once spoken of
love, which greatly embarrassed him. Only once however.
And since the birth and death of the baby boy in Ghent, she
had become like this, indifferent to all things but her religious
practices, her strange dreams and her consuming nostalgia
for Castile.

John climbed into his side of the great bed, glad that space
enough for two separated them.

He heard her whispering in the dark, "Padre, Padre—Padre
mío—" and his flesh crept, knowing that it was not God, but
the ghost of her own father that she supplicated.

Yet Costanza had no tinge of madness. Brother William
had said so, three weeks ago when John had sent him to
Hertford to examine the Duchess. "Disorders of the womb
do ofttimes produce excitable humors in the female," the
Gray Friar had reported. "I've given Her Grace a draught
which may help her, but her Scorpio is afflicted by Saturn—
That is not all that afflicts her," added the friar with stern
unmistakable meaning.

"Her Grace is nothing disturbed by my—my association
with Lady Swynford!" John had answered hotly. "She has
never suffered from it, nor does she care."

"Maybe not, my lord. But God cares—and the sin of
adultery you live in now is but the stinking fruit of the viler
crime which gave it birth."

"What's this, friar?" John had shouted in anger. "Do you
join my enemies in the yapping of vague slanders—or is it
that your bigot mind sees love itself as such a vileness? Speak
out!"

"I cannot, my lord," said the friar after a time. "I can but remind you that Our Blessed Lord taught that the *wish* will be condemned even as the deed."

"What wish? What deed? You babble like a Benedictine! You had better stick to leeching."

"Do you pray sometimes, my lord—for salvation of Nirac de Bayonne's soul?" said Brother William solemnly.

Until now, when Costanza's behavior had reminded him of Brother William, John had put this conversation from his thought, deeming that the friar, like all the clergy, puffed himself up with the making of dark little mysteries and warnings. He had answered impatiently that no doubt Masses had been said for Nirac in St. Exupère's church in Bayonne, since money had been sent there for that purpose. He had resented the friar's steady accusing gaze and said, "It was not *my* fault that the little mountebank's wits unloosened, or that he dabbled in witchcraft! You weary me, Brother William."

"Ay," said the friar, "for you've a conscience blind as a mole and tough as oxhide. Beware for your own soul, my Lord Duke!"

No other cleric in the world could have thus spoken without instant punishment, and the rage that injustice always roused in John had hardly been controlled by the long liking and trust he had for this Brother. But he had sent the friar away from the Savoy before Katherine came. Sent him far north to Pontefract Castle, where the steward had reported several cases of lung fever.

At the thought of Katherine, John stretched and smiled into the darkness. Tomorrow night she would be here with him again, since Costanza was leaving for Canterbury. Nay —not tomorrow night, for that was sacred to the memory of Blanche and would be spent in mourning and fasting, as always on this anniversary. The next night then. He hungered for Katherine with sharp desire, picturing her as she would be now in her bed—white and rose and bronze, warmly fragrant as a gillyflower.

The Castilian Duchess left the Savoy next morning with six of her own courtiers and a few English servants. She was dressed in sackcloth, her head was powdered with ashes, and she rode upon a donkey, for that was the humble beast used by Our Blessed Lord.

Katherine from her chamber window watched the pilgrimage move slowly from the courtyard through the gatehouse to the Strand, and her eyes shone with happy tears as she turned to her sister. "Blessed Jesu—so she's gone again! God be thanked she didn't stay for the Requiem Mass."

"The Duchess cares for no past but her own," said Philippa dryly. "Now that I've a fortnight's leave," she added considering, "I think I'll go back with Geoffrey to Aldgate. His lodging must be in sore need of my care. Last time he'd let an ale keg drip for days—ruined the floor cloth—and the fleas!"

"Geoffrey'll meet us at Saint Paul's?" asked Katherine, but she knew the answer. He, of all people, would never fail in respect to the memory of Blanche. Katherine too thought of Blanche with loving reverence like that one gave the saints. She saw her, gracious and fair, smiling down through the gold gates of heaven—for surely Blanche had ascended from purgatory long since. The horror of the plague morning at Bolingbroke seven years ago this day had diminished to a small lurid picture such as the monks painted on their vellums to show the agonies of hell. One gazed with mild shock, and then one turned the page.

Later that morning, the Lancastrian procession from the Savoy to St. Paul's Cathedral was led by the Duke. They were all dressed in black and all afoot. Katherine's position was between Elizabeth and Philippa, behind little Henry, who followed his father at two paces.

Katherine and John had exchanged hurried words while the procession formed. He had bent close to her and whispered, "Dear heart, we shall be together again tomorrow," and she had pulled her black veil quickly across her face to hide her unseemly joy.

As they marched across the Fleet bridge and entered the City at Ludgate, the Londoners made way respectfully. The men uncovered, many of the women ducked a curtsy as the Duke marched slowly past. There were cries of "Lancaster" and "The Duchess Blanche, God rest her sweet soul!"

At the corner of Ave Maria lane, a woman's voice somewhat thickened with drink shouted out, "Cock's bones, but the Duke's a handsome kingly wight, belike he'd be no bad ruler for us after all!"

She was shushed by a hundred whispers, but John felt a contented glow. He thought that the temper of the London crowd was for him as it never had been before, and he thought that his poor brother had been right to counsel moderation in the handling of the Commons. "The Good Parliament," the people called it now. And the sacrifice had not been too great, barring the whimperings of the old King, bereft of his Alice. The imprisoned merchants doubtless had deserved some punishment, the Lords Latimer and Neville, too. The new Privy Council which Commons had appointed to the King was harder for John to stomach, and yet here too magnanimity might be shown; for little Richard's sake it might be possible to conciliate and work with even such enemies as the Earl of March.

His softened mellow spirit deepened as he walked down St. Paul's immense nave, through the choir and to the right of the High Altar where he knelt in Blanche's chantry beside her marble tomb. His retinue filed in. The nobles filled the choir, the rest overflowed into the aisles. Philippa, Elizabeth and Henry knelt on purple cushions at the far end of their mother's chantry.

The priests in black and silver chasubles commenced the celebration of the Mass. *"Introibo ad altare Dei—ad Deum qui laetificat juventutem meam—"*

The chanting and responses went on, but for John three words echoed and re-echoed—*Laetificat juventutem meam*, the joy of my youth. He looked up at Blanche's effigy, all but her face covered with a black velvet pall. The twenty-eight candles, one for each of her years on earth, illumined the serene alabaster profile. Joy of my youth—yes. But you would not begrudge me joy now, my Blanche, you know that you've lost nothing that was ever yours in this new love that has come to me.

The candles shimmered before his eyes, a soft forgiving peace flowed over him. He heard Philippa weeping quietly, saw Elizabeth's and Henry's awed frightened eyes at the end of the tomb, and he longed to say to them, "Be happy. She wants us to be happy."

His exaltation grew, and with it a certainty that all would go well with him from now on. His enemies would melt away, success would come in war, in peace. Castile would crumble for him like a marchpane subtlety, and he would build it up anew of strong and shining steel while all of England rang with the glory of his name, as it had once rung for Edward.

*"Requiescat in pace—"*

The Mass was over, John felt exalted, cleansed, much as

he had felt long ago during the sacred vigil before his father knighted him.

He walked down the nave. Throughout the vast church his people rose from their knees to follow him. He stepped out to the porch, and stood blinking in the sunlight, still bemused, and not comprehending why there was a great crowd in the walled close. Again he heard "Lancaster," and he threw his head up to smile at them, thinking they came to do him honor. He checked himself, seeing that there was no answering warmth in the upturned faces. They appeared shocked, some even dismayed, but the strongest impact from those gaping faces was a malicious curiosity.

"Make way—make way!" cried Lancaster Herald, bustling out of the church and brandishing his baton and trumpet. "Make way for John, King of Castile, Duke of Lancaster, and for his meinie!"

The crowd did not move. There were a few nervous snickers, then from the midst of the rapidly swelling throng a man's voice shouted, "Fine sounding titles, herald! But tell us why we should make way for John o' Gaunt, a Flemish butcher's son!"

John stood rooted to the pavement. The sky darkened and across the close the roofs wavered like water. There was a roaring in his head.

Katherine with the ducal daughters had come out on the porch in time to hear a man shout, but at first she was simply puzzled like the others. Then she saw whom the crowd was warily watching: like a great collective beast of prey, uncertain of its quarry's next move. And the Duke did nothing, he stood as if some witchcraft had turned him to stone.

Katherine instinctively moved nearer to him as the vanguard of his retinue began to trickle from the church.

"Ay," cried the same taunting voice, "John o' Gaunt seems wonderstruck! He's not yet read the placard what's nailed on yonder door. The good monk there was passing, and *he* read it to us, my lord, so we maught all share the secret o' your true birth!"

Katherine, utterly bewildered, looked where the crowd did and saw two Benedictine monks hovering near a recess of the church porch. Their faces were sunk deep in their black cowls. As she looked, the monks vanished, slipping through a side door into the church.

The crowd roared, half with laughter at the disappearing

monks, half in the jeering excitement with which they would pelt stones at miscreants in the stocks. Yet some were uneasy. The Duke's motionless figure was uncanny. He stared over their heads as though weird signs were painted on the western sky.

Their spokesman shouted out once more, but in less certain tone. "Will ye not read the placard, m'lord? 'Tis on Paul's door behind ye. It tells strange tidings o' a noble lord what holds his head so high!"

Katherine's heart began to pound. She noted something familiar in the voice and stood on tiptoe to peer into the crowd. She saw a broad red face, a sandy thatch of hair beneath a peaked cap with the badge of the weaver's guild. My God, she thought, 'tis Jack Maudelyn! She glared down at Hawise's husband with some confused idea of quelling him, when Lord de la Pole rushed out on the church porch, crying, "Christ's blood, what's ado here! What's this mob?" His shrewd eyes darted over the scene, and he drew his sword, shouting, "A Lancaster! A Lancaster! Come forth to your lord!"

Inside the church there were startled answering cries. The great doors were flung wide. The Duke's knights and squires came running out, fumbling at their sword hilts.

The crowd wavered and pressed back against the wall, then as though a cork had been drawn they poured, stumbling, scrambling, through the churchyard gates, and fled up Pater Noster lane.

"Shall we after them, Your Grace?" cried a young knight eagerly.

The Duke made no answer. He had not moved on the step while his retinue surrounded him.

De la Pole sheathed his sword. "No," he said to the knight. " 'Twould not be seemly here on this day of mourning. 'Tis no doubt some prentice prank. They've done no harm—" He faltered as he got his first direct look at the Duke. "God's bones, my lord—you've not been wounded?"

The Duke's face was gray as the church stones, and beaded with moisture. His lips were drawn in like an old man's.

Katherine too stared at her love's face, and she ran to him crying, "My darling—why do you look like that? They were but silly japes the man called out."

He shoved her aside, and walking to the church door, shut the half his men had opened. On the door dangling from an iron nail hung a large square of parchment. It was inscribed in English in a fine writing suggestive of the cloisters. The Duke clasped his hands behind his back and read it slowly.

*Know men of England, how ye have been wickedly deceived by one who incontinently plots to seize our throne. The Duke of Lancaster is no Englishman, but a Fleming. He's none of royal Edward and Philippa's blood, but a changeling. For ye must know that once in Ghent, the Queen's Grace was delivered of a son that a nurse overlay. In fear of her lord the King, the Queen did send to find another infant the same age. It was a butcher's son, and he whom ye now call John of Gaunt. This secret did the Queen confess to the Bishop of Winchester, on her deathbed, so it is said.*

The Duke drew his dagger from its jeweled sheath. Its hilt was enameled with the lilies and leopards, tipped with a ruby rose of Lancaster. He thrust the dagger through the parchment and left it quivering there.

He turned to his bewildered courtiers. He saw none of them, nor Katherine, nor his children. His face became one only his fighting men had seen, as his lips drew back in a terrible smile. "They shall learn whether I am Edward's trueborn son."

That night at the Savoy uneasy speculation hummed. In the kitchens and cellars, the varlets whispered together, and the men-at-arms in their barracks. The chancery clerks and the chapel priests buzzed as unceasingly, as did the Duke's squires, or the knights and lords who headed his retinue. The Duke had gone to Havering-at-Bower to see the King. He had put off his mourning clothes and ordered his fastest horse to be saddled. Galloping as though Beelzebub's own fiends pursued him, he had set off for Essex. He had chosen none of his men to accompany him, nor spoken to anyone: he had gone alone. This, a circumstance so unprecedented and foolhardy, that Lord de la Pole, anxiously frowning, spoke of it in the Great Hall that night. "God's wounds! Who can guess what's in his mind! He's like a man bewitched!" He spoke to Sir Robert Knolles, another old campaigner who had served the Duke for twenty years.

Sir Robert gnawed on his grizzled mustache and cried

staunchly, "Why, he will avenge this insult to his honor. What man can blame him?"

"Yet such paltry nonsense," answered de la Pole. "They've whispered far worse of him than this farradiddle about a butcher's son, or even that he plots for the throne."

"Whispered, ay," said the old knight, "but this was *written down*."

De la Pole was silent. He himself, who could read a little, had awe of the written word, but to the common folk writing was a sacred oracle.

"By God!" cried de la Pole, angrily banging his hand on the table. "No one who saw him today could doubt him a Plantagenet! D'you remember Prince Edward's face at Limoges massacre? No mercy, and no quarter when the fury's on them."

"But that was war," said Sir Robert. "His Grace can hardly massacre the whole of London."

"Nay, and our Duke has keener mind than his brother ever had. He'll find subtler means of vengeance. But," he added frowning, "I cannot guess what."

Katherine, sitting at her old place at the High Table, heard this conversation, and her troubled heart grew heavier still. Her hurt that he had no more thought of her than for the rest of his meinie was eclipsed by her suffering for him. She had read the placard. The shock it gave her was not at its absurd content but at the vicious hatred which had prompted it. And she who knew John better than anyone, guessed at some strange uncertainty, or fear. She thought of the night at Kenilworth, when he had said, "I've been tilting with a phantom."

Her unhappiness culminated later in violent anger at Hawise. Katherine turned on her maid the moment their chamber door was closed and they were alone. "It was your Jack, the whoreson churl, who shouted insults at my lord!" she cried. "No doubt you knew it. You faithless slut, no doubt 'tis nothing to you to take the Duke's bounty, while your own man sneers at him and yammers filthy lies!"

Hawise gasped. "Don't, sweeting, don't," she cried. "I didna know till now that Jack had aught to do wi' that scrummage today. And God help me, but I love ye better'n him or mine own child. 'Tis in part for this that Jack do hate the Duke."

Katherine turned and flung her arms around the stout

neck. "I know, I know. Forgive me," she cried. "But if you had seen my lord standing there—alone—on the step—I would have shielded him—I couldn't—"

"Hush, poppet, hush," Hawise stroked the wet cheek and made the gentle soothing sound she used to Katherine's babies. I'll speak sharp to Jack when I see him, she thought, but Jack cared little what she said any more. Since she had left him to serve her lady he had taken some Kentish wench to live with him.

" 'Tis nothing so grave after all, sweeting," she said. "Jack was tipsy, no doubt, and meant no real harm. The Duke didn't know who 'twas shouting?"

Katherine shook her head. "Only I up there would've known him. And my lord was dazed, you could see. Oh Hawise—" She shut her eyes with a long unsteady breath while the maid's thick nimble fingers set to unfastening her brooch and girdle.

"Sleep now," said Hawise, "for 'tis late, and shadows cast by candle are vanished in the sun. The Duke'll be back here wi' ye on th' morrow, I'll take oath on't."

But he was not.

All through that autumn the Duke stayed at Havering Castle with the old King, who received him with delight, clung to him and mumbled gratitude to his dear son. For the Duke at once recalled Alice Perrers. He sent the King's own men-at-arms to fetch her from her place of banishment in the north. He met her in Havering courtyard himself and gave her his hand in greeting.

In jewels and brocades and a whirl of musk, Alice flounced triumphantly out of her chariot, her three little dogs frisking and barking after. She raised her thickly painted face to the Duke.

"This is different, Your Grace," said Alice with her sideways smile as she curtsied, "from that time at Westminster when you did bow to Commons and send me away. I thought you could not mean it." Her wooing voice caressed him, she squeezed his hand softly.

He withdrew his hand. "Dame Alice, much has changed since that day in the Painted Chamber, and now I bow to no man—or woman." He looked at her in such a way that she was frightened, and she nodded quickly.

"My lord, I'll do your bidding in everything. I've some influence in my own fashion; but I—I—I do beg of you one
more boon."

He inclined his head and waited.

She breathed sharply, her green eyes narrowed. "I crave
the head of Peter de la Mare," she said, watching the Duke
closely yet sure of her ground. "I did not like the things he
said of me, my lord."

The Duke laughed, and Alice involuntarily stepped back.

"The Speaker of the Commons already lies in chains in
Nottingham Castle dungeon," he said. "I shall decide what's
to be done with him after I deal with other matters. You may
go now to the King."

One by one and day by day the Duke of Lancaster reversed all the measures which the reform Parliament had put
through in the spring. He summarily dismissed the Privy
Council that Commons had appointed. The Lords Latimer
and Neville were released from their confinement and reinstated at court. The merchants impeached by Commons were
released from gaol.

The old King signed whatever papers his son gave him,
much pleased that his beloved Alice and John were now in
agreement, and mistily aware that he was helping to punish a
pack of upstart rebels who had dared to interfere with royal
prerogatives.

The Duke stayed in Essex at Havering Castle with his father, but after the first  few days of inner frenzy, his mind regained control. His purpose became a staunch ship, steered
by his skilful brain, and gliding relentlessly forward along the
cold channel of his fury.

He had the force of the King's authority and the King's
men behind him, and backed it by his own equally powerful
Lancastrian feudality. He summoned key men of his retinue
to Havering, he kept messengers galloping in a constant
stream between Havering and the Savoy. He sent them farther afield to the far-flung corners of his vast holdings. From
Dunstanburgh in the north to Pevensey in the south, from his
Norfolk manors in the east to Monmouth Castle on the
Welsh border—the stewards and constables were alerted to be
ready in case of need.

But there was no need. Commons had dissolved long ago.
The members had scattered to their homes all over England.

Their Speaker was imprisoned, and the lords and bishops who had given them support now wavered one by one and attached themselves to the winning side.

All but the Earl of March and Bishop Courtenay of London.

The Duke let the bishop be, for the present. Courtenay he would deal with later, and he had a special weapon in mind. But for the proper punishment of March, one ally was essential. The Duke summoned to Havering the powerful Border lord, Percy of Northumberland, and in an hour's secret conference, showed him plainly where self-interest lay and how worthless had been March's promises.

The frightened little Earl of March thereupon was ordered to leave the country on foreign service. He refused. Assassination on shipboard or in Calais seemed to him quite as possible as the already accomplished imprisonment of his steward in Nottingham dungeon. Instead he resigned his marshalship of England and fled across the country to barricade himself in Ludlow Castle.

The Duke rewarded Percy's rejuvenated loyalty to the crown with the abandoned Marshal's staff.

These measures it soon appeared were but preliminaries.

At the end of October, the Duke attacked William of Wykeham, the Bishop of Winchester. He summoned him before the new Lancastrian Privy Council on charges of graft, and robbery of the public funds.

So one morning the corpulent fifty-four-year-old bishop stood before the King, the Duke and the members of his council, facing them all with more bewilderment than anger. He had always been in high favor at court, he had been the King's chaplain, the King's architect, the Queen's confessor, and Chancellor of the Realm. He had had no enemies until now.

His pudgy fingers tightened on his crozier; beneath his gorgeous red satin cope his portly belly rumbled with nervousness.

"I cannot understand, Your Majesty," he began his defense to the King, but seeing that his old patron's wrinkled eyelids had shut and the gray, crowned head was nodding, he turned to the Duke. "Your Grace—these charges, they're outrageous! They deal with matters ten years gone."

"But they were *true*—my Lord Bishop?"

"By the Blessed Virgin, how can I remember after all this time *how* I came by every groat? 'Tis impossible, my lord."

"Maybe your memory will sharpen if you be relieved of the clogging burden of your revenues and temporalities," said the Duke. "Holy poverty is much desired by the clergy, I believe." He glanced to the corner of the chamber where stood a priest in plain dun-colored robes, John Wyclif, whom the Duke had called here from Oxford. They exchanged a grave slight smile.

The bishop's mouth fell open. His jowls quivered, his voice was shrill as he cried, "Your Grace, why do you persecute *me?* There are many other bishops—you've always shown me favor before—"

The Duke's eyebrows raised slowly. He folded his hands on his lap and gazed back at the flushed sweating face beneath the jeweled miter.

"It cannot be," cried the bishop, suddenly perceptive, "that you believe I had aught to do with that preposterous changeling story!"

"The scroll said that you had this secret of my true birth from Queen Philippa on her deathbed." The Duke spoke so soft, the members of the council strained to hear, and the bishop stared with stupefied eyes.

"But the Queen confessed no such thing, Your Grace! 'Tis all a lie!"

"That I know, my Lord Bishop. But someone started this lie. Your name was written."

"By the Holy Trinity, it wasn't I. You must believe, Your Grace, it wasn't I!"

The Duke shrugged. "Yet you've admitted your memory is faulty." He glanced at his council. "The trial will proceed."

It proceeded and soon ended. The Bishop of Winchester was stripped of his rich manors, and his coffers full of gold. At one stroke all his worldly possessions were removed from him—though his episcopal office, even the Duke could not touch, for that had come down through St. Peter from God.

The Duke's retinue rejoiced. They swaggered and boasted of their lord's power. They laughed openly at the whole lot of discomfited bishops. In the taverns and halls and on the streets they jeered also at the commons, and at the cocky bantling Peter de la Mare who had thought to defy the Duke and now found himself rotting in a dungeon.

Alone of all Lancaster's knights, Baron de la Pole had reservations. He had expressed them to the Duke and been sent away from Havering for his pains. On a November morning in his chamber at the Savoy, he was gloomily letting his squire array him in hunting costume when his page announced Brother William Appleton, and the barefoot friar walked in.

"Well now, Brother," cried the baron heartily. "I'm glad to see you. How was it at Pontefract, are you just back?"

"Some time ago," said the Franciscan. "I've been staying with my brethren at Grayfriars. I hear strange things of His Grace."

"Not so strange!" said the baron, instantly defending his Duke. "He but vindicates his honor like any noble knight!"

"I hear," said the friar, "that no act of the last Parliament has been suffered to stand, that the Speaker is imprisoned, the Earl of March banished."

"It is so," said de la Pole.

"I hear that the Bishop of Winchester is homeless, virtually begging his bread from door to door."

"Like a friar, my dear Brother, like a friar!" de la Pole laughed. " 'Twill do the fat bishop no harm! And remember," the baron leaned forward, "it is to little Prince Richard that he gave all the bishop's confiscated lands. That should stop their foul talk of plots against the child."

"Nothing but a miracle will stop talk. The Duke's acts are frightening the people."

The baron sighed and sitting on a stool held his legs out for his squire to put on his leather hunting shoes. "He no longer cares. He wants only revenge."

"Has he not had enough?" said the friar sternly.

" 'Twas that placard. He knows not who put it there, or wrote it. So he strikes out blindly. 'Twill be Bishop Courtenay next. A tougher stick to break than Winchester was, and for this he's using Wyclif."

The friar nodded. He had heard how Wyclif had been preaching in the London pulpits, preaching his doctrine of church reform and church taxation so that the burden of the people's own taxes might be lessened.

"An honest man, Wyclif," said the friar thoughtfully, "and his teachings touched by Holy Truth, I think, but they may dangerously inflame the commons—"

"Lancaster too is an honest man!" broke in the baron, "though hot of temper like all his race. And still he's shown forbearance. *Mind you*, Sir Friar, there's been no bloodshed! He's even checked the King's whore in her clamor to kill de la Mare."

"Bloodshed—" The friar smiled faintly. "Blood is all you knights understand. There are far worse sufferings. But 'tis not of that I'd speak." He glanced at the baron's squire who was polishing the tip of his master's spear. The baron took the hint and waved dismissal.

Brother William sat down on a stool and explained. "All this that we've been saying is common knowledge. I'll not spread any rumor that is not. 'Tis about that placard. I believe I know who wrote it."

"God's nails—" breathed the baron, sinking back open-mouthed in his chair. "Do you indeed? His Grace has sent spies throughout the city to listen in the taverns and question offhandedly, but to no purpose."

The friar hesitated. This knowledge had not come to him through any secrets of the confessional, for if it had his lips would have been as sternly sealed as they were on another matter relating to the Duke. Shortly after his return to London from the north, he had been called to examine a sick monk at St. Bartholomew's Benedictine priory, so great was his reputation as leech that even the monks called on him at times.

As he had left the priory infirmary, he had been shocked to hear drunken voices coming from the scriptorium and a bleating laugh like a goat's. He had been about to hurry past the door, thinking that the prior kept lax rule here, when the same bleating voice called out, "And this one'll hang on Paul's door too, 'tis better than the changeling—"

Someone said "Hist!" and there was a sharp silence.

The friar walked into the scriptorium. Two black monks, their foolish young faces red with the ale they had shared from a mazer, gaped at him blankly. The third man was perched on a high stool at a desk, a quill pen in his hand, a square of parchment under it. His robes and semi-tonsure showed him to be a clerk. His pock-marked face instantly became bland as cheese, but his little eyes fastened on the friar with ratlike caution.

"You make merry in here while you inscribe your scrolls?" said the friar pleasantly, trying to edge near enough the desk to see what the clerk had written. "You treat of merry topics, Sir Clerk?"

One of the monks in evident confusion said, "This clerk is none of us, he but lodges here at the priory. He has lately come from Flanders."

"Nay, I'm an Englishman—of—of Norvich," said the clerk quickly in his bleating voice. "Johan of Norvich, I but spent a time in Flanders."

"Johan?" said the monk in surprise. "We've called you Peter—"

"Johan—Peter—both." The clerk slid off his stool, and the friar with keen disappointment saw that the scroll was blank but for two words "Know ye—"

"Is't the custom at Saint Bart's that Gray Friars haf right to nose around and question us?" said the clerk to the monks, and limping to the mazer he took a long draught.

The Gray Friar had made some civil remark and gone, but he had been mulling this matter over in his mind ever since. He had consulted his superior, he had prayed on it, and now, knowing the baron's loyalty and shrewdness, he had come to him.

He told the baron what he had overheard, but added, "There's no proof, they'd say I heard wrong, the parchment with the two words will have vanished. And there is much that's puzzling. Whate'er this clerk may call himself, he spoke with Flemish accent. And never have I seen malice so pure in a man's eyes. What can he have so harsh as this against the Duke? The young monks are fools and swayed by this man though willing enough to spite Wyclif's patron, no doubt."

"The clerk is being bribed?" suggested de la Pole. "By March? Or Courtenay?"

"Ay—mayhap—he had gold rings on his fingers—but the nub of the matter is—shall I go with this tale to the Duke?"

The baron pondered. "Not now. There's no proof, and the Duke may be led to more blind violence. His rage is nearly slaked, 'twill all die down—if nothing further happens. The clerk and Benedictine maybe will bate their tricks, since they must guess you heard them."

Nodding thoughtfully and with relief, the friar stood up. It went against his grain to carry tales that he had got by eaves-dropping and he decided to wait for developments. It might well be too that the Duke would not receive him, since they had parted last on a discordant enough note.

This reminded him of something and he said, "How is't

with Lady Swynford? What part has she played in all this coil
of His Grace's?"

"None at all," answered the baron. "I doubt that he's seen
her since it started." His face softened. "Poor fair lass, she
moped here at the Savoy for days and then returned to Kenilworth, with the ladies Philippa and Elizabeth. And yet it
seems he loves her dearly when he has a mind for love."

"A vile adulterous love," said the friar grimly, pulling up
his cowl and adjusting the knotted cord at his waist. "God
will scourge them for it."

# XIX

KATHERINE kept Christmastide alone with the children at
Kenilworth. The Duke divided his festivities between his
father at Havering and his nephew, little Richard, who
remained with the Princess Joan across the Thames at Kennington.

His establishment at Kenilworth was not, however, entirely
forgotten. In February, the Duke sent belated New Year's
presents to everyone, and a silver-gilt girdle for Katherine
herself, but the accompanying note was stilted, though it indicated that she should return to the Savoy for a visit with the
Lady Philippa, that there was an envoy coming from the
Duchy of Luxemburg who wished to see Philippa with a view
to possible marriage negotiations.

It was an official missive, dictated, and there was no private message to Katherine. He sent the note and the gifts by
a new young squire Katherine did not know, a Robert Beyvill, who was to escort the ladies back to the Savoy.

Katherine received the letter while she sat amongst her
household in Kenilworth's beautiful new Hall. She kept rigid
control of her face as she read and thought, Dear Mother of
God, he has then really ceased to love me or he could not
write thus. I shall not go—I'll refuse. Even as she thought
this, her heart began to deny it. His love had been buried but

surely it was still there despite the evil demon, or whatever the incubus was, that drove him. She must not let her pride strike back at him, since he had again summoned her, no matter how coldly. She would go to London.

And underneath ran bitter realization. What choice had she but to obey? This castle was his, the bread she ate, the clothes she wore came from his bounty. Like the hundreds in his retinue, like his children, like this young squire who stood waiting respectfully before her, she had no course but submission.

Suddenly she thought of Kettlethorpe. That place was wholly hers, her widow's rights had been confirmed. How small and mean it was compared to these lovely castles where she lived now here, now there, at the Duke's whim; and yet that crumb of far-off Lincolnshire was the only thing in the world entirely her own.

The thought was fleeting. She looked at her little Swynfords—Blanchette's golden curls bent over a grubby bit of embroidery while Philippa gravely helped her, Tom whittling an arrow on the hearth—both well grown, finely clad, and educated better than most nobles' children. And she thought how much they had profited by their mother's situation. She turned her eyes to the young squire and said quietly, "Then we must make ready to leave for London, must we not? What are you named, sir?"

"Robert Beyvill, my lady, but mostly I'm called Robin."

"Robin," she said with her sudden enchanting smile, thinking him well-named. He had sharp eyes, a curly brown head, and his tunic was a bright rusty red. He was tall and merry-looking. Altogether far more pleasing a squire than Raulin d'Ypres had been—or Ellis.

Katherine rose abruptly and poured wine for Robin. She never allowed herself to think long of Hugh's erstwhile squire. She had seen Ellis once in Lincoln when little John was born. She had met him by chance as she walked up Pottergate to the house the Duke had leased for her. Ellis had stopped squarely in front of her, his heavy Saxon features twisted to a mask of loathing. "Whore!" he had cried, and spat directly into her face. She had not told the Duke the whole of it but she had seen to it that Ellis de Thoresby was sent off to his estates in Nottingham.

"I daresay Lady Philippa and I shan't be gone long," said Katherine sitting down again and addressing her household.

She spoke soothingly, for she knew there would be bad moments with Elizabeth, who adored the gaieties of London and resented being left out of anything. Worse than any tantrums Elizabeth might have was the stricken look in Blanchette's eyes as the little girl raised them to her mother. Plain as speech they said, And so you leave me again—for him.

"Come here, darling," said Katherine to her. "Shall we sing Havelock the Dane? Will you play it on your lute?" That was the child's favorite ballad, and it used to be that to the point of weariness she begged Katherine for it.

But Blanchette shook her head and lowered it over the embroidery. "No, thank you, Mama," she said in a dull flat little voice.

Katherine, Philippa and Robin Beyvill, the squire, left for London on the fifteenth of February, accompanied by the usual escort of men-at-arms, varlets and baggage carts, while Hawise, and Philippa's waiting women were stuffed into a wagon with their mistresses' traveling coffers.

Robin enlivened the way by telling the two ladies all that had been happening in London, but Philippa did not listen as she rode sedately along on her white mare. She was praying to the Blessed Virgin, supplicating that understanding Lady with conflicting petitions. First, that the marriage negotiations with Luxemburg would come to naught and second, that she would always have the will to obey her father. But Katherine listened eagerly to the squire and learned more about the Duke's activities than she had ever known. Robin had an uncritical admiration for his lord, whom he had served four years, though only recently promoted to be one of the Duke's own personal squires.

There was plenty of time for talk as they wended along the frozen muddy roads, and Katherine's interest was enlivened by feminine amusement when she discovered that Robin was casting her in the classic role of the unattainable lady fair.

He had too much humor to sigh and groan, as the love-stricken squire should do, but he demonstrated the other signs. His hand trembled when he helped her to dismount, he blushed when she looked at him, and once when she dropped a sprig of holly which she had been wearing on her bodice, she saw him stealthily pick it up and, kissing the red berries, slip the whole twig into his pouch.

Katherine's sore heart was warmed by this adoration, in

which she saw no danger; after all, the lad was barely twenty, and she full twenty-six. She relaxed with him and enjoyed his company, perhaps all the more so because Robin was not of high blood. His father was a franklin in Suffolk, a prosperous one, who farmed ample lands and owned a new half-timbered house.

Robin went on to say proudly that his father, Richard, was even now sitting in Parliament at Westminster, a new member of the Commons. "For," said Robin laughing, "the Duke has seen to it that *this* Parliament shall be properly packed with his own supporters, so there'll be no trouble like there was last spring."

Katherine knew very little of what had passed last spring except that the two lords she knew, Latimer and Neville, had got into difficulties but were now released. No one spoke to her of national affairs, but since the incident of the placard, she had been shaken into more awareness.

They jogged out of Buckinghamshire towards Woburn Abbey, where they would sleep that night, while she considered what Robin had said and she spoke thoughtfully. "So all goes well with His Grace now? He has no more enmities to fight against?"

"God's body, lady, I wouldn't say that!" Robin laughed again, then sobered and turned sharply in his saddle. "There's still the bishops! May the devil's pitchforks prick their fat rumps until they've bled out all the gold!"

"Robin!" cried Katherine.

Philippa looked up from her vague gazing at the road. "Are you a Lollard, Sir Squire?" she said stiffly; her long mild face showed a flash of Lancastrian hauteur. It was only in matters of piety that Philippa dared differ from her father's views.

"I ask your pardon, my lady," said Robin to Philippa, "I spoke too crude." But his eyes never lingered on the girl, and they returned at once to Katherine as he explained eagerly, "I but feel as Wyclif does, and our lord the Duke. We've had the 'poor preachers' come to our home in Suffolk—they're good honest men, lady."

"Welladay," said Katherine, uninterested in Wyclif's preachers or indeed in Wyclif. "What is it between the Duke and the bishops now?"

"They most damnably defy His Grace!" cried Robin, his brown eyes flashing. "The Bishops' Convocation has dared to

summon Wyclif for trial at Saint Paul's on Thursday. 'Tis
Courtenay's doing."

Katherine could see no reason for Robin's vehemence. The
bishops were powerful, of course, everyone knew that, but
the Duke was omnipotent—all that Robin had told her
proved it, and some struggle over Wyclif seemed to her of
scanty importance. She now thought that she had been overly
frightened for the Duke when he had faced the mob that
jeered about the placard; and as they drew nearer to London
she began to wonder with increasing anxiety what was really
in her beloved's heart, and to suffer a miserable, vague jealousy, not of Costanza; but there were plenty of designing ladies at court. And he had apparently been seeing much of
Alice Perrers—and the Princess Joan.

John was not aware that he had neglected Katherine.
There were times when he longed for her and desired her,
but these emotions took place at the back of his attention and
were overwhelmed by the obsession which had come to him.
The demonstration of power was a drink heady as the strongest metheglin ever the wild Saxons brewed, and yet continual imposition of his will did little to appease the pain which
drove him on to further fight.

This pain smoldered like a hidden coal in his breast, and
sometimes at night it became an actual fiery lump that rose
into his throat and stuck there, so that he choked and gasped
and sweated as he tried to swallow it down. Alone in his
great State Bed, he would roll in shameful distress, clenching
his fists and struggling for each breath, until at last he fell
back exhausted and the thing dissolved. Then he would think
of witchcraft and pull himself from bed to pray at Blanche's
prie-dieu in the corner of the chamber.

In the mornings he could barely remember what had happened, and would awaken with increased passion to outwit
his enemies.

On Wednesday, February 18, he rose after a badly troubled night and angrily shouted for his squires to come and
dress him. His head ached and he was annoyed at the late-
ness of the hour. Parliament would open today at eight, and
he must hurry to Westminster. This docile Commons was vot-
ing as it should, but they needed constant guidance.

Just as he was leaving the Savoy he remembered to summon the chamberlain, and told him to prepare rooms in the

Momouth Wing for Lady Philippa and Lady Swynford, who might arrive today from Kenilworth. The chamberlain looked startled. The Monmouth Wing was not where Lady Swynford had lodged before, and it was half the length of the Savoy from the Duke. The Duke caught the flicker in the man's eye, and some realization of Katherine's feelings pierced his preoccupation. But nothing on earth would induce him to let anyone see him in those humiliating nightly attacks, and besides he had no time for love.

He flung himself onto his horse and pursued by two of his squires galloped along the Strand to Westminster.

After the day's session, he dined in the Hall with many of the lords. Percy of Northumberland sat on his right. They had much to discuss about Wyclif's trial tomorrow at St. Paul's, and the showdown with Bishop Courtenay.

"But," said the Duke, sipping without relish some very fine malmsey, "we must be temperate, Percy. Wyclif should be his own best advocate."

Northumberland irritably hunched his massive shoulders, while he speared himself a gobbet of smoking sturgeon from the platter offered him by his kneeling son, who was acting as his squire. The baron crammed his mouth full, sputtered with pain and spewed the fish out onto the rushes.

"Sweet Christ! M'tongue's burned off!" He clouted young Percy violently on the ear.

His thirteen-year-old son had a temper to match. " 'Tis not my fault, my lord, an you gobble like a swine!" he cried throwing down the platter.

Father and son glared at each other. The blue Percy lions on their surcotes jigged in and out with their fierce breathings. Then the baron thwacked his heir across the shoulder, upsetting him into the filthy rushes. "Hotspur, Hotspur!" he roared, slapping his thigh. He turned to the Duke, "Saw you ever such a game cockerel—dares flout its own sire!"

"Certainly your young Hotspur shows a spirit which will be useful to keep the Scots in order," said the Duke dryly, thinking of his own Henry's excellent manners.

"Ay—the Scots—" said Northumberland, rinsing his blistered mouth with wine. "First we must keep *London* in order."

"You cannot tamper with the City's liberties," said the Duke firmly. They had been through this before. Percy, as

new Marshal of England, was continuously annoyed that the
City did not admit his jurisdiction.

"Hen piddle!" cried Percy. "That pack of baseborn trades-
men—what right have *they* to liberties? Let the mayor stick
to his needles and threads, 'tis all he's fit for."

"If you abolish the mayoralty and take to yourself the ruling of the City, do you think the Londoners'll submit?"

"By the rood, they'd have to! Jam the bill through Parliament, through their own Commons. They've awe enough of
that!"

The Duke turned away. His ally's loud voice rasped on
him. The headache which had plagued him all morning
began to throb. He longed for sleep, and roused himself with
an effort.

Later that afternoon as London church bells were ringing
for vespers the Duke and Lord Percy rode into the City
bound for the latter's town residence at Aldersgate. This
mansion was but a few hundred yards beyond St. Paul's, and
it had been decided to use it for headquarters.

En route from Westminster to the City, the Duke had
stopped at the Savoy to pick up certain of his men and
Brother William Appleton. The Franciscan, now fully reinstated in the Duke's favor, was to be one of Wyclif's advo-
cates. The other three—a Carmelite, a Dominican and an
Austin—were to meet them at Percy's "inn."

A bleak wintry drizzle began to fall as the Duke and Percy
preceded their followers up Pater Noster lane along the wall
of St. Paul's close. The little ecclesiastical shops were boarded
for the night, and the streets were nearly deserted, for the citizens were at home by their firesides.

They crossed the wide market place at West Chepe. All the
booths and stalls were battened down now, and only the low-
ing of penned cattle from the shambles disturbed the quiet.
They entered St. Martin's lane, and at the bend where it narrowed by the Goldsmiths' Hall, the Gray Friar suddenly saw
three figures in the gloom ahead. Startled, he stood up in his
stirrups and peered over the Duke's shoulder. There was still
light enough to recognize two black-habited monks and a
third shorter man in a dark cleric's robe. The three figures
paused and wavered in a moment of obvious confusion, when
they saw the horsemen approaching. Brother William caught
the flash of something white and stiff being thrust into the
clerk's sleeve.

"My lord!" cried the Gray Friar, "we must catch that man!" He kicked his mule and clattered past the astonished Duke. The two monks swiveled and, hiking up their robes, pelted as fast as their legs would take them towards Aldersgate. The clerk limped frantically behind, while his head jerked this way and that searching for cover.

The friar overtook the hobbling figure as it was about to dart into an alley, and swooping down with a long arm, collared a handful of cloth.

The Duke galloped up as the struggling clerk had nearly freed himself and, leaning from the saddle, grabbed the man's wrist. "What's this, Brother William?" cried the Duke with some amusement, his powerful grip tightening on the plunging wrist. "What games do we play with this wriggling little whelp? I never knew you so sportive."

The friar had flung himself off his mule, and plunged his hand into the clerk's sleeve. He brought out a roll of white parchment and squinted down quickly in the waning light.

"This is the man, my lord, who wrote the placard on Saint Paul's door," he cried.

The Duke started, his grip loosened, and the clerk, twisting suddenly free, would have made off but a score of retainers had come up, and he was surrounded. He stood still in the central gutter and pulled his hood down over his face.

"Bind him," said the Duke in a deadly quiet voice. A squire jumped forward with a leather thong and tied the clerk's wrists behind his back.

"Take him to my inn!" cried Lord Percy. "We'll deal with him there."

The clerk suddenly found his voice. "You can't!" he shrilled "You haf no right to touch me! I know my rights. I claim the City's protection!"

In windows of houses past the Goldsmiths' Hall a few heads peered out cautiously.

"Hark at him!" roared Percy. "Hark who speaks to the Marshal of England. Take him, men!"

The clerk was picked up and rushed down the street to Percy's gate. The Duke and Percy followed. The courtyard gate closed behind them. They dragged the clerk into the house and flung him down on the floor of the Hall. He hitched himself slowly to his knees, then to his feet. He stood swaying; his chin sunk on his chest, his bound hands opening and closing spasmodically behind his back.

The retainers of both lords crowded around, staring curiously, eager to inflict more punishment. As it was, blood dripped from the long ferrety nose, and a lump big as a chestnut rose from the bald spot in the tonsure.

"We'd best flog him, afore he's put in the stocks," said Percy with relish. "What's he done, by the way?" He looked at the Duke, who was standing six feet from the clerk and regarding him fixedly.

The Duke held his hand towards the friar without answering, and brother William gave over the large square of parchment.

"Bring me a light," said the Duke. A varlet ran up with a torch. The rustlings and murmurings ceased, the Hall grew still while they watched the Duke read, until he raised his head and said, "This time it seems that I—John of Gaunt—for reason of my base birth am therefore without honor, so have made secret treaty with King Charles of France to sell him all England."

There were a few gasps, Percy's red face grew redder, but nobody moved. The Duke took the torch from the varlet and bending down held it near to the prisoner.

"Let me see your face!"

The clerk's knees began to quiver, he hunched his shoulders higher around his ears and the sound of his breath was like tearing silk.

The Duke knocked his head up with a blow of the fist beneath the chin and stared down by the torchlight. Suddenly he reached out and yanked the clerk's collar from his stringy throat. A jagged white scar ran from the jaw to the Adam's apple.

"And so it *is* you, Pieter Neumann," said the Duke softly. He handed the torch back to the varlet. "You still bear the mark a boy made on you thirty years ago at Windsor."

"I don't know what you mean, Your Grace. I am Johan, Johan Prenting of Norwich. This scar is from a wound I got in France, I fought well in France for England, Your Grace. I know not what is on the parchment, it vas the monks at Saint Bart's wrote it. I've done no harm—"

"He lies, my lord," interrupted Brother William solemnly. "For I myself saw him writing on the parchment."

"He lies—" said the Duke. "As he always lied—lied—" he repeated, but in the repetition of the word, the friar heard a wavering. He noted this with astonishment. What could it be that the Duke doubted, what uncertainty had caused that stumbling inflection, and what earlier association could there have been between these two?

"We'll hang him!" cried Lord Percy, who had finally comprehended the situation. "Haul him out to the courtyard!" Four of his men sprang forward.

"Wait—" The Duke held up his hand. "Take him to some privy place, put him in the stocks. I would talk to him alone first."

Percy's men hustled the clerk through the kitchens and below stairs to the cellars, where in the darkness there was a small dungeon. The clerk's wrists and ankles were clamped into the holes in the wooden stocks, and the men pulled savagely on his twisted leg to make it fit the hole.

The Duke had followed them. He watched impassively while the prisoner groaned and cursed and tried to ease his dangling rump on the dungeon paving stones. Then he said, "Leave a torch in the bracket and go." Percy's men obeyed. The Duke, clanging shut the iron door, leaned against the wall.

"You suffer now, Pieter Neumann," he said, "but you will suffer far more than this before you die, if you don't speak truth to me. Where have you been since that day at Windsor Castle when you did steal your mother's purse and ran away?"

Pieter's eyes slithered to a heap of rusty chains and fetters and he said sulkily, "In Flanders."

"Where?"

"In Ghent gaol and at the Abbaye de Saint Bavon vere you were born, Your Grace. The monks taught me to write." A sly hope came to him as he noted a change in the Duke's face when he mentioned the abbey. He rested his chin on the rough plank top of the stocks and waited.

"What brought you to London?"

Pieter considered quickly. He had fled from Flanders after stealing a gold chalice from the abbey church, landed off a fishing boat in Norfolk and made his way here knowing there would be more scope for his talents. He had not been disappointed. "I longed to see England again," he said, "the country vere my poor mother died—Isolda, who nursed you and loved you so, my lord—" he added in a sort of hissing whine.

The Duke's breathing quickened, he bent over crying,

"And who has paid you now to write these placards? *Who?*"
He clutched the skinny shoulder, his fingers dug in until the
bones crunched.

The clerk whimpered and twisted, finally gasped out,
"Courtenay."

The Duke straightened up. "By God—" he said under his
breath. "Would even the Bishop of London stoop so low?"

"If you set me free, my lord, I could write another placard," whispered Pieter. "I could say that after all you're no
changeling, that—" He broke off and screamed, "Ah—Your
G-grace—haf mercy—nay, nay don't!" Plain in the torchlight
he had seen murder leap in the Duke's eyes.

John folded his arms and leaned back against the dripping
fetid wall stones. "Did you think that the King's son would
kill you as you hung there trussed like a fowl on a spit, my
poor Pieter? Nay, 'tis not so you shall die—though *how* you
shall die I've not yet decided." He smiled quietly and turned.

"Your Royal Grace, dear sweet lord, don't leaf me here
like this, I-I'll crawl on my hands and knees, I'll kiss your
feet, I'll—"

The Duke opened the iron door and going out into the cellar, banged the door behind him and shot the bolt. He walked
down the passage between rows of piled wine casks until he
reached the steps up to the kitchens. From there he could no
longer hear the echo of Pieter's hysterical cries.

Katherine and her companions duly arrived at the Savoy
that afternoon. The bowing chamberlain met them in the
Outer Ward and informed them that His Grace would not be
there this night, he was staying with the Lord of Northumberland in the City. The chamberlain had been given no special messages for either lady, and doubted whether His Grace
would even return on the morrow, since it was known that he
intended to sup in the City after the trial at St. Paul's.

Philippa let out a long sigh of relief. No marriage talk for
the present anyway.

But Katherine followed the chamberlain to the Monmouth
Wing with a dragging step. If this banishment to a part of the
Savoy so remote from him were truly a symbol of the way he
wished it to be between them, why then had he summoned
her here at all?

She did not leave her chamber again that night, but lay

sleepless on her bed, staring into the shadows with hot aching eyes.

The next day she sent Hawise to fetch Robin from the squire's dormitory and when he eagerly presented himself, she told him that she wished to attend the trial today in the cathedral and asked him to accompany her. She felt that she must see John again, no matter what the circumstances, and that then perhaps she would know what was amiss between them.

Robin assented blithely. His eyes sparkled at the thought of escorting her anywhere, but particularly to a spectacle which promised some excitement.

Hawise was grimly disapproving. "You're full young and brash, m'lad, to have the care of our lady here, there'll be a rough crowd jammed into Paul t'see the fun. Can you keep her from harm?"

"That I can, you old mulligrubber," said Robin, chucking Hawise under the chin. "You know well," he said, giving Katherine a soft yearning glance, "I'd give my life for her gladly, if t'were needed."

"Humph," said Hawise with an unwilling smile, "sheep's eyes, calf talk—nay, lady dear, ye mustn't wear that gown!"

Katherine, hardly listening to them, had pulled the gorgeous apricot velvet robes from her traveling coffer and was smoothing down the ermine bands. She looked up astonished, then flushed. She had been following instinct in planning to make herself beautiful, but she knew that Hawise was right.

"The old gray woolsey, and your plain russet mantle," said Hawise with decision, lifting these garments from the coffer and shaking them out. " 'Twere best ye be not noticed, an ye *must* go." She did not add that she had a sharp foreboding, augmented by having seen a raven perching on the Duke's great coat of arms that hung over the gatehouse. She understood her mistress's heartache and frantic desire for action, but she was uneasy. When she sent Katherine forth with a quick hard kiss, she crossed herself and on rare impulse went into the palace chapel for a prayer.

Katherine and Robin arrived early at St. Paul's, but it was already jammed. The mayor and his aldermen, and their wives, filled the choir aisles; while packed around them stood members of the great guilds: the vintners, the goldsmiths, the mercers, the grocers, all recognizable by their banners.

The nave overflowed with a surging restless mass. There

were prentices in their leather jerkins, tavernkeepers and ale-wives, clerks and a goodly sprinkling of monks. There were professional archers with metal breastplates and long quivers, and heavily bearded seamen who happened to be in home port between voyages. There were whores with ray hoods, and bandaged beggars with crutches. The largest nave in England had St. Paul's, but it would not hold all the Londoners who wished to see their bishop defy the Duke of Lancaster. Folk clambered on the tombs, they clung to the window ledges and the carved-stone traceries of the pillars, but still more kept pressing in.

Robin shoved and coaxed and threatened until he got Katherine nearer to the Lady Chapel. Here all the bishops were assembled around Sudbury, the gentle old Archbishop of Canterbury, who looked and doubtless felt distressed, for he was ever a man of peace. Robin put his hands around Katherine's waist, and blushing a little at this liberty, lifted her to a high perch between two iron bars of a chantry.

Katherine looked first towards Blanche's tomb, and could see the brightly painted stone canopy and the wrought-iron grille that enclosed her chantry, but not the lovely alabaster face. Still she felt a little comforted by her nearness to Blanche.

They waited a long time, and the crowd grew restless. There were stampings of feet and impatient whistles, when high in the tower above them Paul's great bell began to clang.

Katherine craned forward and saw William Courtenay, Bishop of London, appear majestically on the choir steps. He helf his crozier at arm's length to rest the tip on the tapes-tried carpet, and stood like a Roman general, awaiting the homage of a conquered people.

Then she heard shouts at the great door. Her head turned with a thousand other heads to look down the nave. She saw a stocky man in armor covered by a surcote embroidered with blue lions. He waved a white staff and shouted, "Get out o' the way, you scurvy knaves." His arms threshed like flails, and she saw him pound someone's head.

"Who is it?" Katherine whispered.

Robin, standing on tiptoe answered, "Percy, with his mar-shal's staff. The people won't give way for him."

The Bishop of London descended the choir steps and called out angrily to Percy, "What entrance is this you make into the House of God! Throw down your staff or by Saint Paul himself I'll have you thrown out!"

Katherine did not hear the answer, for behind Percy and topping him by a foot, she saw John. The Duke stood where a ray of amber sunlight streamed through the painted glass of the western window onto his head. The blue and red velvet of his sleeves, the three ermine tabs on his chest, the lilies and leopards of his surcote, the gold of his coronet all glowed in a soft yellow nimbus, while his face seemed to shine. Humility struck Katherine, even shame that she had dared to expect love from such a man as this.

But then the Duke strode forward, pushing past Percy, and hurried to the choir steps. She could hear nothing that was said, but she saw that he shouted something to the bishop, who shouted back, and that there was great wrath between them.

The Duke plunged again amongst the muttering people and led forward Wyclif and four friars. The priest walked sturdily with downcast eyes and the crowd fell back, for many of them had listened to him preach and many admired him. It was not Wyclif that they feared.

Wyclif entered the Lady Chapel and the people surged forward again. They climbed up onto each other's shoulders so as to see. Katherine's view was blocked but not her knowledge of what was taking place, for those in front called back to others and murmurs blew like wind throughout the church. "The Duke demands a seat for Wyclif! Our bishop will not allow it!"—"Now Percy shakes his fist in the bishop's face."—"The archbishop seems to plead and try to calm them but no one listens."—"*Now* by God's body—Lancaster—"

"Oh, what's happening?" cried Katherine in an agony. She heard nothing but "Lancaster" as a sullen roar like mounting surf beat to the vaulting of the church.

Robin cried, "I cannot tell. Sweet lady, I must get you out from here—" But he saw no way to move her through the throng.

A great fellow in a leather jerkin called out, "The Duke threatens our bishop—Jesu, he's drawn his sword—Lancaster would kill—"

"Kill—kill—kill—" Like the senseless repetitions of a nightmare, a thousand voices bawled the word. There was a sharp crack of wood from the rood screen as the mob heaved against it. The tapers rocked in their holders. A woman screamed.

"Quick!" cried Robin, "we'll try for that door." He scooped her off her perch and holding her tight in his left arm edged backward along the wall to a small recessed door. Sweat broke out on his forehead when he found that it was open. He pushed Katherine through. They were in the cloisters. From here a gate led to the churchyard and through the gravestones on to Watling street.

Katherine had obeyed her squire blindly, so frightened by that roaring mob that she could not think. But on the street she clutched Robin's arm and cried, "What will happen to him? Jesu, we can't leave here like this."

"No harm can befall our Duke," cried Robin fiercely, wiping his forehead on his sleeve. "I must get you to safety—'twere madness to stay in there, 'twould do no good—"

"Yes, yes," she cried, "then take me to the Pessoners in Billingsgate—'tis near. Hurry, Robin, hurry—so you may go back—"

He nodded instantly and they ran together through the streets towards the Bridge until they came to the fishmonger's half-timbered house on Thames street.

"Lady Katherine!" cried Dame Emma in amazement as she opened to their frantic knocks.

"Let me stay here," panted Katherine. "Robin, run back and see—then tell me—" She sank onto the settle by the bright fire and struggled to catch her breath.

Dame Emma was alone, the children were working on the fish wharf, the maids all in the brewhouse grinding malt. The dame let Katherine recover on the settle while she went to the still room for a bunch of dried sage, prime remedy for nervous upsets. When the brew was cool enough, she brought it to Katherine and made her drink it with the same kind firmness that Hawise had inherited.

"Cock's bones, m'lady, what's ado?" she said then, her smile as warming as her applewood fire. "Is't some trouble at Paul's?" she added, and her smile faded, for her husband Guy, and Jack Maudelyn too, had gone to see the trial.

Katherine explained quickly and Dame Emma shook her head. "There'll be cracked pates and brasted bones if no worse, the City's been heaving like a pot o' porridge these past months. This'll boil it over. I pray me goodman keeps his wits, though I've scant hope o' Hawise's Jack—sore as a bear on a chain—is Jack."

Katherine did not answer; she twisted her hands together and looked continually towards the window hoping for Robin's return. She sipped the sage brew, she wandered about the cheerful low-ceilinged room, presently she sat down by Dame Emma and despite the good dame's protests helped her with the cracking and picking out of hazelnuts. Dame Emma thought how those white soft hands had once been rough and red with chilblains, and of the frightened fifteen-year-old bride who had so touched her heart and Hawise's.

"Lady Katherine, how does my wench?" she asked suddenly. "Does she serve you well?"

"Oh, Dame Emma, I cannot *tell* you how well! She's my sister, my friend—indeed I—I—" Her eyes, though shadowed by worry, shone with wistful gratitude.

The goodwife patted the slender wool-clad shoulder and thought that she understood why Hawise so loved this fair woman, though Hawise's father did not. Egged on by Jack, Guy himself had taken to grumbling lately, to saying that Hawise had better come back to her family and leave the shameful service of the wicked Duke's leman. Nor was he so awed as he used to be by the salary and benefits Hawise received, since he himself was prospering. Yet even Guy must grudgingly admit they could not do for the ten-year-old Jackie what Katherine's influence had. The lad was gone for a page in a Kentish knight's home, and a chestful of clothes with him that would not disgrace an earl's son.

Katherine threw down the cracker and pick amongst the tray of rattling nuts and wandering to the window peered out again. "Robin's coming, he's past Saint Magnus' church!" She opened the door and flew out to the street.

They came back in together and Katherine cried to Dame Emma, "All's well with the Duke! Thanks be to God and His Holy Mother—Tell—tell what happened, Robin."

The young squire laughed and picking up some hazel meats crunched them in his strong teeth. "When I got back, His Grace and Lord Percy had already left the church with Wyclif. I talked to one of Percy's squires, he thought it all a rare good joke. With the turmoil and the shouting, and a score of bishops darting here and there, the folk got confused; and then the rood screen tumbled down and frightened them so they rushed back into the nave."

"And then?" cried Katherine.

"Why then the Duke and my lord Percy simply walked out through the Dean's door, mounted and rode off towards Cornhill, where they are to sup with Sir John d'Ypres. Percy's squire said my lords were cool as spring water and very tickled at the breakdown of the trial."

"There's a-many won't be," said Dame Emma, frowning. "God's nails, 'tsounds a disgraceful brawling all around."

Yes, it is so, Katherine thought bitterly. She sank down on a little three-legged stool within the hearth and rested her forehead on her cold hand. She closed her eyes and saw John as he had stood beneath the amber light of Paul's great window, when she had thought him a god. Now she knew that he had never been less godlike. Hot temper he had always had and arrogance, but not like this. She thought of the furious shoutings and the clash of a sword next to Blanche's quiet tomb.

The fire leaped up, and in its flames Katherine saw far different pictures of him. She saw the gentleness of his face as it had been at Les Landes when they first came together in love; she saw the tender laughing way he had played with their babies when he had last come to Kenilworth. But aside from these personal things, she thought of how he had so often shown a true compassion. Of a happening in Leicester town three years ago, when they crossed the street at Southgate, and an old crazed man had darted out from the gate's shadow. In snatching at the ruby brooch that clasped the Duke's mantle, he had gouged John's cheek open with filthy fingernails. The wretch was one of the Duke's own serfs, and yet John had dealt with him pityingly, soothed the slobbering terror when the guards would have seized him, and taken the old man to a room in Leicester Castle, there to be tended and sheltered until he died at last while blessing the Duke's name.

Yet there now seemed in John nothing but hatred.

The squire and Dame Emma looked at the brooding, desolate figure on the stool within the hearth. Firelight shimmered on the burnished head, on the lovely lines of the brow and straight nose and round cleft chin, and they glanced at each other.

Robin yearned to kiss the little hand that plaited and unplaited a fold of the gray skirt, to implore her to smile.

The goodwife's impulse was more practical. "Sir Squire," she said, "since me men folk're out, do ye go down cellar t'far corner behind a keg o' malmsey. Ye must move the keg to reach a stone crock o' peach brandywine I put down last Lammas. Fetch the crock an ye'll be so kind, 'tis prime cure for low sperrits."

When Robin had made off into the courtyard, bound for the passage that led to the cellars, Dame Emma reached up to a shelf and taking down her two engraved silver cups began to polish them; for she never served her famed liquor in ordinary mugs. Dame Emma had but dipped her cloth into the powdered pumice when she heard the pound of running feet outside, and a banging on the door. In the excited shouts she recognized Jack Maudelyn's voice.

Dame Emma jumped up and yanked the settle around so that it hid Katherine. "Stay there," she whispered, and pulled the bolt. Her son-in-law shot in.

"Out of me way, old mother," he cried, dancing with impatience. "I want me headpiece and bow and quiver, Master Guy too, get down his pike and sword." He flung open the door to the passage where the Pessoner weapons were kept, began to pull them feverishly off the wall pegs.

"Not so hot, not so hot, me lad!" cried Dame Emma, grabbing his arm. "What's all this coil? Where's Master Guy?"

"He's coming." He shook her off as he grabbed a handful of arrows from his quiver, "Where's longshot? Where's me best goose-tipped shaft? The devil take it—who's been meddling here!—and this pike's dull as wood—no matter, 'twill serve—" He thrust his sandy shockhead into the helmet, slung the quiver over his shoulder.

"Serve for what, Jack Maudelyn?" cried Dame Emma in a great voice.

"Why, to pierce the Duke's black heart, if God gi' me that honor!" He was fumbling with the leather lacings of his headpiece and did not hear Katherine's gasp from behind the settle, but Dame Emma ran to the hearth as though to mend the fire. She held her finger to her lips and shook her head violently.

Katherine had started up but she sank back onto the stool. The dame returned to the passage and said sternly, "What d'ye mean by that wicked speech, ye rascallion!"

Jack seized his longbow, shouldered his pike and cried exultantly, "I mean that John o' Gaunt and that whoreson Percy'll never see another sunrise! Men o' London're roused at

last! They've gone off to Percy's now—then we're on to the
Savoy after Lancaster!"

"Jack, Jack!" cried Dame Emma starting back, "ye
couldna do this fearful thing an ye would, the Duke's own
guards—"

Jack broke in contemptuously. "The Duke's own guards'll
not stand against two thousand men! Hush your blab, old
'oman, I'm off, tell Master Guy to hurry after—" He dashed
through the kitchen and the slam of the front door shook the
house.

Katherine stood up. Her face had gone pale as the plaster
wall. "Call Robin, quick!"

The dame obeyed.

The squire had been tugging at the malmsey keg but he
heard the frightened voice, ran up to the court and into the
kitchen. Katherine stood in the center of the rush-strewn
flags, her looks so white and strange that Robin cried out in
alarm. She shook her head impatiently to still him and spoke
with tense restraint.

"Listen—a mob two thousand strong is after the Duke.
They would kill him—but they think him at the Savoy. You
know where he *is*?"

Robin gaped, but the control with which she spoke con-
veyed urgency quicker than if she had shouted. "At Sir John
d'Ypres' in Cornhill," he whispered. "But Lady, how know
you this—"

"No matter. Hurry, Robin, warn him—my God—" Her
voice rose suddenly. "But where can he go—tell him west out
of the city—"

"He would not run from a rabble, lady," Robin, breathing
fast, had now caught the full impact of her news. "Not our
Duke, and with this reckless spirit he has shown."

She nodded, biting her lips, frowning with the force of her
desperate concentration. "Then tell him little Richard is in
danger too, that he must get across the river to Kennington
and protect the boy. *Make him go!*"

Robin turned with his hand on the latch, when Dame
Emma ran up with a paring knife. "Best take this off," she
cried and slicing the stitches, yanked the Duke's badge from
Robin's shoulder.

The squire grunted and dashed out. While the door was
opened both women heard the distant roars of the mob.
"They must be at Ludgate," whispered Dame Emma.

"Christ's blood, but they've gone mad—and you too Guy le Pessoner!" she shouted, for her husband came lumbering along the street, his moon face purple, his paunch heaving beneath his guildsman's tunic.

"No, you don't," she cried pushing him down on the settle, as he started for the armory passage. "Ye'll not go out again to join those ribauds!" The dame, arms akimbo and eyes snapping like sparks, glared down at her panting husband. "Ye big fool, what's got into ye—our roistering and murdering—" She grabbed the poker and brandished it in her husband's face.

"Emma, forbear," stammered the fishmonger. "Ye don't know what they're doing to us. They aim to make us serfs here, to take London's liberties. They've a bill at Westminster ready now, to put that stinking marshal over us. Already he's ta'en a prisoner he'd no right to, had 'im mewed up in a dungeon. We freed the knave and burned the stocks they'd put him in. We searched for Percy—"

"And did ye find him? Nay, stay there," Dame Emma thrust the poker at her lord's belly and he sank back on the settle.

"Not yet—he'll be at the Savoy wi' t'other traitor—Peter —who's this?" The excited fishmonger had just caught sight of Katherine standing like a church statue beyond his angry wife.

Katherine walked forward around Dame Emma, and looked down at the fishmonger. "What has the Duke of Lancaster ever done to you, Master Guy, that you should requite him like this?" she said.

The fishmonger dropped his eyes. "What does Lady Swynford here?" he muttered, twisting his leather-shod feet beneath the settle.

"Fled here for shelter from ruffians like you," cried Dame Emma. "Would ye deny it to her—"

Master Guy swallowed, he waggled his head distractedly. At length he said, "Nay," and sighed. "Ye can put the poker down, Emma. Me blood's cooling. But wrong's been done us —great wrong. Would ye have us take these wrongs like gelded conies?" He reached to the hearth for a flagon of ale and his wife, putting down the poker, brought him a cup. He drank, then looked at Katherine. "Ay, poor lass, I've had bitter thoughts of you, many a time, but now I've room for pity. Me blood's cooled down to be sure—but out there—I doubt

they'll be slaked until they've slain your—" The word he
would have used was paramour, yet there was something in
Katherine's face which checked him. "Until they've got Lancaster," he finished looking down into his cup.

Katherine shuddered, yet still she spoke with biting calm.
"They'll not get him, Master Guy. For they say God is just,
and will know that the Duke has suffered wrongs as much as
you have."

"Brave words, my dear," said the fishmonger. "At least in
this world he has *you* to speak for him."

"And cares not—" she whispered, turning away.

## XX

KATHERINE SLEPT that night of the riots at the fishmonger's. After a few hours of exhaustion, she awoke with a
jump of panic when St. Magnus' bells rang for Prime
and hurrying down to the kitchen was received kindly by the
Pessoners, who told her the latest tidings.

Little harm had been done after all, yestereve. The Duke
and Percy both had somehow escaped, said Master Guy, and
here Emma made a private signal to Katherine, for she had
not disclosed Katherine's part in warning the Duke.

It seemed that Bishop Courtenay himself had finally appeared and berated the mob leaders, saying that they had carried their disorders too far and that he was ashamed of his
flock. So one by one they had slunk off to their homes, con-
tenting themselves with reversing the Duke's coat of arms
wherever it hung outside a shop and then pelting the blazons
with mud and excrement.

"And I'm glad enough now, no harm came to the Duke,"
said Guy, donning his leather apron which was plastered with
fish scales, " 'Twas a good night's work as 'tis, in especial that
we let loose the wrongfully held prisoner from Percy's inn.
The marshal'll not try those tricks again."

"What prisoner was that?" asked Dame Emma, coaxingly pushing a dish of fried eggs towards the silent Katherine.

"Some fellow from Norwich. I didna see him. 'Twas said he was in mortal fear o' the Duke. Th' instant he was freed, he hared it off for sanctuary in Saint Paul's."

Dame Emma sighed. "And think ye, chucklehead, that this is the end o' London's trouble? Can ye get it through your numb skull that violence but breeds violence? D'ye think the Duke will smile and thank ye for this night's work?"

The fishmonger thrust his lip out and said stubbornly, "He should not a tampered wi' our liberties, he should not a set hisself against the commons."

The goodwife sighed again. "Ay, commons've no friend at court these days." She bustled over to pat Katherine's shoulder. "Ye don't eat, my lady?"

"No," said Katherine rising, "forgive me but I can't. I must get to the Savoy. God be thanked the Lady Philippa and Hawise seem to've suffered no harm. I had forgot them last night."

Ay, poor lass, you forgot all else but one man's danger, Emma thought as she said, "Ye canna go alone. Go wi' her, Guy, she'll be safe wi' you."

The fishmonger grumbled that a load of herring awaited him at the wharf, that his prentices must be chivvied to work, that there was a mess of cod to be delivered to the Guildhall, but finally he took off his apron and mounted Katherine behind him on his great bay gelding. He was a goodhearted man, and he admired Katherine's fair face, but he was increasingly convinced that Hawise's devotion to this woman was unfortunate, even dangerous. The mortal hatred aimed at the Duke might well glance off and hit those near him, as indeed it already had; and though no coward, Guy did not like certain remarks he had heard last night which reflected on his own connection with the Duke through that of his obstinate daughter.

He rode along in gloomy silence until they had crossed the Fleet bridge, then he said, "How long d'ye look to be down here, m'lady?" For he thought that since Hawise could not legally be forced to break her service indenture to Lady Swynford, and would not if she could, at least the farther away they went, the better.

"Not long," said Katherine with a cold vehemence that astonished the fishmonger. "I shall see to *that*, Master Guy."

"To Kenilworth, then, or Leicester?"

"No," she said, "to Lincolnshire, to my own home."

"By Saints Simon and Jude!" Guy twisted his fat neck around to stare at her. "Will the Duke allow it? Are ye not contracted to him as governess to his little ladies, as well as by other—other ties?"

"I believe the Duke will not hold me," she said, sitting stiff and straight on the pillion. "And by the Blessed Virgin, I am no serf, to be bound against my will!"

"Welladay!" cried Guy, thinking that the riot had very properly frightened her into caution. " 'Tis a sensible plan."

Katherine did not answer.

The gelding jogged along the Strand past St. Clement's little church. Katherine had passed the church fifty times without special notice; today as she glanced at it, eleven years slid away. She saw in the porch a priest and a knight with crinkled hair, and a girl with a wreath of garden flowers on her head. Handfasted, they stood, the girl and the knight, while the priest intoned, "To have and to hold from this day forward to love . . . and to cherish . . . till death. . . ."

She turned away from the church and stared down the Strand ahead, until they came to the Savoy, then Master Guy started and cried, "By God, see what they did here!"

Katherine looked up at the gatehouse. They had wrenched off the Duke's great five-foot painted shield and hammered it back again upside down.

" 'Tis what they do to traitors!" said Master Guy and chuckled suddenly. "Them leopards look mortal silly astanding on their little heads awaving of their little legs." His chuckles grew into a rumble.

"For the love of Christ—stop it!" Katherine cried, shaking his arm. "Can't you see what you're doing to him? What man could stand the vile lies—the hatred—you *know* he's not a traitor. Oh God curse the lot of you!" She jumped down off the horse.

The fishmonger's jaw dropped. He stared after her while she was challenged by two men-at-arms who barred the way with crossed spears, then he saw her pass and disappear into the Outer Ward. He shrugged his thick shoulders and rode slowly back to town.

That afternoon, unable to come to rest anywhere, Katherine went out into the Savoy gardens. It was chilly, the clipped yew hedges and the shrouded rosebushes were drenched in gray mist, but she had flung a warm squirrel-lined cloak over the gray woolsey. Nor would she have felt the cold in any case, while she paced the deserted brick paths and thought of her new-found decision.

She could leave here tomorrow. She and Hawise and the Kenilworth servants who had come down with them would return there at once. She would pick up her children and hasten to Lincolnshire—to Kettlethorpe.

John might be momentarily annoyed at her taking their two babies from the luxury of Kenilworth, but since they obviously no longer interested him any more than she did herself, his protest would be a formality. He should have no cause to reproach her for negligence in her duties to Philippa and Elizabeth either. Until he should appoint a new governess, Lady Dacre here at the Savoy would be delighted to wait upon Philippa—and delighted to get rid of me, Katherine thought. Well she knew that most of the ladies treated her with contempt when the Duke was not around. Secure in his love and protection she had always ignored these slights.

Now this was changed.

Back and forth she walked between the frosty yews and thought harsh practical thoughts. She would keep the wardships and annuity he had already given her if he allowed her to, for she owed it to his children, that Kettlethorpe might be made habitable for them. But she needed nothing more. She would be invulnerable again and alone, with this wicked unwanted love walled out of her heart.

Suddenly she looked down at the ring he had put on her finger in the ruined chapel in the Pyrenees. Betrothal ring. She stared at the round translucent sapphire, the stone of constancy.

Her lips tightened as she twisted the ring from her finger and walked to the riverbank. She stood on the marble pier and holding the ring outstretched in her hand, gazed down at the black lapping waters.

"Nay—I cannot," she said, after a moment, turning from the river. She slipped the ring into her scarlet purse that was embroidered with her arms, Swynford boars impaling the Catherine wheels; the blazon he had made for her.

Am I then nothing of *myself?* she thought with anguish. Can I not live apart from memories of him—

She sank down on a stone bench, and stared out across the

river to the barren stony hummocks of Lambethmoor. The mists grew thicker and downstream the pale lemon light faded over London. One by one from its churches the bells rang out for vespers, near at hand the Savoy chapel gave forth its sprinkle of silvery chimes. She stirred restlessly on the bench. The bells' familiar summons disturbed her. Since Sunday she had not been to Mass, nor partaken of the Blessed Sacrament in weeks, for it no longer gave her comfort; things of the spirit had grown as empty and cold as her love must grow.

The bells drowned out the sound of approaching oars on the river until a barge appeared out of the mists quite near the pier. Katherine started for the steps, unwilling to be gaped at, when an eager voice called out, "My Lady Swynford, is it you?"

She turned and recognized Robin's feathered cap and rusty tunic as the squire waved from the barge's prow. She came down the steps and waited while the oarsmen steered up to the pier. "So you've returned," she said quietly. "Your errand last night, Robin, was well done, I've heard."

The youth jumped to the pier and cried, "I've been sent for you, my lady, to come to Kennington. You're to come back with me at once!"

"No—" said Katherine, unsmiling. In the shadow of her hood her face gleamed hard as pearl, her eyes were cooler than the mists.

Robin was dismayed that the lovely laughing girl who had been his most precious charge was transformed into a stern woman with a stranger's eyes. He stammered, "But my lady —'tis a command—you are *summoned* to Kennington Palace."

" 'Tis kind of His Grace," she said. "You may tell him that I know he has never been lacking in courtesy when he thinks there's cause for it, but in sending you to warn him I did nothing that his lowliest varlet would not have done."

Robin blinked, and looking down at the toe of his leather shoe, said unhappily, "It is not His Grace who summons you."

The bells ceased their ringing and there was silence on the pier. "Who does then?" said Katherine.

"The Princess Joan, my lady—she commands in the name of Prince Richard that you shall come at once."

"Whyfor?" said Katherine, in a less sure tone. "I've never

met the Princess, what could she want of me? Robin, is His Grace not at Kennington too?"

"Ay—he *was*—locked into a chamber with Percy, I believe. I've not seen him since we crossed the river last night. Lady dear—I beg of you to hurry, the Princess was most anxious."

Since there was now no queen in England, Princess Joan was sovereign lady and must be obeyed. Katherine reluctantly let Robin help her into the waiting barge. The oarsmen bent their backs and pulling sturdily against the current moved their craft upstream. They passed Westminster and crossing to the Lambeth bank landed at the Kennington pier.

They went up a terraced path to the fair small country palace where the Prince of Wales had died. Robin led the way through a courtyard and upstairs to the Princess Joan's bower, where a waiting woman admitted Katherine at once, then left her alone.

The room was gaudy as a jewel box; the walls hung with painted silks, the floor covered with bright woven flowers in a Persian carpet. The furniture was gilded, and in a gold cage studded with crystals two white birds twittered.

As Katherine looked at the birds the Princess entered hurriedly, in a rush of pink velvet and a wave of heavy scent, crying with warm impetuosity, "Welcome, Lady Swynford, I've been awaiting you!" She held out a fat dimpled hand so loaded with diamonds that Katherine, as she curtsied, could scarce find space to kiss.

"I have come, madam, as you commanded," said Katherine distantly, and rising, she waited.

"Take off your mantle and sit down, my dear," said the Princess, while she settled her billowing hips into a canopied chair. Katherine obeyed, wondering what was wanted of her, and her pride hardened still further, for she thought that she could guess.

The Princess was like a large blowzy rose. Katherine noted the dyed hair, the excessive plumpness of the rouged cheeks, the charcoal blackening the scanty lashes, and thought how the nuns at Sheppey Convent had admired this fair maid of Kent, and of how she had once heard a knight say that when Joan had married the Prince of Wales she was "la plus belle femme d'Angleterre—et la plus amoureuse."

Perhaps his brother thought so still.

The Princess cleared her throat and leaning forward said,

"My dear, you're not at all as I expected. I see now why—yes—I'm glad I summoned you." The girl looked highborn and well-bred, Joan thought in surprise, most lovely features. The firm cleft chin showed character too. She was relieved at this new view of Lancaster's mistress, for gossip had it that the little Swynford was an upstart strumpet, and some said that she kept him from his Duchess by the use of black arts.

Joan smiled, the gay confiding smile which had won many a heart, and said, "I have something to ask of you, Lady Swynford—'tis a delicate matter."

"Perhaps I may save you embarrassment, madam, by telling you that I intend to leave the Duke's service tomorrow, and shall go to live permanently in my own manor in Lincolnshire," said Katherine. "Is that far enough away?"

The Princess's eyes grew round as turquoise disks. "Blessed Saint Mary!" she cried. "Did you think I asked you here to beg you to give up the Duke? Great heaven, child, it is quite the opposite!"

"What!" cried Katherine sharply. "Madam, you are jesting." For the Princess was laughing in small muffled spurts.

"Nay, listen," said Joan wiping her eyes on her pink velvet sleeve. "Forgive me, I don't know whether I laugh or weep, for I am frightened—frightened—don't stare at me with those great angry eyes—my dear, I need your help." The Princess rose and walking to Katherine cupped the girl's chin in her hand and gazed down earnestly. "Do you really love my brother of Lancaster?" Katherine looked away, and her color rose. "Ay, I see you do."

"He loves *me* no longer," said Katherine very low. "He's had no thought of me in months—there are many signs—it is finished."

The Princess sighed and wandering to the carved mantel absently traced the pattern of acanthus leaves with her finger. "I believe you're wrong," she said, "and for two reasons. I lived fifteen years with his brother and in many ways they are like as two cockleshells. Edward never ceased to love me and come back to me, and yet when the dark violent fits were on him—"

She shook her head. Her hand dropped from the mantel and she sat down again. "And the other reason is this. Three weeks ago we held a Christmas mumming here for my Richard. John came, of course, with many others to do Richard honor, and late that night when we had all retired I could not sleep for missing my own dear lord and fearing for the future of my little son. Then I heard a strange noise in the State Chamber which is next to mine, and where John slept. It was a sound of outcry and struggle. I opened the door between and listened fearfully, meaning to shout for the guard, and then I knew that he was in the grip of some frightful dream. He choked and panted and cried out your name. 'Katrine! Katrine!' He cried it with a frenzy that would wring your heart. I went to him and woke him, and he was angry with me and bade me get out. We did not speak of it again."

The hardness in Katherine's breast dissolved a little, and she said with a faint smile, " 'Tis something to know that he yet thinks of me in dreams. But what is it you would have me do, madam?"

The Princess, gripping her chair arms violently, cried, "Go to him! Go to him—and somehow, make him listen—make him stop these dreadful things he's planning—Christ's mercy! I think he has gone mad!"

The girl got up and ran to kneel by the weeping Princess. "Dear lady, he is not mad, I know he's not—but he would never listen to me, never has he told me his plans."

The Princess, gripping the chair arms violently, cried, "Go to him! Sir Simon Burley—Richard's guardian—pled. I even summoned the old archbishop here, John would not see him, do you know what he means to do?" She shuddered, and her tear-blurred eyes grew fixed. "He means to muster an army, his own people and Percy's from the north, he means to march it onto London! Civil war! Worse far than what my dear lord dreaded. There'll be no England left for Richard."

Katherine sank back upon the carpet. Her heart beat heavily and her thoughts ran together in confusion.

"And this gathering of an army is not all," cried the Princess. "He proposes this night to violate sanctuary—to seize some prisoner who has fled to Saint Paul's—to drag him out from the altar—hang him."

"Jesu, no!" cried Katherine in horror. For this sacrilege seemed to her the worst of all that the Princess had said. The right of sanctuary was God's most sacred law and to violate it meant damnation.

"Ay," said the Princess with a groan. "*Every* man's hand would be against him then. John will be killed. He was saved last night, Katherine, but after this nothing could save him. As surely as his grandfather was murdered in Berkeley Castle, so will John be killed and thousands of others with him."

"This prisoner," cried Katherine, "who is he?" In the blackness of her confusion, there was a glimmering. An intuition.

"Some knave who did write placards about the Duke, so Percy said." The Princess spoke with weary impatience. She thought this a foolish question indeed when the welfare of her son and England was at stake.

But Katherine's intuition grew stronger. In some way the prisoner held the key to John's unreason. All these things which he had done to so inflame the people dated from the time he read the placard at St. Paul's. Of a sudden her prideful hurt and anger vanished, and her love flowed back on a wave of pity, while she felt in her own breast a vibration from the wild submerged pain he had been suffering. She saw that the Princess Joan was right, and that she alone had love enough for him to wrestle with his demon.

The bower door opened and a child walked in, a lad with curling flaxen hair and a face so delicate that but for his parti-colored hose and royal blazoned surcote he might have been a girl.

"Dickon!" cried the Princess holding out her hand. "Come to me, love. Here, Lady Swynford," she said as the child stood by her knee, "is England's hope." She looked at Katherine with pleading, praying that the girl's hesitation would be finally resolved by the sight of this fair royal child.

Katherine started from her thoughts and curtsied. Richard bowed to her in a courtly manner, and said, "Mama, my lord Uncle John is leaving—he's on the stairs—I thought you didn't wish him to go—"

"Dear God!" cried the Princess jumping up, "he must not go. If he leaves here—Katherine—can you stop him—for I know that I cannot."

"Perhaps," whispered the girl. She shut her eyes. Her mind formed no prayer, she importuned no saints nor even the Blessed Virgin for help, and yet it seemed that some new calm strength came to her.

The Princess rushed to the door. They went out together and down the newel stairs to the courtyard.

The Duke, in brass helmet and full armor, his hand resting on his sword, stood by the river gate shouting last instructions to Percy: "Then by dawn we'll have raised a thousand men between us, 'twill do for now. The Savoy—" He stopped and stared, as Katherine came up to him.

"My lord—"

So full was he of his new plans that at first it seemed he did not know her. Beneath his lifted visor his face was set and haggard, his eyes the sharp ice-blue she had always feared.

She looked at him softly, but she spoke with the force that had come to her. "My lord, I must see you alone *now*."

"Katrine!" he said bewildered. "What do you here? You were at the Savoy—nay, in Billingsgate—I remember Robin Beyvill said you sent him. 'Twas not well done, they were in no danger here at Kennington. I would have faced them down in London, they'd not have dared to touch me."

"My dearest lord," said Katherine, looking steadily up into his face, "I wish to see you alone."

"What tiresome folly!" He jerked his mailed hand on his sword hilt. "I'm off to the Savoy. My men are gathering, and I've other work to do this night."

Percy had drawn off frowning, the Princess and the boy stood watching by the palace door, while along the edges of the court the grooms and retainers were peering openly, wondering at this lady who dared delay the Duke.

Katherine drew herself high, her chin lifted and she said inflexibly, "All this will wait until you've talked with me. I command it, my lord."

*"Command!"*

"Yes," she said unflinching. "By reason of this you gave me." From her purse she drew the sapphire ring and held it out to him on her palm. "And this is the first thing I have ever asked of you, my lord."

He looked at the ring, and then at Katherine.

He turned impatiently to Percy. "You go on ahead. I'll follow shortly. Now Katrine, what *do* you wish of me?"

The Princess saw that the first battle had been won and came forward hastily. "There's a fire in the State Chamber, my lord, you can talk to Lady Swynford there. I'll send food and drink to you, for you've not eaten all this day—" She saw his face darken, and added with the desperate guile she had often needed for her Edward, "Supper will give you more strength and a clearer head for whatever it is you plan to do tonight."

John frowned, but he walked over to the stairs without

comment. The women followed, while the Princess pulled Katherine a little behind. "God help you, child," she whispered, "and Saint Venus help you too. You'll have need of every help to turn him from his purpose. Make him drink much—and—by Peter, I wish there were time to dress you in one of my silk chamber gowns, though 'twouldn't fit—no matter, you must know the ways to make him think of love. Woo him, cajole him, weep—"

"Dear madam," whispered Katherine, "I'll do what I can." But not for you nor me, nor England, she thought, but because he is destroying his own soul.

She entered the State Chamber and the Duke turned sharply to her. "What would you say to me, Katrine—I've little time."

"Time enough to rest a bit though, my lord. And I can't talk to a man standing in full armor, 'tis frightening." She gave him a gay coaxing smile, though her heart beat fast.

He grunted and sat down on the wide oak chair where his brother had used to sit. She went to him and quickly unhooked the latchet of his brass helmet and lifted it off his head. "And you can't eat in these," she said, unbuckling the straps that fastened his mailed gauntlets. "Here comes Robin with wine—won't you let him take off the rest of your armor? 'Twill be quickly donned again when you wish to leave."

The young squire had entered with a flagon of the strongest wine to be found in the Princess's cellars; a server followed bearing a silver platter loaded with eel jellies, white bread rolls and a steaming oyster pie.

She gestured to Robin, for still John did not speak.

He was fighting a great weariness that had come on him when he sat down. He had not slept in two nights, the first at Percy's Inn, the second here. His head swam, and because it blunted his purpose, he fought off too the realization of how strongly he had responded to Katherine's touch as she drew off his helmet.

He suffered Robin to unbuckle the other sections of his armor and hang them with his great sword from gilded wall pegs where the Prince of Wales' black tilting gear still hung. Then he took the cup of wine that Katherine brought him and drank quickly.

As he had hoped, it cleared his head. "What are you doing at Kennington?" he said scowling. "Why didn't you wait at the Savoy to see me?"

Katherine considered quickly. Robin and the server were gone and she was preparing a plate of food. She had never lied to him, nor would she, but she knew that she must choose all her words with care.

"It is not always so easy to see you at the Savoy, my lord," she said pulling a corner of the table over so that he might eat in comfort, "nor for *me* to see you at all—of late." She smiled, with no hint of reproach, and sat down close to him on a stool. "You look very tired, won't you eat, please? Alas that 'tis only Lenten fare, but these oysters are well roasted."

He started to protest hotly, to say that if she had forced him to delay his start simply to babble of oysters, he would be gone this instant, but instead, and to his astonishment, he said a very different thing.

"Why don't you wear the ring I gave you, Katrine?" She had dropped it back into her purse as they left the courtyard.

She was startled too, but she answered evenly, "Because I thought that it had lost its meaning."

A quick dull flush mounted his thin cheeks. "Nay, how could you think that, lovedy!" The little pet name he had so often called her slipped out as unawares as had his question, yet he felt aggrievement. Whether he saw her or not, he had known her ever there in the background—waiting, like his jeweled Order of the Garter, seldom worn, yet the possession of this most special badge of knighthood was of steady importance to his life. "I have had matters to think of," he said roughly, "but these matters had nothing to do with women."

"Yes," she said, filling his cup, "I believe that *now*, my lord."

She brushed against his shoulder as she put the flagon back on the table, and he smelled the warm fragrance of her skin. His arm lifted of its own accord to slip around her waist and pull her closer to him, but she moved away before he touched her and sat down again.

His arm dropped. He drank, and spooned up the oysters, eating fast, for he found that he was famished and this the first food in weeks that had had savor for him. While he ate, he felt another new factor, a quality of rest and lessening of strain. He resented the thought that this easing came somehow from Katherine, who sat beside him quietly, gazing into the fire. He had forgotten too how beautiful she was, nor did he wish to think of it now.

He picked up the gold-handled table knife and cut himself

a slice from the bread loaf, while pulling his mind back towards his purpose. They were massing at the Savoy, men-at-
arms from his near-by castles at Hertford and Hatfield.
They'd be there by now since he had sent messengers off at
dawn, and the King's guard from Sheen too. It would take a
month to gather all his forces from the whole of England,
but already he had sufficient fighters to back the first move
that he would make.

Pieter Neumann— He threw down the bread and his fingers gripped the hilt of the knife. This time he would kill Pieter with his own hand—no mercy.

Yet as he thought this, a spasm of nausea gripped his
stomach, and his throat seemed to thicken and close.

It had not been so this morning when a messenger brought
the news that Pieter had been freed by the London mob, and
had fled to sanctuary in the cathedral. Then his rage had
been so violent that he had lost all control for a time, he had
been shaking and shouting with fury, and he had seen alarm
in the faces of those around him, Joan and Sir Simon—even
Percy, who was angry enough himself at the outrages.

Katherine had turned to look at him as he threw down the
bread and gripped the knife and she forced a long steady
breath to master her dismay. She saw that he had lost awareness of her, his skin had turned the color of mold, he swallowed hard and painfully, and in his eyes as they stared at
the knife the pupils had swollen so that there was no blue.

Katherine felt a shock of recognition. Somewhere there
had been a child who looked like that, an uncomprehending
terrified child. She searched hard for the memory, and when
it came it seemed to her so incongruous that she rejected it.
The reminder was of her little John. Last summer he had
wandered into the cow-byre at Kenilworth, and a playful calf
had galloped at him, knocking him down. The child had believed the calf to be a werewolf, fitting it someway into a
horrible tale a serving maid had told him.

Katherine had reasoned with her boy, had made him pet
the calf, and got him to laugh at his terror, yet a month af-
terward the child had had a nightmare from which he awoke
to scream that the calf was after him with the slobbering
fangs and blood-red eyes of a werewolf, and still when he
saw a calf he trembled and grew white.

It were folly indeed to make a comparison between the
thirty-six-year-old Duke of Lancaster and a four-year-old

child, and yet—in both she had seen the same intrinsic shape of fear.

The Duke stirred and put down the knife, he wiped his lips on the damask napkin. "I—I must go," he said in a voice that wavered. He stood up and glanced towards his armor.

Katherine rose too, and took his hand in hers. "Why must you go, John?" She looked up solemnly into his resistant face. "Is it to kill the man who is in sanctuary at Saint Paul's? Is it to do sacrilegious murder, that you must go?"

He snatched his hand from hers. "How do you know that! And if it were, what right have you to question me! Katrine, you've never before—get out of my way!" For she had backed up so that she barred the way to the armor, and the door.

Her wide gray eyes fixed on him with compassion, but her tone was cool and searching as when she rebuked her children. "Of what, my dear lord, are you so afraid?"

He gasped, and raised his hand as though to strike her.

"No, dear," she said. "To hit me'll do no good. All these last months have you not been striking out, and has it eased you? You know that it hasn't. I believe that to *speak out* might ease you. I love you, John, trust me."

He listened, looking at her and then away. "No man or woman has ever thought me a coward," he whispered. "And now you, who say you love me—"

"Holy Christ, my dearest, you're no coward. I know well how you lead your men in battle, and how you've risked your life a thousand times, and yet there *is* something that you fear."

The angry force drained from him. His big shoulders sagged, and he said in a listless voice. "Witchcraft—witchcraft— The man must die this night, for he has cast on me a monstrous spell." He made the sign of the cross and turning, walked to the cushioned banquette beneath the window, sat down and rested his head in his hands.

Katherine too crossed herself, but without conviction. There were sorceries and devilish spells, of course, and yet she did not believe that here they were the answer. She went to John and sat beside him on the banquette. "Who *is* this man that you fear?" she said gently.

"Not him, I don't fear him, the sniveling crippled little shavepate—" he muttered, nor seemed aware that he contradicted what he had just said.

"What then?" she persisted, "What is it that so troubles you?"

"Katrine, for God's sweet sake! Why must you naggle at me? You know what they've done to me, they seek my life, they reverse my shields, they lie and slander, they doubt my —my honor!"

"Ay—" she said hesitating, for almost she sensed the something deeper than this, something that she began to think he did not see himself. "They've done terrible things to you, but it is because *they* are afraid; and you have made them so. Don't you see this, my lord?"

He did not answer. She saw his brown hands clench and unclench, and then the fingers fall lax. She watched his hands which she had always loved. The palms were square and calloused from much handling of the lance and sword, but the fingers were long and sensitive as those of Hankyn, his chief minstrel, whose soul was filled with poetry, and John's touch at times could be tender as a woman's. She saw now that these hands were trembling, and she ached to put her arms around him, to kiss and comfort him, as she had her babies, but she knew that he would push away in anger, as surely as Tom or little John struggled in manful pride against ill-timed caresses, and she spoke again in a clear sorrowful voice.

"You are the strongest, the most powerful man in England, my dear lord, so can you not be merciful?"

His head twisted around and he looked at her strangely. "Isolda said that! When we vowed in the chapel. But she did not keep *her vow*."

Blessed Virgin, he's drunk, she thought, trying to check her terror that this might be worse than drunkenness. "Isolda?" she questioned as steadily as she could.

"Isolda Neumann—my foster mother." And having said it, he sighed and added in a tone of wonder, "In all these years I've never spoken her name." He reached over for the flagon and his crystal cup, poured until the rich golden wine splashed on the table and drank.

Katherine was amazed. She guessed that she was circling nearer to the answer, but what was this of his milk-nurse, and vows in a chapel, and why had he never spoken the woman's name? She dared not question too much, fearful of rupturing this quieter mood.

The courtyard clock had struck eleven long ago, though he had not heard it. It was black night out, and if he would but

stay until the wine took full effect, she might yet persuade
him to the rest he so badly needed.

She glanced frowning at the State Bed, where the Prince
had died—still hung with gloomy sable mourning velvet—
when John spoke again.

"The man you asked me of, the one I shall kill, is Pieter
Neumann, who was Isolda's son."

"Ah," Katherine breathed, still more startled and trying to
understand this revelation. She ventured on what seemed at
first sight to be likely. "And he injured his mother in some
way? And you, loving her very much perhaps, have not forgiven?" She stopped, for as she spoke this sounded too weak,
too pat.

Yet John said, "Yes," with a peculiar quickness. "Yes, that
was it." He had glanced off from the truth, she knew. What
was it the Princess had said of the man in sanctuary? "Some
knave that wrote placards about the Duke." The placard on
Paul's door—the ridiculous changeling slander.

He stood up suddenly, swayed and caught at the table.
"Late," he said thickly, "must go. Don't like your eyes—Ka-
Katrine—gray eyes that lie—break vows—she said she'd
never leave me but she did—she vowed something else—else
—vowed Pieter had lied—" He rolled his head back and
forth as though to rid it of a weight, and stumbled a few
steps.

Katherine ran to him and flung her arms around him.
"Here, dear love, you must rest."

He stumbled again and by wedging her shoulder beneath
his armpit she got him to the bed. He fell prone onto the
black coverlet amongst the embroidered argent ostrich feathers.

Katherine had never seen John dead drunk, for his tastes
were temperate, but she had had much experience with
Hugh, and she thought now that either he would be very sick
or sink at once into a snoring stupor. But she was wrong.

As she brought a candle to the bedstead and herself
climbed up beside him, pulling her furred cape over them
both, he rolled over onto his back, and he began to speak in
thick disconnected sentences.

She leaned over him and listened while her heart pounded
with her desperate effort to understand what he would tell
her. At first she thought he did not know that she was there
and that these were only drunken ramblings, but his eyes

opened, and he looked at her with recognition, though his speech was so slow and heavy that she could scarcely follow the words.

Vows in the Chapel of St. George at Windsor, broken vows. He said it over and over. Isolda had betrayed him.

"How, darling?" Katherine whispered at last, "how did she betray you?" and thought she should not have spoken for he grew silent, and turned his head away, gazing vaguely at the black folds of the bed curtains.

But after a while he spoke. "She went away that night, though she vowed she'd never leave me. She died," he added in a fainter voice. "She died of plague."

"She lied in that—" said John. Suddenly he struggled up onto his elbow and staring into Katherine's white face he said with a remote and terrible quietness, "So perhaps she lied when she denied what Pieter said at Windsor."

"What Pieter said—" repeated Katherine. "What Pieter said?"

"Changeling," he muttered. His lips drew away from his teeth and he fell back on to the pillow.

"Jesu—" she whispered. "Jesu—now I see—"

She twisted up onto her knees and crouching over him she cried, "And you believed it then, that you were naught but a butcher's son? Part of you believes it now! It is for this that you must prove to England—to yourself—John, look at me!"

She took him by the shoulders and shook him. "Wake up and listen! It's the foolish frightened child in you that believes this. As your son believes that a playful calf is a were-wolf!"

He gazed up bewildered at her gray eyes shining in the candlelight. They were desperate in her desire to reach him. The fog cleared a little in his mind.

"Isolda told you the truth!" she cried. "Oh John—you who are most like the King of all his sons, so like that men say you are twin to what he was when young. How *could you doubt* your birth?"

He moistened his lips and gave a curt harsh laugh. "I did not know that I doubted it—until tonight." His hand moved gropingly and caught a fold of her skirt, and his eyes closed.

She stretched herself beside him and took his head against her breast. He did not know it, though he moved as though seeking the position in which they had so often lain together. His breaths grew quiet and even.

The Duke slept nearly the clock around, and for many hours without stirring.

When the palace bells rang for morning Mass, there was a knock on the door of the State Chamber. Katherine, slipping her arm carefully from beneath John's head, hurried from the bed.

She opened the door and held her finger to her lips.

The Princess stood in the passage round-eyed and anxious. "Is all well?" she whispered, noting Katherine's dishevelment: the gray gown twisted and wrinkled, the great coils of bronze hair that had tumbled on her shoulders, the white tiredness of the girl's drawn face.

Katherine stepped out in the passage. "I hope so, madam," she said gravely. "He sleeps."

"God be thanked," said the Princess. She carried her gold beads on her wrist for she was on the way to Mass, and she kissed the crucifix. "Poor lass," she said, touching Katherine's hand. Her plump rosebud mouth quivered with sympathy, for she remembered the exhausting violence of Plantagenet love-making. "Come to my bower. A sage femme in Bordeaux gave me a philter, 'twill restore you—" She bent closer and whispered.

"Nay," said Katherine smiling faintly. " 'Twas not that, madam. He has been carrying a strange and torturing burden. Please God, 'tis lightened." She put her hand on the door. "I must stay near him lest he wakes."

The Princess, enfolding Katherine in a smother of soft scented flesh, kissed her impulsively. "Ah my dear, if you *have* by any means brought him out of these fits of mad revenge, God will bless you as I do." She went down the passage towards the chapel thinking that all the rumors she had heard about John's leman were false, and that it was a sorry shame that Katherine could not have been born Queen of Castile instead of that cold dark foreigner at Hertford Castle.

All that day, while the outer world hummed and messages went back and forth to the Savoy, Katherine stayed in the State Chamber watching over John as he slept. Robin brought food and drink to the door, and she took a little. Sometimes she rested, far on the outer edge of the bed so as not to disturb him. And she thought long and hard about this secret thing that had so deeply troubled him. She saw on what twofold foundation the whole structure of his early life

had been built: Isolda's love and the sacred privilege of royal
birth. And that when to the child's view these two had
dropped away from under him together, a part of him had
shattered as truly as though a mine had exploded at his feet.

Yet he was strong and tough as had been his father, and
most of the royal Norman line; while from his mother he had
staunch Flemish common sense. So time had passed and he
had built his world up again, and forgotten this shock that
had so frightened him once—until the placard brought it
back, hideously grown because now the whole of England
witnessed it. Since then this buried dread had gripped him
and he had fought back as a child does with blind fury. And
yet because he was not a child but a man, composed by now
of as many colors and shapes as a painted glass window,
there had been deep-seated struggle in his soul. For he was
merciful, by nature, never had he killed senselessly or
maimed even in war, as his brothers had done, and of all Edward's sons he was the most sensitive.

Katherine thought this and much else throughout the long
day. She thought of the fearful power of a lie, of all evil—
and she thought of her own children, and how she had believed herself capable of guiding their lives rightfully, of easily salving their hurts, and that by providing for their mind
and body nurture she had fended off all harm.

Now she was uncertain, and dismayed. Little John's mis-
conception about the calf was minor enough, and would pass
in time; but what other concealed demons might not be prey-
ing on a child?

And with a painful twisting at the heart she saw Blanchette's stricken eyes as she had looked up from her embroidery the last day at Kenilworth. It was useless to deny that
her firstborn and dearest child had lost her old happy confidence and was drawing away into some bitter, jealous little
climate of her own.

But what can I *do?* Katherine thought despairingly. She
glanced towards John as he lay sleeping still. Her love for
him had grown tenfold since he had trusted her last night
with a glimpse of his naked soul. Yet yesterday she had been
swamped with a resentful pride, even with the hatred that
seemed welded, like the obverse of a shield, to love. What
then *was* certain? What was there that would not shift and
veer at the mercy of the winds of feeling?

Sanctity, the clergy said. Prayer. The practice of religion. The benevolence of the holy saints. The Grace of God.

Katherine rose and walked to the Prince of Wales' prie-dieu in the corner beyond the armor. A gilt, elaborately enameled triptych hung above the prayer desk. The center panel depicted Calvary, the side ones showed various tortures of the damned. These were intricately detailed: naked bodies writhed in orange flames, and from severed limbs and seared eyes dripped ruby gouts of blood. The Christ's face on the Cross expressed only contorted agony and above the panels was written, "Repent Ye!"

She gazed at the triptych with repulsion. Here was no message of steadfastness. Here naught but warning and more fear. Her rebellion grew, and she wondered, What guidance do we truly get from the saints or even from the Blessed Mother and Her Son? Why did not they, or Saint John, protect my lord from harm?

What of the vow she herself had made to St. Catherine in the storm at sea? Had the saint in truth really saved her? And this vow she now felt had had nothing to do with heavenly guidance. The necessity of faithfulness to Hugh, however bitter, had sprung from her own self-esteem, her own integrity. For I believe, thought Katherine, there is nothing beyond or above ourselves.

At once—and for an instant she was frightened—she heard plain in her head how Brother William would cry "Heresy!" in his stern tired voice. Then she forgot her painful questions and ran to the bedside, for John stirred and said, "Katrine?"

"My lord," she whispered, bending over him.

His eyes were clear as the sky of Aquitaine, and the smile he gave was one she had not seen in long. He reached his arms up and pulling her down kissed her hard on the mouth. Then he sat up and yawned and said, "Christ, what a sleep I've had—" He looked at the curtained window. "Is't dark still?"

"Again!" she answered smiling. "You've slept the day through."

"By the rood! And did I then?" He scooped his hair back from his forehead and stretched prodigiously. He ran his tongue around his mouth and said, "Dry as tinder. It seems that I was drunk last night—it seems to me too that I babbled much nonsense." He quirked his brows and looked at her half laughing.

"You don't remember?" she said softly.

"Nay—only that you were near me, and most patient. And that I love you, sweet heart." He pinched her cheek and grinned at her. "I shall prove it soon—but not in this gloomy bed. Lord, what a dismal room. We must get back to the Savoy."

He got up and walked into the garderobe. She heard him whistling beneath his breath and the splashing of water. "Send for food, lovedy," he called to her, "I'm famished."

She picked up the hand bell and rang it. There was a pause before it was answered, for the page, who stood ever ready in the passage, had been given orders.

When the door opened, it was the Princess who came in, and with her was her chief advisor, Sir Simon Burley, a grave-eyed conscientious man whose grizzled beard waggled anxiously as he said, "The Duke's awake?"

Katherine nodded and gestured towards the garderobe. John walked out, his face and neck still aglow from the vigorous sluicing he had given them. "Good evening, Joan," he said to his sister-in-law. "Did you think you had old Morpheus himself for guest?" He turned to Burley, "And you, Sir Simon, I see by that long face that there's more ill news. Can't it wait until I'm fed?"

"My lord, of course, but you should know that a deputy of Londoners have gone off to Sheen, to the King's Grace to beg him to reconcile your quarrel with the City. They know your troops are massing at the Savoy. The people are affrighted."

"And so they should be," said John with calm sternness, "And shall make just reparation."

The Princess and Burley glanced at each other, both remembering the terrible rage of yesterday, the threats of war, of violation to St. Paul's, of murdering revenge.

"What is just reparation, my lord?" said the Princess nervously.

"By corpus' bones, Joan! I'll decide that when I've got to Sheen and heard what they offer. Certain it is our poor father won't know what to do— My sweet sister, have your cooks all been drowned in the Thames? Or shall I roast a leg of yonder chair myself over the fire?"

The Princess laughed and called orders to the hovering page.

"My lord," she said, her fair fat face all aquiver with relief, "you sound yourself again. Your sleep did great good."

Impatience, arrogance and sternness he showed as always, but she saw that the wild consuming unreason had left him, and she sent Katherine a look of deepest gratitude.

## XXI

NEITHER KATHERINE nor the Duke ever mentioned the night at Kennington Palace, though it had an immediate effect on their relationship.

His need for her deepened, he talked to her more freely about all his concerns, and he kept her with him constantly, showing her many public as well as private signs of his love.

Katherine bore herself with discretion, but all those of the Duke's meinie, and soon many others outside, grew aware of her new status. At the Savoy, her lodging was changed from the Monmouth Wing, nor was she put in the small room near the Privy Suite which she had occupied on earlier visits. She was given the Duchess's small solar adjacent to the State Chamber, while her nights were spent with John in the Avalon Chamber's ruby velvet bed. At the High Table in the Hall her seat was shifted to one next the Duke, and though decorum was observed by the vacancy of the Duchess's place to his right, it pleased John to order made for Katherine a chair no less magnificent than his own, with gilt carvings, topaz velvet cushions, and her embossed Catherine wheels for a headrest.

These elevations naturally set many spiteful tongues to wagging, but they wagged in secret, not only for fear of the Duke, but because the Princess Joan made plain her tolerance of the situation and treated Lady Swynford with marked favor.

To the Duke's close friends, such as Michael de la Pole, the Princess did not hesitate to attribute the Duke's new restraint to Katherine's influence. This de la Pole inwardly doubted, but he smiled and made some vague remark about the softening power of fair womanhood. Still, whatever the cause, the baron was pleased to see that his lord had reverted to his normal temperament and handled the aftermath of the riots with justice.

The Duke had received the frightened London deputy at Sheen and after listening to their apologies and extenuations, had exacted mild enough punishment: a public penitential procession to St. Paul's in which the City dignitaries should carry a candle painted with his coat of arms, and had ordered that the unnamed instigators of the disturbance should be excommunicated. When these orders had been grudgingly obeyed, he saw to it that the obnoxious parliamentary bill to curtail the City's liberties was quietly dropped. When the people demanded a fair trial for Peter de la Mare, who was still imprisoned in Nottingham, this was granted. In the course of some weeks the Speaker of the Commons was released and rode in triumph back to London.

Against William of Wykeham the Duke's hostility lasted longer, since he was not averse to making an example of the bishop as a lesson to the episcopal party.

Upon finding the Duke implacable, Bishop Wykeham bethought him of another method to regain his rich temporalities, and by the promise of a colossal bribe to Alice Perrers, convinced that lady, and through her the King, of the injustice of his pitiable poverty. King Edward duly signed a bill for Wykeham's restitution.

John when he heard this was displeased, but he shrugged and let the matter rest. This happened in June when the King was obviously failing and there was a great deal else to be thought of besides the chastisement of one fat bishop.

Katherine was interested to hear of these various clement measures and gradually began to understand something of the conflicting ambitions and turbulence which made difficult any clearcut policy. But in the matter of Pieter Neumann's fate she felt vivid personal concern. And on this one topic, John would not speak to her. She saw that the hidden wound, though purged of its prurience and healing rapidly, yet would always leave a sensitive scar, and she forbore any mention of Pieter, though she ached to know what had been done with him.

She found out at last in Eastertide, on Maundy Thursday after the foot-washing ceremony. On this Thursday the act of humility in imitation of the Blessed Christ was performed throughout the Christian world in palaces, monasteries and manors, and at the Savoy the line of beggars began to form in the Outer Ward directly after Mass. It was customary to number the poor by the age of the lord who would humble himself to them, but the Duke magnificently augmented his own thirty-seven years by the ages of his three Lancastrian children, thus making forty additional ragged and filthy candidates to be honored.

The ceremony took place in the Great Hall and Katherine stood watching at one side of the dais where the paupers, looking both proud and frightened, were seated on benches, and tittered nervously as the great Duke of Lancaster commenced the washing of their dirty scabrous feet.

The Duke was dressed in a humble russet tunic devoid of ornament. Two squires held silver basins of warmed rose water, and Robin held a towel. The Duke smiled gravely at his paupers and worked quickly and conscientiously. He made the sign of the cross on each foot, then kissed the toes, while murmuring the words of humility.

Upon dismissal the owners of the feet went on to material rewards. On a table by the kitchens stood vats of broken meats and bread, from which the paupers were permitted to fill large sacks, and at the door the Duke's almoner doled out pieces of maundy silver.

It was a solemn ceremony, but Katherine had trouble keeping her face straight as she watched the ducal children perform their ablutions on their own forty of London's poor.

Elizabeth had been brought down from Kenilworth for Easter, and was wild with excitement at her release from the country but she had protested hotly at this penance. "I won't do it!" she cried angrily to Katherine. "Their feet stink and their fleas and lice come jumping out all over me!"

Elizabeth had not, however, actually dared to flout the yearly custom, but her performance of it was scarcely penitential. She held her nose with one hand while she made a hasty dab at an outstretched foot with the other, and she had finished all of her paupers before Philippa had thoroughly washed and dried one pair of feet.

Philippa alone truly seemed to enjoy this act of service, Katherine thought, watching the girl's exalted face. Pity it was she could not follow her obvious vocation. But at least the marriage offer from Luxemburg had been refused, so she had been happy lately.

Katherine turned to watch the Duke's son do the ablutions.

Little Henry imitated his father as closely as a stocky ten-year-old boy could imitate the graceful motions of a tall lithe man. Henry dipped the towel in water, rubbed, crossed and kissed with a good deal of the Duke's imperturbable dignity. But he would never have his father's debonair charm.

When the ceremony was concluded and the gratified paupers had begun to gabble and bicker amongst themselves, the Duke came to Katherine and said, "Shall we visit the mew, sweet heart? 'Twill smell far better than in here, and we must see how your little merlin does."

Katherine assented gladly. Falconry had become a passion with her, and she was as eager as the Duke for her merlin to be trained, so that they might ride out again to hawk in Moorfields.

Arnold, the Duke's head falconer, met them at the door of the mew with a finger to his lips, and the sad tidings that Oriana had some puzzling ailment. The great white northern falcon had drooped upon her perch for days, she had refused gobbets of raw meat, and even tiny newborn rabbits with which Arnold tempted her.

The falconer glanced back into the darkened mew where fifty hawks of all degrees set up a restless fluttering and tinkling of their silver leg bells. "They be tittuppy," said Arnold anxiously, "hearing voices. Your merlin does well, m'lady," he added to Katherine. "She now flies boldly to the lure, but Oriana—" He turned back to the Duke shaking his head.

John, instantly concerned—for his royal gerfalcon had no peer in England, and aside from his affection for her, was worth nearly two hundred marks—had framed a question as to her medication, when he was interrupted by Brother William Appleton.

The Gray Friar on his mule had trotted through the gatehouse into the Outer Ward and on seeing the Duke standing at the door of the mew, dismounted and walked over. "My lord," he said gravely, gazing at the Duke from beneath his pointed black cowl, "it is done. The ship sailed from Pevensey on Monday." He glanced coldly at Katherine.

She saw John draw a long shaking breath while he said very low, "Chained in the galleys?"

"Even so, my lord. He'll not trouble you again."

"And the Benedictine monks?"

"Have been stringently disciplined by their prior."

John sighed once more, and into his eyes there came a

vague look, as though he listened to an echo. "Good," he said at length. "You've done well, and I thank you." He clapped his hands together once, then let them drop, and turning to Katherine said, "Wait here, lovely. I must see Oriana, but 'twill disturb the birds if you come too."

He entered the mew with Arnold, and the Gray Friar made as though to leave, but Katherine cried out, "Brother William, I beg you!"

The friar paused and examined her. She wore a new gown of emerald brocade so lavishly furred with ermine that it befitted royal rank, and the gold fillet that bound her hair was jeweled and scalloped like a noble's coronet. "Lady Mede," he thought angrily. "Pride be painted here and pomp of the world." It was Alice Perrers that Long Will satirized in his "Piers Ploughman" as Mede, the corrupt courtesan —Yet here was another such, and worse, by reason of the crime which had exalted her.

"What do you wish, Lady Swynford?" he said with fierce emphasis on her surname.

She felt in his gaze some deeper meaning than the abhorrence of an ascetic friar for the sin of unhallowed love. He frightened her, but she persisted urgently. "This man of whom you spoke to the Duke, the one shipped in one of the galleys, is it Pieter Neumann? I've a right to know—" she added sharply, as his lips tightened, "for my dear lord's sake. Ay, I know you think me worthless and lewd, but by the Holy Blood at Hales, my love for him has not harmed him, it may even be that it has helped him at times." She ended on a note of quivering hurt.

The friar, opening his mouth to cry that no good could come from evil, and that she was a fool to think her love had caused no harm, yet did not speak. The candid innocence of her eyes restrained him, and he felt that there was still some good beneath this wicked flaunting beauty. After a moment he said curtly, "It *was* Pieter Neumann, deported on a ship bound for Cyprus where he'll remain in exile—if he survives the voyage."

"But he was in sanctuary—"

"And stayed there the allotted forty days," answered the friar seeing that she knew more of this matter than he had supposed. "All was done with due regard for the laws of sanctuary. I myself was present at his hearing, and have just seen that the sentence of banishment was duly executed."

"Bishop Courtenay didn't try to save him?" she asked quickly.

"No—" said the friar startled. "Courtenay's now ashamed of his tool, and rightly so."

"Did the Duke not see Pieter?"

The friar hesitated, but again he answered her. "No—I believe he did not trust himself."

"God in his mercy be thanked," said Katherine. "My dear lord is then truly and honestly rid of his fardel."

She spoke with simple fervor and more to herself than the friar, but Brother William was softened. He bent close and spoke in a tone he had not used to her since the night of Hugh's death. "My child," he said earnestly, "rouse yourself before it's too late. I believe you have the strength!"

"Rouse myself?" Her mobile face hardened and she stepped back from the friar.

"Give up the Duke—and this unclean love of yours! Uncleaner than you know—" His sunken eyes blazed a warning, then he checked himself.

"Ay, to you all earthly love's unclean," she said bitterly. "You threaten me with hell, I suppose. It may be so—but I don't believe it. I have come," she said looking at him defiantly, "to believe only in my self, and my love."

He shook his head and looked at her with sadness. "You speak foolishly, Lady Swynford. Disaster will come to teach you better. Nor do I mean hell fire—but in this life—disaster!" he repeated on a sharper note and suddenly he clutched his crucifix.

He stared down at the pavingstones, his face half hidden by his cowl.

As happened sometimes during his strict Lenten fasts, strange dreams had come to him of late, dreams so vivid that almost, in his pride, he had thought them holy visions. But the dream last night must have come from Satan, so full of senseless horror had it been, of glaring bearded faces gibbering, of the smell of smoke, and blood. When he had said "disaster" now, he remembered that he had seen Katherine's tearful tender face bending over him in his dream; and that she and he had been linked together in fear.

"*Christe eleison,*" he whispered, much disturbed by the memory of this dream and the foreboding that had come with it, disturbed too that he should have dreamed of Katherine, for it was long since the devil had injected a woman's face into his sleep.

"*Benedicite*," he muttered, abruptly, and walked rapidly away towards the chapel.

Katherine waited by the mew for the Duke to come out and the discomfort Brother William had aroused in her soon melted in the warm spring sunshine. Presently she wandered towards the mossy old bargehouse. Clumps of violets and the yellow celandine had rooted in scanty pockets of earth between the stones, and she touched the little flowers as she passed. Through the water gate she could see an arch-shaped bit of the Thames glinting sapphire beneath the warm blue of the sky where rooks cawed and wheeled towards their nests in the elms across the river. She walked down to the landing and breathed softly. The air smelt of new-turned earth and the budding greenwood.

With the slapping of oars, sounds more melodious than the rooks floated to Katherine from a wherry filled with young folk. A shock-haired lad in scarlet jerkin tootled on his pipe while the others caroled merrily,

> *Oh Lenten is come wi' love to town—sing hi! sing hey!*
> *Wi' blossom and wi' birdies' rune—sing hi! ho! hey!*

They drifted out of earshot, but Katherine, smiling, gazed after them.

When the Duke, having finished inspecting Oriana, walked up behind her on the pier she had a lapful of violets and like an absorbed child was flinging them into the river to watch the little purple specks go bobbing away over the ripples while she sang in her sweet warm voice, "Oh Lenten is come wi' love to town, sing hi! sing hey!"

He laughed and kissed the top of her bent head. "Moppet," he said, "you've forgotten your weight of years and many children?"

Katherine giggled and rising from the step saw that no one watched except the old bargemaster. She flung her arms around John's neck and kissed him heartily. "Many children, my lord, but not yet a full bevy," she whispered against his ear.

The Duke looked startled as he took her meaning. "Is it so, my Katrine?" His eyes darkened and he looked down at her anxiously.

"You aren't pleased?" she asked while her smile faded.

"Ay, I shall welcome it. You know that. But you were very ill last time, lovedy—two nights I didn't sleep and prayed until I wore down the cushions at the altar rail."

"Ah, dear heart—" she whispered turning her cheek against his shoulder, for she had not known of that. When Hawise had finally nursed her through the childbed fever into full consciousness again, he had been gone from Kenilworth and on his way to Bruges to negotiate the truce—with Costanza.

"Nay, but all will go well—this time," she said quickly. "I'm a fruitful woman and shall bear you *another* brawny *son.*" She could not forbear the little note of triumph, for the scale dipped heavy on the other side and she could hear voices sniggering, "What, again a Beaufort bastard! Surely shame itself must blush by now!"

John, too, thought of Costanza and with a glacial repugnance which must be controlled. During Lent he had had no need to visit her at Hertford, nor would she have received him since she observed the penitential season in strict solitude. But she had sent him an Easter summons, so worded that it would seem that her pilgrimage to Canterbury had resulted in a cure. No doubt Costanza again had hopes that she might bear an heir for Castile.

He looked down at the lovely curved cheek that rested trustfully against his russet-clad shoulder, and taking her hand he said in a harsh voice, "Thank God, Katrine—you wear my betrothal ring again."

He started to tell her of the pain he felt for her and all that he would do in recompense; of his Nottinghamshire manors that he would give her and a necklet of rare Eastern pearls a Lombard goldsmith had sent word of to the palace. But she stopped him. "Nay, darling, I know. You needn't fret yourself like that. See, it's for this I had you engrave the raison on my brooch." She touched it, "It is as it is."

"Cold comfort," he said roughly beneath his breath. He drew her tight against him and they stood silent on the pier watching the quiet Thames flow by.

On the twenty-first of June in his palace of Sheen at Richmond, the old King died at last. He was in the sixty-fifth year of his life and the fifty-first of his reign, and most of his subjects felt that both had lasted too long. The glories of Crécy and Poitiers were far in the past, and many now thought that those victories were negated by the interminable warfare that succeeded them and was not yet ended. The very week of the King's death the French were harrying the coast of Sussex.

Yet even those who despised the King for his insensate lust to rule France at whatever cost to England, and for his extravagance and blind follies, were shocked by his end.

The King was alone with Alice Perrers when he was stricken with an apoplexy. She had been sitting on his bed, casting dice with him, and provoking him to delighted titters by the outrageous stakes she demanded—the Archbishop of Canterbury's miter, the province of Gascony, the crown regalia—when the King gave a loud cry and began to gobble in his throat. His staring eyes swam with red, one lip drew up in a snarl, as half of his face was turned to stone.

Alice screamed and jumped off the bed. The King fell back on the pillows. He gave forth great snoring gasps as she watched him, horrified. She saw that he must die and that her long power was at an end. She bent quickly and pulled three richly jeweled rings from off his flaccid fingers.

She thrust the rings in her bodice and backed off trembling, then she turned and fled from the chamber, pausing only to shout at a page that he must get a priest. She ran from the palace to the river, had herself ferried over, and by bribing an innkeeper on the western bank secured a horse and set out for safety to a nook in Bedfordshire where a certain knight owed her return for many favors.

The old King died soon and alone, except for a friar that the frightened page had found. His sons and little Richard, who was now the King of England, did not reach Sheen for some hours.

England mourned courteously for the King, the people wore sad clothes, black cloth shrouded their windows, and Requiem Masses were said throughout the land. Edward's funeral procession and burial next to Queen Philippa on the Confessor's mound in Westminster Abbey were conducted with doleful pomp. The dirge-ale was drunk to the accompaniment of decorous sighs. But everywhere eyes turned with hope and rejoicing to the fair charming boy who would be crowned on the sixteenth of July.

It was useless for wry-faced oldsters to grumble that unlucky was the land ruled by a child: a chorus of rebuttal drowned them out. Richard of Bordeaux was their own. They had loved his father, and Joan of Kent was as English as the hawthorn.

Angers faded. The bishops checked their fulminations against Wyclif and the Duke of Lancaster, the Lollard preachers turned their sermons from the injustices done to the poor and spoke on Isaiah's text, "A little child shall lead them." The great nobles ceased their jealous strivings, and the London merchants amicably prepared to spend a prodigious sum upon their share of the coronation festivities.

On the Feast of St. Swithin, July 15, the day before the ceremony in Westminster, Richard's procession from the Tower through the City surpassed in magnificence any civic celebration ever seen.

Katherine viewed the procession from a tier of wooden benches which had been erected on West Chepe for the accommodation of privileged ladies. The Princess Joan sat on a dais, flanked by two of her sisters-in-law, Isabella of Castile, Edmund's frivolous and empty-headed wife, who was as unlike her sister Costanza as a chaffinch to a raven, and Eleanor de Bohun, the great heiress, Thomas of Woodstock's bride. Eleanor was a high-nosed girl with a mouth like a haddock, who fussed so loudly over some matter of precedence that Katherine could hear her acid complaints from where she sat at some distance from the royal ladies, with Philippa, Elizabeth and her own Blanchette. The Swynford children had been brought down from Kenilworth for this extraordinary occasion, and her little Tom by special favor of the Duke had been permitted a place in the procession amongst the nobly born boys of approximately Richard's own age.

St. Swithin, doubtless propitiated by countless prayers, had in the morning duly cleared some threatening rain clouds from the sky, and the afternoon was as dazzling as the white silk banners and the cloth of silver draperies that were festooned along the line of march.

On the Chepe the great open conduit, new-painted in blue and gold, gurgled pleasantly near the grandstand, and the heat grew such that Katherine sent a page over with a flagon to be filled. The conduit, for the three hours of the procession, ran with wine. Good wine, and even young Philippa drank thirstily before resuming her sedate composure.

Elizabeth fidgeted and yawned as detachment after detachment of the commons walked past by City wards, all garbed in white in honor of the child king.

Blanchette sat quietly beside her mother. Her wondering eyes moved from the marching men to a gold-painted canvas tower where four gold-costumed little girls of her own age were perched in the turrets and in great danger of falling out as they hung over the flimsy parapets.

The commoners had all disappeared down Pater Noster lane and the men of esquire's rank were filing past when Blanchette leaned forward and said, "Th—there's Uncle Ge—Geoffrey," with the little stammer in her speech which had developed during Katherine's last absence from Kenilworth.

"So it is, darling!" her mother answered staring at the rotund figure in the white linen over-robe that made him look comically like a Cistercian monk. She had not seen Geoffrey in months, for he had been again in France on King's business. As his file of esquires passed the ladies' stand, he looked up and waved at them, then peered quickly along the benches looking, no doubt, for his wife. But Philippa Chaucer was not there.

The Duchess of Lancaster would attend the coronation tomorrow and was even now en route from Hertford with her ladies, including Philippa, but a secular parade did not appeal to her.

The knights and knights' banneret followed the squires, then the aldermen, and the new mayor—the wealthy grocer, Nicholas Brembre. He complacently curbed his prancing horse with as much negligent skill as any knight, while he bowed to the stand where his lady mayoress Idonia was ensconced on silver cushions at a place of honor near the Princess Joan.

"He looks almost a gentleman, except he's so greasy and sweaty," said Elizabeth of the mayor in a shrill astonished voice.

"Hush, Bess," said Katherine sharply. "Gentlemen sweat too, in heat like this."

"Not my father's grace," retorted Elizabeth pointing proudly. "He's never slobbery, no matter what."

Katherine bit her lips against a laugh, for Elizabeth was quite right. The lesser earls and barons had passed by and Richard's uncles, led by the Duke, had appeared at the curve by Chepe Cross. In cream velvet trimmed with silver and riding on a snow-white horse, John gleamed as immaculate as an archangel. His brothers, the pale slouching Edmund, and the swarthy bull-faced Thomas, seemed to Katherine like a couple of nondescript rustics by comparison.

She had no opportunity to admire John as she wished nor to respond properly to the bow he sent in their direction, for as the little King approached in a blare of herald's trumpets and the rattle of drums, the ladies surged to their feet amidst cheers and roars of "Long live Richard!"

The small girls in the canvas castle were prodded from below and in a sudden frenzy began to fling out gold florins and tinsel leaves across the King's path. Someone hidden in the tower pulled a string so that a canvas angel with jerking arm brandished a crown over Richard's passing head.

The boy looked up, startled, and laughed, a high fluting tinkle audible even through the tumult of his acclaim.

The ten-year-old Richard was pink and white and delicate as an appleblossom. His thistledown curls were yellow like a new-hatched chick. His shoulders seemed too slight for the vast white and brilliant-studded mantle they had draped on him, albeit he sat his horse sturdily and pricked it angrily with his golden spurs of knighthood when the beast lagged.

"By corpus, he looks like a maiden," cried the irrepressible Elizabeth, examining her cousin critically. "I trust he'll cease to be such a mollycoddle, now he's King!" She had scant use for Richard, who was poor at games, liked only to mess about with little paint pots or to read, and clung to his mother's skirts when teased.

"Tomorrow he will be God's anointed," said Philippa severely, frowning at her sister. "You must not speak like that of the King's Grace."

Elizabeth subsided, faintly awed, so that Katherine could give her whole attention to the group of lads that followed Richard on foot. She singled Tom out first and showed him to Blanchette, aware that the child had drawn back and ceased to look at the procession as the Duke rode by. "Look, sweet," she said taking her daughter's hand, "how bravely our Tom marches with all the young lords." And how much he looks like Hugh, she thought with a pang. The dusty-looking crinkled cap of hair, the square Saxon face, the forthright stride—these were all from Hugh, so was the boarhead-crested dagger that dangled on his hip. The Duke had given him a far handsomer dagger, but Tom obstinately preferred his father's.

"He's m-much t-taller than L-lord Henry, though he's

younger," said Blanchette. Katherine squeezed the passive little hand and agreed, but she sighed. Blanchette's pride in her
brother was natural enough, yet this remark, like nearly everything Blanchette said, showed her animosity to the Duke
and all who belonged to him. Well, she would have to get
over it, thought Katherine with sudden impatience.

The two Hollands came cantering up at the tail of the
procession, waving their great swords and crying to the
people to stand back and wait until the King had passed the
cathedral before they rushed to the wine fountains. These
two young men were the Princess Joan's sons by her first husband and, beloved as Joan was, no one felt that they did her
much credit, except apparently Elizabeth, who had recovered
from Philippa's reproof and pointing at the younger Holland,
John, said, "There's a comely lusty-looking man! 'Tis Jock
Holland. He picked up my glove when I dropped it t'other
day at Westminster. Nan Quilter," she added admiringly,
"says he has more paramours than any other man in London."

"Elizabeth, you're disgusting!" cried Philippa. "Must she
forever tattle servants' gossip, Lady Katherine? You must find
some way to refine her tastes."

Before Katherine could speak, Elizabeth tossed her dark
curls and said, "In truth, 'tis not my lady here should chide
me that I speak of paramours."

Katherine felt herself go crimson and heard a little gasp from
Blanchette.

"This is not the moment to discuss your rudeness, Elizabeth," Katherine said mastering her voice with difficulty, "but
I must remind you that whatever your opinions may be, your
father's grace has put you in my charge."

Elizabeth flounced, but she looked down and began to
twiddle with a loosened pearl on her bodice.

Philippa put her hand on Katherine's knee, shook her head
and said gently, "I ask pardon for my sister." Her pale eyes
rested on Katherine with sorrowful affection.

"God's blood, what a fuss about naught!" cried Elizabeth,
suddenly giggling. "I meant nothing." She looked up through
her lashes at Katherine. " 'Tis too joyous a day for long
faces," she said coaxingly. "Oh, my dear lady—*please*—
mayn't we buy some of those comfits?" Elizabeth's giddy eye
had caught sight of a sweets vendor who was pushing
through the crowd.

Katherine silently drew some silver from her purse and gave it to the page, who darted after the vendor. Elizabeth had been insolent certainly, yet bitter it was for Katherine to realize that she could hardly be punished for stating a simple truth.

But what of Blanchette? Could she at ten know the meaning of "paramour"? Or had she gasped only because she saw that in some way Elizabeth was attacking her mother?

Katherine looked down with an aching tenderness at the little head with its silken crop of flaming curls and was dismayed to see that the round chin was trembling. "Here, darling," said Katherine brightly, taking a sweet from the plate the page proffered, "you love marchpane. Look—'tis made like a perfect little crown in honor of the day."

"I c-can't, Mamma—" said Blanchette shrinking. "I feel sick." She clapped her hand over her mouth. Katherine jumped up and putting her arm around the child rushed her down off the stand to a street gutter.

Poor lamb, thought Katherine, holding the clammy little forehead. It was the heat and excitement. Hawise must make a wormwood physic for her when they got back to the Savoy, and Katherine would make time somehow to pet the child and sing her to sleep.

Even the Duke's influence was not sufficient to procure for Katherine a good view of the actual coronation ceremonies in the Abbey. As High Seneschal of England he had been ruling on hereditary claims and matters of precedence for days, and therefore honor demanded that he show no favoritism. Katherine was accordingly jammed into a section halfway down the nave amongst other wives and widows of obscure knights.

Her pregnancy was not yet obvious when she hid her slightly thickened waist under a green silk mantle as she had today, but hours of standing or kneeling were an ordeal, and she would have begged off from attending the ceremony, except that the Duke wished her to be there, had wanted her to share with him, no matter how imperfectly, in this tremendously moving occasion.

But there was another reason besides her condition which had made her reluctant. At the margin of the sanctuary dais, on a gilt carved and velvet throne as splendid as the Princess

Joan's, sat the Duchess of Lancaster, holding, by right of her claim to the kingdom of Castile, a small lion-headed scepter.

The Duchess had duly arrived at the Savoy last night, Katherine having retired some days past to the Monmouth Wing with her children. John had spent the night at Westminster Palace with Richard so that Katherine had not had the anguish of the thought of him with Costanza. A humiliating anguish which she each time believed to be conquered. She knew that there was no love between them and that whatever union they had resulted from a sense of duty. And yet—

Today in her coronation robes, a sparkle of jeweled crimson and ermine, the Duchess was a handsome woman. At this distance, anyway, she seemed imbued with a dark slender majesty that dominated the other royal wives, and even the Princess, who appeared to be an enormous mound of periwinkle blue surmounted by an orange blob of hair. Katherine closed her eyes and leaned her aching back against a pillar.

Outside to the sound of trumpets and tabors, the solemn processional wound its way from Westminster Palace to the north door of the Abbey along a carpet of striped red worsted. The Duke carried the great blunted sword of mercy, Curtana, and behind him, his enemy, the Earl of March, whose baby son was Richard's heir, carried the sword of state. The bitterness between March and the Duke was abeyant just now, like other enmities, and John had gone out of his way to conciliate the nervous, spiteful little earl. The Earl of Warwick followed with the third sword; Edmund of Langley and Thomas of Woodstock carried the orb and scepter.

Over Richard's bare head, the barons of the Cinque Ports, by ancient right, upheld a cloth-of-gold baldequin supported by four silver poles. After them came old Sudbury, the Archbishop of Canterbury, his wrinkled face working with emotion, his blue veined hands trembling in his crozier—and after him the bishops and the abbots and priors and monks.

As they entered the Abbey and Richard was placed on a platform halfway between the choir and the High Altar, the clergy burst forth in a great anthem, "Firmetur Manus Tua."

Katherine's eyes filled, the people around her wept as the glorious singing mingled with the exultant organ and the Abbey was awash with beauty of sound, enclosed by the beauty of stone.

She could see very little of what took place, but in the suddenly tense, quiet church she heard a quavering boy's voice repeat the coronation oath and when the archbishop turned to the people and asked if they would have and hold Prince Richard for their King, she cried joyously with the thousand other voices, "Ay, we will have him!" while her spine tingled.

The ceremony progressed: the Veni Creator, the Litany, the Collects. Then the King was anointed with the holy oil and invested with all the ceremonial robes and the regalia. Finally he was crowned and installed upon his throne. The archbishop commenced the Enthronement Mass, and first of all Richard's subjects, the Duke of Lancaster, knelt before the child to do him homage.

Katherine could see John's bowed head by craning on tiptoe, since all the people were kneeling, and she saw that Richard smiled sweetly down at his uncle.

"Ah, our little King's one of the Blessed Virgin's holy cherubim," whispered a voice behind Katherine, "and he'll bring a bit o' paradise to England—and peace, God willing."

Richard's reign started with bright promise. Only the most superstitious thought ill-omened two small occurrences.

The little boy drooped and had gone very pale when the Mass and homage were at last over and he walked down the transept to quit the Abbey. He swayed giddily as he stepped into the North Porch. His old tutor, Sir Simon Burley, was watching. He swooped the child up in his arms and ran with him towards the Hall, where Richard still must endure the banquet. When Burley lifted him, one of the King's red-velvet consecrated slippers flew off and must have been seized by some knave in the watching crowd, for it was never seen again.

So soon had Richard lost part of his kinghood.

And at the banquet in Westminster Hall, the child complained that his head ached dreadfully from the weight of the crown. His cousin Henry sat opposite him in his father's place, since the Duke and other lords were riding their horses up and down the Great Hall, keeping order.

"Feel the thing, Henry," said Richard, pushing at his crown. " 'Tis heavier than an iron helm."

Henry curiously reached his stubby little hands across the board to try the crown's weight, but the Earl of March intervened violently and snatched the crown from Richard. "*I* will hold it for Your Grace," said the Earl, "so that you may eat in comfort."

Henry shrugged and returned to his roast peacock, of

which he was very fond. This pother about the crown seemed
to him silly, and Richard was always whining about something, anyway. Henry wondered if he could get Tom Mowbray off in a corner for a wrestling match pretty soon, and
then remembered that he couldn't.

Richard was going to make Tom Earl of Nottingham after
the banquet, and make a lot of other new earls too. Lord
Percy would turn into Northumberland, Uncle Thomas of
Woodstock was finally going to get a title of his own and turn
into Buckingham. The old King hadn't cared much for his
youngest son and had done mighty little for him, not even a
title. But small wonder, thought Henry, Uncle Tom's a
mump.

Henry chewed his peacock, drank some wine and yawned.
This was a frightfully stately banquet, no dogs to play with
under the table, and nobody to talk to but Richard, who was
half asleep. Out of sheer boredom, Henry counted up the
people whom he didn't like. Uncle Thomas *and* Aunt Eleanor
headed the list, both scowly mumps. And Robert de Vere,
whom Richard thought perfection. Robert had a nasty mind,
and there were other things—though Richard was such a
baby he didn't understand.

That about finished the lists of dislikes, except maybe his
stepmother, the Duchess. But you couldn't really feel much
about her one way or the other, nor that lisping little dolt of
a Catalina, for he almost never saw them.

This thought naturally brought him to Lady Swynford and
her two children of whom he had seen quite a bit lately.
Well, he liked them. Blanchette was pretty and no nuisance,
Tom Swynford wrestled and tilted better than most boys, and
as for Lady Swynford—Henry suddenly realized that in a
vague sort of way he thought of her as his mother.

Then he thankfully forgot this dull pastime. The minstrels
and the tumblers had arrived.

In a tapestry-hung gallery at the far end of the great Hall,
the Princess Joan ate with the royal ladies and a few selected
peeresses. She had soon given up making conversation with
the Castilian Duchess, who responded in polite monosyllables
while pecking at her food and sipping her wine with what the
Princess, who adored eating, considered maddening affecta-
tion.

Joan was therefore thunderstruck when the Duchess lifted

her head and, turning her huge black eyes, said somberly, "La Sweenford, es vero que—zat she is wiz child again?"

Joan for all her experience did not know how to take this, and her instinct was to protect Katherine. She answered, "Why—I know nothing about it, Duchess." Though she did.

Costanza gave the Princess a shrewd stare from under her thick white lids. Beneath the ermine cape her thin shoulders sketched a shrug. "I do not inquietarme about hees—bastardos," she said, "excepto—" She stopped, obviously searching for words, and the Princess, embarrassed but curious, suggested that French might be easier.

Costanza's eyes flashed. It was the perfidious French who had been supporting the usurper Trastamare on the throne. She never spoke French.

She continued frigidly, "La Sweenford she make heem—el duque—*soft*. He forget—Castile!"

And a very good thing too, thought the Princess, who began to get the drift of this, as Costanza's dark glance moved down the Hall and rested on Richard's little golden head. Joan had no intention of using her new influence to take up the cudgels for Castile. The French depredations in Sussex were quite enough worry. So she ignored Costanza's real meaning and said with her charming sunny smile, "Oh, I don't believe the Duke has grown soft, in any way. On the contrary, I think he's showing great wisdom lately. We must straighten out the tangles in our own land first, don't you think?"

Costanza understood enough to realize that there was not the ally she had hoped for; a curious blankness like a mist obscured her brilliant eyes. Her lips quivered, and she muttered passionately in Spanish, "Why will not God let me bear a son?" She clutched at the reliquary on her chest.

Poor lady, thought Joan, recognizing anguish of spirit, even though it did not seem to spring from anything as natural as an unloved wife's jealousy.

Joan was not introspective, nor given to moral judgments, and her own youth had contained a decidedly questionable love escapade. But it did occur to her that whether Costanza really minded or not, she was being increasingly wronged by this flagrant affair of John's with Katherine, and that probably the Duchess suffered more than her colossal pride would let her admit. Joan's facile fondness for Katherine slipped a little.

Spurred by her ever-alert watchfulness for Richard's safety, she viewed John's liaison with sudden alarm. Look how the old King's prestige had waned because of Alice Perrers, how the commons had almost lost reverence for royalty and actually rebelled against the crown.

In truth it would be wiser for John to be more discreet in regard to Lady Swynford. Not cast her off, of course, no need for that. He could send her to one of his northern castles, Knaresborough, Pickering, or better yet, to Dunstanburgh on the Scottish border. There people would forget her and he could visit her in secret.

Joan decided to take up this matter tactfully in a day or so when they had all recovered from the fatigue of the coronation, and she had no doubt that John would soon see the wisdom of her advice.

She was destined to be completely disappointed.

# PART FIVE

## (1381)

"Forth, pilgrim, forth! Forth beast out of thy stall!
Know thy country, look up, thank God for all;
Hold the highway, and let thy soul thee lead;
And truth thee shall deliver, it is no dread."

BALLADE DE BON CONSEIL

# XXII

It snowed softly in Leicester on Christmas Day of the
year 1380, and to the hundreds of guests sheltered at the
castle and the Abbey of St. Mary-in-the-Meadows, and in
other foundations and lodgings throughout town, the pure
white drifts were good omen for young Henry of Bolingbroke's wedding to little Mary de Bohun.

Of all the Duke's country castles since he had abandoned
Bolingbroke, Kenilworth and Leicester were his favorites,
and the latter was the more fitting for the marriage of the
Lancastrian heir.

The Duchess Blanche had been born here and her father,
the noble Duke Henry, was buried here in the beautiful
Church of the Newarke which he himself had built to en-
shrine his most treasured relic, a thorn from Christ's crown of
martyrdom.

This joint celebration of Christmastide and a wedding had
turned Leicester to feverish pitch. Each night mummers
came to the castle dressed as bearers and devils and green
men, to scamper on their hobbyhorses through the Great
Hall. And each night a fresh boar's head was borne in to the
feasting and greeted by its own carol, "Caput Apri Defero."

The halls and churches were bowers of holly, bay and evergreens. On every hearth a yule log burned. The kitchens
overflowed with mince pasties, lamprey stews and plum porridge. A stream of servers could not keep filled the wassail
bowls with their "lamb's wool" froth of roasted apples.

And, this Christmastide was a feast of light and music.
Scented yule candles burned all night, while the streets of
Leicester were extravagantly lit by torches that cast their rosy
flames on the snow. The waits sang "Here We Come a-Was-
sailing" in the courtyards, the monks chanted "Veni Emman-

uel" in the churches, and in the castle gallery the Duke's minstrels played carols without ceasing.

On the night of the wedding there was a riotous banquet in the castle Hall. Katherine's sides ached from laughing at the Lord of Misrule, who was dressed in a fool's costume, ajingle with tiny bells, and wore a tinsel crown on his head to show that he was king and must be obeyed. The Lord of Misrule had been chosen by lot, and happened to be Robin Beyvill, though one soon forgot that, because he was masked. Robin's nimble brain thought of many a comical jape, and he won laughter even from the frightened little bride when he seized a peacock feather in lieu of sword and solemnly knighted Jupiter, the Duke's oldest hound.

Katherine sat beside the Duke, but they were not in their usual seats of honor, for those were given to the bride and groom—and Richard.

The King and many of his meinie, including his beloved Robert de Vere, had come to Leicester for his cousin's wedding, though not his mother, the Princess Joan. Joan sent polite messages to Katherine occasionally but they had not met since the coronation. To this wedding invitation Joan had answered that her aching joints and swollen leg veins confined her to Westminster. This avoidance had hurt Katherine for a while, and then she accepted it, with a certain defiance. The Duke had told her of the Princess's request that he hide Katherine away in one of the northern castles and of his indignant repudiation of the idea, adding with tenderness, "It seems Joan has forgot what love is, sweet heart, or she couldn't suggest such a thing."

In fact, Joan's intervention had but increased his ardor, and far from hiding Katherine during these three and a half years, he had taken her with him on all his journeys throughout England. The constables of his Yorkshire castles, Pickering, Knaresborough, and the gloomy Pontefract, of the High Peak in Derbyshire, of Newcastle-under-Lyme and Tutbury in Staffordshire, as well as of Kenilworth and Leicester, had grown accustomed to receiving Lady Swynford in the Duchess's place.

Nor during that time did these constables ever see the Castilian Duchess. She remained at Hertford in retirement. Rumor said that she was sickly, a little crazed. Certain it was that she bore no more children—which could not be said of Lady Swynford. There were four Beaufort bastards now, the last, a year-old girl, christened Joan for her father. The Duke appeared to dote on all these babes as wholeheartedly as though they had been fair-born.

The three little Beaufort boys, John, Harry and Thomas squatted now on stools by their parents' knees, gaping at the antics of their elders, while the Duke caressed the curly yellow head of his namesake and asked Katherine some laughing question with all the fond domesticity of a contented husband.

No one else took much notice of the Duke and Katherine, all eyes were turned on the Lord of Misrule, the bridal couple and the King; but Geoffrey Chaucer watched his sister-in-law with sharp interest.

Geoffrey had eaten and drunk a bit too much. He pushed back from the table, unloosed his girdle and the lower buttons of his pearl-gray surcote, which was too tight a fit. He had not worn it since the coronation and felt much easier in his usual semiclerical robes, but the occasion demanded ceremony.

By the rood!, thought Geoffrey, settling back in slightly tipsy contentment, little Katherine had thoroughly tamed that fierce Plantagenet leopard! It must be nine years that she had enthralled him, and to judge by the Duke's attitude now, his passion for her was strong as ever. That was a long time for the sweet fire to burn so bright, Geoffrey thought with a touch of envy, yet he had always deemed Katherine an exceptional woman. She had borne six children, she must be about thirty, but her beauty was undimmed, though it had acquired assurance and lost the touching wistfulness. The new quality was not brazenness certainly, Katherine could never be that. Yet there were changes. Her gown was low-cut as that of Edmund's promiscuous Isabella, and Katherine leaned openly against the Duke's shoulder as she had never used to do. Still, her gray eyes were clear as crystal, her high white brow smooth as a girl's and the new-fashioned Bohemian headdress gave to her a look of shining delicacy. Though on many women the balanced crescent moon above their faces unfortunately suggested a horned cow. It was so with his Philippa.

Geoffrey glanced sideways at his wife, on whom the wassailing had taken effect: Philippa was breathing hard and staring glassy-eyed at her heaped silver plate as though daring it to accuse her of being drunk. Thanks to Katherine, she was as well gowned as any of the noble ladies, but her horned headdress had slipped over one ear and its blue gauze veil trailed in the sauce.

Philippa would be very cross in the morning. Ah well, 'tis Christmas and a wedding too, Geoffrey thought.

It was a year of weddings and matchmaking. The Duke, single-hearted in all that he did, having turned his mind to domestic matters, had now married off two of his children in ways most advantageous to their prosperity if not their happiness. However, nobody expected happiness from marriage and least of all the Duke, though he had achieved it once. Even now, though Geoffrey was fat and forty, his staid heart felt a springtime thrill at the memory of the Duchess Blanche.

The Duke had procured for his Henry another great English heiress, such as Blanche had been, but the marriage of these two children promised no such felicity. Henry was thirteen and his bride twelve. Up there at the High Table, in her glittering finery, one could see the child trembling like a little white leveret. But she would return to her mother's care tomorrow. The Duke had no intention of prematurely taxing the breeding powers that would eventually produce the next Lancastrian heir, though some less wise fathers threw the children into bed together at any age and accepted whatever consequences might arise.

"She's an ill-tempered vixen," asserted Philippa suddenly, enunciating with great care. "She's scowling at me."

"Who?" asked Geoffrey, looking around and trying not to laugh, for his wife's dignity was much impaired by the further descent of her headdress.

Philippa raised her spoon and pointed at the hawk-nosed Countess of Buckingham. "Her. Bride's sister."

Geoffrey said, "Nonsense!" soothingly. " 'Tis simply that she dislikes this wedding, scowls at everyone."

Though it was true that Eleanor de Bohun's angry eyes rested on Philippa's dishevelment with disgust, her fish mouth was set in continual disapproval anyway. Thomas of Woodstock's wife vehemently agreed with her husband, and resented the Duke's perfidy in snatching her little sister from the convent where they had sent her to be a nun. Mary's return to secular life and marriage to Henry reinstated her as co-heiress to the vast Bohun fortune and correspondingly halved Eleanor's share.

Only an uneasy desire to keep an eye on the proceedings, lest worse befall, had brought Eleanor to the wedding at all, and she made no effort to be civil.

"She glares at *me*," retorted Philippa belligerently, "because she dares not be rude to Katherine. Oh, I *heard* her in the garderobe, squawking to her ladies that I'd no right to be seated above the salt. She called me a pantry wench married to naught but a scribbling wool-counter."

"The Lady Eleanor spoke some truth, if not all of it," murmured Geoffrey, but not loud enough to further inflame is wife, who suddenly forgot her grievance at discovering the sauce stains on her veil and began to rub them furiously.

Geoffrey recrossed his legs and considered with amusement the Lady Eleanor's contempt. Scribbling wool-counter no doubt he was, but a much traveled one on the King's secret service. Peace negotiations, royal marriage negotiations, in France, in Flanders, in Italy, he had acquitted himself well in these. Though general recognition might be pleasant, its absence was not upsetting.

> *"I wot myself best how I stand*
> *For what I dree, or what I think*
> *I will myselven all it drink. . . ."*

He had written that in his poem on the unreliability of Fame, verses he had started at Kenilworth and never quite finished. He had abandoned it before the end since the royal "love tidings" he had meant to celebrate had not materialized. The little Princess Marie of France had died before she could be betrothed to Richard.

There were love tidings aplenty now to celebrate. He glanced again at the new-wed couple. Henry, chunky and serious in his white velvet suit, was politely trying to entertain his pop-eyed bride by carving a horse out of bread. And Geoffrey looked at the King, whose betrothal to Anne of Bohemia, sister of the Holy Roman Emperor, would soon be public.

Richard at barely fourteen still resembled a golden meadow full of pink and white daisies. His German bride-to-be, a year older, was reputed to be lumpish and brown as a nut. It was hard to fit either the flowery conceits of courtly love, or the forthright pleasures of mature mating to these dynastic marriages of children.

Geoffrey's eyes veered to the Lady Elizabeth, the Duke's younger daughter. Her marriage yielded even less inspiration. At Kenilworth last summer when Elizabeth was sixteen she had become the Countess of Pembroke by means of an eight-year-old husband, John Hastings, who had promptly suffered an attack of measles and returned to his mama for nursing.

There was grave doubt that Elizabeth would wait until the years should bring virility to her little husband. At this moment her cheeks were flushed, her dark eyes bright with wine, or lechery, as she lolled against John Holland and teased him with pouting lips. The King's half brother was no Joseph, and his repute for wenching was great. It was a wonder that the Duke did not curb his wild young hoyden, but the dallying pair were hidden from his sight behind a festoon of hanging bayleaves, and none so easily hoodwinked as a fond father— except a husband.

There remained the Lady Philippa. Decorous as always, she sat smiling quietly at some quip made by her Uncle Edmund. Her pale hair was braided in the old manner at either side of her cheeks. She had much of her mother's gentle dignity, but never Blanche's beauty.

Of Philippa there had been many, abortive, love tidings. Scarcely a prince in Europe but had been mentioned for her husband, but none found to be suitable. So Philippa at twenty-one was as yet unwed, and happy that she was still virgin, Katherine had said.

Geoffrey's eyelids drooped as he thought with sudden impatience that though poetical eulogies of royal matings often produced pleasing rewards, he no longer felt the requisite chivalric fervor to do them justice. St. Valentine concerned himself with common folk as well as courtly ones, and the saint's influence on all folk was humorous enough to the onlooker. Yet it was no saint, nor Venus or Cupid, who moderated the affairs of love. No one but Dame Nature. And a gathering of amorous birds would serve to show various kinds of love as well as any gallant knights and languished ladies. The turtle-dove, the falcon, the goose, the cuckoo and the eagle—he thought, much entertained with his idea—fowls of every kind, a parliament of fowls.

He started as a wand of jingling bells thumped him on the shoulder.

The Lord of Misrule stood on the inside of the board grinning down at him beneath a red-spotted half mask.

"Ho, Dan Chaucer!" shouted Robin. " 'Tis crime to doze when all make merry! In punishment we decree that you give us a rhyme. Come tell of love, my master! Tell us of love!"

Geoffrey laughed and rose. His loosened girdle fell off with a clatter of sword, another button popped off his surcote. "I am undone, Your Majesty," he twinkled to Robin. "Your pardon."

"Ay—granted—ay—" cried the young squire, shaking his fool's scepter threateningly. "But sing to us of love!"

The young people on the dais ceased chattering as the King stood up, hushed the minstrels and watched expectantly. Richard had an eager appreciation of poetry as of all the arts and though he preferred French, had read one or two of Master Geoffrey's English translations with pleasure.

Katherine rose too, and seeing that it was Geoffrey that Robin teased, walked a few steps down the Hall and smiled at him encouragingly.

Geoffrey bowed, lifted his arm in solemn invocation, and declaimed,

> *"Since I from Love escapéd am so fat*
> *I think no more to be in prison lean*
> *Since I am free, I count him not a bean. . . ."*

He sat down.

There was a startled roar of indignation. "For shame, for shame," called Richard on a trill of his high childish laughter. "My Lord of Misrule, you cannot pass so ungentle an offense! What penance will you give him?"

Robin waved his scepter as he considered. "By Saint Venus, I command that he shall kiss his wife!"

Philippa bridled at the shouts that greeted this, but Geoffrey promptly rose again and, seizing her by the chin, kissed her heartily on the lips. " 'Tis naught so great a penance," he cried, and her indignant sputterings died away.

Then Robin's usually level head forsook him. This brief time of power had made him drunker than the wassail. By all the rules of Christmas, no man could gainsay him, and he shouted exultantly, "*Now* shall each man kiss the lady of his heart!"

He whirled, and before she had the faintest conception of

what he would do, Robin had covered the few steps between them and, grabbing Katherine around the waist, pressed his eager young mouth passionately to hers.

Few people saw it, because Robin's command was being obeyed, in a whirl of fumblings and giggles and coquettish screams.

Katherine was so astounded that for a moment she could not move. She had continued to treat Robin as a boy and had come scarcely to notice the adoring looks her gave her, but this was no boyish peck. It was a man's kiss, hot with desire, and when she finally jerked her head away, he whispered, "Three years I've waited for this, my heart's life. I shall die if you be not kind to me!" and he kissed her again.

"Jesu, my poor Robin—you're mad," she whispered, pushing at his chest that was covered with gilt bells. Robin held her tighter and muttered a torrent of love words against her cheek. She gave him a great terrified shove—as a voice spoke beside them.

"Here's a pretty little piece of Christmas mumming! 'Twould seem you play your parts well." The voice of stone, the eyes of murderous blue flint.

Robin's arms slackened.

She released herself and cried wildly, "To be sure, my lord —why not? The King of Misrule must be obeyed, it seems he feels most sportive, and has just told me he would kiss *all* the ladies."

"No!" cried Robin, past all caution, and still gazing at her through the mask. "I want only—"

"The Lady Isabella," cried Katherine, seizing the arm of Edmund's light-minded wife, and thrusting her at Robin. "Here's a king dies of love for you, my lady!"

Isabella giggled and preened herself, her voluptuous Castilian eyes gleamed at Robin. She hiccuped gently and clutched at the young squire's arm.

"My lord," said Katherine to John, moving quickly, "shall we not join the dancing?" Here at Leicester a special chamber had been built for dancing. The King and the bride already were gyrating hand in hand in the popular Pavo.

"Nay, my lady," said the Duke, "I do not feel like dancing."

"You're tired, my dearest lord, come to our solar, we'll rest awhile."

"I feel no need of rest." He did not look at her, the corners of his nostrils were dented white. He swung on his heel and strode under the minstrels' gallery towards the guardroom, where his men-at-arms were feasting.

Katherine ran after him in great fear. She had forgotten in these three quiet years that his eyes could look like that—

"My lord," she cried desperately, "You *cannot* be angry at a boy's tipsy yuletide kiss. 'Tis unworthy of you."

At first she thought he would not heed, but at last he stopped by a torchlit recess and turned on her. "Tipsy—ay! Wine makes a window for the truth. I marked well how little you resisted, no doubt because these kisses are not so unaccustomed."

Her own eyes blazed as hot as his, but she knew that Robin's safety depended on her control. "I must believe that this outrageous slur gives proof of your love," she said trembling. "If you have lived so long with me and cannot trust, then all our life is mockery."

John's fists fell slowly open. Her bitter voice spoke to his heart but yet he was deafened by the shock he had felt when he saw her in another man's arms. A new shattering pain, since never by word or deed had she given him cause for jealousy. He had seen how men admired her, but so sure had he always been of her love that no doubts had troubled him.

"If you did not welcome his kisses, why did you babble that folderol to protect him, and thrust Isabella at him?" he cried. "And why didn't you strike his foul slobbering face?"

Why not? she thought. Why, because she liked Robin and love is not so plentiful in this world that one should receive it anywhere with odium. But this she could not say, so she told part of the truth.

"I spoke for fear of you, my lord. What you would do—"

"You think you need to guard my honor?" he cried with new fury. "This yeoman churl that I hired as squire, did you think I'd challenge him to knightly combat! Indeed Katrine, 'tis your own peasant blood that speaks—'tis perhaps the bond between you two."

"Ah—Your Grace?" said Katherine, flatly, staring at him. After a moment she continued, "I thought you would set your guards on him—though your chivalry might well breed mercy to such lowborn folk as Robin—and me."

There was no sound in the passage, except the Duke's harsh breath. Music and the gliding of feet came from the dancing chamber, the dissonance of befuddled voices from the Hall. The torch sputtered and flared brighter.

Katherine's eyes stared into those of the Duke.

At last he sighed and dropped his head. "I'm sorry, Katrine," he said unsteadily, "but the sight of you in that ribaud's arms—" His hands shot out. He grabbed her shoulders and yanked her towards him. He bent and kissed her savagely. "Were his kisses sweet as mine, lovely! Did your mouth open for him too?"

His fingers dug into her shoulders until the skin sprang up livid. She gave a sobbing laugh. "You know that you are my whole life—you know it—"

"Dear Christ, that I should love you still like this," he said through his teeth. "That I can desire you now, as much, nay, more than I did in Bordeaux—do you feed me love potions, Katrine?"

"No, do I have need to?" she whispered. They stood looking at each other, breathing as though they raced with time.

He caught her round the waist. "Come," he said, and pulled her down the passage towards the solar stairs.

"No," she cried, "we've been gone long now. What will they think? You cannot so slight the King!"

He laughed in his throat. "The King will wait on love as well as any man."

In the partially emptied Hall, the varlets stacked the trestle boards and renewed the candles. Geoffrey still sat on, warming himself at the fire. His Philippa had gone to sleep in a chair and snored softly, with her hands folded on her stomach. Some knights and squires slept too against the walls, while others diced or pitched pennies.

Geoffrey had seen what passed between Katherine, Robin and the Duke, and made a shrewd guess as to its meaning. But he had seen something else as well—the look on Blanchette's face when Robin kissed her mother.

He was fond of his pretty niece, but she puzzled him as he knew she did Katherine, who treated the girl's dark moods with an anxious forbearance. Blanchette's marigold curls and dimples, her small delicate body, belied the intensity of her somber slate-gray eyes. Girls of about fourteen were often flighty, but Blanchette's brooding silences, her stammering speech and unwillingness to join with other young folk in any pastime seemed stranger than the normal humors released by puberty. Throughout the banquet, Blanchette had sat next to a stalwart knight called Sir Ralph Hastings, who was cousin to the Earl of Pembroke. Sir Ralph owned much land in Yorkshire near Pontefract, he was one of the Duke's most able knights—and a widower. Recently he had become enamored of Blanchette and had asked Katherine for her, who had told the Chaucers of it.

"A splendid marriage!" Philippa had cried. "By Saint Mary, what luck! Why, she'll have *noble* kin—she'll be cousin to the Lady Elizabeth! Speed the matter, Katherine, lest Sir Ralph change his mind. 'Tis not everyone would want a sulky little snip like Blanchette, and no heiress either."

"She has income from the Deyncourt wardship, my lord granted her," said Katherine slowly, "and her share some day in Kettlethorpe. But the child says she hates Sir Ralph."

"Rubbish!" had cried Philippa sharply. "She but hates whatever you, or His Grace, tell her to do. 'Tis the very thing for her, a wise older man'll soon straighten out these dumpish moods. You humor her too much."

"Maybe—" Katherine's smooth brow had creased in a worried frown. "My lord thinks so. Yet it twists my heart to force the child—"

Blanchette had however been forced to the extent of sitting next to Sir Ralph at the banquet and sharing his cup. A comely man, Sir Ralph, with high florid color, and curling brown beard. Blanchette sat beside him with downcast head, until Robin began to jingle and caper along the Hall between the trestles. Then her great clouded eyes had fixed on Robin and at the moment when he kissed Katherine, Geoffrey had seen the girl start back and whiten. She had left the table at once, gliding out into the courtyard. Nor had she returned to the Hall.

Was that violent flinching because the girl had some special feeling for Robin? Was it because she felt her mother besmirched?

It was hard to tell what Blanchette felt. But, Geoffrey thought pityingly, there was a fey quality about the girl, not sulky as Philippa and many others believed—but tragic.

On the morning after the banquet, John and Katherine lay late in bed, as did most of the castle inhabitants. The winter sun had risen to its full brilliance, and the folk of Leicester town were already out skating and sliding on the frozen Soar

before Katherine awoke. She listened to the shouts of the hol-
idaymakers on the ice, and seeing a strip of orange-colored
light through the brocaded bed curtains, murmured that it
would be a fine day for the stag hunt in Leicester forest, and
yawned voluptuously. In the great enclosed bed it was warm,
snug as a walled garden. She lazily kissed the corner of
John's jaw, and nestled against him, savoring with drowsy delight the hard strength of his muscles.

He acknowledged her caress with a smile and a gentle
pinch on the satin skin of her hip, but he had been awake for
some time, and thinking.

"Lovedy," he said, "Robin Beyvill must go. I'll not answer
for my temperance, if I see him making calf eyes at you now,
and besides there's another reason."

Katherine blinked. She had quite forgotten Robin. "Yes,"
she said thoughtfully, "it were better he leave here—but not
in disgrace, my dear lord. He's served you well."

"Not in disgrace. But he shall go today. To the Scottish
border—to my fortress of Liddel. There he may cool his ar-
dors by taming the Scots, who are rampaging as usual. God
bless them."

John chuckled. He still had affection for the violent brood
that harassed the Border, affection born of his early visit with
his father when he was a lad, and which was incongruously
enough returned. He could arrange truces with the Scots,
when no one else could. Certainly not Percy, who had deliberately provoked the latest Scottish hostilities. Percy be
damned, John thought. The Earl of Northumberland had
taken to snorting and pawing at the Lowlands again, regardless of England's safety—and need. At last a new approach
had opened towards the seizure of Castile, to the final victory
over France. This was no time for enraging the ancient rival
to the north, as well.

Two incredibly fortunate deaths had given England her
chance to strike. Last year the usurping Castilian bastard,
Trastamare, had died, leaving the throne to his degenerate
son, Juan. And now Charles the Fifth, the wily avocat who
had so long plagued the English, was gone too. His successor,
Charles, was but a boy of twelve, and subject to fits. Spain
and France were both, therefore, virtually leaderless, plunged
into turmoil. And Portugal had risen as an English ally.

"Ay," said John aloud on a note of solemn exultation,
"*This* time we'll succeed. I know it."

Katherine stiffened inwardly. She had no need to ask what he meant. Nowadays he told her freely of his plans, and she had never but once requited his confidence with the intrusion of her personal fears.

That once she had said, "But what will happen to me, my lord, if you enter at last into your kingdom?"

And he had answered in surprise, "Why you'll come too, Katrine, after Castile's affairs have settled down. There's a litte castle on the Arlanzon outside of Burgos where you shall be installed."

She had said no more and tried to forget the pangs this prospect gave her, and the bitter misgivings.

As anointed Queen of a Castile which she herself had brought to John, would Costanza show the same forbearance she showed now when she was but a penniless alien in her husband's country? And already there had been a change. Philippa said that when the Duchess heard the news of Trastamare's death, she had laughed loud and shockingly. She had decreed a three-day festival at Hertford, her chapel bell had pealed from dawn to dusk and her jewel-studded statue of the Virgin was carried through the streets to the accompaniment of Spanish hymns of thanksgiving. And she had summoned the Duke to Hertford, where he had stayed a week—all matters it were better not to think of.

"Thank God, darling," said Katherine at last, sighing, "that at least you don't leave England soon. 'Tis something I couldn't bear."

He frowned. Her remark pressed on a subject of deep concern. His brothers Edmund and Thomas were to be the vanguard of the new campaign. But he himself must remain at home for a while to strengthen domestic affairs, and cope with both Scottish and Welsh disorders. Richard's council, the Princess Joan and his own judgment had concurred in this policy, though it irked him and he had little trust in Edmund's diplomacy in Portugal.

"I'd not stay here, lovedy," he said gravely, "if it weren't wiser in the long run."

"Nay," she said with a sharp laugh. "I know your love for me could never keep you here—nor should it," she added with quick penitence. "Forgive me."

He turned and looked at her: the luminous eyes between their thick black lashes, the straight little nose, the voluptuous red mouth above the cleft chin, the transparent rose of her cheeks, the tumbled bronze of her fragrant hair, and the blue veins and white curves of her firm full breasts.

"By the Holy Rood, Katrine," he said, half angry, half rueful, "I *hope* it's not you who keep me here. That were shame indeed."

There were those who thought so; Costanza did. He had denied it furiously and with truth. No woman, not even Katherine, could turn him from his goal. As the Castilian throne drew nearer to his grasp its lure shone even brighter. But he had learned prudence in these last years, and the need for careful planning. Money must be raised for an army, and sporadic little bursts of rioting, not only on the borders, but in English shires, must be put down with a firm hand— And *then* Castile.

Katherine heard his deep breath, and knew that he was thinking of those sun-baked plains that he had shown her from their mountaintop in the Pyrenees. She understood now better than she had then why that faraway land was the summit of his dreams.

She no longer wondered that he was not satisfied with being the greatest nobleman in England and its virtual ruler. Not when he could be a veritable anointed king, king of a country nearly twice as large as England. What complete answer that would be to continuing slanders that he plotted for Richard's throne! And, thought Katherine—that other thing. The ghost of the changeling story had been laid, even his enemies had forgotten it, and John could now refer to it with no more than the passing scorn he gave to all rumors about him. But the scar was there.

The King of Castile would be far above all rumors.

"We must get up, slug-a-bed," said John with sudden energy pushing down the ermine coverlet. "Ring the bell." There were two more days of merrymaking before Richard and the other guests would leave. Stag hunt this afternoon. Bullbaiting and some jousting tomorrow. The season had unfortunately made it impossible to hold a tournament.

Katherine reached an arm through the curtains for the hand bell which would summon Hawise and a valet of the chamber. The bell made her think of Robin, who as body squire had often answered it, and she said, "My lord, you spoke of a second reason why Robin must be sent away?"

"Lollard," said John succinctly, thrusting one leg out of bed.

"But," she protested, "you've never been against the Lollards!" Half the court, the Princess Joan and until recently John himself had subscribed to most of Wyclif's doctrines.

"The Lollards now go too far," said John impatiently. "Their preachers are inflaming the people. And you know very well that I can no longer champion poor old Wyclif. I think his wits've addled. Though I'll not let his enemies harm him either. He shall propound his dreadful new hersies in peace at Lutterworth, but I want no active Lollards in my meinie."

The chamber valet came in and drew back the curtains while another poked the fire into a blaze. A squire presented his lord with a silver tankard of ale. Another held John's scarlet velvet dressing gown.

Hawise delayed a little in coming to her mistress. The baby Joan was teething and Hawise had been up with the nurse, rubbing the little gums with clove syrup. Katherine could not spring naked from the bed when the chamber was filled with men, and as she snuggled in the warm hollow to wait for Hawise to bring her robe, she thought briefly about Wyclif, knowing that the reformer had sharply disappointed John.

Wyclif against the bishops, and the corrupt clergy, had been worthy of help. Wyclif against the Pope, particularly that now since the schism in 'seventy-eight there were most confusingly two popes, had merited many an intelligent person's approval.

Wyclif against the spiritual teachings of the Church was another matter. John had been sympathetic with the Englished Bible which Wyclif wanted given to the people, there was no harm in that, and the Duke believed in learning. He had been patient with the fiery black-robed doctor's arguments against the idolatry of saints, the folly of pilgrimage, the futility of confession.

But lately Wyclif had attacked the sacredness of the Mass itself, had dared to deny the miracle of transubstantiation. He had actually stated that the consecrated wafer and the wine did never change at all into the Blessed Body and Blood, that they were merely symbols. He had said it was better to worship a toad than the Sacrament, for a toad at least had life. And here John's long tolerance had shattered.

Perhaps, thought Katherine, Brother William had had something to do with John's revulsion against Wyclif. The Gray Friar himself no longer had the least sympathy for the reformer. And as for me, thought Katherine wearily, I cannot care either way. The observance of her religion had become dim, meaningless, boring.

John was truly devout in a hearty male way. He believed as his father and mother had believed, so Wyclif had ended by horrifying him. And yet, she thought, it was like him to continue to protect Wyclif despite their quarrel.

His enemies misunderstood as usual. They gave him no credit for the loyalty that was his strongest trait. When he showed mercy they called it cowardice. But welladay, thought Katherine, what use to dwell on gloomy things? Today we'll have the stag hunt and tonight we'll dance, my lord and I. She smiled, for their bodies were attuned in all ways and they danced so well together that even the most spiteful were forced to admire.

"God's greeting, my lady," said Hawise popping her broad face through the curtains. "You look gay as a goldfinch. My lord too—" She gestured with her white-coiffed head towards the garderobe, where the Duke's voice could be heard singing

*Amour et ma dame aussi*
*Votre beauté m'a ravie!*

while his squires rubbed him down with an herb-steeped sponge. "His Grace is in good spirits, I hear. 'Twas not his mood last night in the Hall, by corpus!" She enveloped Katherine in a chamber robe, encased the slim feet in embroidered kid slippers.

"How do you know that?" asked Katherine startled.

"Even common folk've eyes, sweeting. 'Tis known through the castle that fool of a Robin bussed you too hotly last night, and the Duke went black as iron. Some thought he'd beat you to a jelly with a pikestaff, some that Robin's bloody corpse'd be found afloating in the Soar; but *I* never fretted. You can do anything with his grace nowadays."

The two women walked into Katherine's garderobe. It was warmed by a charcoal brazier and smelled agreeably of smoke and Katherine's amber essence. The stone latrine was shut off by a heavy tapestry, much to Hawise's disapproval. She considered Katherine's nose too squeamish. The stench of latrines was well known to be the best preventive of moth, and without it Katherine's perch-hung rows of fur and wool garments were in grave danger.

Katherine sat down on a stool and Hawise commenced combing out the long tangled hair.

"Robin leaves today for Cumberland," said Katherine, while soaking her hands in a basin of warm cream. Still every winter she had to fight recurring chilblains.

"Ay—I'm not surprised. Poor gawk. He lost his head, but small wonder. He's been panting for you like a thirsty dog, this age past."

"I didn't know—at least I never thought much about it," said Katherine ruefully. "Half the young squires're sighing and languishing after somebody, it's the fashion."

"*Truth* is—ye're blind as a midday bat to all but the Duke," said Hawise chuckling. She began to rub separate coppery strands with a silk cloth to increase their sheen and added in a different tone, "Yet there's one who'll be heart-stricken that Robin's to be sent off."

"Who?" asked Katherine idly, patting her hands dry on a linen towel.

"Blanchette, m'lady—nay, I see ye'd not guessed. The poor little wench keeps a button he wore under her pillow, and I've seen other signs."

"Blessed Saint Mary—" cried Katherine on a long note of mingled pity and exasperation. "That child. What am I to do with her? Still it can't be serious, she's too young, and Robin's shown her no special notice, has he?"

"Nay. Robin's had eyes for no woman but you."

Katherine sighed. This then was one explanation of Blanchette's increasing hostility. Lately she had hurt Katherine by her silences, her stubborn refusal to comply with any of Katherine's requests, though Katherine had shown tolerance in the matter of the betrothal to Sir Ralph. The Duke had even been annoyed with her about it. Blanchette could scarcely hope for another such offer, and Sir Ralph was not the man to be kept dangling.

"Robin'd be no match for her, even if he'd have her," said Katherine slowly. "She must look higher than a hobbledehoy Suffolk yeoman. God's blood, I don't know what ails the girl. She cares nothing about all we've done for her!"

Hawise was silent while she began the elaborate braiding of her mistress's hair. She sympathized with Katherine's worries about this child who never smiled any more. Hawise wound and netted the thick braids at the back of Katherine's head in readiness for the moony headdress later, and offered thoughtfully, "She seemed brighter on that visit to Kettle-thorpe than I've seen her in donkey's years."

"Kettlethorpe!" repeated Katherine with disgust. She put down the mirror, and frowned at the unpleasant memory.

A year ago in November, after she had recovered from the baby Joan's birth, the Duke, having business in Lincoln, had decided that they should visit Kettlethorpe and see how Katherine's property did. They took Tom and Blanchette in their train, so that the Swynford children might see their birthplace, and they had stayed at Kettlethorpe for three very uncomfortable days.

The Duke had long ago appointed a resident steward under the direction of his Lincolnshire feodar, William de Spaigne, so that the manor had been kept in repair and was being as efficiently run as possible. But to Katherine, Kettlethorpe had presented a picture of bleak desolateness. It was so small and draughty and damp. Comforts which she had come to take for granted were entirely lacking, a dense November fog chilled the bones, and she, who was so seldom ill, promptly came down with violent chills, streaming nose and a racking cough. She had viewed her erstwhile home through a haze of physical and spiritual dis-ease.

They had held a love day and ale feast in the manor Hall. Herded by the steward and a new reeve, her serfs had filed through and apathetically knelt to do her homage, while little Tom stood by her chair with a proud smile, savoring this parade of his own future possessions.

But Katherine thought the serfs a poor-spirited mangy lot, and wondered that she had ever been afraid of them. Mil-burga had turned into a shrunken old woman with crippled joints, Will the cook trembled with palsy and had been ousted from the manor kitchens. Only Sir Robert, the priest, was much the same, fat, untidy and garrulous; but Molly, his hearthmate, had died.

There had been many deaths since she was here before, some bowel complaint had carried off half of Laughterton. Then there had been three runaways. Odo the ploughman's twin lads had taken to their heels and disappeared in Sher-wood forest. Cob o' Fenton, the former spit-boy, had refused to pay his heriot fine on his father's death, and made off too, but he had been caught at once and brought back. His prop-erty confiscated, he had been branded with an F on his left cheek, for "fugitive," and was even now in the village stocks as an example.

The steward reported that the unrest and disaffection amongst the serfs was truly shocking. Also, and here the steward had grown even more gloomy, there had been thefts and poaching. Hare and even a fat roebuck had been taken from Lady Swynford's own enclosure. Sheep had been stolen from her flocks. Two of the culprits had been caught by the smell of roasting mutton in their cots. And hanged.

The steward had walked Katherine to the village green, where a gibbet had been set up, beside the stocks where Cob the runaway was being punished. Cob had changed little since the old days.

Still small and flaxen-polled, though he must be thirty. Between white lashes his pale eyes had stared at Katherine sullenly—while the branded F reddened on his cheek.

She turned quickly from him, and recoiled as she saw the gibbet. Two rotting half-naked bodies dangled from the nooses. Katherine took one shrinking look and recognized—despite the bloated livid features—the long skull and jaw of Sim Tanner, the reeve. She gave a horrified cry and the steward said, "Ay, my lady. Sim took to thieving and poaching as soon as I turned him from his reeveship. Had got used to little luxuries no doubt, and wouldn't give 'em up."

So Sim had escaped Nirac's dagger so long ago, to end finally like this. The fog swirled thickly in from the Trent, Katherine's teeth chattered with another chill and she had hastened back to the dubious warmth of the Hall. Later she had ordered that Cob be freed from the stocks, and that his plot of land be restored to him, for she had been sickened by all the sights on the village green.

Dear Mother of God, how she had detested Kettlethorpe, and been in a frenzy to get away again.

But now she remembered that Blanchette had not. The girl had visited all the haunts of her childhood, the Broom hills, the mill, the river ford and a little pool where she had once played with village children. As though some inner sluice gate had been raised, Blanchette had asked a spate of eager, shy questions about her father. Was it here in the Hall that his armor had hung? What had been his favorite horse's name? And she had said, "How old was I, Mama, when Father kissed me goodbye here on the mounting b—block, the last d—day I ever saw him when he left for Aquitaine?"

Katherine had answered that Blanchette must have been about three and it was a wonder she remembered.

"I d–do remember," said Blanchette with a sad yet excited little smile. "God rest my dear brave father's soul."

Katherine, lightheaded with her own illness and profoundly discomfited by all these sights and memories, had paid little attention. She realized that both children thought Hugh had died of wounds sustained in glorious battle, since no details had been given them. But it was true enough the dysentery had been a kind of battle wound. There was no falsehood in that.

"Ah—I remember now," said Katherine finishing her thoughts aloud to Hawise, "that Blanchette wept when we left that odious place. But I feel 'tis morbid. She has everything to make her happy now in this new life the Duke has given her. I'll certainly take a firmer hand, as he wishes."

Katherine's face cleared and she waved away the huge gauzy gold-horned headdress that Hawise lifted up. "Let be, for now—" she said, smiling. "One would think I'd no other children but that naughty little wench. I'll not frighten the babies with that foolish thing, and I'm off to the nurseries. How are Joan's gums, poor mite?"

"Sore as boils, I'll warrant, from the uproar she do make," answered Hawise dryly. "She yells louder'n any o' her brothers did."

Katherine laughed, and the two women walked down the passages to the nursery wing. John and Harry had long since gone out to play in the snow with other castle children, but her two latest-born were sitting on a bearskin rug by the fire.

Thomas, so christened because he had been born on St. Thomas à Becket's Day, but called Tamkin to differentiate him from his half brother, Tom Swynford, was engaged in playing some private game with a set of silver chessmen the Duke had given him. Joan was solemnly chewing on a bone teething ring. Both children squealed with delight when they saw their mother. Tamkin jumped up, and the baby held out her arms.

Katherine settled down on the bear rug with them, and kissing them both, pulled the baby into her lap. Joan immediately clutched at her mother's necklace and succeeded in getting the whole of a balas ruby pendant into her mouth.

"Nay—greedy one—" said Katherine extracting the pendant. "Hush," for the little pink mouth opened wide for a roar. Katherine put her finger on the reddened gum and rubbed gently. "Fais dodo—fais dodo, chou-chou, mimi, brebis—tout fait dodo—" she crooned. Joan gave a fat pleased chuckle and quietened.

Joan was an obstreperous and comical baby. Her brown hair grew in little wisps like a hedgehog, her eyes were purple-black and round as bilberries. She was the only dark one of all Katherine's brood and she bore some resemblance to her Aunt Philippa Chaucer. Or could it be to another dark and Flemish Philippa?

"Did you know, my poppet," said Katherine smiling down and tweaking the button nose, "that your grandmother was a Queen?"

The baby gave a protesting squeal at the removal of the comforting finger, and Katherine gave her the teething ring.

"Me too!" cried Tamkin, waving La Ferce, the queen of his chess set. "And my grandsir was a *king*. Hawise telled me." He trotted the plumed king on Katherine's knee, and made a clicking hoof noise with his tongue. "When I get big, *I'll* be a king."

"No, Tamkin—" said Katherine softly. "Never." She looked at her small son. A true Plantagenet like the other boys. They all had the wavy hair, long fine nose, flat high cheekbones, light eyes; though none quite so vivid a blue as their father's.

"Then what'll I *be?*" Tamkin rolled over on his stomach and began to stuff the tiny pawns into caves he poked in the bear fur.

"A knight, darling—*that* you can be. A splendid brave knight." She spoke with bright confidence and felt it for a moment, when it was fractured by a thrust of fear.

If anything should happen to John, what would become of the Beaufort bastards? She crossed herself and sat staring into the fire, while the baby gurgled drowsily on her lap, Hawise and the nurses came and went at their tasks, and Tamkin, tiring of his game, ran off to find his greyhound puppies.

Even with the Duke's all-powerful protection, what future did they have? The boys might be knighted in due course by their father, and make their own way as best they could with the appointments he could give them, but they might not aspire to honors. And the baby Joan—

It would take a stupendous amount of dowry to get her

married properly. Few worthy noblemen would overlook the stain of bastardy.

But if it should happen somehow—in terror, her mind veered from facing the actual thought again—that John could not see to their future, who would protect them then? Not the childish, self-centered Richard, nor the Princess. Certainly not the Earl of Buckingham. Edmund might make a feeble gesture, but when did Edmund's vacillating impulses ever persist for long? It was a treacherous marshy ground over which she had so blithely walked, thinking it firm as granite.

She looked at the baby in her lap, at Tamkin, who was trying to teach one of his puppies to beg. She thought of her two handsome gently bred older boys, who were being reared like young princes. But they were not. They had no legal name, no certain inheritance of any kind, and no sure future but herself. Blessed Mary, she thought, and what could *I* do for them, alone?

She stilled her panic and forced her mind to a practicality that was repugnant to it. Deliberately she scrutinized the total of her few possessions. The Duke from time to time had given her property, which she had accepted with reluctance, disliking the idea of payment for her love. The private income that these brought her she had scarcely heeded, it was but an insignificant trickle of pocket money compared to the lavishness in which she lived.

She had the meager Swynford inheritance, of course, though it was distasteful to her. Besides, it would belong eventually to Tom. She had a yearly hundred marks as governess's recompense, but that would shortly stop, since Elizabeth was married and Philippa beyond the age. She owned houses in Boston, which brought in a small rent. She had two wardships, including the Deyncourt one for Blanchette, some perquisites from the Duke's Nottingham manors, and that was all, except her jewels.

We could never live on that, thought Katherine, frightened. We'd have less than yeoman status. And she determined at least to accept the new wardship and "marriage of the heir" John had semi-humorously offered her.

" 'Twill be appropriate, Katrine. A neat turnabout for the insolence he showed you."

Ellis de Thoresby, Hugh's erstwhile squire, had been killed in a drunken brawl three months ago, leaving a two-year-old son. It was the fat annual fee for guardianship of this son that John offered her, and she refused sharply. She had neither seen nor heard of Ellis since he spat at her in the streets at Lincoln. She wanted no reminder of him.

Ah, but I must be practical, thought Katherine. I've been a soft fool. It was not mercenary to try and protect her children's future, and when the right moment came she would talk to John about it. The moment must be chosen, for though he was generous, he preferred to think of such things himself, and she knew that he might be angered that she should seem to question the provision he intended some day to make for all his children. And he would be right, she thought with sudden revulsion. She could not appear to grasp and scheme as though she had forebodings for him. There was no danger that could threaten them when she had the certainty of his love. She would go on as she had been, nor worry about the future.

Katherine picked up the baby and put her in the cradle, then looking around to find the source of an exceptionally wintry draft, saw that Tamkin had opened the leaded window and was hanging halfway out.

"Tam," she called, "what *are* you doing? Shut the window!"

The boy did not hear her, for there was much noise outside. The nursery windows looked down on Castle street, where a cluster of rustics and townfolk had gathered, while a man in a long russet gown stood on a keg and harangued them.

Hawise came in bearing a pile of the baby's breechclouts as Katherine went over to her son.

" 'Tis only some Christmas mumming," said Katherine impatiently, shutting the window.

"Nay," said Hawise peering over the little boy's shoulder, " 'Tis that Lollard preacher, John Ball, just come to Leicester, I hear. He's been jabbering and havering since Prime. I don't much like the look o' it."

"Whyever not?" said Katherine in surprise. "No harm in preaching."

"They keep singing something, Mama," said Tamkin, "over 'n' over, 'n' shaking their fists."

"They do," said Hawise grimly. "D'ye know *what* they sing?"

Katherine looked out again more curiously. She saw that the preacher had a fiery red face between a black beard and a crop of black hair on a round head, that he waved his arms violently and sometimes struck his russet-clad breast, pointing up to the sky, and then at the castle. Now and again he would stop with both arms wide outflung, when all the crowd of folk would stamp their feet and chant something that sounded like the rhythmic pound of a hammer on a smith's anvil.

"What *do* they sing?" Katherine said and opened the window wide. The hoarse pounding shouts gradually clarified themselves into words:

> *When Adam delved and Eva span,*
> *Who was then the gentleman?*

"What nonsense!" began Katherine—and checked herself. "What do they mean by that?"

"They mean trouble," said Hawise. "This last poll tax has really roiled 'em, and John Ball's doing his best to keep 'em roiled—throughout the land."

"Oh," said Katherine shrugging as she turned from the window. "The poll tax is hard on folks, no doubt, but wars must be paid for, Hawise. Why must they show so much hatred?"

" 'Tis easy to hate, lady dear, when you be poor and starving."

"But they're not!" cried Katherine, her eyes flashing. "Nobody starves in Leicester, or any of the Duke's domains. The kitchens often feed three hundred a day."

" 'Tis not everyone wants to be beggars, sweeting," said Hawise chuckling. "And there's mighty few who like to be unfree."

"The Duke has freed many of his serfs when they deserve it," retorted Katherine hotly. "The eve of Christmas he freed ten in honor of Lord Henry's marriage."

" 'Tis true," said Hawise. "But there be ten thousand more in bondage. Ye needna look so fierce—'tis not *my* thoughts I'm giving—'tis what that John Ball yammers out there."

"But what can they *do?*" said Katherine, frowning towards the window, where again the doggerel pounded its inane rhythm.

"Oh, they'll not do anything," Hawise shrugged. " 'Tis naught but talk. England be a great place for windy grumbles. 'Twill all die down like stale ale."

# XXIII

THE LANCASTRIAN household held their May revels at
the Savoy. The early spring had been stormy but by the
end of April, days of warm sun and nights of gentle
showers enameled the countryside with green luster. The
Savoy servants trundled in barrowfuls of primroses and violets from the meadows near Tyburn, and made garlands to
hang in each of the hundred rooms. They cut thick dewy
branches of the rose-budded may and fastened them to torch
brackets and above doorways. The kitchens and Great Hall
were strewn with new rushes and fragrant herbs.

Every nook was spring-cleaned. The myriad windowpanes
sparkled like diamonds set in lead; the cream and beige tile
floors were polished smooth as eggs, and the silk carpets and
the tapestries of the State Chambers were scrubbed and
flailed to their pristine glow. Gilt, vermilion and azure were
brushed on the stone chimney carvings, while new-painted
fleurs de luce powdered the vaulted ceilings between polished
timbers. The offices of the chancery, the Great Treasure
Chamber, the smithies, the barracks, the armorer's shops, the
falcon mew, even the cellars and the empty dungeon received
new coats of whitewash and were decorated with greenery.

A gilded Maypole had been set up in the river gardens on
a square of turf which was enclosed by the famous Provençal
rosebushes, already tipped with coral buds. Each afternoon of
May week, there was dancing around the great shaft, while
the multicolored ribbons wove up and down against a drift of
pear blossoms.

There were May Day games—the younger lords and ladies
played at Hide-and-Seek in the maze, or at Hoodman Blind
and Hot Cockles. At night there were bonfires built along the
riverbank, and the Duke's barges, festooned with streamers
and lit by torches, raced across the river while wagers were
placed on each contestant.

449

No one could be melancholy during these days of Maytime brightness, and the Duke shut his mind to impending problems and enjoyed himself wholeheartedly with Katherine.

On May 12, he was to set forth for Scotland again. The King's Council, much pleased with his handling of earlier Scottish disorders, had commissioned him to ride north and negotiate for a prolongation of the truce and cessation of the new hostilities. Percy's touchy sensibilities would have to be soothed. The Lord of Northumberland felt that Border matters were his own exclusive concern, and passionately resented interference from Westminster. But a combination of tact, flattery and sternness would doubtless pacify the Border lord as they had before.

Everything contributed to the optimism born of Nature's own gaiety.

Parliament had finally voted an appropriation, and the poll tax was being raised, albeit there had been some trouble. The first collectors, through laziness or venality, had failed miserably to hand over the average shilling a head that was required. In March the system had been tightened and a fresh staff of collectors commissioned. The chancellor, who was now old Sudbury, Archbishop of Canterbury, had been scolded for his slackness; and a new treasurer, Robert Hales, Prior of St. John's, put in charge of the dilatory revenues.

The common folk might grumble—to be sure, taxes always caused grumbling—but a democratic effort had been made to distribute this tax fairly, "with the strong to help the weak." It was true that the levy of a shilling might wreak some hardship amongst laborers and servants, since their wages seldom reached fourteen shillings a year; but on the other hand, the glorious prospects of eventual victory in France and Castile should certainly move the people to patriotic sacrifice. Besides, this new tax, for the first time, spared no one over fifteen years of age, even a baron or a bishop was assessed at a pound a head.

What could be fairer than that, thought the Peers, while the Royal Council and Parliament agreed.

Katherine had been a trifle uneasy since she had heard John Ball preaching at Leicester, until the Duke told her that Ball had been imprisoned in Kent by Archbishop Sudbury.

"No need to fret, lovely," said the Duke gaily. "With that ranting little firebrand quenched in jail, the people'll quiet down. They've no real cause for grievance, anyway."

Katherine was reassured. Yet she did say hesitatingly, "But the villeins *aren't* reasonable. My steward writes that at Kettlethorpe, Cob o' Fenton has run off *again!* Though I freed him from the stocks and gave him back his land."

John shrugged. "No doubt they'll catch him, Katrine. 'Tis always hard to judge when leniency be wise. Some serfs would have shown you greater gratitude."

She had accepted this and ceased to think of it. Each lovely day must be enjoyed to the full, especially as she and John would so soon be separated. Yet she had little fear for him on this march to Scotland which he anticipated with pleasure, nor should it take more than a month or so. She was to await him at Kenilworth with their children, and Kenilworth was a happy summertime castle.

On Sunday she would leave the Savoy with the Duke, who would drop her and her household off at Kenilworth while he continued north. But before they left there was a small private matter to be attended to.

Sir Ralph Hastings would accompany his lord to Scotland, and Blanchette's betrothal should be solemnized. It had been delayed after Katherine's decision at Leicester because Sir Ralph had been at Pontefract, but now he had arrived at the Savoy, eager to claim the girl.

This was on Wednesday, the eighth of May. The Duke and Katherine were sitting in the rose garden watching a troupe of Cornish tumblers and gleemaidens who were cavorting on the lawn.

Sir Ralph strode through the garlanded archway into the garden, and walking to the Duke's chair knelt and kissed his hand. "God's greeting, my lord," he said, and bowed to Katherine. "I'm here a day before I thought to be, but love is a sharp spur, by Peter!" He chuckled and swaggered in his violet brocaded cote-hardie. A well-made man was Sir Ralph, and had spared no expense in clothing himself as finely as any young dandy at Richard's court. Blanchette's aversion to him he had assured himself sprang from charming modesty, being quite certain of his attraction. He was thirty-five and looked younger. He was an excellent horseman and jouster, and had been forbearing to the old wife he had been married to for twelve barren years until her lung complaint released him.

Blanchette had no excuse whatsoever for her behavior,

thought Katherine, smiling at Sir Ralph, who was asking after the girl.

"I'll get her—" said Katherine rising. "In truth, Sir Ralph, you must have patience with her. Woo her gently. I confess she's sometimes of a heavy spirit."

The knight frowned a trifle but he spoke confidently, "Oh I'll soon gentle the little burde, once she's mine. 'Tis natural she should be shy."

"Natural, maybe," said the Duke smiling. "But she's played the coy long enough. We'll have the betrothal tomorrow, a merry climax to May revelry. Here in the arbor—and some jousting to follow. Blanchette shall be May Queen for the day."

Katherine bestowed a loving glance on John as she hurried from the gardens in search of Blanchette.

The girl lodged in a chamber in the Monmouth Wing, and could seldom be persuaded to leave it. Here she carried on many little occupations of her own. She had wooden puppets that she dressed in scraps of silk and velvet and played some secret game with, though she was well past the age for such toys. She strummed her lute and sang melodies of her own devising that were hushed at once if anyone came to the door.

And there were her birds. Almost daily Blanchette sent the page who waited on her to the market. He fetched her singing birds—linnets, thrushes, skylarks and sometimes nightingales that had been netted by fowlers and were offered for sale. She had a ritual with these. She left them in their cages only one night; while she talked to them softly as though they were Christian souls. At the dawning she would free them through her window and Godspeed them as they winged out of sight.

A harmless enough pastime, but while Katherine stood at the girl's door she heard the low voice inside singing a plaintive tune, and the twittering of a bird. As she put her hand on the latch, Katherine's throat constricted while a memory assailed her—of the Lady Nichola in the tower room at Kettlethorpe. Nay, but the child is in *nothing* like Nichola, Katherine thought with vehemence. She pushed the door and found it locked.

"Let me in!" she called sharply. " 'Tis your mother." After a moment the door opened slowly and Blanchette stood as though to bar the way, her hands clenched together between her breasts. Her copper-gold hair cascaded in loose ringlets down her back. She wore a dove-gray chamber robe, unadorned. Never would she willingly wear any of the costly trinkets that the Duke or Katherine gave her. She was still shorter than her mother but her slight body showed the curves of womanhood, though her face had not lost its baby roundness and a few freckles still peppered her nose.

"Come, child," said Katherine more gently, "why must you always act as though I'd harm you? I love you, and wish you nothing but good. It hurts me when you act like this."

The girl stood motionless on the tiles, her somber eyes fixed on Katherine.

A tiny green linnet hopped and twittered in a wooden cage though the cage door had been opened. The lute lay on the window seat next to a quill pen, wet with ink, and a piece of parchment on which there were some straggling characters. Katherine moved to examine them, thinking to please Blanchette with praise for practicing her writing. She read the childish letters at a glance.

> *I sigh when I sing*
> *For sorrow that I see.*
> *Robin is gone*
> *And thinks naught of me.*

Blanchette with a muffled cry rushed over and swooped up the parchment. She crumpled it in her shaking hand, while fury flashed in her eyes. She turned on her mother and gasped, "What d–do you w–want of me, my lady?"

Katherine sat down on the window seat and shook her head. "You mustn't blame me, dearling, for things I can't help," she said quietly. "You must believe that all sorrows pass, and what you feel today you won't in a year. And you must believe that I know what's best for you."

The girl said nothing. Her eyes moved from her mother's pleading face to the green linnet, her mouth set in an ugly line. Her fingers clenched the crumpled ball of parchment, and she flung it on the tiles.

She that was the sweetest and the gentlest of children— Katherine thought—dear Lord, why is she like this now? Ay, it must be I've spoiled her. She sighed, then spoke with decision. "Blanchette, Sir Ralph has come. He's in the garden with my lord. Your betrothal shall take place tomorrow."

Blanchette raised her eyes. "I'll n–not," she said through her teeth. "I'll—run away. You'll n–never find me—" Her voice shrilled and the stammer left her speech. "I'll not do what he says, ever—I swear it by my father's soul!" She crossed herself and her face went white as clay.

"This is wicked folly!" cried Katherine. " 'Tis not what the Duke says, 'tis what *I* say—"

She gasped, for Blanchette flung out her arms and shouted, "You lie! And I hate you! You are naught but his creature, you and the scurvy pack of bastards that you bear him!" She turned wildly and stumbling across the room flung herself on her bed.

"Jesu," whispered Katherine. She sat rigid on the window seat. A black wave submerged her and at length retreated, leaving behind a jutting rock of anger as refuge. She rose and stood by the bed. Blanchette's face was buried in her arms, her shoulders shook but she made no sound.

"This, Blanchette, is too much!" Katherine said in a voice of icy control. "God knows if I can ever find it in my heart to forgive you."

Blanchette quivered. She twisted her face slowly around and stared up at her mother, and seeing there anger for the first time in her life, she gave a frightened moan. "Mama," she whispered.

Katherine moved away. Ay, she thought, my patience is at an end. I've put up with her humors, with the hatred she shows to John and me, and her jealousies of my babies. She blames me too that Robin did not love her, and now she speaks to me like that.

"Since you are lost to decency and make wicked threats, Blanchette," she said, "I shall see that you are strictly guarded night and day. One of my serving maids shall stay here with you, and a man-at-arms remain outside the door. Tomorrow at noon there will be your betrothal to Sir Ralph, and after that I'll send you to a convent until your marriage. You may be thankful that I don't beat you as you deserve."

She picked up the hand bell and rang.

"Mama—" whispered Blanchette again. She slid off the bed. Her eyes were dark with fear. "I d–didn't m–mean—"

Katherine answered frigidly, "Think not to wheedle me into softness as you have so often. I've been soft with you too long."

Blanchette drew back a step. She turned her head from

side to side, her eyes moved from the green linnet to the window, then back to her mother's face. But Katherine did not look at her.

One by one Katherine took the measures for Blanchette's imprisonment. She summoned a serving wench, a taciturn Lancashire lass called Mab, and told her not to leave the girl alone a moment. She stationed a man-at-arms outside the door, telling him to enter if the servant should call. She herself bolted the door on the outside as she left. Then she went back to the gardens and told Sir Ralph that he would see Blanchette on the morrow at the betrothal, but that the girl was indisposed at present. The knight was not pleased.

In the Avalon Chamber Katherine tossed and turned that night until John anxiously asked her what ailed her and suggested that a warm sleeping posset be sent for. She reassured him and kissed him. But she did not tell him of what had passed with Blanchette, for never did she disquiet him if she could help it. He held her close in his arms and after a while she slept, soothed by the familiar comfort of his love; but her sleep was filled with confused bitterness.

Blanchette acted throughout the morning of her betrothal like one of the jointed puppets that she played with in her chamber. She let the Lancashire wench and Hawise array her in a gown of myrtle-green satin and embellish her with jewels, her own and Katherine's. She raised her arms and lowered them when they told her to. They twined flowers in her flowing hair and garlanded her with lilies. She never spoke at all nor seemed to know what they were doing, but once, when Hawise stood back admiringly and said, "God's blood, my poppet, I vow you're near as fair as your mother was on her bridal day!"

Then a strange look came into Blanchette's eyes—of pain, of fear, of revulsion, Hawise could not tell, but it was a relief to see some awareness there, for the girl seemed as thickwitted as though she had been drugged with poppy juice, for all that her eyes glittered glassy bright and her cheeks were crimson.

When Blanchette was dressed, Hawise went to fetch Katherine, who had stayed inflexibly away from her daughter.

"She's ready, my lady," said Hawise, "but I fear she's sickening with something. Her skin's hot as fire to touch, and she do seem strange. even for Blanchette."

"Bah!" said Katherine, "there's no more wrong with her than ill temper that she's being made to obey at last. 'Tis not the first time she's acted illness when she wanted her own way."

Hawise knew that this was true, but still she was uneasy and she said hesitatingly, "I hear there's some sickness in t'Outer Ward."

Katherine, who was examining her face in the mirror, preparatory to descending to the garden for the betrothal ceremony, looked up and caught her breath. "Not plague!" she whispered sharply.

"Nay, nay," Hawise crossed herself. "Saint Roch protect us! Some pink-spotted fever 'mongst the children."

"Oh measles, no doubt," said Katherine returning to the mirror. "I think Blanchette had them long ago, nor has she seen anyone to catch them from. Hawise, you croak like an old raven today."

" 'Tis the toothache," said Hawise gloomily, exploring a jumping molar with her tongue. "I've said all the charms, I prayed to Saint Apollonia, but 'twon't stop. The barber'll have to pull it, like the others, God help me." An agonizing prospect sufficient to cause Hawise's general apprehensions, but she had not told Katherine all that she knew of the sickness. It might be measles, but not like cases she had nursed. A little spit-boy had died in the night, screaming with head pain and scarlet as a boiled crawfish, and the page who waited on Blanchette was said to have come down with the fever this morning.

The chapel bell began to ring, in the Outer Ward the clock manikins clanged out the first twelve strokes.

Katherine jumped up and hurried to the Monmouth Wing.

Blanchette was waiting. She looked once at her mother and then at the window, while Katherine said "Come" sternly and took the girl's hand, which was certainly dry and hot as a hearthstone.

They walked through the courtyards and the archway to the gardens. Amongst assembled lords and ladies, Sir Ralph and the Carmelite, Walter Dysse, waited by a portable altar in the rose arbor. The Duke stood resplendent beside them, dressed in his gold and pearl embroidered tunic, wearing the chain of Castile and the Order of the Garter.

Jesu, how handsome he is, Katherine thought as she advanced gravely, holding Blanchette by the hand. The girl moved like a sleepwalker, but suddenly as Katherine started to place the little hand in the outstretched one of Sir Ralph, Blanchette gave a strangled cry and sprang back, releasing herself. She clutched up her myrtle-green skirts and ran frantically away through the archway.

"By God, what's this!" cried the Duke, while Sir Ralph flushed crimson, staring after Blanchette.

"She shall be beaten for it," cried Katherine, herself trembling with anger. "Nay, my lord," she said to John, "I beg you let me deal with her—" Angry as she was she must still protect Blanchette from the expression she saw in both men's eyes.

The Duke hesitated before he shrugged. He gestured to the minstrels and said with formal courtesy to Sir Ralph, "I've a troupe of gleemen may divert you from this shameful behavior."

The knight bowed silently, biting his lips, while Katherine hurried back through the archway, and saw Blanchette at once, behind a yew tree, on the inner side of the wall. The girl was doubled up on the ground and had been vomiting.

Katherine stared, and her anger became fear.

"Oh my poor child," she cried running to her.

Blanchette gazed at her mother without recognition. "Hurts—" she muttered hoarsely, putting her hand to her head. Her fingers touched the garland of lilies and she pulled it off. "White swans," she said, wrenching at the lilies and throwing them up into the air. "I must let them fly away home like the others."

Dear God, thought Katherine, with a stab of terror. But as she touched Blanchette, trying to raise her, she knew that this was the madness of fever, not lunacy. The girl's body gave off heat like an oven, her face and neck, even her chest, were scarlet, and her teeth began to chatter in a convulsive chill.

Katherine called out repeatedly for help. In the garden they did not hear her, the minstrels were playing and the company were dancing. But the Savoy's sergeant-at-arms, Roger Leach, was berating the lazy porter at the Beaufort Tower and he heard her, and came running. In response to Katherine's gesture he picked the girl up and carried her to the Monmouth Wing.

" 'Tis what they call the scarlet sickness, my lady," said the burly soldier pityingly as he put the moaning, struggling Blanchette down on her bed. One of his own babes had had it a fortnight past. "They mostly goes out o' their heads wi' ut for a while."

Katherine threw her headdress on the window seat and twisted up her long silver sleeves. She dipped a napkin in a flagon of water and held it as best she could to Blanchette's tossing forehead. "Get me Hawise, quick!" she cried to the sergeant. "Then fetch Brother William Appleton—nay, I don't know where he is—at Grayfriars maybe. But get him!"

The sergeant bowed and hurried away. Katherine sat on the bed and tried to quiet her delirious child.

On Sunday when the Duke departed for Scotland, Blanchette was better. The fever persisted but now she did not cry out and toss so much. Her body was covered with a mesh of tiny scarlet dots, and she seemed to feel less pain. Brother William had bled her and had her rolled in cool cloths. He had given her febrifuges and opiates. He said that now though she was still in danger, he had great hopes of her recovery.

Katherine could not leave Blanchette alone, so Hawise and the Beaufort babies were to travel up to Kenilworth without her.

The Gray Friar would not allow Katherine to say farewell to her smaller children. This disease lived in the breath, Brother William said, and breath was so subtle an element that there was no telling what it might permeate. So he had a brimstone candle burned in Blanchette's chamber. But there was little danger for older people, their breaths were strong and could fight off the evil miasma.

The Sunday morning when Katherine said goodbye to the Duke there was a storm as they came out of the chapel after Mass. The sky grew purple, lightning forked through black clouds and thunder rocked the palace. Rain fell in torrents and drenched the waiting cavalcade. The knights and men-at-arms were already mounted in the Outer Ward, the baggage wagons and the chariot with Hawise and the Beauforts already crammed in, were lined up for the start.

Katherine spoke apologetic words to Sir Ralph, who received them courteously, but it was evident his ardor had cooled when he remarked that no doubt he would see Blanchette again sometime, after his return from Scotland. Katherine sadly gave him the stirrup cup, and turned to wave to her children in the chariot. The little boys waved back and

Hawise held Joan up and made her kiss her hand to her mother. Katherine tried to smile. She went away quickly to follow John into a little anteroom below the Avalon Chamber.

He was dressed in full armor, the squire outside held his latten battle helmet in readiness. Katherine raised her arms to him, gazing at him piteously. Tears ran down her cheeks.

"Lovedy," he cried kissing her, "you mustn't weep. Blanchette will soon be well, and you'll come to Kenilworth and meet me later, as we planned." He smiled down at her.

"Ay," she said, but another crash of thunder rattled the windowpanes and she jumped and shivered. " 'Tis evil omen," she whispered. "Sunday thunder. 'Tonnerre de dimanche est tonnerre de diable!' " She crossed herself. "John, there's danger—I feel it. A blackness in my heart black like the sky out there. John, *must* we be parted now?"

He crossed himself too, but impatiently. He was eager to be off, and he had scant faith in omens when they did not accord with his wishes. "The storm'll soon be over, Katrine. Already 'tis lifting. It must be strain from nursing that coddled, vexing child gives you dark whimsies. Come, smile, lovedy—I'd not take the memory of a dismal face to Scotland!"

She tried to obey him but she could not. She saw that he had already gone from her in his thoughts, and knew that it was natural. His men were waiting in the court for word to start, days of hard riding were ahead and already the storm had delayed them.

He bent to kiss her again and with finality, but the oppression in her breast sharpened to panic. "John," she cried, "I'm afraid. Something threatens our love. I know it!" She threw her arms around his neck, pressing her face to the harsh steel links of his gorget.

He had never seen her so excited and unreasonable. He stroked her head as she clung to him sobbing, and said tenderly, "Hush—hush," mastering his impatience because he loved her. But as she continued to weep he took her hands and pulled them down from his neck. "Farewell, my love. God keep you." He strode out of the anteroom before she could stop him.

She watched from the window while his squires held his stallion and he mounted. The rain had stopped. Brightness flowed into the sky above the Lancaster pennant on the pin-

nacle of the Monmouth Tower, his brass helmet glinted as he
turned and waved goodbye.

She leaned from the window and slowly waved her silver
scarf.

He spurred his horse, which leaped ahead through the
gateway to the Strand. The cavalcade formed after him and
clattered two by two through the arch. The chariot and baggage train filed after.

Katherine watched until the stableboys returned to their
tasks and the great Outer Ward was empty. Even the yapping
dogs had slunk back towards the kitchens. Quiet fell on the
whole great Savoy Palace three-quarters emptied now. The
subdued drowsing state that it would show until its lord returned to it again.

And its lord, as he cantered along the country road
through the village of Charing Cross, suddenly reined in his
stallion and looked back to gaze at the fair white palace
which was more completely home to him than any of his
country castles. It sparkled in the after-storm sunshine. He
smiled tenderly at Katherine's dismalness, and thought that
the Savoy set off her beauty like a great ivory frame. He
jerked the tasseled bridle and spurred his stallion, which
bounded northward. No premonition told the Duke that he
had looked his last on the Savoy.

Throughout the rest of May and the first week of June,
Katherine lived in a seclusion as complete as though she were
on an island. She moved into the Monmouth Wing, and for
the days of Blanchette's danger slept in the chamber with her
child. She saw no one but Mab, who shared the nursing, the
varlets who brought food and Brother William, who came
daily to examine the patient.

Blanchette improved gradually, the rash faded, her body
no longer burned with raging heat; but a succession of complications bedeviled her. For some days her throat was so
swollen that she could not swallow, and when this abated she
suffered from excruciating earaches until the drums burst and
prurient matter ran out on her pillow.

During this time the girl reverted to her childhood and
looked to her mother for everything, weeping and fretting if
Katherine left the room, and calling for her constantly. The
conflict between them was as though it had never been, and
Katherine poured out a remorseful love. It was nothing but
coincidence that Blanchette had come down with her illness

on the day of her betrothal, and yet Katherine could not quite rid herself of guilt, and she thought now that Blanchette's outrageous insolence on the day before had stemmed from the beginning of the fever, too, and was sorry that it had made her so angry.

As the girl finally improved, Katherine knew that all her strong love for this child was now augmented by the crisis they had passed through together. Blanchette had gained the added preciousness of something nearly lost which one has oneself saved from destruction.

On the ninth of June, a month after the onset of her illness, Brother William pronounced Blanchette definitely on the mend.

It was in the long golden dusk that the Franciscan friar came to visit his patient and found the girl sitting propped up in the window seat with Katherine beside her. Blanchette's head rested against her mother's shoulder, her little face was pinched and white, and she seemed shockingly diminished because the lovely hair had begun to fall out in handfuls, and Katherine had resolutely cut it short to strengthen the new growth.

Huddled up in her dressing robe, cuddling against her mother, and with the little shorn head, she might have been a child of five, and the Gray Friar upon entering felt an unwelcome softness. As a humane physician he had answered Lady Swynford's frenzied plea for his services. Indeed he could not have refused, since he was retained by the Duke, but he had had to conquer a deep reluctance.

He had entirely avoided Katherine since the day in the courtyard by the falcon mew, and pleading his own ill health, had spent more and more time in his cell at Grayfriars in town, leaving the routine care of the Duke's meinie to two secular leeches. He had been troubled with no more wicked dreams of Katherine since the one in which she had been linked with disaster, and he wished to forget her and her continuing relationship with the Duke. He had done his duty by Blanchette and treated Katherine with rigid impersonality during the girl's illness, but he had been forced to admire the mother's devotion. Tonight he saw that Katherine was as pale and listless as her daughter and while he looked at Blanchette's tongue and felt the slow pulse in her neck, he spoke in a warmer voice than usual.

"Lady Swynford, we shall have you ailing too, if you don't

take care. I'll brew you some parsley water, and," he glanced around Blanchette's chamber, "this place holds unhealthful miasmas. Now the lass is better, I think you should move."

Katherine looked up, pleased by his kindly tone, and said eagerly, "To Kenilworth? But sure she's not well enough yet for that?"

"No," said the friar frowning. "I meant that you might move to another chamber, one with more air and light."

Katherine nodded thoughtfully and after a moment said, "Then we'll move to the Privy Suite. Those apartments are by far the most comfortable." And I, she thought, will sleep in the Avalon Chamber again. In the ruby velvet bed where she had passed so many ecstatic nights, and where John would seem nearer to her.

She was aware at once of the friar's withdrawal. He said stiffly, "There are many other rooms at the Savoy."

Blanchette too stirred and said in her weak little voice, "Oh Mama—don't let's leave here."

"Sweet heart, 'twill do you good," said Katherine briskly. "There are beautiful tapestries for you to look at, I'll tell you stories about them and you can watch the boats on the Thames, and there's the Duke's collection of little ivory saints —you'll like to play with them."

Blanchette drew her breath in, and Katherine realized that it was the first time the Duke's name had been mentioned since the girl's illness, yet surely all that resentment had been dissolved in the renewed love her child gave her. She was reassured when Blanchette murmured, "As you will, Mama."

Brother William frowned, but there was nothing he could say. The Duke's suite was certainly the most comfortable accommodation in the palace.

"Please sit down and sup with us," said Katherine gently. "You seem wan yourself, good Brother. There's no fresh sickness about, I hope."

"No more than usual," said the Gray Friar. "No new fevers at any rate. Ay, I am awearied." He sat down abruptly. "I'll take some wine." For months now there had been a gnawing in his stomach, but he did not bother to give himself remedies, he simply fasted more stringently and ignored it.

Katherine's ring of the hand bell was answered somewhat tardily by a servant she had never seen before, a pimply gat-toothed youth with scabs on his scalp. The points of his hose were untied and his blue and white livery was stained with grease.

"Where's Piers?" she said surveying the uncouth servant with disapproval.

"Piers be took wi' a colic," answered the lad staring at the ceiling. "So I come in his stead. I be called Perkin. What's your wish, m'lady?"

Katherine was slightly disturbed. Lately since Blanchette no longer required her every thought she had noticed a subtle unrest amongst the varlets, nothing so crude as insolence, but slight deviations from the smooth level of service she was accustomed to. The Savoy had been left with a skeleton staff, since the vast army of servants required to wait on the Duke and his retainers naturally moved with them from castle to castle. Katherine's own servants had traveled to Kenilworth with Hawise and the little Beauforts, and none of the family remained at the Savoy.

Elizabeth had gone to visit her mother-in-law, the Countess of Pembroke; the Lady Philippa was spending three months of retreat with the nuns at Barking Abbey; Henry divided his time between his little wife's ancestral de Bohun castle and the King's court at Windsor; and her own Tom Swynford was now formally attached to Henry's retinue.

The Savoy's ordinary maintenance staff was therefore ample for the needs of Katherine and Blanchette, but it seemed to her that this had grown uncommonly lax.

She gave the scabheaded Perkin the order for meat and wine and determined to question the chamberlain about the servants, when Brother William, who had been examining the lad intently, said, "Since I'm here, I'll have a look at this Piers' colic. Where does he lodge?"

Perkin's eyes shifted to the Gray Friar and he said, "No need of that, Sir Friar, 'tis but the common gripes."

*"Where is he now?"* repeated the friar, fixing his stern gaze on the reddening face.

"How should I know, sir?" said the lad sullenly. "He maught be lying in t' kitchen passage, or he maught've ta'en his pallet to the cellars, or he maught—"

"Have left the Savoy altogether on some errand of his own?" said the friar with chill emphasis.

The lad thrust out his underlip and did not answer, then seeing that there were to be no more questions, disappeared quickly.

"What did you mean by that?" asked Katherine frowning. "The varlets can't leave the castle wards without permission."

"There's a deal being done just now without permission," said the friar dryly. "There's rioting in Kent."

"What sort of riots?" asked Katherine after a moment. "Is it the poll tax again?"

"That and other grievances, all most ably dinned into the peasants by a priest called John Ball."

"But he's in gaol!" she cried. "My lord told me so and said the commons were quieting down."

The friar crossed his lean shanks, and resting his gaunt tonsured head against the chair back said with patience, "He *was* in gaol, but the Kentishmen have released him. There's been violence down in Kent, and Essex too, I hear."

Katherine thought of the russet-clad preacher she had seen at Leicester and the pounding ridiculous couplet the mob had chanted, and felt again a vague apprehension, though not of any personal danger, for rioting in Kent seemed nearly as remote as fighting in France. And it was not, thank God, like that black night in 'seventy-six when the people of London had gone mad with rage against Percy and the Duke. This seemed to her a matter of diffused and wearisome theory, and she had learned by now that there were always malcontents about.

"But what is it that the commons *want?*" she said impatiently. "Or rather," she amended, for well she knew the impossible things that the human heart could want, "what is it, in sanity, that they can hope to *get* by their riots?"

The friar raised his lids and looked at her. He smiled faintly. "They want the equality of man. They want freedom. You speak truth when you say that they cannot, in sanity, hope to get it—and especially by violence."

"Then they are mad!"

"Nay—not mad. Ignorant and desperate and oppressed. They're tired of paying for unsuccessful wars, they're tired of serfdom or unfair wages for their labor. They're tired of eating black bread while the manor lords, baron and abbot alike, eat venison and fat capons. It's natural, and a change will come in time, I believe."

Already there had been changes, the friar thought, since the Black Death in 'forty-nine had halved the population and thereby made a scarcity of labor. The old feudal system was crumbling gradually of its own weight without the explosions

that were designed to hasten its destruction. Yet Wyclif's re-
forms had done good, up to the point where the devil had got
hold of him and forced him into blasphemy. Even this fanati-
cal hedge-priest, John Ball, spoke truth in many of his rantings, though hatred and class war were dangerous double-
edged weapons.

Katherine had been considering the friar's remarks with
more attention than she had ever given to this problem of
bondage and privation and need of change, and she struggled
to express a feeling that the argument she had given for the
commons' side were not entirely just.

"But, Brother William," she said at last, "is it not also true
that in most cases the villeins are better off on the manors
where they were born and their forebears too?" She paused,
feeling some unease as to her own administration of Kettlethorpe, yet there they were handicapped in many ways and
the steward did the best he could. And the Duke's manors
were notably well run.

"A good manor lord *cares* for his serfs," she continued.
"He gives them ale feasts, and alms. In time of trouble he
protects them, feeds them, and he administers justice for
them that they have not the understanding to do for themselves. They're like his children."

The friar gave his rare chuckle. "You voice the arguments
for slavery that are old as Babylon and have satisfied many.
There are however others who prefer freedom to any benefits
—I don't know," he added half to himself, "what is *God's*
law."

He picked up his wooden crucifix and stared down at it. "I
only know that our Blessed Lord was a carpenter, and that
He said it was easier for a camel to go through the needle's
eye than for a rich man to get into heaven, and that the Holy
Saint Francis enjoined upon us poverty—which vow I've
tried to follow."

He sighed. It was true he had never broken his vows. He
kept none of the annuities the Duke gave him, but expended
them on charity or returned them to his order. And yet, was
he perhaps as much a parasite of the great Lancastrian feudality as that fat Carmelite, Walter Dysse? Or as the hundreds of retainers who battened off the Duke, or as— He
raised his eyes and looked at Katherine. If God would but
show me the way to save her, he thought in confusion. And
the Duke too, of course, from certain damnation; but the

Duke's fate did not touch him so nearly. Why not? *Domine libera nos a malo*—it surely could not be because of her cursed female beauty that he thought first of her—

Brother William's chair grated on the tiles. He shook himself to his feet. "The food is long in coming. I cannot wait. I'll be back in a day or so. Send if you have sooner need. *Benedicite.*" And he stalked out.

Katherine was used to his abruptness and did not try to stop him though it was lonely now at the Savoy, and she had been glad to talk to him. She had long ago accepted his disapproval, but she had had perfect trust in him and his leechcraft, as she had had at Hugh's bedside in Bordeaux.

Poor Hugh, she thought, faintly pitying. So long ago now and she could recall nothing of Hugh's face except the shape of the scar on his cheek.

Blanchette had spoken of her father while the fever clouded her wits. It seemed that she relived the moment when she had bade him goodbye at Kettlethorpe, repeating as Hugh must have said it to her, "Be a good little maid till I return and I'll bring you back a gift from France." It had sent tears to Katherine's eyes to listen to Blanchette's high excited voice as she quoted her father, and had made her think more gently of Hugh than she ever had. It was true that he had shown a shamefaced warmth for his little daughter, though Katherine had scarcely noticed it at the time, so eaten up with miserable love had she been for John.

She summoned Mab to help her get Blanchette back to bed, and while she washed the girl with cool rose water she thought with joy of the letter she had received yesterday. It had been sent from Knaresborough last week. John said that he was leaving at once for the Border, that Hawise and the babies had been duly dropped off at Kenilworth and were well. He missed her and expected to be back with her in a month or so. She carried the letter in her bodice next to her heart.

In thinking of it and in singing to Blanchette, who quickly fell asleep, she forgot for some time the extraordinary dilatoriness of the varlet she had sent for food, until hunger reminded her and brought sharp annoyance.

Katherine jangled the bell and after a while a sleepy little page appeared. "Fetch me the chamberlain at once!" she commanded. The boy bowed and scurried off. He returned in

a few minutes not with the chamberlain but with Roger
Leach, the sergeant-at-arms.

Katherine raised her eyebrows and the big soldier explained. "Chamberlain's gone to Outer Ward, m'lady. He'll
come to ye directly, but there's a party o' roving gleemen
come into the castle for night's lodging."

"Since when does the chamberlain concern himself personally with the vagabonds who take shelter here and give them
precedence over *my* summons?"

The sergeant looked uncomfortable. He pushed back his
helm and scratched his head where the leather caused it to
sweat. "Well, 'tis this, m'lady, chamberlain thought he best
hear what's going on. Some o' the varlets's packed theirsel's
round the gleemen, seeming so 'tranced wi' their songs, no
work's being done."

"No work's being done anyway," said Katherine. "I ordered wine and meat two hours back, nor has it come yet.
Have the varlets turned unruly, sergeant?"

"Nay, nay, m'lady!" Leach was shocked and his pride hurt.
Though he was directly responsible only for the men-at-arms
left at the Savoy, a dozen or so at present, he also aided the
old chamberlain and the butler and the master cook in keeping a disciplinary eye on the servants. " 'Tis but midsummer
giddiness 'mongst the young folk. A few switchings'll
straighten 'em out."

Katherine looked at him thoughtfully. "I think I'll go down
and listen to these gleemen's songs."

"Then I'll go wi' ye, m'lady," said the sergeant adjusting
his helm and squaring his shoulders under his padded leather
hauberk. "These gleemen shouldna been let in, 'twas that nid-
dering gateward done it."

From this Katherine gathered that the sergeant was a trifle
uneasy despite his denial. Travelers of all sorts, from beggars
to bishops, frequently came to request night's lodging and the
gateward could hardly be blamed for admitting a troupe of
gleemen.

She left Mab in charge of Blanchette and walked downstairs to the Outer Ward, where some thirty of the servants
were gathered in the angle between the chapel and the stables. They were very quiet, listening intently to five gleemen
with harps and bagpipes who were grouped around a well
and singing. One of the men stood on the well curb and
seemed to be the leader. Katherine stared at him searchingly,

half expecting that it might be the rebel preacher John Ball;
but it most certainly was not. This was a pretty lad in a loose
blue and scarlet minstrel's jerkin, and the song he sang had
nothing to do with Adam and Eve. It sounded rather like a
nursery rhyme.

The gleeman sang in a clear flutelike voice and his fellows
hummed the melody, which was plaintive and charming:

> *Jack Milner asketh help to turn his mill aright.*
> *For he hath grounden small, small, small*
> *The King's son of heaven he payeth for all.*
> *With might and with right, with skill and with will*
> *Right before might, then turns our mill aright*
> *But if might goes before right then is the mill misadight.*

" 'Tis gibberish," said the sergeant contemptuously. "No
sense to ut."

As he spoke the intent crowd became aware of Katherine.
There was a murmuring as heads were turned. She saw Piers,
her usual servitor, the scabheaded Perkin and others. They
looked at her from the corners of their eyes, and one by one
began to melt away towards the kitchens and the stables.

The young glee leader on the well curb made Katherine a
little bow, and called out in a pleasant voice, "Shall we sing
for *you,* fair lady? We know many a dainty love tune. Or
shall we juggle for you? By the rood, there's no gleemen in
England can do more jolly tricks than we."

"Nay, not tonight, I thank you," she answered. He was a
comely youth, and she could not believe that his miller's song
had any sinister meaning. Minstrels sang on many topics, and
if that jingle had some political reference that escaped her,
still a song could do no harm.

She found that the chamberlain agreed with her. He had
been listening too from the shadow of the bargehouse and he
hastened to join Katherine and the sergeant.

She spoke sternly to the chamberlain about the neglectful
servants, and he stammered and begged her forgiveness while
tugging unhappily at his spare gray beard.

Katherine returned to Blanchette and at once Piers came
to the chamber with her belated supper. He apologized for
his attack of colic and for the stupidity of Perkin, who had
come in his stead. He waited on her with his usual smooth

efficiency, and Katherine felt that she had been unduly nervous. She did however summon the sergeant once more.

"Can you find out about these gleemen?" she said to him.

"I have, m'lady," answered the sergeant complacently. He had shared a mazer of ale with the young leader and found him a courteous merryhearted youth who was even now entertaining the varlets' hall with a series of good old-fashioned bawdy songs that everyone knew, and could understand.

"They be good lads," said the sergeant with confidence. "No harm in 'em at all. They've come from Canterbury, where they played for the Princess Joan who was on pilgrimage, and they're bound for Norfolk to play at some lord's bridal feast."

"Yet I hear there's rioting in Kent, sergeant," said Katherine, uncertainly.

"Ay, m'lady, so I've heard too," he said soothingly. "But what o' that? There's no danger here at the Savoy wi' me an' me men to guard it. Them churls down Kent way'll never come to Lunnon, an' if they did they'd not come here—why should they?"

To be sure, why should they? thought Katherine. She saw from the twinkle in the sergeant's eye that he thought she was being silly and womanish and that whatever misgivings he had had earlier were now gone.

"Very well," she said with a smile. "I know I couldn't ask for a better protector. His Grace has often told me of your courage."

The sergeant flushed with gratification. A simple man was the sergeant, and passionately loyal to the Duke, under whom he had served in battles as far back as Nájera. He thrust out his chest and said beaming, "Thanks, m'lady. And how's the little maid now?" He glanced at the bed where Blanchette was sleeping.

"Much better. We'll leave here for Kenilworth next week, I hope."

"Ay—ye'll be longing to see your other little ones. 'Tis a good mother ye are, m'lady, I was saying that to me old wife only yestere'en—" The sergeant gulped and stopped, remembering his wife's pithy retort which had to do with the highly irregular status of Lady Swynford's motherhood. "I'll be off to me duties, if you please."

Katherine sat on for a few minutes in the window seat. The chamber was cool and dark, the long June twilight had

at last faded and only the watch candle burned in its silver
sconce by the bed.

A good mother? Katherine thought. The sergeant's blunt
compliment touched her.

She walked to the bed and drawing the curtains looked
down at Blanchette. The small face beneath the cropped curls
seemed pinched and defenseless, the childish hands were
curled open on the fine linen sheet.

Blanchette stirred and murmured something, her fingers
plucked restlessly at the sheet. Katherine lay down beside
her and the girl sighed and grew quiet. Katherine drew her
against her breast, Blanchette nestled as she had used to do
long ago, the whole of her slight body lax and trusting in her
mother's arms. A warm blissful tenderness flowed over
Katherine and she rested her cheek softly against the clustering curls.

Suddenly Blanchette started and giving a moan, sat up and
opened her eyes.

"What is it, darling?" Katherine cried. The girl's eyes were
dazed, and Katherine repeated her question. Since the bursting of her eardrums, Blanchette did not hear keenly.

Blanchette licked her pale fever-chapped lips, and gave a
frightened little laugh. "Dream—" she said, "horrible dream
—I was drowning and you—" She stared at her mother's
anxious face and stiffened, drawing away. "By Sainte Marie,
how silly to be frightened by a dream," Blanchette said in a
strange tight voice. She crossed herself, then as though the familiar protective gesture had suddenly developed meaning,
she said, "Mother, do you ever pray any more?"

"Why darling, of course I do," said Katherine much startled. "I've prayed for your recovery, I went to Mass this
morning—"

"But not the way you used to. I remember when I was little, at Kettlethorpe—it was different. And you're right: prayers
do no good. I don't believe Christ or His Mother or the
saints care what happens to us—if indeed any of them really
exists."

"Blanchette!" cried Katherine, much shocked to have the
child voice the wicked doubts that she had felt herself.
"These are sick fancies—"

She went on for some time, to speak of God's omnipotence
and the efficacy of the saints, giving arguments and reassurance that sounded hollow to her own ears, and saw with dis-

may that the shut-in look of before her illness had come back to Blanchette's face. But at last the girl spoke gently. "Ay, Mama, I know." She sighed and pulled herself to the far side of the bed. "I'm so tired—I cannot listen any more."

# XXIV

THE NEXT DAY, Monday, June 10, Katherine and Blanchette moved over to the Privy Suite. Blanchette had never before been in the ducal apartments, and despite her scruples the girl could not withhold wondering admiration when Katherine helped her walk into the Avalon Chamber. It had been a lovely tower room to start with, but each year the Duke improved it, spending lavish sums on its enhancement. The mantel of rose Carrara marble, brought by galley from Genoa, had been placed last month, and had taken a master mason two years to carve it with a frieze of falcons, roses, castles and ostrich feathers to embrace all the Duke's emblems.

The window on the Thames had been enlarged, and deepened to an oriel. Along the top half of its three lights ran exquisite tinted scenes of the life of St. Ursula with her eleven thousand virgins, though below the panes had been left clear to show the river view. The prie-dieu in a corner niche was of ivory and gold, cushioned with white satin, and it had come from Castile. The red velvet bed was unchanged except that its curtains and tester had been freshened with new embroidery: the Duke had ordered that a sprinkling of her tiny gold Catherine wheels be cunningly inserted amongst the seed pearl foliage, and this had pleased Katherine mightily.

And still beside the bed hung the great Avalon tapestry, with the dark mysterious greens of the enchanted forest and the luminous figures of Arthur, Guenevere and the wizard Merlin.

Katherine never saw the tapestry without remembering what John had said of Merlin's castle when she first came to this room twelve years ago, "It reminds me of one I saw in Castile."

Little had she known then of how much that meant to him.

In seeking to divert Blanchette, Katherine told her a little about the tapestry, but the girl was not much interested, she preferred to sit in the window and watch the river flow by, and as Katherine had hoped, she was delighted with the finger-high ivory figurines of the saints. St. Agnes with her lamb, St. Cecilia with her dulcimer, St. Bartholomew with his flayed skin draped gracefully over his arm—all were carved with an amusing fidelity to life and were, like the little faces on the corbels of churches, obviously portraits of people that the artist had known. The figure of St. Apollonia, holding pincers and a large tooth as symbols of her martyrdom, was so realistic in its swollen jaw and twisted mouth that Blanchette laughed outright.

"Ah, poppet," said Katherine smiling, "you'd not laugh if you'd ever had toothache; it seems 'tis no laughing matter."

"Have you, Mama?" said the girl, putting down Apollonia.

"Nay, I've been lucky, I've all my teeth yet. Though the Duke—" she hesitated. But with Blanchette now, God be thanked, one no longer had to tread gingerly and avoid mention of everything that had once disturbed her. "The Duke has suffered cruelly with toothache at times, and Hawise, too—as you know."

"Poor souls," said Blanchette absently. She had picked up the figure of the North Country saint, Columba, who held a dove. She touched the dove's tiny head and looked up at her mother. "What happened to my green linnet?"

"It's well, I've fed it myself. We'll send for it so you can hang it in your room."

The girl's gray eyes grew thoughtful, and she said, "I left the cage door open, didn't I—the day I sickened? Didn't it fly away?"

"No," Katherine smiled. "But I've shut the door now. So you may free the bird yourself, as you love to do."

"Perhaps it's happy in its cage, after all," said Blanchette slowly. She looked out of the window towards the line of trees across the river where the rooks were circling. "Perhaps it would be frightened out there."

"It might be," said Katherine. Her heart swelled with gladness. Blanchette was better in every way, not only recovered from the illness, but from all the strange dark rebellions that had preceded it for so long. At last, the girl gave voice to some of her thoughts, and the stammer in her speech had almost disappeared. Soon, Katherine decided she might speak frankly about Robin Beyvill and Sir Ralph, find out what the girl really felt, and help her to understand herself.

Blanchette's pale face flushed suddenly, she looked down at the window seat and busied herself with standing the saints carefully in a row while she said, "You've been good to me, dearest Mama."

Katherine caught her breath while her arms ached to hug and shelter, but she knew that she must not force this new delicate balance. She contented herself with a quick kiss. "And why not, mouse!" she said lightly.

Tuesday and Wednesday they had a happy time together. With windows wide open to the soft June air they passed the hours in songs and games. Blanchette played her lute, and Katherine a gittern. Katherine taught her the gay old tune, "Hè, Dame de Vaillance!" and they sang it in rondo. They played at Merelles and at "Tables," the backgammoning game, with silver counters on a mother-of-pearl board. They asked each other riddles and tried to invent new ones. Katherine, in persuading her child to lightheartedness, found gaiety herself, dimmed only by a worry over Blanchette's hearing, but that would certainly soon improve.

Piers brought them up delicious food, Mab waited on them methodically, the chamberlain reported that all was running smoothly with the servants and they saw nobody else. Each found rich reward in this companionship and forgot the painful disagreements that had chafed them before.

Blanchette visibly gained much strength. She could walk about their chambers without help, she was eating well, and some color had returned to her thin cheeks. Next week they could certainly leave for Kenilworth, Katherine thought joyously—and not very long after that she might begin to look for John's return.

On Wednesday evening the courtyard clock beat out seven strokes as they finished their supper in the Avalon Chamber. Blanchette munched on marchpane doucettes, especially made for her by the head pastry cook, while Katherine sipped the last drops of the rich amber wine that remained in her hanap. These goblets that they were using were their own, and exceedingly beautiful.

Blanchette's hanap of silver-gilt with her cipher was the

one given her so long ago as a christening present by the Duke, and Katherine's was a recent New Year's gift from him, a hollow crystal banded with purest gold. This hanap was called Joli-coeur, because a garnet heart was inlaid in its gold cover, and Katherine thought that the goblet always gave to its contents a savor as delicate as its name.

"Brother William hasn't been here since Sunday," said Katherine idly. "Maybe he'll come tonight—though you scarcely need his skill any more, God be thanked." She put down Joli-coeur and pushed back from the table with a contented sigh.

"I hope he does," said Blanchette reaching for another doucette. "I like him. He looks ugly and grim, yet his hands're gentle. He was like a kind father while I was sick. 'Tis pity he mayn't have children of his own, isn't it?"

Katherine assented, faintly amused at the thought of the friar in a fatherly role. Certain it was that Brother William never had been a secret father, whatever irregular paternity might be indulged in by the rest of the clergy. "He's an exceeding righteous man," she said with some dryness. There was a knock on the door, and she called "Enter!" thinking that it might be the friar come now.

It was a page who announced that there was a tradesman below in the antechamber who wished to see Lady Swynford. A Guy le Pessoner.

"Master Guy!" exclaimed Katherine. "Show him up, to be sure," and to Blanchette said, " 'Tis Hawise's father."

The fishmonger came in puffing and mopped his glistening moon face on his brown wool sleeve. He bowed to Katherine, glanced at Blanchette and wheezed, "Whew! 'Tis warm for one o' my port to be ahurrying."

Katherine smiled and indicated a chair. "A pleasure to see you."

Master Guy's great belly gradually ceased to heave. He put his thick red hands on his knees. "Where's Hawise, m'lady?" he said abruptly.

"At Kenilworth with my little Beauforts. She left a month ago when the Duke went north."

"Ah—" said the fishmonger. " 'Twas what I be telling Emma, but she made me come anyhow."

"Why?" asked Katherine. "Is anything wrong?"

"Nay—not what ye might call *wrong*," he shrugged. " 'Tis more that me dame's a dithering old 'oman." Master Guy stuck his thumbs in the armholes of his jerkin and frowned.

These last two days there was no doubt that the rebellion had become more serious. The Kentish mob had advanced as close as Blackheath across the river, while Essex men neared London from the North. Dame Emma had kept badgering him to go and make sure that Hawise was out of possible danger. She had heard a rumor that Lady Swynford remained at the Savoy, though the Duke had left.

"What does Dame Emma dither about then?" asked Katherine anxiously.

"She thinks if them ribauds over on Blackheath should cross the river into Lunnon, there maught be a bad time. I tell her 'tis folly. The King'll calm 'em down. All they want is to set their grievances afore the King. Besides they can't *get* into town. The drawbridge's up, and the gates all closed." He paused. True, the gates were closed and the drawbridge up now, but there were aldermen who sympathized with the rebels. John Horn and Walter Sibley, a fellow fishmonger who was responsible for holding London bridge. You couldn't trust either of 'em far as you'd throw a cat. They'd veer either way they thought to their advantage.

"Devil take the lot o' them!" said Master Guy irritably. His hotheaded days were over. All he wanted was to be left in peace with his prosperous business. But there were plenty in London as well as out who clamored for change, clamored murderously—like Jack.

"I know nothing of all this, Master Guy," said Katherine slowly, "except that there were riots in Kent. I thought the King was at Windsor."

"He's in the Tower now—wi' the Princess Joan and a mort o' the lords and Mayor Walworth. They've got t' old archbishop with 'em and Hales, the treasurer, too, which be canny, or the rebels'd 've strung them two makers of the stinking poll tax up to the nearest trees."

Katherine considered this with astonishment but no particular fear. So the King was in the Tower of London, the strongest fortress in England. Was this from prudence, or because it was easier from there to negotiate with the peasants?

"Has the King talked to the rebels yet?" she asked.

"Nay, he went down river by barge this morn from the Tower to Rotherhithe, but he didn't land. They scuttered back to the Tower again. 'Tis said some o' his lords turned poltroon when they saw the great mob that was awaiting on the bank."

"The poor lad," said Katherine, thinking of the sensitive delicate boy she had seen last Christmastime at Leicester. "He's overyoung to make decisions."

Blanchette had been listening eagerly, straining to hear. Now she leaned forward and spoke with a spark of humor, "The King's not so very young, Mama. He may know better than his elders."

"For sure *you'd* think so, since you're both fourteen—a great age!" said Katherine smiling. She turned back to Master Guy. "I understand from what you say these rebels are loyal to the King?"

"Oh, ay—'tis so." The fishmonger nodded ponderously. "They fly his banner with that of Saint George on Blackheath."

"Then there can be no great danger from them," said Katherine confidently.

She rose and poured ale from a silver flagon into a mazer and handed it to Master Guy, saying, "Forgive me that I did not offer this sooner, but I forgot in the interest of your news. How's Hawise's Jack, by the bye?"

The fishmonger drained his ale and cried, "Spleen! God's wounds, but there ne'er was such a churl for grudges'n spleen. I've had me bellyful o' him. He's still hot against the Duke, o' course, but 'tis the Flemings he chiefly cries out 'gainst now. The Flemish weavers've cut into his trade. I warrant he'd slice all their throats an he could. A bloodthirsty knave is Jack, I begin to think Hawise well shed o' him." He lumbered up out of his chair, belched heartily and said, "Well, m'lady, I'll be off. 'Twill not be easy even for me to get back through Ludgate if I linger."

He hesitated, knowing that he had not given the full urgency of Dame Emma's message. "If Hawise be there or Lady Swynford, tell 'em to hasten north while they yet may." But he deemed his wife overfearful, and actually if rumor were true, no roads were safe that led to London. There were stealthy uprisings all about. Besides, commons didn't war on women and these two were better off here in this great walled palace than anywhere, come trouble. He salved a prick of conscience by saying, "Warn your men-at-arms to be on guard and make sure the water gates're lowered, then ye needna have a care. I'll warrant anyhow 'twill all blow over."

Katherine thanked him for coming and sent her love to Dame Emma. When the fishmonger had gone, she summoned Sergeant Leach and repeated Master Guy's advice.

"Have no fear, m'lady," said the sergeant brightening. The possibility of a little action pleased him, though he had scant hope of gratification now. What could a handful of farmers do, armed as he had heard with picks and staves and scythes, and led by an unfrocked priest and some tiler called Wat?

The tiler may fling his tiles at us, thought Leach grinning to himself, and the villeins may brandish their ploughshares—a lot o' good it'll do 'em.

He went off happily to alert his men-at-arms, to order the great crossbarred portcullis lowered at the Strand, and to check on the security of the water gates. He issued extra arms from the well-stocked armory: maces, battle-axes, swords, breastplates and shields, and instructed the assembled varlets in their use in case his bowmen should need reinforcement.

There were three barrels of gunpowder stored near the armory and there was a small brass cannon mounted on the gatehouse, but the sergeant had no faith in either. Firearms were unreliable and in his opinion worthless. No newfangled weapon could equal an English bowman, and his men were skilled veterans of the French wars.

When dusk fell, the sergeant threw himself down to sleep in the guardroom with a mind as quiet as the evening air.

Katherine too felt secure after re-examining Master Guy's scanty information. Blackheath was seven miles away in Kent, and by morning no doubt the King and his advisors, the Archbishop Sudbury or the mayor, would certainly have decided on some course of action, and appease or quell the rioters.

She knelt on the seat cushion and looked out of the window, up and down the river, but she could see no sign of disturbance anywhere. Water lapped softly on the stone wall below, the sundown sky above Westminster was stained with cool after-tints of lavender and saffron. Through the angled righthand light of the oriel she could see a corner of the gardens, where fireflies shone their fitful little lamps against a bank of Provençal roses. The rose fragrance drifted up to Katherine on a lazy breeze.

She inhaled deeply and turning with a smile to Blanchette quoted from the "Romaunt."

> *Me thinketh I feel it in my nose*
> *The sweet savour of the rose!*

Blanchette sat up, her eyes bright and responsive. She
thought a moment, then proudly added another quotation,
for reading of romances had been her chiefest pleasure during the last lonely years.

> *Always be merry if thou may;*
> *But waste not thy good alway,*
> *Have hat of flowers as fresh as May*
> *Chaplet of roses of Whitsunday!*

They looked at each other and burst out laughing.

"Ah, we're a couple of giddy queans!" cried Katherine,
shaking her head. " 'Tis wrong of me. I should be giving you
moral precepts, as the good Chevalier de la Tour Landry
does to his daughters. Fie upon me!"

"Ay—Mama," said Blanchette with the new, charming glint
of pert humor that delighted Katherine. " 'Tis naughty indeed
that you don't."

"Well, at any rate, it's time for bed, poppet," said Katherine pinching her cheek. "You're sleepy and so'm I—you
know, I believe 'twill be fair tomorrow. We might dare your
strength as far as the gardens."

"Ay, that I'd love," said Blanchette eagerly.

When Katherine helped the girl to bed and smoothed down
the sheet, they kissed each other a warm, happy good night.

Down and across the river at Blackheath, the rebel mob
had grown larger hour by hour until ten thousand desperate
hungry men surged back and forth across the trampled gorse
and heather. They quietened only when John Ball clambered
on a tree stump and shouted to them. By daylight and then
by torchlight they could see his lank figure in the russet
robes, his arms upraised as he called on God to help them;
and many could see the wild crusading light in his eyes.

He told them that their hour had struck at last. "John Ball
hath y-rung the bell!" he cried in a great exultant voice.

All over England they were ready. The members of the
"fellowship" had been traveling for weeks, they had whispered in the manors, they had sung "Jack Milner" in the halls

and village greens, and all who were in sympathy would understand.

John Ball preached his great sermon to them there on Blackheath, telling them how God had created all men equal in the days of Adam and Eve, and how there were then no rich lords or bishops—and there were no slaves.

Like the pounding of ocean surf, the couplet he had given them roared out from the thousands of throats: "When Adam delved and Eve span, who was *then* a gentleman?"

He waited until they finished, stilled them with a gesture. "My poor friends," he cried in a voice that was hoarse and cracking from strain, "things cannot go right in England, nor ever will until everything shall be in common. And there shall be no more lords and vassals! How ill they've used us! Ragged starvelings that we be, we swink in wind and rain that they may loll in furred velvet, warm in their snug manors, glutting their bellies. Ay, by the Holy Rood, my poor friends, we shall change that now!"

They had heard all this many times before, but never with the growing frenzied hope. Now as the fierce preacher's voice trembled and failed him, their leader Wat, the tiler from Maidstone, climbed up on the stump and rehearsed to them their last instructions.

A hairy, powerful grim man was Wat, and thirsting for revenge—some said because his daughter had been raped by a tax collector—but no reason was needed to swell the torment of blind hatred in all their breasts. They would kill their enemies as men have always killed in warfare, and for far more righteous cause.

They had sent to the King a list of the men who must be delivered to them for vengeance. The traitors who were deluding and defrauding their little King.

They had demanded the heads of Simon of Sudbury, the archbishop-chancellor who had instigated the poll tax and who had imprisoned John Ball; of Robert Hales, Treasurer of England and prior of the hated Templars of St. John, where sly money-grabbing lawyers were bred. They demanded the death of twelve others whom they had cause to hate—and the head of John o' Gaunt. They all greatly feared the wicked Duke who was so bloated with lands and power, and yet who traitorously craved to be king—as everyone knew. A monster of villainy, they thought him. Like the first John who had

plotted against another royal Richard and ground all England
into misery.

Wat shouted out the list of heads that they had demanded
from the King, and at each name the crowd roared until the
doors rattled in the rustic cots along the heath. They stamped
until dust rose in clouds as thick as the smoke of their bonfires and torches.

But when he named John o' Gaunt, sharp cries mingled
with their uproar. " 'Tis sooth, by God, we'll have no king
called John!" "Never more a king called John on English
soil! We shall slay that traitor first and pull his castle down
about his ears!"

When they simmered down and listened again, Wat went
on to remind them yet once more of the cornerstone that
supported all their purpose. Soon, he said, there would be an
answer from King Richard, who would surely meet them for
a parley this time. Here they groaned. They had been sorely
disappointed when the King's barge turned and put back to
the Tower without greeting them this morning.

"Yet all must be seemly done in our revenge!" cried Wat.
"No plundering, no ravishing! Commons be not thieves, remember! Commons be honest men who right a fearful wrong
as surely as ever a knight went on crusade!"

They stamped and bellowed and waved their St. George
pennants. Wat reached over from the stump and seized the
King's standard, he raised it high into the sky until all could
see the royal lilies and leopards. "And commons be *loyal!*" he
shouted. "Our little anointed King'll be our true liege leader
like his blessed princely father was, God rest his soul!"

Wat put the standard down and cupping his hands around
his mouth, he roared out, "With whom holdes you?"

In one mighty voice they answered with the watchword.

"With King Richard and the true commons!"

Wat nodded heavily and got down off the stump. He
glanced at the preacher, whose face was upturned to the pale
new stars and saw that John Ball was praying, open-eyed,
while slow tears ran down his cheeks.

"Christ's mercy, but I hope them aldermen'll soon open
the Bridge," Wat murmured.

The peasant army had had no food that day, would have
none until they got in to London. It was cruel hard to hold in
check so wild and mixed a mob. Here were not only angry

farmers and bondsmen, but outlaws and gaolbirds too, aplenty.

Even as Wat spoke, a voice cried out, "To the Marshalsea, men!" and another called, "Yea! Burn the Marshalsea and on to Lambeth! The city cravens see what we'll do on *this* shore, they'll not tarry in coming to terms!"

The rabble shifted and wavered, a dozen broke away and began to run towards the western road. Others followed brandishing torches, some armed with rusty old swords, with picks and hoes and cudgels; here and there a bowman, but the bows were warped and aged, the arrows nearly featherless.

The crowd grew dense that thundered off towards Southwark, and Wat watched uneasily. "An they do more harm'n we meant," he growled, biting his lips, " 'twill mayhap hurt our cause."

John Ball started. Hearing the tiler's words, he lowered his head and looked to see what was happening.

"Not so," he whispered hoarsely. "Naught can harm our cause, for it is God's. They'll but root out the noxious weeds that choke our crops— Mind ye, tiler, what the Blessed Christ has said! 'I came not to send peace, but a sword.' *He* will guide us aright."

Wat's misgivings were silenced, and he thrilled to the confidence that John Ball inspired, but Wat was a man of action, and his mind darted to practical matters. "What of Jack Strawe, Sir Priest?" he asked anxiously. "Think ye his men've entered the city yet by Aldgate?"

This was their plan, long agrowing and ripe at last, that the men who had rallied in Essex should broach London by her eastern gate, while the southern army crossed over on the Bridge.

"If they have not, they soon will," answered the preacher with calm certainty. "We shall succeed in all our aims!"

Katherine awoke suddenly and for no reason in the dawn hour of that Thursday, June 13, which was the Feast of Corpus Christi. She listened drowsily for some time to the sound of distant bells and thought that the church processions were starting early in honor of the Blessed Sacrament, and that this day she would certainly go to Mass. She had been lax too long.

Gradually it seemed to her that the rhythm of the bells was

somewhat violent and clamorous to be the usual summons to
Matins, or yet to signalize the start of a procession. She sat
up in bed and pulled the velvet curtains back. Already the
brief June hours of darkness had faded; gray light sharpened
the forms of the furniture, the gilt carved tables and chairs,
the ivory prie-dieu. She glanced towards the window and
was mildly surprised to see the sky flushed with redness. It
must be later than she had thought if this were sunrise.

She started to ring for Mab, who slept on a pallet in the
passage, but instead she slipped out of bed, and flinging her
chamber robe around her, padded on naked feet across the
tiles and peered curiously out of the window.

She blinked and stared again.

Downriver, in the neighborhood of Southwark, the sky was
lurid, and dense smoke billowed up against pale lemon-colored streaks of dawn. While nearer in a different place to the
south past Lambethmoor, she saw high leaping tongues of
flame.

"Jesu—" she whispered. "The Surrey bank's afire!" She
flung open the leaded window and thrust her head and shoulders out. Still too dazed by sleep and astonishment to com-
prehend, she thought, Can it be Lambeth Palace burning, or
Kennington? Nothing else to the south could cause so great a
fire. She looked again downriver and saw a shower of sparks
wing up into a brick-red sky.

She shut the window and turned uncertainly back, staring
into the familiar, beautiful room. Her bare feet were cold on
the tiles and she shivered, then walked to the bedside, where
her brocaded slippers lay. Thank God the fires're safely
across the river, she thought. I must send some of our men
over to help.

She jumped as there came a banging on her door. It flew
back and Brother William stalked in.

Katherine's chamber robe dropped open as she whirled
around, the friar averted his eyes from the glimpse of white
nakedness, and said, "Dress yourself quickly, Lady Swynford
—and the child—there's danger."

She clutched her robe around her. "What's happened?" she
whispered. "There's fire out there."

The friar glanced towards the window's ruddy light and
said grimly, "There's a deal more than fire. The peasant
army's pouring into London. Hasten—don't waste time in
chatter!"

She stared into his eyes, saw that his haggard face was as gray as his habit, yet that he breathed fast as though he had been running. She obeyed him blindly, forcing her hands to quietness as she dressed herself in the garderobe. Where's Mab? she thought, and forgot the woman. She put on a linen shift, and by instinct pulled down from the perch the plainest of her gowns, an old loose one of dark green wool in which she had nursed Blanchette during the worst of the illness.

"Hasten!" called Brother William fiercely as she was plaiting her hair. Her heart jumped and she bundled all the loose bronze mass into a net and bound a white coif over it. She clasped on a woven girdle and attached her blazoned purse, then she ran to arouse Blanchette.

"I know, sweet," she answered as quietly as she could to the girl's sleepy protest, "But Brother William's come. He says we must get dressed."

While Katherine was gone, the friar stood by the rose marble mantel staring down at the hearth, listening for the first sounds that should announce that the London mob had arrived at the Savoy gate. He knew that he had not outdistanced them by long.

He had seen the London prentices and rebels begin to rally. Aldgate had been opened and the Essex men already overran the streets and joined their partisans inside the walls. In the milling throng and darkness no one had noticed the hurrying Gray Friar, while they dragged some wretched screaming Fleming from his bed and butchered him with howls of glee, and the friar had heard other shouts on the fringes of the crowd. "The Savoy first—ay—'tis Lunnon's right to get there first afore them Kentishmen can do it."

The friar had kicked and pounded his nag to get here in time.

In a few minutes Katherine came back with Blanchette. The girl was dressed in her dove-gray chamber robe, since her daytime clothes had been packed away during her illness. Both women were pale, but the friar saw in one sharp appraising glance how much his little patient had improved: she walked unaided, albeit slowly.

"Good," said the friar. They were both well shod in leather shoes, their wool gowns were practical enough. "Take hooded mantles," he said to Katherine. "Put your jewels in your purse, and have you any money?"

"Two or three nobles—" she answered steadily. "Brother William, what is it—what's happening?"

He raised his hand. "Hark!"

From far off on the Strand by the Outer Ward they heard confused noises, a medley of shouts and a dull roaring. As they listened, the sound swelled and rose.

" 'Tis like the bellowing of penned bulls," said Blanchette cocking her head. "Are there bulls near here, Sir Friar?"

Down Katherine's back ice flowed. She had heard that roaring before as she stood on the step of the Pessoner home five years ago.

"Sweet Christ," she whispered, "what can we do?"

"The sergeant and his men'll hold the gate," said the friar. For a goodish while at least, he thought. But he had seen that the sergeant had had no inkling of the numbers or temper of the rebels. "We've plenty of time to get you away by barge —upstream to safety, past Westminster. No cause to fear," he said to Blanchette who gazed at him dumbly.

"The privy stairs," cried Katherine, her mind working fast, " 'tis quicker."

She scooped some jewels at random from her casket and seized two mantles for herself and Blanchette. The friar put his arm around the trembling girl and they went along the passage to the Duchess Blanche's old garderobe and through the door behind the arras, down the steps to the hidden door that opened behind the empty falcon mew. They stepped into the Outer Ward near the bargehouse, and stopped aghast.

The great portcullis of the gatehouse slowly lifted as they stood staring into the court. Roger Leach had ranged himself with his men-at-arms on the inside of the gatehouse. He gave a loud cry of astonished rage as the portcullis lifted and sprang forward with his sword upraised. His bowmen had their arrows notched ready in the thongs, drawn back for shooting. But they had no time to take aim. The mob poured through the gate in a cataract and were on top of them.

The bowmen flung down their useless bows and fought hand to hand with mace and sword.

The sergeant shouted with what breath he had, while he laid on desperately right and left, but this vanguard of the horde were armed Londoners, not starveling peasants. He shouted for help from the Savoy varlets, but only a handful rushed up in answer, and they were soon overwhelmed.

The other servants stayed in their hall, crouching, waiting,

some laughing hysterically as they heard the battle rage outside. Like the gateward and his helpers who had raised the
portcullis, they gibbered with triumphant excitement and
chanted, "Jack Milner is grinding small, small, small—John
Ball hath now y-rung the bell!"

The Gray Friar and his two charges stood flattened, petri-
fied, across the sunlit court against the plaster wall of the falcon mew. The mob did not notice them. Leaping and shouting, it pounded past the chapel towards the Inner Ward, and
above their heads the tall friar saw a fountainspurt of blood
spray the buttress of the gatehouse. He saw the sword
knocked from the sergeant's hand and another flash of steel
as Leach's helmet was sent spinning from his head. He saw
the sergeant's body spitted high in the air on a spear, and
twirling before it fell to the paving stones, where it was trampled by the insurging rabble.

Three of the men-at-arms fought on against some of the
London prentices, but the mob—now near a thousand strong
—streamed past them indifferently to plunge into the Great
Hall, into the chancery, to batter on the Treasure Chamber.

"*Christus!*" cried the friar, grabbing the two women's arms.
"Back! We must get back upstairs!" No hope now of escape
by barge. The water gates were closed and there was none to
help. He thrust the women behind him towards the little hidden door, and as they stumbled panting into the arch, a sandy
shock-haired man in leather helm and breastplate veered
away from the main stream of the mob.

It was Jack Maudelyn, who had special knowledge of the
Savoy and greater personal hate than any of the rebels. His
sharp questing eyes had seen the friar and recognized him.
Jack charged down the courtyard, flourishing his pike. "Ho!"
he shouted, his yellow teeth bared in a wolf grin, his freckled
face twisted like a devil mask. "So 'tis the puling friar what
sucks gold from the paps o' Lancaster and licks the arses o'
the rich! But I'll mend your ways for ye!" He raised his pike.

The unarmed friar stood rigid, barring the archway, where
behind him Katherine gasped, fumbling frantically at the
doorlatch.

"What's that!" cried Jack, catching the shadow of movement behind Brother William. The weaver shoved the friar
violently aside and, peering into the archway, cried, "By God,
'tis John o' Gaunt's whore! Here men—" he yelled, whirling

back into the courtyard. "Here's merry sport. Here, here to me!" His cry ended in a grunt.

The friar's great bony fist had shot out and landed full center of the weaver's face. Jack staggered and lunged forward with his pike. The lance-shaped point slashed down across the friar's chest, it tore through his habit and pierced deep beside the breastbone. The friar's fist hammered out again and caught the weaver on the left corner of his jaw. Jack reeled, spitting out a tooth, and fell down. Bunching his habit with one hand against the welling blood from his torn chest, the friar picked up Jack's pike.

Still the Londoners and Essex men rampaged through the gate following the others. None had heard Jack's cry. The friar turned and ran into the archway, where Katherine had got the door opened at last. They shut and locked it behind them, and stumbled up the privy stairs back to the Avalon Chamber. It was Katherine who from instinct led them back there where she felt safest. The friar and Blanchette followed.

Brother William helped Katherine shoot the great iron bars through the hasps on the oaken door that led to the Presence Chamber. They locked the small door to the Duchess's bower where Blanchette had slept and pushed the massive table up against it.

"Now we're secure. They can't get in here," whispered Katherine foolishly. She knew not what she said, nor understood quite what had happened. From the shadow of the arch she had seen Jack's exultant leer and seen him fall, but she did not know that the sergeant and his men were dead, nor had she seen what a multitude had thundered through the wards.

Blanchette sank down into a chair, dazed and shivering. Katherine poured ale from the silver flagon and gave her some, then turning to the friar she started and cried, "Jesu, Brother—you're hurt!"

The friar swallowed. He stood hunched and doubled over, holding his hands to his breast, while scarlet oozed down the gray habit. "Ay," he said in a far-off voice, "ay."

She ran to him and pulled him to the bed. He lay down without resistance. "Staunch it—" he said. "A clean cloth." There were towels in the garderobe but that was barred from her now. She pulled a corner of the sheet from under the friar and wadded it into the gaping wound, pressing it down as he told her.

" 'Twill serve awhile," he said. His cavernous eyes opened wide. He looked up at her as she bent over him. He saw the lovely, pitying, frightened face of his dream.

A moment he gazed upward, before he turned his head and shut his eyes. "Disaster—" he whispered. "The ill-starred day has come that I saw long ago. I shall die," he said with dull certainty. "No matter."

Beneath the torn cassock and the bloody wad of sheet, his emaciated chest heaved painfully, he struggled to his elbow and looked at her again. "But first you shall hear the truth at last!"

"Brother—good Brother—I beg you to lie quiet," said Katherine, pushing him gently down on to the bed. "You won't die. For sure 'tis not so deep a wound as that."

He lay quiet again beneath her soft hand, his lips moved in the Miserere, though he scarcely knew it.

Katherine started up crying, "Blessed Jesu!" For suddenly the tumult outside grew louder, though yet distant. There were shouts and shrieks and a muffled sinister thumping. "Oh, that my dear lord were here!" she cried. "My dearest love—to protect us—" She clenched her hands staring into the Avalon tapestry, as though it might channel the force of her desperation and summon him.

The friar made a sharp motion with his arm. Strength flowed into him. He shoved her aside and rose from the bed. He clutched at his crucifix and cried to Katherine fiercely, "So now, graceless woman, you call out for your paramour! Fool, fool—don't you yet see that it is because of your sin— and his—that this disaster comes?"

"Nay, Brother—" she murmured wearily. Surely in this time of danger she might be spared castigations.

"Do you know what they write of you in the abbeys?" he cried. "That you have bewitched the Duke to sodden lechery with your enchantments! And 'tis for this he suffers the hate of all men."

"That is false!" She colored hot, and anger choked her. She forgot, as he had, the shoutings of the mob. She forgot Blanchette, who stiffened in her chair. "How dare you speak to me like that! I've never done him harm. I love him."

The friar drew a rasping breath while red froth bubbled in the corners of his mouth, yet he went on inflexibly, as though she had not spoken.

"Ay—they write of your lechery, these Benedictine monks. They little know that they might also write of *murder!*"

A convulsive shiver shook his lean body. He raised the crucifix and stared down into the woman's white uncomprehending face.

"Katherine Swynford, your husband was murdered. Ay—and in God's sight, you and the Duke murdered Hugh Swynford in Bordeaux as truly as though you had yourselves procured the poison that killed him."

"You're mad," she whispered gazing at him in horror. "Brother William, your wound has made you mad."

From behind them in the chair there came a stifled sound. They did not hear it.

"Nay, not mad but dying," the friar said solemnly. "May God forgive me that I break the vow of the confessional—but I'll not die with this vile secret on my soul, nor shall *you* lack chance for repentance."

Katherine drew back from him, slowly, until her shoulders pressed against the gilded bedpost. "I don't understand," she whispered. "Hugh died of dysentery. You were there."

"Ay—fool that I was. 'Twas Nirac de Bayonne who put the poison in Sir Hugh's cup, this he confessed to me on his deathbed, but 'twas you gave your husband the draught to drink."

"The cup—" she said. Her mind swam in a heavy blackness. She looked down at her hand and saw in it the shape of the little clay cup of medicine that she had held to Hugh's mouth. She dragged her eyes up to the friar. "But I didn't know! Before God, I didn't know!"

"You didn't know! Nor did the Duke, who cast his poor tool aside when it had blindly committed the foulest of all crimes for him. But can you take this crucifix and kiss it, while swearing that you did not long for your husband's death? Nor rejoiced in your secret heart when it had happened? *Can you?*"

She did not move.

The friar's body blotted out a burst of sunlight through the window behind. He held the crucifix towards her with a shaking hand. Dark and terrible as a wall painting of God's judgment wrath he stood over her, then another shudder seized him. The crucifix rattled down the length of its beads beside the knotted scourge.

He slumped forward and stumbled to the ivory prie-dieu.

He knelt on the white satin cushion which crimsoned with a spreading stain. He clasped his hands together, and raising his face to the golden images of Christ and St. John the Baptist in the niche above, he began to chant, *"Ostende nobis, Domine, misericordiam tuam—"*

Katherine sank slowly to her knees beside the bedpost. Her wide-straining eyes fixed themselves on the round white disk of the friar's tonsure, her lips moved in mindless echo of his prayers.

Blanchette was huddled in the chair, her face sunk on her breast. She did not stir, she made no sound, but deep in her brain a voice cried on two notes senselessly like the cuckoo. It said, "Murder—murder—murder," and sometimes it changed its cry and said, "She gave poison to your father—father—father."

Below in the Outer Ward the Kentish rebels had arrived with Wat the tiler at their head, though the exhausted priest John Ball remained behind in a friendly alderman's house to regain his forces. Wat saw by the raised portcullis and the swarming figures near the chancery building and the Great Hall that his men had been forestalled.

But he cared little for that, the more there were to help, the quicker would be the act of vengeance and destruction. He knew by now that the Duke had escaped them, but they would wreak what vengeance they could, on his possessions, as they had on those of other traitors.

Already on the way here they had torn open the Fleet prison. And they had fired the Temple, burning the legal rolls and records on which the cursed ink strokes gave leave to strangle all the rights of common man. A detachment of Wat's force remained there now to watch the razing of the Inns of Court, to see that no vestige remained of that Temple of Iniquity.

Here at the Savoy, Wat saw that his predecessors had achieved but little yet. The Essex peasants had broken into the famous cellars and broached the vintage tuns and vats. They gulped and sloshed the wine, wandering stupidly and singing, bemused by the feel of this rich liquid in their gullets that had never known anything but small ale.

Wat took command at once. Some of the Londoners still pounded at the iron-bound Treasure Chamber door. Wat and his men added their strength to the timber battering ram, until the hinges burst, and they were free of Lancaster's treasure. They dragged out coffers full of gold and silver and piled them unopened in the Great Hall. They took the coronets, the jeweled chains, the diamond-crusted scabbards and broke them up in the courtyard, then ground the jewels to powder beneath great paving stones.

"We be not thieves!" roared Wat, as he spied a lad who stuffed a silver goblet in his jerkin. He killed the lad with a thrust of his sword and threw the goblet on the mangled pile that grew in the center of the Great Hall. Some of them as the frenzy grew, ran into the gardens trampling on the flowers, uprooting the rosebushes. The place was accursed, no part of it should remain.

When Wat seized a torch and set fire to the Hall, they roared with joy. It burned but slowly at first, and they threw in the records of the chancery and pieces of furniture that they brought from more distant rooms. They scattered to the other buildings. Someone fired the Monmouth Wing, another threw his flaming torch into the Beaufort Tower.

They turned to the Duke's privy suite. They had left it to the last for it was nearer to the Outer Ward and gate where they must leave in safety themselves. The fires smoldered behind them, licking at the massive timbers of the floors and vaultings, daunted for a while by thickness of stone wall and coldness of tile.

Wat stayed by the Great Hall to see to the burning of its massed treasure.

It was a slobbering whey-faced Londoner who led a band up the great State Staircase. A weaver by the badge of trade on his arm, his nose was smashed, his jaw had been knocked awry and stuck out comically beneath his left ear, so that they could understand little of his furious gabbling; but they followed him gladly for he seemed to know the way.

A short and meager little man in tattered leather jerkin went in this band too, his flaxen poll was matted thick with sweat and dirt. A branded F was on his cheek, half hidden by the grime. He was one of the outlaws who had crept down from the north and joined the Essex men.

They swarmed up to the Presence Chamber, hacked at the furnishings, flung silver sconces and candlesticks out of the window. They found the Duke's garderobe where some of his surcotes hung from the perches. Jack Maudelyn grabbed one down, a cloth-of-gold cote, emblazoned with the Duke's arms. They stuffed it out with folded cloths, they set it on the Duke's throne in the Presence Chamber, and put a silver basin on its head for a crown. They fired arrows at it, they spat on it, they pissed on it. They shouted that here was a fine king called John. The weaver danced and gibbered round the effigy, and the little outlaw from the north emitted a burst of shrill excited laughter.

Tiring of that, they slashed the surcote into shreds and stuffed the tatters down the open hole of the latrine, where they fell into the Thames below.

And still Jack urged them on with gestures. They swarmed down a passage past a shut door to a suite of empty rooms where they destroyed the furnishings, but the weaver was not satisfied, he pointed back and made them see that they must get inside the shut door they had passed.

They began to batter at the door, but they had scant room to exert leverage in the passage and the door held firm. The weaver beckoned again and they ran into the Duchess's bower and heaved against a small door with the massive headboard of the bed.

Inside the Avalon Chamber, the friar prayed on, through the pounding and the shouts outside the doors, but Katherine rose from her knees, pulling herself up by the bed curtains. She saw the little door begin to give and that the table that was shoved against it quivered.

She walked to Blanchette and put her arm around the huddled shoulders. "Don't be afraid, darling," she whispered. Blanchette started and recoiled. She twisted out from under her mother's arm and sprang back, in her eyes there was a look that caused Katherine to cry out in anguish.

The table rocked and slid. The small door burst open and a huge red-bearded Kentish peasant stepped in first, brandishing a sickle, which he lowered in confusion when he saw two women and a praying friar. "Cock's bones——" he muttered, but the other men shoved past him, Jack and the outlaw and twenty more.

The friar heaved himself to his feet and grabbed the pike he had taken from the weaver, he backed tottering against the fireplace.

"Kill! Kill!" Jack screamed in a voice they all understood. He rushed forward with his sword. The friar parried the thrust feebly with the pike, which dropped from his hand.

Jack raised his sword again, and the friar stood motionless.
He looked past the weaver.

"God in his mercy help you, Katherine!" he cried.

The sword swished like the spitting of a cat, came down
with a dull thud. Blood and brains spurted high then spattered on the marble and on Blanchette's skirt. The friar
gasped once, fell down upon the tiles, and was still.

Again Jack lifted his sword; this Lancastrian friar's head
would be carried on a pike to London bridge with those of
the other traitors. The men had held back watching silently,
but now the outlaw ran forward and held Jack's arm. "Not in
here—" he said, "not afore *them*." He jerked his chin towards Katherine and Blanchette, who stood transfixed against
the wall on either side of the fireplace.

Jack furiously shrugged off the restraining hand, but the
huge red-bearded peasant seized the friar's feet, the outlaw
shot back the bolts on the big door, they dragged Brother
William's body out into the passage.

Katherine did not look at what they dragged, she gazed at
the flaxen-polled little outlaw. 'Tis Cob o' Fenton, she
thought, my runaway serf. Soon he'll kill us too if Jack Maudelyn does not first. It seemed to her strange that Cob should
be there, when she had last seen him in the village stocks at
Kettlethorpe. It seemed to her almost ludicrous—cause for
gigantic laughter. She felt the laughter swelling, choking in
her chest. It rose into her mouth and she leaned over and
vomited.

The men cast sideways glances at the two women but did
not molest them. They set to work, running around the room,
flinging open the hutches and cupboards, following the system which they had used in all the other buildings. They
found the saints' figurines, and the lute and gittern and game
boards, and cast them into the river. They found the two
hanaps, Blanchette's and Joli-coeur. They shattered them with
axes. Joli-coeur's crystal splinters gleamed like diamonds in
the pool of jellied blood on the hearth, its garnet heart rolled
loose into a corner.

Some chopped up the sandalwood chairs, some the
gilded table. The ivory prie-dieu gave them more trouble but
they wrenched it apart and piled it in the center of the floor
with the rugs and the ruby velvet bed hangings and the
wooden portions of the bed. They pulled down the Avalon
tapestry and hacked it into strips for easier burning.

Soon the bearded Kentish peasant came back into the room with Cob, leaving Jack in the passage to finish with Brother William's body. The man from Kent seized the pike the friar had tried to use and amused himself with shattering each of the tinted windowpanes, one after the other, proudly counting as he did so, "Oon, twa, tree, four—" He had learned no higher than ten, so he started over again.

He had still two panes left when they heard the shouts of their leader from the passage and Wat Tiler strode into the chamber crying, "Come, lads, come. Get on wi' it. What's keeping ye so long?" The acrid smell of smoke came with him, charred gray flakes had floated from the fires and settled on his sweat-stained jerkin.

Jack Maudelyn slithered in behind the tiler, mumbling something through his broken jaw. He pointed to Katherine.

"Women?" said the tiler scowling. "What do they here? Who are they?" Not servants by their clothes, he thought, nor noble ladies neither.

Jack's uncouth noises rose to frenzy as he tried to tell who they were. "Kill—" he gobbled again, and he raised his sword.

"Nay, weaver—by the rood—ye've gone daft!" Wat gave him a great shove that sent him spinning. "I canna get a word this brokejaw says."

"Who are ye then?" He turned impatiently to Katherine. The fires were catching fast in the buildings behind them, they must finish this business up, then on to Westminster, and after, hurry back to their camp by the Tower, where surely there would be word from the King.

Katherine could not answer. Her tongue was swollen thick in her mouth. The tiler's form blocked out the sunlight as the friar's had an hour ago. She stared down at the pile of broken furniture on the floor, the strips of the Avalon tapestry, the bed hangings, no redder than the blood pools on the tiles.

Cob will tell him who we are, she thought. And that will be the end. But the little flaxen-haired outlaw did not speak. He cast a slanting look at Katherine, and busied himself with chopping off the carved emblems on the mantel.

"You then!" The tiler rounded on Blanchette, and drew back startled. Almost he made a sign of the cross, the crop-haired girl had so strange a look.

She had lifted a fold of her skirt and dabbled with her fingers in the stains made by the friar's blood, and she was smiling. Smiling as one who knows a sly secret that will confuse the hearer.

"Who are ye, child?" shouted Wat, but more gently.

Blanchette raised her head and gazed behind the tiler toward the shattered window, where drifts of smoke and flying sparks blew past.

"Who am I?" she said in a high, sweet, questioning tone. "Nay, that, good sir, I must not tell you."

Her eyes moved unseeing over the faces of the other men, who had turned to watch. "But I can tell you who I'll *be*—" She nodded three times slowly, and she laughed low in her throat.

Wat swallowed. The men behind did not stir, their mouths dropped open and a shivering unease held them.

"Why, I shall be a whore—good sir," cried Blanchette in a loud voice, "like my mother. A *murdering* whore—mayhap too—like my mother!"

She gathered up her skirts in either hand as though she would make them all a curtsy. The men gaped at her. Like quicksilver she whirled and ran out of the chamber. She stumbled on the friar's dismembered headless body in the passage, then sped on swift as light to the Great Stairs.

"Stop her!" screamed Katherine, dashing forward with her arms outstretched. "Blanchette!"

Jack Maudelyn snatched out his hand and grabbed Katherine by the flying end of her coif. He jerked her back so violently that she fell. Her head hit the tiles. A thousand lights exploded behind her eyes; then there was darkness.

The tiler stared down at the woman who lay crumpled, barely breathing, on the tiles. He stared at the door through which the girl had fled. He looked at the weaver's wry-jawed vicious face. And he shrugged.

"By the rood, I vow they've all gone mad here in this accursed place—" he said. "Well—come lads. Get on wi' it. Where's a torch? Someone carry the woman out. Whoe'er she be, I'll not leave her here to be roasted."

# XXV

ACROSS THE STRAND from the Savoy's gatehouse, there lay an open field that was part of the convent garden belonging to Westminster Abbey. Two of Wat Tiler's men carried Katherine there and dumped her on a grassy bank near a little brook, before dashing off to join their fellows who were streaming out of the burning Savoy, some heading for Westminster, where they would break open the Abbey prison, and many back towards the City.

Cob o' Fenton had followed the men who bore Katherine out of the Savoy and watched from afar as they laid her down. After they ran off, he stood irresolute by the roadside, tugging on his lank tow-colored forelock. He glanced to his left where Katherine's skirt showed as a splotch of darker green against the grass; his eyes shifted to the disappearing bands of rebels.

The Lady of Kettlethorpe was mayhap dying there in the field. Well, let her then! Cob thought with sudden vigor.

What if it was her negligent order that had freed him from the stocks and given him back his croft. What good was that when her steward still exacted the heriot fine overdue from Cob's father's death?—the one ox he owned, and was fond of; company for him that ox had been, since his wife had died in childbed. Then there were the other fines—no end to them: merchet, leyrwite; tithes to the church, "love-work," —and now the poll tax.

"Phuah!" said Cob and spat. He fingered the branded F on his cheek—fugitive, runaway serf, outlaw. Ay, and if he could escape recapture by his own manor lord for a year, he would be legally free. But she could still catch him. Cob glanced again towards Katherine. She could have him dragged back to the manor, and the punishment this time would be far worse than stocks and branding. Cob's watery, white-lashed eyes stared down at the Strand paving stones, he gnawed at an itching fleabite on his finger, when suddenly he jumped and gasped, jerking his head up to look at the Savoy.

An explosion had thundered off behind the walls. A sheet of flame shot up as high as the spire on the Monmouth Tower, where the Duke's pennant still fluttered. The Outer Ward was not yet all afire.

Cob ran back off the road and clapped his hands to his ears, while another explosion rocked the Savoy, and another. A zigzag crack shot down the Monmouth Tower like black lightning. The tower wavered, seeming to dance and sway like a sapling in the wind, it buckled in the middle, and fell with the rumble of an earthquake, in great white clouds of dust and flying stone. Half of the Savoy Strand wall caved in beneath the fallen tower, and the gap filled in at once with raging fire.

Cob ran farther back into the field and stumbling, fell to his knees. Above the roar and crackle of the fire he heard muffled shrieks, demon-like wails for help, different from the screaming whinnies of the terrified horses in the stables.

It was some thirty of the Essex men who shrieked. They had escaped Wat's eye and returned to the cellars and the wine casks, having found a tunnel to the Outer Ward and being sure that they had time to reach it before the fires got too hot. But Wat's men had flung into the Great Hall the three barrels of gunpowder, and the falling of the tower had trapped the rioters in the cellars beneath. It would take long before the fire ate downward to them through the stone roofing of the cellars, but there was now no way out.

"God's passion—" whispered Cob, crossing himself as a deluge of flying sparks fell on him. He scrambled up and took to his heels across the field. He had quite forgotten Katherine, but she lay across his path.

He stopped, and seeing that sparks had fallen on her wool gown and were charring round smoking holes, he reached down and brushed them off. She lay on her back, her face like the marble effigies he'd seen in Lincoln Cathedral. But she breathed. He saw her breasts move up and down.

And Cob, pinching out a spark that still smoldered, saw at her girdle the purse with her blazon. Through Cob's uncertain heart there struck a strange feeling. He stared down at the Swynford arms—three yellow boars' heads on the black chevron. These arms meant home. They were fastened on the manor gate, they swung on the alehouse sign. They meant the fealty that his father had loyally given to Sir Hugh Swynford, and to Sir Thomas before that. They meant the warm smell of earth and ox in his little hut, they meant the mists off the Trent, the candles in the church on holy days. They meant the companionable grumbles of his fellow villeins in the alehouse on the green, and they meant the old stone manor where he himself had done homage to Swynfords—homage to this very woman who lay flat and helpless on the grass.

Cob glanced fearfully over his shoulder and saw that the fire drew nearer them, the buildings in the Outer Ward must now have caught. Heat shimmered out in waves across the Strand, sparks fell thicker and farther into the field.

"Lady!" Cob cried, slapping at her cheeks and shaking Katherine. "Lady, for the love o' God, awake!"

Still she lay limp, and her head fell back when he released her. She was tall, and he undersized and puny. He could not carry her. He took her by the feet and dragged her towards the brook, then cupping his hands, dashed her face with water, crying, "Lady, wake, wake!" pleading with her. "Lady, I must leave ye here an ye not wake soon. For sure ye must know that? Ye'd hardly think I'd cause to burn up wi' ye, now would ye? 'Tis far from Kettlethorpe we are, lady, and I've all but won my freedom. Ye know that, don't ye?"

She did not move. Cob in desperation pulled at her until she rolled into the little brook. He held her head just above the water, and nearly sobbed with relief as she opened her eyes and shuddered. " 'Tis cold—" she whispered. "What's so cold?" She moved her hands in the flowing water, lifted them and stared at their wetness.

"Get up, lady! Up! We must hasten or I vow 'tis not *cold* ye'll be." He hoisted her by the armpits and Katherine slowly rose, dripping, from the brook and stood on the bank, swaying, while Cob held her. She looked down at his matted flaxen hair and the F brand on his cheek, but she did not quite remember him—someone from Kettlethorpe. She turned and stared at the immense roaring furnace across the Strand. A puzzling sight.

"Come! Can't ye walk?" cried Cob impatiently, propelling her along the field. She moved her feet forward, leaning on him heavily. Cob saw that her wet robe clung to her legs and impeded her. He drew his knife from its sheath and cut her skirt off just below the knee. She watched him in vague surprise, then, bothered by her wet hair that flowed loose, she wrung the water out of it and started to braid it.

"No time for that!" cried Cob. "Hurry!"

The flames now licked through the gatehouse; the lower prongs of the raised portcullis began to smolder. The wind blew towards them and bore charring embers with the smoke.

"Where are we going?" Katherine said, while obediently she tried to hurry. The sick giddiness behind her eyes was passing, though her head ached.

"Into town," said Cob, though he didn't know what he was going to do with her. As soon as he had got her beyond the reach of fire, he could dump her on some convent, of course, but he knew little about London.

"Oh," said Katherine. "I've good friends in town. The Pessoners in Billingsgate. Master Guy came yesterday to tell me about the rebels. Are we going to the Pessoners?"

"Might as well," said Cob, relieved.

He dragged her along until they came to St. Clement's Dane. The Temple was burning on the Strand ahead of them. He had forgotten that. "Have to go up there, I think." He pointed up the hill towards Holborn, and turned up the footpath through Fickett's field. "Road's blocked here."

"More fire?" she said, looking at the smoking Temple. "How strange!" The sunny green fields, the fires, the little church were all to her like scenes woven upon a tapestry.

Cob slackened pace, rubbed his sweating face on his sleeve and looked up at her curiously. "Ye don't remember nothing o' this morning, do ye?"

"Why yes," she said courteously. "When I got up and looked out of the window, there were fires on the Surrey bank. I was quite frightened. That was at dawn." She stopped, and frowning, glanced back at the sun. Through the smoke haze it shone high above and a little towards the west. But it's afternoon now, she thought in confusion. What happened to the morning? She tried to pierce through the blankness, and gave it up. "Is the peasant army still at Blackheath waiting for the King?" she said.

Cob shrugged and did not answer. A head blow often wiped out memory of all that had gone before it—for a time. And just as well, poor lady. He wondered what had happened to the Damoiselle Blanchette. A fearful thing the little wench had cried out about her mother, but then the lass had gone

mad from horror when the Gray Friar's blood spattered on
her and knew not what she said. There had been no sign of
her when they carried Lady Swynford out, though Cob had
looked. It seemed likely that in her madness the girl had been
trapped somewhere back in the Savoy, like those whose
screams he had heard. God rest her soul, he thought—she
had been a fair sweet little maid once, some ten years ago, at
Kettlethorpe.

He and Katherine plodded north through the field and
reached Holborn street, where a hundred of the rebels came
marching four abreast and singing "Jack Milner."

A fellow outlaw whom Cob had known in the Essex camp
spied him and called out, "By God's belly—ye little Lincoln
cock! What be ye doing wi' a woman? 'Tis no time for
sport!"

"Nay—true," Cob shouted back, grinning. " 'Tis a poor
affrighted country serving wench has got lost, I but take her
to the City. Then I'll join ye. Where are ye bound?"

Several of the rebels answered him at once. They were off
to burn all Robert Hales' property, his priory at Clerkenwell,
his manor at Highbury. Though the base treasurer himself
still lurked in the Tower, protected by the King.

Katherine waited by the roadside while this interchange
took place and listened without understanding, except that
her companion had called her a country serving wench and
no doubt she looked like one with her green dress cut short
like a kirtle, barelegged, and her tangled hair drying on her
shoulders. Where is my coif? she thought. Didn't I wear a
coif today? Her head gave a painful throb, and she put her
hand on the spot where a lump had formed. I've hurt my
head some way, she thought.

The rebels veered off to the left on the lane for Clerkenwell, and Katherine started walking again when Cob did.
They entered the City at Newgate, which was open and unguarded. They walked down the shambles past the slaughter-
houses with their stench of offal, and on West Chepe came to
the edge of a tremendous crowd who were watching what
took place on a block in the center of the crossways.

Some forty Flemings had been rounded up along with two
richer prizes, the detested merchant Richard Lyons, who had
escaped the justice of the Good Parliament, and a sneaking
informer that the mob had dragged from sanctuary in St.
Martin's. They were all tied arm to arm in a line that had

reached way down the Chepe, but was now diminished as one after the other was dragged forward and flung to his knees beside the block. A man stood there with an axe, and he worked fast. Already a dozen heads had rolled into the central gutter, which ran crimson. Vultures and kites perched high above on the house gables, watching as intently as the crowd did.

Cob shrank. "We must get out o' here," he whispered, grabbing Katherine's arm. He shoved her down an alley until they reached Watling street, which was near deserted. Peaceable citizens were all at home behind barred doors.

"Lady," cried Cob, "where is this Billingsgate to which ye'd go?"

Katherine stopped and stared about her. Those crosskeys on a tavern sign, that bakeshop on the corner of Bread street, the small squeezed-in Church of All Hallows, all were familiar to her. She had passed through here before, running with someone, running from something, from a great roaring mob. Riots in St. Paul's—the Duke in danger. Danger. That day long past slid into now. The two states intermingled, shifting.

"Where's Billingsgate?" repeated Cob, and now his urgency touched her with fear.

"There!" she cried pointing towards the river. "There's rioting again. That crowd on the Chepe. Warn the Duke! We must warn him—run to the Pessoners', Dame Emma'll help!" She seized Cob's hand as once she had seized Robin's, and began to run—around the corner and down Bread street, beneath the dark overhanging gables.

As they passed through the Vintry they saw three hacked and still-bleeding corpses on the steps of St. Martin's. "Sweet Jesus," Katherine gasped, "why does the whole world smell of blood and fire? *Why?*"

Cob said nothing. He hurried her on. They were not molested again. In Billingsgate she saw near St. Magnus' church the half-timbered house and the gilded fish that flapped from a pole over the shop. " 'Tis here," she said with a deep sigh of relief and pulled the door knocker. There was no answer.

Katherine leaned against the oaken doorjamb, and pressed her hand to her head, Cob reached up and banged the knocker again.

The wooden peephole opened and a wrinkle-lidded frightened eye looked out. "What is't?" quavered an old man's creaking voice. "There's no one here. Go 'way."

"Dame Emma!" cried Katherine. "Where's Dame Emma? Tell her Lady Swynford's here, and I've need of her."

"The mistress's not here—no more the master," said the voice. "Be off wi' ye!" The shutter began to slide across the peephole.

"Stop!" Cob rammed his knife between the shutter and its frame. "Nay, don't squeal like that in there, I'll not harm ye. But ye must open the door and let us in!"

"I'll not, nor can ye force me to—the door's iron-barred," the old voice rose high and shrill.

Cob cursed roundly while he thought. His lady looked near to fainting, but that was by no means his chief concern. In this prosperous house there would be far better fare than at the rebel camp they had all been told to rejoin in its new position near the Tower. No doubt tomorrow his lust for revenge and rioting would revive, but for now, he'd had his bellyful of wandering the bloody streets.

Then an idea struck him. "Wait, old gaffer!" he cried as he heard shuffling footsteps retreating. "Wait!" He grabbed Katherine's purse, yanking it from her girdle, and opening it breathed "Holy saints!" as he saw jewels and gold. He fished out a gold noble and waved it at the peephole, snatching it back as a hand reached for it. " 'Tis yours an ye let us in!" Cob shouted. "I'll get it again for ye later," he whispered to Katherine.

"No—" she said faintly, "It doesn't matter."

Doesn't matter, Cob thought, a gold noble doesn't matter! A gold noble was near seven shillings. Half a year's wage for a freeman. As they heard the bolts slowly drawn within, Cob looked at Katherine with an anger he had not felt since he ran in to the Savoy with the mob this morning. He hesitated, but he put the pouch in her limp hand, and her fingers closed automatically around it.

The door opened. Cob shoved it wider, and pulling Katherine with him walked in. Cob shut and barred the door. "Here ye are then," he said roughly dropping the noble in the old man's shaking outstretched hand.

The old man was called Elias, and usually he worked around the fishhouse as nightwatch. He had been left here alone this afternoon to guard the house, for Master Guy had gone to an emergency meeting in Fishmongers' Hall called by Walworth the mayor, who was also a fishmonger and who had hurried from the King in the Tower to confer with his fellows on the rebel crisis which was getting more serious each moment.

"Where's Dame Emma?" said Katherine sinking down on the settle. The kitchen fire was unlighted, the low-raftered room that had always shown a homely cheer was now empty and gloomy behind its drawn shutters.

The old man bit the gold noble between his wobbly remaining teeth before slipping it in some hidden cranny of his stained and fishy tunic. "She's gone," he said eying the two intruders with bleak suspicion.

"But where *is* Dame Emma—isn't she coming back?" Katherine repeated piteously. Dame Emma would have banished the headache and confusion, banished the fear too. Somewhere there was fear, twitching like a bear awakening in a winter cave.

The old man would not answer her.

Master Guy, alarmed at last, had packed Dame Emma and the maids off to St. Helen's priory for safety when at dawn the Kentish rebels had poured over the Bridge, but no need to tell this strange tousled wench that—or anything. Elias folded his arms around his shrunken chest and mumbled with feeble malevolence, as Cob who had been rummaging came back with his finds.

"Ye best eat, lady," said Cob breaking a juicy hunk off a meat pie and holding it out to her. As Katherine shook her head, he thrust out his mug of ale. "Drink then!"

She lowered her lips and swallowed thirstily. Cob held the mug and suddenly chuckled. "Here's something warms me cockles," he said, "to see the Lady o' Kettlethorpe adrinking from the same mug as her serf—ay, there's a sight would dumfounder 'em back home!"

Katherine raised her head from the mug. "Cob—" she whispered, looking at him wonderingly. Cob, the runaway from Kettlethorpe—she knew him now. It was no squire had guided her this day, had told puzzling lies for her. It was her own rebellious serf. Yet not long ago she had dreamed that he was going to kill her. She had dreamed that she saw him chopping the emblems from the marble mantel in the Avalon Chamber. He had given her a strange sideways glance when a question had been asked. What question? "Who are you then?" Had someone asked that? There were others there in the dream: men—and Blanchette. But Blanchette was sleeping in the Duchess's bower—nay, in the Monmouth Wing.

"Cob?" she said. "Do you know where is Blanchette?"

"Nay, lady," replied the little outlaw quickly, and crossed himself. "For sure now ye must rest—old gaffer—" he prodded Elias who was crouching on a stool by the dead fireplace, "where can the lady rest?"

The old man hunched himself. "On the floor, forsooth."

"I know where to go," said Katherine, not hearing him. Why did Cob cross himself? she thought. Behind a flimsy wall a sea of horror surged and pounded, but the wall still held.

"The chamber above the fish shop," she said to Cob, " 'Tis where I've always gone. Ay—I must lie down a while." Her head spun as she rose, and she dragged herself towards the stairs.

"Ye can't go up there, woman!" squealed Elias, jumping up and shaking his fist as he hobbled after Katherine.

"Bung down—bung down, old goat, she'll go where she pleases!" Cob gave him a negligent shove and gestured with his knife. "Me whistle's still dry. Where's more ale? Ye've not earned your noble yet, not by a long shot." He grinned and pricked Elias on his skinny shank. "I'll have that flitch o' bacon too, what's hanging from the rafter, and I daresay ye know where white bread be stored. I've a fancy to taste white bread at last."

While Cob made himself comfortable in the kitchen, Katherine found her way to the chamber loft. The two great beds and the sliding truckle were all neatly made and covered with down quilts. She lay down on the bed which she had once shared with Hawise. Always when she lay down to rest, her longing prayers turned to the Duke. Now for a moment she saw his face but it was far away, tiny and warning, then a hand holding a threatening crucifix thrust up as barrier before John's face, blocking it off. Her head throbbed agonizingly. She moaned a little, and closed her eyes.

When Master Guy returned home, it was near to sundown and the grave issues of the rebellion so perturbed him that he gave scant attention to the presence of a ragged little knave in his kitchen, or to old Elias' stammered excuses.

When he understood from Cob that Lady Swynford was sleeping upstairs, having taken refuge here after the burning of the Savoy, Master Guy banged his pudgy hand on the table in exasperation crying, "By God—why must she come *here!*" But when Cob had tried to go on and tell him of the gruesome happenings in the Savoy and the dangers they had run in London streets to get here, Master Guy interrupted, shaking his fat jowls impatiently. "Ay—ay, I know there's been hideous deeds everywhere this day. Well—let her be—let her be—but I canna concern mesel' wi' her, one way or t'other. Nor ye *neither,*" he said to Cob. "Ye can rest a bit, then out ye go. I want none o' the rebels in here."

Master Guy, drumming his fingers on his ale mug, lapsed into gloomy thought. A black uncertainty, that's what there was, and none knew what the morrow would bring.

Today at the distress meeting in Fishmongers' Hall, first, Mayor Walworth had come to tell his fellow fishmongers that all loyal citizens were to be alerted—here he had glanced frowning at the empty chairs of the alderman who had opened the Bridge and joined the rebels—that since Wat Tiler's early promises of good behavior and no violence had not been kept, and since the rebels were now most threateningly encamped around the Tower and besieging the King, a fierce and sudden counterattack was being planned.

The King's regiment with the Tower would be joined by Sir Robert Knolles' huge force of retainers who were quartered in his inn this side of Tower hill, while all the Londoners who wished to rid their city of the insurrectionists must arm and strike at the same time. It had seemed a good plan to the anxious fishmongers and they had started to organize the runners who would alert the other guilds and burghers while Walworth returned to the Tower.

But no sooner started than the whole scheme had been countermanded. A panting King's messenger arrived at Fishmongers' Hall bearing an official missive. There was to be no attack made on the rebels after all, conciliation was to be tried first. The messenger had been present at the King's Council and amplified his document. He told the fishmongers that the King had ordered the rebel army to meet him at seven in the morning for conference at Mile End, a meadow two miles to the east of town. This would give opportunity for the archbishop and treasurer to escape by boat while the savage mob who howled for their blood were drawn off to parley with the King.

"Before God, I hope it'll work," muttered Master Guy to himself. The howling of the rebel army was plain enough to be heard right now since the Pessoner home was not a bowshot from the Tower. A fearful din it was, too. Small wonder that panic indecision seemed to paralyze the royal party that had taken refuge in the fortress, when those devil howls beat round it like a raging storm beat on a ship.

England's gone mad, for sure, thought the fishmonger, his moon face falling into heavy creases. Still, there was nothing he could do tonight but wait and get some sleep in readiness for any summons.

Master Guy lumbered up to look to the fastenings of his house before going to bed, and was reminded of Cob, who lay curled up snoring on a bench. "Out wi' ye—now," he cried shaking him.

Cob did not protest, for the huge fishmonger was fully armed, besides Cob was rested now and full of food, and not ungrateful. "Ay—I'll be off, thank 'e sir." He yawned and bowed and docilely went out upon Thames street while Master Guy barred his door behind him.

Cob finished out his sleep on a stone bench in St. Magnus' church porch and awakened when its bells rang out for Prime. This Friday, June 14, was another fair warm day, and Cob felt revived interest in the great cause which had brought him into London. He munched on the delicious white bread and bacon with which he had prudently stuffed his pockets and glanced towards the fishmonger's house where Lady Swynford slept, devoutly glad that he was rid of her and wondering that he had taken so much pains to care for her yesterday. Her and her purse full of jewels and gold! A murrain on her and all her kind, thought Cob, bitterly regretting that he had not taken opportunity to steal upstairs and relieve her of that purse before Master Guy came home.

"When Adam delved and Eva span, who had gold and jewels then?" Cob chanted, raking his fingers through his hair and squashing a louse that ran out of it. He trotted off down the street towards the Tower and the rebel camp beyond it on St. Catherine's hill.

Here Cob was swept up by the wild excitement. Their leaders Wat Tiler, Jack Strawe and the priest John Ball were all ahorseback, galloping amongst their forces, which numbered by now nearly eighty thousand men. "Mile End! Mile End!" they shouted. The King was to meet them at Mile End and listen to their plans in person. "Onward march to Mile End to meet the King!"

Cob surged forward with a great multitude of them,

swarming and trampling over the fields until they reached the
meadow where the little King awaited them.

Richard sat pale and stiff upon his brightly caparisoned
white horse. His crown was no more golden than his long
curls, and in Cob's eyes and those of his fellows, Richard's
royal beauty shone round him like a halo. "God bless our
King!" they cried. "We want no King but thee, O Richard!" All bowed their heads, and many genuflected humbly.

The King smiled at them uncertainly and waved his hand in
response, as Wat Tiler rode up to him for parley.

A dozen nobles were gathered behind the King—those
who had been with him in the Tower: the Lords Warwick
and Salisbury and Sir Robert Knolles, grim fighters all three
and of proven courage in war, but this aggression from a
mob of despicable serfs and peasants was so alien to their experience that they had floundered this way and that, quarreling amongst themselves.

The King's beloved Robert de Vere, the Earl of Oxford,
had drawn apart from the others and watched from beneath
raised eyebrows, which were finely plucked as a woman's.
With delicate fingernail he flicked a tiny blob of mud off his
rose velvet côte, and as Wat Tiler approached them, de Vere
sniffed ostentatiously at a scented spice ball that dangled
from his wrist.

The King's Uncle Thomas, Earl of Buckingham, was
there too, his truculent black eyes flashing, his swarthy face
suffused with impotent rage, but even he had sense enough to
hold his tongue and stay his sword arm until they saw what
might be accomplished first by guile—and by a further measure which was even now in progress back in the Tower.

Sudbury's and Hales' attempted escape by boat had gone
awry earlier, ill timed and clumsily executed. The archbishop
had been recognized by rebel guards on St. Catherine's hill
and had regained the safety of the Tower just in time. But
not for long. As the King left for Mile End, Buckingham had
issued certain orders, nor mentioned them to Richard, who
was often oversqueamish. Buckingham had decided that the
safety of England and the crown should no longer be jeopar-
dized by two cumbersome superfluous old men.

The little King gave no sign of fear as he nodded graciously to Wat and after listening a while readily gave the
verbal agreement his advisors had told him to. The abolition
of serfdom and a general pardon for all the rebels—these

were what the tiler demanded first, and "Ay—it shall be done!" cried Richard in his high, pretty, childish voice. "The charters shall be prepared, ye shall have them on the morrow."

This was not all that John Ball and Wat had drawn up as their requirements. It did not answer their demands for the abolition of private courts, for freedom of contract, disendowment of the clergy, land at fourpence an acre rent, but Wat thought it better not to press for too much at once. These other matters could wait, since the greater part of their glorious goal had been so comfortably achieved. He seized Richard's hand and kissed it vehemently. Then he jumped on his horse and standing in the stirrups shouted to the silent straining mob, "The King has agreed there's to be no more bondage!"

In the wild exulting turmoil of triumphant cries and blessings on the King, Cob did not understand at first nor, being short, could he see. He tugged at his neighbor, who was a ploughman from Hertfordshire, and cried, "What is it? What did Wat say?"

"Why man—he said we're free! That's what he said!" cried the ploughman pumping Cob's arm in ecstasy. "King's granted it."

"Free?" whispered Cob swallowing. A shiver ran down his back. No more hiding in the forests or the city. No more heriot fine, no fines, no boon-work. He could go back to Kettlethorpe and do as he pleased on his own croft. He could keep his ox and earn money for his labor. A freeman.

"I didn't rightly believe 'twould ever happen," he whispered. He put his knuckles to his eyes, and a sob rose in his throat. All around him men were leaping, laughing, crying, so that it was hard to hear what else Wat said, but the tall ploughman passed it on.

" 'Twill take a little time to get our charters, the parchment what'll prove we're free. Wat says we'd better wait on St. Catherine's hill."

Cob nodded, for he could not speak.

He and many others took their time about wandering back to the City. The sun shone on them, the earth of the road was brown and warm beneath their feet, and the brooks gurgled joyfully through the meadows. The leaping wild excitement died down and they smiled at each other quietly, their eyes shining. Some sprawled upon the grass apart, thinking with fast-beating hearts of the manors they had left, the anxious waiting wives and children, and how it would be when they got home, free and safe. The King had said so.

Cob heard the martial beat of music as he reached their camp at last and crowded up to watch. A procession came through the postern gate from Tower hill. John Ball led it on his mule, Wat Tiler and Jack Strawe followed on their horses, and behind them came seven proudly grinning members of the fellowship, each bearing a dripping head set on a pole. They marched triumphantly to the blithe rhythm of the pipes and tabors, and they held the heads high so all could see.

Cob wormed his way up to the front and gaped with the others. The first head that went by had belonged to Sudbury, the Archbishop of Canterbury. You could tell that, for they had jammed his jeweled miter down over the gray tonsure, and fastened it to the skull with a long nail.

"How'd they get him?" Cob cried startled; several of the newcomers echoed him.

A Kentishman behind answered them, "We got the old rat in the Tower chapel—when we broke in an hour back. And there's Hales too."

The treasurer's head was mangled and still bled profusely. "That cursed prior sold his life dear," said the Kentishman, "we'd trouble with him."

Four other heads passed by, then Cob stiffened and squinted. "Ah, I know that one," he said pointing to the seventh. " 'Tis from yesterday at the Savoy."

"Ay," said the Kentishman laughing. "They say 'twas John o' Gaunt's own Gray Friar and leech. Some daft broke-jawed weaver had it, and wouldn't give it up, but Wat recognized it and said since we didna get the Duke, we must show off his friar instead."

Cob thought to himself that it was a pity about the Gray Friar, but you couldn't make a custard without breaking eggs. He fingered the brand on his cheek and set to whistling softly.

The rebel camp that Friday night was a happy one. A few charters of freedom began to be delivered from the King, and most of those who received them set off at once for home.

John Ball spent the night on his knees before the cross that was placed on St. Catherine's hill, thanking God for the victories they had won.

The King too and his meinie spent most of the night in prayer, but it was no prayer of thanksgiving.

Richard had cried out in horror when he found what had happened at the Tower in his absence at Mile End, he had wept for the gentle old archbishop and been frightened for his mother, whom the rebels had bespoken roughly but not hurt. She had fled to the royal wardrobe in Carter lane near St. Paul's and here Richard and his nobles joined her, in gloomiest pessimism.

True it was that some of the rebels had gone home as they received their charters, but not nearly enough of them. Thousands still roamed the London streets looting and butchering according to their whims. And a messenger from Wat Tiler made it clear that there were still many points to be discussed, and new concessions to be granted.

On the next morning, Saturday, Richard and his party hurriedly breakfasted in the wardrobe's small congested Hall while they held yet another worried conference.

"Your Grace will have to meet these accursed ribauds again, I fear," said Lord Salisbury gravely. "We'll never rid the city of them else. We must still play for time."

The Princess Joan threw down her wine cup and set up a wail, clasping Richard feverishly to her disheveled bosom. "I'll not let him go out to those fiends again. How dare you ask it, my lord? See how white he is and how he trembles. Jesu, would you *kill* your King?"

"Nay, Mother," said Richard wanly, struggling out from her smothering embrace. "I'm weary, of course, and sick at heart, but there's no cause to fear them. They love me," he said with a faint proud smile.

"God's passion!" cried Thomas of Woodstock, clenching his hairy hand on his sword. "That we were strong enough to wipe them all out now, and have done with them!"

Richard gazed distastefully at his uncle, whom he loathed, and thought that if his eldest uncle, John, was here, matters might not have gone so badly for them as they had. But that it was equally fortunate that Edmund had sailed for Portugal before the uprising, for Edmund was a muddleheaded ass.

"We might risk open fight," said Sir Robert Knolles, knitting his jutting gray brows, "but 'twould be safer to put it off a day or two until we can raise more men. This has come to us so fast—" He shook his head.

"Blessed Virgin, but *how* fast!" cried the Princess beginning to weep again. "Only two days of this terror and it seems—dear God, I can scarce remember when it started."

She wrung her hands, remembering the first moment that she had felt fear, Thursday morning, when she had looked from her turret window in the Tower and seen the Savoy on fire, and then fires everywhere—in Southwark, in Clerkenwell, in Highbury.

"Ay, Your Grace," said Salisbury decisively to the King. "You must meet the rebels again, this afternoon. We'll tell them to come to Smithfield this time, 'tis nearer."

That afternoon Wat led his men towards the new rendezvous at Smithfield. He had been temperate these past days when he knew so much depended on clear thinking, but now with complete victory all but won, he had been lustily celebrating, drinking mug after mug out of a cask of rich vernage that some of his men had taken from a Lombard's cellar.

It had been impossible to continue enforcing the prohibition against all thievery, or to keep a watchful eye on so many men. Besides, the Lombards like the Flemings didn't count. They were lucky if they kept their heads, let alone their wine.

Wat had made himself fine for this second interview with the King. He had donned a fashionable red and blue striped tunic that had belonged to one of the decapitated merchants and a golden velvet cap furred with ermine, such as only lords were allowed to wear; and he carried in a jeweled sheath at his girdle a nobleman's dagger. For now that all men were to be free and equal, a tiler could dress as he pleased to do honor to his King, and his own leadership.

Wat and John Ball rode from the rebel camp at the head of their forces, but Jack Strawe lay sodden in a tavern and did not appear. Wat traversed the blood-soaked pavement of the Chepe and turned up towards Aldersgate and Smithfield. The sun beat down hot, and his face dripped beneath the velvet cap, but the wine bubbled pleasingly in his veins and he began to sing,

> *"The mill is now adight!*
> *It turneth full o' might*
> *Wi' will and wi' skill*
> *We swinked at our mill*
> *Till it goeth right, right, right!*

Good times be acoming for all, m'dear," cried Wat exuberantly turning his flushed face on John Ball, who rode silently beside him.

"Ay, as *God* hath willed it," said the priest solemnly. "Wat, ye're something drunk. Have a care now how ye handle yourself with the King."

Wat grinned. "King and me's good friends. We understand each other. Mayhap King'll dub me a lord this day. Lord Wat I'll be. Lord Walter o' Maidenstone." He chuckled happily.

The priest shook his head and said nothing.

They rode on into Smithfield, where horse markets and tournaments were usually held, and the peasant forces poured in after them to line up in rows along the western side.

Cob was in the vanguard. He shinnied up a little apple tree that stood on the edge of the great parade ground, for he was determined to see all that took place this time, and have a good look at the King. That would be something to tell them in the alehouse at Kettlethorpe. With luck he'd be the first one home with the glorious news. "You're free, men, all o' ye, and I saw the King twice when he said so!" To be sure, nobody from the northern counties had got any charters yet, but Cob didn't see the need of writing to confirm the King's word. He had almost started for home last night, but had waited to see the meeting today when Wat was going to get for them a lot more liberties. Game and forest laws were to be abolished, so everyone could hunt where he pleased, all outlaws were to be pardoned, and a lot more wonderful things that a man had never dared to dream of.

Cob had thought once or twice of Lady Swynford, wondering how she was and if she'd heard the great news which had removed his resentment towards her. He'd work his land and pay her a just rent gladly enough, if he were free not to, ay, that he would, poor lady. Cob clung harder to the tree limb as the swirling dust and the pound of hooves announced that the King was coming.

Richard had sixty men with him today; knights and lords in flashing armor, and as he rode to the east side of the field near St. Bartholomew's walls, his heralds' trumpets sounded with a flourish. Then the King, wasting no time, rode out to the center of the field, accompanied by Mayor Walworth and a squire. The mayor beckoned to Wat, who trotted up blithely and dismounting bobbed his knee to Richard, before seizing the boy's hand in his great hairy workman's paw and shaking it vigorously.

On the edge of the field the watching lords stiffened at this effrontery, and the mayor tightened his grasp on his sharp three-edged cutlass.

"Brother," cried Wat beaming up at the King, "be o' good cheer, lad, here's near forty thousand commons I've brought to ye, for we be staunch comrades, you and me."

Richard withdrew his pale small hand from the tiler's sweating clasp and said with childish earnestness, "Why won't you all go home to your own places?"

Wat drew back and swaggering a little said, "By God's skin and bones, how can we go home till we all get our charters! For sure ye see that, King, don't ye? And there's more grants we must have too!"

"What are they?" asked Richard quietly.

The tiler drew himself up and ticking each off on his stumpy fingers rehearsed all the demands that he and John Ball had been discussing for weeks.

When he had finished, Richard inclined his small, crowned head and said quickly, "You shall have all this. 'Tis granted."

Wat drew a great exulting breath, yet uneasiness penetrated his fuddled wits. The King's young face was unsmiling, the bright blue Plantagenet eyes were narrowed, and not as friendly as Wat had thought them.

"Now I command that you shall all go home," said Richard sternly.

"Sure, sure we will," said Wat, but he was dismayed. The comradeship, the equality had somehow disappeared, and he tried to recapture them. He mounted his horse, so that he should be on a level with the King. "Me throat's dry as a bone, King," he cried. "How about a spot o' wine, how say ye? Shall we share a drink to seal the pact?"

Over Richard's delicate face hot color flowed. He gestured to his squire, who ran and dipped water from a well near the priory and bringing the dipperful back to Wat, held it out to him with sneering insolence.

"Water? Pshaw!" cried the discomfited tiler, seeing that the King had drawn away from him. Wat glared at the squire, slobbered up a great mouthful and with a vulgar noise squirted it out again onto the dust.

"By God!" cried the young squire. "This greatest knave

and robber in all Kent, look at the respect he shows the King's Grace!"

Wat started and his hand flew to his dagger. "What was that ye called me?"

"Knave and robber!" shouted the squire.

Wat pulled his dagger, and kicking his horse, charged—not at the King as it might seem—but past him towards the squire, who ran.

The mayor had been waiting for a chance. He spurred his horse crying, "So ribaud, you'd draw steel against your King!" and with his cutlass slashed sideways down at Wat, carving deep into his shoulder. The tiler staggered, plunging his dagger blindly at the mayor but it glanced off the coat of mail.

Richard's horse reared and snorted, and the boy pulled him in and away from Wat, who lay thrashing on the ground, while Walworth and the squire hacked at him with furious blows of sword and cutlass.

"What's happening?" cried voices from the rebel side. "Wat's down, what is't?" And someone else, seeing a sword flash, cried, "The King is knighting Wat!"

Cob from his tree saw differently. Soon they all saw— Wat's terrified horse galloped across the field dragging the tiler's dying, bleeding body by the stirrup.

"Christus, Christus!" cried John Ball in a voice of agony. "They've killed Wat!"

The rebel army stood gaping, paralyzed. The lords across Smithfield drew back white-faced and murmuring. Richard sat his horse stiffly in the center of the field. Then there was a ripple of movement down the rebel line. Here and there a bowman unslung his bow uncertainly and drew arrow from his quiver. No one else moved. They waited for some signal, but none came.

Richard looked at the bow tips that twinkled in the sun, the arrows being slowly notched and pointing down the field at him. He flung his head back and dug the golden spurs of knighthood into his horse's flanks. He galloped straight towards the rebel lines and shouted, "So now *I* shall be your leader, as you wished me to!"

The bowstrings slackened. The rebels looked at one another, at Wat's body and up at the shining crowned youth who beckoned to them.

"Ay!" they cried. "Our little King is leader! Richard! Richard! We hold wi' *you*, Richard!"

A bondsman from Essex ran out from the crowd, cast himself to his knees and kissed Richard's foot. The King looked down at him and smiled.

The mayor had galloped up behind and pulling his horse near said in a low voice, "Lead them to Clerkenwell, Your Grace, and keep them there. I'll soon be up with reinforcements." He spurred his horse and headed into town.

"Follow me, good people!" Richard called. "Follow now your King!"

The peasant army gazed up at him with confiding trust. Had he not given them their freedom? Had he not shown himself their friend? Richard wheeled his horse and started off up along the Fleet towards the open farmlands, past the smoking ruins of the treasurer's priory that they had fired.

When Walworth and Sir Robert Knolles arrived later with troops and the hastily summoned citizenry, the mayor also bore with him Wat the tiler's head mounted on a pike. The rebels stared at Wat's head in terror and turning again to the King begged for mercy, which he sweetly granted, looking like the young St. George himself as he smiled at them all and accepted their homage.

The peasants' great revolt was ended.

They dispersed fast and were permitted to leave, most of them exceeding joyful, for they had their charters and the King's word that they were free; and when they understood that Wat had drawn a traitor's dagger against the King, they conceded that his death had been inevitable. Nor did those who lingered deem it unfitting when they looked back and saw that the King was knighting Mayor William Walworth.

Only a handful were heavyhearted on that Saturday night and joined John Ball, who fled up towards the Midlands crying that this day's deeds were not as God had willed it, that the fellowship must go on, that its work was but half completed, crying, "Put not your trust in princes!" Few listened to him.

Cob left London too that night. He joined a company of home-going northerners who had not yet their charters, but one of the King's men explained that there was no cause to wait, soon proclamation would be made throughout the land that serfdom was abolished.

So Cob and his companions started on the North road to Waltham, and as they marched they sang.

## XXVI

THE FINE WEATHER broke during that night while most of the rebels were marching home, and Sunday morning in London dawned in a sticky drizzle. The loft above the fish shop was dank and gray when Katherine opened her eyes. She lay quietly for a time on the feather bed looking up at the rafters and wondering exactly where she was, aware at first only of hunger and weakness and that there was a sore place on the back of her head. She knew that a long time had passed since she had been fully aware, though she had a confused memory of wandering through streets with Cob o' Fenton, of lying down up here and waking sometimes to drink water; but mostly she had slept. There had been a confusion of terrible dreams: sinister faces leering like gargoyles—Jack Maudelyn, his jaw jutting out one-sided in a monstrous way, a man with a red beard who, while shattering Avalon's windowpanes with a pike, counted inanely, "Oon, twa, tree—" There had been a huge glowering black-jowled man who kept saying, "Who *are* ye then?" There had been sticky pools of blood with Joli-coeur's crystal splinters glittering in them.

Katherine twisted her head from side to side to throw off the clinging haze of horror, but the dream memories persisted. Now she saw Brother William's pallid doomed face as he cried out, "God in His mercy save you, Katherine!" and heard the dull squashing thud before he fell by the fireplace. She saw Blanchette in a blood-soaked gray chamber robe, smiling a secret smile, curtsying to the man who asked, "Who are ye then?"

Katherine shuddered and sat up dizzily. Her gaze focused

slowly and was caught by the little wooden Calvary that stood on a bracket above a Pessoner clothes coffer. She stared at the cross, which was the size of Brother William's crucifix and of the same dark wood, she stared until it wavered and grew, until it loomed big as a window and blotted out all light behind it.

"No," she whispered shrinking back onto the bed, "Jesu, NO!" She pushed her hands out in front of her as though she pushed against a falling weight. Her breath came ragged and fast. After a moment she pulled herself off the bed and looked down at her green gown. It was cut below the knees and spotted with little charred holes. This is the gown I put on Thursday morning in the garderobe when Brother William came to warn us, to warn me and Blanchette. She lifted the skirt and looked at her shift; there were scorches on it, and red burns in the flesh of her thighs.

"God have mercy on me—" said Katherine aloud, "for those were no dreams." Her nails dug deep into her sweating palms, she stumbled through the door towards the stairs.

An hour ago Master Guy had brought Dame Emma back from St. Helen's priory, the danger being over; and the goodwife was standing by the hearth directing the maids, who were setting the place to rights again.

Dame Emma started as Katherine wavered down the stairs clinging to the rail. "Sweet Mother Mary!" cried Emma running to her, "Guy said ye were asleep—dear, dear." She clicked her tongue as she saw Katherine's gown, the matted tangled hair.

"Blanchette—" said Katherine in a faint dead voice. "I must find Blanchette. She ran away in the Savoy—what day is it now?"

" 'Tis Sunday," said Dame Emma. "But ye can't go anywhere like that, my lady. *Sit down!*" she cried sharply as Katherine swayed. "God love us, what's happened?"

"Happened enough, in truth," said the fishmonger. Now that the revolt was over, he was expansive with relief. "Poor lass's been lying up there mizzyheaded for days."

At his wife's shocked exclamation he said defensively, "Old Elias, he looked to her, brought her water."

Dame Emma poured forth a stream of anxious inquiry, then checked it for more practical matters. She made Katherine sit on the settle and put a pillow to her head. She fed her wine sip by sip until faint color came back to the hollow cheeks.

Katherine did all that she was told and concentrated her mind on regaining strength fast. By noon the swimming feebleness had gone, and she was ready.

"Have you a horse that I may borrow?" she said to the hovering dame. "I must find Blanchette. God help me that so much time was lost." She spoke with a steadiness that silenced the good wife's protests.

Emma docilely commandeered her husband's gelding and had a boy saddle it. She dressed Katherine in one of Hawise's old russet-colored kirtles, but nothing would persuade her to let Katherine go unaccompanied through the streets. The revolt in London had ended but there were still carousing rebels left, and punitive bands of the King's men riding about and restoring order while they searched for Jack Strawe and one or two of the other leaders who had forfeited the right of amnesty. Master Guy had gone to bed exhausted by the last days' events, but the Dame decided that she herself would go pillion behind Katherine. She was motivated not only by kindness but by a lively curiosity.

Secluded as she had been in St. Helen's during the three days of rebellion, she had heard nothing but the wildest rumors of burnings and beheadings, and she thought them much exaggerated. She sympathized with Katherine's anxiety over her child, of course, but she thought that that worry would doubtless be soon resolved. The little lass would be found hiding in some safe nook in the Savoy.

Katherine made no objection to Dame Emma's company, nor to the presence of the armed prentice that the Dame routed out from the fishhouse. She did not speak as they rode in a gray drizzle through London streets towards Ludgate, and beyond it to the Fleet.

Dame Emma's cheerful chatter was soon hushed, her fat comely face fell into dismay and finally to round-eyed horror when they skirted the ruins of the Temple. Ahead of them on the Strand, the Savoy had always loomed in a mass of crenelated walls, of gleaming white turrets and pinnacles with fluttering pennants, and the gold spire on the chapel topping all.

Now there was nothing. No shape against the empty sky —nothing but a vast expanse of rubble behind a shell of crumbling blackened walls.

"Such a thing canna *be*," Dame Emma whimpered crossing

herself. " 'Tis witchcraft. God shield us, is there naught left at all o' that great fair place?" She stole a frightened sideways look at Katherine. "Lady dear—I didna know 'twould be like this."

Katherine did not answer her. The horses whickered nervously, reared, and finally balked some way from the ruins; an acrid suffocating stench hung in the damp air, stench of burned flesh as well as smoke.

Katherine dismounted, while the prentice held the horse. She began to walk towards the ruins, Dame Emma behind her. A little group of folk stood in the fields where Katherine had lain on Thursday. They were gaping at the remains of the Savoy and muttering to each other. As the women approached, a goggle-eyed man greeted them with the familiarity of shared excitement and cried, "It do be a horrid marvel, don't it! There was a score o' rebels trapped in there, they say ye could hear 'em screaming till Friday eve. Be haunted now for sure, John o' Gaunt's Savoy'll be—I'll not go down the Strand after sundown, that I won't."

Katherine walked past the group and turned through the blocks of fallen masonry that had been the gatehouse. She clambered over the still warm rubble into what had been the Outer Ward.

"Lady Katherine," panted Dame Emma, wheezing and clattering after her, "come back—there's naught to find in there—ye can see, and there's danger—that bit o' wall maught fall."

Katherine stumbled on, picking her way over charred fragments of beams and blackened stones until she stood near the falcon mew, which was now a heap of wood ashes. She looked up at the roofless segment of Thames-side wall that stood silhouetted black against the horizon, its vacant window frames showing lancet shapes of the gray sky beyond. She saw high above, the outline of the fireplace that had been in the Avalon Chamber, but the great rose marble mantel had fallen to the paving below and shattered.

Up there, where there was now no floor, they had stood on either side of the fireplace when Brother William was killed —she and Blanchette. On that spot the girl had spoken to the black-jowled leader before she ran from the room towards the stairs. Katherine turned to look for the Great Stairs that had led up to the Privy Suite. From the place where the stairs had been a little cloud of steamy smoke still rose hissing faintly under the rain.

"Sweeting—" said Dame Emma, laying her hand on Katherine's arm, "come away, do. There's naught here but ruin. The little lass'll have run to safety somewhere, ye'll find her."

"To safety?" repeated Katherine. "Nay—she did not think of safety when she ran from me crying that I was—was—oh God—" she whispered. "Dame Emma, go away. Leave me alone awhile. Leave me—" She sank to her knees by a block of burned stone and lifted her eyes up to the empty slits that had been the windows of the Avalon Chamber.

Dame Emma obeyed, so profoundly shocked that she did not heed the blackening of her neat kidskin shoes and the tearing of her fine woolsey gown. She withdrew to the mass of fallen stone at the gatehouse. Heedless even of the rain, she settled herself to wait. She looked back into the distance where she could just see Lady Katherine kneeling, and Dame Emma's eyes crinkled up like a baby's, tears spilled from them.

She shivered as the rain soaked through her mantle and dampened her plump shoulders, and she looked to see if Lady Katherine were not yet ready to leave this dreadful place. Katherine had moved, and was now with bent head walking slowly about the Outer Ward. While Dame Emma watched, she saw the tall russet-clad figure lean over and pick up something, then stand stock-still, holding it to her breast for some moments before coming towards the dame.

Katherine held out an object on her open palm. "Look—" she said in the heavy faraway tone, "do you see this, Dame Emma?"

It was a small silvery half-melted mass. The dame said uncertainly, "Is't a clasp?"

"I think so," said Katherine with stony quiet. "It might be the clasp on Blanchette's chamber robe."

The dame stifled her gasp of dismay and cried heartily, "Nay, 'tis no clasp, and if it were—it means naught."

"It lay in the ashes of the falcon mew," said Katherine. "She loved birds, perhaps she ran there." Then had Blanchette run also to the men who caroused drunkenly in the cellars? "I shall be a whore, good sir—mayhap a murdering whore like my mother." No memory was spared Katherine now of what had taken place on Thursday.

"Blanchette was touched by madness when she ran from the Avalon Chamber," said Katherine in the same toneless voice. "Twas not from the horror of the Gray Friar's blood upon her, but from the horror of what she had heard him say before that."

"Think not o' horrors, dear," cried Dame Emma. "Come away—this does no good."

"Ah, but I *must* think on it," said Katherine. Her eyes were black as the rain-filled sky. "I can no longer hide from truth. Good dame, my friend, you don't know what my sin has been. I did not wholly know, but the Gray Friar did, and God in His vengeance has stricken my innocent child as the first means of my punishment."

"Nay, nay," Dame Emma expostulated, pitying the lady's haggard look, thinking that this morbidness was well explained by all the fearful happenings of the last days, but anxious only to get Katherine back to dryness and comfort.

Katherine said no more, and came with Dame Emma, unprotesting. She mounted the horse where it waited down the Strand. They rode a little way until they came to the Church of St. Clement's Dane, when Katherine pulled up the gelding. "It was here that I married Hugh Swynford," she said.

"Oh ay—I'd forgot," answered the dame, puzzled. " 'Twas so long ago."

"I thought it was long ago." Katherine looped the reins on the pommel. "I know now it was but yesterday." She dismounted. "Dame Emma, I've kept you out enough in the rain. Please leave me here and go home. Nay, I've no need of protection—Jesu, do you think *any* danger could matter to me now?"

"But the services are over—there's no one there," protested the dame staring at the empty little church.

Katherine gave her a faint blind smile. She turned in to the church porch as the dame reluctantly rode off.

Katherine knelt by the altar rail where her Nuptial Mass had been celebrated, and her eyes fixed themselves on the ruby light above the sanctuary. She knelt motionless, forcing herself back into that moment when a man had knelt with her, a man to whom she had given forced unconsidered vows —until at last she reconstructed the presence of that stocky armored figure beside her. She felt the surliness, the roughness that had revolted her then, but she felt plainly too as she had not then, the pathos of the clumsy groping love to which she had made no return but endurance and a pitying contempt. That love of Hugh's had burgeoned again for Blanchette—and had no chance to flower.

Katherine, inflexibly reliving the moments of her marriage, heard the rustling in the back of the church, the clink of golden spurs—she saw the priest hesitate and stop, the leap of flattered awe in his eyes. She saw herself walk down the aisle into the Duke's arms, yielding to him her mouth, her body, her allegiance, in the presence of the husband she had sworn herself to—and in the presence of God.

Here in this church had been the beginning of two long roads, one that ended in a shabby little room in Bordeaux in a death that would not have been except for her; the other road had ended in blood and fire and madness in the Avalon Chamber. Yet were they not the same road after all?

Above in the tower the bell began to toll for vespers, and Katherine arose and pushed aside a leather curtain. It was the priest himself who hauled the rope, and he stared at her in astonishment.

"Father—" said Katherine, "was it you who was priest here fifteen years ago, did you once come from Lincolnshire?"

"Ay, my daughter." He was a mousy ill-fed man with anxious darting eyes, a sickly rash on his face—and in the sparse gray hair of his tonsure. "What is it?"

"I wish to make confession to you."

Father Oswald was at once flustered. He disliked the unusual, and he tried to put Katherine off by saying that it was Sunday, that she was not of his parish, that in any case it was time for vespers.

She replied that she would wait and looked at him with so tragic an urgency that he became still more confused, until she added in a strange voice, "I am a Swynford, Father— Katherine Swynford, Sir Hugh Swynford's widow—ay, I see that means something to you." For he started and the raw scabs on his face blended with its sudden redness. He remembered well the marriage now, it was to Swynford influence that he had owed his living twenty years ago, and he remembered the moment when the great Duke and Duchess of Lancaster had appeared in the back of his church, for he had boasted of it often.

But after vespers when he listened through the grille to the woman's low anguished voice, he was appalled. He could scarce listen to her for fear of the things she told him, dreadful secrets that he did not wish to know. Murder of Sir Hugh, her husband—said the voice—not deliberate but murder in God's sight, a Gray Friar had said so, Brother William Appleton, who had himself been murdered. Ten years of adultery with the Duke of Lancaster resultant upon this murder. And she spoke of a child, who had been driven mad, who might be dead too.

"Cease, daughter!" said the priest at last in a trembling voice. "I cannot grant you absolution, no priest could—"

"I know," said Katherine. " 'Tis not of my own soul I'm thinking. It is of my child's. Father, surely a merciful God will accept from me some penance that will save Blanchette, wherever she be."

"Penance—ay, what penance?" stammered the little priest, wanting only to be rid of her. Now it came clearer to his panicking mind that this woman was protected by the Duke, the Duke who was all-powerful and might remove a meddlesome priest as easily as he would squash a fly. On the other hand the Duke's great palace had been burned by the rebels and he was hated by the common folk whose vengeance also might include a priest.

"True contrition, give up your evil life, make reparation, mortify your senses—" he gabbled quickly. "Daughter, I cannot tell you what else—go to your own priest. Go— Go—" and he pulled the shutter over the grille.

Katherine walked from the church with dragging steps. She went again down Fleet street through Ludgate. By St. Paul's close she stopped and gazed up at the cathedral spire. After a while she entered the huge shadowed nave and walked down it to the chantry by the Lady Chapel, where two candles burned on the little altar and shone on the serene alabaster face and the long white hands that were upraised in perpetual prayer.

Katherine knelt beside the tomb and reached out to touch one corner of the sculptured robe while she spoke to the Lady Blanche. Dearest lady—if I have wronged you too, forgive, but you know that I never meant wrong towards *you*, and you knew what it is to love him, as I have loved him. So forgive—and tell me how to save my child who is your namesake.

The lovely face shimmered in the dimness of the chantry, it floated, high off, pure and cool as a star. A spirit. How should it give comfort to one who had denied the spirit these long years, who had been sufficient unto herself, who had lived for nothing but her own desires?

Outside the cathedral the gray light waned and the rain blew harder. Along the choir aisles a verger passed from time to time and stared curiously at the woman in simple russet gown and goodwife's coif who wept beside the Duchess of Lancaster's tomb. At last when Paul's bell began to ring for Compline, Katherine raised her head and spoke to Blanche again. Lady, I see now that it was yet one more wickedness that I should ask you to help me. And she struggled up from her cramped knees.

Then it seemed the candlelight brightened on the alabaster features, and in Katherine's head she heard the echo of a soft voice that said, "Walsingham," while she saw the Lady Blanche's living face as it had been that Christmastide at Bolingbroke, radiant with fruition for that she bore in her womb Henry, the heir of Lancaster; and Katherine remembered what Blanche had said "Someday you must make pilgrimage to Our Lady of Walsingham, who is especially kind and merciful to mothers—"

It was Blanchette that Katherine had borne within her as she had heard those words long years ago—and surely it was for Blanchette's sake that the Lady Blanche had given Katherine some answer at last.

Katherine remained until the following Saturday with the Pessoners, and each day searched for Blanchette. Master Guy sent forth two of his prentices to cry through the streets that there would be a reward for any information respecting a little maid of fourteen with cropped copper-toned hair, and dark gray eyes, whose Christian name was Blanche; while Katherine herself visited the convents where the child might have taken shelter. They went all through London and over to Southwark and as far as Westminster, but no one had seen the girl. Steeling herself and telling no one of her purpose, Katherine made yet other visits—to the stews along Bankside, where the whoremongers received this pale grave woman kindly enough when they understood that it was a mother searching for a crazed girl, but nobody knew anything of Blanchette.

On the Friday evening before Katherine's departure on pilgrimage to Walsingham, the Pessoners had an unexpected visitor.

Katherine was upstairs in the chamber above the fish shop when Dame Emma opened the door to a knock and greeted with pleased surprise a plump little man with a forked brown beard. "Why, Master Geoffrey, welcome! Guy," she called over her shoulder, " 'tis Master Geoffrey Chaucer come to see us!"

Geoffrey came in with appropriate greetings, accepted a mug of ale, then said in a tone of anxious wonder, "Is it really true that Lady Swynford is here?"

"That she is, poor thing," said the fishmonger, settling down with his own ale, and preparing for a pleasant chat with the Controller of the Customs, who was an important man in London and one Master Guy respected. "Ay, Lady Katherine's here, and a fearful time she had o' it last week in the revolt. Burned out o' the Savoy she was—and her lass gone daft—or—" said the fishmonger shaking his head, "dead more like. We begin to think, Emma and me, the child never got out o' the Savoy, certain 'tis there's no trace o' her— And if she did, crazed as she was and not rightly well from scarlet fever, there's little chance either. Cock's bones!" he broke off as he saw Chaucer's change of expression, "I clean forgot the little maid was your niece."

"Yes," said Geoffrey soberly, "and I'd no idea of any of this until I heard your streetcrier today and questioned him."

Geoffrey had returned from a trip on the night before the revolt and had been snugly ensconced in his rooms over Aldgate when Jack Strawe and his Essex men had streamed and bellowed through the gate beneath him. And there he had stayed unmolested, reading and writing, during the three days of the violence, being a peaceable man and temperamentally indifferent to political factions. But on his emergence he had been shocked by the extent of the destruction, and now more shocked to find that Katherine and Blanchette had been at the Savoy.

"Where is Lady Swynford? I'd like to see her," he said.

"Ye'll find her sadly changed." Dame Emma came bustling up with a dish of her saffron buns. "She's shaved off her hair, and fasts like an anchorite. Seems like she blames herself for the loss of her child—and for the Gray Friar's death too." The dame slammed the plate on the table and her eyes snapped. "But 'twas that cursed Jack Maudelyn really killed the Gray Friar, I got that much out of her. The devil's own spawn is Jack, but Beelzebub'll soon get him, I hear, and a good thing too."

"Wife, wife—" said Master Guy shaking his head. " 'Tis Hawise's wedded husband, ye shouldna wish him damned, no matter what." He turned to answer Chaucer's exclamation. "Jack he run around for all the days o' the hurling time with his jaw broke and now his head's swollen up like a melon and he can't breathe but what the good monks at St. Bart's hospital stick a straw down his gullet, and they say he won't last the day out."

"I'll buy no Masses for *his* soul," snorted the dame. " 'Twas he gave Lady Katherine the blow on her head too."

"By the rood, but these are fearful matters!" cried Geoffrey horrified. "I dread to think what this'll mean to the Duke when he hears. Why hasn't Katherine gone north to meet him then?"

Dame Emma shook her head. "I believe that is no part of her plan. I tell ye, she's much changed. More happened to her than we know on last cursed Thursday. She goes off tomorrow on pilgrimage but where to she won't tell."

Geoffrey's concern increased at each thing he heard, and when Katherine finally came into the kitchen he could not repress an exclamation. She was dressed in a coarse rusty black gown of woven hemp such as the humblest widows wore. Her slender white feet were bare and dusty; around her neck there was a wooden rosary, and on her forehead a great smudge of ashes. Her shaven head was tightly bound with a square of the black cloth. She had beauty still, the thinness of her flesh but exposed the grace of her bones and sinews, but the great brooding eyes were circled by umber shadows and the thick black lashes seemed too heavy for the weary lids.

"Katherine, before God, what does this mean, my dear?" Geoffrey cried, kissing her on the cheek.

"Geoffrey," she said with a faint smile, "I'm glad to see you, and I know that you'll help me."

"Ay, for sure, little sister, but—" He hesitated, at a loss for words. Religious-minded Katherine had never been. These past years with the Duke she had been a warmly vibrant creature of dancing and laughter, with an aura of hot sensual love about her; and in matters of devout observance he had deemed her of a most indifferent turn of thought. This strict penitential garb and talk of pilgrimage was surely some passing derangement, and if he could not change her mind, the Duke most certainly would.

"How can I help you?" he said as she waited, looking at him soberly.

Katherine read some of his disapproval in his face and made an effort to understand it. So dense and high a barrier reared up between this Katherine and the old one that she could barely perceive how strange she must seem to him.

"Come outside with me, Geoffrey," she said, "I must talk to you alone, and show you something."

They went out to Thames street into a golden June evening, and Katherine turned towards the Bridge.

"Your sister has been in danger too during the revolt," said Geoffrey with a hint of reproach as he walked beside her and she did not speak. "On that Wednesday when the trouble began Philippa was at Hertford with the Duchess but they were warned and fled in time to the north. Only today I got word that after a perilous journey they were safe in Yorkshire. During this time of the 'Grand Rumor' it seems that all belonging to him are included in this senseless unjust hatred of the Duke."

"Senseless?" said Katherine pausing and staring at the street. "Unjust? I thought so once. But now I know it's all God's punishment for our great sin."

"By Christ's holy wounds, Katherine, this is sickly talk! Your fleshly sin was not so great as that of many of the monkish fellows who accuse you of it, and *yours* is redeemed by a true love."

She gave him a dark sad look and walked on, guiding him up the wooden step onto London bridge. They passed along the Bridge between the clustered overhanging houses until they came to a small tower with spikes set up around it and vultures wheeling and screaming around the many decaying heads upon the spikes.

Geoffrey's steps faltered; he tried to protest, but Katherine pulled him on until they stood below an eyeless skull on which the drying maggoty flesh hung in ribbons. A skull whose bleaching brainpan had been cleft nearly in two. A piece of parchment had been tied to the spike below this head, and Katherine, seeing Geoffrey's look of shocked incomprehension, said, "Read."

He bent and peered at the parchment, then drew back

sharply, crossing himself. "Brother William!" he whispered. "Ah—may God rest his poor soul."

"Yes," said Katherine, "Brother William! He died because he came to the Savoy to protect me, and he died trying to save *my* soul."

Geoffrey swallowed while a prickle ran down his back. He turned from the rotting head to lean against the Bridge's stone balustrade and stare down into the swirling yellow waters below. At length he said, "But Katherine, you can buy Masses for him. 'Twas not your fault—"

She drew her breath in harshly and answered in a voice that jangled like an iron bell, "I can buy Masses for him, and for Blanchette—and I can buy Masses for my husband Hugh —who was murdered. Ay—*murdered,* Geoffrey. You may well whiten and shrink from me! Now do you still think the sin in which the Duke and I have lived so light a one?"

"Hush—for the love of God, Katherine," Geoffrey cried staring at her. He glanced quickly at the people who passed by on the Bridge. "Come over here, where we'll not be overheard." He drew her to an angle made by the tower buttress, and gazed with incredulous pity into her haunted eyes. "Now tell me," he said quietly.

In the morning when Katherine set out on foot for the North road that led to Walsingham, Geoffrey too left London, bearing a letter from Katherine to the Duke—wherever he might be. An unwilling messenger was Geoffrey, none of the hundred missions he had fulfilled on King's service had been as difficult as this. He knew what Katherine had written, and he suspected that not even the destruction of the Savoy and Hertford Castles nor any as yet unreported catastrophe would shock the Duke as this letter would.

While Geoffrey hurried north on his white palfrey, he could not help delighting in the beauty of the English countryside, the oak and beech studded greenwoods, the lush meadowlands, the fragrance of the hedgerows, the innocent twinkling faces of the little white and red daisies that he loved so well. When he refreshed himself and his horse at alestakes or taverns along the way, he noted as always the quaint oddities of people, and his mind teemed with stories that he wished to tell.

It was his way to finger voluptuously and without moral

judgment, all the multicolored skeins of experience that folk spun for themselves—yet now he was disquieted.

Katherine's revelations and her agony of penitence had startled him into shame. He felt that he had himself been drifting into light-minded worldliness. He thought with remorse of the pagan delight, the immorality, he had written into his "Troilus and Criseyde." They had read this love story at court, Richard had been charmed with it, the frivolous Duchess of York had wept over it, Katherine herself had heard portions of it, never suspecting in how many tender ways she had been Criseyde's model.

On this trip to the north, while bearing Katherine's despairing letter, conscience rode with Geoffrey. He knew very well that his writings were enjoyed by and influenced many who were bored by the moral Gower's homilies or Langland's fierce indictments, and in his light-minded treatment of carnal love he had most certainly ignored the Church's teachings. He had not pointed out that the devil's hand with the five fingers of lechery gripped a man by the loins, to throw him into the furnace of hell.

Instead of writing of penitence and punishment he had dallied with lewd levity. Was it, Geoffrey thought, because tragedy had never touched him personally before and because his whole nature shamefully recoiled from grimness and heavy accusations?

The Troilus should be abandoned for the present and later if he worked on it again he would make it clear that he had written only of "Pagan's cursed old rites," and he would warn young folks to cast their visage up to God. And he felt how he had wronged Katherine in thinking of her in terms of his compliant and fickle little Criseyde.

# XXVII

ON THE SATURDAY night of June 20 that Katherine set out on pilgrimage to Walsingham and that Geoffrey left for the north, the Duke was impounded on the Scottish side of the Border outside the walls of Berwick-upon-Tweed.

While he furiously paced the rough ground beneath a hastily erected tent, two of his most devoted knights, Lord Michael de la Pole and Sir Walter Ursewyk, watched him anxiously, but neither of them dared speak. The two knights had withdrawn to a far side of the tent and, seasoned worldly-wise men though they were, they found incredible this new humiliation that had come upon their Duke.

"I can't believe it," whispered Ursewyk to de la Pole. "Denied entry back into his own country, and at this time. That even Percy should have so villainous a heart!"

"May God strike Percy dead for this!" growled the baron, clenching his gnarled fists. "Could I but lay hands on the whoreson—" Angry breaths whistled through the gaps in his teeth, his great bearded jaw knotted.

Three hours ago, the Duke and his men had marched here from Scotland heading with all possible speed for home, frantic to find out what had actually happened during the revolt, of which the most hideous rumors had reached the Duke while he treated with the Scottish envoys. The frightened messenger who bore the secret news said that he believed all England was in rebellion against the Duke, that he had heard all of his castles had fallen into the peasants' hands, that the fate of his family was uncertain. The messenger had further added that the King—hiding in the Tower—had been forced to repudiate his uncle, had denounced him as a traitor and was thought to side entirely with the peasants.

De la Pole had never so much admired his Duke as he had then. The Scottish truce negotiations had been at the most delicate concluding point when John privily heard this news of total disaster, but no trace of fear or the torturing uncertainty had shown on his handsome face. He had given the Scots no inkling that now in this hour of England's civil war had come Scotland's golden moment to strike, and overrun the weakened torn south. He had suppressed all his personal concern until the Scots had signed an advantageous three-year truce, then he turned and hurried back towards England.

And England would not receive him. At least Percy, the Lord of Northumberland, would not permit him to cross the Border. The gates of Berwick were closed. Percy's forces were massed along the Tweed and planted throughout the Cheviot hills and he had sent word by Sir Matthew Redmayne, Warden of Berwick, that this outrage was done in obedience to the King's orders.

Here in a tent outside the city walls they had been confined these last hours while the cold rain hissed on the painted canvas, and while the Duke paced up and down like a chained bear. Suddenly he turned on his heel and confronted his friends. "Michael," he cried to de la Pole, "how many of my men are left here now?"

De la Pole gnawed his grizzled mustache and said with weary despair, "Not a hundred, my lord—not now." Many of the Duke's small band had melted away when Northumberland's position had become known. "We cannot fight, my lord," said the old campaigner bitterly. "Percy has a hundred thousand knaves to back him." And our luggage train as well, he added to himself. The Duke's main supplies had been trustingly left in Percy's charge at Bamborough before the Duke entered Scotland.

"Why do the hundred stay?" said the Duke through his teeth. "Why do *you* stay with me, de la Pole—and you, Ursewyk? 'Twill profit you nothing to cling to a ruined leader, an exile whom all the English wish to kill, whose King has turned against him— Go join Percy like the others—"

"My lord John—" said de la Pole softly. He rose and taking the Duke's cold hand kissed it. "We are not weather vanes, Ursewyk and I, nor Marmion either, nor Le Scrope and many another that you well know. Nor, my lord, do I believe that the King has given this order. I think it's entirely Percy's malignant invention. You know well he's jealous of your power."

"By God—it seems he has no need to be. Betrayed by my countrymen, sacrificed by my King—and Jesu—what has been happening to my family—to Katrine—" he added beneath his breath.

John threw himself down on a folding campstool, and leaning his elbows on the rough plank table bowed his head against his clenched fists.

His two friends glanced at each other. They both racked their brains for an answer to this stunning new reversal, but it was the wise de la Pole who found it first.

"Write to the King, my lord," he said after a moment. "Ask him his true intention. 'Tis the only way to deal with this."

John lifted his head and said grimly, "And are you fool enough to think Percy'll let my herald safely through? Has Percy shown allegiance to any honor?"

"Nay, I'd not count on it," answered the baron, "but I think Percy'll not dare to stop *me*, my lord, for he knows the King has trust in me."

The Duke looked startled. "Ay, mayhap you're right, 'tis worth a chance. I should have thought of it; though in truth, I'm loath to have you leave me, Michael." He looked with deep affection at the older man who had been his friend and counselor for so many years, and the baron's bluff weather-beaten face flushed with an answering emotion.

John called for pen, ink and parchment, wrote his letter. He handed it silently to de la Pole for reading. The old warrior's eyes misted as he laboriously spelled out the sense of the brief message. The Duke had written that if it were indeed his King's wish that he should remain in dishonored exile, he would obey, albeit with a heart so heavy that he would care no more for life. Or if the King had need of him, yet had been incontinently brought by wicked counsels to fear his uncle, then would John return alone with no one but a squire to attend him. But that he most piteously prayed his King and lord, no matter the decision, to have mercy on all those in England who were dear to Lancaster.

The baron handed the letter back with an embarrassed approving grunt. Surely even that highly strung and unpredictable young King would recognize here the authentic note of much-tried loyalty, though it was doubtful that Richard would have the wisdom to see how sorely tried that loyalty was, not if his other uncle, Thomas of Buckingham, were pouring poison in his ears. But, thought de la Pole, the Duke had at his hand a measure that would right all the wrongs he had suffered, that would take him in triumph back into his own country and might very well lead him to the throne itself, if he were so minded.

"Your Grace," said the baron, leaning near the Duke and speaking very low, "the *Scots* love you; they respected your kingly father but they love you for yourself. You've but to speak the word and the Earls of Carrick and Douglas would back you with an army of their Scots, you've but to lead them south through England to London itself. There's no need to grovel before your capricious nephew."

The Duke pressed his signet ring slowly into the hot wax, and raising his head, stared into his old friend's watchful eyes. "Do you suggest that because I'm so often called a traitor, I should now become one, Michael?" he said at last with a weary smile. "Ay—I see that you were jesting, or testing, and I should be angry that you dare. But I've no belly now for games, or anger either." John sighed and gazed down at his humble letter to the King. " 'Tis true the Scots are my friends—and I shall have to prove their friendship now since I'm not permitted to leave their land. But need I tell you, Michael, that I've never yet broken oath or vow? Twice I've sworn fealty to Richard, once by his father's deathbed, again at the coronation, and I'll do my best to serve him 'till I die."

"Ay—I know," said the baron gruffly. "But I wanted to hear you say it, for the devil has sent you a temptation now that would shatter any common man." His voice shook, and he reached hastily for a mug of wine and drained it. "My lord," he went on in a different tone, "my squire's a canny lad. Once we're in Yorkshire, at Pontefract or Knaresborough, I shall know more of what's really happened, and'll send him back to you with news. He can worm his way somehow through Cumberland border out of Percy's reach."

John nodded while a quiver passed over his haggard face. " 'Twill be bitter waiting," he said. He rose and walked to the tent door to push back the flap and gaze out into the black teeming night. After a moment he beckoned to the baron who came close to him. "I have a foreboding," murmured the Duke, "a heavy foreboding." He twitched his hand on the tent flap.

"Not your children!" cried the baron quickly.

"Nay, not of my children, dear as they are to me, but about someone who—God forgive me—is dearer yet."

The baron was still. He could think of no easy words of

comfort, nor doubt whom the Duke meant, though it seemed to him very strange that at such a time when his whole life might well be ruined, the Duke should waste thought for a woman, and one who was not even his Duchess. This one aspect of the Duke, Michael had never understood.

"I'll not neglect to make immediate inquiry for Lady Swynford when I get south, my lord," he said quietly.

De la Pole was successful in his mission. He found Richard, who shed impulsive tears over his favorite uncle's letter, and cried out, as the baron had suspected, that the closing of the Border had been entirely Percy's doing and without the slightest royal sanction. It was clear that Percy, infuriated that the Duke had been given a commission over him to treat of Scottish matters, had hopefully exaggerated all the rumors and guessed wrong as to the King's intent.

The fleetest royal messengers were accordingly dispatched at once to the north bearing the King's writs, and de la Pole followed after.

The Duke had spent the anxious days of waiting in Edinburgh with his Scottish hosts, who treated him with chivalrous courtesy. And the Scottish earls cheered generously when the royal messenger arrived from Richard and made it plain that all the Duke's embarrassment had been caused by Percy alone, whom they loathed. The Earl of Douglas gleefully offered the Duke eight hundred men-at-arms to aid in the immediate punishment of Percy, and the Duke accepted them as a guard of honor, but only as far as the Border.

"Once in England, my good friend," he said to the Scottish earl, "I'll need no help in dealing with the scurvy Lord of Northumberland, now that I know my King's true intentions." The Duke's voice was at its harshest, his eyes their iciest, and the admiring Earl of Douglas applauded this knightly conduct, even while he regretted giving up so good an excuse for fighting.

The city gates of Berwick were not closed when the Duke arrived there this time, in fact he was met at them by his own retainer, the old Lord Neville of Raby with his entire Westmoreland force of men, and by the trembling warden, Sir Matthew Redmayne, who had refused to admit him earlier.

The moment after the Duke had ridden through the gates into English territory, he lifted the visor on his brass battle helm and looked down at Percy's tool, the cringing, bowing warden. "Where is your master?" he cried, cutting across Sir Matthew's flow of apology.

"At B—Bamborough Castle, Your Grace," stammered the warden. "He waits to make you welcome, he prepares great feastings for you."

"How gracious of him!" said the Duke. "You, Redmayne, hasten now to Northumberland, and tell him to come here to me at once. Tell him I'll meet him across the river in the Tweed bank field. I would—speak with him."

Sir Matthew gulped and changed color. "But—Your Grace—"

The Duke's full mouth curled into a faint smile, while his eyes sharpened until the warden felt them like two piercing daggers. "In case," said the Duke through his smiling lips, "that message is not sufficiently clear, take him this too!" He drew his heavy leather gauntlet from his right hand and flung it on the muddy street at Sir Matthew's feet. It fell with the Duke's embroidered arms upward, the royal arms of England and of Castile.

The unhappy warden, who knew very well that he himself would be made to suffer for bearing so unwelcome a message, stammered something and picked the gauntlet up between two fingers; gloomily mounting his horse, he rode away down the street towards the road to Bamborough.

Neville of Raby slapped his thigh and burst into an excited guffaw. "Oh, well done, my lord! Well done!" he wheezed, while beneath the chain mail shirt and emblazoned jupon his belly jiggled. "God's wounds, but this'll be a rich sight. Percy has as much skill at knightly combat as a goaded bull. 'Twill be rare sport to see him slashing and stomping against the best jouster in the land!"

The Duke did not answer, he spurred Morel, his powerful new black stallion, and galloped through the town, across the bridge to Tweed bank field while his retinue streamed after him. Once arrived there, his squires set about erecting his tent and bringing him food while he settled down to wait for Percy to come from Bamborough near twenty miles away.

It was here that Michael de la Pole found his Duke that afternoon, when there had been as yet no sign of Percy.

The baron had delayed his return trip north. Knowing that the royal messengers bore documents that would relieve the Duke's immediate crisis, de la Pole had taken time to find out the exact state of Lancaster's personal affairs.

When he saw the Lancaster banner flying over a striped red and blue tent near the Tweed bridge, he had ridden into camp and heard at once from the excited retainers of the Duke's challenge. The baron walked to the painted tent and announced his presence to a hovering young squire, whereupon the Duke called out in a glad voice, "Welcome, de la Pole! Come in!"

The Duke had been reading in a favorite volume of Ovid's Metamorphoses when the baron walked into his tent. He flung the book on the table crying, "By the Virgin—but I'm glad to see you, Michael, and deeply grateful too at the way you accomplished your mission!" He shook his friend's hand warmly, smiling. "The only person I would rather see is Percy, whom I await right eagerly."

"Ay—so I hear," said the baron with some dryness, sitting down on a campstool and gazing ruefully at his duke. "You seem in uncommon good spirits for a man who has challenged another to mortal combat."

"Why not? I'm sick of restraint and battling with shadows! I long to come to grips with a worthy foe. God's blood, you know what I've endured from slander, from whispering lies —'twould not have been so in my father's heyday. Ah, but times are sadly changed."

"'Tis so—" said the baron thoughtfully. "Times are changed. I've been seeing the evidence with my own eyes. That the commons should have *dared* to commit the outrages that they did—" He shook his head.

The eager light died from John's eyes. He sighed. "Ay, tell me, Michael. Your squire when he came to me in Edinburgh much relieved my mind when he said Katherine and her children were safe at Kenilworth."

The baron gulped and John, reading his face, said sharply, "What is it? Out with it!"

"I was misinformed in Yorkshire," answered the baron slowly. "Oh, your little Beauforts are safe enough at Kenilworth, for I saw them. But Lady Swynford was never there."

"Where is she then?" John's voice was strident.

"Nobody knows, my lord. I asked at court, I asked your Lancastrian children, Henry, the Ladies Philippa and Elizabeth—*they* are all safe and well, though you've no idea of the times of danger they passed through unscathed, thanks be to all merciful God."

"Ay—ay—I know they're safe, this I've heard already—

but my God, where then is Katherine? I left her at the Savoy, but she must have been warned as the others were—" John stopped. "In what condition *is* the Savoy, Michael?" he said carefully.

The baron bowed his head and plucked with a blunt finger at a loosened thong on his greave. "There is nothing left, my lord, nothing. It was entirely gutted by the fire the rebels set."

John shut his eyes and rising walked away from the baron. Tonnerre de dimanche est tonnerre de diable. He saw Katherine's piteous frightened face the morning that he had left her for Scotland. He felt the clinging arms that he had loosed from his neck and the touch of her beseeching lips on his. He thought of the foreboding he had had before the walls of Berwick and which had been set at rest by the baron's mistaken message. Lovedy, he thought, my Katrine—nay! He checked the rising fear.

" 'Tis ridiculous to speak as though she might have been in danger!" he shouted angrily. "There were plenty of men-at-arms to guard her, Roger Leach the best sergeant in England, there were all the house carls, and above all there was Brother William, who would never let her, or anything belonging to me, come to harm!"

The baron flushed and plucked harder at the leather thong. They knew well enough in London what had happened to the Savoy's men-at-arms, and he himself had seen Brother William's head stuck to a spike on London bridge. "Ay, to be sure," he said quickly. "No use to worry about her. No doubt at all she got away in time. The Savoy is the only gross destruction, my lord," he said forcing a light cheerful tone. "Some damage at Hertford but easily repaired. Your people on all the other manors remained loyal."

"Except the craven steward at Pontefract," said John lifelessly. "I'll soon deal with him when I get there, he shall regret refusing to admit the Duchess."

The baron lifted his head and gave John's shut face a thoughtful look. News of the Duchess Costanza had been the one entirely certain bit of information he had been able to send to the Duke by his squire, for Michael had seen the Duchess himself in Yorkshire on the way south. The poor lady had had a terrifying time of it, fleeing first from Hertford with the rebels actually at her heels and then upon arrival at the Duke's great stronghold of Pontefract, being denied shelter by a frightened addlepated steward, fleeing again through the night to Knaresborough Castle.

"The Duchess awaits you most anxiously at Knaresborough, my lord," said the baron. "She is praying night and day for your safety."

"I suppose so," said the Duke in the same dull tone. "Costanza is very skilled at prayer."

The baron felt a rare spurt of irritation towards his Duke. Consuming love for a woman was a thing which had never come his way, and there was such a thing as justice too; the Duke's total lack of anything more than formal interest in his Duchess struck him as unfair. It was not as though Costanza were old and withered either. She was younger than Lady Swynford and while obviously not as beautiful, yet she appeared to the baron to be an attractive woman. Moreover she had brought to the Duke Castile, and a famous name. If something had really happened to Lady Swynford—here the baron secretly crossed himself—it might well be an ultimate blessing. The scandal of the Duke's open relations with his paramour had not helped his popularity.

"My lord," the baron ventured, "the poor Duchess was much shaken by her harrowing experience, she was actually stoned by the rebels. 'Tis a miracle that neither she nor your little Catalina was hurt."

John frowned and nodded. "Thanks be to Sant' Iago de Compostela." But he spoke without feeling. Even this little girl of his he did not care for deeply, the baron thought, though he was fond of all his other children, and the bastards most of all.

They sat in silence for some minutes until the baron with his Duke's good at heart tried once again. "My lord, when you see the Duchess in a few days' time, will you not receive her warmly and comfort her, that is your much-tried wife?"

John's head jerked around. "By God, de la Pole, if this came from anyone but you— Do you suggest that I'm deficient in respect towards the Queen of Castile? Do you dare to criticize my bearing?"

"No, my lord," said the baron imperturbably. "Your bearing is always correct. I but suggest that she is perhaps more worthy of your affection than your preoccupation elsewhere has permitted you to realize."

Even the baron flinched before the look in the Duke's eyes, and nobody but the baron—and Katherine—would have so braved the ferocious Plantagenet temper, but before the Duke could answer, both men started and listened. Clearly in the distance they heard the blare of an approaching herald's trumpet.

"Percy, at last!" cried the Duke, his thunderous face clearing. He shouted, and two of his squires darted into the tent and began to accouter their lord in his engraved-steel tilting armor, while another tested yet again the lance's point; and in the field the black stallion Morel, already in full battle harness, was led rearing and snorting towards the tent.

The baron went out and, shading his eyes against the westering sun, watched the approach of Northumberland's herald and four armored men who escorted a figure in a helm crested with the blue Percy lion. De la Pole frowned and blinked his farsighted eyes, as Lord Neville walked up to join him.

Both men stared at the advancing Northumbrians, until Neville said, sourly, "Has the devil shrunk Percy of a sudden? Yon figure seems small indeed to me."

"Ay," answered the baron, "so I am thinking."

They turned and silently mounted their waiting chargers when the Duke came out of the tent. Neville and de la Pole though not so heavily armored as their leader, yet had needed help from their squires, but John still kept the lean muscular strength of his youth and he mounted into the gold and velvet saddle unassisted. He spurred Morel, who bounded forward, then checked him to a decorous gait and rode down the field towards the newcomers. His barons and knights followed.

"So, Percy," cried the Duke as he rode up to the stiff short figure in the blue lion jupon, "come forth to do battle for the insults you've offered me!" He struck sharply once with the side of his lance against the other's armplate. Whereupon the Percy lifted his visor and disclosed the small red truculent face, not of his sire, the Earl of Northumberland, but of little Hotspur.

"By God and Saint John!" cried the Duke staring. "What does this mean, lad? Where's your father?"

The boy had hot yellowish eyes like a boar's, and they shifted uncomfortably. "My father cannot accept your challenge, my Lord Duke," he said sullenly. "A painful malady has struck his right shoulder, he cannot move it, he could hold neither sword nor lance."

There was an instant's silence while the Duke's men craned to hear, then they let out a roar of derision. "It seems," said Lord Neville loudly in his grating voice, "that the Earl of Northumberland is lily-livered; this, at least, I had not guessed!"

"No," screamed Hotspur. " 'Tis not true!"

John sat still in his saddle gazing at the flushed boy. "D'you mean that you've brought the earl's full apology for his dishonorable treatment of my person?"

"No!" cried Hotspur again. "He makes no apology. He will meet you next month before the King to see then who is in the right. I've come to take up the challenge now, I shall fight you in his stead!"

"God's wounds—" whispered the Duke. Discouragement dragged him down like a millstone tied to his feet. "I cannot do battle with an undergrown boy of sixteen," he said wearily, pulling on Morel's bridle and turning the horse.

De la Pole glanced at his Duke with sharp sympathy. It must be writ in his stars, thought the baron, naught else could explain the checks and bitter disappointments that constantly assailed poor Lancaster.

But young Percy would not leave it so. He furiously spurred his horse and galloped up to the Duke. "But I will fight, I *will!*" he shouted. "I demand my right to do battle in my father's stead. 'Tis the law of chivalry."

"And what do Percys know of chivalry, young cockerel?" said Lord Neville with a contemptuous laugh.

"Ay, but he *has* the right," said the Duke slowly, reining in his horse. He shrugged beneath his steel epaulettes. "Be it so. To your end of the field, Percy—"

Lancaster and Northumberland heralds ran out to the open space and blowing on their trumpets announced the contest. The Duke waited listlessly until he saw the white batons raised and dropped and heard the heralds call "Laissez-aller—!"

With lances braced and horizontal the two horses pounded down the field from opposite directions. As they crossed each other the Duke negligently parried the boy's wild thrust and on this first course forbore to take advantage of Hotspur's unguarded left flank. But on the second course he shattered the boy's spear and though his own lance point was broken off by the shock, he swerved Morel and coolly slanting the butt of his lance into the boy's armpit beneath the breastplate, lifted him frmm the saddle and deposited him on the ground.

A wild cheer went up from the Duke's men, but John raised his visor and shook his head frowning. "Have done!" he cried sternly. "There's naught to cheer in this shameful contest."

He dismounted and walked over to Hotspur, whose squire was unbuckling his helmet. When it was off, the boyish face was seen to be wet with angry tears.

"You acquitted yourself bravely, young Percy," said the Duke. "You may tell your father so. Now get back to him, and tell him too that since he skulks and runs from me here I shall certainly confront him later in the presence of the King —unless of course some apt malady of limb should prevent the earl from traveling!"

Hotspur screamed out a trembling defiance, but John turned on his heel and did not listen. He strode back to his tent, while Percy's disgruntled men rode silently away beside their little chieftain.

The Duke and his meinie started south that night and on the sixteenth of July they reached Newcastle-upon-Tyne. A fair prosperous town was Newcastle, albeit a smoky one, for folk here burned the coals they laboriously dug from the surrounding hillsides. The Duke rode at the head of his men to the old Norman castle that overlooked the Tyne. He entered by the Black Gate and pausing in his chamber in the keep only long enough to remove his armor and cleanse himself, walked down the twisting stone stairs to the beautiful little chapel.

Here he lit a candle to the Virgin and knelt down to pray, hoping as he had each day since Berwick to lift thereby the oppression in his heart. He would whisper the Ave over and over like an incantation and often found comfort in it, but the painted wooden features of this Virgin had in them something of Katherine in the demure lowered lids, the faintly cleft chin, the high rounded forehead, and he turned away from Her in sharp pain.

There was no image of St. Catherine in this chapel so he could not properly renew the vow he had already made, but he repeated it at the end of his prayers. "If I find my Katrine safe and unharmed, I vow to build a chapel to Saint Catherine on any place in my lands that the Blessed Saint shall designate." He kissed the crucifix on his beads and rose.

He went restlessly upstairs to the Hall, where his knights had gathered, some drinking, some dicing, while de la Pole and Neville were engaged in an acrimonious game of chess. The Hall was fetid and smoky from the old-fashioned fire over which the varlets were roasting a bullock; John, glancing in, changed his mind and continued up the stairs to the leaded roof of the keep. The watch, a burly man-at-arms with pike and longbow, was circling it slowly, but John dismissed him. He wanted to be alone.

He leaned his elbows on the parapet in one of the square towers, breathed deeply of the fresh summer air and let his disconsolate gaze wander from the golden furze-covered moors to the north, to the shipping below in the harbor, and on down the pewter-colored ribbon of the Tyne as it wound into distance towards the sea. He turned slowly to the west where he could see the straight grassy ditch, the mounds and scattered stones of the Roman wall, and he thought of the ages that had streamed by since it was built, and wondered with drear melancholy what had become of the men who built it. Where were their plans and hopes now, what difference had their joys or sufferings made to England? He thought of those of his own blood who had gazed at this ancient wall, his father—all the Plantagenets, and far back to the days of King Arthur himself. In Arthur's reign there had been love-longing and wanhope too and there had been evil to be conquered. But the old tales told of glorious battle against these evils, for there were dragons and giants to be fought in those days, not creeping little jealousies and darting slanders that scurried like spiders into cover when one tried to confront them. He thought with great bitterness of the humiliating, ludicrous outcome of his challenge to Percy, and there rose in him a loathing of Fate that constantly blocked him and denied his deepest wishes.

The sun turned red as blood above the Roman wall and sank down towards the wild desolate moors behind, leaving a sudden chill that struck through John. He turned away and looked down into the castle ward, where his eye was caught by something familiar in a figure that was mounting the long flight of outside stairs into the keep beneath. He leaned over the parapet and stared again, then shouted in amazement, "Ho there! You in the brown hood and cloak, look up!"

The man paused on a step, stared around to find the voice until finally, raising his head, he saw the Duke and waved. It was indeed Geoffrey Chaucer, and John's heart beat faster. "Come up here to me!" he called. Geoffrey nodded and disappeared into the keep, and presently came out onto the tiles through a tower door.

The Duke's hand trembled as he held it out; Geoffrey kissed it while he bent his knee, saying with a faint smile, "Your Grace, I've been a long time afinding you."

"Indeed?" said John, afraid now to ask the question that beat against his lips.

"Ay, my lord. A fortnight ago when you were—ah—detained in Scotland I tried to pass into Northumberland, but was turned back. I waited at Knaresborough until word came that you were at last on your way south."

"Knaresborough," John repeated, and could not hide his bitter disappointment. "To be sure," he said dully. "Your wife is there, I suppose, in the Duchess's train."

"She is, and I've spent some time with Philippa, but 'twas not for that I came north. My lord—" said Geoffrey slowly, touching the pouch that hung from his waist, "I bring you a letter from Lady Katherine."

The Duke's indrawn breath was sharp as tearing silk. He grabbed Geoffrey by the shoulders. "She's well then? And unharmed?"

Geoffrey nodded, but looked away because he could not bear the leap of joy and sudden glistening in the blue eyes.

"Thank God!" the Duke whispered. "Thank God! Thank God and the Blessed Saint Catherine!" He seized Geoffrey's hand, "Oh, Chaucer, you shall be well rewarded for this news. Name what you like. Never did I know how dear she was to me till these last days. In fear and suffering I've longed for her—longed—" He broke off. "And where is she now?"

"I don't know, my lord," said Geoffrey, looking down at the leaded tiles. He unbuckled his pouch and drew out a folded parchment. "You would better be alone when you read this," he said quickly. "I'll wait in the little wall chamber in case you should want me."

The happy flush died on the Duke's lean cheeks as Geoffrey disappeared into the tower. He broke the seal on Katherine's letter and read it by the light of the dying sun.

Geoffrey waited in the wall chamber until Newcastle's bells

rang out for curfew and the sky through the arrow-slit window showed amethyst. He heard his name called at last and went back up to the tiles.

In the evening light the Duke's face now loomed white as ashes, his voice was thick and halting as he said, "Do you know what's in this letter?"

"Ay, my lord. But no one else does, nor ever shall."

"She cannot mean to give me up like this. She cannot! I don't believe it. She says farewell—that we must never meet again. This coldness, these incredible commands! She who was so warm and soft, who has lain so often in my arms, who has borne my children!" The hollow voice faltered, after a moment went on with a sharper edge. "She speaks of Blanchette. You'd think she had no child but Blanchette!"

" 'Tis I think, my lord," Geoffrey ventured, "because of the terror she feels for the little maid, who may be dead. She has not forgot her other children, but they are in no need."

"But *I* am in need," cried the Duke. "She thinks not of that!"

Geoffrey, profoundly disliking this whole coil and his unwilling part in it, yet forced himself to go on. "It is because she loves you that she must give you up. Brother William told her this before he was killed. She believes it. And I, my lord, have come to believe it too. The load of sin, and now the knowledge of murder done would crush you both in the end."

John turned away from Geoffrey and looked out over the parapet into the night of shadows. So it was Swynford's murder that the martyred Gray Friar had meant in all those strange allusions through the years. Nirac, poor little rat—a monstrous sneaking crime in truth—poison—the coward weapon. Sickening. And yet—so long ago, and Nirac had been shriven of his crime by the Gray Friar. The little Gascon's soul was not imperiled. It was Katherine's and his souls that were in danger—so Katherine believed.

"By God," he said roughly, crumpling up her letter, "if fate wills it that we are to be damned, then we shall be damned. I'll not give Katherine up. Where is she, Chaucer?"

"Gone on pilgrimage, my lord."

"Ay—but *where?*"

"I don't know, upon my honor. She would not tell. She doesn't wish you to find her."

"Then God help me, she may have set out for Rome—for Jerusalem even!"

Geoffrey was silent. He thought it possible that Katherine had set forth on the longest and harshest pilgrimage of all. He cleared his throat unhappily, for he had not yet discharged all of Katherine's anguished message. "Your Grace —one more thing she bade me tell you. It is not in the letter because she could not bring herself to write it." He stopped, remembering how her control had broken down at last after she had given him the letter to the Duke, how she had covered her face while the tears coursed down between her fingers.

"What is that one more thing?" said the Duke's voice from the shadows.

"She prays you, my lord—by the love you have borne her —to—to ask the Duchess to forgive her. Yes—I know, my lord," said Chaucer quickly as he heard a sharp exclamation, "but this is what she said. Matters have gone badly with you for a long time, and that is the earthly punishment for murder and adultery. The murder cannot be undone but the adultery must cease. She says that you both have wronged the Duchess—who she thinks loves you in her fashion, as truly as Hugh Swynford was wronged who loved Katherine too—as best he could."

"Blessed Jesu! Now I know you lie! Before God, Chaucer, 'tis not for naught you are a spinner of tales!"

Geoffrey stepped back quickly, the Duke had turned on him as though he would strike.

"I've not invented her letter, my lord," Geoffrey cried.

*"Her letter!"* The Duke's voice shook with fury, he crushed the parchment between his hands and flung the ball violently away from him over the parapet. "That I should live to see Katherine treat me like this! Dismiss me like a thieving scullion, with rantings about morality! She dares send *you* to prate of love that Swynford bore her! By God, 'tis late times to think of that. What has she been doing there in the south when I thought her tending to her child? She found some pretty youth like Robin Beyvill maybe to while the time away. 'Tis because of him she can turn me off so lightly!"

"My lord, my lord," whispered Chaucer retreating farther along the roof while his palms began to sweat. "You do her terrible wrong."

"Wrong, wrong!" shouted the Duke. "All this babbling of

wrong. She vowed she'd never leave me—she has broke it—
as did Isolda—lies! She cozened me all these years with lies.
It's plain now to see she never loved me. Ah," he said with a
laugh like the crackle of burning briars, "Katherine Swynford
has no need to hide from me, no need at all, for I shall never
forgive this, nor try to find her."

The next morning the Duke and his retinue left Newcastle.
Chaucer rode at the end of the line and kept far out of the
Duke's way, knowing that it would be long, if ever, before he
was pardoned for bringing Katherine's message. Geoffrey
bore no ill will. It was natural that a man like Lancaster
should convert the blow to his love and pride into rage, but
Geoffrey had not expected so dreadful a rage and he pondered on what could lie behind it, and at the reference to
Isolda that the Duke had let fall. There was no woman of
that name had ever been mentioned in regard to the Duke
whose fidelity, indeed, to Katherine had been remarkable.
There was no doubt that he deeply loved her, the very violence of his actions proved it. And what a miserable quick-
marsh these two ill-starred lovers had plunged into.

When they had reached central Yorkshire and the Duke's
own lands, at last they approached Knaresborough, and saw
the castle high on its crag above the river Nidd. While they
wound through the limestone gorge with its honeycomb of
caves, towards the ford, Chaucer looked up and saw a
procession of eight women, amongst whom he recognized the
Duchess and his Philippa, slowly wending down the twisting
cliffside from the castle. The Duchess was dressed in garnet
satin embroidered with flashing gold, and she wore her jeweled coronet above a flowing gold veil.

The Duke and his retinue forded the river and when they
all reached the grassy bank, the Duchess came walking slowly
forward, a tentative beseeching look in her dark eyes and a
faint flush on her ivory face. She waited trembling while the
Duke dismounted, but as he came towards her the Duchess
threw herself headlong on the grass and began to sob convulsively.

The Duke leaned over and lifted her up, and she seized his
hands and covered them with kisses. "Mi corazón—" she
cried and went on in gasping Spanish, "I have been so frightened, and I thought never to see you again!"

A peculiar shuttered expression dimmed the Duke's eyes, a

muscle by his mouth quivered. He bent and kissed her on the forehead. "Well, now we are together and all will be well," he answered in Spanish. "Where is our little Catalina?"

"At the castle. I kept her back, my lord. Sometimes you do not wish to see her."

The Duke bent his head, beneath his richly embroidered cote his broad shoulders sagged. "I am eager to see her."

"We may stay here a few days, may we not?" she said timidly. "But indeed where can I go now? Hertford is destroyed—ah, Santiago—it was terrible—you do not know how frightened we were."

"Pobrecita," said the Duke. "Poor Costanza—" He pulled her hand through his arm and they walked off together up the path to the castle.

Chaucer too dismounted and went over to his own wife. "God's greeting, Pica," he said pinching Philippa on the cheek. "Here I am again. I vow we ne'er saw so much of each other in the south."

Philippa nodded and gave him a brief preoccupied smile. "Did you give His Grace Katherine's stupid letter?" she asked quickly. Philippa did not of course know what was in the letter except that her sister had gone off on pilgrimage and would tell nobody where.

"Ay. And he was much angered."

"Small wonder," said Philippa twitching. "She's no more sense than a sheep. I've always said it. She'll lose him with this monstrous behavior and *then* where will we all be! What if she was frightened at the Savoy! Now *that* one—" she jerked her head towards the disappearing figure of the Duchess, "she was frightened too, but it's made her softer, gentler. She's taken pains to please him again. Bathes each morning, has us rub her with scented oils, and put on silk shifts instead of that hair shirt she used to wear. I tell you, Geoffrey, since the Castilian king who murdered her father is dead, she's been changing. She thinks more about the Duke. Katherine better not play fast and loose or she'll lose out."

"Yes, my Pica, she may," said Geoffrey in the quiet edged tone that always daunted her. "I think you must make up your mind to it. We are all out of favor with the Duke."

# XXVIII

ON THE TWENTY-THIRD of June while the Duke was yet in Scotland, Katherine was housed in the pilgrim hostel at Waltham Abbey where she had limped in, sore-footed and deadly tired, two days ago. It was not for the luxury of rest that Katherine lingered these two days, but because Waltham was part of her penance. She spent hours in the abbey praying for the repose of Hugh's soul and asking his forgiveness, while she knelt on the exact spot where his sword had clattered down before the black cross. She went to the inn, The Pelican, where she had passed her wedding night, and forced herself to relive the degradation and the hatred she had felt. Worse than hatred, Katherine thought now—a smoldering secret contempt that had shriveled in time Hugh's self-respect, and his manhood.

Remorse, guilt and punishment—Katherine steeped herself in these by day, and at night her dreams were of spurting blood.

There were no other pilgrims at the hostel; though June was usually prime month for journeying to shrines throughout the country, the revolt and its consequent dangers had quenched most folks' wish for the open road.

Instead, the hostel housed several of the homeward-bound peasants. In the dingy low-raftered hall where all travelers might buy ale and brown bread for a penny a day, Katherine heard much anxious talk.

A penitential pilgrim in widow's weeds was a common sight along the various palmer's ways and drew only respectfully indifferent glances, while she was plunged so deep into her own misery that she noticed nothing. But when after Mass she broke her fast on the Sunday morning that she intended to set forth again towards Walsingham, the loud troubled voices of the men around the trestle tables aroused her attention. She heard them repeatedly mentioning the King.

There had been a proclamation. The King was coming here today, to Waltham.

What was he coming for? cried a blacksmith. Why, to hand out the rest of the charters of freedom, of course, answered someone against a chorus of uneasy assent. It was known that in London the King's men had punished some of the rebels: Jack Strawe had been caught, tortured and beheaded—still, that was natural, for they said he had confessed to treason. Jack Strawe's end could not affect the freedom from bondage and general pardon that the King had granted at Mile End.

"Nay," cried the blacksmith in hearty reassurance, "by this Holy Cross of Waltham here, we must ne'er forget how true a friend our little King did prove himself. He gave us his royal word: 'tis as good as Holy God's."

Katherine listened for some time without attending. She had no interest in the rebels now, though she had put to them one question on her arrival here. Had any of them taken part in the burning of the Savoy? They all said "Nay" except one Suffolk lad who proudly said that *he* had, and a rare fine sight it had been, too.

"Did you see anything of a little maid with close-cropped hair, a lass of fourteen in a gray chamber robe?" Katherine asked, as she had asked this so many times already.

But the Suffolk lad said "Nay" again, though there was such a mort of people running about he wouldn't know one from t'other. The maid she asked about would be one of the house carls no doubt? 'Twas certain they had all fled long before the place was fired.

Katherine had thanked him with weary patience.

Suddenly now at mention of the King's name, her detachment was pierced by a forlorn hope. Might it be that Richard had heard something of Blanchette? True, he had seen the girl but once, at Leicester Castle, yet there was a chance.

When the band of peasants surged from the hostel towards an open heath in Waltham forest, Katherine followed, as did a crowd of villagers. The open heath was shaded by the close-pressing greenwood with its lofty hornbeams and beeches, and the people had need of shade from the broiling sun, for they waited long, before they heard the royal trumpets and the pound of galloping hoofs approaching down the forest road.

But when Richard came at last, there were no more doubts

or hopeful self-deceptions as to his purpose. He galloped up like an avenging whirlwind amongst an army of four thousand soldiers. As he saw the group of peasants waiting, he shouted exultantly to his Uncle Thomas, the Earl of Buckingham, "Here's another foul nest of traitors!" And to his men cried, "Seize them! Seize them!"

Men-at-arms swarmed over the heath with spears and battle-axes. The bewildered peasants could not resist. The armored men—who had already been at this work since dawn—grabbed them, bound their ankles with leather thongs and flung them to their knees on the trampled grass near the King.

The village women and Katherine were not harmed, though they were shoved roughly out of the way, but Katherine, as dumfounded as the helpless rebels, presently pushed through the milling mass of soldiers, intent on speaking somehow to Richard, when she saw amongst the captives who had been caught earlier that day, the matted flaxen hair and meager body of Cob o' Fenton. Cob's wrists were tied and he had a rope around his waist that was fastened to some soldier's saddle. He had been dragged behind the horse for several miles, sometimes on his feet, more often on the ground. His jerkin and leather trunks had been torn off him, his dirty little body, bruised and bleeding, was quite naked.

"Cob!" Katherine cried, trying to get closer to him, but one of the armored men pushed her back and told her to shut up, adding out of deference to her pilgrim habit, "Can't ye see the King is speaking!"

She did not hear what the King had said, but he had pushed his gilded visor up and she could see a cruel half-smile on his girlish pink and white face, and she heard what one of the new captives, the blacksmith, called out from the ground. "But sire, ye gave us all our *freedom* at Mile End! Don't ye remember? Ye promised us we'd all be free. See, here's the charter they gave me!" The man waved a ragged piece of parchment towards Richard, who began to laugh and turning, said something to his Uncle Thomas, who also laughed. Richard backed his horse around, then standing high in the stirrups, shrilled out, "What fools ye be—what dolts—ye traitorous ribauds be!" His high voice crowed with triumph. "You thought to frighten your King! You had it all your way for a time, did you not? That time is past!"

Richard spurred his horse and cantered near the bound

blacksmith, he leaned over and plucked the charter from the blacksmith's hand. Richard drew his jeweled dagger and sliced through the parchment until he could tear it to a dozen fragments. He flung the fragments over his shoulder. "Now you see what use I make of your charter!" he cried. He touched his horse's flank again and rode up and down along the line of kneeling men. "Serfs you are, and serfs you shall remain till doomsday! Is that through your thick skulls now?" He tossed his head and shouted, "Some of you'll return to your own manors and whatever punishment your lords wish to mete out to you. But those of you who've dared defy me openly shall be brought to trial today—and dealt with—ah— *fittingly*, that I promise."

The King's words rang out into a deathly quiet, but when he finished speaking there came from the bondsmen a long sobbing gasp. Katherine saw Cob put his hands up against his face and slump forward on the rope that held him.

Her heart pounded in her throat, sweat prickled her scalp. She darted around the man-at-arms, who had forgotten her, and ran out into the open space by the King.

"Your Grace!" she cried. "Sire! A boon!"

Richard looked down in amazement at this poorly clad widow with the pilgrim scrip and staff.

"What is it, dame?" His squires drew near fingering their swords' hilts.

"Your Grace," said Katherine, "I want that serf that you've got tied to yon rope." She pointed at Cob. "He's mine!"

"By Saint Jude, the woman's crazed," said Buckingham contemptuously, beckoning to his page for wine. "Get rid of her, Richard. 'Tis hot here, and we've much to do."

"You don't know me—Your Grace?" said Katherine very low looking steadily up at the King. "Yet last Christmastide we shared wassail at Leicester Castle." She saw blank impatience in Richard's eyes. She opened her scrip, fumbled quickly inside and brought out the Duke's sapphire signet ring. "You remember this, my lord?" She held it up so that only he could see the carved Lancastrian crest.

Richard stared at the ring, then into her wide gray eyes. "Christus!" he cried pleased as a child that has found answer to a riddle. " 'Tis Lady Swy—"

"Your Grace, for the love of God, don't name me!" She

whispered frantically. "No one must know—it is for penance."

Richard's capricious fancy was caught. He would have questioned her except that it was forbidden to infringe upon a penitential vow and brought ill luck to the offender, but he leaned down close from the saddle and whispered, "You want that naked churl? Is he truly yours, lady?"

"Ay," Katherine said, "from Kettlethorpe, a fugitive. I would deal with him myself."

"*I* would have drawn and quartered him, and hope you do," said Richard, his eyes sparkling. "When my men caught him back there in the forest, he screamed out all manner of treason. But you shall have him."

"Grand merci—most Gracious Majesty—" whispered Katherine. "Wait, my lord, I pray you. I have a daughter, Blanchette, of your own age. Do you remember her at Leicester?"

"I think so," answered Richard, puzzled and losing interest. "She was small with ruddy curls."

"Have you seen aught of her since then?"

"Nay, lady, I have not—how odd a question."

"Forgive me." She curtsied and kissed the boy's gold gauntlet. "Christ's blessings on your generosity, sire."

Richard smiled graciously.

There were murmurs of astonishment and one of sharp protest from Buckingham as the King ordered that the end of Cob's rope be untied from the saddle and given to the pilgrim widow, but Richard, who loved a secret, did not explain except to say that it was part of a penitential vow. Buckingham, who had as little as possible to do with his brother of Lancaster, had never seen Katherine close, and suspected nothing.

No one impeded her as she led her stumbling dazed serf away from the heath, and they were at once forgotten when Richard and his army returned to the congenial punishment of the captured rebels.

She led Cob out of sight and off the road into the forest, until she saw a rain water pool in a glade of holly bush and beeches. The pool was fringed by a mossy bank, dappled with golden light that filtered through the rich leaves of a huge sheltering beech. Katherine gently tugged at the now resistant Cob's rope, and pointing to the soft turf said, "Rest here, Cob."

His pale-lashed eyes stared at her with numb hatred. But

he collapsed on the edge of the pool and plunged his swollen purplish-black hands in the water. The leather thong that bound his wrists had bit so deep that the flesh was puffed in ridges. He rested his elbows on the turf and bending his face to the pool lapped up water avidly while the knobs of his little backbone struck out like walnuts beneath his dirt-caked bleeding skin.

Katherine unclasped her scrip again. In it she carried all that she possessed, the few jewels she had seized that Thursday in the Savoy, the change that remained from the gold nobles, a comb, a coarse towel, a cup and a bone-handled knife.

She took out the knife and kneeling by Cob said, "Keep your arms steady—Sainte Marie, I pray this knife is sharp enough."

Cob jumped back, staring in terror at the knife. He tried to get up on his quivering legs, but the dangling end of his waist rope caught in a holly bush and yanked him down.

"Oh Cob, Cob—poor wight," said Katherine. "How *can* you think I'd harm you? I want to cut that thong for you."

He sucked at his lips, darting at the surrounding forest glances of beastlike wariness, his hands drew up tight against his scrawny chest.

"Look at me, Cob," said Katherine. His eyes shifted slowly and raised to her grave sorrowful face. She smiled at him, took his bound hands in hers and pulled them away from his chest. He held himself quiet, ready to spring. Katherine slid the knife carefully between his jammed arms and working it upward sawed on the thong. It frayed at last, and she threw it on the turf. "When you can use your hands again," she said, "you must help me get that rope off you too."

Cob swallowed, staring at the cut thong. Then he winced, his teeth began to chatter from the pain that throbbed through his freed hands. "What d'ye mean to do wi' me?" he gasped. "I'll get away from ye again, I'll—" He clamped his lips on the threats he had nearly uttered. For sure, she'd not be so calm did she not have men hidden behind the beeches over there, or the King's men might have followed. That was it. What else had she been whispering to the King? God's blood, the clodpolls they'd all been to have believed the Kings word: SERFS YOU ARE AND SERFS YOU SHALL REMAIN! 'Twas clear enough now. Swynford serf. Her serf. Just as it had always been. Branded once for running away, and this time there'd be an end to it—a length of rope from the gibbet on Kettlethorpe green, like Sim the reeve. Unless—Cob glanced at the knife Katherine had left lying on the bank by a clump of purple bell flowers, while she soaked her towel in the pool. He tried to flex his throbbing fingers but they were still useless.

Katherine came to him with the wet towel and began to cleanse the blood and dirt off his little trunk that was sharp-breasted and bony as the carcass of a squab. Cob hunched himself tight. She cleaned as best she could the raw abrasions, the stone cuts on the taut skin and said at last, "Oh Cob, Cob, have you had naught to eat? We must get you food at Waltham."

"*Eat!*" he cried twisting out from under her hands. "Ay, I've had crusts from the monks and fern fronds i' the forest, and thought me well fed, whilst I still had me freedom!"

She sank back on the turf looking at the matted sweat-darkened tow hair, the naked little body, the F brand on the stubbly cheek next to the sullen shifting eyes. Cob chafed his numb hands desperately.

"You *are* free, Cob o' Fenton," said Katherine in a low clear voice. "A freeman from this moment."

Cob's muscles jerked. His hands ceased moving. He peered into her face, then quickly down the shadowy glades between the beeches. In the silence, wood doves cooed, and crackling in a thicket told of a red deer that stared at them, and scampered off as Cob cried, "Ye think to diddle me, lady, wi' yet another trick! Tis sport for ye, belike. Ay—shout ye now for King's men, sure they be near—string me up at once, and ha' done wi' it. See, here's the noose—all ready." He pounded his fists on the rope about his waist.

"Small wonder that you'll not believe me," said Katherine sadly. "Yet, Cob, *could* you think me so ungrateful for what you did that day the Savoy burned that I would so cruelly fool you? I've longed to thank you, was glad you had your freedom from the King. Since it seems that you have not, *I* give it to you, Cob."

"And if 'twere true," he cried in a shaking voice, "who'd believe it! Think ye I could go home—to Kettlethorpe, in peace, to your steward—d'ye know what *he'd* do to me?"

"Yes," said Katherine sighing and rising, "I know. You shall have a writ of manumission under my seal, and this the steward will obey."

"*Another* charter—" Cob whispered. "And if it prove false as the King's—"

" 'Twill not prove false, Cob. I swear it on the cross." She kissed the small rough crucifix that hung from her hempen girdle.

It was many hours before Cob believed, though he came with her back to Waltham under cover of her cloak; though she bought him food, ale and a long woolen smock to cover his nakedness. She enquired from the hostelkeeper where she might find some man of law, and was directed to a learned clerk who lived by the bridge on the river Lea.

The clerk was at home, standing at his desk and copying out a land grand when Katherine and Cob were ushered in. When the clerk understood that the widow had money for a fee, he pulled out a fresh parchment from a pile and shoved a Bible towards Katherine. "Do you kiss the Book and truly swear that this serf is your property? Yours to dispose of as you will?"

"I do," said Katherine while Cob shrank into the shadow behind her.

"And what disposition would you make of him?"

"I wish to free him."

The clerk lifted his scraggy eyebrows. "Is't one of the rebels? Has he been intimidating you? There's no need to fear them now the King is enforcing law and order."

"I know," said Katherine. "I wish to free him."

"For what reason? It must go on the deed of enfranchisement."

"For the brave and loyal service he has rendered me, beyond his bondage duty," she said softly.

The clerk shrugged and scribbled rapidly, asking at the proper place for names. Katherine gave hers with reluctance, but the clerk had never heard of her. He sanded the writing, watched Katherine sign her name, heated red wax and waited. She pressed the sapphire signet ring into the seal, praying that he would not recognize the Lancaster crest, though this crest made it certain that her steward would honor the writ.

But the clerk was incurious, and busy. He stamped his own notary seal beside hers, demanded his fee and thrust the parchment out to Cob, saying briskly, in the traditional phrase, "By the grace of God and your manor lord—serf, native, villein, bondsman, *this* you are no more. Hail freeman of

England!" The clerk pulled over the land grant and began to write on it again.

Cob, making a hoarse sound in his throat, stood rooted to the floor. Katherine put her arm around his shoulders and led him out of the house. "Here, here," she said smiling, "Cob—you dolt, you've dropped your writ of freedom, sure that's no way to treat it!" She picked it up and starting back cried, "Ah no—don't—" for the little man had thrown himself on the road and was kissing her muddy bare feet.

"My lady, my lady," he sobbed, "I'll serve ye till I die, I'll never leave ye. And to think I meant to kill ye, and I nearly robbed ye back there in London—and 'tis from that very money that ye paid the clerk for my freedom. Oh my lady—what can I do for ye—" He raised his stained wet face, looking up at her with worship.

"Pray for me, Cob," said Katherine, " 'Tis all that you can do for me."

Cob and Katherine parted that afternoon at the fork where the North road branched off the Palmer's way to Walsingham. Cob begged to go with her but she would not let him: the penance must be suffered alone, and too she saw how much Cob longed for home. He spoke constantly of Kettlethorpe, of his ox and his little cot, and of a lass in Newton, a freeman's daughter that now he might wed. There was no happier man in England that day than Cob in his new smock and shoes and scarlet hood, with the fine hunting knife Katherine had given him, pennies in his pocket for the journey, and his writ of manumission sewed to his smock against his skin.

His joy could not help but lighten Katherine's heavy heart for a time, but when they had parted and she took up her pilgrimage again, night fell on her spirit as inexorably as it fell on the darkening ridges of the Essex hills. She had listened to Cob's talk of Kettlethorpe with the old shrinking distaste, a revulsion that had spread to include all the scenes of her past life. The taint of corruption had spoiled every memory from the day that she left Sheppey's convent and set out for Windsor. Self-loathing filled her, of the fleshly beauty she had fostered, of the sinful thoughts that she had refused to recognize. The past was evil, the future blank and menacing.

She had no goal but Walsingham and the miracle, when the All Merciful Lady there would tell her how to find Blanchette, how to make reparation.

As she limped towards the hospice where she would spend the night, fresh pain tormented her. It was Midsummer Eve, the Vigil of Saint John, and through the dusk on every hill the boon fires flared against the sky as they had done on this night since the time when England was young, to placate the fairy folk and elves, in honor too perhaps of some fearsome Druid sun god who had once exacted sacrifice.

Last year this night she had been at the Savoy with John. From the Avalon Tower they had watched together the boon fires twinkling around London, when a wild enchanted mood had come to them, born of the magic of the rose-scented June dusk and of the wine they had drunk in celebration of this eve of John's own saint's day. They had called for horses and galloped off into the country, until they came suddenly upon a hidden patch of greensward beside a brook, and a grove of silver birches.

They had dismounted, laughing, amorous, and Katherine on finding a fairy ring of mushrooms in the grove had cried that by means of this enchantment on Midsummer Eve she would bind her love to her forever, so that he might never once leave her side.

Nor had he left her that night, though a great company awaited the Duke at the Savoy. They had lain together, hot with passion, under the birches while a belated nightingale sang to them from a thicket.

Katherine stumbled on the road to Walsingham while her remembering body betrayed her with an agony of longing. My dear dear love, I cannot bear it. At once answer came, in Brother William's voice, *"Dignum et justum est."* It is meet and just that you bear it.

Katherine clenching her hand on her staff went forward along the road. "It is meet indeed and just—" the preface to the reception of the Holy Sacrament from which she was debarred by sins so loathsome that there was no absolution. Sin that had been ever compounded and augmenting. That carnal pagan night beneath the willow tree she had thought of nothing but her adulterous love. She had indeed kept John with her, and the next days too, though the Duchess awaited him at Hertford Castle for the solemn celebration of his saint's day which he had always spent with her in ceremonious observance.

Katherine had laughed with Hawise at this slight put upon the Duchess. God forgive me, Katherine thought, for still she was glad that he had not gone to Costanza. She stumbled on a rock that jutted up from the road, and welcomed the sharp pain that shot through her wrenched ankle.

The days and nights merged into a long gray plodding. The ankle swelled, Katherine's feet festered until she could not walk, and she lay over at a convent where the nuns were good to her. After some time her feet and ankle healed, she gave the nuns her last jewel, an emerald-studded buckle, in gratitude, and they sent her on her way again, begging that she would remember them in her prayers at Walsingham.

It was a searing hot day that Katherine at last reached Houghton-in-the-Dale, a mile south of the shrine, and stopped as did all pilgrims at the little stone slipper chapel. Here she encountered a noisy party of mounted men and women who had left London but a few days ago, though Katherine had been weeks on the road. They were a gaily clad group of young merchants and their wives, and it was apparent from the ribald tune that one of the men played on his bagpipes, from the flask of wine that they passed from hand to hand, and from their noisy laughter, that this pilgrimage was but pious excuse for a summer junket.

Even the casual pilgrim however was required to leave his shoes at the slipper chapel and walk the last mile barefoot. Many were the little shrieks of pain, and giggles, as one by one the London wives filed into the chapel, and came out treading like cats on hot bricks.

Katherine, who had no shoes to remove, drew apart, waiting on the brink of the little river Stiffkey until she might go in and say a prayer in peace. So near at last to journey's end that she could not believe it, she dared not let herself think of the Holy Sight which lay ahead of her, nor of the miracle that she was certain would take place.

They glanced at her incuriously as they passed her by, the Londoners all bright as popinjays in their scarlets and blues and greens, and one of the men—a grocer it would seem by the scales embroidered on his shoulder badge—said crossly in a loud voice to the others, "You shall see what mummery all this'll prove to be. Hurry on, Alison, and let's be done with the bowing and scraping. By God, 'tis not the Virgin's milk I long for, 'tis good brown Norfolk ale!"

"Hush, Andrew!" cried his wife angrily. "Here's no place for your wicked Lollard talk!"

Andrew grumbled and walked on.

Katherine heard, and something in her cringed: a doubt, a fear, darted and was gone. She prayed in the chapel and was filled with exalted hope. Her lassitude and headache vanished, she sped along the sacred mile beside the river. Her skin no longer reddened under the fierce sunrays, the soles of her feet were as tough and calloused as a friar's. She did not feel the torturing fleabites nor the sweat that bathed her body under the hair shirt and the heavy black robe, nor the sore pains in her gums and loosened teeth, pain that had lately made so difficult chewing of the coarse bread, which was all she had allowed herself to eat since starting on pilgrimage. Foul-smelling little sores had broken out on her legs but she had made no effort to poultice them. These afflictions were all sent by God to prove her true contrition, and would insure the Blessed Lady's favor.

As she neared Walsingham, other penitential pilgrims joined her on the road, clad in sackcloth, wearing the wide palmer's hat, with ashes on their brows. These kept their eyes fixed on the ground as Katherine did, they did not glance at the little booths which began to line the way, though the owners of these stalls cried their wares incessantly in hoarse pleading voices.

"Come buy my Walsingham medals—all personally blessed by Our Lady!" Or rosaries, or souvenirs, or gingerbread images of the Virgin, or tin replicas of the vial that held Her Holy Milk.

The town itself was crammed with pilgrim hostels, cookshops and taverns; by the time Katherine reached the abbey gate she was one of a great throng, amongst them many cripples, and sick folk borne on litters by their relatives. Voices hummed around her speaking in a score of accents, not only the strange dialects of remoter parts of England but in the French tongue, and Flemish, and others that she did not recognize.

Beneath a miraculous copper image of a knight, there was a small postern in the abbey gate, and one by one they filed through under the watchful eye of an Austin canon from the priory which had charge of the shrine.

Katherine's heart beat fast, she wanted to hold back, to think and pray again before entering the sacred enclosure, but she could not. Canons ranged on either side the pilgrim path hurried the folk along, while behind her new pilgrims kept pressing through the gate. They were herded first through a little chapel, where they knelt and kissed a bone, big as the shank of an ox. It was the finger-bone of St. Peter, the attendant canon told them, watching while the pilgrims put pennies in a box.

They left the chapel and went through a covered way into a shed thatched with reeds and garnished with flowers. Here on the ground there were two holy wells, side by side. The monk in charge waved the people back, for a child had been laid in the little space between the twin wells.

The child was a boy of about four, but his head was big as that of a grown man, his tongue lolled from his slack spittle-dribbling mouth, his dull swollen eyes were mindless as a dead lamb's. The mother knelt beside him, to pull his arms apart so that one little hand should touch each pool. Her lips moved in desperate prayer while the monk made the sign of the cross over the child. The pilgrims watched, holding their breaths.

The child struggled, trying to jerk his hands from the water, then let out a long sobbing animal wail.

The mother gave a great cry and gathered the child up in her arms. "A miracle!" she cried rocking the child. "For sure, it is a miracle! He had made no sound in months. Our Blessed Lady has cured him!"

While the people gasped and fell to their knees, the monk smiled, laying his hand on the boy's head. Tears ran down Katherine's cheeks, she turned away and could not look at the mother's wild hopeful face. When her own time came to kneel between the holy wells and plunge her hands at once in each, she could form no proper prayer. She saw nothing but Blanchette's trusting, adoring eyes, as they had been long ago.

Our Lady of Walsingham's shrine adjoined the church. It was a small chapel without windows, nor needed any, for its hundred votive candles glittered on walls lined with gold and silver offerings, while the Blessed Image, larger than a woman, was crusted so thick with diamonds, rubies, pearls and other precious stones that the eye was blinded.

Katherine had waited long outside the shrine for her turn —though most pilgrims went through in groups, those who wished might worship alone—but before she finally knelt by the dazzling image a priest in white chasuble came up to her to ask what offering she would make to the Queen of Heaven.

She opened her scrip and taking out the Duke's betrothal ring held it up, whispering, "This, Father."

He took the ring, glanced sharply at the gold and sapphires. "It will be acceptable to Our Gracious Lady, my daughter."

He drew aside while Katherine kissed the statue's golden beringed foot, staring up through clouds of blue incense at the smooth painted wooden face beneath a diamond crown.

In the moments that she knelt there, Katherine prayed with the pent-up violence she had not dared to feel before, she prayed in desperation, she supplicated, she commanded. "Give me back my child! Show me the way to forgiveness. Lady, Lady, you who are all-merciful, tell me how Hugh's murder may be forgiven. Tell me where is my child!"

And there was no answer. The white and red painted face, the round upward-staring eyes remained as before, bland, wooden, indifferent.

Still she knelt, until the priest touched her on the shoulder. "There are many waiting to come in here, daughter."

She gave him so frantic and despairing a look that he said, "Come, come, would you gaze on the precious relic? It works more miracles than any other in Christendom!"

She bowed her head, and he waited, glancing at her scrip. "I've but a few pence left, Father—" she said in a strangled voice. "And this—" She held out four silver pennies and the tarnished silver brooch the Queen had given her at Windsor.

"Ah?" said the priest in a flatter tone. "Well, since you have already donated—" He took the pennies, and ignored the tawdry brooch. He unlocked a small diamond-studded door beneath the Virgin's feet, exposing a crystal vial mounted in the center of a gold and ivory crucifix. The vial seemed to contain a whitish powder.

Katherine gazed at the vial. It was said that when the Virgin was inclined to answer a pilgrim's prayer, the Holy Milk would leap and quiver within the crystal. She strained her eyes until they blurred with pain, her body pounded, but there was no sign from the relic.

The priest closed the reliquary and locked it, he hurried to the exit door on the other side of the shrine; held it wide open for Katherine to leave.

She went out along another covered way and through a gate into the brilliant sunshine of the street. Something pricked her hand and she looked down at the Queen's brooch which she still clasped. "Foi vainquera" was the motto on that brooch—a lie. Faith had conquered nothing. Our Lady had neither heard nor answered. There were no miracles. Her hand dropped slack. The brooch fell into the filth of the gutter.

A man passing behind Katherine on the street saw the brooch drop, picked it up and lumbered after her, as she wandered blindly along the outside of the abbey walls.

"Good pilgrim dame," said the man, "you dropped this nouche."

"Let it be," she said in a muffled voice, not turning. "I do not want it."

The man looked up into her dead-still face, then peered closer at the brooch and read the tiny letters. Because he had suffered very greatly himself, and because his heart was filled with tenderness, he guessed something of what must have happened to this widowed penitent at the shrine. He put the brooch in his pouch and followed Katherine at a distance. People crossed themselves as he walked by them, but some reached out and touched him for luck. He was a hunchback.

Katherine walked until she came to the market square where there were benches along the garden hedge of the Black Lion Tavern, which was jammed with pilgrims who had already visited the shrine, and were now celebrating. Serving maids ran out from the tavern with strong ale and meat pasties. The party of London merchants, each now wearing the Walsingham medal, were clustered at a table by the hedge, talking at the top of their voices.

Katherine's throat was parched with thirst, her stomach gnawed. To gain favor from the Miraculous Lady of Walsingham, nothing at all had passed her lips since vespers yesterday. I shall have to beg for my bread now, she thought. She looked at the food the Londoners were guzzling, and was sickened. Pain throbbed in her sore mouth, in her head. Black swimming weakness crushed her. She slumped down on a bench and shut her eyes.

The man with the humped back paused by the market cross some way off, and watched Katherine with compassion.

The voices behind the hedge rose higher. They were shouting London gossip in answer to eager questions from provincial pilgrims. They were recounting with relish the horrors of the revolt in London two months ago, while a Norfolk man insisted that they had had a worse time of it up here than any Londoner could know.

"But 'tis over now for good, that's certain," cried the grocer called Andrew, "since John Ball was caught at Coventry."

"Ay," agreed a self-important voice, "and I was there. With my own two eyes I saw it when the King's men gelded him and gutted him, and he watched his own guts burn—afterwards they quartered him so cannily, he took a rare long time a-dying."

There was laughter until Andrew cried, "Stale news, *that* is, my friend—but have ye heard the latest of the Duke o' Lancaster?"

Katherine started and opened her eyes. She clenched her hands on the rim of the bench.

"John o' Gaunt's renounced his paramour, that's what! Shipped her off to France, or some say to one of his northern dungeons. The King commanded it."

"Nay—but—" said a woman giggling. " 'Tis well known he was tired of her anyway and has found someone else, the wicked lecher."

"He'll not dare flaunt his *new* harlot then, for a Benedictine told me the Duke made public confession of his sins, called his leman witch and whore, then crawled on hands and knees pleading with his poor Duchess to forgive him when they met up in Yorkshire."

Katherine rose from the bench and began to run. The hunchback hurried after her.

She ran north from the town towards the sea and along the banks of the river Stiffkey, until it widened at one place into a mill pond. Here on the grassy bank by a willow tree she stopped. The mill wheel turned sluggishly, as the falling waters pushed on it splashing downward, flowing towards the sea. Katherine advanced to the brink of the pond. She gazed down into the dark brown depths were long grasses bent in the rushing water. She clasped her hands against her breasts and stood swaying on the brink.

She felt a grip on her arm, a deep gentle voice said, "No, my sister. That is not the way."

Katherine turned her head and her wild dilated eyes stared down into the calm tender brown ones of the hunchback. "Jesu, let me be!" she cried on a choking sob. "Leave me alone."

His grip tightened on her arm. "You cry Jesus' name?" he

said softly. "But you do not know what He has promised. He said *not* that we should not be tempested, nor travailed nor afflicted, but He promised, *Thou shalt not be overcome!"*

A little wind rustled through the willow fronds, mingling with the sound of the river water as it splashed against the turning mill wheel. She stared at him, while a quiver ran down her back. She did not see him clearly, his brown eyes were part of the beckoning dark depths of the pond. "That was not said for me—" she whispered. "God and His Mother have cast me out!"

"Not so. It is not so," he smiled at her. "Since He has said, *I shall keep you securely.* You're as dearworthy a child of His as anyone."

Katherine's gaze cleared and she recoiled. Now she saw what manner of man it was who was speaking to her.

A hideous little man with a hump, whose head was twisted deep into his shoulders. A man with a great purple bulbous nose, scarred by pits, and a fringe of fire-red wisps around a tonsure. She crossed herself, while terror cut her breath. An evil demon—summoned by her from the hell depths of that deep beckoning water. "What are you?" she gasped.

He sighed a little, for he was well used to this, and patiently answered, "I am a simple parson from Norwich, my poor child, and called Father Clement."

Her terror faded. His voice was resonant as a church bell, and his unswerving look met hers with sustaining strength. He wore a much darned but cleanly priest's robe, a crucifix hung from his girdle.

She stepped uncertainly back from the pond, and began to shiver.

"I'll warrant," he said calmly, "you've not eaten in a long time." He opened his pouch, took out slices of buttered barley bread, and a slab of cheese done up in a clean white napkin. "Sit down there," he pointed to a flat stone by a golden clump of wild mustard. "The mustard will flavor the food." He chuckled. "Ah, I make foolish jokes that nobody laughs at but the Lady Julian."

Katherine stared at him dumbly; after a moment, she sat down and took the food.

He saw her wince as she tried to eat and brought her water from the pond in which to soften the bread. He briskly cut the cheese into tiny slivers. While she slowly ate, he pulled a willow whistle from his pouch and with it imitated so perfectly the twitterings of starlings that three of them landed at his feet and twittered answers.

Katherine's physical weakness passed as her stomach filled, but despair rushed back. She folded the white napkin and handed it to Father Clement. "Thank you," she said tonelessly.

"What will you do now?" he asked, putting the napkin and whistle in his pouch. From the bulbous-nosed, pitted face his eyes looked at her with an expression she had seen in no man's eyes before. Love without desire, a kind of gentle merriment.

"I don't know—" she said. "There's nothing for me—nay —" she whispered flushing as she saw his question, "I'll not go near—the pond again. But there was no answer for me here at Walsingham, no miracle was wrought—" She went on speaking because something in him compelled her to, and it was like speaking to herself. "My fearful sins are yet unshriven—my love—he that *was* my love now despises me, and my child—"

Father Clement held his peace. He cocked his massive head against his humped shoulders and waited.

"The cloisters," Katherine said after a while. "There's nothing else. A lifetime of prayer may yet avail to blunt His vengeance. I'll go to Sheppey, to the convent of my childhood. I've given them many gifts through the years. They will take me as a novice."

Father Clement nodded. It was much as he had guessed. "Before you enter this convent," he said, "come with me to the Lady Julian. Speak with her awhile."

"And who is the Lady Julian?"

"A blessed anchoress of Norwich."

"Why should I speak with her?"

"Because through God's love, I think that she will help you —as she has many—as she once did me."

"God is made of wrath, not love," said Katherine dully. "But since you wish it, I will go. It matters naught what I do."

# XXIX

At dusk of the next day when Katherine and the humpbacked parson, Father Clement, rode into Norwich on
his mule, Katherine had learned a little about the Lady
Julian, though she listened without hope or interest.

Of Julian's early life in the world the priest said nothing,
though he knew of the pains and sorrows that had beset it.
But he told Katherine of the fearful illness that had come to
Julian when she was thirty, and how that when she had been
dying in great torment, God had vouchsafed to her a vision
in sixteen separate revelations. These "showings" had healed
her illness and so filled her with mystic joy and fervor to help
others with their message that she had received permission to
dedicate her life to this. She had become an anchoress in a
cell attached to the small parish church of St. Julian, where
folk in need might come to her.

She had been enclosed now for eight years, nor had ever
left her cell.

" 'Tis dismal," murmured Katherine, "yet by misery perhaps she best shares the misery of others."

"Not dismal at all!" cried Father Clement, with his deep
chuckle. "Julian is a most happy saint. God has made a
pleasaunce in her soul. No one so ready to laugh as Dame
Julian."

Katherine was puzzled, and distrustful. She had never
heard of a saint who laughed, nor a recluse who did not dole-
fully agonize over the sins of the world. It seemed too that
though Dame Julian followed the rules prescribed for anchorites, yet these allowed her to receive visitors at times, and
that Father Clement had seen her often, when he wrote down
her memories of her visions, and the further teachings that
came to her through the spirit.

Visions, Katherine thought bitterly. Of what help could it
be to listen to some woman's visions? The bleak empty years

like a winter sea stretched out their limitless miles before
Katherine, and she had no will to live through them. Though
the frenzied impulse by the mill pond had passed.

She could not put upon her children the shameful horror
of a mother who died by her own act, yet the small Beauforts
would never have known. And it were better if everyone
thought her dead. The Beauforts then would be less embarrassment to their father. Hawise would care for them, the
great castle staffs would care for them, and the Duke, not-
withstanding that he had reviled the mother, would provide
for them. Tom Swynford was a nearly grown lad and safe-
berthed with the young Lord Henry. There was but one child
who needed her—and Blanchette was gone.

I will hide me away, thought Katherine, at Sheppey—until
I die. Nor would it be long. She felt death near in the increasing pains her body suffered, in the blurring of her sight,
and the dragging weakness.

Sometime before they rode through Norwich to the hillside
above the river Wensum where Father Clement's little church
stood, the priest had fallen into silence. He felt how grievous
was the illness of body and soul that afflicted Katherine, and
he knew that she was no longer accessible to him.

Guided by Father Clement, Katherine reluctantly entered
the dark churchyard behind the flint church. The sky was
overcast and an evening drizzle had set in. On the south side
beyond the round Saxon church tower, she dimly saw the
boxlike outline of the anchorage which clung to the church
wall. Breast-high on its church yard side there was a window,
closed by a wooden shutter. The priest tapped on the shutter
and called in his bell-toned voice, "Dame Julian, here is
someone who has need."

At once the shutter opened. "Welcoom, whoe'er it be that
seeks me."

Father Clement gently pushed Katherine towards the window, which was obscured by a thin black cloth. "Speak to
her," he said.

Katherine had no wish to speak. It seemed to her that this
was a crowning humiliation, that she should be standing in a
tiny unfamiliar churchyard with a hunchback and commanded to reveal her suffering, to ask for help, for some unseen woman whose voice was homely and prosaic as Dame
Emma's, and who spoke moreover with a thick East Anglian
burr.

"My name is Katherine," she said. Through her weary pain resentment flashed. "There's nothing else to say."

"Coom closer, Kawtherine." The voice behind the curtain was soothing as to a child. "Gi' me your hand." A corner of the black cloth lifted; faintly white in the darkness a hand was held out. Unwillingly Katherine obeyed. At the instant of contact with a firm warm clasp, she was conscious of fragrance. A subtle perfume such as she had never smelled, like herbs, flowers, incense, spices, yet not quite like these. While the hand held hers, she smelled this fragrance and felt a warm tingling in her arm. Then her hand was loosed and the curtain dropped.

"Kawtherine," said the voice, "you are ill. Before you coom to me again, you must rest and drink fresh bullock's blood, tonight, at once—and for days—"

"By the rood, lady!" Katherine cried angrily, "I've tasted no flesh food in months. 'Tis part of my penance."

"Did our moost Dearworthy Lord Jesus gi' you the penance, Kawtherine?" There was a hint of a smile in the voice, and Katherine's confused resentment increased. Everyone knew that the sinful flesh which had betrayed her must be mortified.

Suddenly the voice changed its tone, became lower, humble and yet imbued with power. Katherine was not conscious of the provincial accent as Julian said, "It was shown to me that Christ ministers to us His gifts of grace, our soul with our body, and our body with our soul, either of them taking help with the other. God has no disdain to *serve* the body."

For a startled moment Katherine felt a touch of awe. "That is strange to me, lady," she said to the black curtain. "I cannot believe that the foul body is of any worth to God."

"And shall not try tonight," said the voice gently. "Father Clement?"

The priest who had drawn away, came up to the window. Julian spoke to him at some length.

Katherine was given a chamber reserved for travelers in the rectory across the alley from the church. She was put to bed and cared for by Father Clement's old servant, a bright-eyed woman of sixty, who adored him.

They brought Katherine fresh blood from the slaughter-house, and a bullock's liver, which they chopped up raw and blended into a mortrewe with egg, they fed her boiled dandelion greens, minced so that she need not chew. They made

her eat. Katherine for the first day thought this a worse penance than any she had undergone, but she was too weak to
protest or even to wonder that Dame Julian had said she
should not be bled, that it was not sensible to put in blood at
one place and take it away from another.

Father Clement twinkled as he told Katherine this, and she
smiled feebly, wondering how it was that a man so hideous
and deformed always seemed happy. He labored tirelessly for
his parish, yet was always unhurried. He never scolded, nor
questioned, nor exhorted. There was a sunniness about him
that shone through all his clean shabby little rectory.

In four days Katherine had gained strength, her pains were
less, the bluish sores on her legs had ceased oozing. She
began to worry about the expense that she was giving Father
Clement, but he laughed at her, saying with truth that the
odd things Lady Julian had prescribed for her to eat were to
be had for the asking at the shambles, while the greens came
from his own garden.

"Never did I think that I should be destitute as I am now,"
Katherine said on a long sigh. Yet it had become a dream—
the glamor and the lavish bounty of all those past years. A
guilty dream.

The priest looked at her softly. "Destitute? Perhaps 'tis that
you've always been. For our soul may never have rest in
things that are beneath itself."

"Ah see—" she cried bitterly. "Now at last you speak like
a priest. 'Tis what Brother William would have said—God
keep him—that was killed because of me—he, and others."

The priest seemed not to notice. "The Lady Julian waits
for you," he said quietly. "She believes you well enough to
come to her today."

Katherine had thought much about the anchoress during
these days of recovery, and been astonished to find a longing
to speak with her again. She went back that afternoon to the
little churchyard and knocked at the cell window. The voice
through the black cloth told her to come in at the door which
had been unlocked.

Katherine entered Julian's cell nervously, puzzled, curious.
It was but six paces long and wide, and curtained down the
middle with fine blue wool. There were two windows, the
parlor window to the churchyard, and above a wooden prie-
dieu a narrow slitted window that opened into the church.
Through this, Julian could see the altar and take part in the

Mass. There was a small fireplace, a table and two wooden chairs on the warm brick floor. The bumpy flint walls had been painted white.

A moment after Katherine shut the door, Julian came around the blue curtain. A plain little woman neither fat nor thin, with graying hair beneath a white coif. She wore a soft unbleached linen gown. A woman nearing forty and so ordinary that one might see a hundred like her in any market square, except that as she took Katherine's hand and smiled, the cell filled with the undefinable fragrance, and at the touch of the square blunt fingers, Katherine felt a strange sensation, as though there had been an iron fetter around her chest that now shattered, to let her breathe a light golden air.

"So you are the Katherine Father Clement brought," said Julian in her comfortable slow voice. She sat down in one chair and motioned Katherine to the other. "The pains're better? Can you chew? 'Twould be a shame to lose those pretty teeth, and tell me—" She asked several frank physical questions, which Katherine answered with faint amusement and disappointment. She had come for the spiritual guidance that Father Clement seemed so certain of, and Lady Julian talked of laxatives. Yet there was still the strange sense of freedom.

"This sickness that you have," said Julian, "I too had once, when I had fasted overmuch. And was in great trouble and pain, so near death that my confessor stood over me." She glanced towards the crucifix that was mounted on her prie-dieu, and said simply, "God in His marvelous courtesy did save me."

"By the visions—" said Katherine, sighing. "Father Clement told me of them."

"Ay—by the sixteen showings, but I don't know why they were vouchsafed to me. Truly it was not shown me that God loved me better than the least soul that is in grace. I'm certain there be many that never had showings, nor sight but of the common teaching of Holy Church, that love God better than I."

"It's very hard to love God," said Katherine below her breath, "when He does not love us."

"Oh Katherine, Katherine—" Lady Julian smiled shaking her head. "Love is our Lord's whole *meaning!* It was shown me full surely that ere God made us He loved us, and when we were made, we loved him."

It was not Julian's words, which Katherine barely heard,

that brought an odd half-frightened thrill. Like the first time
Katherine had climbed to the top of the minster tower at
Sheppey and seen the island stretching out for miles to other
villages and blue water in the distance, a landscape she had
not dreamed of.

She stared unbelieving at the homely broad face beneath
the graying hair and wimple, for suddenly it looked beautiful,
made of shining mist.

"Lady," whispered Katherine, "it must be these visions
were vouchsafed to you because you knew naught of sin—
not sins like mine—lady, what would *you* know of—of adultery—of murder—"

Julian rose quickly and placed her hand on Katherine's
shoulder. At the touch, a soft rose flame enveloped her, and
she could not go on.

"I have known all manner of sin," said Julian quietly. "Sin
is the sharpest scourge. And verily as sin is unclean, so verily
it is a disease or monstrous thing against nature. Yet listen to
what I was shown in the thirteenth vision." She moved away
from Katherine. Her voice took on the low chanting note of
power.

"I had been thinking of *my* sins, I was in great sorrow.
Then I saw Him. He turned on me His face of lovely pity
and He said: *It is truth that sin is cause of all this pain; sin is
behovable—none the less all shall be well, and all shall be
well, you shall see yourself that all manner of thing shall be
well.* These words were said to me tenderly, showing no kind
of blame. And then He said, *Accuse not thyself overdone
much, deeming that thy tribulation and thy woe is all thy
fault; for I will not that thou be heavy or sorrowful indis-
creetly.* Then I understood that it was great disobedience to
blame or wonder on God for my sin, since He blamed me
not for it.

"And with these words, I saw a marvelous high mystery
hid in God, which mystery He shall openly make known to
us in heaven; where we shall truly see the cause *why* He
suffered sin to come. For He made me see that from failure
of love on our part, *therefore* is all our travail, and naught
else."

Julian looked at Katherine and smiled. "Do you understand?"

"Nay, lady," said Katherine slowly, "I cannot believe there
could be so much comfort."

Julian sat down and spoke again, simply and quietly.

When Katherine left Julian's cell that day, she did not know how long she had stayed, nor clearly remember the things that had been told her, but for the time she had ceased to question. As she walked out into the little churchyard, it seemed lit with beauty. She stood bemused in a corner by a dark yew tree and saw meaning, blissful meaning, in everything her eye rested on: the blue floweret of the speedwell, the moss on a gravestone, an ant that labored to push a crumb through the grass—all these were radiant, as though she looked at them through crystal.

She picked up a black flint pebble that seemed to glow with light like a diamond, while some of Lady Julian's words came back to her. "In this same time, our Lord showed me a spiritual sight of His homely loving. A little thing like a hazelnut, in the palm of my hand, and I thought what may this be? And it was answered: *It lasteth and ever shall, for that God loveth it.*"

During that moment that she held the pebble, Katherine understood this, and why Julian had said, "After this I saw God in a point, by which sight I saw that He is in all things, be it never so little. Nothing is done by hap or adventure—if it be hap or chance in the sight of man, our blindness is the cause."

These words echoed in Katherine's mind as she held the pebble, joy shimmered through its black flint, there was joy in the grass, the yew tree, the gravestones, the moss. Slowly it faded, and a great sleepiness came over her. She dropped the flint. She scarcely could drag her heavy limbs across the alley to her chamber in the rectory. She laid herself on the bed and slept the night through. There were no dreams.

Each day Katherine went to Julian's cell and listened, each day came back refreshed by glimpses of a love she had not known existed, though the exaltation of that moment in the churchyard did not return.

She argued sometimes, at times cried out in disbelief, unable to hide her doubts, and then indeed Julian once sighed and looked sad and humble, as she said, "All this was shown me in three ways, Katherine, by bodily sight, by word formed in my understanding, and by spiritual sight. But the spiritual sight, I *cannot*, and I may not, show as openly as I would. I trust in God that He will of His Goodness make you take it more spiritually than I can, or may, tell it."

Humility. Katherine saw in those days how far she had
ever been from truly feeling it. She saw that she had never
known the meaning of prayer. Her prayers had all been violent commands and bargainings—dictated by fear.

To Lady Julian, prayer was communion. "Prayer oneth the
soul with God." And it was thanking. Giving thanks even
without reward. In the fourteenth showing, Julian had heard
the lovely words, *I am the ground of thy beseeching.* And
with these blessed words had been seen a full overcoming
against all our weakness and all our doubtful dreads.

Katherine, ever quick to take guilt, had then berated herself for the wrongness of her former prayers, and Julian patiently repeated, *"Accuse not thyself overdone much*—I am
sure that no man asks mercy and grace with true meaning,
but if mercy and grace have been first given to him."

There came a day when Katherine could no longer listen
without pouring out all her anguish to Lady Julian. She did
not know what she said, she only heard her own voice calling
out the names of those who meant for her the sharpest pain
—Hugh, Blanchette and John. When she said the last name,
she buried her face in her hands and sobbed.

Now she saw that though she had meant her letter of re-
nunciation, and honestly thought to spend her life in penance,
yet she had not really believed that John would let her go.
Always she had felt that the miracle would happen at Walsingham, in return for her suffering, in return for giving
John's betrothal ring to the shrine. She had been sure that in
some way Blanchette would be restored to her, her sins forgiven, and—

"That your old life would start again?" asked Julian smiling. "That it would by miracle become fair and clean in all
men's eyes, in God's?"

"Ay—ay—I see now that I thought so. Is it wonder that
God is so angry with me!"

"Truly, Katherine, in all the showings, I saw no manner of
wrath in God, neither for short time nor for long. I saw no
wrath but on man's part, and that He forgives in us."

Then Katherine cried out that if God had no wrath, why
should she fear sin?

And Julian answered ever patiently, "Because as long as
we be meddling with what we know is sin, we shall never see
clearly the blissful countenance of Our Lord. And this is to
break us in twain. For we are all in Him enclosed. And He in
us. He sitteth in our soul."

Then Katherine talked of Sheppey, the convent where she would cloister herself. "—or even to be an anchoress like you, lady. So with true prayer I might come some day to know Him as you do—and to help others."

For the first time, a hint of sternness showed in Julian's face, for the first time she referred to herself apart from the visions, and she said quietly, "When I came here, *I* had no one left of my own."

Katherine did not understand her meaning then, nor why she said a moment after, "It was shown to me that we may never come to full knowing of God till we know first clearly our own soul."

That night, she saw what the Lady Julian had meant. Katherine awoke suddenly from deep sleep, and the little rectory chamber seemed to be suffused with a soft iridescent light. This light was peace. It bathed her, permeated her flesh, her bones, until her being was made of light. The confusions, the gropings, the struggles for escape were all dissolved in that light. In their place came certainty—the answer so simple, so right and inevitable, and so hard.

It would be hard, but now she did not feel it so, for the light sustained her, and in her heart she heard repeated the words the Lady Julian had told her, that He had said: *My darling, I am glad thou art come to me: in all thy woe I have ever been with thee; now seest thou my loving.*

The next morning Katherine sought out Father Clement. He was sitting in his garden under a mulberry tree, while five children from the parish capered in front of him. He was teaching them the parts they were to play at the pageant of the Nativity of the Blessed Virgin next week. He acted each part in turn for them, now squealing through his huge empurpled nose, now growling in imitation of a bear, now flapping his hands on either side of his hump for a crow. The children shrieked with laughter, and called him Bo-Bo, a pet name that they had for him. They did not think him hideous, nor did Katherine. She no longer saw his deformities, as she no longer heard the burr in Lady Julian's speech.

He hushed the children as Katherine walked over to them, and looked at her with gladness.

She had washed her pilgrim's weeds and borrowed a clean white coif and shift from his servant. Her hair had grown long enough so that bronze tendrils escaped beneath the coif, and curled at her temples. She was sparkling and fresh, and

smelled of the lavender she had rubbed onto her skin. Her
illness had nearly left her; the priest saw that she was a lovely
woman.

She stopped beneath the clustering purple mulberries, and
gazed long at the children. "Father," she said, "I'm going
back to Lincolnshire. To the place where I should be."

"Aha?" he said, cocking his head. "And was it not that,
you told me on the road here to Norwich, that you could
never, never do?"

"It was," she said. "I was wrong. Father, tonight will you
hear my confession? I dare to hope that—that tomorrow—at
Mass—" Her voice faltered, she drew a deep breath, and
smiled tremulously into his compassionate eyes.


The next morning in the little flint-walled church, from Father Clement's hands, Katherine received again at last the
Holy Sacrament. Julian kneeling by the narrow church window of her cell shared in the Blessed Communion and watching Katherine's rapt face, humbly knew that once more God
had used her as a channel to touch another soul with the
message of her visions, and a glimpse of His meaning when
He had said, *It is I, that thou lovest, that thou enjoyest, that
thou servest. It is I that thou longest for, it is I that is all.*

Exaltation would fade, the wanhope and doubtful dreads
of the world would seep back, but whatever befell, Katherine
would never be totally bereft again. This Julian knew.


Later that morning, Katherine set out on the road west
across Norfolk, bound for Lincolnshire. She rode on Father
Clement's mule. The priest and Lady Julian had lent her
money for food and housing on the journey. This money and
the mule would be returned after she reached Kettlethorpe.

In the leave-taking, Katherine tried to tell them of her
gratitude, but they would not let her. Instead, in the tiny fragrant cell, Lady Julian had given her a hearty kiss on the
cheek and much practical advice about proper diet and rest.

Father Clement, while he stood on the stone step outside
his rectory, had been equally bracing. He cracked his little
jokes and eased the difficult parting moment with brisk directions as to the best road and what to do when Absalom, the
mule, balked.

Katherine was turning to put her foot in the stirrup when
the priest said in the same brisk voice, "And here is something that once belonged to you—will you take it now?" He

held out his open hand. On the palm lay the Queen's little silver brooch.

"But I cast it away," she cried, "in Walsingham."

"Ay, and I picked it up. 'Tis yours."

She flushed. Pain had gone from the memory of that day in Walsingham, but yet there was a taint of shame. " 'Twas because of the motto I threw it away," she said.

He nodded looking up at her quizzically, his head pressed back against the hump. "So I thought."

She stared at the brooch, thinking of the anguish she had suffered and of that moment by the mill pond. She looked from the little lathe and plaster rectory across to the church-yard, where she could see Lady Julian's cell outlined against the blue September sky.

She reached out and took the brooch, remembering what Julian one day had said of faith: "For it is naught else but a right understanding, with true belief, and sure trust of our Being; that we are in God, and God in us." No more. No demands for proof, no promise that sorrow would be banished. Nothing but sure trust of our Being.

She pinned the brooch at the neck of her black habit, and looked down at the little humpbacked priest, at his purple-pitted nose, the bristly red tonsure on his misshapen head, the long apelike arms and the merry tender brown eyes.

"I remember, what you quoted from Dame Julian's visions, that afternoon by the mill pond," she said. "I did not know that I heard it then, but I've thought much on it since."

"And I," said the priest laughing, "do not remember *what* I said. This often happens with me. Alas, I fear I talk too much. 'Tis a parson's failing."

She shook her head, thinking how strange it was to feel pure affection, and how that never until she had come here had she received or given an entirely undemanding love, nor known the lack. "It was this you said, and Lady Julian has told me too. 'Our dearworthy Lord said *not*, Thou shalt not be tempested, thou shalt not be travailed, thou shalt not be afflicted, but He said, *Thou shalt not be overcome!*' Father Clement, of all the teachings, this seems to me the most beautiful."

Glowing strength stayed in Katherine's heart that day, while she rode her mule along the fair Norfolk road towards King's Lynn. It was Michaelmas. The crisping air sparkled like a fountain, it smelled of wood smoke, and of the succulent geese that were roasting in many a brick oven for the feast. In the woods and thickets, the leaves were flecked with gold or russet, beneath the beeches and giant oaks pigs snuffled greedily, rooting for the acorn mast, between clumps of creamy woodbine.

The following day she entered the Breckland heaths. These chalky wastes teemed with rabbits and pheasants so tame that they did not hide while the mule clopped by between the outspread brilliance of the orange gorse, the fading pink and mauve of heather.

Near Castle Acre with its hostel where she would find night's lodging, Katherine's road crossed the Palmer's way to Walsingham. She had been alone for some time on the westbound road, but at the crossing a band of pilgrims came along and greeted her courteously. They wore shiny tin W's fastened to their broad hats, and lead medals of the annunciation on their chests, for they had visited the shrine and were homeward bound. They assumed that Katherine was en route there, and they vied with each other in shouting out the glories she would see.

"No wonder like it, in this world!" cried a small dark woman with shining eyes. " 'Tis Our Lady Herself, you know, has taken up Her home in Norfolk, when the infidels forced Her to flee from Nazareth, no one has ever been to Her but She did help. Look, Dame Pilgrim!" cried the little woman. She rolled back her gray sackcloth sleeve to show a shrunken withered arm. "See!" she cried again while her birdclaw fingers moved one after the other. "Since I was a weanling and God smote me with sickness, these fingers've not moved, but whilst I knelt before Our Lady and gazed at the Holy Milk, the miracle happened. Life tingled in my hand."

"For sure you were most blessed," said Katherine, bleakly.

The pilgrims passed on southward, Katherine flicked the mule with her staff and continued towards Castle Acre, but the peace which had sustained her ever since Norwich, was gone. She remembered this crossroads and how she passed here at dawn of the day she got to Walsingham. How certain she had been that there would be a miracle for her! The woman with the shrunken hand had said, "No one has ever been to Her but She did help." There had been no help, at all, nothing but further suffering. Ay—what horror would have happened to me had it not been for Father Clement?

Then of a sudden she heard the priest's laugh, and she

heard Dame Julian speaking as she had the first day in that little cell. "Katherine, Katherine—well I saw that nothing is done by hap or chance, but by the foreseeing wisdom of God. 'Tis our blindness when we do not see that."

Blindness! Once again it was as though a shutter opened. For there *had* been miracle at Walsingham. The Blessed Lady had answered with a marvel as great and yet as simple as any She had ever wrought. What else but marvel was it that Father Clement had that day ridden to the Austin priory in Walsingham on behalf of one of his parishioners in Norwich? That he had seen Katherine drop the Queen's brooch, and understood and watched over her, that he had taken her to Julian for cure of body and spirit?

What a weary time it took to learn how homely and direct the answer was, that it needed no thunderbolts and flaming wonders for Him to fulfill His promise, *I will keep thee full securely*. That He had as many ways of loving as there were droplets in the ocean, the ocean that was yet all one sea.

Katherine rode her mule through the sunset of the quiet rolling heaths, and her heart filled with thanking. Three times, in three different ways, the sure light had come to her: in the churchyard, in the rectory chamber and now on the Norfolk road.

The fourth day after, Katherine crossed the fens and mounted the high ridge way that led to Lincoln. Already she could see the rooftops on the distant hill, and the triple spires of the cathedral against the cloud-massed sky.

She turned off the road at Coleby and rode through the gates to inspect her little manor. She had not been near it for nine years. The reeve that her Kettlethorpe steward had put in did not know her and jeered when she said that she was Lady Swynford.

"Ye're crazed, widow. Lady Swynford don't go riding about barefoot on a mule! Why dame, Lady Swynford's the Duke o' Lancaster's doxie, and goes clothed in jingling gold —leastways she did, I've heard tell in Lincoln that the Duke's tired of her—but that's as may be, get ye gone. We've no room for tricksy beggars here. Some hostel in Lincoln'll take ye."

Katherine went on her way. Soon the clouds merged and dipped lower. It began to rain, a cold October rain that soaked through her mantle. In time she entered the familiar village of Wigford, the Lincoln suburb that lay on the near

bank of the Witham. On the left, in the center of the long
high street, there was a handsome stone mansion, with elegant carved corbels, an oriel window, and above the door a
shield with the Duke's coat of arms painted on it. Katherine
knew this house, she had dined here with John on the miserable visit to Kettlethorpe two years ago. It belonged to the
Suttons, the wealthy wool merchants whom she had first met
on the road of Bolingbroke in the plague time when the
Duchess died.

She looked up at the Lancaster arms. The Suttons, having
none of their own, proudly blazoned those of their feudal
overlord. She hesitated, unable to control a coward shrinking.
Tomorrow would do as well. She still had a few pence, and
could spend the night in town. One more night before plunging back into all the humiliating things that must be done.
Besides, she thought with feeble self-deception, like the reeve
at Coleby, the Suttons might not know her.

Katherine got off the mule and tied it to the hitching ring.
Of course, the Suttons would know her: they had seen her
many times. The Suttons were Lincoln's foremost citizens.
They had been mayors, members of Parliament. Thomas the
clerk was now Chancellor of Lincoln Cathedral. They knew
everything that went on in town and could best answer the
questions she must ask.

She knocked. The door was opened by a liveried varlet,
who did not hide his astonished disapproval at her appearance and was reluctant to admit her until she gave him two
pennies, whereupon he thawed. He said that old Master John
had gone to Calais on business for the staple, and Master
Thomas was at the bishop's palace, that Master Robert was at
home. But occupied. A deputy of woolmongers were with
him.

"Tell him please that 'tis Lady Swynford, and I will wait."
Katherine sat down on the wayfarer's bench in a cubbyhole
beside the door.

She waited a long time. When Robert Sutton came at last,
walking ponderously from his counting house to the corner
of the Hall where Katherine sat, she saw that he was embarrassed and uncertain how to greet her. Above his glossy dark
brown beard, his plump cheeks were flushed. He took one
scandalized look at her bedraggled robe, her feet, the wet
limp coif that covered her short hair, and his eyes slid away,
their thick lids lowered. He fingered the gold chain around his
neck, he twitched a fold of his maroon velvet, squirrel-furred
sleeve. " 'Tis a surprise, lady—"

A very great surprise, since he had heard that the Duke had bundled her off abroad, sealed her away in some French convent. He had spent the last ten minutes, not with the woolmongers, but alone, wondering if he should receive her.

Katherine drew a deep breath and laced her hands together. The last time she had seen him, he had been deferential, charming, his eyes moist with covert desire. Now his full handsome face was wary, and he tapped his scarlet shoe impatiently. Ay, it will be like this, she thought. From now on.

"Master Robert, I shall not take much of your time. There are only a few questions I'd like to ask you. I've been a long while on pilgrimage, and know nothing of what has happened in the world."

He flushed again and hawked in his throat.

She saw that he wondered if she even knew of the Duke's renouncement and spoke quickly. "The Duke and I have parted, it was our mutual wish and decision."

He did not believe the latter, but he grunted uneasily. Her low voice softened him and her dignity. As she spoke he began to see glimpses of the beauty he had so enviously admired. But she must be thirty now, he told himself sharply, and a discarded mistress—and if it were money that she wanted—

"Master Robert," she said quietly, "have you heard aught of my children?"

"The bastards?" he said startled.

"The Beauforts," she answered.

He swallowed. "Why I believe they're well—at Kenilworth." His wife, in fact, had been buzzing, since the juicy news about the Duke and Lady Swynford had filtered to Lincoln. Delighted with Lady Swynford's downfall, she had triumphantly garnered every tidbit that travelers could tell them.

"How does my manor of Kettlethorpe?" said Katherine. "I know our wool goes through your warehouse."

"The manor does fairly, I think," he said frowning. "At least the clips are up to standard. By God's nails, lady," his jaw dropped, "you don't mean to come back and live at Kettlethorpe!"

"Ah, but I do," said Katherine smiling faintly. "Where else should I go but my own manor, where my people have need of me? Where else should I bring my children, who have no honest claim on anyone else in the world?"

The wool merchant was dumfounded. "Surely you mean to

sell?" And then take the veil, he thought, far away where no one knows her.

"I will not sell the Swynford holdings," said Katherine, "that were my husband's and belong to my Swynford children—children—" she repeated on a lower wavering note.

Sutton looked at her. "I heard the little maid Blanchette was betrothed to some great knight, and already she had a dowry from the Duke. She'll not need Kettlethorpe."

Katherine could not answer. She could not force herself to say, "I don't know where Blanchette is, no one knows but God. But the home she loved and that I took her from will be always waiting."

"Nevertheless," she said, "I shall live at Kettlethorpe. And now, Master Robert, I do humbly beg one thing of you."

He stiffened, crossed his velvet arms over his great barrel chest. "What is it, Lady Swynford?"

"That you will write in my name to the Duke. He has respect for you. He would not accept a letter from me. But I know that he listens to justice. Will you tell him what I propose to do, and will you request in my name that he send me my Beaufort children? Tell him that when this is done, he shall never be troubled with me again."

Robert Sutton demurred for some time. He pointed out the impracticality of her scheme. Her steward was in the Duke's pay and would undoubtedly be withdrawn. It was folly to think she could run the manor herself, especially since her serfs were known to be unruly—why even here there had been a taint of the iniquitous revolt. Only the most violent suppressive measures had kept the villeins in their places. No doubt she understood nothing of this, having been on pilgrimage so long, but he assured her it was so. Katherine made no reply, except to say that nonetheless she would try to run Kettlethorpe herself.

Then Sutton with increasing embarrassment hinted at the discomfort of her position here, she would be ostracized. The goodwives of Lincoln would be outraged at the reappearance of so notorious a woman, and with her bastards too. Moreover, the bishop was a narrow, strait-laced man with a horror of scandal.

Katherine grew paler as he talked, her gray eyes darkened. But she remarked only that Kettlethorpe was isolated enough, and she would try to trouble no one.

Sutton ended by doing as she wished. He summoned a clerk and dictated the letter to the Duke. When he had finished, a much warmer feeling towards Katherine came over him. He could not help but admire her courage, and too—a woman in her position would be grateful for a friend, for a discreet protector. Ay, it was true and fortunate that Kettlethorpe was isolated, but not so far away that a trip might not be made occasionally. He looked sideways at the slender bare ankles, the faint outline of high firm breasts beneath the hideous black robe, at the cleft chin, the wide voluptuous mouth.

When the clerk had gone, Sutton glanced back into the Hall, saw no one there but servants laying the table. He put his damp hot hand on the bare arm and squeezed. His beard brushed her cheek as he whispered, "You can count on Robert de Sutton, sweet heart, I'll see that you get along."

"Thank you for all your kindness," she said moving away. "I must go, Master Robert, go home."

"But you shall rest first! Nay, you must sup with us—that is, the page'll bring you wine," he amended, knowing very well what his wife would say if she found Lady Swynford supping with them.

Katherine declined everything. She was not hungry, the rain had lessened, she must be on her way. She spoke in a light casual tone, neither chilling nor inviting.

Blessed Mary, it would be hard, she thought, as she rode Absalom across the Witham bridge and turned west along the Fossdyke for Kettlethorpe. She needed the Sutton good will, for business reasons, as well as for mediation with the Duke. And on the whole she had always liked Master Robert. Yet would it be possible to keep his good will, and still deny all the reward which she saw that he would expect?

Hard. The radiance of those revelations had inevitably receded. It shone still, but behind a veil on outer life with its niggling annoyances, worries, hurts. She was no longer simply "Katherine," she must adjust again to the various labels that the world would give her, and the demands fair and unfair that it would make.

She turned north at Drinsey Nook and saw the black forest ahead. The forest where Hugh had hunted, the forest at which she had gazed from the dank solar for so many unhappy years. Soon in the winter the wolves would howl again. She rode through the iron gates that marked the manor road. The mile-long avenue of wych-elms was unchanged; she noted the flocks grazing on her demesne lands, heard a shepherd's shout and the barking of his dog.

Ahead on the right stood the tithe barn and the little church where lay Nichola, Gibbon—and Hugh. To the left, the shabby manor house where Blanchette had been born, where John had come that morning and saved the baby from Lady Nichola.

The bridge was up, the manor dark. When had it ever welcomed her? She pulled the mule over to the old mounting block, and stepped out of the stirrups. She stood there with her hand on a corner of the gatehouse, looking at the church, at the huddled row of cots that were the village.

You've but to call out to the gateward, she thought. But she did not call. She stood there until a small boy came trudging down the lane with an enormous load of faggots on his back. He started and crossed himself when he saw a black figure standing on the mounting block, and Katherine said, "Don't be afraid, lad, I'm Lady Katherine Swynford, this is my home."

The boy gave a sort of snuffling cry, dropped his faggots, and pelted towards the vill, shouting out something Katherine could not hear. That load is too heavy for a child like that, she thought, staring at the faggots. The rain changed to mist. Raw white fog curls floated up from the Trent. Her fingers gripped tight on the rough cold stone beneath her hand. She descended from the block and walked around beneath the gatehouse window. She called, "Gateward! Ho, gateward!"

There was some movement in the gate loft, a man's voice answered, but it was lost in the pound of running footsteps from the vill. A little man with flying light hair ran towards her and others followed him. "Welcome, dearest lady. Welcome. For sure I told 'em, ye'd be coming back some day, would they be patient."

"Cob," she whispered. "Ay, I've come back—"

"They've been praying for it every day." He jerked his head towards the group behind him. She could not see their separate faces, but she felt their quivering expectancy.

"When I told 'em what ye did for me, what ye'd been through in Lunnon, I told 'em ye went on pilgrimage—oh lady, they've been waiting for ye. 'Tis bad here now—not for me that am a freeman," Cob interjected proudly, "but the unfree—steward's mostly drunk. 'Tis cruel—"

Katherine lifted her head and looked past Cob to the crowd of her silent, watchful people. "I shall try to make you all glad that I am home," she said.

# PART SIX

## (1387–1396)

And after winter, followeth green may.

TROILUS AND CRISEYDE

# XXX

On Lincoln town's high hill the raw March wind blew
incessantly. It chilled bones, reddened noses, afflicted
with snuffles and coughs the venerable bishop and the
worshipful Mayor John Sutton as well as the ragged beggars
who whined for alms in the minster's magnificent Galilee
porch.

Wind or no wind—and the citizens were used to it—folk
were all out in the streets, frantically nailing banners, greens
and colored streamers to the fronts of houses. It was the
twenty-sixth of March, 1387, and King Richard and his
Queen Anne were coming to Lincoln that night, the first time
that Lincoln had ever been so honored in the ten years of
Richard's reign. The excitement was tremendous. The ostensible reason for this visit was that he and the Queen were to be
admitted into the Fraternity of Lincoln Cathedral on the
morrow. The actual reason, as many knew, was that Richard
had set out on a good will tour through all his land. He had
felt his popularity slipping, he had been having trouble with
commons and lords alike, and with his Uncle Thomas of
Woodstock, now Duke of Gloucester—particularly since his
Uncle John, the Duke of Lancaster, was at long last in Castile, had been there for a year with Duchess Costanza and
their daughter, and his two girls by the Duchess Blanche.

Richard's arrival affected Katherine too. During the six
years since her return, she had seldom left Kettlethorpe, nor
would have cared to do so now, but the King had commanded it.

On this bleak, windy afternoon, Katherine was sewing by
the fire in the pleasant Hall of her town house on Pottergate,
just inside the cathedral close. Her lap was filled with a sapphire velvet pool while she put the finishing gold stitches on

585

the mantle she would wear to greet the King. Her sister Philippa sat in an armchair, propped with pillows, listlessly pleating a fine gauze veil. Hawise stood behind the kitchen screen pounding almonds into honey for a marchpane while keeping a watchful eye on the housemaids. Little Joan played on the hearth with her kitten. For some time there had been silence, except for Hawise's pounding and the crackle of the fire. The wind howled outside but there was no draught. A good snug house, Katherine thought contentedly.

This was the same house that the Duke had taken for her fifteen years ago when their John Beaufort had been born here, secretly. Three years ago she had decided that the elder boys, John and Harry, would benefit by spending the winter months in Lincoln, where the priests at the newly established Cantilupe Chantry took day scholars. So she had leased this house again. Whereupon the outraged citizenry had shown their displeasure by breaking into her walled close, looting, and beating her servants.

This was the culmination of many unpleasant incidents, which Katherine had borne with patience. In truth her burdens during these years had been even heavier than she had anticipated. Though her parting from the Duke was known to everyone, she continued to be reviled. Not only moral indignation motivated the folk of Lincoln, but resentment because of city quarrels between the Duke's constable at the castle and the town.

Katherine held herself apart, tried to administer her properties wisely and do the best thing for her little Beauforts. But the vandalism to her Pottergate house was another matter, since it had endangered the boys. She appealed by letter to the King. Richard responded promptly and gallantly, had sent a commission to investigate the charges, and fine the offenders. After that, she had been let alone. Entirely alone. Lincoln folk looked through her when they saw her on the street.

It might be because of that incident three years back, or because Richard had been intrigued by the little mystery when she met him outside Waltham and rescued Cob, or because he thought special notice of her would annoy his enemies—one never knew with Richard— In any case, he had sent word that Katherine was to dine at the bishop's palace on the morrow when the royal party would be there.

The three women in Katherine's Hall were all thinking of

the royal visit. "Oh—doux Jésu—Katherine—" Philippa sighed, lifting her thin, vein-corded hand and letting it fall despondently. "If only he would present you to the Queen. Then, then, your position might be better here."

Katherine put down her needle and looked at her sister with deep sorrow. Philippa faded daily. Sometimes she suffered much pain from the canker lump in her breast. Her rosy face was shrunken, her eyelids purple, feebleness had blunted her decisive nature. "But the King would not do that, you know, Pica chérie," said Katherine gently. "I don't mind, and I shall at least see her. I'll tell you all about her."

Philippa sighed again. "Anne, Anne, Queen Anne," she said fretfully. "They say she's ugly, with her fat German cheeks, her thick neck. Yet they say he adores her. 'Tis strange—and no heir either—five years—Richard, of course —one always doubted he *could*—" Her voice trailed off.

Joan, who had been quiet with her kitten, suddenly looked up at Katherine with big-eyed earnestness. "Mama, *why* does Sir Thomas hate the King?"

Katherine laughed as mothers do when their children say something precocious, a little embarrassing. "Why, I'm sure he doesn't. What an idea!" She bent down quickly and tied a wisp of blue velvet around the kitten's neck. "There, look at Mimi, isn't she pretty!"

But Joan was not a baby, to be so easily distracted. She was eight, intelligent and practical. A dark pansy-eyed child, round and red-cheeked, she looked much as her Aunt Philippa had, years ago, though she was prettier and had her mother's wide full mouth. "Thomas *hates* the King," she insisted. "I heard him say so, last year when he was here. He said the King was womanish, soft-bellied and double-tongued as an adder."

"Joan!" cried mother and aunt sharply. The child paid no attention to her aunt, who was usually cross, but she had no wish to provoke her mother's rare displeasure. She hung her head and picked up the kitten.

Katherine, who was always just, stroked the dark curls. "Whatever you heard, mouse, forget it. You're old enough to understand that it's dangerous—and discourteous—to say such things about our King. Come, here's a needle for you, let me see what nice stitches you can make."

She gave the delighted child a corner of the velvet mantle and some gold thread. She resumed her own stitching and thought resignedly that the remark sounded like Tom, though she scarcely saw her eldest son, and knew little of what he thought.

Thomas Swynford was almost nineteen now, and a knight. He still served Henry of Bolingbroke, and what emotions he felt seemed to be for his lord. Tom had made two visits to Kettlethorpe since Katherine had come home, had approved, on the whole, her management of his inheritance, loftily ignored his bastard brothers and sister, and been off again. Katherine knew that he had a dutiful fondness for her, and was also much ashamed of her reputation. He was taller than Hugh had been, but he had the same dusty ram's wool hair, the same secretiveness. They had one clash. Tom had been angry when he arrived at Kettlethorpe and found that Katherine had been freeing her serfs. She knew better than to argue with him or put forth idealistic reasons, had given him proof instead that a manor worked by free, and devoted, tenants, produced more efficiently than one run on the old servile system. Tom had grudgingly scanned the accounts, and ultimately agreed.

Yes, she thought, Tom is a good enough lad. None of her children had given her real anxiety—except —The years had passed without word. All reason demanded acceptance of Blanchette's death in the Savoy—and yet the ache, the void and the question were still there.

The minster bell began to clang for vespers. "The boys will soon be here," said Katherine gladly.

"Ay." Hawise stuck her head around the screen. "And I'd best be hiding me marchpane, them lads'd steal sweeties off the plate o' God himself—Lady," she said severely to Katherine, "put by your sewing, ye mustn't redden your eyes, when ye very well know who's coming to see ye—"

"Oh Hawise," protested Katherine, with a laugh that mingled affection and exasperation, "you make pothers over nothing."

Hawise snorted rebelliously. Stouter, redder, and nearly toothless; nonetheless, Hawise was an unchanging rock. Stubborn as a rock too, at times.

"Ye'll not keep him dangling, I should hope!" she cried, wiping her hands on her apron, and stalking up to Katherine.

"By the Virgin, even Katherine couldn't be such a fool!" said Philippa with sudden energy. "Not if she really gets this chance." Philippa and Hawise were at one on this issue. Since the former had come to live with her sister two years ago, these determined women had learned to respect each other.

"Why—you both should think he calls here for—for any special reason, I'm sure I don't know," said Katherine, defensively, and as they both opened their mouths for argument, she indicated Joan and shook her head. "Please—"

Hawise shrugged, gathering up the mantle. "I'll do the last stitches—sweeting, ye're not going to wear that coif! It hides your hair. I'll bring ye the silver fillet."

"Thank God, Hawise has sense," sighed Philippa, lying back on the pillows. "It comforts me to know you'll have her, after I'm gone."

"Don't, dear—that's foolish," said Katherine quickly. "You'll be better when you've taken that betony wine the leech left."

Philippa shook her head and closed her eyes.

Katherine sighed deeply. I shall have to summon Geoffrey soon, she thought. He was living in Kent and dabbling in politics. He and Philippa were happier apart, but the separation was amicable as always, and he would be deeply shocked when he heard of his wife's condition.

Katherine picked up a distaff and began to spin abstractedly while she faced another more immediate worry. What shall I do about Robert Sutton, what is best? She had no real doubt as to the purpose of the wool merchant's announced visit this afternoon. The last time she had seen him he would have declared himself had she not managed to put him off, speaking—as though casually—about his wife, who was then but two months dead. God had helped her through these years. After an embarrassing time with Robert at the beginning, when she had thoroughly dashed all his amorous hopes, they had settled into a friendly business relationship. Not truly friendly on his part, for Katherine knew he had fallen as deeply in love with her as his cautious, pompous nature would allow.

Katherine twirled the spindle and tried to think coolly. Marriage, honorable marriage with one of Lincoln's foremost citizens. The slandering tongues would be silenced, in public anyway. The lonely struggle would be over, she would be rich, secure. And the children—would it help them? Hawise and Philippa said "Of course." Katherine was not so sure. Robert was a possessive man, her anxious eye had seen indications that he resented the children. Still, she thought, it might be that she had imagined his resentment. All her inmost self constantly sought arguments against this practical decision.

Her heart cried out that she did not love him, that the thought of lying in his arms sickened her. Reason answered that at thirty-six she should be finished with youthful passions and love-longings, that stubborn fidelity to a dream long past was stupid.

By day, it was only when she saw his traits in his children that she thought of the Duke. Young John looked most like him, the tawny gold hair, the arrogant grace of movement. But Harry had his voice, deep, sometimes sarcastic, sometimes so caressing that it turned her heart over. They all had his intense blue eyes, except Joan.

But by night, sometimes she was with him in dreams. In these dreams there was love between them, tenderness greater than there had really been. She awoke from these with her body throbbing and a sense of agonizing loss.

She had had no direct communication with him in these years, but he had been just, as she had known he would. There had been legal documents: severance papers sent through the chancery, which allowed her to keep the properties he had previously given her, and made her a further grant of two hundred marks a year for life "in recognition of her good services towards my daughters, Philippa of Lancaster and Elizabeth, Countess of Pembroke." No mention of his Beaufort children, but Katherine understood very well that this generous sum was to be expended for their benefit and scrupulously did so.

Finally, there had been a fearsomely legal quit-claim in Latin, which the Duke's receiver in Lincoln translated for her. Its purport was a repudiation of all claims past, present and future which might be made on Katherine by the Duke or his heirs, or that she might make on him. Merely a matter of form and mutual protection, explained the receiver coldly, and added that His Grace with his usual beneficence had ordered that two tuns of the finest Gascon wine be delivered at Kettlethorpe as a final present.

So that was how it ended, those ten years of passionate love. A discarded mistress and her bastards, well enough provided for; a repentant adulterer who returned to his wife. A common tale, one old as scripture. The Bishop of Lincoln had not failed to point this out in a sermon, with a reference to Adam and Lilith, and a long diatribe about shameless, scheming magdalenes. This sermon was preached at Katherine during the first hullabaloo after her return.

She could not have endured the cruel humiliations that continually assailed her without the memory of Lady Julian, and the golden days in Norfolk. "This is the remedy, that we be aware of our wretchedness and flee to our Lord: for ever the more needy that we be, the more speedful it is to us to draw nigh to Him."

Yet on this problem of Robert Sutton she had received no answer. The serene certainty which she had come to rely on after prayer failed her in this.

That afternoon, in anticipation of the wool merchant's visit, Katherine kept her three boys with her. Though they were wild to get out on the exciting streets to watch the preparations for the King's procession, she had asked them to stay awhile, partly because they gave her protection, partly to observe closely how Robert would treat them.

John understood at once. The moment she mentioned her expected visitor, he drew his mother away from the younger boys and putting his hands on her shoulders looked steadily into her face. "Are you going to consent, my mother?" he asked. He was almost fifteen, taller than she was now, broad-shouldered and manly in his school uniform of gray cloth. But she knew how he longed to change it for armor, how he longed for knighthood and deeds of valor, for the life he saw his legitimate half brothers lead, Henry of Bolingbroke and Tom Swynford.

"Johnny—I don't know," she said sighing. "What *shall* I do?"

" 'Twould make it easier for you!" he said slowly. Under the new golden fuzz his fair cheeks flushed. "I can't yet protect you, as I would." He gulped and flushed redder, began to twiddle with the flap of his quill case. "But I will! Wait, you'll see! I'll earn my knighthood some way. Mother, I can best all the lads tilting at the quintain. Mother, let me enter the Saint George Day's tournament at Windsor, let me wear plain armor—no one shall guess that I'm—I'm—" Baseborn. He did not say it, it hovered in the air between them.

"We'll see, dear," she said, trying to smile. John's dreams were impractical, but he should at least be attached to some good knight as squire, someone who would honor his royal blood and not take advantage of his friendless position.

And the two other boys. She looked at Harry, sprawled on his stomach by the fire, reading as usual. He had ink on his duckling yellow forelock, ink stains and penknife cuts on his grimy hands. A true scholar was Harry, with a keen shrewd mind beyond his years. He gulped knowledge insatiably, and yet retained it. He was determined to go to Cambridge, to Peterhouse, and train for minor orders at least; any further advancement in the clergy would take great influence—and money. A bastard could not advance in the Church without them. Bastardy. How often had she tried to console the elder boys as they had grown into realization of the barrier that held them back from their ambitions, pointing out that they were not nameless, that their father had endowed them with a special badge, the Beaufort portcullis, and a coat of arms, three royal leopards on a bar. She reminded them that William of Normandy, England's conqueror, was not true-born. These arguments seemed to comfort the boys. At least they had both ceased to distress her with laments. But they were thoughtful of her always. In their different ways, they loved her dearly.

Tamkin was still too young to fret about his birth. He was a happy-go-lucky child anyway, and at ten lived in a boy's world of sport and play. A healthy young puppy, Tamkin, and at the moment engaged in teasing Harry by rolling dried acorns across his book. This ended in a scuffle, and then a roughhouse. Chairs were overturned, the floor rushes flew about the pommeling, shouting whirl of arms and legs when Robert Sutton walked in.

"By God, lady!" he cried above the rumpus, " 'Tis like the mad cell at the Malandry in here! Your lads show you scant respect."

Tamkin and Harry disentangled themselves abruptly. They stood up panting, red-faced. "We mean our lady mother no disrespect, Master Robert," said Harry arranging his torn tunic, and eying the wool merchant coldly.

Robert, glancing at Katherine's watchful face, changed his tone. "Good, good. I'm sure you don't. Boys will be boys, ha? I've brought you lads something." His full swimming eyes veered to include John who stood very stiff and quiet beside his mother. "It, or they rather, are in the courtyard, waiting for you."

"Oh what, what?" cried Tamkin jumping up and down.

"Go and see," said the merchant benevolently.

John and Harry gave him a restrained, considering look, but they went off with their excited little brother.

"My best hound bitch, Tiffany, has lately whelped," Sutton explained to Katherine, sitting down opposite her. "I've brought each of your lads a pup. The strain have the keenest noses in Lincolnshire."

"That's very good of you, Master Robert," said Katherine with sincere gratitude. The boys had no blooded hunting dogs, and made do with the Kettlethorpe mongrels.

"And I've brought Joan a little yellow singing bird that came from the coast of Fez. She must keep it warm and tend it well."

"Ay—and thank you. It'll delight her," said Katherine.

He was not normally perceptive, but with regard to Katherine this middle-aged passion that had come to him made him observant. He saw a shadow in her lovely gray eyes, and a tightness about the mouth which still retained the curves of youth. He put his pudgy hand on his velvet-draped knees and leaning forward said anxiously, "What troubled you, just then, sweet heart?"

He *is* good, she thought, he *is* kind, if the boys are jealous they'll get over it. I'll say yes, but I must be frank with him in all things first.

"It was this," she said speaking with effort. "I had a child —once—who loved singing birds—Blanchette—"

"To be sure, and I remember the little red-haired maid, years ago at Kettlethorpe," said Robert heartily. "Too bad she died, God rest her soul." Pity it wasn't one or more of the bastards died, he thought. Ah well, one must take the rough with the smooth.

As Katherine did not speak but gazed into the fire, he said on a brisker note, "You must forget the past. It does no good to brood."

"No, of course not." She turned and looked at him. At the sleek curls of beard on his well-fed jowls, at the network of tiny purple veins in his cheeks, at the heavy gold chain around his massive crimson velvet shoulders, at the badges of office on his arm—former mayor, member of Parliament, master woolmonger—at the heavy-lidded, slightly bloodshot eyes that answered her gaze with kindling eagerness.

"It does no good to brood," she repeated, "and I try to forget the past."

"I'll make you!" he cried thickly. "Katherine, you know

what I've come to say. We're not children— You shall be
Mistress Sutton. By God, you shall be *mayor's* wife next year
—when Father's out and I'm re-elected. You shall hold your
head up in this town, and be damned to all of them. They
dare not gainsay a Sutton. I'll not say I haven't thought twice
about it, and my father and brother—well, no need to go into
that, they'll do what I tell 'em to. We Suttons stick together
and they had to admit 'tis not as though you came to me penniless. Nay—I've shown 'em that the Beauforts are provided
for, and you have property, a tidy parcel. You'll soon see
how your manors'll flourish when I've full control. Not but
what you've acted cleverly enough for a female. As you
know, I was against your freeing the serfs—but it's not
worked out so badly, I'll admit, long as they pay their rents.
But you can get more out of the manors than you do. There's
a new breed o' Cotswolds I shall try at Kettlethorpe, I think
the pasturage near Fossdyke'd suit 'em, and—" It occurred to
him that women being what they were, this was perhaps not
the most effective of wooings. He cleared his throat and said,
"Well, 'tis no secret to you that I've long wanted you in my
bed, and if you'll come no other way, I'm willing to wed."

Katherine laughed.

The merchant was divided between delight at the pretty
sound of it and a natural annoyance.

"What's so funny?" he said stiffly. " 'Tis not, my dear, as
though you had noble blood, to be sure you'll be plain Mistress Sutton, instead of 'Lady'—but I hardly think—"

"Nay, nay—Master Robert," she put her hand on his knee,
"I've no thought like that, I come of simple yeoman stock,
and will be grateful to be Mistress Sutton—"

"Then you will?" he cried. He lumbered to his feet and
caught her up around the waist. He kissed her hotly, hard
and insistent.

'Tis not so bad, she thought. He smelt of pomade and
cloves, the feel of male strength and of desire, after so long a
chastity, was not disagreeable. As he kissed her, her pulses
quickened a little. Ay, I might learn to love him, at least
enough—she thought. I shall try.

Next day the royal procession to the cathedral justified all
Lincoln's hopes of gorgeousness, it also justified mounting rumors of Richard's unbridled extravagance, but today nobody
bothered about that.

John Sutton, the mayor, in his scarlet robes came first, his aldermen followed, and the guild members with their banners, and the Church dignitaries, culminating in the bishop, aging now, but as haughty, tight-mouthed and supercilious as ever. These were familiar sights to Lincoln and hardly worth standing out in the cold for; but the King and Queen and their retinue were another matter. Never had anyone imagined such a dazzle of cloth of gold, of pure silver tissue, such yards of ermine to trail in the muddy streets, such flashing of jewels.

Thanks to Robert Sutton's influence, Katherine watched from a bench in the minster nave as the procession moved sedately along between the clustered marble columns towards the northeast transept and turned left for the chapter house, where the ceremony would take place.

She watched with emotions more painful than she had anticipated when familiar figures marched by. Michael de la Pole, whom she had seen so often with the Duke. He was Richard's advisor now, had been created Earl of Suffolk, had been Chancellor of England, but there was trouble, how grave she did not know, except that he had been recently ousted from his chancellorship, and disgraced by the Lords in Parliament. He looked old, she thought with a pang, his shoulders stooped under their ermine cape, his hair was white as the ermine.

And Lord Neville of Raby, the fierce North Country warrior: he looked not only old but ill, his steps dragged and he leaned heavily on the arm of his stalwart good-looking son, Ralph.

Next came a giggling, mincing group of young men in skintight hose that showed their thighs, and more, and who wore velvet shoes with points a half yard long—Richard's contemporaries and cronies; and the Bohemian lords and ladies who had come over with Queen Anne. And young de Vere, once Lord Oxford, Richard's favorite, whom he had created Duke of Ireland.

At de Vere's faultlessly handsome face, Katherine gazed with revulsion. Even at Kettlethorpe she had heard of de Vere's incredibly stupid conspiracies against the Duke, three years ago, the subtle plans to have John poisoned, the foul story of a mad Carmelite friar who had been subjected to hideous torture as de Vere's scapegoat. Ay, there was perversion of all sorts dwelling behind those tinted beardless cheeks,

the gold-powdered curls, the tall slender body that bore itself
so haughtily in violet brocade which gave forth a wave of
scent as he passed.

Was it not in great part because of the dark silken influence de Vere had always had on Richard that the reign
that started so auspiciously ten years ago had now degener-
ated into quarrels more violent than any known in Edward's
time, and that Richard, so soon, had come to be loathed by
most of his people, peers and commons alike?

And yet perhaps Queen Anne might save him, many hoped
so.

The royal couple came on alone, after an interval. Katherine and all those crowded into the nave fell to their knees.

Richard had filled out, and blurred. The appleblossom
cheeks were plump, there was roundness beneath the tunic
that was so thickly crusted with gems that one could not see
the gold beneath. Even the white hart badge on his chest was
made of pearls. Queen Anne was equally ornate, and at
first glance because of the horned moon headdress she appeared to tower over her husband. She was no beauty, certainly. This daughter of the Holy Roman Empire would, in a
kirtle, have passed for any stout healthy farm girl, but her
face was kind, and as she whispered something to Richard,
her smallish eyes sparkled agreeably.

They were so young, Katherine thought, only twenty, both
of them, their characters not yet all formed. It might well be
that this pleasant-looking young woman would prop the too
delicately bred Plantagenet flower.

When the royal couple disappeared down the nave, Katherine stood up and stretched her cramped legs, noting that
some of Richard's meinie had not gone into the small chapter
house but were walking back into the nave to wait.

She must go home, she thought, and dress for the banquet.
Also to tell poor Philippa exactly what everyone had worn
and what the Queen looked like. Philippa was happier, even
though in pain. Hawise was happy too, both were delighted
with Katherine's acceptance of Master Robert, though it was
to be a secret until the first banns were read on Sunday.

She wandered down the nave towards the Galilee entrance
and paused in the transept beneath the rainbow shower of
light from the round glass window called the Bishop's Eye.
She had always loved this cathedral, and thought it the most
beautiful in England with its west front of warm apricot-col-

ored stone, its wealth of carvings, some humorous, like the preaching fox in the wooden choir stalls or the tiny imp hidden in the stone foliage of the retrochoir, some inspiring like the musical angels on St. Hugh's shrine. The cathedral had gracious dignity that inspired a reverence peculiarly its own. Yet since the bishop's unkind sermon she could never feel welcome here, fancying that even the sacristans and chantry priests stared at her sardonically.

Today there were so many strangers that she did not feel conspicuous. While she gazed up at the Bishop's Eye, someone spoke her name. She turned and saw that it was Michael de la Pole.

"Why, God's greeting, my lord," she said uncertainly. She had met none of the Duke's close companions since the parting.

"Lady Swynford—" said the old earl smiling. "Fair as ever, I see." He sighed, she saw that his blear eyes held a dragging weariness. " 'Tis good to see something that doesn't change."

"Oh, my lord," she protested, "indeed I have."

He shook his head. "I'm not being gallant, lady—if you remember, pretty speech was no art of mine. You look no older than you did six—ay, six years ago at Leicester Castle —by the Mass—that seems another life, another world."

"It was," said Katherine quietly. "For me."

Never during the long association with this woman had Michael quite understood the Duke's passion for her, but suddenly he did so now, perhaps because he had himself been suffering.

"My lady," he said, smiling ruefully, "I've the infirmities of age, alack—d'you know of a good near-by tavern where my page can go for wine? My belly shrinks and gnaws unless I keep it filled."

She nodded, "But my lord, if you would consider—my house is there, a few steps away—if I might offer you—?"

"The very thing! An hour's quiet will hearten me—immeasurably. Yet, lady," his sunken eyes glimmered with bitter mocking light, "are you sure you wish to receive a man who has been accused of embezzlement, of cowardice, a man dismissed from office in disgrace?"

"You ask this of *me?*" said Katherine. They looked at each other half smiling, with a poignant understanding, before they turned and went together out of the cathedral and across the close to her house.

Hawise and Philippa were vastly fluttered by the arrival of the great Earl of Suffolk, little Joan caught the excitement and stared at him with awe, but the boys were all out enjoying the freedom of this gala day.

Katherine mulled wine herself over the fire for de la Pole while they settled down comfortably in the two cushioned chairs. He drew a sigh of relief. "This is good. Quiet. It takes youth, and strength—and, and—the wariness of a stoat to be around the King."

Philippa and Hawise had tactfully withdrawn, taking Joan with them. The two were alone in the pleasant room where the fitful sunlight glowed on Katherine's plain well-polished furniture, on the fresh sweet-smelling floor rushes. She picked up a tapestry square and began to stitch, thinking that he might prefer not to talk.

He watched her awhile, wondering if she ever thought of the old life and how things went with her here in Lincoln. She *had* changed, he thought, not her features, but in the atmosphere she emanated. There had used to be an undertone of intensity, of striving about her, now she seemed peaceful: serene and deep as a mountain tarn.

"Lady Swynford," he said suddenly, "do you ever think of the Duke?"

Her needle paused, quivered, then plopped through the canvas, trailing its load of crimson wool. "It would do no good if I did, would it?"

"Nay—those times are long past, and well passed, I suppose, yet I don't doubt he thinks of you."

She raised her head. In the gray eyes the pupils enlarged slowly. "I'm sure you're wrong, my lord, unless it is with hatred."

"Hatred?" De la Pole was astonished. "Oh, he was very angry for a while up there in the north when you disappeared, 'twas natural enough. But it was not hatred that made him build a chapel to Saint Catherine near Knaresborough."

Katherine put down her tapestry and stood up; her chair scraped on the hearthstone. "Chapel to Saint Catherine?"

"Ay—in fulfillment of a vow he made to her for your safety through the revolt."

She turned to the fire, pressing her fingers on the mantel's rim. "When did he erect this chapel—not after he publicly renounced me—and returned to the Duchess?"

De la Pole frowned. "Why yes, I'm sure it was, quite a while after he was reunited to the Duchess at Knaresborough. But my dear, there was no public renouncement that I know of. I was with him for some months at that time, and I don't believe he ever spoke your name."

"Yet all England gossiped of how he had reviled me—calling me," she paused, went on steadily, "calling me witch and whore; this I heard that summer in Walsingham."

"And believed it?" cried de la Pole. "By God, lady, didn't you live long enough at court to discount slander? 'Tis the Benedictine chroniclers have been putting out all manner of lies about him—and why? Because of his association with Wyclif, because of the persecution he briefly gave their monasteries after that embroilment in the changeling story, because he has always favored the friars—Christ only knows the reason for malice—but *you* should have known him better than that."

"Ay—I should. Perhaps I did. But I have heard no direct word from him—since then."

De la Pole shook his head, and sighed. "Need I tell you of his pride? And more than that, I believe he saw as you did, that it was best you two should part."

Katherine began to walk up and down across the hearth, she bent to poke the fire, she moved an andiron, she poured more wine into the mulling pot. "My lord, I almost wish you hadn't told me this," she said at last. "I do not wish to think of him—too softly."

Ay, perhaps I should not have mentioned him, thought the old earl. Meddle, meddle—'tis all it seems to me I do nowadays, at least so my enemies think. A lifetime of service to the Duke, to the crown, and at the end nothing but hatred and ingratitude. Gloucester was the real enemy, and Arundel of course. Impeachment, accusations. Michael had suffered both. They said he was nothing but a tradesman, a Hull merchant far too rich to be honest. They said he was a coward because he had influenced Richard towards peace, towards making an end of this senseless, crippling war with France. And now it would soon be exile. No doubt of that. And his one staunch friend, far away in Castile.

"How is it with the Duke?" said Katherine. She had sat down again and picked up her tapestry. She bent her face low over it. "He is gaining at last his long ambition, isn't he? the Castilian throne he so much wanted."

"By the rood, I fear not," answered de la Pole sadly. "At least not as he wanted it. His daughter will sit there, not he."

"Daughter?"

"You've not heard of the marriages?"

She shook her head. "People do not speak to me of him."

"Why, Philippa and João I were married last month in Oporto, she is now Queen of Portugal."

How strange, Katherine thought. Philippa the grave, sedate, virginal girl who had longed for the cloister, now wedded at twenty-six and a queen in a far-off land.

"And little Catalina," said de la Pole, "she is to marry Enrique of Castile, I believe. It is she who will sit on Castile's throne in her parents' stead—and that will mean the end of war at last."

The end of the Castilian dream at last, Katherine thought. Not in failure, but not in glory either. There must be humiliation for John in this denouement. The prize achieved by compromise, by dynastic marriages, but never really his. Always second, she thought, never first. All his life.

"Oh, he still fights," continued de la Pole, who had been following the same thoughts. "He hasn't given up yet. But we hear that his army is fearfully afflicted, there's some disease runs through them and kills. The messenger said that the Duke himself was very ill with it— Nay, lady, I talk too much, a tongue-wagging old man," he added quickly seeing the look in Katherine's eyes. "He'll recover. He has great strength."

She put down the tapestry and said in a choked voice, "My lord, forgive me if I leave you for a time." She walked from the Hall and upstairs to her solar, where for some moments she sat alone.

When she came down again, she found that Master Robert Sutton had arrived to escort her to the banquet. He and de la Pole were standing at the hearth making polite conversation.

The earl came up to her at once and took her hand. "I've trespassed too long upon your kindness, my dear lady, and must hurry back to my duties by the King. Forgive me," he added lower, "for talking so much." He kissed her hand. "It's been good to see you again. God bless you."

He went out, while Robert turned to Katherine with complacence. "It seems my Lord of Suffolk thinks well of you, sweet. Were he not so old, I'd be jealous. You might—" he continued, brightening, "through him even be presented to the Queen. He still has influence with Richard. Did you think to ask him? Maybe we should announce our marriage at the banquet after all."

"No," said Katherine slowly. She sat down and indicated the other chair so lately quitted by de la Pole. "Robert, I cannot marry you. Forgive me."

The wool merchant's ruddy cheeks paled, he stared at her. "Katherine, what whim is this! I ne'er thought you a woman for sly tricks and coquetry."

"It is no trick, or coquetry. It is that I was a fool to think I could forget the past—" She hesitated a long time while he looked at her with dismay and dawning anger. "It is this, you see," she said at last. "For me, it's not the past—it's still the present. Call it folly, madness if you like—but it seems I am so made that I can give myself to no other man."

He argued with her, he stormed at her, he pled with her. Tears filled her eyes, finally she wept in contrition, in pity; but she could not accede. During the moments alone in her chamber, the certainty had come to her at last. For her there could be no comfortable fresh start, no easier way permitted in the following of her destiny. The love that she had felt, she would always feel, and in itself brought dedication, regardless of return. Without de la Pole's revelations she would not have married Sutton, that had been a temporary clouding. But the thought of John suffering, in danger, had hastened the realization.

When Sutton left at last, furious and acid-tongued, she sat on alone in the Hall, nor did she attend the King's banquet. She sent word that she had been taken ill.

# XXXI

THE FEAST of St. Catherine—November 25, 1395. Katherine awoke at Kettlethorpe in an unusual mood of depression and unaccountable loneliness. The old solar was far snugger than it used to be, she had gradually achieved modest comfort in her home. The walls were hung with Lincoln-made tapestries, there were bear rugs and sheepskins on the plank floor. The wooden shutters had been replaced with casements of leaded glass, and the remodeled fireplace made it possible to warm this room that used to be a vortex of draughts. Nevertheless, Katherine shivered when she awoke and listened to the hissing of sleet on the windows. She found in herself a dismal reluctance to face the day: a holiday for all her manor folk, who had planned profuse festivities in her honor.

There was to be a procession, and a Catherine dance and spinning contest for all the village maidens, and a speech given by Cob, who was a great man in Kettlethorpe now, a sort of unofficial mayor. Her tenants would bring her little gifts, at the end there would be feasting in the Great Hall, while she sat on the dais and was crowned with a prickly wreath of pine and holly that Cob's children had made for her. These ceremonies were heart-warming. They had occurred every year, with increasing elaboration, since her return. It would be ungrateful indeed not to rejoice at the affectionate respect that they evinced.

But on this morning her head ached dully. While she waited for Hawise to come in with the morning ale, she could think only of worries. Two of her best ewes showed signs of murrain, the shepherd had sent to the witch of Harby for a charm to prevent the plague from spreading. That was one worry. Janet was another.

Janet Swynford, Tom's wife, who would soon be here from Coleby with the twins, to do her mother-in-law honor. Born a

602

Crophill of Nottingham, Janet was precisely the right wife for Tom, self-effacing, thrifty and plain as an iron pot, so that there was no danger whatsoever in leaving her at Coleby alone during the lengthy periods that Tom was off serving his Lord Henry of Bolingbroke. But Janet talked interminably in a thin martyred whine, and she bored Katherine. The year-old twins were sweet, Katherine longed to enjoy her only grandchildren, but they were delicate, little Hugh coughed incessantly, Dorothy had a weak stomach.

Katherine, who had borne and raised six healthy children, continually choked off advice that Janet would plaintively resent—and ignore.

Ah well, a familiar enough problem, and not worth fretting over. Joan's unhappiness was far more harrowing. Joan, her baby, was now sixteen, and a widow. Not that Joan had loved the fat shabby old knight to whom last year she had been so briefly married; but she had endured the discomforts gladly in return for the improved standing he gave her and the glimpse of the great outer world that poor Joan so longed for. Sir Robert Ferrers had taken his little bride to Leicester Castle and the gay household of Henry's wife, Mary de Bohun. Joan had had a few weeks of excitement before her widowhood and Countess Mary's death thrust her back to her mother and Kettlethorpe. Worse than that, during that brief, brighter time the girl had fallen desperately in love—with Ralph Neville of Raby, the handsome young Lord of Westmoreland, son to the old warrior who had died soon after his visit to Lincoln with Richard. The Nevilles of Raby did not marry bastards. Bitter heartache for Joan, to which Katherine applied the standard palliatives as best she could: so young; she'd get over it; some other suitable husband would turn up, and she would certainly forget young Neville when the babies came.

Joan had gazed at her with the round pansy-purple eyes and said quietly, "Did you, Mother? Did you ever forget my father even while you bore the Swynfords?"

The shock of that was still with Katherine, and the fear of the girl's instinctive comparison, which Joan had seen and allayed most painfully. "Nay—" she had whispered in a choked voice, "I shall never be Neville's paramour, though he begged it. Do you think I, who know what it is to be baseborn, would inflict that on another human soul? Ah, forgive me, Mother—"

They had both turned away in tears, nor referred to it again.

This new unhappiness of Joan's had awakened the dormant pain for Blanchette. Fourteen years without word. Requiem Masses were said for her in the church here on June 13, the day she disappeared, and yet Katherine had not quite accepted her death.

It was true that life was harder on women, but why, Katherine wondered, should it be her oldest and youngest children that seemed marked out for special suffering? To this question, as to many others, there was no answer.

*I am the ground of thy beseeching. How shouldest thou not then have thy beseeching?* Ay, she believed that. Many times comfort had been given her, and a glimpse of grace. Yet there were arid spaces like now when the light dwindled into grayness, and she fell into the sloth and doubt that Lady Julian considered the only true sins.

The door to the outside staircase flew open with a bang. Hawise came in on a stinging blast of cold air. "Cock's bones, but 'tis fine weather for friars!" she slammed the door shut and blew on her fingers. "No matter, sweeting, 'tis your saint's day, and I've laced your ale wi' cinnamon special as ye like it. Bless ye!" She leaned over the bed and gave Katherine a kiss. "Peter, what a long face! What's a matter?"

"I don't know—I've got the dumps." Katherine tried to smile. "Hawise, do you know how old I am?"

"I ought to." Hawise poured steaming ale into a cup and poked at the fire embers, "I've not lost me memory yet, let alone that all the kitchen folk're busy painting red ribbons 'round forty-five candles for your feast tonight."

"Forty-five," said Katherine flatly. "Jesu, what an age!"

Hawise came back to the bed holding out a rabbit-lined chamber robe. "Well, ye've not gone off much, if that's any comfort. Cob was boasting only yestere'en that the Lady o' Kettlethorpe is the fairest woman in Lincolnshire."

"Cob is partial, bless him," said Katherine with a rueful laugh. She looked down at her long braids, thick as ever but lightly frosted with silver, while at her temples she knew well that there were two white patches springing up with startling effect against the dark bronze.

"Ye're still firm as an apple," said Hawise casting a critical

look as she enfolded Katherine in the chamber robe. " 'Tis all
the work ye do, Saint Mary, I'd never've believed it in the old
days—brewing, baking, distilling, churning along wi' the
maids—running here, running there tending to the cotters—
gardening, even shearing. Lord, what busyness!"

"Well, I've had to," said Katherine bleakly. There had
been a bad couple of years after Sutton withdrew his advice
and support. She had run the manor entirely alone, but they
struggled through to modest profit again. Sutton's outraged
feelings had eventually been soothed by marriage with the
daughter of a wealthy knight. And it all seemed very long
ago.

She went mechanically through the process of washing and
dressing, allowed Hawise to bedeck her in the gala robe of
deep crimson velvet edged with squirrel and fasten the bodice
with the Queen's brooch.

"Seems strange too," said Hawise, adjusting the clasp,
"what coffers full o' jewels I used to rummage in afore we'd
find one to your liking—and now there's naught to wear but
this thing."

Katherine sighed and sat down by the fire. "So much has
changed," she said sadly. "Hawise—I think of my poor sister
this morning, God rest her soul. So many deaths—"

"Christ-a-mercy—lady—" cried Hawise crossing herself.
"What a way to talk on your saint's day!"

"What better day?" said Katherine. "Since I am thinking
of them—" She fell silent, staring into the fire.

Ay, o' *one* death especial, thought Hawise as she shook her
head and started to straighten the bedsheets. The Duchess.
Last year had come a strange smiting on the highest ladies of
the land, the Lollard preachers had seen God's vengeance in
it, and folk had been afraid. Between Lent and Lammastide,
they died, the three noblest ladies in England. Queen Anne,
she died of plague at Sheen Castle, and the King had gone
out of his mind with grief. Mary de Bohun, Lord Henry of
Bolingbroke's countess, had died in childbirth, Christ have
mercy on her, thought Hawise, remembering the frightened
twelve-year-old bride at Leicester Castle the winter before the
revolt.

And the Duchess Costanza had died, here in England, of
some sickness in her belly, they said. When the news got to
Kettlethorpe, Lady Katherine had been very quiet for many
days, her beautiful gray eyes had taken on a strained, waiting

look, but nothing had happened at all, except that the Beaufort children had all been sent fresh grants through the chancery. In truth, through the last years, the Duke seemed to have taken a concealed interest in them; at least he had not interfered with the marked favor and help that his heir Henry had occasionally showed them.

But, thought Hawise, tugging viciously at a blanket, wouldn't you think the scurvy ribaud might have sent my lady some kindly word, at last? Instead he had gone off to Aquitaine again as ruler. And was still there, God blast him, and why hadn't she taken that Sutton when she had the chance, though to be sure he might not of made her happy. Men, men, men, thought Hawise angrily, then seeing that Katherine still sat in dismal abstraction, she went up to her coaxingly. "Read some o' those merry tales in the book Master Geoffery sent ye, now do. They always cheer ye."

Katherine blinked and sighed. "Oh Hawise—I fear 'twould take more than tales of junketing to Canterbury to cheer me today—poor Geoffrey—" He was having a hard time, she knew, though his letters were philosophical as always, yet he was in financial difficulties, his health not good, and he was lonely in the Somerset backwater where he had been consigned as Royal Forester. I wish I could help him, she thought. Perhaps when the accounts are all toted up, there may be a shilling or so to spare here—

"Hark!" said Hawise suddenly, pulling a wry mouth. "There's my Lady Janet with the twins." They both listened to the familiar clatter of hooves in the courtyard, and heard the peevish howling of babies.

"Yes," said Katherine rising and reaching for her mantle. "The day's festivities most merrily commence."

That's not like her, Hawise thought gloomily, while she continued to straighten the solar, that dry bitter inflection from one who had shown of late years a nearly constant sweetness and courage. Hawise paused by the prie-dieu and picking up her mistress's beads said a rosary for her. Still dissatisfied, she hunted through Katherine's dressing coffer until she found a little brass pin which she threw into the fire with a wish, and felt better. "Cry before breakfast; sing before supper," she quoted from Dame Emma's collection of comforting lore.

Hawise's prayer and wish were granted, though not before supper and by nothing as simple as cheerful song.

The villagers had finished their feasting, the boards had been cleared, and stacked with the trestles in the corner of the Hall. Cob had made his speech. He had sent hot color to Katherine's cheeks, mist to her eyes with his eulogies, and her tenants had cheered her exuberantly. Two ne'er-do-wells from Laughterton had even brought her some back rent that she had despaired of getting, and there had been copious donations of apples, and little cakes baked by the village wives.

Now Katherine sat on in the hour before bed strumming her lute, while Joan sang and Janet listened vaguely. The twins were asleep in their cradle by the hearth. Hawise sat by the kitchen screen mending sheets. The house carls had all gone off to the village tavern to wind up the day. The forty-five big candles still burned, and shed unusual brilliance in the old Hall.

"I wonder where my brothers all are tonight?" said Joan in a pause between songs. "Lord, I wish I was a man."

Her mother's heart tightened. So dreary for the child here in this middle-aged woman's household, such tame distractions to offset the cankering hidden love.

"Well," said Katherine lightly, "we know Harry's studying in Germany and Tamkin is *supposed* to be at Oxford, though I wouldn't count on it." She smiled. Tamkin was no scholar like Harry, who had already risen farther in the Church than had ever seemed possible. There could be no doubt that their father's secret influence had helped them all. This had often comforted her. Young John had achieved at last his great ambition and been knighted, after he traveled with Lord Henry to the Barbary coast. A lovable fellow Johnnie was and had made his way as a soldier of fortune, despite the hindrance of his birth. Even Richard liked him—so far any way—and had taken him with the army to Ireland last year.

"I don't know where Thomas is," said Janet suddenly in her plaintive whine. "I hope he gets home for Christmas; he never lets me know *anything*."

"Poor Janet." Katherine put down the lute and sighed. "Waiting is woman's lot, I don't suppose I'll see my Johnnie for a long day, either."

Janet's small pale eyes sent her mother-in-law a resentful look. A blind mole could see that Lady Katherine preferred her baseborn sons to her legitimate one, and Janet considered this shameful. Her discontented gaze roamed around the Hall, which was larger and better furnished than Coleby's.

She indulged in a familiar calculation as to how long it would be before Tom inherited. But Lady Katherine seemed healthy enough and looked, most infuriatingly, ten years younger than she was, manifestly unfair reward for a wicked life.

"I think I'll go to bed," said Joan yawning. "With you, I suppose, Mother?"

Katherine nodded. The arrival of guests always meant switch of sleeping quarters. Janet, nurse and twins would occupy Joan's usual tower chamber—that had once been Nichola's.

Hawise put down her mending and began to blow out the candles. There were still twenty to go when the dogs started to bark outside. The blooded hound, Erro, that Sutton had given young John over eight years ago had been lying by the fire with his head on his paws. A dignified aristocrat, Erro, who did not consider himself a watchdog, and usually ignored the noisy antics of his inferiors. It was therefore astonishing to have him raise his head and whine, then leap up with one powerful bound and precipitate himself uproariously against the door.

"Strange," said Katherine running to hold his collar. "There's only one—Saint Marie, *could* it be?" she added joyously.

And it was. Young John Beaufort came into the Hall on a swirl of soft snow. He caught his mother in his arms, kissed her heartily. "God's greeting, my lady! Sure your saint might have sent better weather to a son who's been hurrying to you these many days!"

He kissed his sister, Hawise, and, less enthusiastically, Janet, before quieting the ecstatic Erro, who barked fit to raise the dead in the churchyard across the road. John stood by the fire while the women fluttered around him removing his mantle, brushing snow from his curling yellow hair, unfastening his sword, and the gold knight's spurs of which he was so proud, heating ale for him in the long-handled iron pot over the fire.

"Oh dearling," Katherine cried, quivering with pride—surely there was no comelier young man in England—"and you remembered your old mother's feast day! Johnnie, this is the pleasantest surprise, the goodliest thing that's happened to me in an age. I thought you abroad!"

"Well, I was." He sank into a chair with a grunt, held his steaming red leather shoes towards the fire. "Until three weeks ago. In Bordeaux. Mother—" He turned and looked directly into her face. "I was not the only one there who remembered your saint's day."

Katherine's look of contented pride slowly dissolved, to be replaced by tenseness. She said slowly, "What were you doing at Bordeaux, Johnnie?"

Hawise's hands, which had been rubbing lard into John's wet shoe leather, suddenly stilled. Janet ceased jiggling the twins' cradle and raised her head, not understanding the odd tone in her mother-in-law's voice. Joan looked from her mother to her brother and began to breathe fast.

"I was *summoned* by my father!" cried John triumphantly. "I spent a week with him and have brought you a letter from him. He wanted it to reach you today."

In Katherine's head there was a rumble like far-off thunder, while she felt a peculiar coolness as though the snow outside were melting through her veins.

"So you have met the Duke again," she said speaking from the depths of the coolness. "How does he seem?"

John's surprise that she did not at once ask for her letter was shared by Joan and Janet, but Hawise understood. She returned grimly to the shoe leather and thought, Now what does that accursed Duke want?

"He's very tired, I think," said John, "and lean as—as Erro here, anxious to be back. His work is finished in Aquitaine, and Richard has summoned him home, much to Gloucester's fury, I believe."

"Ah—" said Katherine.

"By God," said John eagerly, "of course, that stinking Thomas of Woodstock wants our father's grace kept out of the country, so he can have free hand with Richard and the foul plottings and warmongerings that Father holds in check. Richard's fed up for the time and is pro-Lancaster now."

"Ah—" said Katherine again. "Far off as we are here, we've not followed court policies, or the King's whims. The Duke of Gloucester, that was Buckingham when I knew him, I thought to be in favor."

"Well, he's not now, and I think the King's afraid of him. That's why he wants Father's help. Mother," said John, unbuttoning his surcote and pulling a parchment from his breast, "don't you want your letter? I'm in a fever to know what's in it!"

"And I," whispered Joan, putting her hand on Katherine's

arm. Katherine took the letter and looked at the superscription: "Lady Kateryn de Swynforth, Kettlethorp, County of Nicole," in John's own decisive heavily stroked black writing. It is fourteen and a half years since I have seen this writing, she thought. But it looked quite unchanged. She turned the letter over and examined the crimson imprint of his privy seal. In this there was change. The royal arms of Castile and León no longer occupied the dexter half. So he admitted at last the extinction of the great Castilian myth. Yet his daughter Catalina sat on the throne. He and Costanza had accomplished that much.

"Lady mother," said her son beseechingly, "for the love of Christ, read it! He told me nothing of what he wrote, and my father's grace is not a man one can question—yet he seemed pleased with me. He watched me joust and seemed very pleased."

Katherine smiled faintly. "You shall know soon what's in the letter." She rose. Under the disappointed looks of her children, she retrieved her mantle from the perch and went out into the snow, up the outside stairs into her solar. She bolted the door and put the parchment on a table while she replenished the fire. When the flames burned well, she went to her prie-dieu and knelt for some time. Then she lit a candle at the fire and placed it carefully on its iron pricket. After a while she picked up the letter and sat on a stool by the hearth. Her fingers were cold as the icicles that hung from the thatched eaves when she at length broke the crimson seal.

There was no greeting. It began abruptly, in French, as he had always written to her.

*Recently I visited Château la Teste in Les Landes. Poignant memories were aroused of a time long ago. I am weary of many things, each day my life becomes more irksome to me, and in the light of this weariness I view many bygone actions differently from what I used to. I shall be back in England at Christmas time, and I wish to see you again. I beg of you to forget all past bitterness, to look courteously across the great chasm that opened between us, and to grant my request. I also wish to see Joan, who is with you, I understand. Harry, I have summoned from Germany and should be on his way home. Our Thomas I shall visit at Oxford before I come to Lincolnshire. John, who has brought you this*

*letter, will remain with you until I arrive, about the first*
*of the year. He is a son to be proud of. You have done*
*well with him, and with the others too.*

*God and His Blessed Mother have you in their keep-*
*ing.*

JOHN, DUKE OF LANCASTER . . .
Bordeaux, November 5, 1395

"So—" said Katherine aloud, putting down the letter. She
repeated a sentence slowly: "Je vous emprie d'oublier toute l'a-
mertume du passé—" Yes, bitterness should be forgotten. She
no longer felt bitterness, but there was a sharp reluctance. It's
too late, much too late for us to meet again. Middle-aged
people—almost old. John was fifty-five. She could not hinder
the children, since their father was at last taking an open interest in them. But as for me, she thought—far better if I'm
not here when he comes. She could go to Janet at Coleby.
Ah, let me alone—she said to the letter, looking at the words
"Château la Teste dans les Landes . . . des souvenirs poign-
ants": the round room in the donjon tower, the sea air, the
mewing of gulls—and ecstasy that can come but once.

She had made a new life; usually there was content. She
had learned the pleasure of little things: the glint of May
sunlight on a cluster of bluebells, the smell of white bread she
had herself baked, quiet companionable talk with some of the
village wives, whose pungent humor she had come to appreciate.

Had she not earned freedom from turmoil? From fear and
pain? The letter brought both. Fear not only of emotional up-
heaval, but of practical troubles. She had gradually become
acceptable to Lincolnshire, time had somewhat regularized
her position. The old buzzings and scandals would inevitably
start up again upon the Duke's visit. Worse than that was the
fear of anticlimax. Far better to keep the memory of a great
love—as it had once been—than have it cheapened forever
by disillusionment. Indigne—she thought in the French word
—unseemly, even perhaps ridiculous. No, she would not meet
the Duke.

She persisted in her decision until the arrival of Harry on
Christmas Eve. He had been studying at Aachen when his fa-
ther's summons reached him, had hurriedly embarked from
Holland and just landed at Boston. He arrived in a state of

bright-eyed excitement. "What does this mean, Mother? Before God, I can't understand it, but surely it can't be for ill tidings he's summoned us!"

A large forceful young man of twenty, Harry had become; sleek as a pigeon in his plum-colored cleric's robes. He had a hearty laugh, a fine resonant voice obviously made for the pulpit and a quick legal mind. In time he dissuaded Katherine from her flight, saying that she had no right to anger or balk their father in any way, since it might prejudice him against the children. John and Joan, who were inclined to humor their mother, had not used this argument, but Katherine saw the truth of it.

When Janet eventually went back to Coleby without her, Katherine had achieved resignation much strengthened by inner certainty that she was doing right. Glimpses of the light returned to her during that Christmastide, the channel of communication which had seemed blocked ran clear again and gave her serenity.

She noticed that her three children often gathered in corners whispering, and looking at her with excited speculative eyes, but the whispers stilled at once when she came near, and no hint of their purport reached Katherine. She had no idea that, led by Harry, her Beauforts were allowing themselves an incredible hope. One so preposterous that they were ashamed of it, even while they could not help referring to it in broken phrases: "If—"; "Could it be?"; "But Blessed Christ, it's impossible—"; "Nay, his letter was cold, there was nothing to build on. He means nothing like that." Katherine, to quiet their clamorous questions, had shown them the letter.

When a herald came on New Year's Day to announce the Duke's arrival on the morrow, Katherine was far calmer than her children. She looked at the Lancastrian arms on the herald's tabard, at the blue and gray of his trunks, at the falcon badge embroidered on his blue cap—the familiar panoply of Lancaster—and thought how long it was since she had seen it. Once she had been borne along on a raging current that all those symbols stood for, and she vowed that she would not permit that turbulent river to submerge her again.

The next morning, she was touched and a trifle exasperated by Joan's hovering anxiety. "Mother, let me do your hair, Hawise is clumsy at it! Mother, please wear the gold brooch Sir Robert left me, it looks far better than that silver thing. Oh Jesu, if you only had a new gown, he'll think you so old-fashioned in that sideless surcote, and shoes are far more pointed now in London—at least," she added slowly, "they *were* when I was there nineteen months ago." She sighed.

Katherine looked at the pretty dark head, the charming face that was bleak with longing, and said gently, "You shall make me as splendid as possible, darling, but truly it's of no consequence, one way or the other."

Joan picked up a vial of lavender water, fiddled with the lead stopper, and said, "It is because of his love for you, and yours for him, that we exist at all—isn't it?"

Katherine was startled and confused. "That was a very long time ago, Joan," she answered with some difficulty. "Human love dies. You must face that, dear—" She bit her lips, for she saw that Joan was crying, quietly, proudly, big tears slipping down her pink cheeks.

Long before the court dogs began to bark, they heard the winding flourish from Lancaster Herald's trumpet as the Duke's cavalcade turned off the highway on to the manor road. At the well-remembered sound, Katherine's heart at last took up a hard-measured pounding, while Joan ran up to the tower roof to watch the approach over the sparkling white-gold snow, down the avenue of bare-branched wych-elms.

Katherine walked slowly across the courtyard and the drawbridge to stand by the old mounting block. Her two sons held back nervously in the court, where Joan joined them, saying, "Tamkin came with him. O Blessed Mary, make everything go well!" She crossed herself and lifting her beads began to whisper a rosary. Her brothers drew closer to her. The three stood waiting.

The Duke reined in his black stallion when he came to the church. A watchful squire ran up and held the horse. The Duke dismounted. He was not armored, he wore an enveloping violet-colored mantle trimmed with ermine, an intricately draped furred hood concealed most of his face. As he advanced towards her across the trodden snow, Katherine curtsied deeply and said, "Welcome to Kettlethorpe, my lord."

He pulled off his jeweled gauntlet and took her bare hand in his. "Am I truly well come, Katrine?" he said in a harsh thick tone.

She raised her eyes to his face. Deep new lines on the forehead, lines from the nostrils of the long nose to the corners of the set, thin-lipped mouth. Gray hairs in the tawny eyebrows above the eyes of a quieter blue, sad, questioning eyes.

A long white scar ran from left ear to forehead and had puckered the eyelid. Dear God, so much change, she thought. Yet it was still the face she had so greatly loved.

"You are well come, my lord," she repeated evenly, though she felt the touch of his hand like a burn. "Our—the Beauforts await you most eagerly."

He glanced where she did through the gatehouse to the courtyard, where his children were grouped by the hall door. "Ay," he said, "and I've brought Tamkin. But I should like to see you alone first."

"Why for, my lord?" she said drawing back her hand. "What have we to say alone now?"

"Katrine, I beg you!"

"'Tis not so easy to be alone at Kettlethorpe," she said with a faint cool smile.

"The church?" he suggested. "'Twill be empty at this hour?"

She inclined her head and preceded him through the lych gate. The church had been decorated with holly and evergreens for New Year's; the nave, which was the village hall in winter, was still cluttered with small tables from the "church ale" and fair they had held here yesterday; the rushes were strewn with candle wax, nut shells, crumbs. Five children stood by a thatched stable which enclosed crudely painted home-made figures of the nativity, and loudly disputed whether the Baby were smiling or not.

The Duke glanced at them, removed his draped headdress and said, "Farther up in the choir—surely 'twill be quieter." He walked around the rood screen.

Candles burned before the statue of the Blessed Virgin, and a wall painting of Sts. Peter and Paul, the church's patrons. Four long tapers flickered in a small chapel Katherine had built behind the Swynford choir stall. They shone on a tomb with the brightly tinted effigy of a knight in armor.

The Duke paused by the tomb and looked down at the knight, at the boarhead crest on the helm, the shield with three boars' heads on a chevron, the bearded face, which bore little resemblance to the original since it had been carved in Lincoln from Katherine's description, only a few years ago. Slowly the Duke crossed himself. "May God comfort and keep his soul," he said, and turned to Katherine, who stood at the entrance of the chapel, her hood pulled far over her face.

"Katrine—" he said, "is this to stand between us, forever?"

In the moments during which she did not answer, the voices of the children in the nave rose louder until one cried "Hush!" in a frightened voice; there was a scamper of feet and the west door banged, leaving silence.

"There is far more than Hugh that stands between us, my lord," she said in the silence.

He made a gesture, impatient, resigned, letting his hand fall slack. He left the tomb to stand beside her in the aisle. Suddenly he raised his hand and brushed back her hood, staring down at her face, into the wide gray eyes that met his steadily, without bitterness; but neither did they soften under his long gaze, they held detachment, a watchful calmness that daunted him. He reached out his finger to touch the white streaks at her temples. "Age on you has but added swan's wings to your fairness," he said wryly, "while I'm grizzled and hacked like an old badger—"

"You do yourself injustice, my lord. Badgers are hunched, lumpy creatures, while you are still straight as a lance." She spoke in a light social tone, as he had heard her chatting with knights of his retinue long ago. She replaced her hood, and glanced down the nave towards the door, obviously checked only by courtesy from suggesting that they leave.

In that instant, John forgot that he was Duke of Lancaster, while his last doubt vanished. From the deepest springs of his being, words bubbled to his lips, so that he stammered like a pageboy. "Katrine—Katrine—you make this so hard—my God, is there nothing left for me at all? We can't be forever thinking of the dead. We're getting old, 'tis true, but we're still alive—and if you feel nothing for me—if too much has passed since we were together—then think of our children, for them at least it's not too late—"

He stopped, trembling—his close-shaven cheeks had turned a dull brick-red, he was breathing fast, painfully.

Katherine swallowed, she saw his flushed pleading face through a fog and spoke with remote sad scorn. "Is some bargain still necessary between us, to aid my children's advancement? Has our age, at least, not removed incentive to further shame!"

He gasped as though she had struck him, and stared at her. Then he clenched his fist, banging it on the wooden rim of the choir stall. "Christ, Katrine! I'm asking you to *marry me!*"

The dusky little church, the candlelight, the evergreens spiraled around her.

"It must have occurred to you?" he said with more control, astonished at her dazed face. "Surely when Costanza died—and now when I've summoned all our Beauforts here—Katrine, I could not come sooner—the King sent me to Aquitaine—" He had entirely forgotten the doubts and uncertainties he had felt, how he had not been entirely sure until he saw her again.

"It did not occur to me," she said in a wooden voice. "After your Duchess died, I hoped for a word from you, then even that desire passed. I received you today for our children's sake. There's much you can do for them—if you will—" She could not think, there was no feeling but shock, and dislocation.

"What better can I do for them, than have them legitimated?" he said, half smiling. "This, Richard has agreed to in the event of our marriage, and the Pope will confirm it."

"Legitimated—" she repeated, "legitimated—I've never heard of that. Jesu—the stain of bastardy cannot be wiped out!"

He nodded slowly. "It can." Legitimation was an unusual procedure. There had in fact never been a precedent entailing circumstances quite like these. But English law permitted it, this he had verified. "With the King decreeing their legitimacy in the temporal realm, and the Pope as Christ's vicar in the spiritual, how can anything in heaven or earth then gainsay their true birth?" he said gently.

Her face crumpled like a child's. She raised her twisted hands to her mouth and walked rapidly down to the nave, seeking to be alone—to integrate herself. This sensation was as shattering as pain, indistinguishable from it.

After a time he came down and stood beside her. "Katrine," he said touching her shoulder, "it is necessary that we be married first, you know. I trust this is not too great a hindrance. Have you any thought for me—as well as the children?"

"I don't know yet—" she said, staring at the rushes. "I can't realize. My lord—the Duke of Lancaster does not wed his paramour, and one of common stock—how could the King countenance this?"

"Well, he has," said John dryly. Richard at present would

countenance far more than that to please his eldest uncle and annoy his youngest one.

"I thought you hated me," she said. "Your love was over long ago."

"You yourself decreed our parting. I hated for a while. Then I saw that you were right. I made Costanza as happy as it was in her nature to be happy, but you've never been far from my deepest thoughts. I swore once that I'd love you till I die, it seems that I'm so made, that I must keep a vow—Katrine, can you doubt this? My dear, I have had other mistresses, other bastards too, years ago—so has every other noble in the land. I am offering *you* marriage, and the true birth of our children."

She rose slowly from the chair and looked up into his face, into the sad, questioning, tender eyes.

Katherine and John were married, very quietly, on January 13, beneath the stone carvings of the angels in the retrochoir of Lincoln Cathedral. A January thaw had set in during the days of waiting since the Duke had come to Katherine at Kettlethorpe, but on the marriage morning snow blew again over the fens from the North Sea and slapped softly against the cathedral's tinted windows while four junior vicars clustered around a lectern and chanted the office.

The subdean, John Carleton, celebrated the Nuptial Mass. The Duke had requested that the bishop should perform the marriage, and the bishop had refused. "For which," the Duke had said with the old glinting icy look, "he will soon be exceeding sorry." His gaze rested speculatively on Harry. "Old Buckingham shall see how unchristian have been his many insults to my lady. It's high time Lincoln had a young and intelligent bishop, don't you think so, Harry?"

Harry's rapturous agreement was but one more note in the combined Beaufort joy. They lived now in bewildered glamor. A sorcery as marvelous as any of Merlin's was transforming all four of their young lives. During the ceremony while they knelt on velvet faldstools behind their parents, they were giddy with exultance. That very morning a letter had arrived from the King, who sent his blessings and said that as soon as the legitimations were confirmed by the Pope, John Beaufort was to be created Earl of Somerset, Harry to be appointed Dean of Wells Cathedral in transit to a bishopric, Tamkin to be knighted; and as for Joan— Already her father, upon discovering her despairing love, had opened negotiations with young Neville, the Lord of Westmoreland—an excellent alliance. Without a doubt there would be another wedding soon. Joan had been ill from joy and as she watched the tall figures of her parents at the altar, there was such a shaking in her chest that she could not follow the service.

At noon the nuptial bells pealed out over Lincoln, and Katherine arose from her knees to find herself the Duchess of Lancaster. Her children, unable to contain themselves, were surging around St. Hugh's shrine, while Joan sobbed hysterically. Katherine saw the awed face of Mayor Robert Sutton, who hovered in the aisle with an alderman. She saw Hawise's massive shoulders quivering, her face buried in a new scarlet silk skirt, and as realization came to Katherine, she swayed and caught at the altar rail. Blessed Christ, she thought, in terror. Against the triptych behind the crucifix she saw the lovely face of the Lady Blanche—and the enigmatic dark look of Costanza.

The Duke's strong hand closed on her arm. "Kiss me, Katrine," he said. She raised her mouth blindly. He brushed her lips with his and whispered, "Don't look back. We must be happy for the little time that's left."

He pulled her hand through his arm and turned from the altar. They walked together down the steps, stood on a cloth-of-gold rug, while their children ran up to them weeping, kissing their hands and their cheeks. Emotion almost too great to be borne and fortunately broken by a small, hoarse, crowing cheer.

Everyone looked around for the source of the cheer, which was Cob o' Fenton. He ran out from behind a pillar, flung himself to his knees while clutching a fold of Katherine's gown.

"Oh lady—I couldn't help cheering. Ye *said* the manor folk could come. Lady—that is, Your Grace—we're all here, down in the nave. Oh lady, this is a great day for Kettlethorpe!"

"A great day for *Kettlethorpe?*" cried Harry Beaufort, throwing back his head and gulping. "Oh in truth, by God, a great day for Kettlethorpe!" Suddenly they all dissolved into wild laughter. The Beaufort boys gasped and wheezed. They thumped little Cob on the back, who did not understand but grinned and chortled happily. The Duke and Katherine laughed.

Robert Sutton, watching from the aisle, was shocked, but the peculiarities of great folk must be tolerated. He smiled feebly and stared at Katherine as he had throughout the ceremony. A beautiful woman still, regal-looking in her green velvet and ermine and a silver-gilt veil covering her hair. "Christ's wounds!" Robert muttered suddenly to his alderman, "d'you know what this day's work makes of her—until King Richard marries himself that little maid in France—this makes her," he nudged his fat chins towards Katherine, "first lady of England!" His jaw dropped while he assimilated his own discovery.

"So it does," said the alderman thoughtfully. "Well, it's small wonder she wouldn't marry *you,* old trout, what a comedown that woulda been!"

Master Robert did not hear, he was walking ponderously towards the ducal party, whose laughter had died down. With some difficulty he heaved himself to his knees and kissed Katherine's hand. "My homage, Your Grace," he said in a toneless, deliberate voice. "Your liegeman, in life and limb—" Under Katherine's startled gaze he methodically completed his feudal oath due to the rulers of Lancaster.

By tacit consent, Katherine and John avoided all the places where they had previously been together for their wedding night. Until the snow started, they had thought to ride to his near-by castle of Tickhill, but since that was now impossible, he commandeered rooms in the constable's quarters of Lincoln Castle. The flustered constable sent his men scurrying hither and yon around Lincoln to find furnishings worthy of this occupancy, but the result at such short notice was not impressive.

" 'Tis not what I wanted for you, my Katrine," said John looking around the two small rooms, with their hastily hung arras, crude rugs, squat oaken bed.

"What does it matter?" she said softly, smiling. "It's true one should not look back too much—but I find now that I can't help remembering the hundreds of nights we've spent together—and in so many different places."

They sat at a small table before a rather smoky fire; neither had eaten of the food a squire had brought them, nor drunk of the claret.

Hawise had dressed Katherine in a plain blue chamber robe, to which John had fastened a brooch he had ordered from a Lincoln goldsmith. It was enameled in full colors with her new blazon, the de Roet Catherine wheels impaling the royal lilies and leopards of England. Never shall I get used to that, she thought. She looked down at the brooch and shook her head. "I pray you'll never regret giving me the right to wear it," she whispered.

"I never will, lovedy."

He knew what a furore this marriage would cause in England, and in all Europe. He had weighed the disadvantages coolly enough before he saw her again; now he did not care. Since Blanche's death there had been no other woman for him—though he had tried hard enough to forget Katherine. And even Blanche—that had been different, to Blanche he owed his power, his enormous wealth, there had been loving gratitude. When he died, he would be buried beside her in St. Paul's as she had long ago requested, but now for what time was left, he would please his heart at last. He watched Katherine as she sat across the table from him, her graceful head a little bent, gazing into the fire as she so often did, and wondered if part of the enduring love he had for her sprang from the fact that she had given him nothing but herself. She had brought him no wealth, no power, no hope of foreign thrones. Always with her, he had been the donor.

A dreamy contentment came to him, an absence of strain. But I'm happy, he thought in amazement. When have I ever been happy before?

"Come here to me, darling," he said. When she obeyed, he drew her down onto his lap, with her cheek in the old place against his shoulder. "How shocked our children would be, if they saw us," he said smiling into her soft hair. "They think us too old for this—I've thought so myself. Now I don't." He kissed her hard on the lips. "It's not like Château la Teste," he said, "that it can't be—there's not youth—nor the fierce heat of passion—"

"Thank God, it's not Château la Teste," she whispered. "We paid for that, John—both of us—and others—"

He was silent, his arms tight around her. The snow hissed and slapped on the horn windows; distantly from the castle ramparts the nightwatch called out some challenge.

"Yet I believe you were no less my wife then, than you are tonight, Katrine," he said in a wondering voice.

# XXXII

KATHERINE DINED in the Great Hall at Windsor on the July night of the banquet to the French envoys who had come over to arrange final details of the meeting between the French and English kings.

In October, Richard would take formal possession of his eight-year-old bride, Princess Isabelle of France, and ratify the treaty of alliance at long last to be sealed with the ancient enemy—much to the fury of Gloucester and his warmongers.

Katherine sat on the dais to the right of the King's throne. She was encased in stiff cloth of gold and so burdened with necklaces, bracelets, clasps, rings and the heavy jeweled coronet of Lancaster, that natural movement was impossible, even if the meticulous ceremony which Richard exacted had not made any impulsive action unwise. Richard reserved the right of impulse for himself.

The King was dressed in a new tunic of white brocade peppered with diamonds. His yellow hair was tightly curled and scented, his little tufted beard did not quite conceal the softness of his small pointed chin. At the moment he was idly toying with a jade butterfly the French nobles had brought as a gift from their King. The butterfly had originally come from the mysterious dragon land of Cathay, and as Richard's plump almond-white fingers caressed the soft jade and his polished pink fingernails ran along the exquisite lines of the carving, he smiled at the butterfly as though it were a loved child. He ignored a dish of roast larks and ginger fritters which a kneeling squire presented to him. The squire continued to kneel, and the King to caress his bauble.

On Katherine's other side, sat her Duke, imperturbably, frigidly courteous, while he made small talk with Eleanor de Bohun, his sister-in-law. But the Duchess of Gloucester was far too angry to be civil in return, though from fear—of the King, whose sparkling malicious eyes darted her way now and then, of Lancaster who had that very morning corrected her behavior towards Katherine with a controlled but menacing wrath—she managed to grunt, and say "Ay so" and "No doubt" occasionally.

When news of the Duke of Lancaster's extraordinary marriage had burst on England, it had caused a furore as great as John had expected, though the outcry was not all hostile. From cot to castle the news had been mouthed voluptuously, but many of the commons and middle class had been amused, even pleased. Their hatred of the Duke had gradually given place to hatred of Richard and his favorites. They had come to consider Lancaster as the only sage restraining hand on his nephew's headlong rush into mad extravagance and contempt for his people. Moreover, the Duke's elevation of a woman who was born a commoner appealed to popular sentiment, while most feminine hearts were touched by the romantic apotheosis of a fallen sister.

The noble ladies at court were not so tolerant; while Eleanor, upon realizing the magnitude and implications of the news, had gone into an actual frenzy, beating her breast, tearing her hair and shouting for all to hear that her heart would burst with grief and shame if she were asked to give precedence to such a lewd baseborn Duchess! Which had delighted Richard, who detested his aunt nearly as much as he hated and feared his domineering Uncle Thomas. By all means, let Eleanor's heart burst, he said, and so much the better, but until it did she would have to witness the exaltation of the new Duchess of Lancaster. Not only here in England, either, but in France, where Katherine was soon to travel with the King and court and, as first lady of England, take official charge of the new little Queen.

The night was warm, the banquet tedious, the minstrels played listlessly. Richard yawned, put down the jade butterfly, and said to the quiet gold-clad figure on his right, "Why do you continually glance down the Hall towards that table near the door?"

Katherine started, then smiled. She answered frankly in her low sweet voice, "I am seeing there, Your Grace, a dazzled little convent girl of fifteen who wears an ill-fitting borrowed gown, and stares up at this High Table and its line of glittering Plantagenets as though they were the Holy Angels ranged beside God's throne."

"Ah yes," Richard smiled, after a puzzled moment. "And now you're one of them. It must be very strange."

"I pinch myself and still can't believe it! 'Tis thanks to you, Your Grace, and to my dear lord—" She looked at John's averted head, seeing that he had given up struggling with Eleanor and was talking around her stiff back to Mowbray, the Earl Marshal, who was an enemy. Or had been. Mowbray had lately made his peace with John, whom he had consistently denounced during John's absence in Aquitaine.

With the exception of Gloucester, who had refused to come to this banquet and remained at his castle of Plashy, pleading ill health, the court had taken its tone from Richard and welcomed Lancaster with ostensible rejoicing. But beneath the scent of costly perfumes and strewn flowers in this Hall, the air was thick with hidden enmity. One had but to look at the King's ever-present bodyguard ranged along the walls—enormous armed ruffians imported from Cheshire, and their white hart badges apparently gave them unlimited license to rape, steal and murder, unchecked. All England was afraid of them, and no king before Richard had thought such protection necessary. God shield us, Katherine thought.

But in time the banquet would finish, and she and John would be alone. She anticipated each night when they were freed from court duties as eagerly as she had long ago. Now it was not for bodily passion that she yearned, though they were still tenderly responsive to each other. A different bond had become more satisfying. He might be discouraged, irritable, tired—and sometimes she thought with fear that he seemed to be losing strength, sudden lassitude would overpower him—but yet, when the door of the great Lancastrian state suite was closed at last, a warm deep content came to them. There was no need for talk or love-making, they were at rest.

Richard, while he played with his golden fork and nibbled a slice of porcupine seethed in almond milk, had been considering Katherine's explanation of her glances down the Hall. It was charming as a variant of the old tale of the prince and the beggarmaid; and pleasing as an example of the omnipotence of anointed kings.

And those who dared challenge that divine power would bitterly repent their folly! His lids drooped as he glanced down the Hall towards the ranks of helmeted heads—his Cheshire archers. Two thousand of them in here and outside in the court, waiting, always ready. Had I had them sooner, he thought—his hand trembled on his fork, the two tines rattled on the gold plate.

Now and again fears swooped down like vampires in the night, especially since Anne had died. She had held them at bay. The vampires must be fought alone now and exterminated cunningly, one by one, Gloucester, Arundel, and there were others—who had thought themselves strong enough to defy a king. And had succeeded for a time. They had exiled the one beloved friend, de Vere, who died over there alone in France; they had exiled good old Michael de la Pole, who also died; they had actually murdered Simon Burley, the kind tutor of his childhood. By the Blood of Christ, who was to know for sure that they had not murdered Anne? Plague could be caused by witchcraft, poison could counterfeit plague—

Be careful, said a voice in Richard's mind. Don't let them guess what you are thinking. Remember those suave watchful Frenchmen over there. Wait until after the marriage with little Isabelle, until we are at peace with France—and then—

He turned suddenly to Katherine, mustering all his eager boyish charm. "I'm much interested in what you said of that night here thirty, is it, years ago. Ay—a year before I was born. Whom were you sitting with?"

Katherine was startled. Unpredictable as a cat, one never knew where he would pounce next. "Why," she said, "it was with my sister Philippa, Your Grace, and her betrothed, Geoffrey Chaucer."

"Chaucer?" said the King raising his plucked golden brows, and twirling the stem of his goblet. "Have you seen the scurrilous verses he dared write to me?"

Katherine had seen them. Geoffrey had imprudently taken it upon himself to chide the King for "lack of steadfastness" and it was no wonder that he had been reduced to a penury that she had immediately relieved, with John's help, when she became Duchess.

"Geoffrey's getting old," she said uncomfortably, "and is in poor health. He served His Grace, your grandfather, most loyally."

Richard laughed and took a sip of iced wine. "Oh I forgive him, because of the pleasure some of his poems had brought me." And he shrugged, dismissing Chaucer. "Tell me," he said smoothly, "that day in Essex when I was putting down the revolt and you were on pilgrimage, what was the vow you made?"

This was so unexpected that she colored. Jesu, he forgets nothing, she thought, every detail, every smallest thing. Every slight too, Christ pity him. For there was pathos in Richard, one felt the misery of his distrusts and deep uncertainties, sometimes there was a plaintive frightened sweetness about him. She had come to see this in the last months. But he was undisciplined, childish, vengeful—and dangerous. John was in high favor now, but if— She dismissed these rushing thoughts and answered with the only part of the truth it was safe to tell him. "I had a daughter, Your Grace, Blanchette —you remember I asked of her that day? She was injured, disappeared when the rebels fired the Savoy. I took the pilgrimage in hope that Our Lady of Walsingham would find her for me."

"Ah—" cried Richard, his eyes lighting, "those whoreson serfs. I soon dealt with them, didn't I? Well, did Our Lady send you Blanchette?"

"No—" said Katherine slowly. "I've never heard what happened to her."

"And there's pain still, after all these years?" asked Richard curiously.

"Time never entirely heals the loss of a child, Your Grace," said Katherine incautiously. The King's round pink and white face hardened. The Plantagenet glint flashed in his pale blue eyes.

Richard's failure to produce an heir, and the choice of his new Queen, whose age made it impossible that she could even be bedded for years, was the common whisper of England. Anything that Richard might construe as the obliquest reference to his peculiarities was unwise.

He paid her back at once by smiling his small purse-lipped smile and saying, "Alas, I have as yet no way of knowing these parental sensibilities, have I, my lady? Young Mortimer is still my heir. 'Tis pity indeed," he said softly, watching her closely, "that your new husband's good and *prolific* Henry of Bolingbroke may not succeed."

Blessed Mother, thought Katherine. The sudden claws, the threat that jumped out when all was most charming. She cast about for politic answers and instinctively rejected them for frankness.

"Henry has never coveted the throne, Your Grace, any

more than has my dear lord his father, and this you know right well by long years of proof."

Richard stared at her, astonished by positive rebuttal. Of late, and barely recognized, for he was fond of his Uncle John, there had been growing in Richard a dislike of Henry: so solid and masculine a man, so excellent a soldier and jouster—and so popular with the people. "I've never doubted my Uncle of Lancaster's loyalty, no matter what they said—" he murmured half to himself, looking beyond her to the Duke.

"Nor need you doubt his son's, Your Grace." Katherine smiled, still a lovely warm smile, with white teeth and a hint of her youthful dimple. In both the smile and her sincere voice, there was for Richard something maternal and reassuring. She was nearly of the age at which he best remembered his mother, the Princess Joan, and that memory brought ease.

With one of his characteristic volte-faces, Richard laughed and patted Katherine's hand. "I shall believe you, my fair new aunt," he said mischievously. "At least for tonight! God's blood, but the minstrels play badly. This banquet bores me." He stood up, shoving his plate away. Like released bowstrings, the two hundred diners jumped to their feet and waited. The Cheshire guard sprang to attention.

Richard airly waved the Flemish lace handkerchief he always carried. "Clear the Hall. There shall be dancing now!"

The half-eaten food was whisked away. The subtleties not yet presented were returned to the kitchens.

Richard looked up at Katherine, who topped him by some inches, crying loudly, "My first dance of course will be with the Duchess of Lancaster." He winked at the Duke, as Eleanor gave an unmistakable anguished choke.

On the day after the banquet, the Lancasters traveled back to Kenilworth to enjoy a few days of privacy before leaving for Calais and the state meeting there with the Dukes of Berry and Burgundy—more preliminaries to peace with France.

As the ducal retinue cantered along the side of the mere towards Kenilworth, Katherine looked ahead at the red sandstone battlements with fervent relief. This was the castle which in the old days had always been home to her, its warm ruddy fabric was interwoven with memories of her children's babyhood, and of the more peaceful stretches of her love.

The watch had seen them. The trumpets blew a salute, and

the Lancaster pennant ran hastily up on the Mortimer Tower. The Duke's retinue pulled their horses down to a walk, and Katherine presently said to John, "Oh my dear lord—how delicious it will be to rest here a few days."

He placed his hand on the jeweled pommel to turn and smile at her. "Your new duties are exacting, lovely! And I fear it won't be all rest now. There's Saint Pol to be entertained. The tenants have planned celebrations for you, and all the chancery officials are here, since we have much business to discuss before going abroad."

"Oh well—I know—but that's all simple compared to court life. Sainte Marie, but these last few days at Windsor were grueling. 'Be gracious to the Siéur de Vertain, but remember that he's outranked by Saint Pol. Remember that Lady Arundel will repeat everything I say to Gloucester, and Lady Salisbury to her husband, who will tell the King, and above all be careful what you say to the King.' I never knew how hard it was to be a great lady—"

"You do it superbly, Katrine," said John with sudden seriousness. "I've been very proud of you and of the way you ignore malice and slander."

She blushed and said quietly, "Malice and slander are accustomed things to both of us, darling. One learns to live without their hurting overmuch."

"Ay," he said, "they never disturbed me but once—that foolish changeling story. Ah Katrine—never during the long time of our separation did I quite forget what your love did for me then."

They both fell silent as they rode through the two gates and under the raised portcullises of Mortimer's tower into the base court, where they were greeted by the usual confusion of scurrying stableboys, barking dogs and children. It was a different set of children now who ran in great excitement down from the inner court, escaping from nurses and governesses to precipitate themselves perilously near the rearing, snorting horses. These were John's grandchildren, Henry's brood, who summered at Kenilworth. Little Henry of Monmouth, nine years old, did not wait for the Duke to dismount, but swarmed up the flank of his grandfather's great charger, and sure of indulgence, wedged himself between the pommel and the Duke crying, "Grandsir, Grandsir, did you bring me the peregrine you promised? Did you, my lord?"

John smiled at Katherine over the child's head. "Here's a

naughty mannerless lad, who thinks of nothing but falconry! Get down, you little savage, get down, you'll find out in good time." He scooped the boy out of the saddle and deposited him on the flags. "Now stand back and show the Duchess and me proper courtesy."

"Ah but not too much ceremony, my lord," said Katherine laughing, as the boy, who had no awe of his grandfather, made a pert face. "It's good to have a pack of rowdy children around again!"

She glanced up at the weather vane on the stable roof remembering the day Elizabeth had clung to it. Elizabeth, now at last married none too happily to the John Holland of her earliest passion, the King's lustful unprincipled half brother. Katherine walked through the arch after the Duke and saw the stone bench by the keep where Philippa had said gravely on that same day, "Nay, I don't mind that my father should love you—but I pray—pray for your souls."

Philippa was now Queen of Portugal with five children of her own. She had written Katherine a gentle affectionate letter of congratulation upon receiving news of the marriage.

There had been another child on that old mossy stone bench that day. Katherine had an instant vision of the upturned dark gray eyes and dismissed it sharply. It was morbid to dwell on the one sorrow when the other five children were secure now in positions never imagined in her most daring dreams.

The next morning when Katherine awoke early in the State Bed of the White Chamber, John still slept. He needed more rest than he used to, and though she tried to deny it to herself, nor even let him guess that she noticed, she knew that his heart was tiring. He must mount stairs slowly, or struggle to breathe; at times his mouth had a pinched bluish look, and there was an oppression in his chest.

Yet on this summer morning he looked well, the deep grooves on his forehead and cheeks were smoothed by sleep, the scarred eyelid less puckered. He was thin but still hard and muscular, the hairs on his chest were golden as they used to be, though his head was streaked with gray. He slept tidily without sound, the fastidiousness that she loved in him never failed. She thought of what Elizabeth had said when she saw her father in Richard's coronation procession, "He's never slobbery, no matter what," and smiling kissed him on the shoulder, then slid out of bed and summoned Hawise.

Hawise was a person of consequence now, and not sure that she liked it. She had four waiting women under her, besides a score of maidservants, and her new position required that she dress in heavy flowing woolen robes no matter the temperature.

Katherine gestured towards the garderobe, and the women went in there so as not to disturb the Duke.

"I've brought ye spiced hippocras the butler sent up," said Hawise crossly, putting a chased gold ewer down on the toilet table. "We're all far too grand to drink honest English ale of a morning any more."

Katherine laughed. "Don't tell me you miss Kettlethorpe, my lass?" She swallowed a cupful of the cool sweet wine and began to wash herself with rose water.

"Not sure I don't—" grumbled Hawise, mixing powdered coral and myrrh for the tooth cleaning. "Doesn't take five women to wait on you, when I've done it well enough alone these donkey's years—that Dame Griselda Moorehead, Dame Muttonhead *I* call her, telling me it's her *right* and privilege to attend ye at your bath, that I know naught of etiquette. I'll right-and-privilege her, may Saint Anthony's fire burn me if I won't. 'Fishmongress' she calls me, as though Father's trade was aught to be 'shamed of!"

"Have some hippocras," said Katherine pacifically, putting the cup in Hawise's reluctant hand. " 'Tis really delicious. We must both put up with changed conditions for ill or well—I suppose."

"Ah sweeting—" cried Hawise, her broad freckled face crinkling, "ye know I don't mean it. God's belly, there's not an hour in the day I don't gi' thanks for the marvelous thing what's happened to ye—when I think o' the black past—well let be—we won't think on it."

They looked at each other, while the memory of all the years they had shared together hovered between them, then spoke of trifling matters while they proceeded with Katherine's elaborate toilet. John wished her to be always richly dressed, and to wear the new jewels he had given her. He took great pride in her mature beauty and liked her to enhance it by the artful application of unguents, rouges and perfumes.

After Hawise had adjusted a light seed-pearl coronet over a veil of rosy gauze, Katherine glanced into the bedchamber and said, "My dear lord sleeps late, I'm afraid I should wake him. He must sign those letters to the King before the Comte de Saint Pol starts back for Windsor."

"Let His Grace rest, poor soul, he seemed dreadful weary yestere'en." Hawise had indulgence now towards the Duke and did not even mind his teasing her for her jealous wardship of her mistress.

Katherine nodded, walked rapidly through the passages of the Sainteowe Tower into the beautiful Great Hall which John had now completed. It was crowded with retainers, lords, knights, squires and their ladies, all waiting for her to come so that they might sit down to eat. As she entered, the men bowed, and the ladies curtsied. The chamberlain ushered her unctuously to the dais, where her own squire, kneeling, presented her with a damask napkin.

"Good morning, Roger," she said smiling at him, while the company seated themselves. "You look very merry, you won at dicing last night?"

The lad blushed, and bit his lips to keep from laughing. "Dame Fortune favored me, Your Grace," he admitted.

He's like his grandfather, she thought—Roger de Cheyne with the bold wooing eyes, the pretty chestnut curls—my first love, I suppose, or I thought so—Jesu, how long ago. Thirty years. She thought of the tournament, the knight with the nodding iris stuck in his helm—poor Roger, who was killed so shortly after that at Nájera. Blessed Mother, how many were dead that had witnessed Saint George's tournament at Windsor. She crossed herself, and turned abruptly to the French nobleman on her right, the Comte de St. Pol. "Vous vous amusez bien ici en Angleterre, monsieur, ça vous plaît?" She embarked on the courteous chitchat which was constantly required of her now.

"Parfaitement, madame la duchesse," replied the count, delicately wiping his long black mustaches, and thinking that despite the scandal of this marriage, the new Duchess had far better manners than most of the English barbarians and the further advantage of speaking pure French—which he would report to his own King Charles in good time.

The stately breakfast proceeded. Katherine longed to go out to her pleasaunce where the peaches were ripening and the new Persian lilies were in bloom, but she allowed herself no impatience. It would be hours before she could enjoy the garden. There must first be interviews with the chamberlain and the steward. She must arbitrate a quarrel between the village and castle laundresses, she must dictate answers to a dozen letters, and as most of them were begging letters, there would be conference first with the clerk of her wardrobe.

When she rose at length, a page came up to say that two nuns had just arrived at the castle and craved an audience. "Certainly," said Katherine wondering which convent it was this time that required a benefice. "Tell them I'll receive them presently." And hoped that whatever it was they wanted, she could manage to gratify them herself from her privy purse without bothering John.

By the time she had finished her necessary morning routine, it had grown very warm, and she sent a page to the nuns to convey them to the oriel of the Great Hall, where a faint breeze blew through the opened window. John was up at last and had gone to the chancery office with St. Pol. Except for her own women who were embroidering and spinning by one of the empty fireplaces, the Hall was deserted for the present.

Katherine seated herself in a carved gilt chair and surveyed the two nuns with polite indifference as they bowed before her. White nuns, Cistercians, shrouded in snowy wimples and habits, a tall one and a short one. The former turned away at once and seemed to be examining the embroidered Venetian wall hanging. Katherine had had only a glimpse of a pale unsmiling profile.

The short nun began to talk in a weak insistent voice, her heavy-jawed, middle-aged face twitched with nervous little smiles. "Most kind of you, Your Grace—forgive this intrusion, really I hardly know how to explain it. Oh, I'm the prioress of Pinley—a very small foundation, you know where we are? Only a few miles from here, near Warwick—but of course we're not on Lancastrian land, Your Grace wouldn't know us—"

What is all this about, Katherine thought faintly amused. "Is there some help I can give you, my lady prioress?" she said, glancing in some perplexity at the rigid white back of the other nun, whose marked withdrawal was surely peculiar.

"Well—" said the prioress, chewing her lips, "I don't rightly know. It's Dame Ursula there who *would* come. She's my sacrist and librarian, not that we have many books, I

think it's maybe *that* she wanted, wondered if—but Dame
Ursula, she talks so little, sometimes we think she's very odd,
though not the way she used to be—"

Katherine raised her eyebrows and drew them together.

"Oh," said the prioress, "she's quite deaf, I doubt she can
hear me."

But it seemed that the other nun had heard. With a slow
almost languorous motion she turned and looked full at
Katherine, whose heart began to pound before her mind
knew any reason for it, who gazed blankly at the triangular
wedge of face enclosed by the white wimple, then at the
slate-gray eyes that looked at her with hesitant enigmatic
question.

"You do not know me?" said the tall nun quietly in the flat
toneless voice of the deafened.

Katherine stared again. She pushed herself up from the
chair, gripping the armrests. She tried to speak, but the blood
drained from her head, she fell back sideways—and slipped
off the chair.

The blankness lasted only a few moments, though it was
long enough for the page on hearing the prioress's frightened
cry to have summoned Katherine's women. When she opened
her eyes, she had been laid on the rug, Griselda Moorehead
was sponging her forehead with wine, Hawise was burning a
feather beneath her nose and there was a chorus of female
speculation: "What happened? The Duchess swooned—but
she never does—what can be amiss?"

The prioress had drawn back and was wringing her hands,
crying that it was no fault of hers, that she didn't know what
happened, that Dame Ursula—

Katherine pushed Hawise and Griselda aside, she struggled
to her elbow and saw that the tall white nun knelt by her
feet, the wimpled head was bowed and there were tears on
the pale cheeks.

"Go away please, everybody—" said Katherine in a shaking voice, "all but Dame Ursula. I'm sorry I was so foolish.
The heat, perhaps—" The women reluctantly obeyed her.
Hawise made them after she had helped her mistress to her
feet and shot a long startled unbelieving look at Dame Ursula, who continued to kneel with her head bowed.

When they were alone, Katherine leaned down, took the
clasped thin trembling hands in hers. "Blanchette—" she

whispered. "Oh my darling—I always knew— Dear God, I knew you'd come back—"

The nun raised her head at last. "I had to see you again," she said through stiff pale lips, "I could no longer live with my hatred."

There were only two people in the castle who understood why the Duchess were closeted in her bower all that day with the Cistercian nun. These were the Duke and Hawise, who saw to it that she was not disturbed, while the mystified prioress was made welcome in the Hall.

The mother and daughter could not speak much for a long time. They wept together quietly and after a while they prayed on Katherine's prie-dieu. It was only bit by bit that Katherine comprehended her daughter's story. Blanchette was unaccustomed to talking, and her deafness, result of the scarlet fever, had increased her withdrawal into an interior world which satisfied her.

She made this clear: the convent life contented her, she wished for no other, there was no doubt that she had a true vocation. She was grateful to the nuns, who had sheltered the wild half-demented child who had come to them fifteen years ago, and who had accepted her as a novice later, though she had no dowry and pretended that she did not know her name. "I never told anything about myself—" said Blanchette. "I couldn't. My soul was eaten up with fear, fear and hate. Mother—" she took a sharp breath and looked deep into Katherine's eyes, "did I hear wrong that day in the Avalon Chamber?"

It was as Katherine had suspected all these years, the added pain that had lain at the core of her anguished bereavement. Blanchette had misinterpreted the Gray Friar's accusation and had believed that her mother deliberately poisoned her father.

Speaking distinctly, her lips slowly forming each word, Katherine effaced this horror for Blanchette at last. And the grave twenty-nine-year-old nun received the truth and understood, as the frightened child could never have.

It was the news of the marriage which had stirred Blanchette from her long self-containment. She had begun to remember her mother's love for her, to see Katherine as a woman who could never commit the hideous crime that the child had believed in. "And—I thought, I felt, that you could not have married the Duke if it were true."

Later Blanchette, speaking with even greater effort, told of how she had escaped from the Savoy; though that time was for her now a dim fantastic memory. From the Avalon Chamber she had run to hide in the falcon mew. "How long I don't know, the hawks in there frightened me, I had forgotten you, forgotten what was happening to the Savoy. I thought only of my green linnet in its cage upstairs."

She had gone back up the secret stairs to the Privy Suite to find her bird. The bird lay dead on the bottom of its cage which the rebels had tossed in a corner of the Duchess's garderobe. As Blanchette picked up the cage, the passageway burst into flames behind her, and she jumped from the window into the Thames. The wooden cage had held her up until a boat came by. It was rowed by a Fleming, who was flying from the massacre of his people that was taking place in London. He hauled Blanchette on board with him and rowed on desperately up the river.

"I don't know where he put me ashore," said Blanchette, "nor where I wandered for some days—but I think I was trying to get here to Kenilworth, to you as you used to be. One of the Pinley serfs found me lying exhausted in a field, he brought me to the convent. They thought me daft for a long time, I would not talk and could hear but little, while in my heart was—oh Blessed Christ—" She turned from her mother and clasping her long delicate hands on the white wool of her habit stared out through the window to the placid mere.

"Ay—" she said after a while, "it was He and His love that held me, when all other love was twisted into hate." She got up and kneeling down by Katherine looked up into her face. "Mother, I shall be an anchoress. Ay—I've thought much about it, but I had to be free of hatred first. A cell dedicated to God where I shall never more see the outer world."

"No, darling, no!" Katherine cried below her breath. "I can't give you up again." She had been thinking of what might still be done for Blanchette to make up to her for the gaiety and youth she had missed. Of how by special dispensation, Blanchette might visit Kenilworth from time to time, that she might even travel to Kettlethorpe as she had once so longed to do.

Blanchette did not hear the protest, but she saw her

mother's recoil. "It's right for me to become a recluse," she said gravely. "God has stopped up my ears, so that I may better hear His voice. By His grace, my prayers will be of stronger help to others than aught else I can do. You must not doubt this, Mother, for I know it is so."

I know it is so. What dear-bought treasured certainty that was. It seemed to Katherine that above Blanchette's halting voice she heard the Lady Julian speak. "I saw full surely that it needs be that we should be in longing and in penance until the time that we be led so deep into God that we truly know our own soul."

This had happened to Blanchette, she could not doubt it. For this child of hers, the sanctified life of a recluse was right, as it would have been wrong for Katherine, who had so desperately wished to renounce the world during the time of rebellion and anguish in Norfolk.

Katherine leaned down and kissed her daughter's forehead, while she thought with humble gratitude of the guidance that had sent her back to the long years of struggle and humiliation. Of the grace that had been shown in the end to help her children to their birthright, to ease the lot of her manor folk at Kettlethorpe—to give of herself to John.

The women spoke but little more together, nor had need to. They went to vespers together in Kenilworth's chapel, and afterwards kissed each other a long tender farewell. They would meet once more at the convent when Katherine came back from France, before Blanchette's final enclosure.

The prioress had watched all these extraordinary happenings with popping eyes, and was told the truth before the two nuns set forth with their servant back to Pinley. She was also told to keep silence on Dame Ursula's identity, a promise which she gave the more readily when she realized the advantages resultant upon the Duchess of Lancaster's new interest in the little priory. Blanchette's original Deyncourt dowry should be paid them at once and there would be other rewards for the Christian kindness they had shown the girl.

The Duke stood beside Katherine in the courtyard, while they watched the two white figures disappear through the Mortimer Gate. He looked down at his wife's face and said softly, "I believe this has given you more happiness than I have ever done. I think I'm jealous of that look in your eyes."

"Ah my dear love," she said, turning to him, "don't you

see that it's more than thanksgiving for the safety of the child I so deeply wronged? It's that this means forgiveness, at last — We are forgiven all that we've done to harm others. I feel it." He could not share her certainty, though during the months that they had been together again, he had often been touched by the quiet fearless faith, which she had never used to have.

This day he had received sinister news. A rumor that his brother of Gloucester had been overheard making bloody threats against the King. Whom I shall protect as always, God help me, John thought bitterly. He had pity for his unhappy, confused nephew, and certainly Richard had no one else left who could protect him now.

Yet during the past night, John had had a frightful dream of Richard. In the dream, the King's plump girlish body had been clothed in a leopard's hide, and the cruel yellow eyes had been covertly watching Henry, John's firstborn and heir. Treachery. The word had been on John's lips when he finally awoke this morning. The dream fear faded soon, but it merged into a haze of sadness and foreboding. He had lain in bed for some time, thinking of the failures in his life, the injustices and stupidities and of the clouded threatening future.

He had meant to tell Katherine, the voicing of his thoughts to her would bring relief, but now he could not damp the great joy that had come to her.

When the two nuns had gone she had moved instinctively towards the pleasaunce gate and he followed her silently. They walked into the evening quiet of the privy garden. Bees hummed still over the white Persian lilies and the clove gillyflowers, whose fragrance had deepened in the summer dusk. Against the warm brick wall espaliered apricot and pear trees held up green hands studded with golden fruit. The crystal waters of the fountain splashed softly into a mossy marble basin, near the carved oak bench where Katherine and John sat down together and gazed out across the mere. Swans glided by with their cygnets, the fringing rushes quivered under the first harbingers of the evening breeze.

The sweetness of the garden had begun to lull John into Katherine's mood of deep unexpectant peace, when suddenly from the castle ward behind them there erupted the shrill fanfare of a trumpet; dogs barked, and there were shouts of greeting.

Katherine stirred, rousing herself reluctantly. "Now who could that be arriving."

John's farsighted eyes had seen a galloping horseman streak by along the causeway. " 'Tis a King's herald," he said in a down-dragging voice. "Richard will have had some new idea for the French envoys, or discovered some new conspiracy—or worse—I don't know—Katrine, I have a foreboding—there's danger ahead."

She turned to him on the bench, seeing the tight lines of his mouth, the discouragement in his eyes.

"It may be so, darling," she said slowly. "It may be that there is danger—" She paused and said more softly still, "There was no promise that we should not be tempested and travailed—but there *was* a promise." She smiled and did not go on as she saw that he was not really listening. She put her hand over his, and waited until his clenched fingers relaxed and clasped hers. Hand-fasted they sat looking out across the darkening lake into the forest beyond.

Presently comfort came to him, and he thought that she had always given him of her strength though he had never quite realized it until now.

Glory had passed him by, fame too perhaps would not endure, it might well be that the incalculable goddess would decree ill fame as his due. Perhaps there might not be included in his epitaph the one tribute to his knighthood that he knew he deserved: "Il fut toujours bon et loyal chevalier."

But whatever the shadowed years might bring, as long as life should last, he knew that he had here at his side one sure recompense and one abiding loyalty.

## AFTERWORD

THE FOLLOWING YEAR, 1397, Richard effected the murder of his uncle, Thomas, Duke of Gloucester, at Calais, while Lord Arundel was beheaded for treason. Shortly thereafter, Richard cruelly and inexplicably exiled Henry of Bolingbroke.

John, Duke of Lancaster, died a natural death on February 3, 1399, at Leicester Castle, with Katherine by his side. They had been married three years. Upon the Duke's death, Richard wantonly confiscated all the Lancastrian estates and heritage, and Henry soon returned to England to fight for his rights.

By popular acclaim, Richard was forced to abdicate in favor of his much wronged cousin, who thereupon became King Henry the Fourth of England, while Richard was imprisoned in Pontefract Castle, where he soon died. Katherine's son Thomas Swynford was at that time constable of Pontefract and it was said that by starvation he murdered Richard.

After her Duke's death Katherine returned to Lincolnshire, where she lived quietly four years and died on May 10, 1403. She was buried by the High Altar in Lincoln Cathedral, where her son Harry Beaufort, later cardinal and chancellor, had duly become bishop. Katherine's tomb is there now, with that of her Joan.

From the Beauforts, the royal line of England eventually descended. Through John Beaufort (Earl of Somerset, Marquis of Dorset), who married Richard's half niece, Katherine became the ancestress of Henry the Seventh, and the Tudor line, also of the royal Stuart line of Scotland. Through Joan and Ralph Neville of Raby (Earl of Westmoreland), Katherine was great-grandmother to Edward the Fourth, and Richard the Third.

Surely John of Gaunt and Katherine de Roet, the herald's daughter, fulfilled the ancient prophecy, "Thou shalt get kings though thou be none."